Praise for *The Lays of Anuskaya*

"The Lays of Anuskaya is a... ...ncluding volumes in the history of epic fantasy."

—Justin Landon, Staffer's Book Review

"All in all, The Lays of Anuskaya series is dark, ambitious, complex, and populated with a great cast of characters that leap off the pages. If you are looking for a quality read that's different from everything else on the market today, this series is definitely for you."

—*Pat's Fantasy Hotlist*

"In remarkably short order, Beaulieu has marked himself as an epic fantasist that any reader of the subgenre should take a look at."

—Paul Weimer, SFSignal

"*The Flames of Shadam Khoreh* is the capstone of a landmark series full of intrigue, swashbuckling, betrayal, sacrifice, and love."

—Amazing Stories

"A marvelous accomplishment. I am so impressed with how [Beaulieu] tied everything together, giving everyone such a satisfying, noble, and strangely uplifting ending. Well, almost everyone. Let's face it: This third book was a *bloodbath*."

—Eugene Myers, Author of *Fair Coin* and *Quantum Coin*

"Beautifully written and delicious to read. It's not that often that a series of books sweeps me away, but these books did. Highly recommended."

—Brenda Cooper, Author of *The Creative Fire* and *Mayan December*

"Intricate yet fast-paced, full of Byzantine politics, unexpected alliances and high-stakes action, *The Flames of Shadam Khoreh* is an outstanding capstone to a fully realized epic."

—Rob Ziegler, Author of *Seed*

Praise for *The Straits of Galahesh*

"Beaulieu presents a [...] vividly realized tale of heroes torn between duty and love."
—*Publisher's Weekly*

"Dark, ambitious, complex, populated with a great cast of characters that leap off the pages, *The Straits of Galahesh* is just what the doctor ordered if you are looking for a quality read that's different from everything else on the market today. *The Winds of Khalakovo* turned out to be one of the very best SFF works of 2011. Somehow, Bradley P. Beaulieu has raised the bar even higher for this sequel, making *The Straits of Galahesh* a "must read" speculative fiction title for 2012."
—*Pat's Fantasy Hotlist*

"If you're the kind of reader who enjoys Steven Erikson's approach of throwing readers into a setting without too much guidance and letting the story do the job of explaining the details as it progresses, you should have a great time getting to know this fantasy universe. While that happens, you'll be treated to healthy doses of feudal and international politics, strong characters, unique magic, romance, spectacular battles on land and in the air, and a story that continues to broaden in scope. The Lays of Anuskaya is shaping up to be a fine fantasy trilogy."
—Tor.com

"If you read *The Winds of Khalakovo*, then you will want to read *The Straits of Galahesh*. If you haven't, then buy and read them both."
—Adventures Fantastic

"Reading Bradley P. Beaulieu's The Lays of Anuskaya series is like traveling through grand undiscovered country. [...] *The Straits of Galahesh* continues the breakneck pace of a fight for an entire world, touched by passion, love, and loyalty. As a reader, almost every chapter added to my sense of wonder and realization. I can't recommend this fabulous fantasy series highly enough. Read it."
—Brenda Cooper, author of *Wings of Creation* and *Mayan December*

"With *The Straits of Galahesh*, Beaulieu returns to the vibrant fantasy he introduced in *The Winds of Khalakovo*. A gritty book packed with big ideas and Byzantine politics, and inhabited by compellingly flawed heroes, *Straits* is the sort of fully realized epic one can sink into for days. It sings with action, magic, and heart—the perfect second act in a brilliant series."
—Rob Ziegler, author of *Seed*

Praise for *The Winds of Khalakovo*

"Sailing ships of the sky! Bradley P. Beaulieu's *The Winds of Khalakovo* is an energetic, swashbuckling novel with a distinctive flavor, a lush setting, and a plot filled with adventure, interesting characters, and intrigue. Exactly the kind of fantasy I like to read."
—Kevin J. Anderson, *New York Times* bestselling author of *The Saga of Seven Suns*

"Overlaid with the rich feel of Cyrillic culture, Beaulieu's debut intro- duces a fascinating world of archipelagic realms and shamanic magic worked primarily by women. Verdict: Strong characters and a plot filled with tension and difficult choices make this a good option for fantasy fans."

—*Library Journal*

"Elegantly crafted, refreshingly creative, *The Winds of Khalakovo* offers a compelling tale of men and women fighting to protect their world. Politics, faith, betrayal, sacrifice, and of course supernatural mystery—it's all there, seamlessly combined in a tale driven by intelligent and passionate characters whose relationships and goals a reader can really care about. A great read!"

—C. S. Friedman, bestselling author of the Coldfire and Magister trilogies

"Bradley P. Beaulieu is a welcome addition to the roster of new fantasy novelists. *The Winds of Khalakovo* is a sharp and original fantasy full of action, intrigue, romance, politics, mystery and magick, tons of magick. The boldly imagined new world and sharply drawn characters will pull you into *The Winds of Khalakovo* and won't let you go until the last page."

—Michael A. Stackpole, author of *I, Jedi* and *At the Queen's Command*

THE FLAMES OF
SHADAM KHOREH

Also by Bradley P. Beaulieu

The Lays of Anuskaya
The Winds of Khalakovo
The Straits of Galahesh
The Flames of Shadam Khoreh

Short Story Collections
Lest Our Passage Be Forgotten & Other Stories

Novellas
Strata (with Stephen Gaskell)

Forthcoming in 2014 from DAW Books

The Song of the Shattered Sands
Twelve Kings in Sharakhai
The Inverted Thorn
The Thirteenth Tribe

THE FLAMES OF
SHADAM KHOREH

BRADLEY P. BEAULIEU

NIGHT SHADE BOOKS
NEW YORK

10 9 8 7 6 5 4 3 2 1

Library of Congress Cataloging-in-Publication Data is available on file.

Cover art by Aaron J. Riley © 2013
Cover design by Bradley P. Beaulieu
Interior art by Evgeni Maloshenkov © 2013
Maps by William McAusland

Visit the author on the web at http://www.quillings.com

Print ISBN: 978-1-59780-550-6

Printed in the United States of America

For Rhys, my dear son.
Through you, I relive my own childhood,
and this is a gift I can never repay.

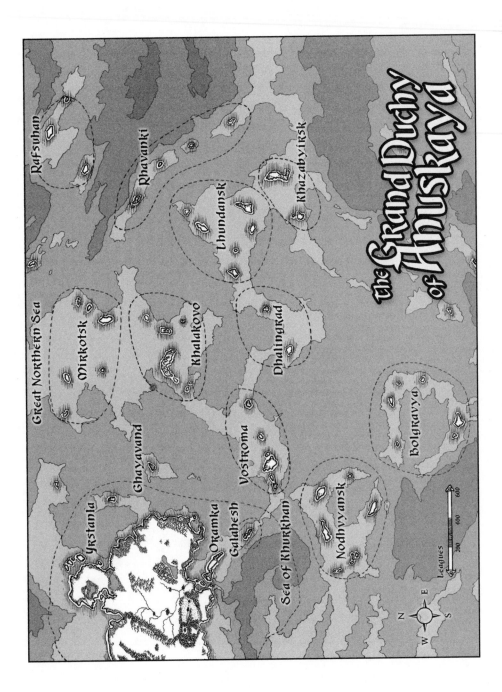

The Grand Duchy of Anuskaya

Rafsuhan

Ghayankt

Lhundansk

Khazabyirsk

Great Northern Sea

Mirkotsk

Khalakovo

Dhalingrad

Bolgravya

Ghayavand

Vostroma

Yrstanla

Oramka

Galahesh

Nodhvyansk

Sea of Khurkhan

N
W   E
S

Leagues
200 400 600

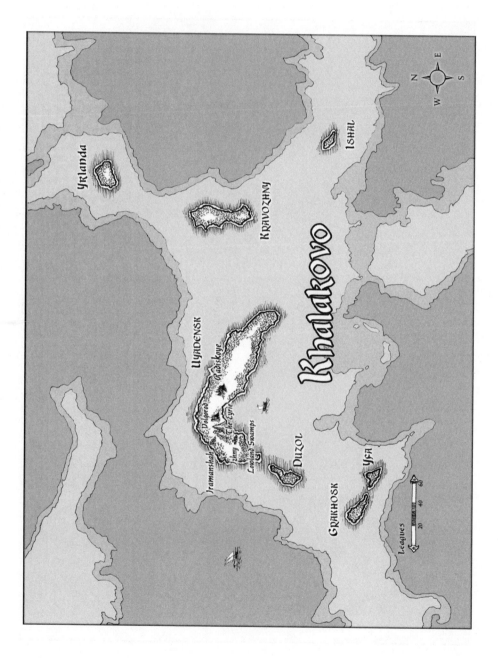

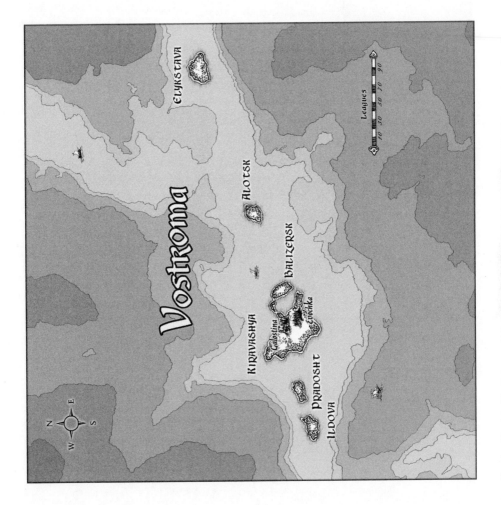

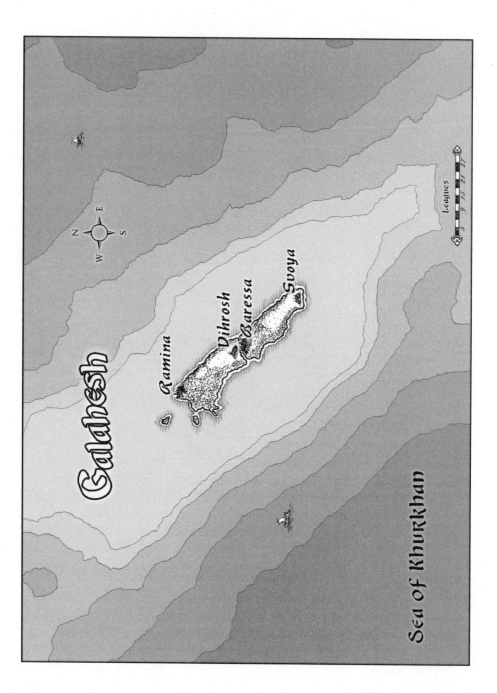

DRAMATIS PERSONÆ

Prince Nikandr Iarosloav Khalakovo: youngest son of the Duke and Duchess of Khalakovo.

Princess Atiana Radieva Vostroma: daughter of the Duke and Duchess of Vostroma.

Nasim an Ashan: an orphan Aramahn boy with strange abilities to commune with elemental spirits.

Styophan Andrashayev: a komodor of the Khalakovan staaya.

Ashan Kida al Ahrumea: one of the arqesh (master of all disciplines) among the Aramahn.

Soroush Wahad al Gatha: leader of the northern sect of the Maharraht.

The Duchy of Khalakovo

The Duke and Duchess
Ranos Iaroslov Khalakovo
Yvanna Antoneva Khalakovo

Others
Saphia Mishkeva Khalakovo: mother of Ranos, Nikandr, and Victania
Princess Victania Saphieva Khalakovo: sister of Ranos and Nikandr.
Isaak Ylafslov: the seneschal of Palotza Radiskoye.
Rodion: cousin to Styophan and a trusted soldier in his command.

The Duchy of Vostroma

The Duke and Duchess
Borund Zhabynov Vostroma
Nataliya Iyaneva Bolgravya

Others
Radia Anastasiyeva Vostroma: mother of Borund, Atiana, Mileva, and Ishkyna.
Princess Mileva Radieva Vostroma: daughter, sister to Atiana.
Princess Ishkyna Radieva Vostroma: daughter, sister to Atiana.
Katerina Vostroma: a Matra of Vostroma: Zhabyn's sister.

The Duchy of Bolgravya

The Duke
Konstantin Stasayev Bolgravya
Grigory Stasayev Bolgravya: Konstantin's brother.

The Duchy of Dhalingrad

The Grand Duke and Duchess of Anuskaya
Grand Duke Leonid Roaldov Dhalingrad
Grand Duchess Iyana Klarieva Dhalingrad

The Royalty of the Other Duchies

Duke Yegor Nikolov Nodhvyansk
Duchess Kseniya Zoyeva Nodhvyansk

Duke Yevgeny Krazhnegov Mirkotsk
Duchess Polina Anayev Mirkotsk

Duke Andreyo Sergeyov Rhavanki
Duchess Ekaterina Margeva Rhavanki

Duke Heodor Yaroslov Lhudansk
Duchess Rosa Oriseva Lhudansk

Duke Aleg Ganevov Khazabyirsk
Duchess Zanaida Lariseva Khazabyirsk

The Al-Aqim

The Al-Aqim were three legendary arqesh who lived on Ghayavand. Together, they caused the sundering three hundred years ago and were trapped on the island for many years.

Sariya Quljan al Vehayeh: gifted with the ways of the mind and the aether.
Muqallad Bakshazhd al Dananir: gifted with the ways of Adhiya, the spirit world.
Khamal Cyphar al Maladhin: gifted with the ways of Erahm, the material world.

The Aramahn and the Maharraht

Ushai Kissath al Shahda: a woman of the Maharraht who travels with Soroush in search of Nasim.
Anahid: Nikandr's dhoshaqiram (master of the stuff of life), the cousin of Jahalan.
Fahroz Bashar al Lilliah: The woman who taught Nasim after he was returned to himself in the ritual performed by Soroush.
Bersuq Wahad al Gatha: Soroush's dead brother, once the leader of the Maharraht.

People of the Yrstanlan Empire

Selim ül Hakan: the young Kamarisi Hakan ül Ayeşe.
Hakan ül Ayeşe: the former Kamarisi of Yrstanla, now dead.
Bahett ül Kirdhash: the regent to Selim ül Hakan, former Kaymakam of Galahesh.

People of Hael

Brechan son of Gaelynd: King of Kings among the Haelish.
Elean: the wife of Kürad, queen to the people of Clan Eidihla.
Kürad son of Külesh: the King of Clan Eidihla, a tribe of the Haelish people.
Datha: a stout Haelish warrior of Clan Eidihla.
Aelwen: a wodjan of Hael, a mystic who uses blood to scry the fortunes of others.

A Summary of *The Winds of Khalakovo*, Book One of the Lays of Anuskaya

As the story opens, the islands of the Grand Duchy are under siege from a blight to their crops and a deadly wasting disease that strikes royalty and peasants alike. A prince of the islands, Nikandr Khalakovo, is set to be married to Atiana Vostroma, a princess from a neighboring duchy. A pall is cast against the nuptials, however, when a fire spirit attacks and murders the Grand Duke.

The gathered royalty demand justice, and Nikandr is sent to investigate. All signs point to a young autistic savant named Nasim, and it is this boy's mysterious past that Nikandr becomes entangled with. Nikandr believes Nasim is not to blame for the attack. He believes instead that he was used as a tool by the Maharraht, a ruthless sect of the peace-loving Aramahn that want nothing less than the destruction of the Grand Duchy. As escalations rise over the murder of the Grand Duke, Nikandr and Nasim escape to the island of Ghayavand, a place that holds many secrets from Nasim's past.

Meanwhile, Atiana is pressed into service as a Matra, a woman who submerges herself in ice-cold water and enters the astral realm of the aether, where she can project herself to tend to the defense of the Grand Duchy and to communicate with other Matri. While doing so, Atiana comes face to face with Rehada, Nikandr's Aramahn lover. Atiana later learns that Rehada has only been posing as Nikandr's lover, and that in reality she is a spy for the Maharraht. Not only has she been feeding the Maharraht information about the Grand Duchy for years, she's been in league with Soroush, a sworn enemy of the Grand Duchy who hopes to open a rift that hangs over Khalakovo. Tearing open the rift would cause untold destruction to Khalakovo and the other islands of the Grand Duchy, but Soroush cannot do this alone. He must use Nasim and his unique abilities to tear the rift open. Rehada's loyalties, however, are not so resolute as they seem at first. She has come to doubt the path of violence that Soroush and the Maharraht are following, and it is through this doubt that she begins to question her place in the Maharraht.

Nikandr learns more of Nasim's past and returns with him to Khalakovo, hoping to heal the rift, but before he can do so, Soroush steals Nasim away. Nikandr is forced to return home to Khalakovo without him, and he finds that tensions among the nine dukes of the Grand Duchy have reached the boiling point.

A battle between the duchies ensues, providing the perfect cover for Soroush, who takes Nasim to a small keep on the nearby island of Duzol. There he plans to perform the ritual he's been planning for years. Using Nasim as a conduit, he will summon five elder spirits, and when all five have been summoned, the rift will be torn wide.

Soroush doesn't count on Rehada, however, who turns away from the path of violence. She warns Nikandr of what Soroush is planning, and together, Nikandr, Atiana, and Rehada move against Soroush and the Maharraht. Soroush completes his ritual, but Nikandr has come to understand his bond with Nasim intimately. He and Atiana use this knowledge to draw Nasim fully into the material world, an act that heals not only the blight, but Nasim as well. Nasim is now as whole as he has ever been in his life, and he may finally find it possible to learn and grow. The cost, however, is heavy. Nikandr's father is captured by the traitor dukes.

As the story closes, the Khalakovo family cedes control of their duchy to the new Grand Duke, and Nasim is taken away by his people for his own safety. Nikandr, however, knows that the rifts are not permanently closed, and he vows to find Nasim and complete what they have begun.

A Summary of *The Straits of Galahesh*, Book Two of the Lays of Anuskaya

Five years have passed since Nikandr and Atiana saved Khalakovo from widespread destruction, and Nasim has fully awoken. He has been taught the ways of the world on Mirashadal, the floating village of the Aramahn, and gained new purpose. The sundering, a ritual performed long ago by three powerful Aramahn known as the Al-Aqim, was the very thing that caused the rifts and the wasting disease that are now spreading throughout the islands, and Nasim feels that he must heal the damage. He knows he cannot do it alone, however. He doesn't know why, but his powers have been stunted since his awakening, so he recruits two other gifted children to help him: a spirited girl named Rabiah and a reserved boy named Sukharam.

Nikandr, on the other hand, has grown in his abilities. A wind spirit, a ha-vahezhan, is bound to him, and he uses it as he goes to free Soroush from his imprisonment in Mirashadal. He successfully frees Soroush and takes him to Rafsuhan. Nikandr needs Soroush, for Rafsuhan is controlled by the Maharraht, the violent sect of the Aramahn people that wishes to destroy the Grand Duchy of Anuskaya. A new rift has formed there, however, and Nikandr hopes to learn more, perhaps even to heal the rift as Nasim did on Khalakovo, but to do this Soroush must vouch for him. Although Soroush is reluctant to help a man he hates, he eventually agrees, as it may help his people.

Atiana, however, has a different opinion of what's best for the islands. Every day she sees more of the effects from the steady advance of the wasting disease and the rampant hunger caused by the blight. Both, they now know, are caused by the slow spread of the rifts. As noble as Nikandr's goals are, Anuskaya needs help now, so she arranges for a marriage of convenience between herself and Bahett ül Kirdhash, the Kaymakam of the island of Galahesh. Galahesh sits between the islands of the Grand Duchy and the mainland of Yrstanla, and while it has interests in the Grand Duchy, it also holds considerable influence in the halls of Yrstanla's capital, Alekeşir. Atiana's marriage could bring much needed aid to not only her home of Vostroma, but to all of the duchies. Atiana travels to Galahesh, and there she begins to spy on a mysterious woman named Arvaneh, a woman that Bahett fears has grave powers. She discovers, however, that this woman is in fact Sariya, one of the Al-Aqim. She, along with another of the Al-Aqim, a man named Muqallad, are powerful indeed and have survived since the time of the sundering.

As Atiana investigates Sariya's plans, Nasim arrives on Ghayavand with Rabiah and Sukharam. Together they find one of the pieces of the Atalayina, the fabled stone that the Al-Aqim used during the ritual that caused the sundering. They also discover that Ashan has beaten them to the island, and that Muqallad has captured him. Nasim goes there with Rabiah's help. Not only do they fail to recover Ashan, they lose Sukharam as well. Muqallad is holding him hostage along with Ashan until he gets another piece of the Atalayina, a piece he knows is trapped in Sariya's white tower. Nasim preaches patience, but Rabiah, angry with Nasim that they've lost Sukharam, goes to the tower on her own. She underestimates the power of Sariya, however, and is killed. Nasim, devastated by this loss, finds Rabiah's trapped soul in Sariya's tower and frees her. He then continues on to find the stone. Sariya opposes him, but his anger fuels him, and he finds the second piece of the Atalayina. Atiana is also there—she has come through a gateway that Sariya created on Galahesh—and Nasim gives the stone to her so that Muqallad cannot have it.

Nikandr arrives on Rafsuhan and soon discovers that Muqallad has been making plans there as well. He has an ally in Kaleh, a young girl he soon discovers is Sariya's own daughter. Muqallad and Kaleh have been using the children of the Maharraht, people who are loyal to them, for their own gain. Muqallad takes the children and turns them into akhoz, strange, twisted creatures that hardly resemble the children they once were, then uses them in a terrible ritual to fuse two of the pieces of the Atalayina together. Only the third piece, which now rests in Atiana's hands, will keep him from his ultimate goal: to bring about indaraqiram, an event that will destroy the world to begin it anew. With two of the three pieces of the Atalayina now in hand, Muqallad goes to Galahesh to find the third piece, and Nikandr follows.

Atiana, meanwhile, has learned more of Sariya. Years ago Sariya forced the Kamarisi of Yrstanla to begin the construction of a bridge that would cross the Straits of Galahesh. That bridge, known as the Spar, is nearly complete, and Atiana realizes too late that it will allow the windships of the Empire of Yrstanla to cross the straits themselves, a thing once thought impossible. As the bridge is completed, Atiana's father is taken to the center of the newly completed Spar and sacrificed by the Kamarisi of Yrstanla himself. Soon after, windships soar across the straits to attack the Grand Duchy. War ensues, but Atiana makes it away safely by hiding within the massive city of Baressa. What she doesn't realize is that her mind is not her own. She's caught in Sariya's spell, and has been for some time. Sariya forces Atiana to return and surrender the third piece of the Atalayina. With this in hand, Sariya goes to Muqallad and together, in another grisly ritual, they make the Atalayina whole.

The war, however, has reached the shores of Galahesh. The forces of the Grand Duchy, led by Nikandr's father, Iaros, have crossed the treacherous seas and are pushing toward the Spar to prevent Muqallad and Sariya from performing their final ritual, the one that will bring about indaraqiram. They manage to hold off the forces of Yrstanla long enough to reach the Spar, and there, in a final confrontation, Atiana puts Sariya's powers in check while Nasim and Nikandr move against Muqallad. Sariya is killed shortly before Muqallad reaches the center of the Spar. Nasim, however, uses a knife to stab Nikandr in the chest. He does so because of the thread that had been tying them together ever since the two met one another on Khalakovo five years before. This frees Nasim. He is finally able to control his abilities, and he moves to stop Muqallad from completing the ritual. As Nasim and Muqallad battle, a ship piloted by Grigory Bolgravya crashes into the Spar, killing Muqallad and sending Nasim and Nikandr down toward the turbulent waters below. Nasim uses the Atalayina to heal Nikandr, but then he is taken by Kaleh, the daughter of Sariya. They crash deep into the water and are lost.

Nikandr discovers after the battle that his father, Iaros, has been killed in battle. Nikandr and Atiana have now both lost their fathers to this struggle. They fear the worst for Nasim, but they believe Kaleh escaped with the Atalayina. Knowing that powerful stone cannot be left in her hands, they vow to go and find her, wherever the trail may lead.

PROLOGUE

At first light, deep within the massive Palotza Radiskoye, Styophan Andrashayev sat in a chair near the largest bed he'd ever slept in while his wife busied herself around the room, preparing them both for the coronation. Styophan's dress uniform lay on the bed. The pants he already wore, but the white shirt and the silk scarf and the black cherkesska, the one upon which all his medals were pinned, lay there, waiting to be donned.

"Hurry yourself," Rozalyna said.

He slipped one boot partway on and used two wood-handled hooks to pull at the straps inside the boots until his foot slid home. The boots were a deep and beautiful black. They'd been polished by Rozalyna yesterday, hours before the coach had come for them at their home on the outskirts of Volgorod. She polished them again last night after they'd arrived and been shown to their opulent rooms in the palotza's northern wing. She'd tried to do so again this morning, but he'd refused her. "You'll wear them through the way you go at them."

She'd huffed while washing her face in the porcelain basin. "If I left it up to you, you'd go in your long clothes."

After pulling on the second boot, Styophan stretched them, trying to work out the tightness. He'd never had the chance to break them in, and now he'd be limping from blisters on a day that should have brought honor to him and his entire family.

He pulled on his shirt and tied the red scarf tightly around his neck so that the shirt's collar stood up, slipped into his cherkesska, and stood before the mirror. "'Twould be a sight, wouldn't it?"

He could see Roza in the mirror, sitting on the edge of the bed and brushing her long brown hair. The sound of it was like leaves being raked in the distance. "What would?"

"Everyone wearing long clothes to the coronation?"

1

Roza leveled her stare at him, the one that told him she was not pleased, but then she burst out laughing. "Could you see that fat Borund walking in with his stained bed shirt to hand Ranos the scepter?"

"He wouldn't dare take up Iaros's scepter."

"If it's a fancy we're talking about, I'll have that fat slob wearing a stained bed shirt and handing the scepter of Khalakovo to Ranos if I want."

It was his turn to stare, but he couldn't keep it up. He broke down laughing. "Scepter in one hand, ham hock in the other."

Roza laughed so hard her face turned red and she wiped tears from her eyes.

"Be quiet," Styophan said. "You'll wake our neighbors."

It took her long moments of rolling laughter before she could speak again. "I don't think we *have* neighbors, Styopha." She finished her brushing and came to his side by the mirror. She looked him up and down, her pride showing clear.

He tried to see what she saw. But in himself he could only see a soldier that had failed his commander. He looked at the scars along his right cheek, at the patch over his right eye. His bloody right eye. Why did it have to be the right? He could still remember the akhoz—that foul, misshapen child—crawling up his sword and grabbing his jaw and pulling herself along until she was able to snatch his wrist, then his neck, and finally his head. It had all happened so quickly. Her withered hands had grabbed his skull like a gourd, her right thumb piercing his eye. By his father's fathers, it had been agony. What was worse, though, was the realization that he had failed to save his lord, Prince Nikandr, that he'd failed to wake Princess Atiana from the spell that had been put upon her. No matter that they had both lived—it had been no thanks to him.

"Stop thinking about it," Roza said.

He took a deep breath, taking in the coat, the boots, the scarf. He looked a right proper soldier. But he was an impostor. Ranos might be giving him a medal today, perhaps an assignment, but he'd be giving it to the wrong man.

"*Stop it.*" She put her arm around him and pulled him tight. "A prouder wife there never was, and you should be proud, too."

"I may have to go again."

"As you've said, but even if you hadn't, the wife of a strelet at war knows such things."

He drew his gaze down to her. She still wore her nightdress. Through the supple cloth he could see the curve of her hips, the swell of her breasts. He turned to face her and pulled her into a deep embrace, smelling the scent of rosewater on her skin. He drank in the form of her, his hand against the small of her back, his hips pressed tight against hers, his lips against the soft round of muscle just behind her ear. How had he lived so long without her?

And how would he do so again?

Roza tried to pull away. "We're due at the *ceremony*, Styophan!"

"The ceremony can wait." He pulled her tight and together they fell into the bed. She struggled as he kissed her neck, right where she liked it. He slipped one hand beneath her dress and caressed her thighs.

"Stypoha…" She spoke his name—half rebuke, half invitation. She made no move to stop him as he moved his hand slowly up. She drew breath sharply when he reached the silky place between her thighs. A slow moan escaped her as he began stroking her there.

She pushed his shoulders away, but not hard. She closed her eyes, arched her neck back, drew her pelvis higher as her moaning intensified. She regarded him with a slow, smoldering look, and then she flipped him over and straddled his waist. She pressed herself against him, thighs tightening over his hips, hair tickling his face as she bit his ear. "Perhaps it can wait for a bit," she whispered.

He drew her in for a kiss as warm as a winter fire. "Just don't make me take off my boots."

She looked back, confused, and then dissolved into laughter. A more beautiful sound he'd never heard.

As he pulled off her dress and she scooted his pants down to his thighs—going no further than the tops of his tight dress boots—he lost himself in her form. He knew it was partly so he wouldn't have to think about Galahesh—he also knew that in another day he might regret what he was doing, or at least the *reason* he was doing it—but right then, he didn't care.

And then, as she settled down on top of him, a moan escaped *his* lips.

Styophan watched, Rozalyna by his side, as Prince Nikandr handed his brother, Ranos, the scepter of Khalakovo. The two brothers wore their long coats of office—bright medals and the golden seal of Khalakovo pinned over their right breast, epaulets of golden thread resting on their shoulders. Their tall black boots, every bit as polished as Styophan's, glinted under the soft light that suffused the room. They stood on a dais. The ducal throne of Khalakovo rested behind them. Dozens were in attendance, but there were many notable in their absence. Some had been taken by the war, some by disease, some by old age. The courts of Khalakovo were changing, but at least it was back in rightful hands.

Styophan was close enough to the front of the assemblage that he could see Ranos's hands tremble as he held the scepter. There was no expression of joy on his face, no sense of satisfaction that the interloper, Borund, had finally left Khalakovo's shores. His was an expression of sadness, as if he wished for nothing more than to turn and hand the scepter to his father.

And yet, as quickly as this expression came, it fled, and Ranos straightened. He turned to those gathered and raised the scepter and said, "For the throne!"

"For the throne!" the crowd yelled back, and then everyone began clapping while the military men stomped their feet.

Nikandr, standing next to Ranos, cheered along with everyone else, but there was a certain lifelessness in his eyes that Styophan had often seen since the events at the Spar. He didn't know what had happened. He heard something about Nikandr being wounded. Some said he had been stabbed by Muqallad. Others said Soroush. Some even said Nasim had done it, though how this could be, from a boy as gentle as Nasim, Styophan couldn't guess. The one time Styophan had broached the subject, Nikandr had refused to speak of it, so Styophan left it alone, figuring Nikandr would share the story if and when he wished.

Styophan looked to the opposite side of the aisle and saw Princess Atiana. She was smiling—beaming—as she watched Ranos with Nikandr by his side. The joy of it filled Styophan's heart as well. The man who had led Khalakovo through the storm had passed, and now a strong young man was taking his place. As the crowd continued to clap, as the streltsi, young and old, continued to stomp, Atiana turned her head and caught Styophan's eye.

Styophan felt a chill run through him. He could think of nothing in that moment but the princess staring down at him coldly as the akhoz, that shriveled, rotted girl, clawed her way toward his throat. He wondered what had happened afterward. Why had he not been killed? Had Atiana found some small ounce of compassion, or had the fact that he still breathed simply gone overlooked? The look on Atiana's face was not one of apology, but there was something like regret. As the clapping died down at last, she tipped her head, as if she too had felt the victim that cold morning in the streets of Vihrosh.

Suddenly the sharp sound of bells filled the room, and everyone turned their heads. The doors leading to the great room were opened. Servants stepped in carrying small silver handbells. They rang them in time, walking slowly and leading the crowd into the adjoining room where a feast would be held. As he was bid, however, Styophan remained, giving Roza a kiss on her cheek before she left.

She looked up to him, with a smile as wide as the seas. She knew that this was an honor for him. She also knew—for he'd told her—that he would likely receive his next commission at this meeting, whatever it might be. She knew he might be called away, and yet here she was, eyes proud, tears of joy gathering at their corners. She squeezed his hand one last time and then followed the rest.

Soon the doors had been closed and Styophan was left with seven other officers of the Grand Duchy's wind corps, the staaya, as well as Ranos and Nikandr. In turn, Ranos greeted each man, thanking them for their service in the conflict on Galahesh. There was Artur Edikov, a grizzly old officer who led a vicious, even foolish, countercharge when the forces of Yrstanla had nearly routed the

Grand Duchy's troops near the base of the Mount in Baressa. There was Denis Gennadov, a dark-faced hussar with his left arm in a sling, his hand now missing. He had charged through deep ranks of janissaries to reach a cannon position near the straits that had been laying waste to a line of advancing streltsi. He and his hussari on their fearless ponies had laid waste to the cannoneers, allowing the streltsi to advance at last. There was Aleg Kastayov, a young, wide-eyed strelet with a shock of blond hair—he couldn't have been more than sixteen—who had found his commander unconscious behind the enemy lines and had carried him through the city streets until he reached a physic.

And on it went, hero after hero, making Styophan wonder why *he* would be counted among them. He had done nothing. He had failed when it had counted most. His lord had been taken. His men had all been lost.

He caught Nikandr staring at him. His Lord Prince had a look in his eye that Styophan didn't quite know how to interpret. He seemed ashamed, somehow, though whether it was because of his own actions, or Styophan's, he couldn't say.

As Duke Ranos read off the accomplishments of each man, he gave them a medal—in the case of Denis, he received two—and then he took them into tight embraces, slapping their backs and kissing their cheeks. The men bowed and were asked to leave, one by one, until it was clear that Styophan would be the last. No one would be here to see the Duke speak to him—only the Duke himself and Prince Nikandr—which made it clear that for him there would be no medal. For him there would be no honor. Why they would make him watch this ceremony he did not know, but his gut wrenched at the notion that it was for no good reason at all.

Finally, the sixth officer left through doors behind Styophan. As they had for the others, the crowd clapped as he entered. When the door closed, it sounded like a gavel, for the sound in the room dropped to an ominous silence.

Ranos stepped in front of Styophan. He had rarely seen Ranos up close. The Duke was a young man still, not quite forty years old. Grey streaks ran through his closely cut, dark brown hair. His russet-colored eyes were hard. They weighed Styophan while giving little away in turn. There was much of Iaros in him, but his eyes… Those were his mother's.

"My brother has spoken well of you, Styophan Andrashayev."

Styophan bowed his head. "As you say, My Lord Duke."

"He's spoken well of your time together on the winds. You are stout and hard-willed, and yet you listen to your men when needed."

Styophan bowed his head again, trying hard to keep his eyes fixed on Ranos and not Nikandr, who stood on the dais near the throne.

"We've spoken much about those final hours on the Spar, but Nikandr remembers little beyond the time his mind was taken. What can you tell me of it?"

"In truth, My Lord, I can tell you little. I continued to fight after My Lord Prince had fallen, but the akhoz and the Hratha… They were too many, and we were quickly overrun. I was taken by the akhoz, and I thought surely my ancestors had come for me, but I awoke early in the morning, when the great storm was still raging. A woman and her husband were over me, dragging me into their home, to safety." Styophan motioned to his ruined eye, the scars on his face. His heart was pounding, and his eye, though six weeks had passed since those events on Galahesh, was still not fully healed, and just then it hurt terribly. "They bandaged my wounds, helped me as much as they were able, until the following day when the streltsi began to arrive in Vihrosh. I was taken then to a proper physic and eventually brought back here to Uyadensk."

"You have a wife."

"I do, My Lord."

"I'm glad for it," Ranos said. "I truly am. And I wonder if I should give you a choice at all."

Styophan shook his head, confused. "My Lord?"

At this Ranos turned, and Nikandr stepped forward with a shallow wooden box. Ranos lifted the hinged lid and from within cradled a golden medal with a ribbon of purple and white. The medal was fashioned into a hawk, talons bared, eyes fierce.

A medal of valor. For him…

Ranos stepped forward and pinned it onto the left breast of Styophan's cherkesska, above all the other medals. He spoke while adjusting the medal just so. "With quick and decisive action—even despite Nikandr's orders—you saved his life on Rafsuhan. You returned for him, when others might have left. You sent him away on Galahesh after the gunpowder had been taken, and you've protected him in battle dozens of times. This is all reason enough for me to grant you a title and give you a keep here on the islands. And so I wonder if I shouldn't simply grant you that and give you your time with your wife." Apparently satisfied, Ranos stopped fussing with the medal and stood tall, hands clasped behind his back. "But troubled winds lay ahead, Styophan, son of Andrasha. Bahett ül Kirdhash has retreated to Alekeşir. He's ingratiated himself with the Kamarisi's eldest son, and he's been appointed regent. He is already gathering forces so that he can return to Oramka and Galahesh, so that he can retake them either in hopes of returning to his seat on Galahesh or, more likely, to gain a larger title under the newly proclaimed Kamarisi when he comes of age.

"I have need of men like you, but still, I would grant you your title and your keep if you've thought better of your place in the staaya." Ranos motioned to Styophan's eye. "Ancients know you deserve it, and you've been serving our house for nearly twenty years already. No stain upon you or your house were you to decide that is what you wish. It's why I've saved you until last. Whatever your choice, the decision won't leave this room."

"Of course, My Lord."

"So I put it to you. Would you stay here on Khalakovo? Or would you take to the winds?"

Styophan could only stare. He'd never even considered the option of leaving the staaya. Truth to tell, ever since Nikandr had chosen him for service in his own personal unit, he'd never considered leaving his side.

But to be in a keep? A lord of Khalakovo? A lord of Anuskaya? He was stunned. He could live there with Rozalyna. They could have the children they'd always wanted. They'd tried, many times. It seemed to be difficult for her, but if they lived here, he was sure she could have a child. And he could watch his son grow, watch him run along the halls of a keep, or outside it along the snowy grass in winter.

He looked to Nikandr, who had been strangely silent through this whole affair. That same look of shame was on his face, and Styophan was sure it had to do with his assignment, were he to take on a new commission.

"Forgive me, My Lord Duke," Styophan said, "but if I were to accept this new commission, where would I go?"

Ranos cleared his throat. "This is sensitive, Styophan."

"Of course, My Lord."

"One month ago a woman of Hael made her way to these shores. I spoke to her in this very room with Nikandr. She is a wodjan. Do you know the term?"

"I've heard it spoken."

"And what do the wodjana do?"

"In truth I know little. I've heard they perform heathen rituals, and that they act as healers for their tribe."

Ranos nodded. "They're soothsayers. They claim to see the future."

Styophan chuckled. "A lot of good that's done the Haelish."

Ranos shrugged and gave Styophan a smile that told him he'd be foolish to underestimate the Haelish. "Who can say? What might the Haelish have become without their wodjana? Yrstanla is vast and powerful. They may not have wodjana, they may not have Matri, but they have overwhelming numbers. They have gunpowder and they have steel. In any case, this has little to do with why she came. She came to treat with us. She asked us to send rooks to speak with the Kings. She asked us to offer aid to the Haelish so that they might take up their war with Yrstanla, which she says they are ready to put down."

"Why would they abandon a war they've waged for generations?"

The sound of clapping and laughing rose up from the next room. Ranos glanced that way and then regarded Styophan seriously. "She would not say."

Styophan worked this through in his mind. "She came at the behest of the Haelish Kings?"

"I think only the wodjana know. Much as the Matri work here, the women of Hael form their own counsel, and they advise the Kings in their way. She asked that I speak with our Grand Duke."

"And what had the Grand Duke to say of it?"

Ranos smiled a humoring smile. "The Grand Duke thought our ships would be better spent as firewood than giving them over to Hael—or worse, to Yrstanla. He thought any gems we might grant the Haelish would be better served as jewelry for dogs than to give them to the Haelish warriors. He believes them impotent, ready to fade into history, and so he bid me to keep our ships moored, to keep our gems locked away." Ranos paused, running a hand down his trim moustache and beard. "What have you to say to that, Styophan son of Andrasha?"

Styophan was not a man accustomed to the halls of power, but he chose his next words as carefully as he could. "It seems as though the Haelish might prove a distraction, and that however small it might be, it could be worth a few gemstones."

Ranos's smile turned genuine. "Yrstanla will come. They will attack. And in doing so they will all but ignore the Haelish. For now the Kings know little enough of our war, and when they *do* hear of the conflict, they may think it small. They might even think it a ruse formulated by the Kamarisi. But we need them. They must attack the Empire, for in this lies our only hope of blunting the forces of Yrstanla that now gather, preparing to head east. Three weeks ago I sent a rook to the Haelish. Ishkyna Vostroma spoke with them for eleven days. They've agreed to treat with us. I would have you go, Styophan. I would have you fly westward, over the bulk of the Motherland and down along the great mountains until you reach Haelish lands. I would have you tell them what's happening so that they can come to our aid—or their own, as they may see it. Now is the time to strike, for if we wait and simply entrench, as the Grand Duke would have us do, we will be doomed."

"And the Grand Duke?"

Ranos pulled himself taller. "This is why it must go to someone like you, Styophan. The North must tend to Anuskaya if the Grand Duke will not."

"Would I be going with My Lord Prince?"

"You would not," Nikandr said, stepping off the dais and moving to Ranos's side. "There are other places I must go."

"Were I given the choice," Styophan said, bowing his head, "I would accompany you."

Ranos shook his head. "That's not the choice you've been given. You are needed elsewhere." The Duke took a deep breath as someone in the next room began to make sounds like a snorting bull and laughter rose around it. "And so it comes to it. Think on it tonight. Stay here in Radiskoye, and we'll speak in the morning. I will have your answer then."

Ranos did not speak as if this were punishment, but it somehow felt like it, or at the very least as if it had been Nikandr's choice all along. Part of him wanted to take the lordship and be done with this life. But what would he be if he took it and left the Grand Duchy wanting? He could not take the lordship and simply wait as the war raged on. He had to go. He had to see his country safe. Only then could he settle with Rozalyna.

How he was going to tell her, he didn't know.

Please forgive me, Roza. "I can give you my answer now, My Lord Duke."

Ranos paused. He glanced to Nikandr at his side, and then met Styophan's gaze. Again he seemed to be weighing Styophan. "Go on, then."

"I will go west. I will find the Haelish and bring them down like a hammer on the crown of Yrstanla, if that is what you wish."

Ranos's face did not change for a breath, perhaps two, but then he smiled proudly, slapped Styophan's shoulders, and took him into a fierce embrace.

PART I

CHAPTER ONE

Nikandr grunted as he attacked the rocky red slope. He pushed as well as he was able, but he still had several hundred yards before he would reach the summit, so he stopped and leaned against a boulder the bright color of coral. His breath left him so quickly here. A hot wind blew, picking up dust and forcing him to draw his ghoutra across his face. Even so, he had to squint against the dust and the bite of the sand. The wind pulled at his kaftan and the loose pants he wore beneath, until at last the wind died down.

The path he was following was easy enough to spot, but it was also treacherous. It was important he be able to see far enough into the desert beyond, though. Soroush and Ushai had already been gone a day longer than planned, and he'd told Atiana that they would stay only one more night. If they didn't return by tomorrow morning, Atiana, Nikandr, Ashan, and Sukharam would have to go into Andakhara to learn what had become of them.

Behind Nikandr was a vale with a meager stream running through it. They'd timed their entrance to the desert to take advantage of the spring rains, but the gentle weather wouldn't last much longer. It made it all the more important for them to get into the Gaji and out before it became too dry.

His breath had returned. There was part of him that didn't want to complete this climb. He knew what would happen at the top. It scared him, and yet he was unable to deny the urge to go there, to look upon the desert below from such a height, so he took to the path once more. His breathing became labored halfway up, but he pushed now that he was so close. Near the top the slope was not so brutal, but he still found it impossible to catch his breath. Eventually, however, he came to a narrow ridge.

The wind here was cooler. It blew more fiercely than below. Ahead of him, the red desert floor opened up. It went on forever, flat as could be. Who would have guessed that so much land could be amassed in one place? He was so used to the islands, so used to the span of the sea, that he never thought what it would be like to see something so grand and humbling as this. It was a dangerous place, but beautiful, perhaps more so *because* of the danger.

He stared at the edge of the cliff ahead. The ridge was wide in places, but this was its highest point, and also the narrowest. Only a score of paces separated him from the edge.

He stepped forward, feeling the wind against his fingertips.

He took another step, felt the soles of his boots scrape.

He had hoped, in the days that had followed the events at the bridge on Galahesh, that his sense of the wind would return to him. He had hoped that he could once more feel the touch of the havahezhan. He had hoped he could summon the wind as he once had. But the days had turned into weeks, and the weeks into months, and still he felt nothing. He had tried from the towers of Galostina, and later, Radiskoye. He had tried from the mountains of Uyadensk. He had tried from the perches of the eyrie and the decks of windships. But each and every time, he'd felt nothing.

As was true now.

He took another step forward.

The wind gusted, tugging at his clothes.

He breathed deep, swallowing the spit that filled his mouth now that he was so very near the edge.

The desert yawned wider and wider, and yet it was not this he was most aware of, but the sheer height of this vantage.

With one more long step he reached the edge. The wind howled for a moment along the face of the cliff below. The desert seemed as wide as the sky. The ground was rocky, the vegetation sparse. The red floor of the dry plain ahead felt limitless. In the distance, below the cloudless blue sky, was a line of dark mountains, but it didn't feel like they encompassed the desert, or even obstructed it in any way. It felt as if the mountains were merely one small obstacle, and that the desert continued on and on, eating more of the world as it went.

In those mountains was a village named Kohor, an ancient place where they could learn more of the Gaji and the secretive tribes that had for centuries remained hidden from the world. Closer, much closer, was a caravanserai, little more than a few dozen red-stone buildings with a well and a thousand-year-old trade route running through it. It was another stop on their journey toward the mountains, and the place Soroush and Ushai had gone the day before to secure them passage with a caravan.

Nikandr's eyes were drawn to the base of the cliff where a whirlwind rose and twisted on the wind before spinning away into nothingness. Nikandr knew it was a havahezhan slipping momentarily into the world of Erahm, playing with the wind before being drawn back to Adhiya.

He often noticed such things. He didn't want to; he simply did, and it made him painfully aware of the weight around his neck. For weeks after the events on Galahesh, he'd reached for his soulstone and gripped it tightly in his hand, hoping to feel the wind spirit—the havahezhan—he'd been bonded to ever since seeing Soroush on the cliffs below Palotza Radiskoye six years ago. He would eventually release his grip, for he felt nothing, and knew that he never would. His bond to that spirit had been broken the moment Nasim had driven the khanjar into his chest.

He scraped his feet forward. The tips of his boots were now only inches from the edge.

There were days when he wished he'd never gone to Galahesh—days when he wished he could once again feel the touch of the havahezhan, to summon the wind with mere thought—but he knew such hopes to be foolish. Had those events not occurred, Nasim would never have been freed. He would never have been able to stop Muqallad. And the world would have ended.

In the distance, another whirlwind lifted and twisted and fell. He knew it was foolish to think of such things, but still...

He inched one foot forward. He settled his weight onto the other, afraid to lift it from the dry earth lest he do something foolish.

He pulled the ghoutra from his face, pulled the headband from around his head and tossed it to the dirt behind him. With shaking hands, he spread his arms wide, tilted his head back, closed his eyes. He felt the sun upon his face, felt the wind through his hair. He breathed deeply and took in the scents of the desert—sage and baked earth and the strange spiky bushes that smelled like burning cedar.

He could feel the wind running through his fingers, could feel it tug at his kaftan and the white cotton legs of his sirwaal.

He recalled where his journey had begun. Before Galahesh, before Ghayavand. Before Nasim had been healed.

Before Rehada had died.

He had flown above his homeland, the island of Uyadensk. Soroush and his Maharraht had come to gather elemental stones for a ritual. One of them had stood at the edge of a cliff, as he stood now. He had spread his arms, looked up to the sky. And he'd leapt. He'd leapt from the cliffs, and the winds had saved him. They'd borne him upward until setting him gently down like a thrush alighting on a lonely branch.

Nikandr had thought much on that day. That spirit, the one the man had called forth, was the one that had attached itself to him, an elder, a spirit of the wind so old, the Aramahn said, that it had been eons since it had crossed over from

Erahm, preferring, for whatever reason, the world of the spirits to the world of the living. Centuries ago, the Aramahn and Maharraht had no need of stones for summoning spirits. They'd done it on their own, as Nasim and Muqallad did. But before them, when the earliest of wandering desert tribesmen were first learning how to tame the spirits, they did what that lone man on that cliff had done. They gave of themselves. They *offered* themselves to the spirits. They did so in small ways at first. Submerging themselves in water, covering themselves in dirt, running their hands over flames. But as their thirst for knowledge and power grew, they tried things that seemed more and more desperate. Those aligned with water would drown themselves. Those aligned with fire would burn themselves. Those aligned with earth would bury themselves.

And those aligned with wind would offer themselves to it. They would find mountains, cliffs, gorges. They would find the highest points they could, and they would leap. They did so not hoping for a bond, but to *understand* the wind in a way they never had before, and it was this state of mind that the hezhan were attracted to. Many carried fear in their hearts—they were not able to wholly commit themselves—and they died. Those that leapt with complete freedom, however, were rewarded with power beyond anything the world had yet seen.

Nikandr had not known it at the time—how could he have?—but this is what the Maharraht on that cliff had done. He had believed in what he was doing so completely that when he had leapt, an elder havahezhan had come.

There had been times over the past many months that Nikandr had stood at the edge of a precipice like this, and he'd felt, almost, that he could touch Adhiya. It felt near enough that he could step forward and he would become part of it. It felt like it would embrace him, envelop him and protect him as it once had.

He felt this way now. The space before him was so large, so deep and so wide, that it beckoned him.

His feet shifted. He heard the skitter of stones as they fell over the edge and slipped down along the face of the cliff, but he didn't care. Stones might fall, but he would not.

The scuff of leather against stone came to him. The crunch of footsteps on gravel.

Nikandr opened his eyes.

Looked down.

Saw the height from which he now stood, and wondered what it would be like to crash against the stones below.

The footsteps came closer.

He licked his lips. They were dry. So dry. How long had he been up here?

He looked to the western horizon. The sun was lowering. Already it was approaching the distant line of dark mountains.

He'd been here for hours, he realized. Hours. How could time have passed so quickly?

"Nikandr?"

He stepped back. One step, then two. And then he turned around.

Ashan stood some ten paces away, alternating glances between Nikandr and the edge of the cliff a long stride behind him. "You've been gone a long time."

"So has Soroush."

"So he has." Ashan studied Nikandr's face. He sidestepped along the rocky ground toward the edge, always keeping himself square to Nikandr. Only when he'd reached the edge did he look down at the outpost, Andakhara.

Ashan looked old. He looked old and weary. Much had been taken from him on the island of Ghayavand. He still managed to smile—he hadn't lost that—but it seemed to tax him, whereas before it had always been effortless, a spring of good will flowing up from inside him.

"Come," Ashan said, putting his arm around Nikandr's shoulders. "Soroush and Ushai will return in the morning."

Nikandr allowed himself to be led away from the edge and toward the trail. He hoped Ashan was right. The Gaji was a dangerous place. And not only because those who failed to give her respect died.

CHAPTER TWO

Atiana left her tent when she heard footsteps approaching. She wore a shayla, a dress cut in the style of the desert tribes, patterned red and white with tiny silver bells at the hem that jingled as she walked. She wore a veil across her face with a delicate chain hanging down from the ivory outer cloak she wore to keep the sun away. It protected her from the ever-present sand and dust, but more importantly, it did much to hide her origins here in the desert.

She looked toward the trail leading down from the steep ridge above their campsite and saw Ashan and Nikandr walking together. She busied herself at the fire, forming the dough she'd made hours earlier into a circle and setting it onto the stone that had been sitting above the coals to gather heat. She sprinkled the dough with cumin and cardamom and flax, the scent of it filling the dry, desert air as the flatbread cooked. Next to the bread she placed lengths of eggplant. She waited while they cooked, keeping her gaze from Nikandr but seeing him approach from the corner of her eye.

Ashan squatted next to the fire. He rested on his heels and rocked slowly back and forth. It was a position Atiana had never gotten the hang of, but for him seemed every bit as comfortable as lying down.

Without looking at her, without giving any word as to why he'd been gone for so long, Nikandr retreated to the tent he shared with Atiana.

Ashan rested his chin on his knees and stared at the flatbread. "He's only worried about Soroush."

What a strange thing to hear. Years ago, Nikandr might have hung Soroush before speaking to him. Now there was still a certain distance that separated them, but one would be a fool not to think of them as friends. It was telling as well that Ashan had referred only to Soroush and not Ushai. Nikandr would not have wished her to come with them to the desert. Neither would Atiana.

Ushai had been Maharraht. Atiana supposed she was still, but like Soroush, she had set aside her hatred of the Grand Duchy while they searched for Kaleh and Nasim in this vast desert. Despite their misgivings, Soroush had fought bitterly for her place in their party. It went beyond the fact that the two of them were lovers. Ushai had roots in the Gaji. Her father was from Kohor. She'd taken to the winds with her mother, who was Aramahn, when she was only eight, but she still remembered it in bits and glimpses. In the end, they'd agreed that her blood ties to that place could prove useful.

Atiana could hear Nikandr rooting around the tent, no doubt for a mouthful of vodka. Whatever truth there was in Ashan's words—she had no doubt he *was* worried about Soroush—there was more bothering him. One could not be near him and not know of it. It was his link to Adhiya. A year and a half had passed since the events at the Spar on Galahesh, and a day didn't go by when Nikandr didn't seem maudlin or reticent. She tried to find ways to reach him, to pull him from his doldrums—and indeed, there were times when he seemed to brighten, giving her hope—but then a day would pass, perhaps two, and he would return to his yearning.

"How long do we wait for them?" Atiana asked, referring to Soroush and Ushai.

"If they're not back by morning, we'll continue as planned, and hopefully find them at the caravanserai."

Footsteps crunched over the ground toward them. It was Sukharam, the boy Nasim had found and brought to Ghayavand with him. He was gifted—as gifted as Nasim, if Ashan was to be believed—but that wasn't why Ashan had insisted he be brought. *His fate is entwined with Nasim's,* Ashan had said before the journey had begun. *We can no more forget about him than we can Kaleh, or the Atalayina.*

Sukharam was a grown young man of sixteen now. He pulled up the hem of his flax-colored robes and knelt between her and Ashan. He reached for the flatbreads, perhaps to test them, perhaps to steal a bite, but Atiana slapped his hand away. He scowled, but Atiana paid him no mind. She quickly flipped the flatbreads over, each landing on the cookstone with a sizzle.

"I don't like the feel of this," Sukharam said. "Any of it."

Ashan watched Sukharam intently. "There's no reason to think that anything's gone amiss."

Sukharam looked to his right, toward the caravan route that would take them to the plains below. "Those that live here in the desert... They're secretive."

"As much as the people of the desert might isolate themselves, the caravanserais are run by the Empire. They are the Kamarisi's people. We should worry about him, not the locals."

Atiana flipped the eggplant and sprinkled it with coarse grains of salt and pepper.

"You may not see it," Sukharam said, "but they have a distrust of us. I saw it at the edge of the desert. I've seen it in each of the caravanserais we've visited. They may pledge their loyalty to the Kamarisi in the light of day, but in the dark of the night they serve the desert, and the desert does not want us."

"I've been here many times before," Ashan replied. "They watch travelers they do not know, true, but they watch everyone, even people from other caravanserais, other villages."

Sukharam was staring at the cookstone—he was a young man, and young men were always hungry—but then he glanced up at Atiana with a sullenness she'd seen on him often.

Atiana pulled up one of the flatbreads, quickly snatching two of the eggplant strips and folding the bread over it. She handed it to Ashan, whose face brightened as he accepted it. Atiana did the same for the next, handing this one to Sukharam. Only when she'd made the third, and set more dough and eggplant onto the stone for Nikandr, did she turn to Sukharam. "You can say it."

He took a bite of his bread and spoke as he chewed. "You shouldn't have come. You should have left this to us."

By *us* he meant himself and Ashan and even Soroush and Ushai. In his eyes, the four of them had more of a right than Atiana and Nikandr to be here in the desert chasing after the Atalayina.

"Nasim needs us."

"Nasim needs his own people," Sukharam shot back.

Ashan took a large bite of the flatbread, which steamed where he'd bitten into it. He stared at Atiana and then at Sukharam, his eyebrows pinching in concern. "It's that kind of attitude that put you in those mines, Sukharam."

Sukharam's eyes glowed fiercely. "And perhaps if I'd fought back they'd think twice over doing so again."

"The way to vashaqiram is through peace. Only through peace."

"And maybe one day we'll be free enough to find it. But until then—"

"Don't allow Ushai's ways to cloud your mind, Sukharam."

Indeed, Atiana thought. The two of them had been talking often over the course of the past many months. Soroush may have set aside his violent ways—at least for now—but Ushai had not, and she'd been plying Sukharam with them for some time. At first she'd seen no change in Sukharam, but more and more he'd brought up notions like this. Fighting. Resisting. But at what cost?

Sukharam stared at his flatbread as if it suddenly disgusted him. "Haven't you ever thought you might be wrong, Ashan? How would you know the way to vashaqiram? You won't reach it in this lifetime. You won't reach it in the next. We're all of us eons away from oneness with our world. Perhaps the way to vashaqiram is to cleanse the world of that which is wrong."

Ashan had been chewing, but he now stopped. He stared at Sukharam as if he just now realized how dangerously close he was to turning away from the path of peace. He swallowed his mouthful heavily. "You don't believe that."

Sukharam stared at Ashan, then to Atiana. His face was angry, but there was also a look of shame, as if he knew Ashan was right, as if he'd voiced half-formed thoughts without thinking. Without saying another word he stood and threw his flatbread into the dry scrub brush beyond their camp site. His footsteps crunched as he headed beyond the horses and behind the small hill where he'd spent most of the day taking breath.

"So much anger in him..." Atiana said.

Ashan took another bite of his flatbread. "We all have anger, daughter of Radia, Sukharam more than most. It's what we do with it that counts."

"That's what I'm afraid of. What Sukharam will do with his." She paused, letting those words sink in. "I wonder if we shouldn't send him back."

"A desire he leveled against you only moments ago." Ashan shook his head. "Make no mistake. As surely as the sun needs the moon, we need one another. We are bound together, all of us, by Nasim and the events that lay behind us. By the ones that lay before us as well. Now, we have but to carry one another to the end."

"You speak as if we're trapped by the fates," Atiana said, "but that's where you're wrong. We aren't bodies slipping through the firmament with no choice left to us. We are our own. *We* choose our destiny."

Ashan put the last of his flatbread into his mouth, smacking his lips noisily. When he spoke again, it was with a seriousness that surprised her. "Believe what you wish, daughter of Radia. We may try to escape the paths the fates have set for us, but they will have us in the end."

Atiana entered the tent, holding a cup of water and the still-warm flatbread for Nikandr. He was sitting cross-legged on their shared blanket, his eyes distant. She shook the flatbread at him, and he looked up, accepting it reluctantly.

"Eat," she said.

He took a mouthful and chewed as if he knew he needed the sustenance but could barely stomach the taste of it.

"Ashan said we would leave in the morning."

Nikandr stared at the wall of the tent as if he hoped to peer through it to the caravanserai beyond. "Is your sister near?"

Though she had tried to find Ishkyna that morning, she cast herself outward again, already knowing Ishkyna was too busy to speak with her. War was brewing to the northeast. Leonid had months ago secured Oramka and the nearby coast of Yrstanla, and he was now pushing westward to take as much of the continent as he could in hopes of blunting the Empire's response when at last it came. Only in the past few weeks had a sizable force been sent from Alekeşir, the capital of the Empire. More were headed south from the northern reaches. The desert tribes had been called upon as well, but they had long been hoping to throw off the yoke of the Kamarisi, and they'd been slow in responding. Still, the armies of Yrstanla were triple what the islands had so far gathered. Were it not for Ishkyna, Atiana would be worried, but with her and the other Matri, they had a good chance of turning the tide against the counter-assault that was sure to begin soon.

Ishkyna had helped lead them through the desert, and she had promised to find them each fortnight, but Ishkyna had been trying to find Kaleh ever since the events on Galahesh, with no success. Since those fleeting feelings she'd felt in the days that had followed the destruction of the Spar, there had been nothing.

"She won't come," Atiana said. "Not for several days yet."

"We need her to come more often."

"You know she cannot. The war—"

"I know the war's begun, Atiana, but here we are again, ignoring what needs to be done. It's the Atalayina that matters, and Ghayavand, not a hurried grab for power while the Empire marches east."

"I know. And Borund knows."

Nikandr couldn't even bring himself to scoff. He merely stared at her with cold, incredulous eyes.

"He *does*."

"He is a lapdog, as he ever was."

"Do not speak of my brother so! *Dhalingrad* is the Grand Duke, and he will brook no insult, no test of his authority. He's already hung dozens of men from his own duchy, and three from Bolgravya for what he saw as insubordination. Borund must be careful, especially since the spire on Kiravashya is still only half-built. The spoils from Yrstanla are being funneled to the duchies, but the lion's share goes to feed the mouths of Dhalingrad. And don't forget, Borund spared your life."

"How very gracious of him after killing seven innocent men and women in cold blood."

"You left him no choice! The Maharraht should have been brought somewhere else."

"Where could they have gone, Atiana?"

"Anywhere but under Borund's wing. Face it, you were thumbing your nose at him."

"I was saving those that had—"

"Nischka! I've heard it all a hundred times before! You could have brought them to Mirkotsk. You could have brought them to one of the smaller islands, to be ferried to Iramanshah later. By the ancients, you could have let them find their own way, wherever they wished to go. You didn't have to bring them to Khalakovo!"

Nikandr set his flatbread aside as if he were disgusted by it. He picked up a goat skin, realizing only then that it no longer held any vodka. He fumbled around the blankets until he found another, at which point he opened it and took a long pull from the liquor within.

Atiana stared, wishing she knew what to say. He was lost, and yet he was sitting right before her. They'd found a way to be with one another at last, and yet they were more distant than ever.

"Nikandr," she said softly, "this isn't about the hangings, and it isn't about Borund."

He stared with flat eyes and took another drink.

"If Nasim were dead, you'd know." She reached out and gripped his hand. He squeezed back, but it was practically lifeless. "We'll find him."

"I know," he lied.

Late that night, long after the sun went down, they lay on their blankets, their backs to one another. She felt him turn over. He was facing her, waiting for her to turn around. It was then, with that one simple gesture, that much of the tightness within her melted away. She turned toward him, hoping to see his smiling face. And he did smile. But she also saw within his eyes that haunted look. He might never be free of it, she realized. He might yearn for the touch of Adhiya for the rest of his life.

He pulled her close, and she laid her head against his chest. He breathed easier after that, and at last they fell asleep.

CHAPTER THREE

Styophan stood at the helm of the galleon *Vayetka*, one of the ships taken from Yrstanla after the Battle of Galahesh nearly two years ago. Theirs was the lead ship. Behind, trailing by an eighth-league, was the *Graaza*, another galleon, as were the three others in his wing that he'd flown all the way from Khalakovo's great eyrie.

He'd stood upon the decks of all five ships over the course of their three-month journey here, and he'd come to hate their design. They were slow to maneuver and too heavy by far. The shipwrights of the Empire knew little of building windworthy ships, but he had to admit that they were good for flying over land. The obsidian keels were larger than the ones used in the ships of the islands, which made them slow to turn but more capable of picking up the weaker ley lines over land.

"Yvan, take the helm."

Yvan, a broad-shouldered streltsi from Duzol, turned from the gunwales and snapped his heels. "*Da*, Kapitan."

Styophan relinquished control and moved to the forecastle, telescope in hand. When he brought the scope to his eye, he brought it to his right by accident. There were still dozens of things like this, things he used to do with his right eye and still *tried* to do even though the right side of his face was now little more than a ruined landscape of scars.

He adjusted and scanned the horizon ahead. They were flying to the western side of a long range of mountains, the Kuvvatli range. The mountains were tall and black with white caps and sheer cliffs, but they would soon dwindle and widen until they gave way to more open land and tall, rolling hills. This was the land of the Haelish and their tribal kings. They had for long centuries been loosely gathered bands, with many kings throughout their territories, and though there had been wars among them, there had also been peace.

Perhaps too much peace.

When Kamarisi Alhamid, Hakan's great-great-grandfather, reached their lands, he found them ripe for the picking. Yrstanla had ruled over them for a century and a half, but the Haelish did not forget the ruthless way in which they'd been subjugated, nor had they ever taken well to being yoked. They'd learned from the janissaries sent by the Kamarisi to rule their lands, and they'd overthrown them. At least for a time.

The Kamarisi had come again, this time Hakan's father, Ayeşe. He brought war to Haelish lands once more, this one a long, protracted conflict that he left to his son to finish. It was a war Hakan had twice thought won, but each time the Haelish had retreated into the highlands and had come back years later to overthrow the Kamarisi when they took their troops to other fronts and other wars.

And now Hakan's son, Selim, had inherited the war. He was too young to sit the throne, and so had been given a regent—Bahett ül Kirdhash, a man who had fought ruthlessly for the title and had eventually been granted it by Selim's uncles on the promise that Bahett knew the men of Anuskaya best, knew the way they fought and how to weaken them. Whether or not Bahett could deliver on his promises, Styophan didn't know. He was of half the mind that Bahett had simply said anything he could to gain the title and power he craved, but secretly he worried that Bahett was right. He *did* know the islands well, especially those among the south, and if he were any sort of strategist, he would know how weak Leonid had left them to the south. Grand Duke Leonid had piled so many resources along Oramka and the coastal cities.

Bahett didn't have Matri to find these things out for him, but he certainly had spies, and he'd have prisoners before too long. It was only a matter of time before he discovered just how soft Anuskaya's flanks were.

Styophan swung the scope over the landscape carefully, searching, certain that they'd reached Haelish lands but seeing no evidence of it so far. Perhaps the Haelish had been pushed further back than their spies in Alekeşir had reported, or perhaps they were better at hiding themselves than he gave them credit for. But then he saw a thin trail of smoke against the dark green forest. It was near a flat-topped hill on the westward side of the mountains, high enough that they could lose themselves in the mountains if they chose and low enough that they could reach the plains within a day's ride.

"Anahid, bring her down by half. Yvan, three points windward."

Anahid had been his stalwart companion on this trip. She and Avil and Mikhalai were the only ones still flying with him from his time with Prince Nikandr. Truly they deserved their own ships, but Styophan trusted them too much. When this was all done, he told himself, he would see to it that they became kapitans.

Styophan decided to take a single skiff; more and it would be seen as aggression. He loaded it with trusted men—Avil and Mikhalai and his own cousin, Rodion—and then Anahid guided them down. The smoke stopped as they approached, a clear indicator that they'd been spotted.

And now, for a reason he couldn't quite define, Styophan became nervous. He had no idea how the Haelish would view him. It was said that they were little better than barbarians, but Styophan had spoken to Isaak, the Duke's seneschal, in the days before leaving Khalakovo. He'd said that while they had been driven to primitive ways by their long war with Yrstanla, it wasn't always so. They had a rich history, and there were those among them that would remember. Few could read or write among the Haelish, but their history, passed down in song from father to son and mother to daughter, was a thing they took great pride in. If they didn't, Isaak had said, they would long ago have abandoned this war and succumbed to the might of Yrstanla.

They landed the skiff within a copse of linden trees and disembarked. Ten men plus Anahid. They took to the hill, which was thick with willow and oak and birch. Styophan took the lead, with the others walking single file behind him.

"Weapons at the ready," he said, "but no one draws until I say."

"*Da*, Kapitan," his men replied.

Anahid still had her circlet upon her brow, and in the setting there was an opal, glowing ever so softly under the light of day. She was bonded still with her dhoshahezhan. It was a weapon of sorts, but not one he would have her release. He felt better with her bonded to a spirit that might protect them.

When he glanced back at the men, he saw how tight they were. These were hardened men, and yet their eyes darted nervously about the forest. Avil was the worst of them. In a way, Styophan understood. They were as far from help as they could be. But the Haelish had agreed to accept weapons and gems from Anuskaya in return for their help here in the west.

"Avil," Styophan said. "Come with me." He strode ahead, far enough that they wouldn't be overheard. Avil caught up to him with a short jog. "I've seen you fight ten men with no fear," Styophan said to him. "Why do the Haelish affect you so?"

"They're heathens, Styopha. Bloody heathens. They practice foul rituals. When they capture their enemies, they take them to their villages and hang them up by their wrists and gut them while they're still alive. They take their blood and use it to peer into the future, and when they take to the battlefield once more, the misery of those they took find release. The screams of the dead pour from the throats of the Haelish warriors, for the dying had no chance to do so. They worship trees and hills, and they claim wives from their brothers and cousins. We shouldn't walk into their lands like this, a mere handful, weapons sheathed."

"We're here to ask for their help, Avil."

"We don't need help from the likes of them."

Styophan wished that were true. He didn't like coming here any more than Avil did, but there was no choice, and not simply because this had been a direct order from his Lord Duke. The Haelish could help turn the tide against Yrstanla. The Empire might be a wounded lion, but its claws could still rend flesh.

Still, Avil was merely voicing his fears, fears most of the men shared. Fears Styophan shared as well, though perhaps not to the same degree. The Haelish were fierce warriors—they were not to be taken lightly—but tales always grew in the telling. And besides, it was the *Empire* that had to worry about them, not the Grand Duchy.

As they hiked up the slope, the sounds of trilling and strange looping calls filled the forest. Had they not been walking to meet the Haelish, Styophan might not have known, but the timing was too convenient, so he began searching the landscape carefully for the first of them. He found them moments later. Tall men stepped out from behind trees, some near, some far. They wore breeches of thick leather, but no shirts. The skin on their chests and arms and faces were covered with a grey-green mud—even their hair was thick with it—making them difficult to see even though Styophan was staring right at them. They were muscular, these men, not the heavy muscles that landsmen who lifted cargo all day developed, but like windsmen who spent their days climbing rigging. They were lithe, with muscles like corded rope.

They slipped forward through the trees, their gait odd, like a cat's. They seemed barely aware of how carefully they were choosing their course over the leaf- and branch-strewn ground, but he was sure they were perfectly aware of just how silent they were, each and every one of them. Winter was coming—frost was on the ground—and yet they wore no shoes. Styophan was a man closely acquainted with the bitter winters of the islands, but he got cold just watching them approach.

"Hands clear of your weapons," Styophan said in Anuskayan. Then he raised both hands slowly.

Styophan was no small man, but one of the Haelish stood a full head taller than him. This one approached while the others stopped behind him. Styophan could see beneath the grey-green mud that his hair was a reddish brown. His eyes were the green of new summer growth, and though they might not be charitable, neither were they wicked.

"Are you Kürad?" Styophan asked in Yrstanlan.

"I am Datha," he replied in a thick accent, "but the King awaits us." He held out his hand and the two of them gripped one another's forearms in the way of the Haelish. His grip was short, perfunctory, as if he could barely stomach the presence of Anuskayan men in his lands. Datha, after looking over the streltsi, pointed to the crest of the slope behind him. "Come."

Styophan hadn't been sure until that moment whether these men were the ones they were supposed to meet. The fighting Haelish moved so often it was difficult to tell, and with Princess Ishkyna so occupied by the nascent war on Yrstanla's southeastern coast, he'd had no word to verify the final location where they would meet.

They went uphill for a quarter-league and then went down slope into another long valley that doglegged at a pond overrun with cattails. In a section of the forest dominated by twisted oak trees stood dozens of Haelish yurts. Their roofs were made of oiled leather, the walls of woven reed. It was strangely quiet, as if most had been killed, leaving the rest to grieve in silence. Somewhere in the distance a babe cried, but beyond this he heard little more than the soft clatter of the bright beads that hung from the arched entryways to the yurts.

As they were led toward a massive yurt at the center of the village, several children poked their heads around doorways. Some were pulled back by their mothers; others merely stared, their eyes hard as they sized up these strangers who had entered their home.

When they reached the yurt, Datha pulled aside the strings of wooden beads, as if he meant Styophan to enter, but before he could, Datha pointed to Avil and the others. "You may bring one other."

Styophan considered, and then motioned for Anahid to join him. She was the only one who'd been in Haelish lands before, even if it had been when she was young. Plus, she was learned; he'd come to value her counsel.

Together they ducked inside the yurt, where reed mats covered the earthen floor. Bright blankets with curving designs woven into them hung from the walls. Two dozen men and a handful of women sat in narrow chairs with low backs around a small, well-tended fire from which no smoke rose. The men wore thick leggings of leather, as the men outside did, and they also wore no shirts. There was no mud upon them, but several had umber paint in intricate designs over the skin of their chest and arms and neck. The designs reminded him of the traceries of the Aramahn, and though these were more primitive, they had that same feeling of being connected somehow to earth or sky or sea. The paint glittered like liquid gold.

One of these men, the one sitting on the far side, directly facing the entryway, wore a crown upon his head. The crown was not made of gold or silver or even brass, but of thick brown vines with sharp thorns. He wore the umber paint as well. It matched his deep brown eyes and his stony gaze. He was as old as Styophan's father. Like the other men gathered here, like the warriors that had greeted Styophan in the forest, he was lithe and muscular and clean-shaven.

No doubt this was Kürad.

The women wore soft clothes of buckskin and necklaces made from the same auburn-colored beads that hung from the doorways. One of them—the one sitting to the left of Kürad—drew Styophan's eye, for her eyes were sunken. She had hair the color of the beads around her neck, an auburn color so rich it reminded him of the boldest autumn leaves. Her cheeks were gaunt, her skin sallow, and she had that same grim look that Styophan had seen among the islands so often, especially of late.

The wasting, Styophan realized. The wasting had come even here, to Haelish lands.

Kürad stood as Styophan and Anahid approached. He spoke in Haelish, a language Styophan knew nothing of. Anahid said she knew some, but would be unable to reliably translate. The language was heavy and guttural. It sounded like the land here, simple and pristine. Primal.

When he finished, the diseased woman sitting to his right spoke in near-perfect Yrstanlan. "Kürad, son of Külesh, King of Clan Eidihla, bids you welcome. He asks if you've brought the promised stones."

Styophan could only stare. He'd brought them, of course—they'd demanded this of Ishkyna when she'd come to treat with them—but still, he'd expected introductions, perhaps a ceremonial greeting of some kind. Anything but this.

"My Lord," Styophan said, bowing his head to Kürad. "Perhaps we could discuss the state of affairs here in the west, and I could do the same for the war brewing in the east."

"The stones," the woman said.

Styophan reached into the leather satchel that hung from over his shoulder and held it out for the woman to take. She accepted it and brought it to Kürad, who opened the satchel and peered inside. He pulled out one of the tied silken bags within and untied the drawstring.

"Those are but a taste," Styophan said. "The rest are in chests on my ship."

The woman translated, and Kürad glanced over to Styophan, his gaze resting for a moment on Styophan's eye patch, and then he proceeded to spill the opals from the bag onto his upturned palm. He looked at them, tilting his palm this way and that under the sunlight that came in through the smoke hole above. He spoke his guttural tongue, and the woman nodded.

"Are the rest like this?" she asked.

"They are," Styophan said. And it was true. He'd looked at them all himself, and he'd chosen those that went into the bag, making sure they were neither the best nor the worst. The Haelish had for some reason asked for uncut stones. He knew they crushed the gemstones and worked them into paint that they slathered over their skin before battle. It imbued them, it was said, with the abilities of hezhan without communing with them directly as the Aramahn did. Their wicked magic was how they'd survived so long against Yrstanla, but Yrstanla had been successful at taking and holding the land that held much of Hael's gemstone mines, slowly tilting the war in their favor.

The woman, as tall as Styophan himself, gave Kürad his answer. Kürad closed the bag and hefted two of the others before dropping them into the satchel and turning to Styophan. He took one deep breath, and then met Styophan's gaze. His look was like stone—uncaring, resolute—but it wasn't until he nodded to the warrior standing at the beaded doorway that Styophan was certain something had gone terribly wrong.

The warrior turned and left. Styophan heard the call of a bird, the same lonely cry he'd heard earlier in the forest. In the distance he heard it picked up and repeated. And then, barely, he heard it again.

Styophan's pulse quickened. A message was being passed through the forest, no doubt to those who'd been set to watch his ships. Had he done something to offend Kürad?

"My Lord—"

Styophan managed no more than this, for just then he heard the sound of a cannon in the distance. Another came shortly after. And then a barrage of them came, one after the other.

Like the pounding of the drums of war.

CHAPTER FOUR

S tyophan pulled the flintlock pistol from his belt and pointed it at Kürad's chest as a cry from his men outside the yurt filtered in through the doorway.

"Tell them to stop!" Styophan cried.

The cannons continued to boom in the distance.

"Tell them to stop!"

But the Haelish did not listen. They merely stared, especially Kürad. It was as if he were *begging* Styophan to fire.

Styophan pulled the trigger. The shot boomed in the enclosed space and exploded against Kürad's chest, flaking away some of the glittering umber paint. His skin *cracked*, as if it were made of so much stone. Blood seeped through the fissures, but the shot itself—by the ancients who protect—had impacted and fallen with a thump to the reed-covered floor.

Anahid, the gem upon her brow glowing, raised her hands above her head. Between them, white lightning formed. Men ran at her, but before they could grab her, lightning arced out and ran through three of them. They fell to the ground, the first one unmoving, the other two twitching.

Styophan dropped his pistol and tried to pull his shashka to run them through, but the Haelish men nearby grabbed his arms and twisted them behind his back. He struggled as one of the women rushed forward and struck Anahid on the crown of her head with the hilt of her wood-handled knife.

The lightning vanished with a resonant buzz, and Anahid slumped to the ground.

"Leave her!" Styophan cried.

The Haelish men twisted his arms more painfully until he was on his toes to keep them from pulling an arm from its socket.

Kürad, the blood from the wound running down his chest and seeping into his buckskin pants, stepped forward until the two of them were face-to-face.

31

In the distance, the cannon fire continued, some with the sound he knew well—the smaller cannons of Anuskayan windships. And then a massive boom fell across the forest. Gunpowder... There was a store of gunpowder on the *Graaza*.

A score of men had just died from that explosion, and it sounded as if none of the other ships would be spared. The Haelish wouldn't know what to do with the ships in any case.

"You cowardly goat!" Styophan shouted in Anuskayan. "You mongrel dog!"

Kürad responded in Haelish, and the same woman, this time with a flinty look on her face, translated. "You came too late."

Styophan looked between her and Kürad. "What do you mean *too late*?"

When Kürad spoke, it was with clear reluctance, but it seemed as though he would give this to Styophan, this if nothing else. He spoke for a long time. He paused every so often, gathering himself, choosing the right words, and Styophan wondered what could make him open up so.

"Three weeks ago," the woman finally said, "the Empire came and offered us peace. They came with food and gold and an offer of land—nearly all of it that had been taken in the war between us that has lasted generations. Kürad spoke to your crow, to your Matra. The gems you offered were generous, and we would have continued the war, despite our losses..." Now it was the woman's turn to gather herself. "Gripping arms with Yrstanla is not something we would have foreseen even three moons ago. But the withering..." Styophan had seen this look a hundred times. A thousand. It was the look of someone approaching the final days of the wasting who thought the disease a failing, some fault of their own. "Kürad could not allow our numbers to dwindle further, not if we wanted any chance of surviving."

"They're *lying* to you," Styophan said. "They've done this because of the war with Anuskaya. When that is done, they will return."

"That is why Kürad hopes you fight to your last breath. The people of Hael must rest. We must breathe."

"But don't you see? Our only hope is to fight *together*. If you wait, Bahett will take you at his leisure."

"That may be so, but the Lord of the Hills has told us that we cannot fight. And so it will be."

Styophan tried to speak again, but Kürad pointed toward the entryway, and he was led roughly outside. Mikhalai and Rodion and four others were held by the Haelish men. Four more lay upon the ground, unmoving, blood pooled beneath them.

Styophan stared at the face of Avil, young Avil, his eyes slack, lifeless. His lips were already blue. By the ancients who preserve, he was only twenty-three.

"You goat-fucking heathens!"

The man who held him struck him across the back of his head.

"Fuck your mother!" he shouted over the pain as he tried to wrench his arms away.

But their hold on him was as sure as a mainstay. They struck him again and again. Finally one struck squarely. Stars burst before him. He felt woozy. He drew in another breath, ready to fight until they killed him, but the next strike brought with it a deep and utter blackness.

When Styophan woke, he was being dragged behind a horse on a wooden framework. His wrists and ankles were tied to long wooden poles that crossed over the horse's withers. They were traveling through a marsh. The smell of it as the horses' hooves *splooshed* into the muck was foul and fetid. The sled pulled him through the shallow water at a downward angle, giving him a clear view of the Haelish to the rear of the line. He had to lift his head to do it, though, and every time he did it the movement sent a spike of cold iron through his head.

Dozens of horses rode in the line behind him. He could see more sleds like his, but who was on them, he couldn't tell. He'd brought *eighty-nine* windsmen to Haelish lands. How many of them still lived? Four? Five? His head pounded as the weight of it struck him. He felt tears forming, but he stifled his thoughts of regret ruthlessly. He refused to let the Haelish see his tears.

Behind the horses marched several hundred Haelish, most carrying large bundles or baskets on their backs. The entire tribe must have come, he realized. They'd picked up their entire village and went on the move. No wonder it was so difficult for the Empire to pin them down. They had only a handful of permanent settlements, and those were on ground the Haelish considered sacred, places they were especially loath to relinquish to the Empire.

Styophan's vision went blurry. He blinked his eyes, but it wouldn't go away, and soon his head began to hurt worse than only moments ago. His stomach felt like it was twisting in circles, and as a Haelish man came beside him, a nausea struck him so fiercely that he simply threw up what little there was in his stomach.

The man walking beside his sled was Datha, he realized. His eyes were resolute, but there was shame in them as well. He took a length of brown cloth from a sack at his belt and placed it over Styophan's eyes.

Styophan tried to move his head away, fearing what he might do when the blindfold was on him.

"Sleep," Datha said, tying the cloth despite Styophan's feeble attempts at preventing it.

Styophan wanted to spit in his face, but he saw no point in it.

He was so woozy he wanted to throw up again, but whatever small amount of vigor he'd had on waking had already been drained from him, and he fell asleep minutes later.

The next time Styophan woke, his blindfold had been removed. He wasn't sure why. Perhaps they reasoned they were deep enough into Haelish territory, or they'd confirmed that there were no allies near enough to help him. Or perhaps Styophan had proved himself docile enough that they could allow this small amount of freedom. That made him want to struggle once more, to break free if only to take one of them with him before he died, but the truth was he was too weak at the moment to do anything.

They traveled among tall hills still bright with green summer growth. Grasses taller than a man swayed in the wind, making them look alive, as if they might pick themselves up and fall into line with the Haelish on their trek southward. The sky was a nondescript grey. A light snow was falling, casting the hills as something from a dream, as if it didn't really exist beyond the white haze of snow in the distance.

Datha was walking next to him again. As he had in the forest, he wore no shirt, no form of protection from the growing cold. His skin was also covered in something that glistened in the low light. Goat fat, perhaps, as the Matri did before submerging themselves beneath the frigid waters of the drowning basin. No paint covered his chest. This was also true of the other Haelish men that Styophan could see walking in the line behind him. Perhaps they only applied the paint in preparation for battle. It would make sense. To use it unnecessarily would be to waste the stones they found so valuable.

He wondered if they'd scavenged the ships for the stones he'd brought from Khalakovo. Surely they had. He could see several of the warriors bearing muskets. Even from this distance Styophan could tell they were Anuskayan.

Datha glanced down at Styophan, doing a double-take when he realized Styophan was awake. He unslung a skin of water from around his shoulders and held it up to Styophan's lips. The act of lifting his head caused Styophan no small amount of pain, but it was manageable, and he was able to drink his fill.

"You're gutless," Styophan said in Yrstanlan when Datha pulled the skin away.

Datha bristled. "Watch your tongue."

"Worthless."

No sooner had Styophan said this than Datha lashed out and clouted him across the cheek. It was not a particularly hard hit, but with his head wound already throbbing, it made Styophan feel as if his skull were being crushed beneath a wagon wheel.

"Kürad is taking you to Skolohalla. Bahett wished to speak with the one who led the forces of Anuskaya when they came. If you wish for mercy, or any kind-ness at all for the Aramahn woman or your remaining men, you will watch your tongue. No matter what Bahett has offered, Kürad won't hesitate to kill them, or you, if you bring further shame on our tribe."

Styophan had heard of Skolohalla. It was not a place. Rather, it was a meeting, a joining of the various tribes of Hael in one location. They did so at certain times of the year, most often at summer and winter solstice, but this felt differ-ent. It felt momentous. They came together not only to celebrate, but to decide upon things that affected all the peoples of Hael. The Kings would meet and hold council and decide the fate of their Kingdoms, such as they were.

"Any shame brought upon you—"

Datha grabbed Styophan's cheeks and squeezed until Styophan stopped talk-ing. His eyes were bright with anger. "I know who brought shame upon us, and so does Kürad. Why do you think you were allowed into the yurt with your weapons? Why do you think we waited after the sound of cannon was heard through the forest?" He waited for those words to sink in. "Kürad feels shame, but this is a thing he feels we must do. The withering has come, even though our wodjana said it would happen only to the Empire. They said it was in punishment for the Kamarisi's transgressions. They said it would stop when Yrstanla retreated beyond the hills and promised never to return. And we all believed them.

"But then the withering came, more ravenously than it had for the armies of the Kamarisi. Those taken by it die in weeks, not months. *How can this be?* we asked. *How can we be punished more harshly than Yrstanla?* Do you know the answer, Styophan son of Andrasha?"

Styophan couldn't shake his head. It hurt too much. So he merely stared.

"*Hayir,*" Datha said with a sneer. "You have no *idea* what happened. It's been happening for years among the islands and you haven't a clue how to heal it."

Prince Nikandr had healed some who'd been taken by the wasting, but Styophan wondered—now that his Lord had lost his ability to commune with his wind spirit—if he could do so again. Probably not, and even if he could, he could not stem this tide. He couldn't do so on Rafsuhan, and he certainly couldn't do it here.

"Do you want to know what changed Kürad's mind?" Datha asked. "Why he decided, after all our years of war with Yrstanla, to betray his word and give you to Bahett?"

Styophan could see the anger radiating from Datha. He didn't truly wish to trade words with this man, but his curiosity got the better of him. "Why?"

"Because the withering began on the islands. Is it not so?"

The horse climbed a rise out of the swamp, but then rounded the other side and entered it once more. The water was deeper here. It seeped into Styophan's boots and chilled his feet. "We call it the wasting, and it started on the islands, but we didn't cause it."

"You did! And now it has come here. Our warriors and our women die, and the wodjana say that the only way to be rid of it is to give you to Yrstanla."

Datha walked in silence for a time, his footsteps splashing in water covered with tiny green plants. His face had lost much of its anger, and it was replaced with a look of regret, as if he wished Styophan and his ships had never come.

"*They* may believe that," Styophan said, "but *you* don't."

Datha glanced over. "Don't I?"

"If you did you wouldn't be talking to me now."

Datha walked in silence for a time, the snow falling against his dark skin and melting. Toward the front of the line, the sounds of footsteps sloshing through the mud was replaced by soft footfalls against dry grasses, and soon the horse bearing Styophan reached solid ground. They began taking a trail along higher land, and the marsh began to fade into the distance.

"We'll reach our meeting ground in less than a fortnight," Datha said softly. "Four of your men are left, plus the woman."

"Why are you telling me this?"

"So you don't do anything rash. Let Kürad treat with Bahett's men. They'll take you eastward, and if luck shines upon you, you'll be rescued." With that he began walking faster, perhaps to be done with speaking with one of the enemy.

"Wait! How could I be *rescued*? We were betrayed. No one even knows where we are."

If Datha was bothered by the word *betrayed* he didn't show it. "They say you pray to your dead to protect you. Is it so?"

Styophan nodded, ignoring the pain the simple motion brought.

"Then pray to them today, Styophan of Anuskaya"—he glanced up toward the sky—"for one of your ships made it safely away."

CHAPTER FIVE

Nikandr rode at the head of the line, guiding them across a landscape dotted with bushes and the occasional cacti that with the spring rains were blooming with bright yellow flowers. They'd been riding since dawn and were just now, with the sun already past midday, nearing the outskirts of Andakhara. He glanced back to Atiana, who rode stoically behind him on her own mount—an ab-sair of the Gaji. Ashan and Sukharam brought up the rear. Ashan smiled and nodded, but Sukharam merely turned his gaze elsewhere. He returned to the land ahead, staring at the collection of homes in the distance that occupied the center of the wide horizon.

He and Atiana had woken before dawn, the two of them tearing down their tent and preparing for the day's ride silently. He'd apologized to her, the two of them holding each other for a time, but it had felt insufficient. And if it felt that way to him, he was sure it would be trebly so for Atiana.

As he reined his ab-sair over, the beast lifted its head and wailed—a sad sound that reminded Nikandr of the elk herds that ran through the Empire's eastern mountains. The others in the train all did the same. They were strangely docile that way. The beasts were equine, but their shoulders and withers and neck were massive, storing water for their long journeys across the wastelands of the desert and the great, arid plains to the west. They were not fleet, but they were perfect for treks across the Gaji.

He guided his ab-sair until he was riding alongside Atiana. "Good day to you, m'lady."

Atiana remained silent, her eyes fixed on the road ahead.

"Ah, you're upset. I've come without a gift." He kicked his ab-sair forward, riding into the scrub.

"Don't, Nischka," he heard Atiana call behind him.

He continued on, riding toward one of the tall cacti with the thousand arms.

He urged the ab-sair forward and stood up on the saddle.

"Nischka, don't!"

It was a thing easy enough to do on the beast's wide shoulders. He rode forward, feeling the rhythm of the ab-sair's powerful gait, and snatched one of the yellow flowers from an arm that hung well wide of the body of the plant. He guided the ab-sair back toward the group, still holding the flower high, and only then, when he was back by Atiana's side, did he drop down and hold the flower out to her with a flourish.

She made no move to take it. She simply stared at him as if that were the most idiotic thing she'd ever seen.

"They smell like home," he said, shaking it.

"They smell nothing of the sort."

He shook it gently, and waited.

With an annoyed look, she accepted the flower and held it to her nose. Nikandr could still smell it: the scent of jasmine, which grew thick and strong in the gardens of Palotza Galostina, Atiana's childhood home and the seat of her family's power.

"You're little more than a fool child, Nikandr Iaroslov." She spoke the words, but there was a reluctant smile on her lips. She hid it with the flower, taking in the scent again. By the time she lowered it, the look was gone.

"I've been thinking," Nikandr said.

"Have you?"

"I haven't been truthful about the hezhan."

"Do tell."

"Atiana, please, let me get this out."

She took a deep breath. "You're right. Go on."

"I miss the bond. You've known that for as long as I have, perhaps longer. But I think I didn't realize just how much I missed Nasim. I knew him for only a short time before he took to the winds with Fahroz. We were separated by such great distances, and still I felt him. I didn't know it, but he was there with me, all that time. I felt him growing." Atiana made to speak, but he talked over her. "I know it sounds foolish, but I didn't realize any of that until it was taken away from me. I felt him growing over those years. I felt his awareness expanding. I thought it was my own understanding, my own connection to Adhiya and the world around me. But it wasn't. It never was. It was Nasim's, or what little he granted me of it.

"On the Spar, when Nasim severed that connection, when he plunged that knife into me, that was all lost to me. Adhiya. The havahezhan. And Nasim. As strange as it sounds, he was like a son to me." Ahead, the wind pulled up dirt from the desert floor, played with it. Nikandr pointedly ignored it. "While I was up on the cliff, I was thinking only of myself, but last night, lying in the tent, I realized how desperately I want to find Nasim."

Atiana glanced at him, stared deeply into his eyes, and then focused on the way ahead once more. "So that you can forge a new bond with him?"

Nikandr shrugged. "Perhaps. But I think it's more than that. We know that Nasim is one key to closing the rifts over Ghayavand. I felt as though, if I had some connection to him, I also had some power over the fate of the world."

"But you do. That's why we're here, to find him."

"I know, but this is different. There's always been something about Nasim. I can't explain it. It's deep, and ancient. It's power I've never had on my own."

Atiana was quiet for a time. The only sound came from the plodding of the ab-sair's hooves. He thought he'd angered her, and he was just about to apologize for making a mess of things again when she began talking. "I know what you mean. I felt the same of Sariya." She placed the flower behind her ear and urged her mount closer to his. She took his hand and squeezed tenderly. "There are times when I miss that as well."

She meant well by what she'd said, but it only served to remind them both that Sariya was dead. Nasim might be dead as well. They might be on a fool's errand, coming to the desert, chasing Sariya's daughter.

"We'll find him," she said, squeezing his hand one last time.

"I know," he replied, but he wasn't at all sure it was true.

They continued on toward Andakhara, reaching its outskirts within the hour. When they came abreast of the first of the simple mudbrick homes, the ab-sair wailed. Perhaps in answer, a goat brayed, and a bell clanged, and then a female goat heavy with milk trundled out from behind the nearby home. Her two kids followed, ducking their heads and drawing sharply from their mother's teats while the mother stared on. As they passed the house—little more than a single room with a thatched roof—a black-haired girl wearing a blue shayla poked her head out from behind a corner.

Andakhara was more than just a caravanserai. There were enough homes for several thousand. On the edges of the village the houses littered the land like scrub brush—most of them with small fields of wheat or flax or bright orange gourds—but as they came closer to the central well, the houses were more tightly packed, including a cluster of larger buildings.

As they continued down a shallow slope, the road wound back and forth through the homes until they could no longer see the desert behind them. Nikandr watched the houses carefully, expecting to see the barrel of a musket poke out from a darkened window. But nothing of the sort happened, and they made their way to the center of the caravanserai. There was one large open-walled structure there. The well house. A dozen or so men stood beneath the shelter of the roof, talking, but they stopped as Nikandr and the others approached. One of them, a thin man with dark brown skin and a wide smile with several missing teeth, broke away, snapping his fingers at two boys as he came. He wore a cap of embroidered wool and a striped kaftan of bright blue and grey. On his hands were silver rings with yellow gemstones—citrine, perhaps, or beryl.

"The fates are kind," he said in the dialect of Mahndi used in the desert. "Welcome to Andakhara."

The boys accepted the reins of their ab-sair, waiting patiently for them to dismount. They'd discussed it on the way in, that they should not act as if anything were amiss, even if they feared it. The desert tribes did not like outsiders, and if there was any chance Soroush had gone missing for some innocent reason, they needed to find out. So they would follow their customs and remain as wary as they could until they could learn more.

Once they were all down, the boys took the ab-sair toward the watering trough as a well-muscled man pumped the well. He was bald, except for a full mustache and a trim black beard. He wore no shirt, which revealed the latticework of scars running across his shoulders and chest and arms. He seemed proud to display those scars, however he'd received them. The ab-sair emitted their wails and then fell to drinking the water from the trough, nudging one another out of the way as they did so.

Before offering greeting, Nikandr pulled his veil from his face. Atiana did the same with her veil. Then all four of them reached down and took a small amount of dirt from the dry earth. Nikandr rubbed it between his palms and then smudged a bit across his forehead, showing these men that they would share of their land, not simply use it.

When they were done, the wellmaster smiled and bowed his head. "My name is Dahud. Please, what can Andakhara offer you?"

As Atiana and Nikandr covered their faces once more, Ashan answered, "Rooms for the night, perhaps a handful of water before we leave."

Dahud smiled widely and bowed his head once more. "In Andakhara you can set your worries aside, at least for the night. Or more, if you'd like."

Most of the men in the well house had gone back to their conversation, but several were still watching, including the stout man at the pump. Dahud seemed to notice, for he glanced toward the well, and then motioned them toward a large clay building with a thatched roof. "There are few enough who remain for more than a night." He tipped his head back toward the men. "You mightn't guess it from the way they act, but we welcome those who do."

"Another time," Ashan said. "For now, there are places we must go."

Dahud parted the beads that hung from the top of the squared doorway. Inside was a room with a dozen piles of pillows with shishas at the center of each. Two old men in striped kaftans sat on the far side of the room, drawing from the ivory-tipped tubes as a haze of smoke trailed up toward the ceiling. They looked toward the entrance, but then returned to their low conversation.

"Please," Dahud said, motioning to a mound of pillows nearby. "You'll have drink and smoke, and then we can talk."

"We couldn't," Ashan said.

But Dahud already had his hands up. "A drink and a bit of smoke. Then we'll talk."

They waited there on those pillows for a long time. More men came to the smoke house, and then several old couples came in as well. A young woman entered from the back of the building, where Dahud had gone. Another one near Atiana's age followed soon after. They wandered the room, greeting those who entered, bringing them tabbaq for their shishas and araq in deep blue glasses. They all but ignored Nikandr and the others. The sound of conversation and clinking glasses, even laughter, filled the room, and still Dahud did not come.

"We should go," Atiana said after a time, echoing Nikandr's own feelings.

Ashan, sitting cross-legged comfortably, merely patted the air with his hands and told them to wait.

Only after the sun went down did Dahud return. He came with a long-necked bottle. Nikandr found himself more eager to partake of the drink—whatever it was—than he would have guessed. As Dahud sat on the pillows across from Nikandr, the two women whisked in, handing glasses to each of them, including Sukharam, and placing a healthy amount of what smelled like very expensive tabbaq into the bowl of the shisha. After lighting it, they handed tubes to each of them and then left, attending to the crowd that filled the room.

Nikandr smelled the araq and was surprised how complex it was. It smelled of anise, but also of butter and smoke and honey and earth. The taste of it was deep, like a well through the center of a mountain. Nikandr closed his eyes as the warmth of it suffused his chest and gut. Were he alone he would have downed the entire glass and poured another, and perhaps downed that too. But he couldn't. Not with the others watching so closely. He noticed Atiana watching him. He smiled to her, to tell her he was well, but she seemed as unconvinced as he was.

If only to assuage her, he took up his shisha and drew upon it, inhaling the smoke and holding it for as long as he could. He breathed it out slowly, up toward the ceiling as the taste of oak and loamy forest floor complicated the finish of the araq.

Dahud studied Nikandr's face for longer than was polite. "You're a long way from home." Smoke wiggled out from his mouth and nostrils like a drakhen breathing fire. "I'm sure you know your way, but it's good you've come through Andakhara instead of the taking the western paths."

"And why is that?" Ashan asked.

Dahud's smile was wicked. "They aren't so kind among the hills." He was perhaps fishing for information—where were they headed? what was their purpose?—but Nikandr would share none of this, and neither would the others.

No sooner had the thought come to him than Ashan said, "We've come seeking a boy."

Nikandr snapped his head toward Ashan. He shook his head, hoping Dahud wouldn't see, but he didn't understand what Ashan was doing.

Dahud relaxed more deeply into his pillows as if he'd been afraid of their purpose here in Andakhara. "A boy," he repeated as the young serving woman returned with a platter of dates.

Ashan waved to Sukharam. "As old as him, and a girl five years younger."

"Who would they have been traveling with?"

"Only themselves."

Dahud plucked a date filled with goat cheese and pistachios from a wooden tray and popped it into his mouth. "Describe them."

"The girl had dark brown hair with bright blue eyes."

"And the boy?"

"Hair the color of aged oak, and burning brown eyes. He might have worn the clothes of the Aramahn, but he would wear no stones. Neither would the girl."

Dahud shrugged. "There was a girl who came through Andakhara three months ago. She had blue eyes, but she looked older than this young man"—he motioned to Sukharam—"and she came alone." He took a deep pull off of the shisha, holding the smoke for a long time as the conversation and revelry continued around them. As he blew the smoke upward, adding to the layer hanging over the room, he peered more closely at Ashan. "Is there nothing else you're searching for?"

Atiana looked cool, but Nikandr could tell from the way she held her hands tightly in her lap that she was nervous. Sukharam, however, seemed as cool as the winds of winter, and it was *Ashan* that seemed nervous. He licked his lips as if he were dying of thirst and glanced to the people over Nikandr's shoulder.

Dahud leaned in. "I know much, and I know many people far beyond the reaches of this small caravanserai. If there's anything, you need only name it."

Ashan looked as though he were ready to ask a question, but then he suddenly looked down at his shisha tube as if it had offended him. "We seem to be out," he said, motioning to the bowl.

"Ah," Dahud said. "Right away." He turned and snapped his fingers to get the attention of one of the women, the younger. As he did, Ashan nodded toward the crowd. Sitting at another shisha was the large man from the water house. He caught Nikandr's eye and shook his head back and forth while staring pointedly at Dahud, who was still facing away.

The girl slipped off through the smokehouse crowd and Dahud turned back to them. "But a moment... Now, where were we?"

"The boy," Ashan said. "You'll ask after him?"

Dahud nodded. "You'll stay for a day or two, won't you?"

"We leave in the morning," Nikandr replied.

For the first time Dahud gave Nikandr serious consideration. "Why, if you'll forgive the question, are two from the islands here in the desert? This boy must owe you much to come searching so far."

"*Neh*," Nikandr replied. "It is *I* who owe *him* much."

"Ah." Dahud's face became more serious. "I've some of those debts myself." Dahud rose in one smooth motion and bowed deeply to them, doffing his embroidered cap as he did so. "Let me find what I can while you take your rest and prepare for the days ahead."

Ashan stood and hugged him. "We would be grateful."

"One of my boys will take you to your room." And with that he left.

Nikandr looked back to the corner where the large, scarred man had been sitting, but he was no longer there. A boy of twelve or thirteen came to them a short while later and led them outside and to the back of the long building. With the din of the smoke room now filtering softly into the night air, he opened a creaking door to a large room with several pallets. In one corner was a pedestal and a washbasin and above that a beaten mirror hanging from a bent nail. The boy grabbed a fluted, patina-green ewer sitting next to the pedestal and headed for the door. "I'll bring water."

They closed the door and settled themselves. Everyone but Nikandr.

"We can't stay here."

"I suspect we won't be staying long," Ashan said.

"Why?"

But before Ashan could answer, a knock came at the door.

Nikandr thought the boy had forgotten something, but he found instead the hulking man from the smokehouse. Nikandr reached for his shashka, but the man darted forward and grabbed Nikandr's wrist. He did not attack, however. He merely put one finger to his lips and shook his head.

"Who are you?" Nikandr asked.

"I am Goeh," he replied, releasing Nikandr's wrist and stepping inside, "and I'm the closest thing you have to a friend in this place."

"What's happening?"

"Dahud has gone to fetch the Kamarisi's men. They've been stationed at the southern edge of Andakhara, awaiting a summons."

"You're Dahud's man, are you not?"

Goeh turned to spit on the dusty wooden floorboards. "There are men who have no love for the Kamarisi, even less for the lackeys he sends to the desert, or those that serve them."

Nikandr looked to the door, which was still cracked open. "Dahud would have this place watched, would he not?"

"The room is being watched, but not by Dahud's men." Goeh smiled grimly. "Not any longer."

From outside their room a low whistle came, a trilling call like a desert finch.

Goeh's eyes hardened. "There's no time. If you want to find the two who came before you, you must come now."

Nikandr looked to Ashan, who nodded back to him. "The desert, as much as they like to think differently, is still under the Kamarisi's rule, and if that's so, then Dahud, who is essentially the lord of this place, cannot be trusted."

Nikandr turned to Atiana, ready to ask her the same question, but she was staring at the opposite wall, her eyes vacant and half-lidded.

"Atiana?"

She didn't respond.

Again the call of the desert finch came, louder this time.

"Atiana?" Nikandr called again, shaking her shoulder lightly. "Atiana, hear me."

And still she didn't move.

He felt the pulse at her neck. It was slow, like it was when the Matri removed themselves from their drowning chambers.

"We must hurry," Goeh said.

But Nikandr couldn't. His whole body was suddenly tense, and he was frozen in place, for it was clear there was something deeply, deeply wrong with Atiana.

CHAPTER SIX

Nikandr shook Atiana harder, and was about to do so again, to slap her or shout at her or something—anything to wake her—when she said in a voice as cold as winter, "Men are coming."

She said this without moving, without looking at any of them.

"Who's coming?" Nikandr asked.

"Men," she repeated. "Armed men. Along the main road. And more are moving in from the desert."

At last she did turn, but she looked *through* Nikandr as if he wasn't there. She looked through Goeh as well, and then walked past him, out and into the night.

Goeh stared at her, clearly confused, but then he motioned for them to follow. As they left and began taking a slope upward through a grove of lemon trees, men resolved from the darkness.

"These are mine," Goeh said.

There were six of them in all, spread out in a line ahead.

Nikandr took Atiana's arm, but she fended him away. "Do not touch me again, Nischka, and move slowly."

She followed him, with Ashan and Sukharam bringing up the rear, with a slow pace, like a woman sleepwalking. He dearly wished to speak to her of it, but it was clear she couldn't. Not now. For the time being, they simply had to get out of this place before the Kamarisi's men swooped in.

With progress that felt painful, they hiked up the same rise Nikandr had climbed only minutes before, and then continued beyond it, along a gentle slope to a dry stream bed, a wadi, that ran through the easternmost section of the caravanserai. In the height of spring this trough in the land would be alive with rushing water, but now it was as dry and rocky as the surrounding terrain. More importantly, it was lower than the mostly flat ground, and a good way to reach the southern end of Andakhara with fewer eyes watching their passage.

They heard little, only the sound of their own feet crunching over the dry soil, offset by the occasional bell of a goat and the rattle of the beetles flying among the scrub trees lining the wadi.

"They've reached the inn," Atiana said.

She was using the aether, Nikandr knew. He just couldn't understand how. She'd shown this ability only once before—on Galahesh while Sariya had held her spellbound—but those had been very special circumstances. What it was about this place that was allowing her to take the dark, he didn't know. Perhaps Ishkyna was communicating with her in some way. Ishkyna, after all, had grown in her abilities since Galahesh. She'd dealt with the loss of her body and moved beyond it—or so Atiana had said—and this had allowed her to spread herself even further and do things never before seen in the history of the Matri.

He scanned the skies for the gallows crow, the bird Ishkyna most often inhabited, but saw nothing, and he felt for her through his soulstone, but here too he felt nothing save Atiana's presence, a warmth that suffused the center of his chest.

They came to a halt at a copse of scraggly trees at the center of the wadi. Along the bank above them sat a large home with a high stone fence around it. It could be scaled, but surely there were men guarding it.

"There are twelve men on the far side," Atiana said, perhaps sensing his worry. She pointed with deliberate care to the corner of the fence twenty paces away. "Three stand just there. The others are spaced about the interior."

"Are Soroush and Ushai there?" Nikandr asked.

"They're being held within the home." She pointed to the roof, which from their angle could barely be seen beyond the wall. "Two more men are inside. They're janissaries, Nischka, and they're well armed. All of them."

Nikandr felt his fingers go cold. Janissaries. There might be some stationed this far from the lands of the Empire proper, but it seemed out of the ordinary. It could only mean that the janissaries had somehow gotten wind of where they were headed. They had chosen their number carefully—as few as possible—in hopes of avoiding the notice of the Kamarisi and Yrstanla's new regent, Bahett ül Kirdhash.

"Perhaps word of our travels has reached Alekeşir," Nikandr said.

Ashan, whose circlet glowed faintly in the darkness, shook his head. "In time to send men here? Doubtful."

"He can't have guessed our destination."

"There is one more," Atiana said softly, "within the home. A woman. She's kneeling over a dish, rocking back and forth." Atiana's voice went distant and ephemeral. "It's filled with blood. Her own blood."

"The Haelish." This came from Sukharam. "She's one of their wodjana. They use blood to scry. She's trying to find us."

"Then she knows we're here."

"Maybe not," Ashan said. "The wodjana of Hael are not like the Matri. Their scrying is inexact. They find paths to the future—many paths—and choosing the right one is difficult."

"She was skilled enough to find us here." Nikandr took out his pistol, felt the familiar weight of it and the smooth grip. "We can't allow her to live."

Ashan gripped Nikandr's arm. "*Neh*, son of Iaros. We'll not kill her, not unless she threatens our lives."

"She *does* threaten our lives."

"That isn't what I mean."

"I know what you mean, but we can't allow her or Bahett's men to find us again."

Ashan shook his head. "This is the price we agreed upon when Sukharam and I joined you. You stay here. Sukharam and I will return with Soroush and Ushai."

"I can't allow the two of you—"

"We'll be well." Ashan stood, beckoning Sukharam to come closer.

As they strode toward the wall, Goeh crept closer, barely making a sound over the loose stones. "There are stables beyond the house. We should make our way there before Dahud—"

Before Goeh could finish his words, a bell began to ring from the center of the caravanserai. It was coming from the direction of the inn, or perhaps the well house.

"Quickly," Goeh said. "Go to the stables." He beckoned to his men and began heading toward higher ground. "They'll be moving along the road. We'll slow them as much as we're able."

"Thank you," Nikandr said.

Goeh spat at Nikandr's feet. "I don't do this for you."

And with that he was gone, he and his men moving into the night as silently as they'd come.

Nikandr took Atiana's arm, and though she tried to shake his hand away, he gripped her tightly and led her forward. "Atiana," he whispered as the wind began to rise. "*Atiana.*"

She wouldn't respond, but Nikandr had to move.

Ahead, Ashan and Sukharam were only paces away from the wall. Ashan had stopped and was spreading his arms wide. He was communing with a jalahezhan, a water spirit. Nikandr could feel it on the night air, an oppressive humidity that was wholly new to his time in the desert. It made the air difficult to breathe, and it would likely foul any muskets or pistols being fired.

Sukharam continued on to the wall and set his hand against it. Nikandr thought it might crumble, but it did not. It disintegrated as if it were made of sand. In moments, an opening formed, an archway as wide as a cart. The three janissaries standing there shouted. They pulled their muskets up to their shoulders. Nikandr heard them click—the hammer falling against the frizzen—just before Sukharam summoned a wind so fierce that it blew them backward and out of sight.

The wind blew around Nikandr. It tugged at his kaftan and tousled his hair. It lifted the smell of sage from the land around them. But he felt none of this within himself, as he had so often before the events at the Spar.

There was a part of him, a part buried deep inside, that would sacrifice almost anything to feel it again.

But he knew he couldn't. Those days were gone.

Even knowing this, he released Atiana's arm. He closed his eyes and tipped his head back and spread his arms wide.

By the ancients, to feel the wind. To command it…

Nyet. He had never *commanded* it. He had *asked.* He had given of himself, and the wind had returned the gesture in kind. When he had communed with the spirit Nasim had somehow bound to him he had often wondered what it would be like to trade places. What if he were to slip into Adhiya and the havahezhan were to slip into Erahm?

Could they do such a thing? Would he die if he somehow managed it? Or would he live in Adhiya for a time as the hezhan did here when they passed through the veil?

Were he given the chance now, he would take it willingly. Gladly. He would know what the world beyond was like.

"Nikandr!"

Nikandr blinked, tears falling from his eyes.

He hadn't even known he was crying.

He looked up the slope to where Ashan stood in the gap in the wall.

"Go!" Ashan shouted. "Go now!"

Nikandr shook his head fiercely and pulled Atiana with him, along the wadi and toward the far end of the wall where the stables lay.

Before he'd gone twenty paces, musket fire broke out from the far side of the estate—Goeh and his men.

"Atiana, can you hear me?"

She was still unwilling—or unable—to respond.

As the shouting from inside the wall intensified, as the wind continued to blow, they reached the corner of the wall. Just beyond it, built against the wall itself, was the stables. He watched for signs that it was being watched, but he saw no one. Surely they'd been drawn into the estate by the shouts of the men. He led Atiana to a large, misshapen tree in the center of the yard before the stable doors.

He eased Atiana into the crook between two massive boughs. He didn't want to leave her, but he couldn't take the chance that there was anyone waiting in the stables. "Wait here," he said to her.

She didn't respond, but she remained, her eyes heavy and sluggish.

Nikandr ran into the stables and found a dozen stalls. Seven were filled with stout ab-sair. Another three were still saddled, their reins hanging loosely from a post. He grabbed three blankets and looked for the most energetic of the beasts, selecting them quickly and leading them out from their stalls. He threw the blankets over them and began saddling them, but he'd only finished one when the sound of galloping hooves came to him.

Surely it was Dahud's men returning, or the janissaries that had been sent to find them at the inn.

They were already so near.

Nikandr abandoned the two unsaddled mounts and led the four readied ab-sair from the stables. No sooner had he sprinted toward Atiana than three janissaries riding black ab-sair came galloping around the corner and up to the yard. The janissaries wore rounded turbans in the style of the Empire. They wore vests and wide cloth belts and short, baggy pants over tall leather boots.

"Halt," the lead man called to Nikandr in Yrstanlan. He was a tall fellow with a thick black mustache, and the only soldier with a tall horsehair broach in his turban. He held his reins with one hand and a flintlock pistol in the other.

Nikandr nearly reached for his own pistol, but one of the men had spotted Atiana and was pointing his cocked pistol at her.

His heart pounded. It was bad enough he'd been caught by these men, but more soldiers would be here any moment.

"Release the horses," the janissary called with a calm assurance. He would fire if Nikandr didn't do as he asked, no matter what orders he might have received from Dahud or his superiors.

Nikandr released the reins, his mind going wild trying to find some way, any way, out of this.

The janissary swung his horse around so that he was between Nikandr and Atiana. "Now step away."

Nikandr had taken only one step back when the ground began to rumble. From the far side of the wall came a sound like a growing landslide.

The janissary looked to the wall, then to Nikandr. His ab-sair reared onto its hind legs, screaming loudly as if some primal fear had risen up within it. "Easy, boy!" the janissary called as his mount dropped back down. "Easy!"

But the ab-sair began bucking like an unbroken yearling. It rose up again, and when another janissary urged his skittish mount forward and began grabbing for its reins, it clubbed the other ab-sair. Its sharp front hoof caught the other beast's head with a sound like a gourd being staved in. Mount and rider both fell, pinning the janissary's leg. As the soldier screamed in pain, the crazed beast charged over him, its hooves landing heavily on the fallen janissary's chest.

A pistol cracked sharply over the sound of the ab-sair's screaming. Blood exploded from its chest, but other than a momentary pause, it didn't seem to notice. Until the leader of the janissaries, still seated in his saddle, leaned forward and shot the beast point blank in the skull.

The mount collapsed, every one of its powerful muscles going slack in an instant. As the leader leapt free and rolled along the ground, Nikandr darted forward and grabbed the pistol that the fallen janissary had dropped. He pulled his own pistol as well, and trained the two of them on the two soldiers—one mounted, one on his feet, neither of whom had loaded weapons at the ready. "You'll tell your man to get off his horse and you'll run out into the desert"—Nikandr motioned with one pistol out to the southern wastes of the Gaji—"or I'll send you to meet your ancestors now."

The soldiers from Yrstanla stared at him, then each other, but when Nikandr lifted his left arm to aim for the leader's chest, the man raised his hands and ordered his man down from his ab-sair. The two of them ran off into the desert as Nikandr readied the mounts. He was just finishing when Sukharam returned with Soroush in tow. Ashan came behind him, carrying an unconscious Ushai.

"Hurry," Ashan said. His face was wan, even in the white moonlight.

And they did. As beaten as they were, they pulled themselves onto the ab-sair, taking what food and water they could, and rode into the desert night.

CHAPTER SEVEN

A young man trudges through sand the color of ochre. A woman of nearly the same age walks next to him. She wears a flowing desert dress, light and bright and supple as the wind. It is the color of the desert dawn, a pale yellow not so different from the color of a golden tourmaline. She does not wear a veil as the desert women do, nor does she drape a cowl over her head. Her nutmeg hair flows freely down her back, and she lets the sun fall as it will against her olive skin.

He feels foreign in this place, as well, more so than she. He wears no turban. His clothes are cut differently than those of the people who live in this endless desert.

They came here together—he and the woman—but he knows not where they go, or why. He knows only that they will work toward some greater goal. He doesn't think to speak to her of it. To speak would be to waste his breath. She knows where they go, and that is enough for him.

As they take the incline toward the black-capped mountain far ahead, the sand gives way to gravel, and gravel gives way to dirt. The barren scrub brush of the desert floor grow sparser, and in their place comes a wiry grass that will cut skin if one is not careful.

Eventually there come proper, if stunted, trees. As he walks among them, as the endless hike and incline make his thighs burn, he tries to remember his name. There are days when he can remember it, but today isn't one of them. Nor is it one in which he remembers the name of the girl—*neh*, the young woman—who walks beside him.

They stop at a tree whose boughs spiral up toward the sky. The woman moves to the trunk and presses her hands against it. She leans forward and kisses the rough bark. For long moments, nothing happens, but then the bark darkens where she'd placed her lips. It moistens, and soon there is a rivulet of sap draining from a small hole in the tree. She presses her lips against the hole, drinking from it, and he's surprised how similar it seems to the hezhan who feed upon her—and him—constantly.

She finishes and motions for him to drink his fill.

He doesn't wish to, but neither does he wish to die. As powerful as the two of them are, they must still drink, and they have no other source of water. He steps to the tree and presses his own lips against the rough bark. The smell of the wood is as strong as the heat of the desert—they've not risen so high to have escaped that—but the sap is cool, and it tastes sweet, like the juice of a melon, but with earthy, mineral overtones.

When he finishes, he calls upon a spirit of life, a dhoshahezhan. It comes easily, willingly, feeding upon him, feeding upon the tree, even as it does his bidding. The flow of sap stops. The hole mends. And the hezhan is sent back from whence it came, beyond the veil to the land of Adhiya.

"How much longer?" he asks the woman.

She stares at him with bright blue eyes and smiles, but he knows it is forced. The handful of times he's seen her truly smile, it was bright indeed—the moon itself, not the dim and distant star she offers him now.

She points toward the dark peak. "We'll reach the entrance before nightfall."

They rest for a time, eating honey and seeds that had been flattened into a sticky wafer. As they prepare to continue up toward the tomb, he notices a lump within the leather satchel at her side. There is something within that satchel. Something important. He's looked upon it in the past, but for the life of him he cannot remember what it is.

She sees him staring at her satchel, and it is in that one small instant that he remembers the radiance that comes from the stone that lays hidden from his gaze. It is a stone as old as the earth. As old as the worlds themselves. It created them, and one day it will destroy them.

"May I look upon it?" he asks.

For a moment there is mistrust and worry in her eyes, a look that speaks of insecurity, which is strange given the amount of power she wields. "You may not," she says, and with that she turns and resumes her trek up toward the peak.

He follows, wondering what it was he was just asking about.

The sun sets as they come to an easy, upward slope. The peak juts up from this place, climbing quickly, harsh stone and black rock, an edifice that seems fit to house the fates themselves. They trek toward the base of it, and he realizes she reminds him of another. A woman tall and fair, her hair golden, her eyes a beautiful blue.

Her name was Sariya, and she was fearsome and learned and wise.

But she was also dead.

Who then was this woman? Were they related? He remembers her daughter. Sariya's daughter. She was young, a child where the one next to him is a woman grown. They must be the same, but how could this be?

Had so much time passed since...

He remembers a bridge. He remembers falling. He remembers holding a heavy stone in his hand. He remembers healing a man who had come to be a hidden and indescribable part of him, like memories both painful and sweet that shaped a man into the person he was.

He remembers a girl crashing into him. They fell to the waves and plummeted through the sea. Down and down they went. He felt the stone, the Atalayina, slip from his grasp. It had been a moment of terror, not for himself but for the world.

There was a shift. It itched the skin of his face and scalp. Made his bones ache. It brought them to a different place. He could tell, for the light was different, the water warmer. The very *sound* of it was different. When the girl pulled him with an arm around his neck, he let her, and when they broke the surface at last, he found himself in the center of a wide river. The land around him was rich with swaying fields of grass that seemed untouched by the hand of man.

He recalls asking her one simple question. "Where have we come?"

She looked at him, her brown hair plastered to her face. She looked as her mother had, regal and frightening while others would look bedraggled and sad. With that one look, she stole his memories, for he recalls nothing beyond it for long days or even weeks.

As they approach the base of the cliff, more memories surface, mere glimmers of their travel across the Motherland. A village where they bought packs and food for their journey. A forest of alder and spruce whose last leaves were just beginning to fall. A city that lay at the edge of the desert. It was difficult for him to see how she changed over that time, but now, as he looks back, he sees the changes clearly. She was a girl of eleven when they left the Spar. But now she looks to be at least as old as his eighteen years. If he reckons it right, less than two years have passed, and yet she has somehow aged seven or eight. He wonders if her mind has grown similarly, but he tosses the thought aside in an instant. She had always seemed older than her years. Perhaps this was simply the fates allowing her mortal shell to catch up.

Thinking back, he doesn't know why she didn't simply transport them as she did in the sea, but he wonders if it had anything to do with the way she stared into the stone when the two of them were alone. There were many nights when she would simply sit at the edge of their fire like an urchin with a bright new coin. She would stare into its depths, learning or perhaps yearning for things yet closed to her.

She asked him from time to time what he knew of it, and he would answer—he had no choice but to do so—and he would tell her of his memories...

His memories of Khamal. One of the Al-Aqim.

By the fates, he cannot remember who he is *now*—that much is still closed—but he remembers his life as Khamal, and he remembers the other Al-Aqim. Muqallad and Sariya they were named. And with Sariya's memories come memories of her daughter.

Kaleh.

The woman's name is Kaleh.

He told her of his life as Khamal, of what he had done with the stone. She asked not of the time after the sundering but instead of the days leading up to it. Of those days, however, he had very few memories, and all too soon she would return to her contemplation of the Atalayina, and *he* would slip back into forgetfulness. But he would retain *some* of what he'd lost, and he would store it away in a place she couldn't find so that when he woke again he could find it easily and slowly, hopefully, return to himself. It was the only way he knew to break the chains she and the Atalayina placed on him.

At last they come to the face of the tall black cliff. Kaleh walks along its length. Bushes and briars grow at the foot of the cliff, and it is in those dark places that Kaleh stops and hunkers down and peers intently. She finds nothing, however, and they continue on.

As the sun slides behind the westward ridge of the towering peak, the air immediately becomes more chill. They come to a forest of impossibly tall trees. Their bark is greenish-grey, and their branches still hold leaves, as if they refuse to bend to the coming winter. The air is filled with sage, but there is also the scent of antiquity, like the smell of ancient scrolls. Kaleh continues to lead them along the face of the cliff. Sometimes they're forced away by the landscape, but this never seems to bother her. She simply leads them beyond it and resumes her search as they trek westward. The sky darkens, making their path through the trees more difficult to see. She continues until she's practically searching with her hands along the rock.

Finally the sun sets fully. The stars shine brightly and insects chitter among the trees. And Kaleh suddenly steps back.

Ahead there is a looming blackness. Kaleh retrieves the Atalayina from its pouch and holds it high in her hand. The stone begins to glow, first a deep blue like the sun against a shallow sea, and then it intensifies into a cold white brightness that reveals a yawning opening in the face of the cliff. She stares at it for some time, moving the stone this way and that, as if she doesn't quite believe what she's found.

She shrugs off her pack and motions for him to do the same.

He complies—there is no choice but to obey—and he follows her into the opening. It is not deep. They come quickly to the end of it. Creeping vines grow here, and it is clear they're covering something. Kaleh pulls at them. Unbidden, he does the same, and slowly a figure is revealed, a figure carved into the stone itself: a woman, her eyes closed, her arms crossed over her chest as if she's been laid to rest. His first thought is that this is a grave, a marker of someone's passing, but somehow that doesn't seem right.

Kaleh, holding the Atalayina in her left hand, touches the statue with her right. No more do her fingertips brush the statue than the stone begins to crumble. It seems improper to tear down what someone took so long to create, but in mere moments it is done and the rocks look like nothing more than some forgotten remnant of man.

Revealed is a passageway into the mountain.

Kaleh stares into that deep darkness. Her grip on the Atalayina is not merely tight; her hand shakes from it. For the first time he can remember, she seems fearful—truly fearful. For some reason this place has shaken her to her very core. She notices him watching and tries to calm herself, but the strength of her emotions cannot be buried so easily. He can hear it through the quaver in her voice as she utters a single word. "Come." And with that, she heads into the passageway, holding the glowing Atalayina above her head as if it would protect her from whatever dark things lie ahead.

He follows, and the cool night becomes infinitely more chill. It saps his strength, makes him shiver uncontrollably. Something about this place tells him not to call upon a suurahezhan, a spirit of fire. He knows not what would happen—perhaps nothing—but at the moment he's unwilling to tempt the fates.

The passageway slopes upward, then downward, and then it begins to curve until he's sure that they've completed several full circuits. All the while, Kaleh seems more nervous.

"We can return to the forest," he suggests, "and try again in the morning."

She stares at him, the light from the stone shining up and across her face like shadows in a vale. "Do not speak again," she says, turning away and continuing.

At last the passage stops at a dead end. The face of the stone is embossed. It shows the image of the same person who stood at the entrance, except instead of her arms being crossed, they are spread wide, as qiram do when they commune with hezhan. Her eyes are open, and they stare at Kaleh with a look of stony judgment. Kaleh inspects the slab, which is nearly double her height. She presses her hand against it as she did outside, but this time, the stone does not change. Nothing happens at all.

She tries again, her face growing concerned as she does so. Her jaw sets. The tendons on her hand stand out even more than the veins on her forehead. The light in the Atalayina fades and goes black.

For long moments he hears only the sound of her labored breathing. It smells of winter here. Of a cold so deep it might be left from the forming of the world.

The wall begins to glow, a dull orange light centered on Kaleh's hand. It spreads, and the light brightens until there's a yellow burning around the outline of her hand that fades to orange and red and black as it radiates outward. Kaleh is pressing harder than he's ever seen her. Her head quivers. Her shoulders shake. A long groan comes from somewhere deep inside her and it grows as the wall turns white at its center, and then she screams, a sound of pain and rage and frustration, and still she tries harder.

And then it becomes too much.

Kaleh collapses, and the Atalayina slips from her grasp, the stone rolling away with the bright sound of rattling crystal.

CHAPTER EIGHT

I mmediately, the glowing wall begins to dull, but before it dies completely, he kneels by her side and checks her pulse.

"Wake, Kaleh. Please."

The wall is too hot to touch, but the warmth of it is welcome after the frigid confines of this place.

"Kaleh!" He shakes her, then slaps her cheek as the glow continues to fade. The vision of her face before him fades, orange then red then ruddy crimson. And then all is black save the center of the door, which glows like a distant volcano.

Kaleh still breathes, but she does not heed his call nor respond to his light slaps. She doesn't seem to be in danger of dying, and he's unwilling to do anything more harsh to her, so he reaches for the Atalayina. In the near darkness, his hand brushes it. It chimes as it rolls away.

He picks the stone up and stands before the door. What could lie behind it? And why has Kaleh brought them so far across the Gaji in order to find it?

And suddenly he remembers bits and pieces of their time in the desert. Perhaps it's because he now holds the stone. Whatever the reason, he goes rigid, waiting for more of his precious memories to return. He recalls a village, and the wary people who lived there. Kaleh was wise, though. She took her time, waiting until she knew them well enough, and then she began taking them one by one, sifting through their minds until she had the knowledge she wanted.

Of the days that followed he remembers little, only that Kaleh grew more intent. She allowed him to attend her less and less often. He wondered whether it was because she didn't want him to know her true purpose. He was her puppet, doing as she wished, but still, perhaps she knew enough to keep her true thoughts from him, for surely she still hoped to complete what her mother had begun.

And then it comes to him. His name. His name is Nasim.

He has been drowning in his attempts to remember more, even a thing as simple as this. He has felt so powerless. He is largely powerless still, but the simple knowledge of his own name gives him hope.

The door is completely dark now. As he stands before it, he feels the weight of the Atalayina in his hand. It is as large as an apple and as smooth. He cannot feel the seams where the stone was once split into three, and he wonders for a moment if it is less powerful than it once was. He doubts that it is so, for when he touches it with his mind, the way to Adhiya opens up to him. It practically swallows him. How could anything have been more powerful than this?

As Kaleh did, he calls upon a dhoshahezhan, a spirit of life, to light the Atalayina from within. As a soft blue-white glow lights the tunnel, he reaches out and feels the surface of the door, which is still warm to the touch. No more does he press his hand against it than a crack forms. It widens, runs up to the ceiling and down to the floor. More cracks run from side to side like a spider web being spun before his very eyes. Flakes of stone begin to fall away, then larger chunks, and soon the entire massive thing is breaking and crumbling to the floor like a landslide. He pulls Kaleh away as stone falls around her feet. Still she does not wake, so he holds the Atalayina high and steps over the uneven rubble to inspect the passage that has been revealed. Twenty paces in there is a square room. A stone chest the size of a coffin sits at the center. On either side of it are two statues, one man and one woman. They wear the robes of the Aramahn. Their hands are to their sides, and their faces upturned in rapture, as if they've found vashaqiram at last.

Nasim approaches the sarcophagus. Upon it lays a sheaf of wheat, which crumbles in his hand as he tries to pick it up. Who lies within it? Why would a place like this have been built to house them? Most importantly, though, why would Kaleh care? Why would she come all this way and risk her life to find it? And why, by the will of the fates, would this place have allowed him in but kept Kaleh out? He struggles to remember anything of this place or of Kaleh's purpose, but too many of his memories have been secreted away, and he has no idea how to find them.

After brushing away the remains of the wheat, he places his hands on the stone lid. Using the Atalayina, he calls upon a vanahezhan. As deeply buried as this tomb is within the mountain, there are many near, but instead of choosing one himself, he allows one to choose *him*. Strangely, the hezhan do not squabble, as they often do. They seem to bow to one, and though it is strong, it is neither the strongest nor the eldest.

The hezhan approaches, and a metallic taste fills Nasim's mouth. The mineral scents of copper and iron fill his nostrils. He bids the hezhan to warp the stone, to part it that he might see inside. The hezhan, this spirit of earth, has no power over it. The lid does not bend to its will. And yet, he senses something within, not a hezhan, but a soul. A living soul. And it is awakening.

Merciful heavens, what could be alive in a place that has surely remained untouched for centuries?

Nasim suddenly becomes fearful.

The lid shakes. It scrapes several inches toward Nasim. He backs away as a sickly sweet smell fills the room.

The lid moves again, and then a hand rises from within. Nasim lifts the Atalayina, makes it brighten so that he can see more detail. The hand is desiccated, little more than bone covered by a white layer of the palest skin Nasim has ever seen. It isn't just white, it is nearly translucent, revealing veins both large and small.

Another hand rises up, and the lid is thrown aside, forcing Nasim to back away or have it crush his legs. The massive tablet dashes against the floor, breaking into three large pieces.

Dust billows around the sarcophagus, occluding it momentarily as Nasim watches on, eyes wide, heart pumping madly. He can see the outline of a head within. He can see shoulders. There are robes around the form in the same style as those on the statues, but they, just like the sheaf of wheat, crumble as the form pulls itself up and stands within the confines of its coffin.

The thing inside seems to be a woman, though he is not at all sure of this. She is so emaciated that her stomach is drawn toward her spine as if no viscera remain. Her limbs are as thin as the boughs of a yearling tree. Her cheeks are mere hollows, her eyes so sunken they are difficult to see in the depths of their sockets. A golden circlet rests upon her brow, not one of the delicate ones the qiram of Nasim's generation use, but one of the wide circlets of old, more crown than ornament. Five settings adorn it, one for each of the aspects of hezhan, but he is sure that this woman, whoever she might have been, has no need of stones. The qiram of ancient days had not needed to commune in such ways; the use of stones was a recent contrivance, brought on by the inability of later generations to touch Adhiya as easily as their grandmothers and grandfathers had.

The woman turns her head, as if she senses Nasim but cannot yet see him.

He steps forward, holding no fear. She was a woman of knowledge when she was buried. "Here," he calls, waving his hand while holding the Atalayina high.

She turns her head, seeing not him but the Atalayina. She stares directly at it, her sunken eyes squinting against the brightness.

He eases the intensity of the light, and she seems to calm.

Her mouth works. Her lips are drawn back in a permanent grimace, revealing stained teeth and gums that are so severely receded it is a wonder any teeth remain. Her shriveled tongue moves. A sound like a sigh escapes her, and she reaches out with her hand. She takes one halting step forward within the confines of the sarcophagus, and Nasim wonders if she will fall.

"Th—"

The sound is breathy, almost a whisper.

"The aht—"

She is unmistakably trying to speak. She swallows, a thing that seems eminently painful for her.

"All will be well, grandmother. I hear you."

"The atahl—" She works her mouth and tries again. "The Atalayina."

Nasim can only stare. The Atalayina. She knows of the Atalayina. But how? The stone has been missing from the world for three centuries.

"How do you know of this stone?"

She pulls herself taller and stares, somehow regal despite her frail state. "I know..." Her words are hoary with age and disuse. "I know of the Atalayina."

"How?"

"I was there."

"You were on Ghayavand."

"*Yeh.*"

"But..." Nasim didn't know where to begin. "Grandmother, how came you here?"

She considers for a moment, as if reliving those ancient days, but before she can respond, a blast of fire streaks in and plows into the woman. It knocks her aside, flips her over the edge and sends her crashing to the ground. Above the roar of the fire, Nasim hears brittle bones break. The woman cries out, a low moan at first but rising quickly to a fever pitch.

Kaleh stands in the broken doorway, breathing heavily, staring at Nasim as if he's betrayed her.

She stalks forward, keeping an eye on Nasim while moving toward the burning figure that writhes upon the floor.

"Don't!" Nasim cries. He lifts the Atalayina. He calls upon a dhoshahezhan to stop her.

But before he can, Kaleh says one word. "*Insa.*" The Kalhani word for *forget*.

And he remembers not who he is.

Knows not why he's here.

Knows not why there is a slight and ancient woman ablaze before him.

The young woman to his left pours more fire upon her until the crying stops. Until her movement ceases. Until she is little more than a blackened husk.

Tears burn down his cheeks, but the emotions that drive them are buried and unreachable.

He's confused by everything around him, but he knows this young woman. Her name is Kaleh. She is a powerful woman. Fearsome.

He believes in her. He believes that her cause is just. But this is not an absolute belief. For there is now doubt, planted there by the murdered woman who lies at his feet.

And suddenly he realizes that he has been here before. He has witnessed this scene play out in other mountains and other tombs. Other men and woman dying by Kaleh's hand.

He also knows that he was tricked. She could not enter this place. Not on her own. She needed him. Why, he doesn't know, but he realizes now that it was he that allowed her to enter this sacred place so that she could murder the holy woman that lay within this ancient sarcophagus. It was he that allowed her to do this to the others—four or five or a dozen; who knows how many in all? His blind faith in her was yet another of her commands, and yet, even knowing this, there is a part of him that *wants* to believe in her, that *wants* to obey. But there is another part as well, however small, that sees her for what she is.

Kaleh turns toward him, indifferent to the horror that had just played out before her. There is something ancient within her eyes, so much like Sariya that he shivers.

She steps forward and with her left hand touches his forehead. "*Insa.*"

He stands, merely watching, merely waiting. The young woman before him takes the blue stone from his hand. He lets her. He isn't sure why he was holding it in the first place.

He stares at the blackened mound of ash nearby. It stains the floor. The ashes drift about the room as the woman walks briskly away.

At the doorway marked by broken stones, she beckons him.

He follows, and together they walk down the cold, curving hallway.

He doesn't think to speak to her. They have no need for such things. They know where they go. They know where they've come from. To speak would be to waste one's breath.

But within him, there is a spark. A spark of a memory. He doesn't know where it comes from, and it is a minor thing, but he treasures it just the same.

It is only a name, but it is *his* name.

He is Nasim. Nasim an Ashan.

Such a small thing, one's name, but it is a start.

CHAPTER NINE

A tiana's body feels distant, like a memory, or a long-forgotten wish. She hardly feels the powerful strides of the ab-sair as it gallops through the night. She is vaguely aware—and grateful—that Nikandr is seated behind her in the saddle, for if she were alone, she would surely fall off.

She can still feel the woman in the compound over a league behind, but as they ride away beyond the caravanserai and into the desert, the feeling of the wodjan, the Haelish witch, begins to recede. Even so, Atiana can still see her, a diaphanous white against the midnight blue of the aether. The wodjan recovers her censer that had been spilled when Sukharam entered the home. She sets it on the glowing red coals. A blackened remnant of the blood she burned still rests within the censer. She hunches over the fire pit, drawing the rising smoke from her own burning blood toward her as if it is her sole link to life.

Atiana is disgusted, but she knows that this ritual, the burning of the wodjan's own blood, is the thing that both drew her into the aether and allowed her to remain there. She felt it in the room shortly before Goeh arrived, a sudden and undeniable pull toward the aether. She thought it was Ishkyna, her sister, returned from the warfront—for who else could it be?—but it hadn't felt like Ishkyna, nor Mileva, nor any of the Matri. It had felt foreign and raw, not so different than her first time in the drowning chamber those many years ago.

And it had *smelled* wrong. She knows now that it was the blood. It had filled her senses, an acrid smell that even now sickens her.

She slips in the saddle, nearly falling from the charging beast as Nikandr reins it westward along a dry desert path. Nikandr pulls her back up and shouts into her ear, "Atiana, please wake up!"

She can hear the alarm in his voice, but strangely, she does not wish to wake—she must learn all she can about this woman—but soon the woman begins to drift away. The delicate balance the aether demands becomes harder and harder to maintain.

Then it is too much, and she releases a pent-up cry of frustration as she's thrown from the aether altogether.

The sudden shift to the reality of the physical world made Atiana's stomach churn. She leaned forward and retched while Nikandr held her firmly in place.

He spoke calmly, softly, into her ear. "It's all right."

She took deep breaths of the cool night air and tried to draw herself fully into the here and now, but her mind was sluggish. She yearned for the aether, even more so than when she left the drowning basins of Galostina. Why this might be she had no idea. Perhaps because finding herself in the aether here, a place so foreign from the islands, made her yearn for what she missed the most. She also had to admit that it felt freeing to touch the aether without so much preparation and ritual. She had done the same near the Spar, but she had written that off as nothing more than an effect of Sariya's power and the confluence of aether running through Galahesh.

Finally they slowed their pace, giving their mounts some much-needed rest. Nikandr continued to hold her tight. "Can you hear me?"

She nodded, still not trusting herself to speak. If she opened her mouth, she feared her confusion and yearning would be released in one long, uncontrollable wail.

"It's all right," Nikandr said again, and he kissed her cheek.

It felt good, that kiss. It felt not only tender, but genuine, something that had been missing from their lives of late.

That one small gesture pulled her fully into this new reality. She heard the rhythmic canter of their ab-sair over the desert floor, smelled the desert sage, saw the blanket of stars that hung over them, guiding their way.

"Are they safe?" she asked Nikandr.

"They're safe, though Ushai is hurt."

Soroush held Ushai as Nikandr held Atiana—with great care. She wondered, though, whether this was only the heat of the moment speaking in Nikandr. She wondered whether in a day or two he'd return to his distant ways. She hoped not, but she had no reason to think otherwise. He was still broken, somehow, and she had no idea how to fix him.

Two mounts trailed the four they were riding. They held what looked to be a wholly insufficient amount of water for them to make their way across the desert to Kohor. The caravanserais along this route had long fallen into disuse. Too few traveled these paths now. Why, she had never learned. All she knew was that the people of Kohor were secretive and that they disliked strangers who came to their lands. Even Ashan, in all his travels, had never been to Kohor.

But Ushai had. Which was why it was vitally important, despite Atiana's misgivings about her effect on Sukharam, that she be present when they reached that hidden place.

They continued riding through the night. They watched and listened carefully for signs of pursuit. After the moon set in the west, they all felt as though they needed to put more distance between them and the men that were sure to follow, so they continued on, allowing the ab-sair to pick their path through the night with their excellent eyesight.

They stopped every so often to listen for the sound of hooves upon the earth. "I can feel for them," Sukharam offered at one such stop, meaning he could use a hezhan to search for them coming over the desert floor.

"Do not," Ashan replied. "It's best we take ourselves far away before calling upon the hezhan once again. The Haelish woman's magic. I know it not well at all, but she may be able to sense us if we do."

Atiana shivered, and not from the cold. Bahett's men would follow. With the Haelish woman guiding them with her foul magic, the janissaries had already found their trail once; there was no reason to think they couldn't do so again.

"Is there no way to stop her?" Atiana asked.

Ashan turned in his saddle to look at her. "Other than killing her, you mean?"

"*Yeh*," she said, "other than killing her."

"None that I know of."

When the coming of dawn brightened the eastern horizon, they picked up their pace once more. They were exhausted after the chase from Andakhara, but none of them felt safe stopping so soon, so they continued on as the sun rose behind them. They sipped at their water as the heat sapped what little energy they had. Nikandr had found four large bags of water in the stables, but that would only last the six of them two days, perhaps three if they were careful. Finding jalahezhan here in the desert was difficult. Even Sukharam had trouble bonding with them; they were simply too few, and even when he managed it he was unable to use them to draw much water. The best he could do was to draw sap from plants or the occasional acacia, but the process was too slow to try with pursuit so close on their heels. Better to push for the mountains and lose them there.

Atiana only hoped they could make it that far.

As midday neared and the heat became stifling they came to a small, abandoned caravanserai. They were all bleary eyed, and Ushai, sitting in the saddle in front of Soroush, looked ready to collapse. Dried blood matted her hair and marked her left cheek and stained her flax-colored robes. She had trouble keeping her eyes open, but just then she met Atiana's gaze. She did not smile—such was not her way—but when Atiana *did* smile and nod to her, Ushai nodded back, telling Atiana she'd be well.

The ground here offered a clear view of the land eastward, so they decided to rest before continuing on. The caravanserai had three abandoned mudbrick buildings and a dry well. They hid themselves in the largest of the buildings, a place that had surely acted as a communal sleeping room decades ago when the caravanserai had been active.

Soroush said he would have trouble sleeping and asked to take watch as everyone rested. Atiana could tell he was lying. He was embarrassed that he'd been taken hostage in Andakhara, and he wanted to prove to everyone that he was still valuable.

"I can't sleep either," Atiana said. This was no act. She couldn't shake her memories of the woman breathing in the smell of burnt blood.

She sat in the shade of the small mudbrick shed as the sun continued its march. Soroush rested his musket against the wall of the shed and stood, watching stoically. He wore his double robes and an almond-shaped turban, as he always had. The turban's tail hung down and swung lightly in the breeze. She still hadn't gotten used to him wearing one that was white. His black turban had seemed so much a part of him. Somehow, the change to the white one—even though she knew it was because of the sun's heat—made him seem changed. Not impotent, but less threatening.

"You can sit," Atiana said.

He stroked his long, square-cut beard while watching the horizon. "I know."

"Then why don't you?"

He glanced down at her, his serious face cracking a grudging smile, accentuating the ragged scar that ran along the ruin of his left ear and down his neck. "I have burns from those beasts I'll not regale you with now. Suffice it to say I'd rather stand."

He pulled a cloth from the bag at his side and unfolded it. He bent down and held the salt-cured meat within it for her to take. In the past she'd always refused, never having cared for the taste or texture, but today it seemed important that she accept, and so she did.

"Thank you," she said in Mahndi.

"You are welcome," he replied in Anuskayan.

She chewed off a piece from the flat, russet-colored meat. As her mouth watered, she noticed the gamey taste of the boar beyond the layers of peppercorn and fennel and salt.

"How was your Prince while I was gone?" He meant Nikandr's feelings of incompleteness. Of his distance from her and everyone else.

"He went to watch the path you took to Andakhara from our campsite. On top of the ridge." She suddenly found herself unable to swallow the meat around the quickly growing lump in her throat. "Ashan said he found him standing at the very edge of the drop-off. Ashan wouldn't say it, but I think he was ready to jump, to see if a havahezhan would bond with him, as the Aramahn of old once did."

Neither one of them made mention of the time when Soroush's comrade leapt from the cliffs below Radiskoye, but they both knew that the same had been done then, to great effect. It had been on Nikandr's mind ever since Nasim had severed their bond at the Spar, the bridge that stood over the Straits of Galahesh. Suddenly, she felt dizzy. The floor of the desert wavered in the heat. She stood and breathed deeply, hoping the effect would pass, but instead it grew worse.

"What is it?" Soroush asked.

And then she smelled the smoke. It was distant, like the scent of a wood fire carried leagues on the wind. Even as faint as it was she recognized it immediately, the scent of burning blood. The Haelish witch was searching for them again. And already, just as she had the previous night, she felt herself being drawn toward it.

Soroush came to her side. He leaned over, as if he were afraid she would collapse, but stopped just short of touching her. "Shall I get Nikandr?"

She refused to allow herself to be drawn into the aether again, and she fought to remain in place, but in that moment, as she stood halfway in and halfway out of the aether, she felt something, a presence to the south, someone coming toward the caravanserai from out of the desert. A man. A soldier. He felt familiar; surely one of the janissaries from Andakhara.

Atiana managed to pull herself taller, and by taking short, sharp breaths was able to stave off the overwhelming feeling of the aether. She pointed to her right, where a rise hid much of the southern plain. "Someone's coming."

In a blur of movement Soroush snatched up his musket and led Atiana around the corner of the low shed so that they were hidden from view from the southern approach. After making sure she was safe, he pulled the hammer of his musket to full cock, pulled the weapon to his shoulder, and leaned around the corner.

His eyes were alive as he sighted along the barrel. "How many?"

He thought she was still in the aether, as she had been during his rescue. She wished she was. She desperately wanted to know if there were more than just the one man. Surely they would have sent a dozen or more. Perhaps the others were coming from different directions, hoping to surround the caravanserai and cut off any hope of escape, but she had no idea if that were true.

"How *many*?"

"I don't know."

Atiana could smell the smoke. The bloody burnt smell. She *tried* to enter the aether, but of course this was the perfectly wrong way to do it. Both times she'd been drawn in with no effort on her part, so she relaxed, as she did in the drowning basins.

"There's only one," Soroush whispered. "He's walking alone. He doesn't even have a mount."

Atiana couldn't do it. The smoke was too faint, or she was too tense. But the feeling of familiarity in this man remained. She knew him, and he was no janissary.

She heard Soroush take a deep breath, as Nikandr often did before he fired.

"Stop!" she shouted while pushing him away.

The musket fired. White smoke filled the air as Atiana rounded the corner and saw, sixty paces away, a man crouched with a cloud of dirt dissipating in the distance behind him.

She heard the others waking from within the large building.

Soroush reached for his pistol, but Atiana grabbed his wrist. "His name is Goeh, and he helped us to find you. He helped us escape."

Soroush glanced at her over his shoulder, skeptical, but then he nodded and took his hand away from his weapon.

Atiana strode toward Goeh, raising her hands and mimicking the gesture he was giving as he walked forward to meet her. His eyes alternated between her, Soroush, and the communal building, from which the others were just now exiting.

"Why have you come?" Atiana asked him as the others caught up with her.

At last Goeh relaxed and pointed eastward. "They're coming. Fifty or more." He pointed beyond the dry well, where the ab-sair were tied. "You'll never make it to Kohor with just those, and you'll run out of water tomorrow unless you come with me."

"And why would we do that?"

"Because I was sent to watch for you. There are those in Kohor who would speak with you."

Strangely, when he spoke these words he did not look to Atiana. Nor did he look to Nikandr or Soroush.

Instead, he looked to Sukharam.

CHAPTER TEN

Atiana didn't have long to decipher Goeh's obsession with Sukharam, for as quickly as the look had come, it was gone.

"If you wish to live," Goeh told them, "you'll follow me." He told them what lay ahead. The ancient trail they'd been following, the one dotted by caravanserais, remained in the desert pan until finally meeting the foothills five days further, but Goeh said he knew of another path, one long forgotten by the men of Andakhara, that followed the rocky hills to the southwest. It would take longer—much longer—than following the other trail, but there was no choice at this point. Continue as they had and the Kamarisi's men would have them. Had they enough water, they might still have made a go of it, but they *didn't* have enough water, and Goeh said there were hidden wells he could lead them to.

It took them little time to agree. Soon they were mounted again and riding as their shadows leaned out over the land ahead of them. They'd been riding only a short while when Ushai called out from the rear of the train. They all turned in their saddles and saw, at the edge of the horizon, a dust cloud rising. They hurried after that, pushing their mounts faster than was wise. Their ab-sair seemed up to the task, however. These were not the mounts they had purchased at the northern edge of the Gaji. These were Dahud's mounts, taken from his stables. They would be some of the finest the desert had to offer. And so they were. The beasts took to the snap of the reins like newly trained colts, surging forward and maintaining a slow gallop for an hour at a time before they were forced to slow and give them a rest. By the time Atiana and the others had gone deep into the hills late that day, they could see no signs of the janissaries on their trail.

"I don't trust it," Atiana told Nikandr as they sat at the top of a hill, watching the eastern horizon for the telltale clouds that would signal the chase.

"Neither do I," Nikandr said. "Another reason to keep on the move."

He meant beyond finding Nasim, of course, but what he wasn't saying was that when they found Nasim at last—*if* they found him—Nikandr still harbored hope that Nasim could somehow heal him, that he could restore Nikandr's ability to touch Adhiya and commune with his havahezhan.

She didn't have the heart to tell him outright it would never be so. She'd told him obliquely a hundred times already, but there was a part of her that wanted him to keep that hope. Were he to realize the path to the world beyond would never be open to him again he might heal once and for all, but he might also be pushed deeper into despair. She had only to think of the many times she'd seen him staring vacantly from heights—windships, palotzas, eyrie perches and cliffs—to know what might happen. That wasn't something she could face. Not here in this place so far from their island home.

Since the moon was bright, they continued well beyond sunset, stopping only when the moon finally set. They went on like this for days, riding at first light until the hottest time of day—at which point they and their ab-sair would rest—and picking up again as the sun began to lower, continuing until the night stars were fully upon them. True to his word, Goeh found them water. There was a small spring in one of the valleys they passed through, which they used to fill all their skins and drink their fill. Food, however, was scarce. Goeh used a bow to kill the occasional desert hare, and once he even managed to take down an emaciated jackal, but these were rare luxuries. Most of their sustenance came from tiny red berries and fibrous leaves that Goeh said would help keep up their strength.

Nikandr, however, became more and more bleak. He was out of vodka. She knew, because she'd checked all of his skins. He was irritable and his eyes looked more and more haunted. She would catch him staring up at the tops of the hills, but she knew just by looking at them that they weren't tall enough. He needed true height. A sheer drop-off. She thanked the ancients none were available here.

On their third week into the hills, they made camp near a massive acacia, its branches reaching far out, occluding half of the delicate, twinkling sky. Atiana lay next to Nikandr on their blanket. They had no tent. None of them did, their exit from Andakhara being what it was. This was fine with Atiana. She liked lying beneath the stars. It made her feel as if she were near her home of Vostroma, a stone's throw from Galostina, not thousands of leagues away in this infernal place. And, as she felt the warmth of Nikandr lying next to her, it somehow made the distance between her and Nikandr feel less. The grandness of the firmament humbled her, made her petty human problems seem small, and it often made her think of the rifts and the wasting and how bad they'd become.

She and Nikandr made love that night. Atiana took his hand and led him away from the group, moving out and into the darkness until they'd found a bare rock jutting up from the landscape. She laid a blanket down behind it and brought Nikandr down with her. It felt like the days of old, when they would meet several times a year on Khalakovo or Vostroma or another of the duchies—any excuse to see one another and simply touch and kiss and caress. They breathed each other's skin. Nikandr was gentle, but that only made her want him more, and they ended holding one another tightly, sweating and panting as the throes of their love overtook them.

She knew he would return to his distant ways tomorrow, but for now she didn't care. For now, she had the Nikandr of old. She could only hope he would one day return to her fully.

When they returned to the camp, she tried to sleep, but couldn't. She lay awake long into the night and eventually left Nikandr sleeping on his bedroll. Goeh was awake as well. She could see his silhouette as he leaned against the twisted trunk of the ancient tree, and she moved to sit by him. Together, they sat side by side, staring up at the stars.

"Why did they send you, Goeh?"

"I *chose* to come here."

"You were the only one?"

"*Neh.* There are others, waiting in the caravanserai and the villages around the edge of the Gaji."

"Why? Why do they wish to speak to us?"

"It isn't my place to say. The elders will reveal that to you when they're ready."

"So you've said, but there must be something you can tell us. Is it to do with Nasim?"

"I've told you, I've not seen the boy you speak of."

"But the elders might have. Or the others from your village."

"Perhaps, and you'll know that once we arrive."

"Then tell me of Kohor."

Here Goeh paused. The chill night air rustled the leaves of the acacia above them. "It is a beautiful place. It lies in a wide valley of red sands and black mountains. The sun is bright and hot, but the night brings with it a cold that the skin welcomes. Kohor is ancient. More ancient than Tulandan. More ancient than Alekeşir. It is why the Kamarisi Haman ül Veşe became jealous and razed her to the ground. He couldn't stand to have a city older than his own."

"Kohor has been a part of the Empire for more than four centuries."

"Six centuries, daughter of Radia. Six centuries. And she is much, much older than that. Two thousand years ago the first settlement was built. It is a place of learning. A place of sharing." He motioned to Ushai's sleeping form on the opposite side of the softly glowing fire. "Ushai's mother came to Kohor, as do many others, for that is our birthplace—all of us—or near enough to it that it no longer makes a difference."

"Ushai has spoken highly of it, but she also said that it's small."

"There are more measures of a settlement's size than number of people she holds, or the land she occupies. Centuries ago Kohor was a place of high learning."

"It is no longer?"

Goeh remained silent.

"You're very secretive, Goeh."

When he spoke again, his voice was filled with melancholy. "Had your most precious secrets been ripped from your breast, again and again, you would be secretive too."

"But you were sent to us for a reason."

"You speak truth, Atiana Radieva, but I'll not be the one to share our purpose with you. The elders of Kohor will speak with you when we arrive."

Atiana paused, choosing her next words carefully. "Surely news of the wasting has reached Kohor."

Goeh turned his head toward her, but did not look at her. "We know of it."

"Then you also know that time grows short. Disease comes even to the desert if the amount of game we've seen is any indication. That jackal we killed the other day was sickly, and I'd be willing to bet the same is true all over the Gaji. Is it not so?"

"It is."

"Then I would think you'd understand how dangerous it is to withhold information from me, from us. We're here to help. We're here to find our comrades, and with their help, return to Ghayavand and mend what was torn."

She saw Goeh turn to face her, and she suddenly wondered if he could see more than her silhouette in the darkness. "Given what you know about Nasim, about Kaleh, do you think it likely that the elders of Kohor would cast so wide a net and *not* wish to talk to you about them?"

"They have seen Nasim." She knew it was true, and yet she wanted Goeh to tell her of it, to tell her more of the elders' purpose.

But Goeh wouldn't. Not this night, in any case. He merely returned his scrutiny back to the eastern horizon.

Atiana stood. "Play games if you wish. Just know that you, as much as I or Soroush or Nikandr, hold the fate of the world in your hands."

She walked away, but heard him call behind her. "Don't go far."

"I won't," she replied.

She strolled beyond the hill behind which they were camped and took a wide path down to a vale. She went slowly, picking her path among the wiry trees and scrub brush. As she walked, she took out her soulstone and held it in her hand. "Hear me, Ishkyna."

Of all the Matri, only Ishkyna could hear her this far away, and it wasn't merely because she had become more powerful than any of the Matri. It was because she was no longer chained to her mortal shell. Mere days after returning to Vostroma from the battle on Galahesh, Ishkyna's heart had stopped beating. Everyone including Atiana had thought she had died in that same instant, but shortly after, the gallows crow, the bird Ishkyna had used to return to herself, had started cawing madly. It flapped around the room for the better part of an hour. Slowly, it dawned on her and Mileva and their mother, Radia, that Ishkyna was crying. Except she *couldn't* cry. Not really. This was her sister's lament finding its release in the only way possible—in the flapping wings and ceaseless cawing of this one, sad bird.

Atiana began to fear that Ishkyna would die when the gallows crow did. It was irrational, she knew—no one could predict how long Ishkyna would live—but there were times when she found herself wanting to have the crow bound and taken and placed in a cage and cared for. There were others when she reckoned Ishkyna had lived beyond the time given to her, and if that were so—if she'd been granted time by the ancients—Atiana would cherish it and defer to their wisdom.

"Ishkyna, please hear me."

She'd done this every night since entering the desert. They had agreed that they would not talk often. As gifted as Ishkyna was, it was still taxing for her to travel so far. Plus, she was needed at the war front. So they'd agreed to speak only every few weeks, but it had now been more than two months since they'd last spoken.

She gripped her soulstone tighter, and there was a moment when, beneath the smooth surface of the stone, she thought she could feel a presence. Whether it was Ishkyna's or not she wasn't sure, but she wanted it to be, for she was desperately lonely. She thought Nikandr's presence with her in the Gaji would be enough, but the truth was it wasn't. Nikandr was slipping away from her, and she didn't know if she had the strength to support both of them, to find Nasim, *and* to make their way to Ghayavand. Who knew what might happen then? How could they stop the world from tearing itself apart? It all seemed so much bigger than her. Bigger than any of them.

She heard a rustle ahead, perhaps a bird flapping among the branches of a scrub tree. Perhaps the gallows crow.

"Ishkyna?" she called softly.

She gasped when she saw the silhouette of a man wending his way through the trees.

Something deep inside uncoiled and raged at her to run. To flee. To call for the others. But before she could an acrid odor came on the wind. It was the smell of blood. Burnt blood. In an instant she was borne back to the ritual the Haelish woman had used, and she realized she'd misjudged. This was no man at all. It was the Haelish wodjan who was, for whatever unfathomable reason, aiding the Empire.

Running would still be the wise thing to do, and yet Atiana found herself rooted. The wodjan had known Atiana would be here. She was headed straight for her, and she seemed to be alone, which meant she'd come for a reason, and Atiana would know what it was.

"That's far enough," Atiana said.

The wodjan stopped. They stood only ten paces apart. Atiana realized just how tall she was—at least a full head taller than Atiana—making her of a height with Nikandr. She was lithe, but Atiana would not call her thin.

Atiana looked around the hills, expecting the janissaries to come marching out of the dark at any moment. "Where are the soldiers of Yrstanla?"

"Near, but they will not find you." Her accent was thick, and she spoke slowly. Clearly Yrstanlan was still new to her tongue.

"But *you're* here."

"Because I wish to be. I've led the men of Yrstanla near your path, but not exactly. At least for now."

"Are you not their servant?" Atiana asked.

"Hael will never be the servant of Yrstanla."

"Then why have you come?"

"To give you warning. For all of you, but you most of all."

"You make no sense. You're *aiding* them."

The woman paused. She started to speak several times, but she couldn't seem to find the right words. "I brought them because it was needed."

"*Needed?* Why?"

"The wodjana see many paths in our blood. You know this?"

The Haelish believed in the fates, as the Aramahn did, but they also believed their wodjana could use rituals to see their own fate. They even believed they could *affect* their own fates, and the fates of others, if they chose the right paths.

"I know of it."

"The world is in danger, and you hope to fix it."

"We do."

"And so do we."

She said it as if it were explanation enough for what she was doing. But it wasn't. It didn't begin to explain.

"Are you here to help us?"

"I come to put you on the right path."

"Which path?"

"Our path. Your path. The path of the world. You go to Kohor, you and others, but you will not leave as you came."

Atiana felt her blood go cold. The wodjan—her voice, the way she spoke—made Atiana feel as though she'd been caught in something much larger than the two of them. It felt larger than the mere struggle to find Nasim and Kaleh and the Atalayina. It felt as if the decisions she made now, here in this valley in the middle of the desert night, would affect everything, even the fate of the worlds.

But then she shook herself from it. This was preposterous. She couldn't trust this woman. She couldn't. And yet, there seemed to be something in her voice, a confidence that came from a deep-seated truth that was leading her to do this. Either that, Atiana thought, or this woman was a gifted actress, indeed.

Atiana turned and looked back toward the hill. "I should call to my comrades. I should not let you leave."

"Do not." Something glinted in the night—a knife the wodjan was holding above her head. When she spoke again, her voice was low and dangerous. "I saw you next to me, you know." When Atiana paused confusedly, the wodjan continued. "In Andakhara. I felt your desire to enter the dreaming world."

The aether. She meant the aether. "I hoped to find my sister."

"You hoped to enter for yourself. You miss the land of dreams."

Atiana saw no reason to deny it. "I miss it very much."

The knife twisted in the dark, catching the light of the stars. "You can enter again. I can teach."

Atiana took two steps backward without meaning to. The wodjan meant for her to cut herself. To burn her own blood. "I would never."

A wicked chuckle came from the wodjan. "Do not be so quick to refuse. It is in you. I can feel it now, burning. I felt it even before I left Hael."

"You didn't know who I was."

Again the chuckle came. "How little you know of the Haelish." She began backing away. "I will return two days from now. Think on this, daughter of dreams. Think on it well."

"Wait. What is your name?"

The woman paused. "My name is Aelwen." And then she was swallowed by the darkness, and Atiana was alone once more.

Atiana walked back up to their camp, infinitely colder than she'd been on the way down. Ushai was up, leaning against a rock with her bedroll behind her. She looked bedraggled, her eyes sunken and dark, still recovering from her treatment at the hands of the janissaries. "Who were you speaking to?"

"No one," Atiana replied. "I was calling for my sister."

For some reason this seemed to amuse Ushai, for she smiled a patronizing smile and said, "Did she answer?"

"*Neh*," Atiana replied. "She did not."

CHAPTER ELEVEN

For eight days did Styophan travel tied to the Haelish litter. He was untied when he needed to relieve himself, but on these occasions Datha and another Haelish warrior would walk with him. They tied a rope around his neck, which they held tightly and removed only when his ankles and wrists had been secured once more. Datha continued to give him water, but for food, at dawn and dusk they allowed him dried meat and berries and nuts with nothing in between.

He hadn't seen Anahid or Mikhalai or Rodion or the others since the attack inside Kürad's yurt, and though he'd asked of them each day, Datha's only answer was that he would see them when Kürad allowed it.

"And when will that be?"

"Who can say?" Datha would reply.

Styophan came to understand that watching over Styophan was not only a punishment for Datha; it was a self-imposed one as well. He was deeply embarrassed by what had happened to Styophan and his men. His King had betrayed his word to Ranos Khalakovo, but what was worse: Kürad had betrayed his people as well. It wasn't simply a matter of turning on the men of Anuskaya—men they didn't know—nor was it a matter of simply betraying their word to the Duke of Khalakovo. They were deeply shamed because they'd betrayed them for their sworn enemy, Yrstanla.

When night came, Styophan was untied and led toward a clearing where he was forced to help stand up one of the clan's many yurts. The first few nights he had refused, but Datha had calmly told him that Anahid would pay the price if he refused. With Datha waiting patiently, his anger settled. He had no doubt that Datha would follow through on his threat, so he'd agreed. In setting the poles and helping to lay the skin walls and roof of the yurt that he would sleep in, Styophan came face to face with a dozen other men and women. Each night they'd been different, as if whoever happened to be nearby when camp began would help. He even saw Kürad helping to stand his own yurt some distance away. Their eyes had met in that one instant. Styophan found his fury returning, along with a burning desire to kill, but Kürad only stared back impassively and eventually returned to his work as if Styophan and his anger meant nothing to him.

Styophan couldn't help but feel the sense of community among these people. Everyone helped, and everyone seemed skilled at so many things—cooking, weaving, horse handling. Even in hunting the women and older children helped. More than once he'd seen a woman return from a forest with a bow in one hand and a gutted doe balanced across her shoulders.

The yurts were stood quickly and efficiently, with space for a thousand or more of the Haelish. Styophan was always taken into the one he'd helped pitch. There he would lay for the night, untied. He would often lay awake, thinking of ways to avenge the death of his men, but any thoughts of vengeance were tempered by the fact that twenty Haelish warriors slept with him. Some would remain awake, smoking or talking in low voices while most fell asleep, but Styophan woke many times over the days to find all of them asleep. He might have tried to escape, but he had no idea where Anahid and his men were, and he would not leave them. And so he lay there, fuming, wondering why the ancients had so abandoned him and his cause. He couldn't help but think of what Datha had said, that the King had allowed him to approach with weapons even knowing he was about to betray Styophan. He had done so because of their strange sense of justness, perhaps reasoning that allowing Styophan freedom to retaliate somehow evened the scales for what they'd done. Styophan wanted to spit, thinking of it, but he kept his face calm. There would come a time when he learned more, and then perhaps he could leave and find the others and somehow forge a path back to Anuskaya.

He laughed, thinking of how far-fetched that seemed just then.

Datha, sitting near the entrance smoking a pipe, turned and asked, "What do you find so amusing?"

"I only wondered if I'll ever see the shores of Anuskaya again."

"One never knows," he replied, returning his gaze back to stare outside the yurt through the crack made by the entryway's thick leather flaps. "Sleep. For tomorrow we push early and hard to reach the Place of Kings."

Styophan laid his head down, not at all comforted by those words.

Styophan woke with a shudder.

He stared wildly about the dark interior of the yurt, not understanding what had woken him. He shivered again when he realized someone was standing over him—a woman, judging from her outline. She beckoned him with her hand and tread carefully between the sleeping men until she reached the door. There, she pulled the flap to one side and beckoned again before stepping out into the cold.

Styophan stood—adjusting the patch over his right eye, which had slid out of place while he was sleeping—and stepped carefully over the men and into the cold night air. Without speaking a word, the woman walked toward the nearby woods, her feet crunching softly on well-trodden snow. He followed, their footsteps becoming more hollow-sounding as they reached deeper, untouched snow. It was dark as they wound their way through the forest, but with the blanket of snow, it was easy to pick out the trees and the lithe form of the tall woman before him.

When they were out of earshot of the camp, he called to her in Yrstanlan, "Who *are* you?"

She did not respond, but merely kept walking.

He stopped, refusing to be led like this.

She continued on for a time, but then, when she realized he wouldn't follow without an answer, she stopped and turned. "I am Elean, queen of this clan. Now come. The night grows short."

He remained where he was, but she ignored him, heading deeper into the forest. He thought of returning to the yurt, but that would be a thing done in spite only, and he couldn't do that, not if there was more to be learned.

He followed, and soon, far ahead, he saw golden light coming through the trees. When they came closer, he could see a bearskin in the middle of a small clearing with a brass lamp sitting in its center. Elean strode onto the bearskin. Only then, by the light of the lamp, did he realize she was wearing no shoes. He shook his head at the Haelish. Were his shoes taken from him, he would huddle and shiver, as any proper man would, but Elean did none of these things. She seemed completely at ease with the burgeoning winter.

She motioned for him to step onto the skin. He did so and faced her. He knew she was tall, but it didn't quite strike him until he stood eye-to-eye with this cruel yet graceful queen. Her eyes, as he'd seen when they'd first met in Kürad's yurt, were sunken and dark. Her cheeks were drawn. Her appetite would be low by this point. She would keep down perhaps half of every meal she ate.

"You know of the withering," Elean said. Not a question, but a simple statement.

"There isn't a man from Anuskaya who would not."

"You know the signs? You would be able to tell if someone has it with certainty?"

He hesitated, confused. "Of course."

Elean looked to his ruined eye, then stared into his good one. "Would you look at me? Tell me what you see?"

He nearly laughed. "Can there be any doubt?"

She did not laugh in turn, nor did she smile. Instead, her face was stoic, even sad.

"I will look if you wish."

With that she nodded and began removing her clothes. She allowed her clothes to pool at her feet, then she stepped to one side and kicked them away. The queen was well formed. Her arms and legs showed the muscle of long days of shared labor. Her breasts were small, like apples, but they matched her waist and hips well.

Styophan hadn't been around a naked woman other than his own wife in years, and even then it hadn't been like this, a cold offer for him to look upon a woman's body. Seeing his discomfort, she motioned to the lamp. He picked it up, held it close to her face. There was a crust at the base of her eyelashes, which was common. The skin around her eyes, as he'd already noted, was discolored, though now that he was close it had a strange yellow hue to it, and the whites of her eyes were a color that was atypical of the wasting—hers were yellow with a tinge of orange.

He looked to her russet-colored hair, which seemed healthy, lustrous even. He lifted his free hand near her long auburn locks. "May I?" When she nodded, he took her hair and let it slip between his fingers. It felt supple, not dry as he would have expected, and when he tugged gently, only a few strands pulled away. Typically the hair—be it man, woman, or child—would fall out easily at this stage.

"If it please you, would you raise your arm?"

She did, and he looked closely at her armpit. There was no lump. He even felt for it, and found nothing. He could do the same where thigh met torso, but he could already see that the same was true there. The lumps didn't often show early, but they did as the wasting progressed. It was more than passing strange that Elean showed none of them.

He took her hand next, bringing the lamplight close to her fingernails. These, too, showed no darkening, no purpling.

He stared, taking her in anew, utterly at a loss to explain his conclusion. "It isn't the wasting," he said.

She met his gaze with something akin to relief. "You're sure?"

"*Evet.* Too many things are different." He paused before speaking again, even debated whether or not to go on. But he had to. He had to know more. "You knew this already."

She reached down and picked up her clothes. "I suspected."

"Why?"

"Because the other queens have been similarly afflicted. We met eight weeks ago, and we were all healthy"—Elean pulled her long dress around her waist—"but soon after every last one of us had been taken by the withering. The kings thought it a sign of ill fortune, but I was never so sure as they. Think of it. All of the queens struck after meeting to raise one last glass of summer wine—"

Elean stopped, for just then the sound of a breaking branch came from somewhere deep in the forest. Immediately she took the lamp from Styophan. As she lifted the glass and blew out the flame, darkness enveloped them.

"Go," she said harshly, pointing back the way they'd come. "If anyone stops you, tell them you went to relieve yourself. They won't raise an alarm."

"But why?" he asked. "Why did you bring me here?"

She used an arm to shove him easily off of the bearskin. "Go." She folded the skin and began walking toward another part of the camp. "I'll find you again when I'm able."

"But we'll reach Skolohalla in only a few days!" He said it as loud as he dared.

She did not respond, and soon he was left alone in the darkness, the only sound the barely discernible thump her footsteps were making in the snow.

Seeing no other choice, he left and returned to the yurt. There he lay himself down among the sleeping warriors. Surely they'd heard him return. Surely they'd felt the cold as the yurt flap opened and closed. Yet no one moved. No one said a word.

And as he lay down and tried to fall asleep, the yurt remained quiet as a boneyard.

CHAPTER TWELVE

On the ninth day since his capture, as they were heading down an age-worn path through the wilderness, another band of Haelish joined them. They fell into line as if they'd planned all along to meet Kürad's tribe at that very place and at that very time. There was hardly any conversation. There were smiles. Men and women embraced. But beyond this, they seemed oddly content.

Somewhere near the head of the line another king had come. Surely he was already riding beside Kürad, the two of them discussing what would become of Anahid and the soldiers of the Grand Duchy.

Styophan watched for Elean throughout the day. Anytime a woman with auburn hair walked behind the line, or rode past on a horse, he would take note, but none of them were Elean.

Another tribe joined them two days later. Three more came the day following, until it seemed as though an army to match any the Grand Duchy could field was walking through the hills of the Haelish Kings.

On the twelfth day, they reached Skolohalla.

It was set in a vast field between tall, snow-covered hills. The sun was out as the vast line of Haelish entered. Hundreds of yurts were already set up in a great circle around a tall black stone. More were being set up as they approached. Surely by the time Skolohalla was complete, thousands upon thousands of yurts would have been stood.

And the people! Styophan was used to estimating numbers of men—as any man who'd been in the staaya for any length of time would—and he judged that over twenty thousand had gathered already. Thirty thousand or more would be here by the time all was said and done. They wore buckskin mostly, but many wore shirts or dresses made from rough, woven cloth. Feathers and beads were woven into the women's hair. Tails of raccoons hung from the braided belts of the men. Most had simple knives made from dull-looking metal. There were muskets as well, and they appeared to be well kept, but they were few and far between.

The people of Hael stopped as they passed. The women and children outnumbered the men ten to one, and many of the men were old or crippled. Perhaps one in forty was a man Styophan would choose to fight alongside him. Still, they looked upon him with pride on their faces and anger in their eyes. It spoke of their love of this place and their resentment that he'd been brought to such a sacred meeting.

A number of the women, and even some children, had sunken cheeks and hollow eyes. They coughed as they watched him pass, their backs bending under some unseen weight. It was the wasting, Styophan knew, and it was because of the ever-expanding rifts. They'd spread so far in the years since the events on Galahesh. It seemed as though they were becoming more and more voracious, not just among the islands, but throughout the Empire and now here. How long before it swallowed the world?

As they continued, many of Kürad's people left the line, but Datha stayed alongside Styophan, as did several other warriors who led horses with litters. Styophan assumed these were his men and Anahid.

A child—a boy of twelve or thirteen—began to walk alongside the line of horses. His long black hair was braided, much of it in one long tail behind his head. Other small braids hung behind his ear and to one side of his forehead. He was rail thin, and unlike Kürad's warriors he was dressed warmly in multiple layers of supple doeskin.

Another boy, even younger, joined the first. And another, this one a waif of a girl. In little time, there were dozens pacing the horses, the nearest of them staring at Styophan fiercely. The first, the boy with the jet-black hair, whipped his arm forward. A stone flew from his hand and struck Styophan on the forehead. Another boy threw a stone, and another, until Styophan was being pelted from all sides.

"*Kanta!*" Datha yelled at them, waving his arms in a shooing motion.

One close to Datha tried to throw another stone, but Datha caught his wrist and slapped him across the face, sending him sprawling to the snow-covered ground.

Datha pointed back the way the children had come. "*Sihjan!*"

One by one, they left. Styophan felt a warm trickle of blood creep down his forehead, move along his eyebrows and down his right cheek. Datha stared at Styophan, but said nothing of the children, nor did he wear a look of apology on his face. He seemed indifferent, as if this was simply the way of things, like a hare that had narrowly escaped the teeth of a fox.

"Why do you not take the cities of the Empire?" Styophan asked. It was something he'd heard long ago of the Haelish, that they were difficult to pin down. They lived in few permanent settlements, preferring a nomadic lifestyle, but they were fiercely protective of their land. They would fight tooth and claw when the forces of Yrstanla came and took their cities for their own, or took their land for new settlements, and yet they would never venture beyond a certain border, the line they considered to be the true boundary of the Empire. This decision seemed strange, and for some reason the actions of the boys, and Datha's cold stare, reminded him of it.

"We do not take them because they are not ours."

"But they could be."

"*Hayir*, they cannot. If we took them, we would be no better than the Usurpers."

"It would protect your border."

"The border will be protected regardless. We will not allow it to be otherwise."

"You're foolish to believe that. The Kamarisi will push into Hael until there are none of you left or you run so far that you fall into legend."

"We will not run. We will continue to bleed them until they die of a thousand wounds."

Styophan opened his mouth to speak, but Datha raised his hand and pointed ahead. "Enough. We come to the Place of Kings."

The horses stopped, and Styophan was untied and allowed to stand. He'd done this for twelve days, but there was no getting used to the pain that came from having himself free of his bonds once more. His shoulders and elbows were the worst, but his wrists and hips and knees ached as he was forced to limp toward the other horses, where Anahid and Rodion were still being untied.

Anahid did not look ill treated, but she looked haggard. Her long black hair was matted and tangled. Her eyes were sunken and wary. She was worried about what was to come, perhaps more for Styophan's sake than her own. Rodion was of a height with Styophan, but he looked even more bent and broken. His face was bruised along his right cheek. There was a nasty gash near his temple that ran into his chestnut-brown hair. It looked to be healing poorly. His blue-grey eyes had lost much of the luster that had been there when they were sailing the skies over the Great Northern Sea, but when Styophan gave him a look, asking him if he could continue, Rodion nodded.

"Where are the others?" Styophan asked Datha.

"You'll be brought to them soon enough."

Styophan and Anahid and Rodion were led to the edge of a large field free of Haelish yurts. The field looked to be a natural depression in the hills, and yet it was so perfectly formed—more like a bowl than a turn in the land—it looked touched by the hand of man. Had the ancient Haels *made* this place for their Kings? Had they made other places like this as well? Styophan had heard of such things, even as far away as Anuskaya, but it had always seemed like a tale for children. Now he wasn't so sure. If the tales were true, there were dozens, perhaps hundreds, of such places.

The land of Hael was large indeed.

At the center of the bowl-shaped depression was a menhir, a granite column fifty feet tall if it was one. Somehow it looked natural, as if the will of the world had made it this way, but he could see facets of it that made him think of men chipping away at it with hammers and chisels for who knew how long until it seemed perfect to their eyes. Near the menhir were a dozen men and several women. Kürad was striding across the open grass toward them. Elean was by his side. Styophan felt a sense of loss as she walked away from him, as if the chance to speak to her, to learn of the mystery she'd revealed to him in the woods, had been lost forever now that they'd reached Skolohalla.

Some of the men and women near the stone hailed Kürad and Elean, but most did not. They were speaking with a man in a red turban, a man with a tall black plume and bright clothing. A man from Yrstanla.

Styophan knew without being able to see his face—knew from the man's bearing alone—that it was Bahett. Why he would have come this far, he had no idea. It couldn't have been for the ships sent by Ranos. That made no sense. For that, he could have sent his trusted men. He didn't have to come himself.

"You'll wait here," Datha said to Anahid and Rodion.

Rodion looked to Styophan much like Styophan had toward him only moments ago. Styophan nodded. Anahid's eyes were placid—almost too much so—but there was fright hidden in the set of her jaw and in the flaring of her nostrils and the way her thumbs picked at the skin of her forefingers.

Styophan nodded to her slowly, waiting for her to meet his eyes. "I'll return as soon as I'm able."

"Make no promises you cannot keep," Datha said as he led Styophan by the arm down to level land.

They came after a time to the center, and there Datha waited. The menhir looked more impressive from this vantage. The size of this place was skewing his perceptions; that and his nerves and the lack of proper sleep.

Bahett was speaking with several men—Haelish Kings by the look of them. There were nine, and they wore cloth of wool around their shoulders. The cloth was wrapped in such a manner—and clasped with ornate golden broaches—that it left one arm free, their right. The wool wrapped around their left shoulder and arm like a half-cloak, but most of this arm was exposed to the wind as well.

Styophan counted himself tall among the islands, and yet these men towered over him. A few he could almost look in the eye, but most were a half-head taller, and one was a giant even among these men. He stood at least seven feet tall. It was to this man that Bahett was speaking. Upon the heads of the Kings were crowns of thorns or vines with dark, dried berries, but the tall man's crown was more ornate, more impressive than the rest, for clutched between the vines were dark red rubies, glinting in the sun.

Standing behind Bahett were three soldiers of Yrstanla. They wore uniforms similar to the janissaries of the Empire—black boots and baggy pants and thick woolen shirts—but their armor was hardened leather. These were the Kiliç Şaik, the Singers of the Blade. The Kiliç were the Kamarisi's personal guard, but they would guard Bahett, as long as he stood regent, every bit as fiercely as they would the Kamarisi.

To Styophan's surprise, Bahett was speaking in Haelish. Styophan was no judge, but it sounded fluent. Odd for a man that had called Galahesh his home for the first three decades of his life, but Bahett was an intelligent man and had never been above manipulation. He was here, ostensibly, to finalize a treaty that would pit the Haelish against the islands, or at the very least ensure that they would stand aside as Yrstanla brought its army to bear on the eastern coast where the war with Anuskaya was growing more and more intense.

No wonder he was speaking in Haelish.

The tall Haelish king could be no other than King Brechan, son of Gaelynd, the one for whom—for the time being at least—the other Haelish kings took knee. King Brechan did not take notice of Styophan, nor Datha, but King Kürad did. He was standing three men to Brechan's left, and he listened to Bahett's words, but he also looked sidelong toward Styophan. Styophan and Anahid were jewels he wished to display, and Brechan, for whatever reason, wasn't allowing him to do so.

Queen Elean stood to Kürad's side and one step behind. She did not look at Styophan. Not even once. Her attention was fixed on the conversation between Bahett and King Brechan. Her eyes seemed even more dark than they'd been that night in the woods. He could see the orange tinge in them more clearly now, though if he hadn't been directed to examine her, he might not have noted the distinction from the wasting's typical yellow hue. After seeing what he'd seen the other night, Styophan was somehow not surprised to see the other three queens—each to one side and a step behind their king—with similar symptoms. Two seemed no worse than Elean, but the regal woman who stood behind Brechan was much worse. Her cheekbones stood out like rocky promontories. The hollows of her eyes were dark as night. She quivered as she stood, though she did not seem to be aware of it. She coughed lightly every so often, and each time she did, she paused, pulling her shoulders inward and leaning forward, perhaps fighting the pain she felt within.

Small wonder that the Kings had agreed to Bahett's demands if they believed the withering had been caused by some failing of theirs. If the royal born themselves were being struck down like this, what else were they to do? But in Styophan's mind this was strange, indeed. The irregularity of symptoms was one thing. The precision with which it had struck the queens was quite another.

Bahett spoke with the kings, carefully composing his face as respectful yet commanding. Perhaps they were negotiating final terms in their treaty, or perhaps it was something else entirely, but when he finally looked Styophan's way, he looked twice.

He turned then to Styophan, taking him in from head to foot. He took in Datha as well with an appraising stare.

Kürad cleared his throat and stepped ahead of Brechan. "I present to you Styophan Andrashayev, Kapitan of the *Vayetka* and Komodor of the Anuskayan ships sent against us."

Strangely, Brechan watched this exchange not with acceptance exactly—he was outwardly perturbed by Kürad's presumption—but with a forbearance that made Styophan pause. He'd heard of the strange rule of law among the kings, but he had to admit he didn't understand them at all. They would vie for honor— sometimes in battle, sometimes in forethought—and when they managed it, the others, vying for the very same sort of recognition, would bow their head to the one who had proven himself and step back, allowing that king to rule until another took his place. It made for a fluid, somewhat inefficient command, but it allowed them to recover easily when one of their number was slain.

Or taken by the wasting, Styophan thought.

Styophan had never seen Bahett before. He'd heard about him, about his confidence, his sharp mind, the ease with which he played among the Empire's courts. Too often reputations like Bahett's were simply overblown rumors, but in Bahett's eyes he saw a sharpness, a calculation behind his courtly face, that made him think that in this case these were no simple rumors.

"You were Nikandr Khalakovo's man," Bahett said in Anuskayan.

Styophan nodded, seeing no need to hide it.

Bahett stared around them, to the yurts, to the menhir and the vast field surrounding it. "Strange, is it not, to find ourselves here?"

He spoke as if they were cousins, and in a way, they were. They were both from the islands—each knew the other more than he ever would the Haelish—and yet Styophan didn't like the association, nor the fact that this man, the man that had caused the death of dozens of his comrades, was trying to ingratiate himself.

"Thousands of leagues away from our homes," Bahett continued, "and here we are, you a komodor where once you were a soldier, me a single step from the Kamarisi's side."

"Hardly one step if you've been sent to the very edge of Yrstanla."

The kings watched this exchange with mild confusion, and perhaps annoyance that it was being conducted in a language they didn't understand. But they said nothing; they allowed the two interlopers to speak, suffering their presence in hopes that they'd soon be gone.

And here Bahett switched to Yrstanlan. "Listen to my words, Styophan of Khalakovo. There are some things, no matter how high you become, that you must see to yourself."

More likely the Haelish had demanded his presence here, Styophan thought.

Bahett turned to the kings and bowed his head, though as he did, there was a wry hint of a smile that gave proof to his lie. Most of the kings bowed their heads in turn, not nearly so deeply as Bahett. Brechan, however, stood stiffly, like the nearby menhir. There was a rigidity in him that spoke of the sour taste in his mouth. He seemed tight, like the string of a crossbow, or a strained halyard, ready to snap in the gusting wind.

Bahett turned back to Styophan and spoke in Anuskayan once more. "Who sent you?" he asked. "Was it your Grand Duke or the young Ranos?"

Styophan remained silent.

"You don't wish to talk?"

"I have little enough to say, Bahett ül Kirdhash."

Bahett's gaze shifted over his shoulder, a subtle indicator to the guardsmen that stood behind him.

"We shall see, Styophan Andrashayev."

With that he waved one hand—

"We shall see."

—and Styophan was led away.

CHAPTER THIRTEEN

It is morning when Nasim and Kaleh reach the end of the dark mountain tunnel. Kaleh leads the way, taking them deeper into the forest, where the land slopes gently downward. The morning is gentle, pleasant, so different from the memories that play within Nasim's mind. Memories of a dark room, a stone lid sliding back, an ancient woman who had no right being alive burning before his eyes.

He remembers these things, and he wonders whether this is some mistake on Kaleh's part. Has she *allowed* him to retain these memories or has she simply forgotten? It might be the latter. She seems upset enough to have done so. Then again, maybe she doesn't care. Perhaps in an hour or a day or a week she'll simply banish his memories like crows before a storm, and then they'll continue on to murder another soul buried deep in an ancient mountain chamber.

He knows they are going to kill more. What he doesn't know is how many she's already killed. And how many are left.

The horror over what they're doing—at what they've already done—grows by the hour, and yet the thought of defying her is inconceivable. He can no more stop his eyes from seeing than ignore her commands. He need only think of such a thing and the notion twists and turns until it seems like a distant thought, preposterous even to consider. And yet there's a certain awareness of this that he can only wonder about. Does she allow this as well? Or is the mind too complex to subvert in such a way? Perhaps it is another of the hidden gifts handed down to him from Khamal. After all, he was Al-Aqim in his past life—much of this life is a reflection of that—and it may be that Kaleh is unable to overcome it.

Still, even with all these possibilities, the one that seems most likely is simple complacency. Kaleh must surely find this distasteful. She must. He would never have guessed she had the capacity for murder, especially a systematic slaughter of people that had gone to great lengths to keep themselves secret.

They continue their trek throughout the day, moving beyond the forest by high noon and to the base of the mountain by nightfall. They stop near a stream with the barest amount of water trickling down the center of its nearly dry bed. Nasim collects wood for a fire without thinking about it, knowing at the same time that it was an unspoken demand from Kaleh. The land here is dry, the scrub trees sparse, so it takes him some time, and when he returns, he finds Kaleh kneeling next to a large, rust-colored stone. The Atalayina sits atop it, and Kaleh stares into its depths, as if she's lost. Nasim sets the firewood down and chooses a spot for the fire, but as he does, he cannot help but steal glances at the stone, for Kaleh does not often take it from her pack. The sun sets golden on the horizon, and the light reflects brilliantly off the surface of the blue stone. The specks of silver and gold glimmer from within, making it appear deep and mysterious. It's as if by looking into it you can see another world entirely.

"Where do you think it came from?" Kaleh asks as Nasim finishes leaning the wood into a rough cone shape.

He's surprised by the question. Not that she would ask it, but that she asked him anything at all. So often their days and nights are filled with silence; it is a strangely welcome thing to be able to talk, even if it is with his captor.

"You would know better than I," he replies. "Muqallad was the one who bore it from this place."

She turns and with a glance sets the wood afire. He felt no summoning of a hezhan. There was no flame from the palms of her hands. She simply looked, and the wood was aflame. Such was the power of the Atalayina.

"Muqallad would never tell me of his time here, but I heard him once when he was speaking with my mother. He said he'd gone through much to find it." She looks over the Atalayina to the horizon. "*Neh*... He said he'd *sacrificed* much."

"Aren't they the same thing?"

Her eyes twinkle under the burgeoning light of the fire. "You know Muqallad nearly as well as I. Would you say those two things were the same, knowing it was Muqallad who spoke them?"

She's right. Muqallad was a proud man. When he experienced travail, he suffered it with no comment, thinking little of it. But when he *sacrificed*, it implied that he valued that which had been lost, and this was not something Muqallad would do lightly, even in those early days before the sundering.

"*Neh*," Nasim says after a time. "He would not."

From his own pack, Nasim takes out a bundle of cloth. He unrolls it carefully and takes out a piece of the dried snake meat within. He offers it to Kaleh, but she shakes her head, as she often did, and returns to her inspection of the stone.

"Where do you think it came from?" she asks again.

He takes a bite from the salty meat. "What does it matter?"

"I want to know."

"You want to know the truth?"

She turns sharply, perhaps sensing something in his voice. "*Yeh*, I want to know the truth."

"I don't care where it came from. I don't care how Muqallad found it. I don't care that you have it now. What I care about is that it was the cause of the sundering. I care that you're using it to hide me from those I love, people that might help me to unlock its secrets. I care that you're using it to kill."

If she feels surprised or chastised by his words, she doesn't show it. She stares into the stone for a while longer, but then, when the sun has gone down completely, she wraps it in its lambskin and puts it back in the bottom of her pack.

She moves to the fire and then does accept a strip of meat from him. She tears off a hunk of it and begins chewing, staring absently into the fire while crouching as the desert folk do.

"Why are you growing older?"

She doesn't look up as she replies, "Aren't *you* growing older?"

"Not nearly as fast as you are."

"Go to sleep."

He lies down on his bedroll, but for some reason sleep doesn't come. He keeps thinking about the woman burning in that deep, dark place. Had it really been only one night ago?

"Are you worried you'll die before you can work out how to unlock the Atalayina's secrets?"

Kaleh lies down on her own bedroll and stares up at the starry sky. "Go to sleep."

She says the words the same way she did before—the same tone, the same inflection—and yet, this time, Nasim closes his eyes and drifts toward sleep. But one thing is crystal clear in those final moments: if he is to have any hope of freeing himself, he needs to spend time with the Atalayina. He knows he's had these thoughts before, but he's becoming adept at putting them into a place that Kaleh either cannot reach or doesn't wish to go.

This gives him hope, and yet his dreams are both wicked and wretched.

The following morning, they continue their trek down from the mountain and across the desert plain. The ochre sand discolors Kaleh's golden dress, dark near the hem and lighter as it flows upward, as if the desert were swallowing her bit by bit.

By midday, Nasim realizes they're heading for another mountain peak, and it occurs to him that this place, this desert pan, is situated between many mountains. Their dark peaks are spaced unevenly around it, but it still reminds him of a crown. It makes him feel as though they're walking along the pate of a slumbering titan, some ancient and long-forgotten king, or perhaps a consort to the fates, killed when they had no more use for him. Perhaps, he thinks, the Atalayina is not a tear shed from the fates, but their consort.

As is often the case, Nasim walks behind Kaleh. She adjusts her pack, and he remembers that he wants something from within it. It takes him nearly an hour of walking to recall that it is, in fact, the Atalayina.

The ties Kaleh placed on his mind... He cannot sense them, but he knows they are there. And the stone, the Atalayina, will release him.

Ahead, the mountain looms. They'll reach the base of it by sunset, but will not go beyond that, not unless Kaleh pushes them through the night. He would have to get the stone then. He cannot allow another of these ancient souls to die.

Kaleh seems weary. Nasim counts himself lucky for that. It's clear the tomb they left the day before weakened her. Just how much he isn't sure, but it makes him wonder just how many they've killed in this way—he opening the tomb, Kaleh murdering them with fire.

At this, from the corner of his eye, Nasim senses movement.

He turns and looks over the desert wastes, but sees nothing. Nothing but the wiry desert bushes and ochre sand.

He shakes his head and continues on.

They reach a massive outcropping of rock as night falls. A passage takes them through the towering red stone. Beyond is a narrow gorge where the path slopes gently downward. Soon the high walls on either side of them open, revealing a hidden vale. Nasim has never seen the likes of it, a lush green bowl surrounded on all sides by steep stone walls hundreds of feet high. The stone is not craggy like many of the cliffs of the island eyries are, or even the straits that run through the island of Galahesh. These are smooth, as if the fates themselves had formed this place with painstaking care, making sure that each gentle curve fit every other. It feels ancient, and vital, as if it hides the very heart of the world.

The tall spruce stand proudly, staring down at the two of them as if they are interlopers. *And we are*, Nasim thinks. *We're interlopers set to kill.*

Unless he can figure out some way to stop it.

Kaleh seems to know this place, for they continue through the spruce forest until they reach a pool of water. The moon has risen, but it's still hidden beyond the valley walls. Its light comes in at an angle, limning the upper reaches of this valley with subtle silver light. It shines brightly enough that Nasim can see the contours of the pool. The water is placid, so much so that the stone wall ahead is reflected perfectly on its surface.

To the left of the pool is a patch of darkness that Nasim recognizes immediately. A tunnel. Kaleh plans on heading to the tomb immediately. What drives her to such states of exhaustion he doesn't know, but he cannot allow it. He must stop her so that he can steal a look at the Atalayina.

He's about to shout at her to halt, not knowing what else to do, when he again catches movement from the corner of his eye—something in the trees, beyond the pool.

On the desert plain he thought it merely a figment of his imagination, a symptom of his weariness, but now he wonders if Kaleh hadn't noticed it. He wonders if she'd hidden the fact that she had, for this time she stops in her tracks. She turns her head.

For long moments she faces away from Nasim, her back to him, motionless. "We'll make camp," she says.

That simple command is not something he can disobey, but he finds himself more resistant to it than he would have been only days before. He sees this as a good sign, and when he gathers firewood and they light a fire, he can see just how tired she is. Her eyes have dark bags. She can barely keep them open.

He lies down next to the fire and closes his own eyes, hoping she'll be too tired to order him asleep. Across the fire, Kaleh's face is lit in a ruddy glow. He doesn't know why he's never noticed it, but it strikes him just how beautiful she's become. She feels more like a sister to him than anything, and there is a strange sense of pride within him, a pride that she is a woman now, grown from the girl she once was. How he can have such feelings when she's been forcing him to help her commit murder, he doesn't know, but it is there like a candle in the mist, bright yet indistinct.

Kaleh's eyes are on him, and for a moment there is pain within them. "Do you remember the time before the sundering?" she asks.

"I am not Khamal," he replies.

She closes her eyes, annoyed. "I know. His memories. Do you remember the time before the stone was broken?"

He shrugs as the fire snaps between them. "Some."

The look of pain has moved to her face, the set of her jaw. Her eyes close of their own volition. "What do you remember?"

He shrugs again, even though she no longer watches. "It was a beautiful time. A time full of hope."

"Would that we could return to it," she says softly.

Nasim thinks on this for a moment. Would he return, if he could? It was a time of high learning. A time of sharing, at least among the Aramahn. The Maharraht had not yet been born. Many thought indaraqiram was close.

And yet it was all an illusion. They *weren't* close, and the fates were about to play the biggest trick they'd ever played.

"I would not wish—"

He stops, for Kaleh's breathing has become heavier, slower. He remains quiet, refusing to move in hopes that she will remain asleep. He refuses to look upon her, as if his mere stare has the power to wake her. He stares instead into the fire, counting the moments as they pass.

So that when she stirs and says, "Go to sleep, Nasim," his stomach drops. Another night gone. Another opportunity missed.

When they wake once more, they will go to kill.

It sickens him, but there is nothing he can do but lay his head down and close his eyes.

CHAPTER FOURTEEN

Nasim wakes facing the fire, which has burned down to embers, but still gives a bare amount of light by which he can see the trunks of the nearest trees. He doesn't know *how* he knows, but he feels someone watching him from those trees.

He sits up with a jolt, all traces of sleep fading as his heart beats madly. He isn't scared exactly, but he is anxious, and in a moment he understands why. The visions he had, the visions from the corner of his eye… The one who caused them is ahead in those trees.

He peers into the darkness. There, behind one of the massive spruce trees, is the silhouette of a head, a shoulder.

As he sets his blanket aside and inches to his feet, he watches Kaleh carefully. She is sleeping, her eyes moving beneath her lids, her brow creasing as from a dream.

He takes one careful step forward, then another.

And then the form darts into the forest.

Sparing only a quick glance back at Kaleh, he gives chase. The moon is half full, and gives enough light to move by, but the way is treacherous. He trips and falls onto the dry pine needles, but he's up again in a moment, running among the tall trunks, his arms warding before him.

The silhouette darts silently between trees. From the lithe and delicate shape he has the impression he's chasing a girl.

"Stop," he calls.

She continues, but there is something terribly familiar about her. He knows her, or knows someone *like* her. If only he could put his finger on who.

They're coming closer and closer to the sheer walls of the vale. She can't run much further. But run she does. The trees suddenly end a dozen paces from a sheer and imposing stone wall. The form runs toward a crevice. Her shadow hunkers down, lost in an instant among the deeper shadows.

He slows, then creeps forward. "Please," he says. "I only wish to speak."

There is only silence, so he steps forward, peering into the darkness.

"Who are you?" he asks.

His only answer is the sound of the mountain wind sighing through the spruce above him.

One of Nasim's rare memories from childhood is of kneeling at a hillock, staring into a burrow, wondering what lay within. His curiosity was so strong that he reached inside, childlike, to find out. Stronger than those feelings of curiosity was the deep-seated fear that accompanied the simple act. He has the same sort of fear now as he peers into the darkness, hoping to peel it away to see who might be waiting for him inside that crevice. By the time he's within a few paces, his feet respond to his will to move forward by inching across the needle-strewn ground.

He finds that the crevice isn't deep at all. Were he to reach in, he could touch the opposite side. To his relief—and his profound disappointment—he discovers that there is nothing within that place. Nothing at all. He turns and scans the trees. He stares along the wall, wondering if he'd stalked toward the wrong hiding place. But no. There is nowhere else along this wall where one could hide. It has to have been here.

He tries to think of who it might have been. Rabiah, the gifted Aramahn girl he brought with him to Galahesh to help him heal the rifts, is the first person that jumps to mind, but only because she's one of the few girls he's ever truly known. The trouble is this girl doesn't remind him of Rabiah at all. Her shape is wrong, and the way she runs... It just isn't like her.

He finds no answers, nor does he find any new sign of her after searching for long minutes, so he treks back through the forest toward camp. He thinks of continuing beyond it, of walking out from this hidden vale and to the desert beyond to find help among the islands or from the floating village of Mirashadal, but these are fleeting thoughts, things that flutter through his mind and depart as quickly as they'd come. Kaleh's hold on him is not so weak as that.

When he returns to their camp, the embers of the fire glow softly still. Kaleh is asleep, facing away from him, which he sees a favorable sign after the frustrating chase he's just led. He sees her pack resting by her head. She has always kept it thus, trusting that Nasim would be unable to free himself of the bonds she'd placed on him.

He cannot sense the Atalayina—it has a unique way of shedding the attention of man and hezhan alike—but he knows it is there. He creeps forward and kneels by her pack. He pulls back the canvas flap and reaches into it, rummaging along the bottom until he finds it. After unwrapping it carefully from the lambskin that holds it, he cradles it, staring deeply into its depths. The Atalayina is heavy. And even under the bare light of the stars and the nearby embers, it glints as if it accepts what it's given and amplifies it in some way, or alters it so that it becomes more striking to the eye. It is unapologetic, the Atalayina. It has caused untold pain and suffering—it may yet lead to the destruction of the world—and yet it seems coldly indifferent.

The way it acts like a lens, focusing light, is important. It is this, more than any of its other attributes, that allowed the Al-Aqim to use it to create the first rift on Ghayavand. He recalls Khamal hefting this same stone before placing it on the obsidian pedestal at the top of Sihyaan, the tallest mountain on Ghayavand. He recalls Khamal opening himself to the stone, and in doing so opening himself to the other two who stood nearby—Sariya and Muqallad. The three of them were as powerful as any Aramahn had ever been, and still they were humbled before the might of the Atalayina, and the power that the stone in turn opened up for them. It was like pulling back a curtain to see Adhiya in its natural state. But more than this, it opened Erahm as well, and the aether between. All three worlds were brought together by this stone, and Nasim can see for the first time how it might be done again on Ghayavand, except this time it would be to heal the rifts once and for all.

As he stares at this stone, a thought occurs to him. He sits upon the ground, raking his fingers through his hair as the implications sweep over him. Khamal planned his own death. Nasim thought he'd planned for Nasim to return as a normal, if gifted, boy. He thought that surely Khamal wanted him to retain Khamal's memories so that he could go to Ghayavand and there heal the rift that Khamal had a hand in making.

But now—

Nasim pulls his knees up to his chest and rests his head against them.

—he wonders if he's been wrong all along.

What if Khamal *planned* for Nasim to walk between worlds? What if it had been in preparation for Nasim's eventual return to Ghayavand? Might not walking in Adhiya and Erahm, might not straddling the aether, prepare him for holding this stone? Prepare him for understanding it?

If that were true, it could only mean that Khamal had wanted Nasim to return so that he alone could heal the rift. He'd never meant for Nasim to find others. But Nasim had. He'd found Sukharam and Rabiah, and Rabiah had died because of it. He knew not what might have happened to Sukharam after the events at the Spar. He might be dead. Or he might have taken to the wind—to learn what he could on his own as Nasim had done. In all likelihood, he is lost to Nasim.

Nasim feels dizzy. Sick to his stomach. Part of him wants to drop this stone, for it feels as though it controls him, has *always* controlled him, and this is something he cannot abide.

He tightens his jaw, refusing to give in to such feelings. He cannot give the stone more power than it has. He must remain grounded. He must remain resolute. For only in doing this will he have any chance of overthrowing Kaleh's hold on him.

He is just preparing to open his mind to the Atalayina once more when he feels a weight upon him. He knows immediately what it is.

Slowly, he turns toward Kaleh.

And finds her staring at him.

Even in the dim light, she looks fierce. Kaleh has aged unnaturally fast, but never has she looked more like her mother, Sariya.

Before he knows what's happening he finds himself on the ground, writhing in searing white pain. He can think of nothing else. Only the pain. His entire body is alive with it, a burning agony so fierce he twists and writhes on the dry ground. He feels himself roll into the fire, but he has no idea if it was his idea or a command from Kaleh.

The coals burn his back and shoulder. He screams from it, twisting away reflexively, but Kaleh forces him to roll back and he's burned again, this time along his hip and thigh.

He cries out. Pushes away again, and this time he's allowed to remain out of the fire. But the blinding white pain does not ebb.

"Please!" he screams to the night sky. "Please stop!"

Kaleh stares on dispassionately. So much of her emotion has drained that she looks, strangely, not so different from the stone, as if the pain he's feeling has nothing to do with her and is instead a thing completely of his own making.

How long it goes on he is not sure, but finally it ends, and he is left to sob into the bed of needles on the ground beneath him. He lies there for some time. Hears sounds, but cannot understand what they are, not until his cries subside.

It is the sound of preparation, of gathering up the camp. Kaleh is readying them, and even though he finds it difficult to think, he knows exactly what this means.

"Come," she says when it's done.

And there is no choice but to obey. It is a much stronger command than any had been over the last several days. He doesn't understand what happened, but he knows that Kaleh has somehow revitalized herself. Perhaps it is from her anger. Perhaps it is from the sleep she'd managed to find. Whatever the reason, he is held in thrall as they walk down, past the pool and into the shadowed area where Nasim is sure the tunnel lies.

Indeed, when they enter the tall, narrow cave, Kaleh uses the Atalayina to light their way, and ahead, similar to the last tomb, there is a man carved into the stone. His arms are not across his chest, as the woman's were at the last; instead they're at his side, and his hands are balled into fists. His eyes and face, however, project that same feeling of sorrow. Perhaps it has been the same with every tomb they'd come to; he can't remember.

He doesn't know how many are left but has the distinct feeling that the end is near. Kaleh is coming closer and closer to reaching her goals, whatever they may be. He cannot allow her to reach them. He knows this. He just has no idea how to stop her.

Kaleh touches the stone with the Atalayina raised in her opposite hand, and the stone crumbles. It collapses. One large piece falls against Kaleh's leg, cutting her. She stares down only for a moment as blood pools along the length of the cut and runs down her leg.

Holding the Atalayina high, she steps over the stones and walks down the tunnel. Nasim follows without thinking. There is a part of him that wishes to disobey, but like a butterfly the thought is there one moment and gone the next. They move along the cold tunnel, which spirals upward and upward. For hours they climb until at last they come to a door with another sculpture. Here is the man once more, but instead of his hands tight to his side, they are spread wide, as if he's welcoming the morning breeze after a long and listless night.

Kaleh steps to one side and motions to the door. "Open it."

He does. He walks forward, driven like an ox beneath the whip. He accepts the Atalayina. Places his hand on the door, though while he's doing this, he wonders why Kaleh hasn't simply done this very same thing each time they came to a tomb. Why has she resorted to tricking him? She must have played a ruse on him in their previous tombs they'd visited. Why would she do this when she had complete control over his mind?

And then he understood.

As the door crumbles before him, filling the hall with sound and kicking up dust, he knows it is because it costs her. She is already fatigued mentally, no doubt from holding him under her spell for so long. He feels no particular struggle going on within her, but that is probably because she still retained control, but he wonders what it must be like for her. It would be a struggle both night and day to keep someone's free will suppressed as she's doing now. And it would be more difficult over time as her mind began to weaken, to tire. Surely fooling him into doing as she wished was easier than this.

He needs only to look at her face to know the truth of it. She is willful, even angry, but also haggard. The effort she's putting forth is already taking its toll. How soon before she is unable to do this any longer? How long before he can wake from this dream to control his own destiny once more?

When he gives the Atalayina back to her, he has his answer. The load upon her lightens. She draws strength from the stone. The effort weighs upon her, and it's clear that she cannot do this forever, but it will be enough, and Kaleh knows it too. There are only so many tombs, and something within Nasim tells him that they are nearing the end. After only a few more, she will have what she desires: all of these strange, hidden-away souls will be dead. And what then? Most likely she will cast Nasim aside. Kill him and be done with it so that she can be on her way to finish what her mother started.

Despite this burning desire to stop her, he can do nothing but watch as Kaleh steps inside the tomb. He watches, impotent, as the lid slides away from the sarcophagus and the sheaf of wheat lying on the top falls to the cold tomb floor.

This man wears a circlet of gold, five stones set within it. His hair and beard are long and curly. It reminds Nasim so much of Ashan that tears form and slide down his cheeks.

As a blast of fire flows from Kaleh's upturned palm, he lifts an emaciated hand and presses it against the flame. The fire splays where it strikes his hand, flows outward, licking against the low ceiling or the sides of the sarcophagus. The hoary skin of his face is pulled back in concentration. His deeply sunken eyes flare with pain or rage or fear. Kaleh's face becomes more intense as well.

Please, Nasim pleads to the fates, *let him win*.

But that battle is over as soon as it began. As powerful as this man might have once been, he has been sleeping for generations, for eons. How can he stand against Kaleh, a gifted young woman who holds the Atalayina in her hand?

He cannot.

And so the flames envelop his hand, then his wrist, and then his arm. Soon it has wrapped itself around him completely. His hair lights yellow, a contrast to the orange flames that surround him. He screams in pain, a sound so sad and forlorn it fills Nasim's heart with bits of broken glass. When the man falls to the floor of the tomb, a black, broken husk, Nasim stares, raging inside while his body refuses to move. His tears slip wet and warm along his cheek. He feels them patter against his hand, but he cannot look at them, those hands that allowed entrance to this place.

When Kaleh steps from the room, her face is resolute. Emotionless. "*Insa*," she says as she passes him.

And indeed, he forgets, as he did the last time. And the time before that.

As Kaleh marches down the hall, expecting to be followed, Nasim takes one last look into the tomb, and there he sees, cowering behind the sarcophagus, the dim outline of a girl. He peers into the darkness, but the light of the Atalayina is already too far, and he can see nothing but shadows within the room.

He knows not who the girl might be, but the sight of her sparks a memory. And that in turn sparks more. He's confused as to why he's here in this place.

Confused where they might now be headed. But he knows who he is—Nasim—and he knows that the young woman walking down the tunnel is Kaleh, daughter of Sariya and Khamal, and he knows that many answers lie within the glowing stone she carries.

This isn't much, this pittance of knowledge.

But it is a start.

CHAPTER FIFTEEN

Atiana stared into the campfire as Soroush leaned against a rock smoking his pipe while Goeh sprinkled salt over two freshly dressed desert hares. He skewered them with iron spits and set them onto the makeshift rotisserie he'd made from the fresh-cut branches off a nearby bush.

"Can you turn them?" he asked Soroush.

Soroush nodded as Goeh left to scout the trail behind them, as he did every night they camped. Soroush wore the double-robes of the Aramahn, inner robes of grey and outer robes of sage green. He had not yet taken off his white turban, which he often did at sunset. He was the only one with her at the fire now. Ushai was washing at a small stream at the center of the valley. Sukharam and Ashan were taking breath in a small cave Goeh had shown them.

And Nikandr...

Nikandr was riding ahead to check the way they'd take tomorrow. Atiana knew he was becoming overwhelmed by his urges again—she could see it in his eyes and the way he bowed in the saddle when he'd ridden away—but she had not tried to stop him. She had merely waved when he left. There was nothing else to say. Not anymore. She could no more fix him of this malady than she could summon a hezhan for him.

Soroush blew smoke into the air and turned the hares over absently. The sun was setting, but the sky was unnaturally overcast. The clouds were so uniformly grey that it reminded her of the islands. And that, of course, reminded her of the palotzas, the drowning chambers, entering the aether and expanding her mind as she'd done so many times in the past. She'd been away from it for well over a year. She'd missed it terribly at first, but she found that the desire had faded over time to a dull but persistent ache.

The wodjan had changed everything, however.

Now Atiana thought about it every waking moment. It was especially strong when she woke each morning. Those first few moments from sleep felt like waking from the drowning chamber, and when she realized she *hadn't* been in the aether, she became despondent.

"Are you off with Nikandr?"

Atiana started, pulling her gaze from the flickering fire as Soroush turned the skewers. The smell of the hares cooking, the sound of the fat dripping and sizzling against the burning wood, reminded her of the grand dinners she and Mileva and Ishkyna—especially Ishkyna—had all loved so much. She managed to give Soroush a smile.

"Thinking of home." She stared eastward, toward the Grand Duchy. "I miss it terribly."

"*What* do you miss?"

She shrugged. "Many things. The people. The music. The dancing. But most of all, I miss taking the dark."

Perhaps she shouldn't have told him the truth—she didn't want anyone to know about her thoughts of the aether and the wodjan—but it seemed like the right thing to do. The Aramahn tended to be brutally honest, and it seemed wrong, somehow, to lie to one of them, even Soroush, who she still thought of as Maharraht more than Aramahn.

He took a long pull from his pipe. "What do you miss about the aether?"

She thought about it for a moment. It was difficult to articulate. "Everything," she finally said.

"Strange"—smoke trailed from his nostrils and mouth as he smiled wistfully—"when years ago you were petrified of it."

"Petrified?" Atiana laughed. "Perhaps I was. But once you overcome your fears, it is a wondrous place. It connects this world to the one beyond. It runs through all things. I cannot help but marvel at its beauty every time I enter, and when I'm gone from it, a yearning builds within me."

Soroush turned the skewers and adjusted the flaming logs below them with a spare stick. "You've been gone from the islands for eighteen months, and you've been here in the Gaji for nearly a year." He glanced eastward himself. "Why now?"

He was coming dangerously close to the very thing she'd been trying to hide since the wodjan had come to their camp two nights ago.

"I like the Gaji," she said after a pause. "It holds a stark beauty I hadn't expected. But we're coming closer to reaching our goal now. I can feel it. And it makes me wonder if I'll ever see the islands again."

Soroush furrowed his brow and pursed his lips. "You'll see them again."

"Is that so?"

He smiled for her, a wide thing that was strangely infectious from such a reticent man. "I'm sure of it."

She returned the smile. "Then I'm glad."

Ushai returned soon after, and Goeh came an hour after that. They ate in fits and starts, hoping the others would return so they could all eat together. Ushai did not eat of the hare. She merely chewed the bark from a tree that Goeh said would stave off hunger. She did so with her right hand. Her left, a scarred ruin from her time in Sariya's tower on Galahesh, sat cradled in her lap. Ushai, after stabbing Sariya, had tried to grasp one of the broken pieces of the Atalayina, and the ward Sariya had set to protect it burned her badly.

While they ate, Soroush told them of the miserable islands he'd taken breath on during his first circuit of the world, how he moved slowly from desolate island to desolate island, accepting rides on skiffs occasionally from Aramahn who had taken to the winds to circuit the world.

Atiana tore off a strip of juicy meat from the thigh of the hare. "When did you first take to the winds?"

"When I was twelve. My mother left us when I was seven. I remained with my father for five more years until the calling finally convinced me to leave him. Truthfully, though, I felt it years earlier."

Atiana knew of their practices, of leaving their children when they were as young as seven or eight to do as they would, but it never failed to surprise her when she heard the tales. "He simply left you on an island in the middle of the seas?"

Soroush waggled his head while using his fingers to scoop hamma, a bean paste spiced with paprika and cumin and the sour seeds of a wizened fruit Goeh had found for them, into his mouth. "He didn't *leave* me, not as you mean it. I *asked* him to go. It was time."

"Were there others there?"

Soroush shook his head. "Looking back now, it was perhaps a foolish decision. The islands to the east of Anuskaya are mostly barren. There are birds. There are fish. And little else. Only when you near the western border of Yrstanla is there game to speak of." He shrugged. "But I wished to be alone, and I wished for it to be so as long as the fates saw fit."

"Meaning what?" Goeh asked, pausing from ravenous bites he was taking from his own pieces of hare.

"Meaning I had no way off the island."

Atiana stared, unbelieving, but the look on Soroush's face made it clear he wasn't joking. "Did your father return for you?"

"*Neh*, nor did I wish him to. I learned much on that island"—he looked more deeply into Atiana's eyes while the firelight glimmered in his eyes—"not the least of which was patience."

Atiana finished her food and set the bones roughly aside. "I would never leave a child of twelve on an island by himself, much less my own son."

Ushai, who had been sitting quietly and watching the exchange with an amused glint in her eye, sat up straighter. "That's the difference between us," she said. "The Aramahn allow the world to come to them while the Landed wish to take it. The trouble is, the world cares not for your desire to own it. It laughs at you, while we learn."

Atiana stared into Ushai's wide, striking eyes. Her shoulder-length hair was pulled back into a short braid. She wore an Aramahn dress—simple in cut, the cloth dyed the subtle shades of lavender and amethyst. To Atiana it looked like a mask, as if every day she were hiding her true nature as Maharraht and that some day soon she would remove it and stab Atiana in the chest, grinning as she did so.

"And what do you learn by killing?" Atiana asked her.

She had expected remorse from Ushai—some token amount—but in this she was disappointed. Ushai stood, throwing the strip of bark she'd been chewing into the fire. "You learn much from death, Atiana of Vostroma. And you should know. But you and your Landed brothers and sisters are too busy to do even that, aren't you?"

Atiana stood as well, and faced Ushai as her fingers flexed. "We are not proud of death."

"*Neh.*" Ushai spat on the ground between them. "Only of the spoils."

"Enough!" Soroush stood and stepped between them. He took Ushai by the elbow and led her away. Ushai went, but ripped her arm from Soroush's grip. She glanced back once and stared into Atiana's eyes.

The venom Atiana saw there...

Why were they allowing her to continue on this journey? Whether she was born in Kohor or not, they didn't need such an abscess in their midst.

Atiana smoothed down her dress and looked to Goeh, who'd been watching the exchange with a steadily growing unease, but as he studied Atiana, his expression calmed and he smiled awkwardly. "Off to find your sister?"

Atiana nodded. "If she's there to be found."

"Then I bid you luck."

As she was heading downslope, she came across Nikandr. He stopped, watching her carefully. He'd seen the exchange. He'd heard it.

She didn't care. She walked up to him and grabbed his head with both her hands and pulled him into a long kiss.

She loved Nikandr—she felt this more passionately than she had at any time since leaving the islands—and she knew that deep down, beneath the black layer of yearning he wore around his shoulders like a mantle, he felt the same. He had not lost his love for her. It had merely been smothered by his feelings of loss.

She felt the tension release from him like rain. He melted in her hands. He placed his hands tenderly on her hips, kissed her as deeply as she was kissing him. He didn't understand why she was doing this—how could he?—but he was allowing his feelings for her to rise to the surface.

She could drown in this. She wished it would go on forever, but she knew that it wouldn't. This kiss would fade. His feelings would fade. And all too soon he would return to his brooding self, once again a prisoner to the knife that had cut his ties to Nasim and to Adhiya.

Unless she did something about it.

At last she pushed him away, the perfect seal on their lips parting with a smack, and she stared into his eyes.

"You *must* come back to me," she said, still holding his head in her hands. "You must come back." She moved one hand down to his shoulder. The other she placed over his heart. "I know you feel pain. I know that the loss of Nasim is like having a child ripped from your arms. I can't pretend to understand it, but I know this, Nischka. If you continue as you have, you will die. You will lose yourself to the ache that you've been nurturing since the Spar was shattered."

His eyes had slipped down to her hand that was now over his beating heart, but she shook his shoulder until he looked her in the eyes once more. "I'm *here*. I love you. Let me help, because I'll *not* see you throw your life away."

"I'm not—"

She put her hand over his lips. "Say nothing now, Nischka. Think on this carefully before speaking of it again."

He stared deeply into her eyes and nodded. "I will."

And with that she walked away.

She walked downslope, taking a different path than the one Soroush and Ushai had taken. After minutes of walking she came to a place with an outcropping of rock just off the trail that overlooked the valley below. She moved to this rock and sat, dangling her legs over the side, allowing her feelings of anger for Ushai and her ache for Nikandr to play themselves out. All the while she wondered if the Haelish woman, Aelwen, would come as she'd promised. Atiana wondered if Aelwen could find them so easily, but the proof was in their last meeting. She'd known, somehow, where Atiana would be. She'd known that Atiana would be alone as well.

Had she truly used her blood to see her own future? To see Atiana's as well? She said the Haelish saw paths, many paths, and it was up to them to determine the right one. Or perhaps guide others so that the right one was chosen. Is this what the wodjan was doing with her? Manipulating her to find a certain path, one that she and her sisters had determined was the right one?

The right one for whom, Atiana wondered, *Hael or Anuskaya?*

Perhaps both, she thought. She hoped it was both.

"*Tsss.*"

Atiana looked behind her, unsure which direction the sound had come from.

"*Tsss.*"

She looked down and saw a vague outline in the dark. It was Aelwen, standing on the trail only a short drop from where she sat. How had she snuck up without Atiana seeing?

"Come," Aelwen said.

Without a word, Atiana got up, walked down the trail, and followed. They walked until they came to the trough of the valley, and then Aelwen stepped off the trail and into a low cave. Atiana stopped at the entrance. For a moment the scattered brush in the immediate vicinity, the squat and heavyset trees, looked as though they were hiding the enemy. But why would they be? Aelwen hadn't brought them last time, and she had no reason to do so now.

Atiana ducked down and entered.

Inside was a space no larger than the interior of a coach. At the center of it was a dying fire that glowed a dull red. Two small rugs sat on either side of the fire, and on one of them was a brass censer and a knife no longer than the span of Atiana's hand. The hilt of the knife was made of braided gold. It had the look of age about it, as if not just Aelwen had used it, but her mother and grandmother as well.

"Sit," Aelwen said as she moved to the empty carpet.

Atiana complied, sitting with her legs folded under her. She did not touch the censer, nor the knife.

"Are the servants of the Kamarisi close?"

"Not close," Aelwen said, "but not far."

"You could lead them away from us, couldn't you?"

"I could."

"Will you?"

Aelwen's face was dark under the ruddy light of the coals. "Is that why you came? To convince me to lead the janissaries away?"

Atiana took a deep breath and released it slowly. "I don't know *why* I've come."

Aelwen motioned to the knife and censer. "You've come to open a door."

The knife's blade glinted. "I suppose I have."

"Then take it up, Atiana of Anuskaya. Take up the knife and put the censer before you."

Atiana did, feeling as though she were betraying her mother, Radia, and her grandmother, Anastasa, by the mere act of it. Such things had never been taught in the halls of Anuskaya, nor would they ever be. And perhaps for good reason.

This not only felt like she was betraying the tradition of the Matri, it felt as though she were giving Aelwen power over her. She hoped it wasn't so—she would be careful to watch for any sign of it—but if this was something that might help her, or the others, she had to try it.

"Cut," Aelwen said, "here." She pointed to the place on her forearm just below her wrist. "Cut with the point, not deeply, but enough to draw good blood."

And suddenly Atiana was afflicted with the same fear she'd had of the drowning basin years ago. She told herself that it was the bitter chill of the water she hated, but in truth it was the fear of the aether was welling up inside her. Was it true? Had she been gone from the aether so long that she now feared entering it again? It was an exotic and in some ways repulsive method to use, but it was *a* way, and that was what mattered. Wasn't it?

Fear, Atiana thought. She had to master her fear.

After taking a deep breath, she rolled the sleeve of her shayla up and pressed the point of the knife against her skin. She continued to breathe while watching the point press deeper and deeper. She felt the heat from the fire, and also the coldness of the stone through the carpet beneath her. She heard her own breathing. Heard Aelwen's. Heard the strange creaking of the insects in the dry valley outside the cave.

Knowing it would become no easier, she pressed the knife in, felt the bite and the burning sting. Blood slipped from the wound.

"Over the censer now," Aelwen said.

Atiana moved her arm over the round brass censer. Her blood pattered against it, creating strange patterns, red against gold. She continued until the center of it was covered.

"Now place it on the flames."

Atiana complied, and watched as the blood began to bubble and then smoke.

"Draw the smoke over you. Wash your body with it."

Aelwen began drawing the smoke toward her.

"Do not!" Atiana called, louder than she'd meant. "This is mine alone."

Aelwen's eyes flashed, but she sat up straight, motioning for Atiana to continue.

Atiana did. She pulled the smoke toward her, ran it down her chest and over her legs as Aelwen had shown her. She drew it down one arm, then the other. Then she brought it over her head, and as she did so she breathed it in deeply. The smell of it was bitter and acrid and foul. She nearly stopped. She nearly stood and left this cave. But the look on Aelwen's face was one of high anticipation. There was power here. Power in her own blood, and she would know what it was. It was important that she understand if only to understand more about the Haelish and their strange ways.

Slowly her mind began to broaden. She felt more of this cave, more of the surroundings outside. She felt the wiry bushes and the small scrub trees that dotted the landscape. She felt the stream that ran largely beneath the ground.

And soon. Soon…

She is in the aether. She has taken the dark.

She feels the hills around her now.

A valley lies to the west, and more to the south. Is that where they go? Is that where Kohor lies?

She feels more of the Gaji. Its vastness, its varying landscape. She feels Andakhara to the east and many more of the caravanserai that dot the desert plain's massive eastern pan.

She is losing herself. She knows this. And yet she allows it, for this place feels so familiar she's ready to cry.

How she's missed it. Missed this place that once was the place she least wanted to be. While she was in the aether, she felt connected to so much more than in the waking world.

And yet she knows she isn't asleep—not as she is in the drowning basin. She is awake, drawing smoke over her frame to keep herself in this place. It feels wrong, and it makes her notice all the differences. It feels more raw, as though she's becoming part of the stuff from which the world was made. It feels foreign as well, as though it is the domain of the wodjana, not the Matri of the islands, and it is this realization that makes her lose control.

Her mind goes wild, and in her fever she reaches eastward, toward Anuskaya, for help.

Ishkyna, she calls. *Ishkyna!*

But her sister does not hear.

She must leave.

She cannot remain.

With one last act of desperation, she pulls herself inward, back toward the Gaji, back toward the hills, back toward the cave in which she kneels.

And she woke.

Shivering. Her stomach turning at the smell of burning blood, so much so that she leaned forward and vomited over the fire, over the smoking censer.

Before she knew what was happening, Aelwen was by her side, rubbing her back. She realized her wound had been treated, a cloth bandage wrapped around her forearm, near her wrist. How long had she been gone?

"You did well for your first time," Aelwen said. "It comes easier after this."

Atiana was already shaking her head. "I won't be doing this again."

Silence followed, and then a low rumbling sound filled the cave. At first Atiana wasn't sure what it was, but then she realized it was Aelwen. She was laughing. "Will you not?" she asked.

Atiana shrugged off her help and got to her feet. "I will not." As she moved toward the cave's entrance, Aelwen's laughter only grew.

She'd made it outside when she heard Aelwen call. "Atiana?"

She should have kept moving. She should have hiked back to her camp and lain with Nikandr and forgotten all about this.

But she didn't.

She stopped and looked back. "What?"

"I'll come to you tomorrow," came the wodjan's soft voice, "just in case you change your mind."

With her face burning in shame, Atiana walked back up the trail toward camp.

CHAPTER SIXTEEN

The wind blustered as Nikandr and his companions rode their massive ab-sair along the dry hills of the western Gaji. Nikandr was trying to control his breathing, but it was becoming difficult. He was distracted, perhaps because they were nearing the valley in which Kohor lay. The desert overflowed with strange stories about that valley—that in the hills around it one could find the walking dead, that on the darkest night of the month one could speak and hear the fates answering back, that it held a secret place where the makers of the world still slept. Whatever the reason, Nikandr watched his surroundings closely. He became aware of the ground, for as the ab-sair plodded onward, it felt as though their cloven hooves were hammering the earth, summoning from it a sound like the echoes of the forging of the world. He became aware of the dry, mineral scent and the overpowering smell of the flowering bushes—adwas, Goeh had called them.

More than anything, though, Nikandr felt the wind. The air. The open sky above them. Rarely were there clouds, only an open maw of blue so wide and deep it felt as though he would surely fall into it, never to return.

He couldn't help but think of Atiana the night before. The way she'd kissed him. The way she'd held her hand over his heart, as if she held his life in her hands.

And perhaps she did.

She'd been right. She hadn't even said it out loud, but he'd found himself on an overhang, one that had looked down on the shallow valley to the west of their camp. He'd remained there for hours without realizing it. It had felt much shorter, but each and every moment had been filled with that same ache. He'd thought about leaping, thought about calling to the wind to save him. But the hoot of a desert owl, so near he'd felt it on the back of his neck, had jarred him.

He'd returned to camp, shamed again at what he'd been thinking of doing, unsure how to break the cycle. And then he'd walked into Atiana's kiss.

It had jarred him. It made him think over the days since leaving Galahesh, the days on the mainland as they trekked toward and then into the Gaji. As he lay on his bedroll that night he saw his slow slide toward this, what he'd become, and he'd vowed to change it. He just had no idea how. Not yet. But he would find a way.

He began to look for a way to retreat, a way to find himself alone, if only to howl his frustration at the uncaring sky. There was something about being among the others that confused him. He wasn't able to concentrate on his feelings of loss. And for better or worse—no matter how much they might want to help, no matter how wise they collectively were—they couldn't help him. He had to work his way beyond his burning desire to touch Adhiya once more. Atiana could help once he found the path. But he had to get there first.

As she often did, Atiana rode beside him. He could feel her stare. He turned and saw a look upon her face that on the surface was pleasant, but there was that look of concern. She knew what he was feeling.

"If I continue at this plodding pace for another minute," he told her, "I'll go mad." He motioned down to the long, narrow valley on their right. "I'm going to ride hard for a while." He reined his ab-sair closer and leaned in to kiss her. "I'll meet you at the far end."

She held his hand, refusing to let go for a moment. "Be careful. Goeh said we'd be coming close to Kohor today. And the janissaries may not be far behind."

"We've seen no sign of them for over a week," he said. "We're making good time, and with any luck, they've given up the chase."

"Or they're pushing to move ahead of us."

He squeezed her hand back. "Then I'm doubly safe for now."

Just then a gust blew Atiana's left sleeve up, revealing a bandage with dried red blood on the inside of her forearm. Atiana pulled her sleeve back in place quickly, as if she were embarrassed over it.

"What's that?" Nikandr asked.

"Nothing."

"It looks serious."

"It's nothing. I only scraped myself on a thorn."

Atiana had been leaving the camp last night—to try to find Ishkyna, she'd said. "You shouldn't leave the camp for so long."

"We have to find her," Atiana replied easily. "She can tell us much, but she may have lost her way to us. I can't find her with so many of you near." Before he could say anything further, she pointed to the valley below. "Go. Breathe." And with that she kicked her mount to a faster pace, leaving him behind as she rode toward Goeh at the head of the line.

He thought of catching up to her and pressing her on it, but there was no point. They were distant enough without him pushing her to speak of things she clearly didn't wish to speak of, so he pulled his ab-sair to a stop and waited for the rest of them to pass. Ashan and Soroush gave him concerned but understanding looks—they knew, at least to a degree, what he was going through. Ushai barely acknowledged him, and Sukharam merely rode on obliviously, either too lost in thought or caring little what became of Nikandr. When Nikandr had lost sight of them, he pulled at the reins. The beast snorted, champing at its bit and shaking its head, but then it complied.

When he reached the valley floor, the tightness in his chest eased. He was alone, or as alone as he was going to get in this place of wide valleys and dried grass. The way ahead was clear and flat. On either side of him were gently sloping hills covered with grey-green sage and red-brown dirt.

He took out his soulstone and kissed it. "I'm sorry," he whispered to it. In the months since Galahesh, he'd felt more and more as though he had betrayed his past by allowing himself to touch the hezhan. Whether or not he'd had any choice in the matter wasn't the point. He'd done it, and he'd become a pariah everywhere except Khalakovo, and even there, many looked on him with cold and mistrustful eyes when once they would have hailed him, invited him to their homes for warmed vodka and fresh bread.

He felt as though he'd betrayed his heritage by touching Adhiya, and yet he couldn't help but try again, for such was the allure of touching the wind, of opening himself to the sky and its many-faceted currents.

He dropped the reins of his ab-sair, letting it run as it would. It seemed to feel the wind as well, for it fell into a gallop that felt as though it was eager to fly like the vulture that wheeled lazily in the sky ahead. After spreading his arms wide, Nikandr tipped his head back and breathed deeply. He drew in the dry desert air and expanded his mind, at least as far as he was able. He reached for Adhiya, as he'd done so many times in the past, but he did not reach for the same spirit, the same hezhan. He knew that spirit was lost to him, and he would need to find another if he was ever to commune with a havahezhan again.

He wondered if he should try to commune with other spirits, but Ashan had told him that whatever inability he had with touching Adhiya now, he was clearly one who would find it easiest to bond with spirits of the wind. Indeed, he'd tried to feel the earth beneath him, the water running over his hands at a stream, the life held within the leaves of an acacia, but this made him feel *more* distant from the spirit realm, not closer. And there was no denying that he was drawn inexorably, at the strangest times, to the sky and the wind and the way in which it touched everything, be it a light caress or a rude shove.

His arms flounced in time with the ab-sair's gait, and soon he realized it was also in time with his heart. He wondered for a moment if the beast's heart was drumming the same rhythm, but he stopped this line of thinking and merely experienced the moment, for it was grand—the closest he'd come to those feelings of old in quite some time.

Without knowing why, he pulled himself up in his saddle. He stood on the seat, holding himself still, crouching there as his mount galloped lazily forward. He reacquainted himself with the timing of its gait and then stood, placing his feet onto the beast's wide shoulders. Again he paused in a half-crouch, but he already knew he could ride like this as long as the ab-sair would take him. Then, at last, he stood and spread his arms wide. He closed his eyes, feeling more in tune with the world than he'd felt in months. No longer was he at war with it, but neither was he its master. He was simply a part of it, and it a part of him.

He thought perhaps it had to do with the release he'd felt after Atiana had confronted him, *pleaded* with him to return to her. He didn't know if that was true. He only knew it was beautiful, this feeling, and for a moment—a moment only—it felt like it had just before the walls of Adhiya came down and he was able to commune with his spirit. For a moment he simply lived in his skin, feeling these precipitous feelings, urging himself to simply *be*.

But soon his heart yearned for more, and he found himself calling, reaching outward, hoping a spirit would find him.

That was when the ab-sair slowed its gait.

Nikandr tried to crouch down, to regain his balance, but the beast slowed too quickly and he found himself flying over its head. He managed to dive to one side, or he would have been trampled. He fell and dropped into a roll, his shoulder crashing against the earth. After skidding unceremoniously to a stop, he remained still for a moment, counting his wounds, testing his aching shoulder for soundness. "Stupid," he said as he stood and limped after the ab-sair, which had slowed to a walk and finally stopped at a clutch of adwas to nibble at the bright yellow flowers.

"You'll find it difficult to reach it from here."

Nikandr spun and found Sukharam sitting on his own ab-sair, watching with curious eyes.

"Reach what?" Nikandr asked.

"Adhiya. That's what you're searching for, isn't it?"

Nikandr swung up into his saddle in one fluid, if painful, motion. "Why would it be difficult to reach here?"

The two of them urged their mounts into an easy pace, Sukharam coming alongside him as if they were two old friends. Except they *weren't* old friends. Sukharam despised his presence here. Or at the very least thought it unwise.

"This place," Sukharam said. "For the past few days, Adhiya has felt further and further from reach, to the point that Ashan and I are finding it difficult to commune with spirits. He lost one of his bonded spirits yesterday, and now he's released the rest, feeling it improper to keep them bound if Erahm sees fit to deny him."

"It's difficult even for you?"

Sukharam laughed. "Am I not a man? Am I not bound by the worlds as Ashan is?"

"You are gifted."

"Some days it doesn't feel that way, son of Iaros."

They rode in silence for a time. They'd never seen eye-to-eye. For long months Sukharam had seemed like an impudent child, to the point that Nikandr had found himself questioning Nasim's choice—Sukharam so often railed against Ashan's tutelage; he would sulk and he would brood—but then Nikandr recognized, as gifted as this boy was, he was still just a boy. And Sukharam had grown in the time since. He'd begun to accept Ashan's teachings. He'd accepted Soroush's as well, and he spoke often with Ushai, who openly spoke of the ways of the Maharraht, which made Nikandr uncomfortable. Sukharam was impressionable, and he'd started talking as if he truly believed that violence might, at times, be the path to peace.

Were Sukharam not so wrapped up with the fate of the Atalayina and the rifts, Nikandr might have urged Ashan to find another gifted child who might help them, but Sukharam *was* wrapped up with the fate of the stone, more so than Nikandr himself was, more even than Ashan. Much like Nasim, Sukharam was a boy that had a certain weight to him, and it often made Nikandr wonder if their past lives were similar. Who might Sukharam have been? Had he known Khamal in his past life? Had they met in previous lives? Perhaps they'd met many times, their souls meeting again and again in each incarnation.

"Do you think you were meant to touch that spirit?" Sukharam asked as they passed a gnarled tree with winding branches that looked older than the hills they rode through.

"Who can say?"

"*You* can say," Sukharam replied.

"How would I know? It feels like an accident. Nothing more."

"The will of the fates is not always clear, son of Iaros."

For some reason, Sukharam's use of his father's name only served to remind Nikandr how much he missed him. He didn't react that way when Ashan used it, or Soroush. Perhaps it was because Sukharam was so young, and to hear someone speak of someone now gone only reminded Nikandr of his own mortality.

"When I bonded with that spirit," Nikandr said, "I felt free. I felt as if I *were* the hezhan, not that I was merely bonding with one."

"Do you think it felt the same of you?"

"Again, who can know?"

Sukharam turned in his saddle and regarded Nikandr with a look, not of disdain, but certainly disappointment. "*You* can know. Do you think that the Aramahn bond with spirits without considering these things? Do you not think that we share of ourselves even as we accept from the other? It is at those times that we are one, and it is then, in those moments, that we act as mirror for the other, that we are able to take steps forward in our understanding, small as they may be."

He meant steps toward vashaqiram, the state of oneness for the individual. "Do the hezhan also look for vashaqiram?"

Sukharam turned his attention back to the way ahead. They were coming closer to the end of the valley, and soon they'd forge a trail up to find the others. "They must," he said at last.

"How can you be sure? We hardly know them. We hardly know their world, and they hardly know ours."

"They are us, and we are them. It can be no other way."

"Did you ever speak to Nasim of it?"

"What would Nasim know of this?"

"He is gifted, as you are. And he walked between worlds."

"You're assuming, of course, that he's still alive at all, that he still has *gifts*, as you call them."

"He is alive."

Sukharam shifted in his saddle. "I know you must tell yourself this, that he is still alive, and perhaps he is, but I tell you this, son of Iaros—if he has gifts, they are wasted."

"I don't see that."

"Do you not? He, of all the children in the world, is the closest to his prior self. And yet he learned almost nothing until he was freed by you. He could have done so much, but instead what are we left with? Thoughts of what could have been and a world so broken we've nearly reached the end of days."

For a moment Nikandr could only stare. He'd known there had been friction between Sukharam and Nasim, but he never would have guessed that Sukharam harbored such resentment. "It wasn't Nasim's fault that he was lost."

"Perhaps he didn't have the courage to overcome it."

"And that would place the blame on him?"

"Whether or not the blame is his isn't the point. He had failings, and he has them still."

"And yet we go to find him."

"*You* go to find him. I go to find the Atalayina."

"He is part of the Atalayina. Their fates are bound together."

"That's where you're wrong, Nikandr Iaroslov. That's the failing of you and Ashan and everyone that's surrounded Nasim for so long. He is no savior. He is someone who stands in the way of the healing of the world."

Nikandr spurred his ab-sair until it was in front of Sukharam's, and then he reined his mount over, forcing Sukharam to stop. Sukharam stared into Nikandr's eyes, unflinching.

"Nasim *saved* us. Without him, we all would have died at the straits."

"That's to be commended, but that doesn't qualify him to hold the Atalayina. That is only for the pure of heart, the pure of mind."

"And you *are* qualified?"

"*Yeh*. As much as anyone alive is." Sukharam paused but only for the briefest of moments. "I don't blame Nasim for his failings. He isn't malicious." He pulled at the reins and kicked his ab-sair, moving past Nikandr toward the wash leading up the hill. "He's merely unfit."

CHAPTER SEVENTEEN

Late that night, Goeh left the camp to scout to the east. The hills became treacherous around Kohor and the valley that housed it, and he didn't want to risk riding through the night, not unless it was absolutely necessary.

The rest set up their blankets in the lee of an outcropping of hard red rock. The rock shielded them from the east, so they thought it safe to build a small fire. Nikandr, surprisingly, felt at peace with himself. Even though he'd failed to make any major breakthrough while he'd been riding, it had done him good to simply be away from the others; but more than this, it was his conversation with Sukharam that had drawn his mind toward other things.

After a meager meal of water and dried cardamom bread and tart green berries Goeh had gathered on their ride that day, Soroush filled a pipe with tabbaq and lit it using a brand from the fire. "Alas," he said, holding the smoking pipe high for a moment, "the last I brought from Rafsuhan."

Atiana looked around at all of them and then stood, brushing her skirt as if she were overly conscious of the mere act of standing. "I'd better go now."

"Stay until Goeh returns," Ashan said, smiling gently, the breeze tugging at his curly brown hair. "I'd feel better were he to tell us that the path behind us is clear."

"The time feels right," Atiana replied, a bit sharply. "If I hope to find Ishkyna, it must be now."

Soroush offered Ushai his pipe. Ushai, using her good right hand, took it from him. "Let me come with you," she said to Atiana, "and I'll help as I can." She took a long pull. The light from the tabbaq lit her eyes with a mischievous glint as if she knew Atiana would decline and yet wanted to press her anyway.

Atiana stared bitterly back. "You would only get in the way."

Ushai handed the pipe back to Soroush, who took it and drew breath from it as well, though not so deeply as Ushai had. He watched the exchange with cautious concern. Even Sukharam seemed to like it not at all, for he snorted and stood, leaving to climb the rocks which sheltered them.

"Why would I get in the way?" Ushai asked. "Because I'm not Landed?"

"Because you are not my sister, and your presence is invasive."

"Invasive..." She turned to Soroush. "She says that I'm invasive."

Soroush looked at her easily, the golden rings in his ruined left ear glinting under the firelight. "Perhaps you are."

Ushai seemed upset by this comment at first, but then she turned introspective and regarded Atiana anew. "Perhaps I am. Go then, Atiana Radieva, and tell us what you learn."

"I don't need your permission to go, daughter of Shahda." Atiana turned and walked away, but not before calling over her shoulder, "And I keep my own counsel."

Soroush leaned over the fire and offered the pipe to Nikandr. He accepted it and took a breath of his own, drawing on the sweet smoke. He held it for long moments, the scents of loam and leather and hay coming to him the longer he held it. He breathed it out slowly, handing the pipe back to Soroush.

For a spell, they simply smoked and listened to the sound of the fire and felt the cold breeze blow across their camp. But Nikandr was still bothered by what Sukharam had said in the valley. He'd wanted to speak to Ashan alone, but here at the end of the day, he felt less guarded, and he saw no reason not to get the opinion of Soroush and Ushai as well. "Sukharam tells me he no longer believes in Nasim."

"I'm not sure he *ever* believed," Ashan replied.

"But Nasim found him," Nikandr replied, feeling a touch lightheaded. He'd smoked tabbaq in Andakhara, and it was good, but nothing like this. Soroush had a nose for strong and complex leaf. He prized it above food, and rooted out the best sources wherever they traveled. Nikandr didn't mind at all, because Soroush was generous with it, though he had to be careful. If he smoked too much his stomach would turn and his mind would be cloudy for too long after.

"He did," Ashan replied, crossing his legs and staring up at the starry sky, "but I don't know that he ever *believed* in Nasim. Even in those early days, Nasim was not able to share all that he knew. He tried, but he was a boy that had lost his childhood to the choices Khamal had made for him. Fahroz did well bringing to Nasim a sense of normalcy so that he could go on about his life, but Nasim was unprepared for that which followed. And," Ashan went on, "Sukharam was not ready to learn. He was a boy who'd been sheltered from what he might have been by the path the fates had laid before him."

"Do you not believe Nasim is the key to unlocking the riddle of the Atalayina? That he's the key to closing the rifts?"

Ashan shrugged. "I believe that he is *one* of the keys, but who am I to say?" He looked to Soroush and Ushai, a prompt for them to offer their own opinions.

Soroush blew smoke into the night sky. "Nasim has links to Khamal, but does that somehow qualify him to pick up the stone that created the rifts in the first place? That may have been Khamal's plan, but it didn't work out that way. In fact, he may be the wrong person for the very fact that the link exists."

Nikandr shook his head. "That's absurd. He's the only one of us with direct knowledge of the stone."

"Little knowledge, indeed," Ushai said. She was staring into the fire while absently rubbing the scars along her hand and wrist. "He confessed to Sukharam many times that the days of the sundering were lost to him. What little he remembered were only glimpses, flashes of light that paint an incomplete picture."

"But surely that's better than nothing."

"*Neh*," Ushai went on. "His memories are incomplete, almost absent, and yet he feels responsible, and so entitled. He feels that the Atalayina is his to master, that the rifts are his to close. It is not, and *they* are not, and if we decide that he is unfit to hold the stone once again, then it shall be so, for *he* is certainly not fit to decide."

Soroush was staring at Nikandr, trying to read his expression. He was weighing Nikandr, deciding whether or not he was someone who could be trusted when the time came—*if* the time came—to make a decision about the Atalayina.

"This is madness! We already know he used the Atalayina." Nikandr touched his chest, the place where Nasim had driven home Muqallad's knife on the center of the Spar. "I would have died had he not used it to save me."

Soroush nodded, granting Nikandr the point. "That was a peculiar time and a peculiar place, Nikandr. Adhiya had been drawn close by the loss of the spires and the confluence around the Spar. What Nasim did was most likely due to that, something he did out of pure instinct."

Nikandr turned to Ashan. "Don't you preach for Sukharam to follow his instincts?"

"I do," Ashan said. "And perhaps it will be enough. I—"

Ashan stopped, for they heard someone calling. It was Goeh. "They're coming!" he called. Goeh resolved from the darkness. "They've found us," he said breathlessly. "Do not bother to pack. We must go." He pointed beyond Nikandr, to the westward trail they'd been following for days. "Quickly."

As Goeh kicked dirt onto the small fire, Nikandr stood and headed southward, toward Atiana.

Ashan took to the rocks above their shelter, where Sukharam had gone, while Soroush and Ushai ran toward their mounts.

Nikandr moved quickly but silently, listening for signs of the enemy. He heard nothing, however, as he took a shallow decline down to the plateau that continued for some time before dropping off into the darkness of the valley beyond. His eyes had not yet lost the light of the fire, and the moon was only a quarter full, making it difficult to see, but he could see the silhouettes of the sparse trees around him. Their leaves sighed beneath the chill wind of the star-filled night.

"Atiana!" he hissed, though not too loudly for it to carry among the hills. "Atiana!" he said again, more loudly. She didn't respond, however, and his heart began to beat fiercely.

In the distance, off to his left and well beyond their campsite, he heard the rattle of stone slipping down a hillside.

"Atiana, hear me!"

He'd nearly made it to the edge of the plateau when he saw the form of an old woman, hunkered over. Nikandr reached for the hilt of his shashka and scanned the landscape quickly, thinking her the wodjan that had found them in Andakhara, but it soon became clear that this was no old crone. It was Atiana, and by all that was good, she was hurt.

"Atiana!"

He ran to her side. Caught her in his arms. He noticed a strong burning smell in the air. Atiana looked as though she was ready to collapse to the ground, but now he realized she was dazed, for her head continued to roll in a circle as if she'd been struck dumb, or had smoked too much black-hoof. "Can you hear me?"

She didn't respond as her head rolled against his neck and shoulder. As he readied to pick her up, he felt something wet and warm along her left arm.

Blood.

He looked at her arm quickly, at least as well as he was able while holding her up, and realized her forearm was covered in it, her palm and fingers as well. The bleeding seemed to have stopped, for the blood was thick and tacky. Near his feet was a round object that reflected the light of the moon. He kicked at it and found burning red coals beneath it. A censer, and the blood had been burning upon it. What in the name of the ancients had Atiana been doing?

He left the coals as they were. They were dim, but hopefully the wind would brighten them and their pursuers would be drawn here instead of toward the camp.

After taking Atiana up in his arms, he hurried away.

He'd not gone ten paces when a flash came from his right, followed immediately by the crack of musket fire. Another came a moment later, and the ground near Nikandr's feet erupted, spraying his shins and thighs with scree.

The musket fire was at least a hundred yards away. He hurried forward, listening for signs of pursuit. For long moments he heard nothing, but when he reached the beginning of the incline close to their camp, he heard them—two sets of footsteps, running quickly.

He stopped immediately and set Atiana down. *Please, Atiana, wake!* But she did not. She merely lay there, motionless, though thank the ancients she still drew breath.

As the footsteps came closer, he pulled two walrus tusk cartridges from his bandolier and emptied them onto the ground before him. He did the same with two more, piling the powder as carefully as he could.

The footsteps were close now. He could see their shapes bearing down on him.

He pulled his pistol from its holster at his belt and called, "Halt!"

Then he closed his eyes, laid the pistol near the powder, and pulled the trigger.

CHAPTER EIGHTEEN

The flint struck the frizzen. Through pinched eyes Nikandr saw a flash of yellow, a momentary glimpse of the sun, as the pile of gunpowder sizzled and erupted with a sound like snapping stone.

Burning powder seared the back of his hand.

Bits of stone pelted his arm and chest and face.

One of the janissaries cried out in fear or surprise.

Nikandr holstered the pistol and drew his shashka. One of the men had stopped but the other was continuing, sword drawn, perhaps hoping to barrel Nikandr over before he could recover.

But, blinded as he was, it was child's play for Nikandr to step to one side, to hold out his leg and trip the man. He fell face-first to the ground, and Nikandr drove his shashka down through the man's back. He withdrew his sword just in time to meet the rush of the other janissary, who was calling out loudly now and swinging his sword maniacally. He was not, however, running pell-mell as his comrade had been.

Nikandr beat off two hasty swings and stabbed the janissary's sword arm. When the soldier dropped the sword, Nikandr swung his blade across the man's neck.

A gurgling sound replaced the soldier's shouts, and he fell, dropping his sword and grasping his neck in a vain attempt to stem the flow of blood.

Nikandr returned to Atiana and picked her up again. By now he could hear the plodding hooves of the enemy's ab-sair. They were coming from the trail Nikandr and the others had followed just before nightfall.

He could hear Goeh and Soroush and the others preparing their own ab-sair as well. The beasts could sense the danger they were in, for they made a sad sound, like a wracking cough one got in the dark stages of the wasting.

"Here!" Nikandr said as he pushed harder to reach the top of the rise.

An ab-sair with a tall form astride it—Goeh—loomed in the darkness. Goeh bore two ab-sair by their reins, which he tossed down to Nikandr. Nikandr couldn't let Atiana ride alone, however, so he swung Atiana up into the nearest beast's saddle and came up behind her.

Soon after, they were off, kicking their ab-sair into lazy gallops. A musket shot pounded the air behind them. Another came, and Nikandr heard the musket shot whir past him. A third came, and Nikandr heard a grunt from somewhere ahead—Goeh, or perhaps Soroush, he couldn't be sure.

They continued on with Goeh in the lead. As dark as it was, they were largely leaving it to the ab-sair to find their own way. Nikandr knew they were able to see in such dim light, and yet he still found his hands cramping from holding the reins so tightly. There were sheer drop-offs on their right, and every so often Nikandr's mount would lose its footing when the loose trail gave way beneath it. The beasts were sure-footed, though, and each time it happened, the beast would recover, plodding on as if nothing had happened.

They took a curve to the left. Nikandr could see tall hills above them on his left. The inclines were much sharper here than among any of hills they'd been riding through for days. And it became more marked the further they went, until there were imposing peaks towering to their left and more sheer drops to their right.

The musket shots continued for some time, but stopped as the enemy lost distance, making it nearly impossible to get a reasonable shot. Still, whenever there were long unobstructed paths, a few shots would come in, some pelting into the earth on their left or whizzing above their heads.

Nikandr tried to wake Atiana. He called to her. He shook her. He even tried slapping her to jar her to wakefulness, but none of this worked. He feared she was dying, but when he held her close and listened to her breathing and felt for her heartbeat, they were shallow but strong, and remained so as the night led on.

When the moon set, the musket fire stopped altogether, and their progress slowed to a crawl. The beasts could see by starlight, but even they weren't comfortable moving at a pace any greater than a walk. Surely it was the same for the janissaries chasing them. Nikandr hoped they might even call off their chase, preferring to wait for morning, but there came a time about an hour into the darkest part of their ride when Goeh called back to them, "Quiet now. Quiet."

Minutes later, they took a sharp curve in the trail. On their right was a steep drop, as it had been for hours, but the trail had curved so sharply that the trail they'd just been riding along was on the far side of the gap, less than twenty paces away. Nikandr could see the barest outline of the dark hill with the gauze of starlight hanging above it. He thought he could detect forms moving along the trail. It felt as though they were training their muskets on them. He could almost *feel* the stare of their barrels. But no shots came, and eventually they made it to a place where the trail led between two tall cliffs. They moved faster after this, protected as they were on both sides. Plus, the path here seemed wider than before.

Dawn approached. Nikandr could see its light, an indigo brightening of the horizon behind them that illuminated more and more of the landscape. The hills were sharper and darker than the peaks above them. And ahead of them, there was a flat pan.

There, Nikandr thought, was Kohor.

The janissaries were gaining on them, though. There were nearly two dozen of them. Two dozen against their seven. Their only hope was to reach level ground and to make for Kohor as quickly as their weary mounts could take them. But it was already clear the janissaries were gaining. They had extra mounts at their rear. Surely they'd been spelling their mounts by changing every so often.

Ashan was spreading his arms wide while lifting his head toward the sky. Nikandr watched as he did so. He prayed that Ashan would be able to bond with a hezhan—any hezhan—but in the end nothing happened. Surely he was trying to bond with a havahezhan to bring biting wind against their pursuers, or to lift a dust storm so thick they could no longer follow, but the deadening around Kohor must have become markedly worse to keep Ashan—an arqesh of the Aramahn people—from touching Adhiya and bonding with a spirit.

Nikandr couldn't see Sukharam's face, but he too spread his arms, but he did so only for a short time. Either he'd given up or he'd judged that he would never be able to bond with a spirit here.

The horizon continued to brighten the east. They could make out the janissaries clearly now. Goeh was leading the group toward another defile when the first of the musket shots started. A second came, taking Ushai's ab-sair in the flank. The beast tripped, tried to catch itself, and then collapsed, throwing Ushai violently from the saddle.

Soroush slipped off his mount easily and ran back to Ushai, who had fallen hard, but seemed well enough for it. Nikandr steered his ab-sair toward them and threw Soroush the reins of the extra mount, the one Atiana should have been riding.

After helping Ushai up into the saddle, Soroush sprinted to his own ab-sair. They'd lost little time, but even as they continued toward the narrow space between the cliffs ahead, more musket shots came in, and they were coming faster now. The path was wide enough behind them that the janissaries were allowing the men who hadn't fired to move to the front of the line to fire, while the others fell back to reload their weapons.

A flurry of seven or eight shots rained in as Nikandr and the others reached the mouth of the narrow passage. Goeh's ab-sair was struck, though it kept moving, and Nikandr felt a musket ball tug at Atiana's skirts. If Atiana's leg had been grazed, she didn't show it. She was as silent as she'd been since leaving their camp.

Upon entering the defile, they fell into shadow.

They were protected for the time being, but the enemy would be on them soon. Nikandr whistled and waved to catch Soroush's and Goeh's attention. He waved them back, and then he looked to Ashan. "Please, Ashan, take her."

Ashan did, slipping behind Nikandr in the saddle and taking Atiana from him. Nikandr then climbed down and grabbed his musket from its holster behind the saddle and ran to stand beside Goeh and Soroush.

As the others continued down the trail, the three of them waited.

"I'll take the first. Soroush, the second."

Soroush nodded, and just then Nikandr saw the first of them. He thought of taking down the mounts—it was a much easier shot—but with their extras it would be a waste. It was vital that they take men out while they could. As the lead man came more fully into view, he sighted carefully and pulled the trigger. The shot caught the soldier of Yrstanla fully in the chest and sent him reeling back and over the rump of his mount. Even before he'd collapsed to the ground, Soroush fired, taking the second in line. Nikandr was reloading when Goeh took the third.

Nikandr fired again as the janissaries began returning fire. Soroush fired shortly after. Goeh was slower. Nikandr and Soroush were both able to fire one more time before Goeh raised his musket to his shoulder. Just as Goeh fired, the shot striking the red earth of the dry cliffs, the janissaries called a charge.

"Quickly," Nikandr called, retreating toward their ab-sair. "We'll try again ahead."

But Nikandr knew that such a thing would be difficult. They'd dropped only four of the men, leaving at least twenty. And with the speed the janissaries would put on now, there would most likely be no time. They'd be lucky to make it out of this defile, much less reach level ground below.

They rode hard. Their ab-sair were winded, but they'd heard the pounding of hooves behind them; they'd heard the gunfire—they were every bit as scared as Nikandr, and their pace showed a renewed strength because of it.

Even so, it couldn't last long. The winding path through the defile—so close at times his arms brushed the red rock of the sheer cliff walls—took them lower and lower, and then it opened up into a valley of sorts. The rock formations here were strange. Some were short. Others were hundreds of feet tall. Their bases widened and were somewhat rough, but the higher they went the smoother the stone became until they looked like needles ready to pierce the fabric of the deep blue sky.

The janissaries were only a hundred paces behind them now.

They could not outrun them.

If they tried, they would all be killed one by one, or their mounts shot out from underneath them.

Nikandr glanced back. Several janissaries, now that the path had widened, were spaced more widely and were sighting along their muskets once more.

Just then Nikandr noticed, toward the desert plain, a form rising from behind one of the strange rock formations. It was a man wearing robes the same color as the red stone from which the columns were made, the same red as this entire desert seemed to be made. He bore a musket with beads and braided rope decorating the barrel. His face was hidden by a red scarf so that only his eyes were revealed. He lowered his musket and aimed it toward Nikandr. Before Nikandr could react, a white puff of smoke issued from the barrel.

Nikandr ducked instinctively, but shortly after he heard one of the janissaries' mounts scream. He looked back and saw the ab-sair rolling in the dry earth. The rider was caught in the tumble and was lost a moment later to the dust that rose up around them. The other riders steered wide, one of them firing his musket at the red-robed man, but as he did, a dozen others rose up, then more, and more. There must have been forty of them. Fifty.

Unlike the first who had fired, these men bore curving bows made from beautiful black wood. They pulled the strings back, sighting for a moment, before releasing their arrows in tight succession. They took down a dozen janissaries in mere seconds.

The surviving janissaries pulled their mounts to a halt. They looked, wide-eyed, for only a moment before one of them called retreat. The rest needed no convincing. They turned and urged their mounts to head back toward the defile. And soon, they were gone.

Leaving Nikandr and the rest alone with these men from the heart of the desert. These men of Kohor.

CHAPTER NINETEEN

That night Styophan's hands and feet were bound, and he was tied to an iron ring set into the central posts of a large yurt. Anahid was with him. Rodion and Edik and Galeb were brought in soon after, but Vyagos and Oleg were not. Guards were set outside the yurt, but no others stayed inside with them. It was a large space for five people, which made Styophan nervous. Something had changed, no doubt due to the expectations of Bahett, or perhaps King Brechan. Or perhaps it was simply that Kürad felt his debt to the fates had been paid in full, and it was time Styophan be treated like any other prisoner of war.

"Where are the others?" Styophan asked Rodion.

Rodion shook his head, his eyes expressing the worry seething inside him. "They were taken northward through the yurts while we were led here."

Styophan's gut tightened like a skein of wet yarn left drying in the sun. "Why?" he managed to get out.

"They spoke to one another in Haelish, but I don't know what they said, Styopha."

Anahid stared on with a harried look about her.

"Speak," Styophan snapped. "We don't have time to dance around the issue."

She glanced toward the entrance. When she spoke, it was barely loud enough for Styophan to hear. "I've told you some of the details of their wodjana." She licked her lips. "But not all. I never thought it necessary, as I thought they would become our allies. Many men of Yrstanla have suffered greatly under their attention. They use foul magic with the blood of those they take. They bleed them, keeping them alive for hours or days at a time, using them to scry. There are those among the Aramahn that believe the soul of the tortured is drained in this process. We fear that the soul becomes lost, perhaps never to be reborn."

"They won't do that to us."

"They will." Her neck muscles were taut. Her eyes were wild, and her nostrils flared. "They will think me more powerful than the men. They will think you more powerful than me. We'll be saved for last. They'll hope to find what they want, but if they don't, they'll continue with us, one by one, bleeding us to see their future."

"We're too valuable to Bahett." He looked to the men. "*All* of us. He'll take us back with him to Alekeşir, and he'll ransom us back to the Grand Duchy."

"You, perhaps," Anahid said. "Not me. Not Rodion or Vyagos or Oleg."

"I won't let them leave you."

"You are a *prisoner!*" Anahid shouted. "A prisoner! Do you hear me? You have no sway among these people! We came here arms extended in friendship and they cut our hands from our wrists. Do not think that I for my Aramahn blood, nor you for your Anuskayan, will be spared from their attentions. We will not. Look beyond their kings, Styophan Andrashayev. They are guided by their wodjan, and only them, and they will demand blood at a time like this, upon this embrace between Hael and Yrstanla. It can be no other way. And they will use us to do so, for we are at the heart of their troubles."

Styophan had never seen Anahid in such a state. She always seemed so calm and centered. He could only think of shaking her, to draw her away from the horrors in her mind, but all of them were bound to iron rings, separated by leagues though they sat mere steps away from one another.

"They'll—"

He stopped, for just then a wailing carried to them from the direction of the Place of Kings and its menhir. Though soft at first, it was a mere precursor to the outpouring of suffering that followed. It was joined moments later by another voice. He recognized them both. Vyagos's higher voice joined by Oleg's baritone, the two of them rising and falling in a terrible rhythm.

He'd been so sure of what he'd been telling Anahid, but he realized now it had all been a foolish hope. He knew as well as Anahid how cruel the Haelish could be. He just hadn't wanted to give up hope. Not yet.

He fell against the post to which he was bound. He closed his left eye tight—feeling the muscles around his ruined right eye pinch—and knocked his head against the wood, praying to his long-dead father to make this stop. The wailing scoured him from the inside. It gnawed, as if his men were trapped within him and were digging their way out with teeth and nails.

These were his men. His. He had taken them on as his sons the moment he'd nodded his head to Ranos, the Duke of Khalakovo, in his throne room. Dear Fathers, how he'd failed them...

He stood, though it was difficult and awkward to do so. He pulled at his restraints, pulled against the stout yurt pole, yanking again and again until his wrists screamed from it. Eventually the sound clawed its way up his throat and found release in a long outpouring of grief and rage and regret. He threw himself into these simple motions, becoming little more than a beast of bone and muscle, pulling against bonds that utterly refused to release him.

His head tilted up toward the sky as the cries of his men reached a new crescendo. "Leave them!" he cried to the worked leather of the yurt's roof. "Leave them be!"

But the sound of pain continued, on and on and on.

He strained harder than ever. He thought surely his limbs would break, that his joints would fail, leaving him powerless once more, but then the pole moved. A scrape no wider than his thumb showed as the massive pole gouged the earth. This energized him. He pulled again, this time keeping more of his rage pent up within him. A long grunt escaped him, for he could not keep it all bound within, but the pole moved further.

But then one of the voices fell silent.

Oleg. He no longer heard Oleg's cries.

He locked eyes with Rodion and Edik, who stared back with venom in their eyes. Galeb, however, stared down at the hard-packed ground, nostrils flaring, the apple in his throat bobbing up and down, up and down. Galeb was one of the youngest of his men. He'd been a good fighter, and eager to prove himself, but this was more than he could handle. He was completely and utterly stricken with fear.

Before Styophan could speak to him the yurt flap opened and in stepped Datha and three other warriors, each of them dressed in leggings only—no shoes, no shirt, the crushed and glittering remains of yellow jasper spread across their chests in tight, swirling patterns. The warriors were unfamiliar to Styophan. This in itself wasn't strange, but they wore their hair differently than did the people of Clan Eidihla, and their leggings were of a different style, made from different leather. These men were even different from one another. Telling, then, that Datha had come with them. It showed how little power Kürad had when his men could not be trusted to perform this simple task—the gathering of sacrifices to slake the wodjan's thirst for sacrificial blood.

Datha's eyes were bright and fierce and in no way sympathetic. Such a change, Styophan thought, from the long trek to Skolohalla. Styophan could smell upon his breath something earthy, perhaps a tincture given to the chief among this infernal ritual's participants.

"You will come with us," Datha said to Styophan.

Datha and one of the warriors began untying Styophan's restraints while the other two went to Anahid.

"*Nyet!*" Styophan screamed. "Leave her!"

Datha brought his fist across Styophan's cheek. His hand was as hard as stone—it dazed Styophan into silence, and in that moment, he found some small amount of clarity. Datha *could* have struck him much harder.

"Do not speak," Datha said to Styophan. "Not until you're spoken to by the wodjan."

Styophan spit at him, and nearly unleashed a stampede of hatred against him, but there was something in Datha's eyes. Not sympathy, but a concentration, as if he dearly hoped, and not for his own sake, that Styophan would obey, and it made Styophan wonder through his haze of anger whether he'd been wrong. Datha was expressing to him, in the only way he could, the way to save himself. *I cannot save the men who were taken*, he said, *but you might yet be spared.*

He hoped it was so, for if Datha were fooling him, and he was allowing himself to be taken, he would deserve the shame to himself and his family that would follow his death.

The other Haelish took him, their fingers digging into his arm like steel clamps. Despite his struggling they hobbled his legs and tied his wrists and guided him out of the yurt and into the cold night air. They did so with an ease and a disregard that made it clear just how powerless he was to prevent them. He was a lone sapling, they the avalanche, and they were charging down toward the base of the mountain, toward something momentous and terrible.

They wove through the yurts, and soon came to the Place of Kings, the vast depression with its menhir pointing like a single, accusing finger toward an uncaring sky. In the middle ground, circling the menhir, were dozens of massive braziers. Each held a tall wood fire atop it, and the collective light showed the Haelish warriors—hundreds of them—standing like sentinels around the great circle's edge. Their eyes were closed, and they hummed in low tones, the sound of it collecting until it was very much like the massive wooden horns the mountain villages of Anuskaya used to warn one another of danger.

With Datha leading the way, his warriors led Styophan and Anahid toward the menhir. Grouped around the standing stone itself were dozens of wodjan. They wore leather skirts, but like the men, their torsos were bare. Their skin was covered in patterns of black paint that glittered opalescent beneath the light of the braziers. Their faces were covered as well, the bold, intricate lines making them look animalistic. He saw the face of a badger on one, the face of a hawk on another, each with the reddened eyes of a woman who'd been breathing in the heady smoking leaves of the wodjan.

With the deep sounds of the men thrumming through the very air, rumbling Styophan's chest, the wodjan danced. They circled the menhir, some raising their arms to the sky as if begging the knowledge of the stars, while others spun low like a leaf on a windswept pond. Each of them—every one—had darkened hands, but it wasn't the same color as the paint upon their stomachs and arms and breasts. This paint was muddier. Browner. And it slowly dawned on Styophan that it was blood. They had blood upon their hands. Blood from his men, who'd done nothing to them.

As they moved beyond the circling wodjan, the space closest to the menhir was revealed. The Haelish kings stood there, as did many of their queens. Bahett was there with his guardsmen as well, but Styophan paid little attention to them.

For staked to the ground, naked, his middle cut open, was Vyagos.

His arms pulled above his head.

His wrists tied to a wooden stake.

His ankles were similarly tied, but it was the travesty between them that held Styophan's gaze.

A cut trailed from sternum down to his pelvis, opening the cavity and allowing plain view of all that lay within. His viscera had been pulled out and laid upon the ground in a clear pattern, though what in the ancients' names it might mean Styophan had no idea.

On the far side, Oleg was also staked to the ground, though—dear mothers—he *still breathed*. He breathed when his torso was cut stem to stern and his guts were thrown about. A woman stood over him, a bloody knife in her hand, her breasts hanging down as she peered into his eyes and his chest rose and fell as slow as the coming of winter.

CHAPTER TWENTY

The other times harm had befallen his men at the hands of the Haelish, Styophan had been consumed with rage. But here, seeing his men like this, he had no idea what to think. He'd heard of the Haelish's bloody rituals many times. Even in the tent while Anahid pleaded with him to understand, he thought he'd known how cruel they were, but here, standing before Vyagos's lifeless remains, watching Oleg somehow draw breath, he was unmanned.

He nearly tripped, hobbled as he was, but the Haelish warriors on either side of him pulled him up and dragged him before King Brechan. Kürad and Elean stood nearby as well. The mystery of the queen's visitation in the woods, of her strange request to examine her, still haunted him. The other queens were little different—dark eyes with the same color. All but Queen Dahlia, the wife of King Brechan. *Her* eyes seemed more sunken, and they had the proper yellowish tinge with no signs of the strange orange that Elean exhibited. She coughed as Styophan watched, but she bore a defiant look, as if she'd vowed long ago to fight this disease, to win against it. It stood in stark contrast to the other queens, who seemed sick, certainly, but somehow accepting of it. It was a mystery that dogged him, but at the moment he could spare no thought for it.

King Brechan wore an elaborate shirt of leather, braided with horsehair along the chest and arms. His crown of thorns rested upon his head, its hidden rubies glinting beneath the firelight.

"The kings have spoken," Brechan said in low tones. His eyes were hazy as he looked at Styophan. The whites were red. He'd been drinking, not alcohol, surely, but some brew prepared by the wodjan.

Styophan saw to his left Anahid being taken to the northern side of the menhir stone. He nearly called out—nearly surged forward to fight for her—but the words of Datha rang true. He was sure that if he were to speak a single word, the wodjan would kill her, and him, and do so painfully. He would wait, for only in this did there seem to be some small chance of survival.

Brechan continued. "It is judged that you brought the withering here. You and your brothers, the men of Anuskaya. You and your sisters, the women and the Matri. The wodjan have seen it while looking death in the eye, while speaking with her at long length."

Styophan felt sick. He meant the death throes of Vyagos and Oleg. The wodjan had used them to sift through the passages of time, to have questions answered from beyond the grave, from beyond this world.

Brechan nodded to Styophan, his eyebrows pinching, perhaps in pain or confusion from the elixir he'd imbibed. "What have you to say?"

Styophan looked at the gathered assemblage. Was he to defend himself from this? Was he to defend all of Anuskaya from these accusations? What could he say? They'd done no such thing. The *rifts* had caused the wasting. And since the conflict on Galahesh, they'd been spreading, faster and farther than ever before. It wasn't the Grand Duchy that was responsible, but the Al-Aqim. But how could he tell the Haelish this? They would have none of it.

He looked to Queen Elean, who stared on with a look of intense concentration, as if she cared about the outcome of this conversation very much. Her eyes... Her apparent affliction... He didn't even know why he cared, but he did. It seemed part and parcel of his fate—his and the fates of his men.

And then he caught Bahett, this regent from Yrstanla who stood to gain so much from the Haelish. The war between them would be stopped. He could focus his forces eastward to meet the oncoming threat of the Grand Duchy's push onto the continent. He might even gain allies among the Haelish, as Styophan had planned to secure for Duke Ranos. Standing behind Bahett were three swordsmen in boiled leather armor. They stood easily, eyes watching the proceedings lazily, but Styophan knew these would be the very sharpest and brightest of the Kamarisi's swords.

Styophan looked to the other queens. The one to Brechan's right, his wife, had the same dark eyes as Elean. A brazier burned nearby, shedding light on her face, on her eyes, and Styophan could tell that they were the same hue as Elean's. He looked to another of the queens, and another. There were seven of them in all, and he could see it now, plain as day. With the exception of Dahlia, they were all afflicted in the same manner as Elean.

Nyet, Styophan thought. Not afflicted. Suffered. They suffered from this condition, because it was something that had been done to them. They were victims.

He stared into Bahett's eyes. He was staring back with a look of cold discomfort, as if he'd rather this night be done and his treaty signed so that he could return to Alekeşir and resume his role at the Kamarisi's side.

And then Styophan knew.

Cold prickled his skin. A shiver shook him from the mere certainty of this newfound insight.

It was Bahett.

Bahett had done this.

Styophan didn't know how, but he had. He'd poisoned the queens. His resources were considerable, and the knowledge held within the library of Alekeşir and the wise men that groomed it were vast. Could he not find a poison or a venom that could mimic the withering given the right dosage? How else could all of the queens have contracted it? The wasting was indiscriminate. But a poison? *That* could be delivered precisely given the right access, and it would give Bahett exactly the leverage he wanted: a reason for the kings to join him, or at the very least to cease hostilities while he took care of the upstart islands.

As Anahid was laid down on the ground, his mind raced. How? How could Bahett have done this?

Elean was watching him intently. Did she know? Did she suspect where his thoughts were headed? Perhaps she did. Else why would she have called him to her that night in the forest?

And then, for the love of all that was good, he remembered her words. More and more of the picture filled in, and as he looked over Bahett's shoulder, full understanding finally came.

Bahett glanced over his shoulder to where his three Kiliç Şaik stood, curious as to what Styophan was thinking, but then his expression returned to the same look of disinterest he'd had ever since Styophan had arrived—disinterest, Styophan thought, when men had just been put to death in front of him.

Brechan, meanwhile, stared down at Styophan, his face growing angry. He was waiting for an answer to the charges he'd leveled. But how could Styophan respond? He couldn't simply accuse Bahett. It would be discarded as a desperate attempt to free himself and his men.

"The withering started among the islands," Styophan acknowledged with a nod, "but it isn't the withering that stands among you now."

Brechan's face constricted into a look of confusion. "It *does* stand among us, everywhere." He motioned back to where the women stood. "Even the queens."

"*Evet*," Styophan replied, "they *look* as though they have the wasting, but they do not."

Brechan's face grew even darker. "I can see it with my own eyes."

"As can I, but they aren't the symptoms of the withering, King Brechan. They are the symptoms of a poison, rendered to your queen." He stared at each of the gathered Kings. "Rendered to *all* of your queens."

"We are no fools, Styophan Andrashayev. There are hundreds who've taken ill. Dozens have already died from it. Our graves are filled with their bodies, and you tell me that Yrstanla has poisoned all of them?"

"Indeed the withering has come, and surely many *have* died from it. But not your queens."

"How can you know?"

"Because they don't have the same symptoms."

This only seemed to make Brechan angrier. "How can you know?"

"Because I saw Queen Elean. I examined her."

"You lie," Brechan said, his voice rising in volume.

"I do not. I examined her fully as she stood naked before me."

The gathered crowd spoke in low tones until Brechan turned and shouted, "Silence!"

Nearby, the wodjan faltered in their dance. They stopped and stared with scowling expressions. Even the constant drone of the men standing sentinel around the edge of the basin broke momentarily before picking up once more.

All eyes turned to Elean, but she kept her gaze pointed downward, refusing to meet the eyes of Brechan or her king.

Kürad stepped out from the line of kings, and as he did, Brechan backed away with a tilt of his head, an acknowledgement that it was within Kürad's rights to question Styophan. Kürad paused only long enough to pull the long length of steel at his side. The sword's straight blade was nicked from countless battles, but its edge was otherwise gleaming and sharp. Styophan had no doubt it could cleave his head from his shoulders with little trouble, especially from a man like Kürad, whose corded muscles rippled as he gripped the leather-wrapped hilt.

For the first time Bahett was nervous—Styophan could see it in the way he sent fleeting glances among the kings, the way his shoulders had tightened—but he hid it well, and he doubted the Haelish would note that anything was amiss.

Kürad continued until he was nearly chest-to-chest with Styophan, and he spoke low enough for only Styophan to hear. "When did you do this?"

"Speak clearly," Brechan said behind him. "All will hear."

The only response Styophan could see to this demand was a momentary tightening of Kürad's jaw. When he spoke again, however, it was with a strong voice. "When did you do this?"

"In the forest four nights ago, Elean came to me. She brought me to the woods, fearful that something was amiss. And a good thing she did, for it was clear to me that she had not been struck by the same thing I've seen among the people of the islands."

"You cannot be sure," Kürad said.

"I've seen hundreds of cases, oh King. Hundreds. The islands have been struck hard these past years. From the moment we enter the service of our dukes, the men of the staaya are taught to recognize the signs, but in truth such things are unnecessary. Anyone born and raised in the Grand Duchy knows the signs, for all families have been struck. Elean has eyes of the wrong color. Her hair remains lustrous where it should be dry and brittle. There are no lumps in the pits of her arms or the hollow where her thighs meet."

Kürad's nostrils flared at this, but he did nothing to stop Styophan from speaking.

"Look upon Queen Dahlia. Her eyes are the proper color, and her hair is thinning. She will have had trouble keeping her food down, as Elean no doubt has, but Elean's will have come and gone, where Dahlia's would be constant. And the pits of their arms"—Styophan waited until Kürad had turned to stare at Dahlia—"one need only look at the two of them and compare."

The assemblage stared between the two women. When Styophan had first arrived he'd been too blinded to see it, but now it seemed as plain as day.

"The wasting can take different forms," Bahett said.

"Only at first," Styophan replied, loudly enough for all to hear. "In the final stages, all will fall to the same signs."

The kings moved more closely to the two queens. The queens seemed nervous at first, but Styophan was under no illusions. Elean was pleased. It was why she'd brought him into the forest in the first place. Indeed, there could be no greater evidence of this than what she did next. After pulling at the ties that held her buckskin dress closed about her chest, she slipped her arms out of her sleeves and allowed the bodice to fall around her hips. She raised her hands to reveal the pits of her arms. Queen Dahlia, apparently drawing courage from this, did the same, slipping out of her dress to raise her arms. It was strange seeing these two women naked from the waist up, baring themselves for all to see, a thing that would never happen among the islands. Even now, Styophan was embarrassed over it, but he was relieved they'd had the courage to do this, for the differences between them were immediately obvious. Dahlia stared from the deep pits of her eyes, triumphant. Elean looked to Styophan, but then she turned to Bahett, who was watching this exchange with ever growing alarm.

Brechan turned to him next, then Kürad, and then the rest of the kings.

"This is foolishness," Bahett said with a confident air. "Whether they have the wasting or not, it certainly wasn't the Empire that came to Hael and poisoned them. How could anyone have done so?"

"Skolohalla," Styophan replied. "The queens met a mere eight weeks ago to discuss what would be done of Yrstanla's overture given that they'd already accepted the offer from my Lord, the Duke of Khalakovo." Styophan motioned easily to the men standing behind Bahett. "We both know, oh Kings of Hael, how gifted and cruel are the Kiliç Şaik. Could they not have stolen into Skolohalla under cover of night? Could they not have poisoned the wine of the queens as they met?"

The kings would not admit it, but they knew the elite of the Kamarisi's guard could do just that. Over the years, rumors of murders had come even to Anuskaya—the loss of a handful of kings was spoken of openly, and if that were so, it was likely the secretive Haelish had lost even more than this.

Bahett, licking his lips, his eyes darting among the kings, stepped forward. "Surely you don't believe that all could have been poisoned so."

"They meet on the same night as the kings, as I'm sure you know. You've been played for fools," Styophan said to the kings. "He knew that we'd come with an offer of friendship. He knew that you would consider it carefully. He had no choice but to take steps to prevent it, not if he had any hope of winning his war to the east, a war that threatens to run all the way to the steps of Alekeşir."

"This is madness!" Bahett turned his back on Styophan, facing only Brechan. This was a tactical error. He was a full head shorter than the towering King of Kings. "How can you give credence to a man who was about to die at the hands of your wodjan? They were to put him beneath their knives. He was to give me answers, which are as much a part of the bargain as are the gems I've granted you, as is the land I've ceded to you, King Brechan."

Brechan turned to Dahlia and spoke in Haelish. His words were quick and forceful.

Dahlia nodded.

Styophan understood nothing of the Haelish language, but Bahett clearly did, for he interrupted them, shouting, "*How* could they know?"

Brechan turned slowly back to Bahett. "Still your tongue."

Everyone who heard those three simple words knew just how grave Brechan was. Bahett seemed cowed at first. He seemed as though he would do exactly as Brechan wished, but then something strange happened. Earlier that day, when Styophan had first seen him, Bahett had seemed calm beyond measure. He'd seemed much the same even during this savage ritual. But now, as the implications of Brechan's words settled over him, the skin of his cheeks and forehead turned red. His pulse pounded at the base of his neck. The veins on his forehead stood out and were shadowed by the light of the fire. He seemed to notice the eyes that were upon him, but was trying not to show it.

Then his face hardened.

Before Styophan knew what was happening Bahett had pulled a knife, an ornate bichaq, from his belt and stalked forward.

Bahett's arm rose. It thrust forward.

Before Styophan could move something bright flashed before his eyes. Kürad's arm swung down mightily, sword in hand.

Bahett screamed and gripped his wrist.

Styophan stared downward onto the snow-trampled ground. There, swathed in red, was a severed hand, still holding the ornate knife with the finger-slim blade.

Kürad stared on, eyes afire, as if he expected Bahett to retaliate in some way, but Bahett's face had gone white as snow. It was clear that he could do nothing but grip his wrist tightly.

Behind him, however, were his Kiliç Şaik. They drew their swords and advanced until they stood between Bahett and the kings. Kürad moved forward to meet them, but the first of Bahett's men flung his arm outward and a spray of white dust filled the air. Some of it caught Styophan across his face, and he found his eyes stinging. He breathed some of it in, and in mere moments his throat and lungs were burning from it.

He stepped back out of the cloud as the wind carried it over the gathered kings and queens and their retinue. As he fought to clear his lungs and blink away the tears, another of the Kiliç Şaik pointed his arm toward the sky. He was holding a short wooden tube. He pulled a cord and a moment later a hissing sound accompanied a bright point of light that snaked up into the sky. It illuminated all around them, making the menhir look as if it were pointing toward the twinkling point of light in alarm.

The furthest pair of Kiliç Şaik led Bahett away, one of them slipping a length of cord around his wrist and tightening it to staunch the bleeding. Where they thought they could flee with so many Haelish men standing guard Styophan didn't know, but flee they did as the Haelish at the far side of the basin moved in to meet them.

The third of Bahett's guardsmen—the one who'd thrown the powder—was slowed as three of the wodjan intercepted him. He cut one down and kicked another square in the chest, sending her flying backward, but the final one leapt upon him. With a lithe twist of his body, the guardsman spun and brought her to the ground. In a flash, he swung his sword down and across her throat, but the delay had allowed Kürad the time he needed to close in. The guardsman could have run, but instead he turned and met the Haelish king with bright eyes and a flashing blade, as if he dearly hoped to take one of these kings down before he left.

Styophan stared down at the severed hand, at the knife. He liberated the knife from the fingers. If he couldn't have a pistol, he wanted cold steel in his hand. After cutting himself free of his bonds, he stalked forward to help Kürad.

The Kiliç Şaik had broken through Kürad's defenses several times already, but Kürad's skin of stone absorbed these swings with only the smallest of nicks to show for it.

As he approached, the Kiliç Şaik glanced back over his shoulder. He blocked a swing from Kürad and snapped a kick backward. Styophan was ready, however. He leaned away from the kick and then darted in. Kürad swung from on high, hoping to catch the swordsman off guard, but the Kiliç Şaik was too fast, and he spun away. Kürad swung again, and this time, the Kiliç Şaik slipped under the swing and behind Kürad before Styophan could close in again.

In a blink, he had slipped an arm around Kürad's neck. He'd caught Kürad off balance and for a moment had the upper hand, but he couldn't hope to stand against Kürad—the king was too strong and too well protected with the glittering paint laid upon his skin.

How little Styophan knew.

Styophan prepared to stalk around, or wait for Kürad himself to turn so he could bring his knife to bear, but before Kürad could do anything the Kiliç Şaik had pulled an impossibly thin dagger—more spike than knife—from some hidden location and raised it high above his head. He brought it down in one smooth but powerful motion. With a sickening crunch it drove down through Kürad's head until the knife's guard stopped against his skull.

Kürad's eyes rolled up. His eyelids fluttered. The guardsman released him, pulling the knife sharply free. Kürad's head lolled spasmodically before he finally collapsed to the ground.

The Kiliç Şaik stalked forward, sword in one hand, bloody knife in the other. Styophan waited, backing up, acting as if he was ready to turn and run. When the guardsman came too close, he leapt forward, dropping to the ground and kicking the man's legs out from under him. As the Kiliç Şaik came down, his sword swung at an odd angle. It missed Styophan entirely and bit into the cold earth. He tried to bring his knife to bear, but Styophan blocked it with his left arm and drove Bahett's knife deep into the Kiliç Şaik's throat.

As Styophan rolled the Kiliç Şaik off his chest, he heard the sound of gunfire. A few at first, and then a dozen in tight sequence. He stood and saw that the two Kiliç Şaik had sped Bahett to the edge of the basin. Many of the Haelish warriors had moved to engage, but they seemed slowed, perhaps from their ritualistic daze. A dozen horses galloped out from between the yurts and broke through the haphazard line of the Haelish. The warriors, bearing only knives, were unprepared for this organized retreat.

In moments, the Kiliç Şaik had taken Bahett up and onto one of the horses and begun riding with him back through the skirmish. More musket flashes came from the shadows of the yurts. Several of the horses were felled and the guardsmen taken down. Haelish knives rose and fell as they dispatched the men from Yrstanla, but Bahett was carried swiftly away. Moments later, the rest of the horses retreated as well, leaving only cries of alarm and the calls of the wounded.

CHAPTER TWENTY-ONE

As Kaleh climbs ahead on the lonely mountain path, Nasim sees the girl again. She is to his left, crouching behind a stone the size of a sleeping ox. The sun is high but the shadows near the base of the large boulder are dark. He does not look directly at her, for that has never once served him. The only way he can find any additional detail is to look slantwise. He's grown better at this over the past few days. He is able to keep his gaze steady and unfocused so that he can see more and more of her in his periphery.

And then he looks too closely, and she is gone.

His footfalls crunch lightly against soil that is no longer red, but the orange-yellow of dried wood sorrel blossoms. The air is dry, metallic, and there are few sounds, only the occasional sigh of the wind through the sparse bushes, or the skitter of a lizard.

Kaleh trudges ahead. She is silent, as she's been for much of the past three days, ever since leaving the last tomb. They are heading for the mountain's peak, which unnerves him. He cannot recall each of the tombs they'd entered in this lost valley, but all of those he *can* remember were situated near the base of the mountain, not the peak. Why the change he doesn't know, but he is sure that they are coming to the end of their circuit of this valley shaped like a crown. They approach the final few, saved for last for reasons he can only guess at.

As he passes by another stone to his right, there is a subtle shift of shadow: a shape that looks like a head poking out to regard his passage. He can see few details—a thin arm, a swath of rich brown hair—enough for him to know that it is the same girl each time.

Ahead, Kaleh's gait stutters. It is no more than a momentary pause, but the moment she does this, the shape at the base of the stone retreats and is gone.

Kaleh is powerful. More powerful than he would have guessed. But then again, she is born of the Al-Aqim. Why wouldn't she be?

She is also filled with purpose. He can remember times when they were among the red-robed people of another place not far from here—keepers of knowledge, protectors of this very place. He and Kaleh had spent weeks there, and all the while, Kaleh had wheedled information from them. Bit by bit she had found the secrets she'd been searching for, and when they'd left, she had gone to each one and passed the palm of her hand before their eyes. They'd looked at her blankly, and then they'd walked away as if Kaleh and Nasim didn't exist, and he was sure that was the state of things. None of them would remember their passing. None. Leaving Kaleh with the will and the knowledge to come to this valley to commit her murders.

He recalls with vivid clarity the tomb they'd entered last, the ancient and desiccated man rising from the sarcophagus only to be burned by Kaleh's hand. He's long since given up on the question of how many have died. More important is the question of how many are left. He has trouble keeping this question in his mind. It is Kaleh working against him, he knows. One moment he'd be working out where they'd started, and sometimes he thought he almost had it, but then the memories would slip through his fingers like sand. But slowly, as the girl appeared more and more frequently, he began to stitch his days in this valley together.

These ancient tombs held the still-living bodies of arqesh, or their equivalent from centuries ago. The fact that the entombed men and women wore circlets with five stones was telling. The arqesh of today are very different from those of centuries before. Today, men like Ashan *need* stones to commune with their spirits. Not so during the time before the sundering. Then the stones had known affinities with the various hezhan, but they were only used in certain ceremonies, most often at equinox and solstice. The sheaf of wheat is also a clue as to their origin, or at least the time during which these tombs had been built. Wheat was considered good luck for a plentiful bounty, an offering made to the fates, especially during times of drought or famine. They were placed on the graves of the ancient tribes before they'd learned the ways of the hezhan, but they hadn't been used in such a way anywhere since well before the sundering.

Except in Kohor.

Where Khamal spent much of his youth. Where Sariya came from. Where Muqallad traveled and eventually found the Atalayina.

That a sheaf was placed on each of the tombs is an indicator of where this valley stood. It is near Kohor, of that much he is sure. And if he is correct, these tombs were built around the time of the sundering.

He can't help but think of Inan, the mother of Yadhan, the first of the akhoz. She was a loyal follower of Khamal, but over time she became disillusioned. She rallied others to rise against Khamal and the other Al-Aqim for what they perceived as unforgivable acts. It wasn't so much the failure of the Al-Aqim during the sundering as it was the steps they'd taken afterward to halt the spread of the rifts. Changing the children into the akhoz had worked, but in doing so—in the eyes of Inan, at least—the Al-Aqim had taken too much from the world, including the soul of her own daughter, and she refused to allow more to be taken in the same way. And so her fellow qiram created a barrier that prevented the Al-Aqim from leaving. It also suppressed the power of the broken Atalayina, which kept the Al-Aqim from using it to escape or to cause further damage to the world.

To Nasim's right is the valley they've been circling for weeks. As he stares at the remote peaks, he remembers its name. Shadam Khoreh. A hidden place, not merely for its remoteness but for the secrets that it holds. To Nasim's knowledge, no one knows what became of the followers of Inan. No one knows how they had erected their barrier, but he is sure that these men and women of this valley, these many qiram hidden away in tombs, were related.

A chill runs down his frame as the answer comes to him.

These men and women... They are the qiram from Ghayavand, the very ones who witnessed the sundering. They're still alive, in a manner of speaking.

But why?

The answer, of course, is obvious. They must maintain the barrier around Ghayavand by giving of themselves, allowing the magics of it to draw from them to sustain those walls. Why, then, would Kaleh burn them like tinder?

Because she needs those walls to fall. To crumble. To vanish so that she can return to the island and complete her plans.

He must stop her, he realizes.

And he must do so today, while she is weak and he still remembers.

They climb throughout the day, and it becomes clear that they'll reach the peak before nightfall. It may be coincidence, but they'd entered each tomb around the same time. They reach a plateau. The dark peak looms above them, but it's small now. They could reach the summit if they wanted to, but as Kaleh leads them across the flat, grass-covered ground, he sees an arch hidden by the wide shoulders of the peak.

"We should rest," Nasim says.

Kaleh glances back as if he's little more than a shadow. She continues to walk, and the urge to rest vanishes. She's exerting her will upon him, but he's become more and more aware of when she does such things. It isn't constant. That would be like trying to hold a stone at arm's length indefinitely. Eventually the muscles would grow tired, and the stone would fall. And so Kaleh *suggests*. She *pushes* Nasim in a certain direction, and months ago, his mind would simply accept it and continue like a windborne skiff pushed from an eyrie's perch on a windless day.

But now Nasim's will is like a headwind. It is becoming harder and harder for her to nudge his mind in the ways she wants. Soon, unless she rests, he will be free. And Kaleh knows it. She is not so simple that she can't predict the outcome, as he has, which is a disconcerting thing. It means she doesn't care, at least for now, and that in turn is another indicator that she's close to finishing what she came here for.

"We should rest," Nasim says again.

Perhaps it is a foolish thing to say, to invite her to work harder against him, but he considers it a calculated risk. He knows she's tired, and if that is so, she more than likely can't press on into the tomb tonight. She might even wait another full day.

Kaleh glances back at him again, but this time she looks longer. She stares into his eyes—he still has trouble looking upon her and recognizing her as Kaleh. She was once years younger than him and now she appears older by several years.

The fates work in strange ways.

Without speaking, she turns toward a patch of ground with bushes along one side that cut the wind slightly. She slips her pack off her shoulders and sets it down and fairly drops to the ground.

"Build a fire," she says.

He does, piling kindling and stacking thicker branches on top. When he sits, he closes his eyes and opens his mind to Adhiya.

This valley is strange, however. It's difficult to call upon the hezhan, to bond with them in even the simplest of ways, but he's learned—or perhaps Kaleh has taught him—how to reach them. It wasn't that they weren't near, it was that this place made it difficult for the spirits to hear him. He thought at first he would need to shout, as if he were calling to them from within a gale, but that rarely worked. Instead, he called to them more like a bell being struck. A single note, it turned out, was easier for the hezhan to hear.

A suurahezhan approaches, and he gives of himself so that it will do the same. He feels its heat infuse him, and then lends some of that to the gathered wood. In moments, the fire is ablaze, and he releases the hezhan. He feels it floating around the burgeoning fire like a moth, but then it loses interest and slips away from whence it came.

"There are few left," Nasim says, holding his hands out to the fire as night steals over the mountains.

He thinks Kaleh might deny it, but she merely stares into the fire, chin upon her knees, and nods. "There are three."

"And then what?"

"Then we return to Ghayavand."

"They are the followers of Inan, are they not?"

"They are," Kaleh says. Her voice is weary, not from the physical exertion of the day, but from some hidden weight that seems to be bearing down on her more fully than ever before. And there is something in her eyes, a sadness that he hadn't expected. He doesn't recall her ever allowing her emotions to show like this. Why here? Why now?

There is something else as well. Kaleh is young and beautiful, but there is a timeless quality in her gaze. She looks as if she's staring beyond the fire, to ages past, and it is that more than anything that makes her seem not merely old, but ancient.

"But you knew that already." She looks up and locks eyes with him. "Did you not?"

Nasim nods carefully. "They protect Ghayavand. They've *been* protecting it for generations. And now, with so few akhoz remaining, the walls that keep the rifts at bay will crumble."

"It is the only way."

"Do you care so little for this world?"

"I care. But this place"—she sweeps her gaze across the mountains, and it is clear she means not just Shadam Khoreh, but the entire world—"is broken."

"It is as the fates have chosen."

She reaches into her pack by her side and pulls out the Atalayina. "Can you be so sure?" Her face, tickled by the light of the fire, looks not merely forlorn, but guilty, as if she is somehow to blame for what her mother did. But then she lifts her head and stares into Nasim's eyes. There is a desperation he hasn't seen before, a look that speaks of the need for a friend, an ally in the road she now travels. "Have you ever wondered if the fates left us that day? If they abandoned us when the sundering occurred?"

Nasim shivers, and not from the chill of the night. "Of course not."

"And how would you know?"

"I don't," he replies. "I have faith."

She seems disappointed in his answer, but unsurprised. "Sleep, Nasim. Sleep, for this time, I go to the mountain alone."

A surge of fear courses through him, and along with it comes a weariness so complete he cannot hope to stand against it. He tries. He fights to stay awake, but soon the world around him closes in and he falls deep, deep into the valley.

CHAPTER TWENTY-TWO

Khamal stands on a parapet at the edge of one of the tallest buildings in Alayazhar. In his hand he holds the Atalayina, the stone of legend that Muqallad brought back from the desert wastes of the Gaji three days ago. He wears robes of light linen, for the day is warm. His sandals, however, are on the roof behind him. For the moment, they are unneeded.

As he holds the stone, he reaches out to Adhiya. With but a thought, one mental gesture, a suurahezhan approaches. He bonds with it as if it were as simple as a handshake. It has never been so, but with the stone, it is an act as easy as breathing.

Ahead of him, in midair, a ball of flame sparks into being. The flame widens into a disc. He steps off of the parapet and onto the burning disc. Just as the hezhan created the flame from the stuff of Adhiya, it protects his skin.

Khamal marvels. Bonding with hezhan has never been difficult for him, but it has always taken patience and understanding. It has always been important to maintain balance, lest you give too much to, or take too much from, the spirit. This balance is still important, but the stone simplifies it to the point that it worries him. The Atalayina acts as a locus, a place of power between all three worlds, such that instead of trying to keep their mutual bond stable from afar, it made the hezhan feel as close as the air around him, the flame beneath him.

When Muqallad returned from his voyage, Khamal hadn't truly believed his claims that this was the stone of legend. But today that all changed. Muqallad gave him the stone to study, and it was more than Khamal could have ever imagined.

Another patch of flame forms ahead. He steps onto it, and like the last, it carries his weight like a pad of stone. He makes another and another, stepping over the air on circles of flame as if they were stairs ready to take him up to the heavens. Far beyond, over the bright roofs of Alayazhar, stands Sihyaan. He has taken breath there many times, and part of him wishes to continue on, to walk to that very place on these steps of fire. Below him there are those that watch, those who have come to study and learn and teach. But today they have come to see what is already being spoken of in whispers.

Transcendence.

By now everyone in Alayazhar knows why Muqallad left and what he returned with. Muqallad is reticent to share knowledge of the Atalayina, but Sariya seems eager to do so. And Khamal, while not necessarily eager, sees no point in hiding it. All will know soon enough. Why not allow them some small part of it? Why not allow them to share in this as they would the events of the day when the three of them—he, Sariya, and Muqallad—will meet on Sihyaan to bring about the next age of man?

Below, walking along the street, he recognizes Inan. She was at one time his disciple, but she has long since outstripped the need for guidance, and in fact has taught him much over recent years.

He delves deeper into the Atalayina, partly to learn but partly, he admits, to impress his one-time student. The stone is difficult in this way, however. It does not allow its depths to be plumbed so easily. To a certain point, the stone is effortless to work with, but beyond that it becomes unbalanced, and then it's like standing on a log in a lake—it rolls and bobs, twisting the other way when one tries to steady it.

Before Khamal knows it, the discs of fire have disappeared and he is falling toward the ground. He strikes it hard, twisting his ankle and cutting his knee. As Inan and Yadhan rush toward him, the Atalayina clatters to the stones and skitters along the cobbles toward an open doorway.

"Are you well?" Inan says as she kneels by his side.

His ankle feels as though it's been kicked by a pony, while the gash along his knee burns more brightly by the second. Still, it's the embarrassment that pains him. He can hardly look Inan in the eye as he says, "I'll be fine."

Yadhan comes forward holding the Atalayina. The stone's blue surface glints beneath the sun, brighter than it seems it should.

It gloats over its victory, Khamal thinks wryly.

Still, despite the pain, he is glad this happened now. They must discover all they can before taking steps with one another on Sihyaan, where there can be no mistakes.

Yadhan holds the stone, offers it to him. She is shy, but also brave to hand this precious stone to a man she's clearly afraid of.

"Thank you, child," Khamal says, and accepts the stone from her.

Nasim wakes at a soft touch against the skin of his cheek, yet when he sits up and looks around he sees nothing. The fire has gone out. He reaches over and feels the warmth of the coals, judging he'd been asleep for no more than two hours.

The dreams of Khamal are still fresh in his mind. He hasn't had such dreams since before Galahesh. That in itself is a clue, but what is infinitely more important is the fact that it had been about the days before the sundering. And not merely that: the dream had been about Yadhan, the first of the akhoz, and her mother, Inan. It is important, but his mind is too muddy to make any sort of connection.

He remembers Khamal's thoughts and emotions as he worked the Atalayina, how wide and powerful and deep it was. He tries to hold on to the dream, but dreams care not for one's wishes, and soon the memories of Alayazhar are replaced with the dry mountain in the depths of the Gaji.

He thought the touch on his cheek was a part of a dream, but he soon comes to a cold realization. That touch had been all too real.

He stands, peering beyond the bare light of the glowing coals of the fire to the stone where the entrance to the tomb would be found. There is nothing in particular that draws Nasim's mind—no snap of twig, no clearing of throat, no overt movement—but it is then that he notices a form sitting on the far side of the fire. A dark silhouette sits cross-legged, but she is too far from the coals for Nasim to see much.

She is young. This much is clear. Her frame is small and slight—either that or she's drawn herself inward like children do when they don't want to be seen. And there is a scent redolent of sailing over open sea.

He's terrified that the simple act of *showing* that he's noticed her will send her running away, for he knows that this girl is the key to much. But he can already tell that something is different. Whether it's due to the absence of Kaleh or some other thing, he doesn't know, but it's clear that she has come here to tell him secrets. So instead of looking at her askance as he's so used to doing, he stares at her directly. She leans forward as if eager to speak but unsure how to begin.

It is in this moment, as her face leans closer to the fire, that he recognizes her. The scent of the open sea…

Why it took him so long to realize he has no idea, but the scent was the final clue. He remembers that scent from Galahesh. Remembers it when he stood upon the Spar and stabbed Nikandr in the chest. Remembers the crashing of the great ship into what remained of the blackened center of that great edifice.

He was thrown from the bridge, as Nikandr was, as the ruined body of Muqallad was. He drew upon a havahezhan to cradle the Atalayina, to guide it into his hand. He gripped it and used the wind to slow Nikandr's fall. With stone in hand he pulled the knife free. He healed the man that had improbably drawn him up from the depths of his confusion.

And then he was struck from behind. He lost hold of the Atalayina. His soul cried for its loss even as he plummeted into the sea. Only then, beneath the cold waves, did he realize who had caught him.

Kaleh.

Kaleh had found him, but she wasn't alone. There was another within the recesses of her mind.

"Sariya took you," he says to the dark form on the opposite side of the dead-ened fire. "On Galahesh, she took you and made you follow me."

The girl remains silent, but Nasim already knows its true.

All of it is true.

The one before him, this shade, *is* Kaleh, the girl Nasim met on Ghayavand, the girl who transported him a thousand leagues to Rafsuhan, the girl who came to Mirashadal, burned and bruised after the staged attack by Muqallad.

The girl who killed Fahroz, the woman who'd most closely resembled a mother for Nasim.

He wonders whether Kaleh had been herself when they'd fought in the streets of Baressa. Perhaps and perhaps not. What *is* clear, though, is that she was taken by Sariya before she flew down through the air and stole the Atalayina from Nasim before both of them plummeted into the sea. Nasim had forgotten most of those details, but he remembers them clearly now. He remembers the sound of the water crashing around him. They drove deep, and the swirling currents of the straits drew them deeper. Kaleh had not seemed to mind. She allowed it, and when Nasim tried to swim away, she caught his ankle and pulled him down.

He was losing air. The twinkling light above dwindled until it was a blue so deep it was almost black.

And then the world shifted.

He'd felt it before, when Kaleh had forced the walls of stone around him in the village of Shirvozeh. She'd transported him in that instant to Rafsuhan. This time, though, the water merely pressed harder, and it twisted about him like the white serpents of the coral seas.

The water felt suddenly warmer. The sun shone brighter as well. Kaleh was holding his wrist instead of his ankle, pulling him upward while kicking her legs and stroking with her free arm.

They broke the water's surface. Nasim tried to cough, but his lungs had filled too far with water. With but a flick of a finger to his lips, she pulled a thin tendril of water from his mouth. It flowed like honey, bright and clear, more and more of it sliding from his lungs and throat until all of it was gone and he was able to cough and sputter and fill his lungs with air once more.

Only then was he able to take in his surroundings. Gone were the towering white cliffs of the straits. Gone was the tall white bridge. Gone was the falling wreckage of stone and wood and sail. Here there was a calm river with rolling grassland on either shore. From there they headed west. His travels since—their trek through the villages and cities of Yrstanla, their entrance to the Gaji and her desert wastes, their arrival in Kohor and their subsequent journey here to Shadam Khoreh—had not been led by Kaleh at all.

It had been Sariya.

How she could have taken Kaleh's form he doesn't know, but it is clear not only that she had but also that Kaleh herself had survived. She had been pushed aside, shoved to the dark recesses of her own mind—refuse, as far as Sariya was concerned.

"It was you," Nasim says as a new realization dawns on him. "You allowed me to remember."

Kaleh remains silent, a brooding shadow.

"You hobbled her so that she couldn't keep me down, and that in turn allowed you to surface more easily."

"She'll be done with the Tashavir soon." Her voice is exactly as he remembered the young Kaleh, the voice he'd heard on Ghayavand and Mirashadal and Galahesh. "She plans to kill you when that is done."

"How many?" Nasim asks. "How many remain?"

"Five, including the one buried below this peak, but do not think of following her. She is nearly there now. You will never reach the tomb in time. Go, Nasim. Go to the next, and save one. Save two. Save as many as you can."

There is an urge within him, nearly undeniable, to ignore Kaleh's warning and run through the tunnel that would lead to a sarcophagus with a defenseless soul inside, but Kaleh speaks truth. Sariya wants to murder these Tashavir—each and every one of them—and this is something he cannot allow.

He feels no less a coward when he shoulders his pack and prepares to leave. He takes up Kaleh's pack as well. She will not be slowed much by its loss, but any time she spends drawing water or finding food will be precious seconds he can use. He's nearly ready to leave, but he stops and stares at Kaleh, this frail girl who lives now only in his memories.

"How many have died?" he asks.

He doesn't have to tell Kaleh who he means. She knows, and she doesn't hesitate in her response. "Fifty-five men and women followed the words of Inan. Fifty-five returned from Ghayavand to Kohor and then to the valley of Shadam Khoreh. Fifty-five were buried alive that the walls around Ghayavand would remain in place."

Kaleh paused, and Nasim knows why. He can feel it too. A shifting of the wind, a whisper from the earth. Far below, in a tomb made for one, a life has been lost.

When Kaleh speaks again, her voice has grown older, more haunting. "Fifty-five flames, Nasim an Ashan, and fifty-one have now been snuffed. Only four stand before Sariya and that which she most desires. Go. Do not fail in this."

"And where will *you* go?"

"You know better than to ask," she says, retreating until she is little more than a shard of obsidian in a sea of black spinel.

CHAPTER TWENTY-THREE

A tiana tried to open her eyes, but the mere act caused her insides to twist and churn. She was dizzy no matter what she did—eyes open, eyes closed—so she lay still, one arm across her brow, remaining perfectly still, lengthening her breath and waiting for the dizziness to pass. As she lay there, memories began to return. A knife held in her own hand. Burning pain as she pressed the point into her skin. The pattering sound as she held her arm above the beaten copper censer and allowed it to collect. The blood bubbling as she set the censer over the coals.

And the smoke.

It rose in coils, lit by the faint glow of the fire and the bare light from the rising moon. She collected it with open palms, drew it over her arms, down her chest, over her head and shoulders and long blonde hair. The smell of it was pungent and foul, but she hadn't allowed those impressions to affect her. She had welcomed the scent, had allowed it to take her.

She remembered the feelings it had brought on. Just as the wodjan had said. Lightheadedness. A widening of her consciousness. With this, she had one toe in the aether, and it was only one small step from there to submersing herself fully.

Instead of sliding into the aether as she did in the drowning basins, she'd been swallowed by it. She had not *allowed* the aether to take her; it had consumed her, as if a fire had suddenly risen up around her, and it was that reason more than any other that prevented her from remembering a single thing beyond that point. She knew she'd entered the aether. Knew she'd remained for some time. But she remembered neither her immersion nor her return. And yet the feeling within her—like a nightmare whose details she could not recall and yet still haunted her—told her that something important had happened. She'd found something, spoken with someone about something imminent. Something dangerous.

She just had no idea what it might be.

Eventually her eyes fell open of their own accord. Even this, mostly from the sudden bright light, threatened her tentative hold over her stomach, but she continued her breathing, gaining in confidence and control, as she'd done so often in the aether.

Walls of red brick surrounded her. Above was a thatched roof. No one else occupied the single-room home. By the ancients, the janissaries had found them and returned them to Andakhara. But for what? To take them to Alekeşir? It must be so. Certainly Bahett or the young Kamarisi himself would want to question them.

She tried to sit up, but found herself restrained. Belts of leather held her tight against the bed. She wanted to call out for Nikandr to help her, but she was too afraid. She didn't know where she was, who had taken her, and she didn't know why. As she tried to wriggle free of her restraints, the bed creaked mightily. Fear seeped through her, from her chest to her fingers and her toes, fear that she would be caught here alone, fear of what the janissaries would do once they realized she was conscious and able to answer their questions.

She paused, waiting for her heart to calm before she tried to test the restraints again, and as she did, the sensations of this place washed over her like warm summer rain. It smelled different than Andakhara. It sounded different, too. Andakhara smelled of sage and spice and dung, and she could often hear the bleat of goats and the calls of children. The air here smelled like wood being left to dry, and the only sound she heard was a soft chiming sound, as of crystal being struck. It felt for a moment as if she were the only one left in the world, as if this place were both cradle and grave of all that ever was.

She tried to sit up again. The leather restraints creaked and the wooden frame of the bed groaned, but this time, instead of silence, footsteps followed her efforts. A woman entered the home through the archway on the far side of the room. She was old, her face so wrinkled she looked like she'd been drying in the sun for a thousand years. In one hand she held a cloth-of-gold abaya—the outer cloak many women of the desert wore over their head and shoulders—and a length of golden thread. She set this aside and moved to the bedside. She stared down at Atiana, lips drawn as if she had no teeth. Her lips smacked wetly several times as she stared at Atiana's restraints. Her expression betrayed no emotion, but to Atiana she seemed little more than annoyed that she'd awoken.

"*Kaht thadi ab shahn,*" she said.

The words were foreign to Atiana. There was some resemblance to Mahndi, but she suspected this was Kalhani, the mothertongue, a language she knew precious little of. The realization gave some focus to her muddled mind. She was in Kohor. She remembered none of the journey after her ritual had begun, but clearly the others had brought her here.

The woman continued to stare with her deep-set eyes.

"I don't understand," Atiana said.

"*Hahla kir obn ab shahn*," she said, motioning to the leather straps wrapped around Atiana's chest and waist and legs. It sounded like a question, though she couldn't be sure.

"My mind is my own," Atiana said. "I won't harm you."

She smacked her lips, glanced at the restraints one last time, and then leaned over and began unbuckling them.

This simple motion—the leather straps pressing against her, the woman's hands brushing her—was painful in the way the body aches after a bout with the flu, but soon it was done, and the woman helped Atiana to sit up, though she was so ancient it was difficult to provide anything more than a guiding hand.

As the woman turned away and poured Atiana a glass of water from a glazed pitcher the color of burning leaves, Atiana touched the linen bandage wrapped around her own left arm. The inside of it was dark with dried blood. The cut was deep, she knew, enough to draw blood, but not so much that it would threaten her life when she fell to the effects of the smoke coming from the censer. She lay her arm against her lap as the woman handed the glass of water to Atiana with shaking hands. Then she waited, looking Atiana up and down, judging her readiness to do anything more than sit.

"*Kaheth id shahdn vey*," she said, pointing out the doorway. Through it Atiana could see other structures, most of them homes, surely. Beyond them stood an obelisk made from stone that was closer to the color of blood than the rusty red of the Gaji.

"Are they there?" Atiana asked.

"*Kaheth id shahdn vey*," the woman said again. She pointed to Atiana's glass, motioning for her to drink the last of it.

It was a lot of water at once, especially after being unconscious for so long in the desert, but it felt good to drink something. It cooled her insides, brought her more fully into her body and further from the worries that crept in the dark corners of her mind.

The woman took the glass and set it with a thump onto the simple wooden table nearby. When she held out her hands, offering to help Atiana to her feet, Atiana saw the complex tattoos that marked the palms of her hands. They were intricate, swirling. They reminded her of the graceful embellishments the vanahezhan stone masters would add to their creations, but these seemed more primitive, more ancient.

Atiana paused, feeling for a moment as though to take this woman's hands was to step back into another world, a world from aeons past. It felt as though she would be leaving her own world behind forever. It was a foolish notion, and yet it was one she couldn't shake. Even as she touched the woman's soft palms and leaned forward until she was able to stand, she felt as though she were bidding farewell to Vostroma and the halls of Galostina, farewell to the islands and her majestic windships, farewell to her mother and her sister and the blood of her blood spread throughout the duchies.

The woman looked carefully into Atiana's eyes. Her lips smacked wetly, and she smiled purely for Atiana's benefit. She motioned to the doorway, to the obelisk. Atiana nodded, and together they made their way slowly out the door and down to the dry desert ground of Kohor. They were quite a pair, the two of them, the woman so infirm she could manage no more than a shuffling pace, and Atiana in so much pain she could no more than match her. They made their way along a simple path between the homes and eventually came to the large circle where the obelisk stood.

Nikandr stood near its base. Soroush and Ushai stood several paces behind him, but Ashan and Sukharam were missing. There must have been two hundred villagers gathered, the men and women of Kohor. Some were young, but there were no children, and in fact there were few that were old like the woman who'd brought Atiana here. The women wore light-colored shaylas and abayas of red and purple and midnight blue, and veils across their faces. The men wore kaftans the color of flax, with white sirwaal pants and ghoutras over their heads. Except for the few who stood near the obelisk, all of them knelt or sat, some fanning themselves with horsehair fans, others merely watching, their faces intent upon the conversation. They sat in a semi-circle, as they might for a poetry reading, and yet their expressions were serious, serene, as if the decisions to be made here held great weight for them.

Goeh stood next to Nikandr. He was speaking quickly and loudly with a group of men and women—seven in all. Goeh, as tall as he was, towered over them. One older man stood only as high as Goeh's chest, but he had a look about him—a piercing look, like a falcon watching carefully for the leaping jerboa before winging from its roost. This man's igaal, the band that held his ghoutra in place, was golden. Among all the men, only his was this color. The rest were black or white or the darkest purple.

The other men and women were older as well, but they looked hale despite it. One, a woman with stark grey eyes and several delicate golden chains running from her left ear to her rings on her nose, was speaking excitedly with Goeh. She spoke in Kalhani. Atiana could understand a word here and a word there, but it was the woman's attitude that stood out most. She was agitated. Worried.

Their number—seven—was conspicuous. Seven were the number of mahtar, the village elders, in an Aramahn village. Surely this was the same, and this was a council of sorts, a questioning of the newcomers to this secretive place.

As Atiana walked across the village circle, many looked her way. Nikandr didn't notice her, however. He was fixated on the conversation before him. His head turned between Goeh and the woman with the golden chains as if he understood, or *wanted* to understand.

When Atiana reached Ushai's side, her guide bowed her head and motioned her hand, as if indicating that Atiana should take part in the conversation; though whether this was what the woman really meant, Atiana had no idea.

"What's happening?" Atiana asked Ushai in Anuskayan.

"Don't," Ushai replied quickly in Mahndi while glancing toward the Kohori council. "To speak your language would be an insult."

Atiana thought it was from a prejudice against the Grand Duchy—as the Maharraht would have—but then she realized it was simply a question of exclusion. Many of them would understand Yrstanlan and Mahndi, but very few would know Anuskayan, so to speak that language would be to exclude them.

Seeing no reason to deny the request, Atiana nodded to Ushai. "Tell me," she said in Mahndi.

"They are the elders of Kohor. The man next to Goeh, the one with the golden ghoutra, is Habram. He is their leader. The woman Nikandr is speaking with, however, is Safwah, and it is *she*, not Habram, that has been asking the most questions. Nikandr told her of our travels and whom we seek to find, but Safwah never seems satisfied. And when it came to Nasim and Kaleh, she asked many questions."

Soroush glanced over at them with a look that told them to speak more quietly. Nikandr finally noticed her, and he stopped mid-sentence. He smiled stiffly. It wasn't forced, exactly—he was glad to see her up and about—but the two of them had much to talk about. And then he turned back to Goeh and Safwah.

Atiana's mind was still muddled, but this news was a revelation. "Praise the ancients," she said softly to Ushai. "This tells us they know of Nasim and Kaleh, that the two of them passed through Kohor."

Ushai's eyes narrowed while she stared at Habram. "I'm not so sure."

"What do you mean?"

"Safwah spent a good while asking Nikandr to describe them. Their height, their color of hair and skin and eye. Distinguishing marks like moles or scars. Even their smell."

"Their smell?"

Ushai shrugged, apparently confused as Atiana was. "Then she asked of their mannerisms, what they ate, and how. How they spoke, turns of phrase, how they pronounced their names and what other names they might have used. She asked where they came from, their mothers and fathers."

"And how did Nikandr respond?"

"With the truth. What else is there to say?"

It was a discussion they'd had a dozen times as a group—just how much to reveal once they arrived. "And how did they react?"

Without being apparent about it, Ushai glanced at the half-circle of elders. "When they heard Nasim's origins they became animated. These people are closed, daughter of Radia. They do not let their emotions show. But I could tell. They stood straighter. Their stares, not exactly charitable, became even more serious, or perhaps shocked. They seemed anxious over Nasim's rebirth. They know of the Al-Aqim, of course—all three of them have history here—and all of them, even the stoic Habram, asked many questions about Khamal."

"What do we know of Khamal?"

Ushai raised her eyebrows. "You'd be surprised. Your Nikandr knows much. He and Ashan have been talking for months now, and through Nasim he lived as Khamal, if only for a short while. He gave them much of what they wanted to know."

Atiana's head jerked back as if she'd been struck. She watched Nikandr as he spoke with the elders. He was telling them of their flight across the desert and the chase of the janissaries. It was no surprise that he'd spoken to Ashan about his memories of Khamal. She *was* surprised that he hadn't mentioned it to her. It was clearly a part of him that meant much, and yet he'd shared so little of it with her since the events at the Spar. Khamal was a part of Nasim, and Nasim was a part of Nikandr, no matter that they'd been separated when Nasim had thrust his khanjar through Nikandr's heart.

Despite these feelings of distance, she was struck by how majestic he seemed just then. As he told their story, not a shred of his weakness from the loss of his hezhan showed, nor did he bow over his chest wound—the place where Nasim had driven the khanjar—as he so often did when he thought overly long about his inability to touch Adhiya. He stood tall and he spoke with a tone in his voice that sounded like what Atiana imagined the dukes of old would have sounded like, the ones that had forged a new power in the world from the bitterly cold islands they called home.

"And when they learned of Kaleh's past?" Atiana asked.

"This was strange, daughter of Radia. Strange indeed. When they learned that she was a daughter of the Al-Aqim, they became still, so still there was not one of them that moved. They sat and watched as Nikandr told them what we know of her, which isn't much." Ushai's voice became distant, and pensive. "They seemed more worried over her than Nasim, which is strange since his story seems more improbable. But I tell you this, it makes me nervous. They're secretive, these people. They protect Kohor ruthlessly, refusing to let even the forces of Yrstanla within their borders except for a select few days of the year.

You may not remember, but the janissaries chased us to the very edge of this valley. And when they did, the Kohori rose up and shot them with arrows. They protect their secrets carefully, and if that is so, what would they do if they fear that some have been taken from them?"

She was referring to Kaleh's abilities. If she could take one's mind, as her mother Sariya could, might she not have come to this place and stolen their secrets? This place was wrapped tightly with the history of the Al-Aqim and the Atalayina. It made Atiana shudder to think what Kaleh had found. "Look at them," Atiana said. The elders' faces were composed, but there was a tightness in their eyes and lips, and the way they stood was stiff, as if every muscle were tensed. "They're terrified of what Kaleh did while here."

"*Yeh.*" Ushai looked at Atiana as if she'd surprised her. "Terrified is precisely the right word."

"Where are Ashan and Sukharam?" Atiana asked.

"Ashan asked to be taken to the Vale of Stars."

"The what?"

"One of the places of power here in the desert. A place where the mindful can learn much about themselves and the world."

"Wouldn't they want Ashan here?"

Ushai shrugged. "They wished to begin taking breath as soon as they were able, though in truth I think it was to shelter Sukharam."

"From what?"

"From the Kohori. He has many of Nasim's qualities, and for the time being, Ashan thought it best if Soroush and Nikandr sized up our hosts."

"But you don't agree."

Ushai turned to Atiana and stared at her with placid eyes. "What does my opinion matter to anyone here?"

Nikandr was just finishing up their tale, telling the elders of their ride through the night. That was when Nikandr had learned of Atiana's attempt at scrying, her attempt at using the secrets of the wodjan to reach the aether. He went on to relay just how closely the janissaries had come to catching them. Praise to the ancients for seeing fit they'd only lost one ab-sair during that ride. What sobered Atiana more than the rest of the tale, however, was the very end. He described how the warriors of Kohor had risen from the desert itself and struck the janissaries with a flight of arrows and driven them away.

These people were not afraid of death, nor were they afraid to deal it. And Atiana would be wise to remember that.

CHAPTER TWENTY-FOUR

Atiana knelt on a pillow near the round table they used for meals. Before her were dates and pistachios and olives and a soft, sour goat cheese whose taste reminded her of walking through the fields below Galostina during the summers of her youth. And when she spread the cheese on the warm flatbread and tasted it, she was reminded of those times when she would pull stalks of grass to chew on the sweet white ends. There was wine as well, a fruity red that felt unfinished on her palate, and too spicy by far, but she couldn't deny that the sour-sweet taste of currants went well with the rest of the meal.

Nikandr knelt by her side, and Soroush sat across the table, while Vashti, the ancient woman who had helped Atiana after she'd woken, shuffled about the room, setting their table and clearing it when they were done. Atiana had tried to help her the first day, but Vashti had waved her away, shouting in Kalhani and pointing to the pillows when Atiana had tried to take away the plate of spiced flatbread she held in her hands. Vashti seemed a kindly old woman most times, but not when her blood was up—then she was a terror, and she held a grudge, scowling for hours afterward and snapping her fingers when she thought Atiana was moving too slowly or when she spoke out of turn.

Ushai was out in the desert, taking breath, a thing she'd taken to doing for many hours of each day. This place spoke to her, she said, in ways she'd never felt before. She'd been born here, but she and Soroush had still taken to wondering openly whether she'd lived past lives in this place. How else to explain such strong *echoes*, as she called them, of a place that had seen her leave mere months after her birth?

They'd been in Kohor for over a week, and they hadn't been allowed to speak to the elders of the village again. Not since that first day had they seen the bulk of the Kohori. Since then, life had gone on, however tensely. Atiana heard them tending to the goats, saw them walking here and there about the village, but no one had come to speak to them again, and all attempts to speak to the elders had been met with requests to remain in the house they'd been given and to wait to be summoned.

Ashan and Sukharam were the exception. Both had been gone nearly the entire time since they'd arrived. They hadn't seen Sukharam at all, but Ashan had returned twice, and both times it had been for only a few minutes.

"Where have you been?" Nikandr had asked on his first visit.

"With the elders," Ashan had replied, rummaging through his things until he'd found a small, leather-bound journal.

"Do they know anything of Nasim or Kaleh? Where they've gone?"

"I suspect they do," he'd said while walking toward the open doorway, "but they won't speak of it. Not yet. Not until they've come to trust us."

"And how long will that take?" Nikandr had called to his retreating form.

Ashan had stopped in the doorway and turned back. "Who can tell?"

He'd returned three days later, stopping only to tell them that he was making progress, that he believed the elders would soon tell him more. They were speaking at length with Sukharam, which pleased Nikandr not at all.

"*We* need to speak with them," Nikandr had said sternly.

"Give them time," Ashan had replied.

"We've been here for six days and all we've *done* is wait."

"We've come this far, Nikandr, and we've learned much. We know that Kaleh and Nasim both live. We know they passed through this place. And given the confusion of the elders, we can be somewhat sure that Kaleh stole knowledge from these people. Now we need to figure out what. Most likely the elders already know, or at least they suspect, and now they're deciding whether or not to share it with us. Let them come to know us. Let them come to know our purpose, and soon, they'll share what they know."

"How can they know us if they set us aside and refuse to speak with us?"

Ashan had raised one finger, a teacher before all else. "Don't forget how much you told them on that first day. It gave them much to digest."

"If Nasim or Kaleh are near, we *must* go. We *must* find them."

"And where would you go?" Ashan had asked. "They will not tell us. Not until they're ready. And they will not let us leave, not if they think we will betray them or this place."

Atiana hadn't understood what he'd meant by betraying *this place* but the argument had died shortly after and Ashan had been gone since, apparently working with Sukharam or speaking with the elders on his own.

Atiana took some of the bread and dipped it into the spiced sesame oil that set her mouth aflame if she wasn't careful. She'd found the spice offensive at first, but after Vashti's urgings to try it with the wine, she'd found that it brought out the flavor in the fruit, and that the oil itself had subtle flavors of primrose and sandalwood.

After seeing to their meal, Vashti shuffled out, leaving them in peace.

"I don't like this waiting," Atiana said. "There's something happening in this place."

Soroush slathered goat cheese onto a hunk of bread and stuffed it into his mouth. He looked like he was about to speak, but his words died as he looked over Atiana's shoulder to the doorway beyond. Atiana turned and found Goeh walking toward their door. No longer was he shirtless. He wore the light kaftan of the Kohori men, making him seem more menacing somehow.

He stopped in the doorway, blocking it with his bulk, and bowed his head. "May I join you?"

Soroush nodded, and Goeh sat cross-legged before their table. He quickly declined, however, when Soroush waved toward the food. "The elders have spoken," Goeh said after settling himself. "They do not believe what you've told them."

Nikandr's back stiffened. "It was the truth. All of it."

Goeh held his hand up. "I believe you, but they do not. They believe…" Goeh paused, pursing his lips, as if searching for the right words. "This is difficult to explain. Your questions woke in Safwah memories she didn't recall having beforehand. You saw how inquisitive she was with you, and I hope the reason is now clear. You tapped into memories that she now believes were stolen from her when this woman left."

Atiana shook her head. "The one we look for is twelve, perhaps thirteen."

Goeh shrugged. "Perhaps she's the one you're searching for and perhaps she isn't, but she had another with her. A quiet young man that fits your description of Nasim."

"What did he look like? Did she describe him?"

"She did not," Goeh replied easily, "and she won't. Not until she's convinced your intentions are pure."

"We've come to find the Atalayina. We've come to find those who can help to save this world."

Again Goeh raised his hand. "Safwah needs assurances, and she won't get it from your words alone. Among our people, when there is doubt as to someone's honesty or faith, there is a ritual we perform. The one in doubt sits in a smokehouse with the elders, and together, they take of tūtūn. Do you know of it?"

Soroush nodded his head. "It's a special form of tabbaq that makes one … open to suggestion."

Goeh tilted his head, a half agreement. "Open to suggestion, *yeh*, but more importantly, open to telling the truth."

"It *forces* one to tell the truth," Soroush countered.

Again Goeh tilted his head. His expression was one of pained regret, as though he felt the characterization of the tabbaq—and so his people—improper. "Truth is a quality we strive for. But there are times when we lie even to ourselves. Is it not so? Tūtūn allows us to find truths, even those that are buried deep within us."

"And you wish us to take it?" Atiana asked.

Goeh turned to her. "One will suffice." As he said these words, Atiana knew it wasn't a matter of them choosing amongst themselves who should go. The Kohori elders had already chosen, and it was clear from Goeh's dark gaze that they'd chosen her. A chill ran through her at the thought, not because she was afraid of what they would learn about her, but what she would learn about herself.

Before she could answer, Nikandr stepped in. "We won't do it," he said. "We've not harmed the people of Kohor. The elders should be grateful we've come, for ours is a story born of the desert, born of these people. Why should we be paid with suspicion and mistrust?"

"I would not put it so," Goeh replied evenly, though it was clear from his expression he hadn't taken kindly to Nikandr's words.

"*Neh?*" Nikandr asked. "How would you put it?"

"My people value our history. We are part of this land and it is a part of us. We have not often stepped beyond the boundaries of the Gaji, and the last time we did so in any significant way was the exodus to Ghayavand." He motioned widely with his hand, indicating the wide basin in which Kohor was centered. "Many left this valley and the world was nearly destroyed because of it. It is a stain upon us, one we are not yet free of, and we will not be distracted from our cause again."

"And what cause is that?" Nikandr asked.

"Our secrets are our own," Goeh replied easily.

"You speak from both sides of your mouth, Goeh. You ask us to speak truth— you demand it—and yet you'll give no answers of your own."

"It is you that have come to this place asking for our help."

"We'll leave, then, if you'll offer no help to those who are trying to protect you."

Goeh smiled wanly. "Sadly, leaving is no longer a choice open to you. The Kohori have saved your life thrice now. Each of you owes us much. Too much. So we will have our answers, Nikandr of Khalakovo, whether you agree to it or not."

Nikandr stood. "Now you threaten us?"

Goeh stood as well. He towered over Nikandr, but Nikandr didn't move an inch. "We do what we must," Goeh said.

"Please," Atiana said, standing as well.

Nikandr raised his palm to her. "Atiana, sit down."

"I will not," she said, turning to Goeh. "I will take the tūtūn, Goeh."

"You will not!" Nikandr said.

"I will!" Atiana replied, her blood running hot now. "What are more questions when we've already told them the truth?"

Nikandr's hands bunched into fists until his forearms shook. "This is intimidation! Coercion. I won't stand for it!"

"If they asked you more questions, would you not answer them?"

"This is different."

"Why? Because they're asking it of me?"

"It is different"—his tone and the set of his jaw made it clear he felt this a deep betrayal on her part—"because they are not asking. They are demanding, and we've done nothing to deserve it."

"I'm going, Nischka, whether you approve of it or not."

Nikandr's head reeled back. The hurt was plain in his eyes and on the sun-kissed skin of his face, and suddenly she felt as though the two of them were the only ones in the room. "Is *this* what we've come to?" he asked.

He was right to feel hurt, not because she'd volunteered to take the tūtūn, but because she'd been reticent about speaking to him of what had happened in the hills of the Gaji. She'd performed the rituals of the wodjan, thereby subverting her own beliefs and the teachings of the Matri. And then she'd hidden it from him, refusing to reveal the truth when she knew she should. Even here in Kohor she'd declined to speak of it, for she couldn't quite find the words. It wasn't something she was ready to face.

And now she'd agreed to reveal all these secrets to the Kohori, for surely this would come out in the ritual they would perform.

She strode forward until Nikandr was forced to turn toward her, and more importantly turn *away* from Goeh. She placed a hand on his chest and spoke to him in the same way he had—as though they were the only two there. "I'm sorry, Nischka. I should have told you all. And I will. But let me go with Goeh. We know now that Nasim and Kaleh were here. Let me take us beyond this place so that we can find them, or at the very least the Atalayina. Your pride, my pride, is not what's important now. What's important is that we move on, because the more days that go by the more the world slips from our grasp. I can feel it, and I know you can as well. So I will go, and I will put the elders at ease."

Nikandr stared down into her eyes. He stared deeply, and though there was hurt there, she could see in him the love he'd had for her since she'd arrived on Khalakovo those many years ago. She loved him as well. True, there were divides between them, but they would be bridged—of this she was sure.

Nikandr licked his lips. He glanced up at Soroush and Goeh, and then nodded to Atiana.

"When?" Atiana asked Goeh.

"At sunset."

CHAPTER TWENTY-FIVE

The walk to the western end of the village felt strange. The Kohori—at least near where they'd been housed for the past seven days—were so often hidden away, but tonight, as the sun neared the mountains far to the west, they stood in doorways, they watched from windows, making Atiana feel as though they were stripping her bare so that by the time she reached her destination, she would be all but defenseless, both physically and mentally.

Goeh led her, weaving among the redbrick homes, passing the tall obelisk in the village circle. Just as the sun slipped behind the mountains, they reached the edge of the village proper and entered the desert itself. Atiana didn't understand at first where Goeh was taking her. She thought perhaps they would smoke beneath the stars in the immensity of this desert plain, but then she saw it, a hut of some kind, dark and hidden against the backdrop of the dark mountains and the burning copper sky.

The crunching sound of her footsteps against the rocky soil made her feel small and alone and, strangely, more exposed than she'd felt in the village. She didn't like offering herself up to this sort of questioning. She'd been raised in the halls of power. Not until her time on Khalakovo, when Soroush and Rehada had caused the death of the Grand Duke Stasa Bolgravya, had she felt any slip in the control she'd grown to expect. She'd faced that challenge as well as she could, but she'd wondered in the weeks that followed the Battle of Uyadensk if she was made from the same cloth that others seemed to be made of—like Nikandr, or Nikandr's mother, Saphia, or even Nikandr's dead Aramahn lover, Rehada.

Atiana had hated Rehada when she'd first met her, not only because she was Nikandr's lover, but because she was everything Atiana was not. Open. Daring. Welcoming of whatever the fates had in store for her. For years after leaving Khalakovo, Atiana had had difficulty in trying to do more for Vostroma, more for the Grand Duchy. She'd done what she could, but there had always been something inside her that wanted her to pull back.

That had all changed on Galahesh. She knew the very moment the change had come. When she'd been assumed by Sariya, and when she'd assumed Sariya in return, she'd learned much of what Sariya was like. There were some of the things she'd seen in Rehada: confidence, a calm surety that what she was doing was right, a willingness to not only take what the fates would give her, but to forge her own path. Atiana hadn't known it at the time, but those moments with Sariya had been a catalyst that had changed Atiana.

It was this, more than anything, that allowed her to set her fears aside and embrace what lay ahead. The memories of the Kohori watching her from their windows and doorways faded. Her feelings of discomfort dwindled until all that remained was an uncomfortable twinge somewhere deep in her stomach. If this was a trap, then so be it, and woe betide the men and women who'd brought it about.

"How many will question me?" she asked Goeh.

Goeh glanced her way. "Does it matter?"

"Does it matter if I know?"

He chuckled, a sound like the earth must make when it laughs. "Four others will question you, Atiana of Anuskaya. Four others, and you will make five. A propitious number. Do not fear over what they will ask of you. It's best if you let the tūtūn embrace you."

"And if I don't?"

"Then it will fight you. Believe me when I say that this is a fight you will not win."

These words didn't sit well with Atiana, but she kept a steady, trudging pace toward the hut. As they came closer she saw it for what it was—no hut at all, but more of a thicket, a mass of vines wound so tightly that she could barely see the light coming from within, even when she was mere paces away. At first it reminded her of something the Aramahn dhoshaqiram, masters of the spirits of life, might have created, but as Goeh ducked his head and stepped inside, she realized she was wrong. This did not look like it had been made with magic, as many of the wondrous creations of the Aramahn did, but rather as if it had been tended by hand to look just as it did. It lent the simple structure a feeling of acceptance and forbearance that the works of the Aramahn did not have.

When she ducked inside, she found a small coal fire at the center of the hut. As Goeh had said, there were four others, all of them women. Safwah was among them, her grey eyes piercing, the golden chains running from her ear to her pierced nose shining under the light of the coals. She seemed every bit as fierce as she'd been in the village. The others were no different. It felt like a tribunal for crimes she hadn't known she committed—quite the difference from the way

Goeh had described it.

There was something reassuring about them, however. They reminded her of the Matri, and in this she found comfort.

After motioning Atiana to sit on a pillow near the fire, Goeh opened a wooden box near the wall. Within was a lumpy substance that looked like decomposed leaves. It smelled that way as well, but when Goeh sprinkled it over the fire, a scent like autumn fires and fresh-cut cedar and vanilla and chestnuts filled the air. The scent was heady. Much of the smoke trailed up and out through the many small holes between the vines, but when Goeh took a folded blanket, and threw it over the outside of the hut, the air became thick with it.

Atiana's stomach became queasy, and at first she thought she was going to throw up under the critical stares of these old matrons, but the feeling ebbed, and she began to feel wider, and deeper somehow. Her awareness expanded to fill this small space, to fill the space beyond, until she felt as though she were looking down upon this valley, down upon the world.

When she heard words being spoken, she had no idea who had uttered them. She thought at first it was her mother, but she wasn't here, was she? Mother was home, on Vostroma.

She heard herself answer, though she didn't even know what had been asked. She knew from her answers that they were asking her of her past, of her life on the islands before she had met Nasim and Sariya and Muqallad. She gave answer after answer, but for the life of her she couldn't hear them asking the questions. All she heard were unintelligible mumblings that made her chest vibrate.

How long this went on she didn't know, but eventually she gave them an answer that made her fall into a memory she didn't remember having. She told them of her ability to touch the aether, and the moment she did, she recalled her time in the hills to the east of Kohor. She'd bled herself. She'd cut her arm and bled onto the censer away from the others so that she could try to enter the aether as she'd done when fleeing Andakhara.

It was an embarrassment, what she'd done, a betrayal of the Matri and their ways, but she'd already touched the aether once, and they'd been cut off from Ishkyna and Mileva for so long. She had to learn more.

Kneeling over the smell of her own burning blood, she'd felt herself fall into the aether as she had so many times in the drowning chamber of Palotza Galostina. It had startled her, but once she was there, she felt perfectly at ease. Her only fear was that she would be drawn back too soon.

She cast herself outward, searching for the other Matri, and eventually she'd felt the first tentative touch of another. It was Ishkyna, and she felt stronger than Atiana would have guessed.

What are you doing, sister? Ishkyna asked. She was surprised. More than surprised.

Atiana opened her mind to the memories of the wodjan. This was no easy thing. Most Matri could not share memories in this way, even those that had known one another for years, even decades. Most could only share emotions and speak with one another as they would when together. Others, like Grigory's mother, Alesya, could assume another and rifle through their thoughts and memories, but such a thing was a grave insult, and it was a vulgar tool, a bludgeon. Something like this—an exchange of one's own experiences—was an intricate thing and a difficult balancing act to maintain. Any slip on either Matra's part and they might be thrown from the aether, unable to reenter for days or even weeks. But such was Ishkyna's skill, and their familiarity with one another, that they could do this now without much thought.

Ishkyna's driving emotion was for a long time simple shock.

Bloodletting, Tiana?

It is a path to the aether. Another path. And with you gone for so long, I felt it—

Dear sister, Ishkyna snapped. *Have you ever considered it might give her power over you?*

Atiana paused. She hadn't. She'd never considered it might grant the wodjan some hidden power. *I sensed nothing,* she said lamely.

And how would you know what to look for?

She wouldn't. How could she? *I had to reach you, Ishkyna.*

This is a perversion, Tiana! And it's dangerous. You mustn't do it again. Promise me.

You know me well enough to know that it would be a lie.

Ishkyna paused. *Then promise me you'll consider what I've said.*

I will, sister, but tell me what news. They might have tried to do the same thing Ishkyna had just done, but this was no simple thing. Ishkyna no longer had a living body to return to. She had no anchor. She wandered the aether like the currents of the great wide sea, spreading herself wide and thin, or sometimes narrow and fierce. Were Atiana to try to sift through Ishkyna's memories, her awareness would likely be drawn over an area so wide she might never recover.

The war continues, but Yrstanla has brought more to bear. They've pulled their troops from the west, Tiana. Nearly all of them so they can focus our efforts on us.

But the Haelish.

Da. The Haelish. They've made amends, it seems, and no thanks to your precious Nischka.

What could Nikandr have had to do with that?

You should ask him that very thing. Despite Leonid's orders, Ranos sent ships to Hael to treat with them. And what came of it? A front reinvigorated with not only men, but purpose. The war with Hael was a long-standing thing, a thing the Kamarisi and his Kaymakam had long grown weary of. But this? The war with the

Grand Duchy? With Bahett guiding the hand of Hakan's young son, he has come with vengeance and a will to retake his homeland, and the Kaymakam are following him, perhaps even more than they'd followed Hakan. Already they've pushed us back a hundred leagues, fully half of the territory Leonid had taken.

A sizzle within the hut pulled Atiana back from these memories. More tūtūn was being thrown onto the fire, but she couldn't tell who was doing it. The hut was dark, but more than this, she couldn't focus her eyes. She saw little more than an orange glow reflecting against the sweat-lined skin of an old woman. The image swam before her, and her eyes fluttered closed as she heard them asking her about Sariya, about their time together on Galahesh in the city of Vihrosh. She heard herself speak more clearly than her memories felt to her, but she recalled the pain of her deeds. She watched Sihaş die, taken by the ravenous akhoz. Her stomach twisted painfully at the vision of her own hand pulling the khanjar across Irkadiy's throat. Kind Irkadiy. Watchful Irkadiy. *Dear ancients, forgive me for what I've done.*

The matrons of Kohor asked her about these deaths, but they focused closely on the point at which Kaleh had taken Atiana's hand, for it was then that she had fallen to Sariya's will. They asked her of those moments, both before and after, over and over until it felt like a chant, a ritual she was performing for these women.

Why were they so interested in Sariya?

She didn't know, and soon she slipped back to her memories of Ishkyna.

There's more, Ishkyna had said.

Her tone had been serious and grave.

What's happened? Atiana had asked.

It's mother. She's been taking to the drowning basin more often, and staying longer than she aught. For days at a time she goes now, refusing to allow Mileva to spell her.

She misses father, Atiana said.

Ishkyna did not reply. They both knew it was true. She had never been a strong woman, and with father gone, she had fallen into darker and darker moods. Borund had returned from Khalakovo to take up the mantle of duke, but much of his time was spent on Galahesh and sometimes Oramka, seeing to the affairs of the war. When she was out of the drowning basin, Mileva was often in it, and Atiana was in the wastes of the Gaji, lost to her.

And Ishkyna... Well, she and Mother had never had a strong relationship to begin with, and Atiana knew that the few times Ishkyna had tried to console Mother in the aether, Mother had sent her away, sometimes forcibly.

If you were home, it would do her well, Ishkyna said.

We are hunting for Kaleh. For the Atalayina.

They will return to Ghayavand, Tiana. Borund has offered to send ships there to set up an outpost.

Kaleh is here somewhere. You said so yourself.

I said I felt her, but that was just after the Spar was broken. She could be any-where now. You know this.

There are things we can learn.

Be that as it may, Mother could use your presence in the basin. So could Mileva. There are troubled times ahead, and I no longer think it wise to risk you and Ni-kandr and the others over a girl whose trail, even if found, is months old. Come back to Vostroma, Atiana. Let's meet the confrontation that's staring us in the face and prepare for Kaleh's return to Ghayavand. For she will *come. You know this as well as I. We must be ready when she does.*

Atiana was struck by her sister's words, for she was using the exact same argument Atiana had used against Nikandr when he'd gone to Rafsuhan. Nikandr had remained despite her pleas, and she'd been furious with him for it. Was Ishkyna in the right? Should she abandon this and return to her family?

There was sense in what Ishkyna was saying. They risked much by continuing on this path, especially considering how closed the people of Kohor were and how tightly they held their secrets. And her mother *did* need her. Atiana had known that when she left Vostroma, but things had clearly become worse.

She nearly told Ishkyna that she would speak to Nikandr, that the two of them would return to the islands. She felt the words ready to spill from her, but then she realized just how forcefully and suddenly the notion had come to her, and a sudden rage built within her, like oil thrown onto a smoldering fire.

Atiana shoved her away, and like morning fog beneath the rising sun, Atiana's mind cleared. *You would manipulate me? Your own sister?*

To Atiana's surprise, Ishkyna didn't seem chagrined, but instead cross that she'd been rebuffed. *Sometimes people need manipulating, Tiana.*

How many others have you done this to, Ishkyna?

Ishkyna remained obstinately silent.

Dear ancients, you consider this acceptable?

And now, finally, there was some sense that Ishkyna was embarrassed.

Go, Atiana said. *Tell Mother we're close to Kohor and that we'll return when we're able.*

I'll tell her nothing. Any mention of you will only serve to remind her that you're gone. Think on what I've said, Atiana.

These memories faded with the feeling of cool air on her skin. The smoke in the hut was beginning to clear, but this did nothing to clear the haze over Atiana's mind. She floated for hours longer. She felt herself falling, but her head did not strike the ground. Someone loomed over her. The elder, Safwah. She smiled—or was it a grimace? Her teeth looked like tombstones, her mouth like an open grave. Atiana wanted to thrust her away, but she hadn't the strength to do so.

"Sleep," Safwah said.

She'd said it in Mahndi, and it made Atiana wonder whether she knew that language well. Perhaps she did and she'd hidden it from Atiana. Or perhaps she knew only a handful of words.

The roof of the hut, a winding knot of thick vines, distorted and contorted above her. She heard more words, the women speaking in some foreign tongue. Or perhaps it was Mahndi after all—she could no longer tell—she only knew the tone of their voices had risen in pitch, had taken on an urgency that hadn't been present during the questioning. She knew not of what they spoke, but she knew this: whatever she'd told them, whatever they'd gleaned, it had made them nervous.

And that, it seemed to Atiana, was cause for great concern.

CHAPTER TWENTY-SIX

Styophan stood before the grand yurt, the largest of Clan Eidihla's and nearly as large as King Brechan's. Two of Queen Elean's guards stood beside him, but neither had so much as touched him on the walk from the yurt where he'd spent the night with Rodion and Edik and Galeb. Anahid had been led to a different place. *For her own good*, Datha had told her the night before, after it had been confirmed that Bahett had escaped with many of his guardsmen.

Styophan could hear voices from inside the yurt, but they were low enough that he could make out only a handful of words. They were speaking in Haelish, of course, so even if they *were* closer, it would do him little good.

After drawing in a deep breath and smelling the unique tabbaq the Haelish favored, Styophan released it white upon the wind. The day was bitterly cold, the coldest of the young winter. The inland weather was nothing like what they saw on the islands in the depths of winter's chill, but still it seeped beneath his cherkesska, it snuck through his thick leather soles and chilled his feet, and it served to remind him of just how far away from home he was.

He stared up at the arched doorway, where a complex arrangement of deer antlers was hung.

What am I doing here, Roza, when I should be home with you?

His mission here had not seemed foolish when he'd been given it by Duke Ranos, but it seemed foolish now. Nearly all of his men dead. Four of the five ships he'd been granted gone, perhaps the fifth one as well. Two of his men murdered heartlessly for the rituals of these heathens. And why? So that the Haelish could draw attention from the war to the east? He'd rather be leading his men against the endless ranks of janissaries along the coast of Yrstanla, not treating with the fickle kings and queens of a land he cared nothing about.

The leather flaps at the entrance parted. A woman Styophan's age—no more than thirty years old—stood there watching him with dark eyes. She wore the

171

bracelets of a wodjan. Dozens of golden bands ran the length of her forearm, twisting like snakes as she beckoned him. Styophan couldn't help but wonder if she'd been one of the ones to take a knife to Vyagos or Oleg. Had she stood above them and watched while they screamed? Had she pulled his steaming entrails out and laid them out over the ground? He didn't know the answers, but it didn't lessen the urge to gouge her eyes from her head.

See if you can look into the future then.

Had he known for certain, he would have taken her down then and there and strangled the life from her, no matter that the queens had summoned him. But damn him, he didn't know, and so again he could do nothing.

The wodjan's eyes pinched as she beckoned again. Styophan stepped inside and onto the animal skin floor of the yurt. He backed away from the wodjan as soon as he was able, if only to keep his emotions in check. The guards did not follow. For now, he'd be alone with those gathered within, which appeared to be seven queens and a handful of wodjana who stood behind them like a murder of gallows crows.

The queens were kneeling around a brazier that held a low-burning fire. "Please," Elean said in Yrstanlan, motioning to the empty space opposite her.

Styophan complied, glancing at each of the queens in turn. Each wore a crown made from braided wood with emeralds and rubies worked cunningly into them. Elean's crown, however, was different. It took Styophan a moment to recognize it. It had been Kürad's. He had worn it last night in the ceremony at the menhir. It now sat on Elean's head, surely because—for now at least—she would speak for her clan. The fire cast enough light that he could see stains of blood upon the vines and thorns. Why she wouldn't have cleansed it before wearing it he didn't know. Nor did he care to.

Elean watched him expectantly, as if she were waiting for him to bid them greeting, but if that were the case, she would wait until the end of the world, for he would grant these women nothing.

Elean seemed to reconcile with this, for she nodded to him, a gesture so slight it was difficult to recognize it as such. "I regret I could not find my way to you again after the forest."

Styophan blinked. He glanced to the other women—the queens and the wodjana—but none of them seemed fazed by this news. "Surely you could have, had you chosen."

"I might have, but appearances were important."

"Meaning what, you couldn't be known as associating with a man from the islands?"

"Meaning," Elean said, her voice rising, "that no one could suspect that you'd had a chance to look upon me so intimately."

"Because of impropriety?" Styophan found his voice rising in pitch and volume. It was all he could do to remain seated, talking respectfully. "A poor reason, indeed, Queen Elean."

"Not impropriety, Styophan of Anuskaya, but because you *had to* come to the information on your own. The kings *had to* believe your words."

Styophan thought back to that night when he'd inspected Elean on that bear-skin rug in the middle of the snow-covered forest. A branch had snapped only moments after he'd finished his inspection. Convenient, he thought, though he wished he'd recognized it then.

And from there more and more fell into place, until he landed on a realization that should have come to him well before now. It hadn't been Bahett's doing at all. The poisoning of the queens hadn't come from Yrstanla. It had come from Hael, from the queens themselves. "You *wanted* me to implicate Bahett—"

The queens stared on. Brechan's wife, Queen Dahlia, coughed, but she had a look on her face that was just as triumphant as it had been the night before, when she'd bared herself for all to see.

"—and you needed me to come to it on my own," Styophan continued softly, more to himself than these gathered women. "You needed me to convince the kings of Bahett's guilt." He began shaking his head. "But why? If you suspected Bahett of foul doing, you could have simply told the kings of it."

"It wouldn't have worked," Dahlia said. She stared at him from deep-set eyes. "They needed to hear it from a man like you."

"You think they wouldn't have believed?"

"They might have." Dahlia coughed and licked her lips before continuing. "They might have, indeed. But they needed not just to believe. They needed to find the anger in their heart that has been drained by withering and war alike. That flame has now been rekindled, Styophan of Anuskaya. They are men who are once more prepared to go to war."

Styophan stared into the steely gazes of these women.

That was it, then. They'd done all of this so that Hael would once more go to war. "The kings saw the withering and they stepped down from the threshold of war. And you"—Styophan stared directly into Elean's eyes—"you *wanted* war with Yrstanla."

"The kings have grown concerned, deservedly so, over the welfare of our people. We have long been weary of war."

"Then *why*?"

Elean slammed her fist on the table. "Because the Empire is weak! Anuskaya has at long last taken the Kamarisi's attention to a place other than Hael. If we are ever to throw off the yoke of Yrstanla, it must be now!"

"And the kings?" Styophan asked.

"The kings were trying to protect the tribes the only way they knew how. They would have stood by, denying you your treaty, denying Yrstanla theirs as well. They wanted to stand and cower and wait while you and the Empire fought like wounded dogs. Only after the Empire had been weakened would we return and take back our rightful lands."

"So you poisoned yourselves that your kings would find their nerve?"

"Watch your tongue!" Elean said.

Dahlia reached over and touched Elean's arm. "*Hayir*, what he says is true. Our kings are brave, but there comes a time when even they must be wary of the myriad ways that lie ahead. They cannot see all. Even our wodjana cannot see all. They must look to our safety, and to them the safest course seemed to be to wait, to see if the anger of the Hills would pass, to see if our people would begin to heal."

"And you would risk that," Styophan said.

"We must," Dahlia continued. "There is no other time. Whether the Hills would have us or not, we must fight."

"And yet you will not take land from Yrstanla."

"It isn't land the kings are after now. It's blood." The way she said it sent a chill down Styophan's spine.

"What do you mean?"

Elean looked to her left and to her right, taking in the gathered queens. "Such an affront as the regent of Yrstanla committed against us cannot stand. The kings wish for not only Bahett's blood, but the Kamarisi's. They must make it clear to the Empire that Hael will not be treated like a child with a knife—a child who might be dangerous, but who can be left for another time. They are now preparing themselves to go to Alekeşir. They are preparing to lop the head from the Empire before it can turn its attention back toward the west."

"They go to kill the Kamarisi."

"*Evet*. And as compensation for your loss, they will ask that you join them, you and yours, if you wish to go."

This was bold, indeed. It was something the Haelish had never done. Their beliefs had prevented them from taking such a step in the past, but it seemed that time, or the withering, or fear of outright collapse, had forced their hand to do something they'd previously found objectionable.

"And if I don't wish to go?" Styophan asked.

Elean shrugged. "Your ship, the lone survivor, has been spotted to the south several times. No doubt you can find your way back to them if that is your choice."

Styophan's heart leapt. "My ship?"

"You knew that one had escaped our cannons, did you not?"

"I thought it had traveled home."

"Your men are loyal, as you are loyal to them. Would you find them? Would you return home?"

He nearly told her that he would. The words were on his lips, ready to be spoken. And yet he could not. Not so easily.

"Why?" he said instead. "Why would you need me and my men?"

Elean, the queen of her clan, leaned forward, her piercing eyes weighing him more critically than she'd done thus far. "Who would deny that the fighting men of Anuskaya would be welcome in battle?"

"The Haelish have men enough."

Elean leaned back and laughed. "Men enough? Did you see what happened to us last night? Had we men enough, we would never have willingly allowed Bahett onto our lands. Had we men enough, Bahett's Kiliç Şaik would never have surprised us so. Had we men enough, our war with Yrstanla would have been settled long ago and you wouldn't be sitting before me now wondering whether you should join us in battle to fight a common enemy. There are those precious few among every clan who remain—those who have been tested in battle—but so many have died that we are left with the young and the old and the infirm. If we are to send our best into the heart of Yrstanla, we would have those who have seen battle at their side. Are your men battle ready, Styophan of Anuskaya?"

He held his tongue. She was goading him, hoping that a simple appeal to his manhood would win him to her side.

Elean waited for him to speak. Her blood was up. He could see it in the set of her spine, the tilt of her head and the way she seemed to look down on him, but when he didn't respond, some of her fire left her. "Do you not wish to bring home the head of Bahett ül Kirdhash to give to your Grand Duke?"

"You still haven't told me why you need me or my men. Few men though you have, surely there are enough stout men to take up this cause, especially with the respite you've been given."

"A respite that's about to end."

"Be that as it may…"

Elean seemed reluctant to speak further. She seemed, in fact, as likely to order him to be taken from the tent and chased from Haelish lands as she was to speak to him again, but there was a rustling among these queens, a passing of looks with hidden meaning, and Elean was all too aware of them.

"Tell him," Dahlia said softly. She seemed unable to meet Styophan's eyes, though why this would be, he had no idea.

"We agreed," Elean replied.

Dahlia did not respond, but she raised her head and took Styophan in anew.

Her eyes looked deep beneath the flicker of the nearby flames. She coughed. It was a long, wet cough, one that seemed to go on and on, as if her very life were spilling from her. Yet still she kept her gaze upon him.

It wasn't Dahlia that truly drew Styophan's attention, however. It was the wodjana. They'd been silent up until now, but at this exchange, they'd become restless. The one who stood behind Elean—the same one that had beckoned Styophan into the yurt—looked at him with an expression as dour as it was disapproving, but it was her eyes more than anything that gave him pause. Perhaps it was the smoke that ran thick in the air, but she seemed to see through him. She seemed to be staring directly into his soul. She seemed to be weighing his past in one eye, his future in the other. He'd heard strange things of these wodjana, that they could see beyond the day to what might lay beyond, but he'd never given them credence until now.

He broke her gaze with some effort and looked to Elean, who seemed to have been waiting until the exchange had been completed.

"Tell him." This came not from Dahlia, but from the wodjan. Her voice croaked. She sounded like stone, like ancient, fallen wood.

"There's reason for you to go to Alekeşir. The wodjana have seen it."

"What reason?"

Elean smiled, but it was a sad thing. A lonely thing. "Your Lord, the Duke of Khalakovo, sent you here hoping to save Anuskaya despite your Grand Duke's best efforts to hand it to the Empire. You're overextended already, and Bahett knows it. Despite what we've done, Bahett will focus all he has on his eastward flank. He knows, as perhaps you do by now, that he can meet whatever resistance we might be able to muster." She waited for these words to sink in before continuing. "Had the Grand Duchy come ten years ago, or even five, we would have been able to place Yrstanla in a grip they would never have been able to wriggle free of. Now, we are weakened, more than we've let you know."

"What did the wodjan see?"

"They see no one thing, Styophan, son of Andrasha. They see many things, many possible futures, and in one, you join with the men of Hael. You travel to Alekeşir along the hidden trails only we know of. You go to Alekeşir and you find your way through the walls of Irabahce."

"And what happens?"

"The Kamarisi dies. But it comes at great cost."

The words came slowly, but they filled the room with such gravity that Styophan's shoulders bent from it.

"What cost?"

The silence in the room lengthened. The fire snapped loudly.

"What cost?" Styophan said again.

"When you go to Alekeşir," Elean said, "the path there and the path beyond will lead to your graves."

Styophan looked among these gathered women. He'd been in a hundred battles. He'd spent long hours preparing for those days of ache and sorrow. He'd worried over his own life, the lives of his brothers, the lives of the people he sought to protect, but never had he felt sure that he would die.

Not until now.

Now, even as Elean had voiced those words, it felt as though it had been written in stone.

He cleared his throat. "The paths the wodjana find are not always clear."

"That is true," the old wodjan replied. "Some paths continue on, but into darkness, into a fog that even our most gifted cannot penetrate. But in this, the way is clear as streams in spring. When you go to Alekeşir, you go to die, not merely you, but all of your men. Every last one."

The queen glanced to one side, as if considering these words, but then she brushed the buckskin along one thigh, as if what the wodjan had said was of little consequence. "But this is only *one* path. There are others. You may return home."

For some reason, Styophan could hardly breathe. He didn't want to ask. He felt like the mere voicing of the question would submit him to a fate he couldn't bear.

But he had to know. He couldn't leave this place without the knowledge.

"What happens then?"

"I will not lie to you. Either way you choose, the islands suffer. As does the Empire. As does Hael. But when the wodjana saw you return to your islands, you found your way to your woman. Your wife."

"Don't say her name."

"Rozalyna," Elean spoke, despite his plea. "You return to her."

The implication was clear. If he went to Alekeşir, to the heart of the Empire, he would take the life of the Kamarisi, and perhaps save the islands, but in doing so, he would give his own life. And if he returned to the islands, he would find his way into Roza's arms once more.

By the ancients, the Haelish had come by this information by sacrificing his men. For the moment, ancients forgive him, he couldn't think of the Kamarisi or Roza. He couldn't think of the war or Duke Ranos or Grand Duke Leonid. He could only think of Oleg, of Vyagos, and how they'd died so that the wodjana could dance and pick their way through the possible futures of their people like crows pecking among the bones of the dead.

Only when the first tear fell onto his bunched fists did he realize he was crying.

With great effort, he unclenched his fists. The palms of his hands had crescents of blood where his fingernails had torn through his skin. He stared at them for long moments, not truly seeing. His inner sight was back at the menhir, watching as Oleg's chest continued to rise and fall even after what they'd done to him.

He tipped his head back and released one long, primal cry.

Why? Why would the ancients have placed him here? Why would they have put before him such choices?

The gathered women watched as the flames continued to flicker.

"What would you do?"

Styophan shivered. To his surprise, it wasn't Elean who threw these words at Styophan, nor was it Dahlia. It was the old wodjan, and it felt as if she held his fate in her hands.

But she didn't, Styophan said to himself. *He* held his fate. Not them. And he had a choice to make.

He would see his wife again. He would take her up in his arms and make love to her as the cold winter winds howled outside their home. He would give her sons and daughters.

But he could do none of these things if by doing so he placed the Grand Duchy in danger. He had it within him to cripple the Empire, at least for a time, and if that were so—no matter what might happen to him in the end—then he had no choice but to do it.

He stood, though this clearly displeased the wodjana, and spit into the fire. As it sizzled on the burning coals, he turned and strode from the yurt.

"I will go."

CHAPTER TWENTY-SEVEN

S tyophan rode one of the Haelish's tall black stallions toward the crest of
the hill. Anahid had already reached the crest, where she reined her own
horse in and waved back to him. Edik and Galeb came behind, while Rodion, who had clearly taken to these tall horses of the west, rode well behind at
a full gallop. His face while he rode… It was one of exuberance, of unexpected
freedom. Styophan nearly called to Rodion, to remind him he was a soldier
of the staaya, but thought better of it. They had each of them weathered this
storm differently, and if Rodion had found joy in testing the limits of a fleet
and beautiful charger, he would let him.

Styophan and Edik and Galeb rode until they came abreast of Anahid. Rodion
came shortly after, his piebald stallion huffing and shaking its mane and stamp-
ing its front hooves until Rodion stroked its neck and whispered into its ear.

Anahid pointed to the horizon ahead, and there, flying far in the distance
above the hilly landscape, was a windship. The *Zhostova*. The last of the five
ships over which he'd been granted command by Duke Ranos.

Styophan nodded to Anahid. After returning his nod, she slipped from her
horse as if she'd been riding all her life. She wore her circlet, and it held an opal,
a fresh one given her by Brechan, the King of Kings himself. It twinkled softly
in the daylight. One who didn't know what to look for might not realize she'd
bonded with a spirit, but Styophan knew the stones well and Anahid better.
She'd lost her composure on the night of the ritual, but she'd regained most of
it in the days since. And now she had that same sense of control that showed
in her measured movements when she bonded with spirits.

The top of the hill was bald, but nearby there were trees of alder that reached
skyward like the clutching hands of the dead. Anahid knelt, heedless of the
light covering of snow. She placed her hands on top of the snow and pressed
downward. She leaned into it for long moments, melting the snow so that she

could touch her skin to the ground directly. She closed her eyes, but for long minutes nothing happened. Near the horizon, the *Zhostova* was moving away. They were searching for him and the others, whatever survivors there might be. They were brave, these men, but perhaps foolish in the bigger picture. Unless they'd received orders through one of the Matri's rooks, they should have returned to Khalakovo to let them know what had happened. Duke Ranos needed to know that his gambit had failed, that they'd been betrayed by the Haelish.

But the ancients have eyes that see far, he told himself. They must have known what would happen, for even though Styophan would still send them back to Khalakovo, it would be with the knowledge that he would travel with the Haelish on a new mission, one that would hopefully give the islands a respite from the storm. Even if it only delayed Yrstanla by a month, it would be worth it.

Still, Styophan was no fool. He knew the visions of the wodjana were clouded and imperfect. He knew they might be wrong. The Kamarisi Selim ül Hakan lived in a fortress. Only twice had any in the line of Kamarisis been killed within the walls of Irabahce, and both times had been by betrayal. Styophan most likely went to dash his life against the walls of Kasir Irabahce—assuming, of course, they even made it that far—and yet he cared little. The point was not to kill the Kamarisi. With Bahett's return—less one hand—and a bold attack such as this, young Selim and Bahett would pause. They would worry that Hael was coming for them, and they would be forced to shift their attention westward. It would give the Grand Duchy the time it needed to press, or retreat, or whatever it was Grand Duke Leonid thought proper.

But first, for the leaders of the Grand Duchy to be ready, they needed to know. The *Zhostova* was further away now.

"Come," Styophan said to Anahid. "We should ride ahead and build a fire."

She did not move, however. She remained kneeling in the snow, her head upturned.

His men alternated glances at Anahid, the ship in the distance, and Styophan.

"Anahid, come," Styophan said more loudly.

It was then that he saw the cracks in the snow around Anahid's pressed hands. They were small at first, almost indiscernible, but they widened, and dark material was revealed beneath. Leaves, he realized. They were leaves, and they were pushing up from beneath the blanket of snow. Some lifted, twisting, snow falling and leaving pockmarks where it fell. The leaves spun upward, more and more of them, until there were dozens circling in the air above Anahid. Soon there were hundreds, thousands, swirling like bees around a nest.

They flew higher, and they drifted north, toward the *Zhostova*, until they looked like a distant flock of gulls. Not a single leaf fell to the ground, for this was no act of wind. The leaves had been granted life by Anahid, and the kapitan of the *Zhostova* would recognize it as such, or his dhoshaqiram would, and they would come.

"I would know before the men arrive," Rodion said softly.

Styophan turned to him, the snow crunching beneath his boots. "I know, Rodion." He nodded to Edik and Galeb, motioning them closer. "You all deserve to know."

Edik, a man who had served in the staaya for two decades, glanced toward the receding leaves, and then stepped closer. Galeb followed, straightening his cherkesska, pulling himself taller as he did so.

"The ship will come, and some will return home, but I won't be going with them."

"You're not returning?" Rodion asked.

"*Nyet*, I am not."

"And where will you go?"

"I and as many desyatni as can be spared will go east into Yrstanla."

Galeb was stone-faced and silent. Behind his eyes, though, Styophan could see an unspeakable fear. Edik's face, however, turned immediately sour. "Komodor"—Edik stabbed his finger southward—"our brothers died here. Those fucking savages killed them. You saw it yourself. We heard their screams all through the night. And you would send us *home*?"

"I wish for Our Lord Duke to know what happened, and he should hear it firsthand."

The three soldiers exchanged glances. Galeb seemed confused, but Rodion looked angry, and Edik looked as though he would spit upon Styophan's black boots.

"You would take others and leave *us*?" Edik said.

These were the reactions Styophan had been expecting. Edik was a devil of a fighter and smart in battle. Rodion was cool. Men followed him easily. But Galeb. Young Galeb. Was not made for this. He'd been brave when they'd arrived. He'd stood tall when they'd been taken to Skolohalla. But something in him had broken three nights ago when the other men had died at the hands of the wodjana.

"I need but one to go home." All three, even Galeb, seemed ready to object until Styophan raised his hand. "Hold your peace. Those who go to Alekeşir do not go to battle. We go *with* the Haelish, and like a spear thrust at the heart of the Empire, we go to Alekeşir itself, to kill the Kamarisi."

Rodion laughed. "The Kamarisi?"

"Just so."

"We'll be killed, well before we reach Alekeşir."

"The Haelish know the way to the city."

Edik stabbed a finger at Styophan's chest. "You now place *trust* in them?"

Styophan stared down calmly at Edik's finger, and Edik, though his face didn't soften, slowly pulled his hand back.

"If you dare challenge me or another officer in such a way again, Edik, I'll have that finger."

Finally some of the bile left Edik's face, but not the pent-up hatred. That he seemed to bottle up inside, and Styophan wondered if he weren't making a mistake. "*Da*, Komodor."

Perhaps he should send Edik home instead of Galeb. But one look at Galeb showed him the error in that thinking.

"In this I trust them," Styophan said. "Their blood is up, but they are no fools. They know ancient ways into Yrstanla. We will not be found until we reach the city. And then we will find our way into Irabahce itself. And then…" Styophan searched for the right words, but there was only one way to say it. "The queens confessed to me what their wodjana found that night."

Edik's eyes grew confused, and then his lips curled, as if he could hardly stomach the thought. "With Oleg and Vyagos?"

"Those who go to Alekeşir—all of us—will die."

"Komodor—"

"Speak no more, Edik. Whether or not the wodjana are right isn't the point. We have a chance to give Yrstanla pause, and the Haelish are with us in this. If Bahett and the Kamarisi and the Kaymakam who kiss his boots think the Haelish will soon attack in force, they will pull men back from their eastern front. And if we do not join them, it may be that the wodjana will lose confidence in their vision. And if they lose confidence, so will the queens and kings. All of our plans have been turned inside out since we arrived, but this is a chance for us to make a difference, a chance to do what we came to do, a chance—and you'll know this as well as I if you stop to think about it—granted by the ancients themselves. It's something we *must* do. But one of you will go home to tell our Duke of it." He looked over each of them in turn, giving them a proper amount of consideration, enough that Galeb wouldn't be insulted. He saved Galeb for last. "Come, strelet. Let us speak."

Galeb looked to Rodion and Edik. When he turned back to Styophan there was an expression of forced indignance, but there was also relief in the way his shoulders relaxed, the way he leaned forward like a man who'd received news that he would live after a long bout with the black cough.

To the north, the flock of leaves were little more than a dark twinkling against the light blue sky. As Styophan and Galeb fell into step with one another and walked down the snow-covered hill, Styophan put his hand on Galeb's shoulder. "You have a wife, do you not?"

Galeb nodded. "Avita."

Styophan squeezed his shoulder. "Tell me about her."

Wearing the uniform of a janissary commander, Styophan ran through a field of tall grass. The clothes were easy enough to adjust to, but the turban still felt strange on his head, and he hated the fact that the bright green plume attached by a brooch to the front of it marked him so conspicuously.

Ahead of Styophan—running two-by-two—were twenty men of Anuskaya, two desyatni, and behind him three desyatni more. Fifty streltsi running with one hundred of the Haelish leading them through Yrstanlan lands. The *Zhostova* had not been manned with so many, but the ancients had been smiling on them the day the Haelish had attacked with their cannons. Two skiffs had managed to escape the damaged ships before they'd fallen. Nearly seventy men had been saved, and Styophan had taken nearly all of them, leaving only enough to head to the coast and around the great northeastern shoulder of Yrstanla before heading south to Trevitze or Galahesh, where many of the Grand Duchy's ships were now moored.

Like Styophan, his men wore the uniform of janissaries as well. They'd been culled from among the collected effects of the Haelish. Surely they'd kept them for a purpose such as this. The uniforms were all large—large enough to fit the frames of the Haelish men—so they'd needed some adjusting before they'd headed into the lands of the Empire, but they fit well enough, particularly Styophan's and those of his men he might present for inspection to the soldiers of Yrstanla. Datha said they wouldn't be needed for days yet, perhaps weeks, but there was no sense in taking a chance. The element of surprise was one of the few advantages they had.

To their right stood the long line of mountains that marked the traditional border between Hael and Yrstanla—the very mountains that had provided his wing of ships with the ley lines they'd needed to fly south from the Great Northern Sea all the way down to Haelish lands. That range had been crossed many times by the forces of Yrstanla. They had taken land. Forts and outposts had been stood. Even villages and one small city had been erected over the decades that Hael had been held at bay, but eventually Hael had returned to the lands they considered their own, pushing Yrstanla back, sometimes butchering those who had come to build a life.

The rhythmic sound of soldiers running in time and the rattle of their gear—muskets and bandoliers and kilijs at their sides—were the only sounds that filled the air. They'd been running for three days. His men were well trained, some of the best Khalakovo had to offer. They could march double-time for weeks, keep a jogging pace for days at a time, but these Haelish warriors were

tall—nearly all of them a head taller than his streltsi—and their stride was difficult to keep pace with. Plus they were used to overland travel. The Haelish
had horses, but most were saved for the transport of their yurts and for their
royalty. So though his men were ready, the dawn-to-dusk days and the grueling
pace were taking their toll.

Still, despite the long days, it felt good to be among his men, to be in control—as much as one ever was.

Datha marched at the very head of the Haelish column. He was nearing a rise
that marked the southern end of the vale they'd been marching toward all day,
the place—if what the Haelish told him was true—where a small Yrstanlan fort
stood. It was one of many such fortifications the Empire had built along their
long border with Hael. Styophan wondered if they'd received word of what had
happened to Bahett at Skolohalla. In all likelihood they had—the Empire was
careful about such things, sending messages by pigeon—but this was what King
Brechan was counting on. The forts along the border would be on alert, and this
attack, along with four others being conducted this very same day, would make
Yrstanla think that a full-on assault was underway. In some ways, it wasn't far
from the truth. Brechan had decided it was time for as many of the forts and
settlements within a hundred miles of Hael to be burned to the ground. Today
brought the first of those attacks, and if Yrstanla thought the larger western
cities threatened as well, then so be it.

When Datha reached the top of the rise he held his fist high and in one sharp
motion brought it low. Immediately, the warriors behind him slowed and moved
forward at a crouch. They split into two groups, kneeling in the snow-topped
grass and awaiting further orders. Datha waved Styophan forward. The Haelish warrior was not a man easily rattled, but there was a tightness to his wave,
an urgency that made Styophan wonder just what he'd seen in the vale below.

Styophan motioned for Rodion and Edik to join him, and together the three
of them approached Datha's position.

They crawled the last handful of yards until they reached Datha's side. The
vale opened up before them. Below, situated near a dark, stream-fed pool, was
a fort with four wooden towers at its corners and a massive stone keep at its
center. There was a massive gap in the wall. It had clearly been burned, for
much of the remaining wall around the gap was blackened. The gate to the
fort's interior—which faced their position—was still in the raised position. The
entrance to the keep could be seen, but instead of a fortified gate of some kind,
it was little more than a dark, open maw.

"A keep like that would have had a reinforced door," Rodion said.

Styophan nodded. "Look at the char above the door. It would have taken a
long time to burn through."

"Not if a hezhan had crossed," Edik said. "An elder could burn through it like tinder."

They watched for a time, waiting for any sign of life, but there was none.

"We should go before it gets dark," Styophan said.

They were going to wait until shortly after dusk for their attack, but things had changed, and Styophan wanted to inspect this place in the daylight if they could.

Datha nodded and together, their band of men marched down. As they neared the fort, weapons were readied. Styophan held his musket, pulling it to his shoulder and staring with his good left eye along the wall and up to the tower. His men did the same, but they were not met with resistance. They did not, in fact, see a single sign that anyone still resided within this place.

They reached the gap in the western wall. There was a large area where the snow around it had melted, revealing matted, winterdead grass—part of a nearby field—and the brown, singed remains closer to the wall itself. The air smelled strongly of cardamom and myrrh. Just inside were the blackened remains of a dozen men. Some had been burned down to their bones. Others had cracked and charred skin over much of their bodies. Beyond, in the courtyard there were more. They lay scattered here and there. There was little grass to mark the passage of the suurahezhan—for by now it was clear that one had crossed over and attacked the fort—but there were places where the earth was cracked and split like a mud puddle drying in the summer sun. Styophan walked the very same path the suurahezhan had. The remains of the dead lay along its path. Sometimes in ones and twos, and in one case eight men had died together.

To a man, they clutched things in their arms. A few bore muskets, others tools from the smithy, but all were proper pieces of iron. One even held an old wooden shield banded with iron. Only one had a proper dousing rod. They'd been trying to stop the suurahezhan from entering the keep.

Styophan glanced to his left as Datha joined him. "Do you see?"

Datha looked more closely, for he hadn't recognized what had truly happened. "They were trying to stop it."

"They should have been able to." This was from Edik, who knelt and picked up the blackened shield. It crumbled in his hands. "Unless it was an elder, this should have been able to stop it, at least force it to take a different path. But look"—Edik stood and pointed—"its path never wavered."

He was right. The hezhan's path continued straight and up to the keep doors. He locked eyes with Styophan, both of them immediately understanding the importance.

Datha glanced between the two of them. "Speak, Styophan son of Andrasha."

"It's a symptom of the change. Things have been growing worse, but even among the islands, I would have thought this much iron would have stopped the hezhan."

"Yet it didn't," Datha said.

"Even here, the rifts have grown wide. I would never have thought... This far from Ghayavand..." Styophan looked over these men. They'd wanted desperately to prevent the hezhan from reaching the keep. "Come."

They continued past the burned wreckage of the doors where the smell of cardamom became almost overpowering. Beyond, in the great room, they found a large charred circle where the suurahezhan must have crossed back to Adhiya. More of the dead—another twenty, both men and women—lay scattered about the room like forgotten toys. There was one near the back of the room, however, that drew Styophan's attention. It was a man who wore black boots and baggy pants and armor of hardened leather.

Styophan almost thought he recognized the man by his shape alone. It was one of the Kiliç Şaik. One of Bahett's men.

They'd come here, then. After fleeing Hael, they'd come to this keep, and they'd been here—Bahett included—when the suurahezhan had attacked.

"You think we'll find him?" Edik asked in Anuskayan.

Styophan stood and looked more closely at the remains of the other bodies. None had the same leather armor. "Something tells me our friend from Galahesh escaped."

"Bahett?" Edik said as he crouched and looked impassively at the Kiliç Şaik. "Why?"

They continued up to the second floor. At the back of the keep near an open window was the body of a man who'd been burned badly along his right side. He was face down, and he wore red robes of a cut and style Styophan had never seen before.

Styophan kneeled down by him. He had swarthy skin. He looked like a young man, but the deep wrinkles around his eyes marked him as a man from the desert. A man from the Gaji, perhaps, which made a strange sort of sense. It was where Nikandr and Atiana had gone searching for Kaleh and Nasim and the Atalayina. There were no others they'd seen—Aramahn or Maharraht—that might have summoned the suurahezhan. It was possible that the qiram had left with Bahett and the other survivors of the attack, but Styophan had the distinct impression that this man had summoned the spirit. Why he wasn't sure. Nor did he understand why he now lay dead. Perhaps he'd tried to send the spirit back. Perhaps he'd wished to send it into the land of Hael at the behest of Bahett and had lost control.

Styophan would probably never know, but he did know this: the world was beginning to fall apart at the seams. He'd felt it in his heart already, but to see such strange things before his very eyes... It made him feel as though they were already too late, that no matter what they did the rifts would continue to spread and bring about the end of the world after all.

CHAPTER TWENTY-EIGHT

Rare clouds hid the moon, plunging the chill desert night into total darkness, but Nasim could still feel the tomb ahead. He'd opened his mind to Adhiya to draw upon a vanahezhan, and he could feel the earth beneath his feet, the immensity of the peak above him. The lay of the land was open to him, its twists and turns, its hills and valleys. He'd drawn upon a dhoshahezhan as well, and he used it to feel the life around him—the towering spruce and the moss and small ferns that grew upon the forest floor. The sweet smell of the sap that seeped through the bark was heightened, as were the dried pine needles, and the pungent odor of the tiny mushrooms that lay hidden among them. He took the time to draw upon more hezhan. He'd not done so until now for the fear that Sariya would sense him, but he could wait no longer. He was too near the next tomb, and he refused to allow Sariya to catch him off-guard.

First, he called upon a jalahezhan, a spirit of water—difficult to reach in these places but easier now that he had two others to help draw it near. Through it he felt the pathways of water as they slipped down mountain streams and through cracks in this great mountain.

Next, a havahezhan. He called upon one—not the nearest, but the eldest. It came easily. Willingly. The touch of it made Nasim want to soar among the dark clouds above.

Last was a suurahezhan. This was the most difficult. There were few here among the valley. Years ago he might have forced one closer. But he'd changed. He'd grown, in no small part due to the Atalayina; the stone had opened secrets to him that he'd never have found on his own. He stood resolute, beckoning. Not demanding, nor begging, but *urging*—a simple call to an equal. The eldest among them, an old spirit indeed, was intrigued. It drifted closer. Nasim offered himself to the spirit, and for a moment it scoffed. *What need have you of me,* it seemed to say, *when you've called on so many others.*

Nasim shared his need, his will to right the world. Even the spirits knew how unbalanced the world had become, he was sure. Still, it retreated, perhaps ready to move on, to go wherever it is that hezhan go in their ephemeral world, but then it paused. It reconsidered, perhaps sensing something in Nasim it had not seen before, something it would like to taste of. Or perhaps its hunger outweighed its better judgment. Who knew the minds of the spirits?

It reached out.

And Nasim took it.

Suddenly it stormed over Nasim. Tried to consume him.

Nasim fought, but did not push the suurahezhan away. Instead, he embraced it. He allowed the hezhan to feed on him, to feel what the world of Erahm was like. It raged against him, but he refused to allow it thought, instead feeding it the dark sights of the forest around him, the smells, the solidity of the earth beneath his feet, and the touch of the wind that sighed through the needles of the spruce.

Like a child in a world filled with wonder and delight, the suurahezhan lost itself. It struggled only once more. A swirl of flame lit the forest. It twisted and churned, lights of yellow and orange twisting like a flock of starlings, and then it was gone, its energy snuffed as it gave itself to Nasim at last.

Despite this strange response to his offer of communion, of bonding, Nasim held no grudge. He did not command these hezhan. Any of them could leave if they truly wished. But they did not. They had all come willingly.

At last he was ready. The entrance to the tomb loomed before him. He could not see it with his eyes, but through the vanahezhan he could feel the sculpture on the stone. It was of a man, taller than Nasim, his arms folded across his chest. In his left hand was a wreath of mountain laurel, in the other an olive branch. When Sariya had opened the door she'd sent cracks through the stone, weakening it while using the smallest amount of energy she could. Nasim touched the stone with the tips of his fingers and called upon the vanahezhan, asking it to weaken the stone. He asked the jalahezhan to draw the moisture forth. Asked the suurahezhan to heat it. Bit by bit the entrance began to ablate, stone becoming sand and the sand being drawn away by the wind, and soon the way was open.

Nasim entered, but before he'd gone three paces he turned and crouched and picked up a handful of dust. He held his hand high and allowed the dust to slip through his fingers. He called upon the vanahezhan and the dhoshahezhan, both, stone and vitality bound together, and the dust billowed toward the entryway, creating a barely discernible gauze. If Sariya came, she would pass through this, and when she did, he would feel it.

He moved faster now. After a long trek he reached the door to the crypt. He could already sense the bas relief sculpture carved into the door with the senses granted him by the vanahezhan, but he would look upon it with his eyes, so he drew upon his suurahezhan, creating a bright flame that floated in the air near the door. The same sculpture as at the entrance was worked into the stone, but here the man did not hold an olive branch, nor a wreath of laurel. Here his hands were held together near his navel, the place that breath comes from, and cupped there, as gently as a robin's egg, was a stone. It had the same striations of the Atalayina. They even glinted under the light. The stonemason who'd built this door had taken the time to work metal into it, which was very difficult, as most metal was anathema to bonding with hezhan. It took a deft hand indeed to work with it at all, and this man or woman had done it so masterfully that Nasim doubted anyone alive could still do the same.

Sorrow filled him for what he was about to do, but he stepped to the door and touched it as he had the last.

And nothing happened.

He placed his hand on it again, but this time he fed his dhoshahezhan into the stone to a greater degree, and still the stone stood resolute.

Worry grew within him like ivy, creeping through him slowly but surely as thoughts of Sariya's eventual arrival came to him.

He pushed such thoughts away and examined the stone more closely, wondering if it was of some different quality than the last. It certainly *looked* the same—it had the same red color of sandstone—but beyond this, if there were qualities he'd missed, something its maker had granted it, he didn't know what they might be.

It may have been the Atalayina's mere presence that had allowed him to open the others. But if that were the case, why hadn't they opened for Sariya?

Nasim stopped. Took a deep breath and released it slowly.

He was rushing.

He stepped away from the stone. Allowed the light from the suurahezhan to extinguish, plunging the tunnel into pitch darkness.

He stepped forward and placed his hands flat against the stone. Pressed his cheek against it as well, and his chest, so he could feel more of it. He had felt stone before—felt its weight and age and solidity—but he had never done anything like this before, and suddenly he felt the poorer for it.

He slowed his breathing and felt the cool, gritty surface. If this were water, he would have submerged himself in it. If it were air, he would have floated within it. But this was stone. This was earth, and so he made himself rigid. He felt it run through the palms of his hands, through the soles of his feet. He felt his muscles harden, felt his blood slow, felt his breath release under the unrelenting pressure of the weight of the mountain above him. He did not fear this change, but neither did he welcome it. He simply waited for it to happen—like an impending landslide, like the slow rise of the mountains, like the birth of the world itself.

He could feel the hand of the stone's maker. Could feel the magic that ran through it, magic that had been painstakingly crafted and woven into the very warp and weft of this doorway.

He paused in his examination, marveling. By the fates who watch above, the woman who'd done this had woven not just with a vanahezhan, but with a dhoshahezhan as well. He could feel how the spirit had been infused into the stone. It watched over this place still, guarding not just this door, but the tomb within.

The other tombs must have been the same. So why would they have denied Sariya but allowed *him* entrance? The answer was not in the Atalayina—both he and Sariya had held it—so what? The answer must be wrapped up with his very nature—who he was as opposed to Sariya. Either that or it had somehow sensed his intent. The qiram who'd created these tombs would have been gifted enough to do such things, and they might have done so given the importance of this place. But if it had opened itself to him before, why wouldn't it now?

When he thought about it, the answer was obvious. He'd been made simple with the spell Sariya had laid over him, but not only that, he'd had an innocence about him, a curiosity, but little true purpose other than to help the young woman he'd thought was Kaleh. He'd held charity in his heart.

It was no easy thing to hide things from your own mind. It was like trying to keep an image of a blue sky from your mind when someone told you not to. But in this he was uniquely gifted. The first eleven years of his life had been little more than chaos. He'd rarely been able to concentrate on any one thing—either in the physical world or the spiritual—for more than a few moments at a time. He'd grown up confused and unable to relate to those around him. But Fahroz, bless her soul, had been steadfast in her guidance. On Mirashadal, the floating village, she'd forced him to concentrate on things. Some days it was a skiff that was floating away from its eyrie. Other days it was part of the village itself—a bole of a tree trunk or a candle's flame or the long ballast tower that hung below the byways of the village itself. He'd eventually managed to do as she asked to the point that he could consider the object, consider its nature. And then she'd moved on to concepts. When he became proud from completing the tasks she set for him, she asked him to hold on to it, to grasp it and keep it near his center. When he experienced sorrow from the passing of someone in the village, she'd asked him to focus on this as well. Even *anger* she'd asked him to grasp onto and retain for a time—not so much that it was unhealthy, but so that he could ground himself in his own body and make sense of the world around him.

And so it was that he was now able to hold tightly to the same sort of charity he'd felt days ago. He wanted to open this door. He wanted to help the person who lay within. He wanted to heal the rifts and so heal the world. These things he allowed to run through him until they filled him with light.

Only then did he reach out and touch the door with the tip of his forefinger.

A crack as thin as a trail of ink spread from where his finger touched. The crack radiated like lightning strikes until the door shattered and fell with a sound like a mason dumping a pile of bricks. Dust rose and Nasim stepped through it, summoning the flame from the suurahezhan once more. Light stretched before him, revealing a short tunnel that led to a larger room. Inside was the same sort of sarcophagus as he'd seen in the other tombs, and again, on either side stood two statues, a man and a woman, with their hands to their sides, their faces beatific in repose.

Upon the stone lid of the sarcophagus were a laurel wreath and an olive branch. Nasim tried to pick them up, to set them aside and preserve them, but he no more than touched them than they crumbled like ash. With a delicate drawing on his jalahezhan, he made the stone lid slicker than ice, such that when he pushed it, it slid off easily and fell to the floor with a resounding boom.

He looked to the entryway, as the echoes died away, and a horrible thought occurred to him. Sariya was clever. Deceitful. He needed only to look at the times he thought he'd been helping only to find later that it had been Sariya's plan all along. Could it be she was deceiving him even now? Was the echo of Kaleh merely some ploy that would allow Sariya to get what she wanted?

Taking a deep breath, he decided it didn't matter. He didn't know her mind. He knew only his, and he could do only what he thought was right.

He brought the flame nearer until it floated above the open maw of the sarcophagus. Lying within, arms crossed over his chest, was the man whose likeness had been captured in the statue at the tomb's entrance, a likeness almost impossible to discern. He was so emaciated. It seemed as though he would crumble at the merest touch. On his brow was a crown with five gemstones set within it: tourmaline for fire, jasper for earth, alabaster for air, azurite for water, and in the center, raised slightly above the others, opal for life.

The last one had awoken when the lid had been removed, but perhaps she had sensed the danger she was in, whereas this man—this qiram from another age—did not.

"Can you hear me?" Nasim called.

His eyes opened slowly. They focused on the fire above him as his chest rose. He had not breathed before this moment—of this Nasim was sure—but he took breath now. It was long and full and sibilant.

"Come, grandfather," Nasim said, hoping that continued communication would help to bring him back from his long sleep.

That was when Nasim felt her.

Sariya. She'd reached the entrance of the tomb. And she was rushing to this place as quickly as she was able.

CHAPTER TWENTY-NINE

N asim helped the ancient man to sit. "Quickly, grandfather."

The man's eyes blinked slowly. They took in the room around him with a confusion that spoke volumes. Still, there was a glimmer of recognition. Clearly he recognized this place, but his expression looked too confused for him to have gained an understanding of what had passed since he'd slept.

"Grandfather, can you hear me?" Nasim wanted to shake him, but that was his fear of Sariya speaking.

The old, jaundiced eyes met Nasim's. He blinked once, twice, and then he uttered something from his mouth that was half croak, half moan.

"Here." Nasim opened the stopper to his water skin and poured a small amount into his mouth.

Sariya had reached the first of the turns below, and she was now taking the winding way up to the tunnel outside this room.

The old man's throat convulsed as he drank the water. His drawn grey skin beneath his chin waggled as a shudder ran through him. He blinked, staring ahead, but there was intelligence behind those eyes. He was piecing together the events from before he'd fallen asleep. His brow creased. His eyes became progressively more frantic. He took Nasim in anew, then looked to the door and the sarcophagus in which he lay.

He opened his mouth, and again a croak came, but this time, Nasim recognized it as a word. "*How...*"

He'd spoken the word in Kalhani, but Nasim knew enough to recognize it.

"How *what*, grandfather?"

"*How...*" He shook his head and motioned to the water skin with his shoulder. That simple movement was accompanied by a pop and a crack and a grimace that made it clear just how painful it had been. Nasim poured him more water.

"*How long?*"

"Since the sundering? Three hundred years."

The old man's eyes searched Nasim's. He seemed confused. Perhaps he thought Nasim was lying. But then he turned toward the entrance to the tomb. Again snapping sounds accompanied the slow movement. Again he grimaced.

"*One comes.*"

"*Yeh,*" Nasim said in Mahndi. "One comes."

As Nasim watched, a sound came from the tunnel, a sound of earth shifting, of stone cracking. Sariya was near, and he could feel her burning intent, her will to kill this man.

Nasim could not allow it, and yet he didn't know how to stop her. He had hope, however. There was one he could count as an ally...

He reached into the sarcophagus and lifted the old man out. He was light as a bundle of sticks, and it was no trouble at all for Nasim to walk with him. He did not notice before, but now that he was so close he saw that the gemstones in his crown not only glittered, they glowed from within. The glow was faint—as faint as this man's grasp on life—but it was there. The mere thought of it was staggering, a man bound to five hezhan at once. This ancient qiram had done so before he'd entered this tomb, that much was clear. What was also clear was that the hezhan had remained with him the entire time. Three centuries they'd stayed. Three centuries, when today it would be difficult for most qiram to bond with a single hezhan for more than a week at a time. It had been a different time then—the world had been a different place—but this was still hard to believe.

Nasim heard footsteps outside in the tunnel. Sariya was running, but slowed as she sensed him.

Still cradling the ancient man, Nasim stepped out into the hallway—beyond the door that had crumbled at his touch. Once there, he set the old man gently down and turned to face Sariya. He sent the glowing point of flame ahead. It floated in the air between them. It was strange to see her now: Sariya, hiding behind the eyes of Kaleh. The feeling of ages long past was more present than it had been before. In the past he'd written it off to Kaleh's heritage, but now he was surprised he hadn't realized her true nature sooner.

"Hear me, Kaleh!" Nasim bellowed.

Sariya looked down to the Tashavir, the Atalayina held tightly in one hand. She looked haggard. She'd pushed herself for weeks, perhaps months, to arrive at this very place, and she would push herself harder still. It was this very thing, Sariya's unquenchable desire to finish this, that Nasim was counting on.

"Hear me!" Nasim said again, the words echoing down the tunnel.

"She cannot," Sariya said. "She may have found her way to you before, but no longer, Khamal. No longer." She raised the Atalayina over her head, pointed the palm of her other hand toward Nasim just before releasing a blast of fire.

The fire splayed across the shield Nasim had erected. Life and fire were allied spirits, but it was through this bond that one could defend against the other.

"Kaleh!" Nasim called above the flames. "Fight her! She will never be weaker than she is now!"

He staggered back, for the heat was rising.

Sariya stepped forward, her hand still blasting flame. He pulled the stopper from the water skin at his side and called upon the jalahezhan to draw the water forth. He launched it against the flames. It did not douse them, but the entire hall flashed to steam, fogging the area they were in. Nasim then reached out with his hand, causing the stone near Sariya's feet to soften. She sunk into the stone. Tendrils of stone snaked out from the walls and wrapped around her arms and wrists. Encompassed her hands, including the one holding the Atalayina.

The flames stopped. The stone hardened at his command.

Sariya fought against these restraints, but for the moment she was bound.

Nasim brightened his point of flame until Sariya's eyes were drawn to it. "Kaleh, please! Fight her! There will be no other time!"

He had hoped there would be some sense of recognition in Sariya's eyes, but they merely hardened. It wasn't going to work. Kaleh wouldn't, or couldn't, fight her—not when Sariya was fully aware of her attempts to regain dominance.

The muscles along Sariya's arms tightened like cordage. Nasim tried to strengthen the stone that bound her, but in the end she was too strong, and the stone shattered.

Nasim had slowly been returning to himself since leaving the last tomb and traveling across the plain of Shadam Khoreh to this mountain. But he hadn't been fully aware of who he was and what he could do until this moment. He didn't know what had triggered it—perhaps this very conflict. Whatever the case, he remembered what he had done on Mirashadal when Kaleh had murdered Fahroz, he remembered what he had done on the Spar on Galahesh.

And he does so again.

He draws the world in around him, draws it tight, until the mountain above seems to crouch and the heavens seem to stoop.

Sariya slows. The flame in the air shifts slowly, as if caught in amber.

"Kaleh," he says. His voice sounds dead in this place.

Kaleh does not respond. Sariya still holds her tight.

He calls her name again, and now Sariya's eyes *do* change. They soften. Her expression turns desperate, then painful, and soon she is little more than a picture of misery.

She is Sariya no longer.

Kaleh has returned.

"Can you not fight her?" he asks.

The veins stand out along her forehead and her temples. The skin along her neck beats in time as her heart pumps with a violence that makes it clear just how close she is to losing control. Her nostrils flare as she draws in a sharp breath and releases it in halting increments. She swallows hard, blinks away tears, unable to speak, and in the end merely shakes her head.

"Did she reach the tomb in the last mountain?"

Kaleh glances at the withered man lying on the floor behind Nasim and nods.

"How many are left?"

She shivers, as if she's fighting a fever that threatens to kill.

"*How many?*" he shouts.

"Th-three."

A sinking feeling opens up inside him, and it continues to widen, as if the world itself is preparing to consume him.

He turns and looks down at the man, at his shriveled skin, at his watering eyes. Three. Only three of the Tashavir left, and he doesn't even know if he'll be able to save this *one* from Sariya's attentions.

"How, Kaleh? How can I stop her?"

She swallows and grimaces before turning her head toward her hand. That hand still holds the Atalayina, and it hasn't moved since the world slowed around them.

"Should I take it?"

She nods.

Nasim is loath to leave the Tashavir defenseless, but he sees no choice. He steps forward until he's face-to-face with her. He reaches up to touch the stone, but halts mere inches from it. He flexes his hands, inexplicably hesitant.

He should not be apprehensive. This is something that must be done.

"Now," Kaleh says through gritted teeth.

He stares at the stone, at the glittering lines of gold running along its surface. He looks at the fingers of Kaleh's hand, at the tendons, so tight they're ready to snap.

Something is wrong. Too often Sariya has fooled him, and this feels like another trap. Why it is she wants him to touch the stone, he doesn't know, but this time he won't do it.

"Now, Nasim!" she screams.

His only response is to step away.

Sariya—for he is sure it is her now, if it ever *was* Kaleh—changes. Her eyes transform from pained to desperate to enraged. She straightens, and her hand relaxes on the stone.

"Begone, then," she says.

And this time, her words echo along the tunnel.

In that one small moment, the mountain expands and the heavens recede.

And the flame flickered once more.

A blast of wind pushed Nasim and the Tashavir down the tunnel until the two of them crashed against the wall. The ancient man cried out and tried to roll over—perhaps hoping to reach his knees—but he was too weak.

Nasim managed to stand, but he stumbled when he realized his hezhan were gone. They were lost to him, all five, and he now lay defenseless before Sariya, who was inexplicably walking away from him, back the way she'd come.

The cracking sounds came moments later. They were piercing and shrill. But then they became louder and longer. Bits of stone above him fractured away, falling and pelting his scalp and shoulders and arms as he ducked away from the falling debris.

Larger pieces of stone calved away. He could hear nothing but the cacophony of stone shearing and falling. He moved to where the Tashavir lay and threw himself over the old man, hoping at the very least to spare him pain, but as he did, he felt a change. He felt at one with the stone around him. His skin turned rigid, and his mouth nearly burst with mineral taste.

Stones struck him, but he barely felt them. He knew little more than he was being protected, but even despite this the pressure above him increased. He became weighted down. His breath was pressed from his lungs. He wanted to warn the Tashavir, or maybe he simply wanted to speak to someone in these last moments, but if that were so he didn't know what to say. Still, he was glad he would be with someone, and it was strangely comforting that it would be with one who had lived during the sundering. He was born only eighteen years ago, but he felt a kinship with that distant age three hundred years before.

Stone and earth continued to press. It drove him down, and he became light-headed. And then it became too much. And the earth closed in around him.

He woke in utter darkness. He had no idea how much time had passed. He still felt the pressure of the mountain around him, but he also felt *her*—the one who'd protected both him and the Tashavir.

Kaleh.

He could feel her through her vanahezhan. It felt as though she were embracing him.

And then the world shifted.

It felt the same as it had on Ghayavand when she'd transported him to Rafsuhan. And this time he felt how she was doing it. It was like turning a skiff to align with the wind so that instead of being pushed by it, the ship could sidle along the currents of aether to go where it wished. Except instead of using wind, she was using stone.

The ground around him rumbled. A narrow line of star-filled darkness opened up before him. The crack widened like the maw of some ancient and forgotten beast, revealing the moon and the mantle of the heavens above. At last he was able to stand and help the Tashavir out of the hole. They stood on a hill beneath one of the peaks. He could see in the distance more peaks standing out against the starry sky. They were still in Shadam Khoreh, which could either mean that Kaleh hadn't had enough strength to take them farther, or she'd wanted him to continue to the next tomb so he could save another of the Tashavir.

He looked the ancient Tashavir over, but was unable to tell much in the darkness. "Are you well?"

No response came.

"Are you well?" he asked again in Kalhani.

"I am well." The words were spoken in a slurred approximation of Mahndi. He was crooked and seemed barely able to stand on his own, and yet, even though the words were slurred and slow in coming, there was no denying that there was verve in his voice. There was confidence as well.

Nasim bowed his head. "I am Nasim. Nasim an Ashan."

Before the Tashavir could respond, the gap in the earth behind them rumbled and groaned. It closed like a healing wound until all Nasim could see of it was a dark line in the otherwise-unremarkable terrain.

The Tashavir blinked for long moments—he even closed his eyes for a moment, as if sleep were about to take him—but then his eyes snapped open and focused on Nasim. "Tohrab," he said while patting his chest several times. "I am Tohrab Hamir al Nahin."

In the east, the sky was just beginning to brighten. In an hour, the sun would rise, but by then, Nasim would be asleep. He had been going for too long. Much too long. And the weariness he'd felt only in his bones had now caught up to him.

Northward, toward the nearest peak, was the low-lying edge of a forest that ran up the side of the mountain. It was there that they would rest. He was no longer worried about Sariya. Whatever Kaleh had done, Sariya would be hours coming from the tomb, and then she too—even with the Atalayina—would need to rest.

Nasim took the old man by the arm and guided him forward. "Come, Tohrab. We must reach the foot of that mountain, and then there is much you and I must speak of."

Tohrab nodded and shuffled along as Nasim led him toward the mountain.

CHAPTER THIRTY

Nikandr lay awake in bed, the night stars visible through the open window above him. The wind was dry and cold, and it smelled of the desert, but there was something distinct about its scent. It was different, somehow, than the rest of the Gaji. He knew it was foolish, but this place smelled ancient and forgotten in a way the rest of the desert did not.

He stood and began pacing, as he'd done many times that night, stopping at the door and peering into the night, hoping he'd find Atiana returning to him.

"Go out or go to sleep," Ushai said. She slept in the second of the two beds with Soroush.

Without saying a word, Nikandr left. He *couldn't* fall asleep. Not with Atiana still gone.

They'd told him the ritual would take several hours. That they'd most likely be done by morning, but they also said that some fell so deeply into the trance brought on by the tūtūn that they remained until the following afternoon, or even into the third day. Nikandr had no idea if what they were saying was true, but even if it was, it seemed as though Atiana—with all her years as a Matra—would be able to lift herself from the trance quicker than most.

He stared westward, wishing Atiana would appear beyond the mudbrick homes and walk toward him. They'd been distant, he knew, but he wanted nothing more now than to tell her how foolish he'd been, that he'd leave his thoughts of the wind behind him and focus on her, and Nasim, and the Grand Duchy. The two of them would be married after this was over. That much he knew. No one would stand in their way. Not her brother, Borund, not her mother, and certainly not Grand Duke Leonid. They would be married, and he would tell her so.

He waited longer, pacing in front of the home they'd been given, until he could take no more of it. He strode toward the center of the village, but he'd not gone ten paces when three men in robes stepped from the shadows of the homes ahead and barred his way.

"Go back," one of them said in Mahndi.

"I need to speak to Atiana."

"She'll be done by morning, or if not then, by midday."

"I will speak with her." He began walking past them, but the one who spoke, the one in the center, stepped forward and put his hand on Nikandr's chest. His other hand rested on the pommel of his shamshir. The other two were doing the same, and they'd dropped into defensive stances. He had a mind to press them, thinking they'd allow him to go if he showed them he wouldn't be swayed, but the memories of the day they'd risen from the desert and fired their arrows into the janissaries came to him. They'd been cold and calmly cruel, and Nikandr had no doubt that they'd be the same with him, the prince of a foreign realm or not.

He took a half step back so that the Kohori was no longer touching his chest. "If you won't allow me to see her, then take me to Ashan. Surely you can do that much."

The eyes of the Kohori softened. He took his hand off his shamshir and stood straighter, and Nikandr was suddenly reminded of the way he and Soroush used to view one another—as enemies and little more—and yet here was this man, stepping back from the edge of violence. "The son of Ahrumea will no doubt come to you when he is able."

"Are you to keep me from Ashan as well?"

For a moment, the only sound was that of a strange clicking coming from deep within the desert. An insect perhaps, or one of the long, black lizards he'd seen since arriving here in Kohor. It was followed moments later by another, more distant.

"I'll take you to him, if it will calm your heart."

They moved through the village, not westward as he'd hoped but southward. Beyond the mudbrick homes and thatched roofs, Nikandr could see the dark outline of the mountains and the shimmering gauze of night suspended above it. Eventually the village was behind them and they were into the desert itself. He was off to speak with a trusted friend, and that calmed him further.

Ahead, the desert floor twinkled as if stars had fallen and were reaching up, begging to rejoin their sisters. As they came closer, the effect became more pronounced and gained a sense of depth. The ground opened up here, and depressions as large as houses, as large as palotzas, pocked the ground. Nikandr thought they might be the entrances to mines, but as they took a path down into one of them, he got the distinct impression that these formations were simply a part of this place, no different than the dry earth or the mountains that ringed the valley.

"This is the Vale of Stars?" Nikandr asked.

"*Yeh*. One of the rarest jewels of the Gaji."

Nikandr had never seen anything like it. It was beautiful, like the heavens brought low so that mortals could walk among them.

They came to a tunnel of sorts. As they walked, oddly shaped holes provided a view to the interior. Crystals were embedded in the natural earthen walls, uncovered by some unknown working of earth and weather and time. Some tunnels branched off of this main one now and again, heading deeper into the earth, but this wasn't where the Kohori led him. They came to a large cavernous room with lightly glowing crystals all around. The roof—if such a thing could be called a roof—was a porous opening that gave view to the sky above. It was difficult to tell where the cavernous twinkling ended and the heavens began.

Ashan stood within this place with his arms to his sides, staring up. It was too dark for Nikandr to see, but he was sure Ashan's eyes were closed. Sukharam was there as well, facing Ashan and mirroring the arqesh's posture. They did not move as Nikandr came to their side, nor when the Kohori men bowed and took their leave. Only when the sound of their footsteps had faded did Ashan lower his arms and turn toward Nikandr.

"What is it you wish, son of Iaros?"

"I simply wish to talk."

Ashan waved to Sukharam. "We have much to do."

"You're merely taking breath." Nikandr immediately regretted his words. He could not make out Ashan's expression, but the slump of his shoulders told him all he needed to know.

"Would you wish him to be unprepared should we find the stone again?"

"Do you doubt that we will?"

"Answer my question, Nikandr."

Nikandr released his breath in a huff. "I'm sorry, Ashan. I've come because of Atiana. She hasn't yet returned."

Ashan began walking toward the tunnel, and Nikandr fell into step beside him.

"How long?" Ashan asked.

"Since sunset."

They continued on their circular path, treading upward, closer to ground level. Nikandr could still make out Sukharam's dark form below.

Ashan clasped his hands before him as he walked. "Do you know why you can't find the hezhan?"

Nikandr shook upon hearing these words. "What?"

"You cannot find it because you refuse to submit."

"I bonded with the hezhan for years, Ashan."

"What you did was not bonding. The havahezhan, through some trick of the fates, was bound to you. That isn't the same thing at all."

"I did not *command* it."

"You did. I watched you. I felt you. A true bonding is nothing like what you did. What you did was slavery, nothing more."

Nikandr swallowed. "It wouldn't have stayed had I done that. Every qiram I've talked to said the same."

Ashan laughed, a biting sound for all its simplicity. "They didn't know the nature of your bond, Nikandr."

"Jahalan said the same thing."

"As wise as Jahalan was, he was always blinded when it came to you. He cared for you, but in you he saw what he wanted to see."

"*Neh.* He was truthful with me."

"I didn't say he lied. His own mind led him to believe that you were doing as one of the Aramahn might have done, bonding through your soulstone as we do with alabaster. But believe me when I say it wasn't the same."

They left the confines of the tunnel, where the starry sky opened up before them. To the east, the first light of dawn touched the sky.

"Why didn't you tell me this before?" Nikandr asked.

"Would you have listened?"

"I might have." The words sounded hollow even to his own ears.

Ashan stopped and faced Nikandr. "In truth, I hoped you would stop. I hoped you would leave aside our ways and return to your own. I'm ashamed of it, Nikandr, but that is the truth of it, and you deserve to hear it."

Nikandr wanted to send back a biting reply, but how could he, especially with Ashan, a man who had so much caring in his heart? Nikandr could still feel the hole in his chest where the havahezhan had been. It was more physical than emotional, but it produced feelings of yearning, and the longer he focused on it, the worse it became. He felt the cold desert wind on his cheeks. It ruffled his hair. He wanted to call out to the wind, hoping a havahezhan would heed his call, but Ashan's words had shaken him more than he thought. Had he *controlled?* Had he taken and given nothing? "I'll never find another, will I?"

"Perhaps not. Perhaps you should let go of those desires." He reached up and gripped Nikandr's shoulder. "Do the same for Atiana. Do not seek to control the Kohori. They will see the truth, and once they see our hearts are pure, they will allow us to go. They may even help us."

"And if they don't?"

"Then they don't. We will find Nasim if he is to be found. We will find Kaleh and, fates willing, the Atalayina as well. These people know more than anyone of the stone. They'll help us to uncover its secrets."

"Why does any of that mean I should give up the one I love to be questioned like a thief?"

"Do you remember the mahtar who were hung in the garden of Radiskoye?"

He could still see them, swinging in the wind after Borund had ordered the hangman to throw the lever. "Why would you dredge that memory up?"

"Do you imagine—after hearing of such a thing—the people of the island would be easily trusted?"

"I know what you're getting at, Ashan, but—"

"Do not brush this aside, Nikandr. It was your people who did that deed. And here you are, hands clasped, begging the people of Kohor to help you when they know nothing of you. They guard their secrets closely, and you would have them forget centuries of such behavior and grant you your wish upon your arrival?"

"This is important."

"To them as well, more than you know, which is why they must take care."

"What, then? What are they hiding, Ashan? You must know something by now."

"They are hiding their history, which to them is more than simply the past. It is who they are. It is why they live." Before Nikandr could protest, Ashan put his hand on Nikandr's shoulder. "Be at ease, Nikandr Iaroslov."

Nikandr took a moment. He *tried* to listen to Ashan. He released his worries over the Kohori, released his worries over Atiana, and for a moment, with Ashan's hand holding him steady, he was able to breathe easily, to shed some of the tension that had been wound so tightly within him since long before arriving in this valley.

Ashan took his hand away and reached into a bag at his belt, the one that held the stones he used to bond with the hezhan. He held up a pale colored stone—alabaster, the kind used with spirits of the wind. "Do you know why we use alabaster for havahezhan?"

"It is the stone to which they're attracted."

Ashan shook his head. "It's because alabaster lightens the mind. It allows you to truly feel that which lies around you." He took Nikandr's hand, placed the stone into the center of his palm, and then closed Nikandr's fingers around it. "If you're open to it."

Nikandr felt the stone, felt the smoothness and its small imperfections. "Why help me now?"

"Perhaps I was wrong." Ashan shrugged, an apology. "Perhaps the fates wish you to reach Adhiya. Perhaps after all these years it is time to share with those who would accept such knowledge. Who am I to deny them?"

Nikandr didn't know what to feel. He considered Ashan a great friend. A true friend. And yet he'd withheld something he knew was terribly important to Nikandr.

His thoughts were interrupted by movement to his left. Over Ashan's shoulder, at the entrance to the tunnel leading down into the ground, was Sukharam. His white robes stood bright against the glittering background of the dark soil. He said nothing. He appeared to be waiting.

"What is it?" Nikandr asked.

"I've found him," he replied.

Nikandr's fingers began to tingle. "Found who, Sukharam?"

"Nasim," he said. "I know where he is."

CHAPTER THIRTY-ONE

"Where?" Nikandr asked Sukharam. "Where is Nasim?"

Under the growing yellow light of dawn, Nikandr could see the confusion on Sukharam's face. His eyes searched the fading stars, then the desert around him, and finally the long line of mountains in the distance. "To the south"—he lifted his hand and pointed—"Three days' hike, perhaps more."

Ashan studied Sukharam with a look of grave concern that seemed to be less about the news Sukharam had shared and more about the way he was acting.

"What is it, Ashan?" Nikandr asked.

Ashan jerked his head to Nikandr as if annoyed by the interruption, but then he shook his head, which was apparently the only answer Nikandr was going to get.

"What lies there?" Nikandr pressed Ashan. "What lies south?"

"I don't know. We're at the western edge of the Gaji. There are hills, valleys, tall black peaks. All of it barren. There are no settlements that I know of."

"There must be something."

Ashan stepped toward Sukharam, keeping his gaze fixed on the southern range. The sun lit the peaks like brands, making it look as though flaming suurahezhan stood atop them ready to bar passage for anyone who sought to cross. When Ashan motioned Sukharam back toward Kohor, Sukharam merely stared into his hands as if some deep mystery lay within them. He was crying, Nikandr realized. Tears flowed down his cheeks like diamonds.

At last Sukharam allowed himself to be guided away, but not before gazing south one last time. Nikandr knew that look—a look of weighing appraisal, as if he weren't at all sure he wanted to *find* Nasim.

When Nikandr returned to their mudbrick home, he desperately hoped Atiana would already be there. He was disappointed, however. It was an hour past dawn—over eight hours since Atiana had been taken away. Ushai was sitting at the table, eating charred flatbread with pungent goat cheese slathered over it.

"Has she been here?" Nikandr asked.

Ushai shook her head, apparently unconcerned over Atiana and Nikandr's obvious anxiety.

Nikandr moved to his bed and began gathering his clothing and shoving them into his pack. "Get ready."

She took another bite of her bread. "Why?"

"Because we're leaving."

Ushai sat unmoving, chewing her food as if he'd done nothing more than wish her good morning.

Nikandr paused and stood up straight. "Get ready, Ushai, unless you wish to be left behind."

Soroush entered just then, saving the two of them from a confrontation that had been brewing since long before they'd entered the desert. Soroush, his pepper-grey hair hanging down over his shoulder, stared between the two of them while dusting off his robes. "What's happened?"

"Sukharam found Nasim," Nikandr said.

With practiced ease, Soroush twisted his long hair into a rope and rolled it on top of his head and then began wrapping his turban cloth around his head. He was already backing up toward the entryway. "Are you coming?" he asked Ushai.

"I'll be along shortly."

"I'll get the ab-sair ready," Soroush said, not taking his eyes off of Ushai. Then he was gone, moving quickly toward the stables where their ab-sair had been taken.

Ushai stood and left without saying another word, but before Nikandr could call her back, Ashan and Sukharam entered, and they all quickly got to packing their things. Nikandr hadn't seen Ashan this unsettled in a long time, not since their time together on Ghayavand years ago.

And then Nikandr realized. All this time, Ashan had not *truly* expected to find Nasim alive. He'd thought they might find Kaleh and the Atalayina or he wouldn't have followed them this far, but it was clear he'd thought Nasim long since dead, lost in the water below the Spar on Galahesh.

Finished, Nikandr swung the packs onto the table with a crash. "Take those to the stables." He slung his bandolier over one shoulder and grabbed his musket from where it leaned against the wall. "I'm going to find Atiana."

Ashan grabbed his wrist, forestalling him. "I'll go with you, but leave the musket with Sukharam. The shashka as well."

"I must have her back, Ashan."

"You won't, not if you come with weapons at your side, or worse, held in your hands. Let Sukharam take them to the stables and we'll find Atiana together."

Nikandr didn't wish to be without his musket—the mere holding of it made him feel more at peace—but Ashan's words rang true. He handed the musket to Sukharam, then the bandolier and his sword, and then left with Ashan. They'd not gone twenty paces down the beaten path toward the stables when Safwah shambled out from behind two homes further up the trail.

Nikandr and Ashan ran to her. A swath of blood marked one side of her face, and across the bridge of her nose was a jagged gash.

"What's happened?" Nikandr asked.

Safwah's eyes looked straight through Nikandr. They darted back and forth, sifting through a myriad of possibilities, trying desperately to choose the right one. Then her eyes focused on Nikandr, though it seemed to take all her will. "You must follow," she said, "all of you."

"Where's Atiana?"

"Not now."

She tried walking past him, but Nikandr grabbed her by the elbow and spun her around. "I must know."

"She's been taken, son of Iaros. I know not where. And if you remain, you'll be taken too." She jerked her arm from his grasp. "Now come."

Before Nikandr could open his mouth to speak, an arrow came streaking in from Nikandr's right and struck her through her back.

Safwah screamed and fell to her knees, clutching for the black shaft of the arrow that had buried itself just above her right hip.

Nikandr reached down for her as another arrow dug into the dry path near his feet. A third speared through Ashan's robes, altering the arrow's path to send it wobbling into a dry bush a dozen paces away.

Nikandr no more than saw the forms of three Kohori men standing in their red robes with bows drawn back than he felt something strange inside his chest. That old familiar feeling, a feeling he'd thought lost to him long ago, had returned. He had no time to wonder about it, however, for the wind gusted around him. The Kohori released their arrows—so quickly after their first volley!—but Nikandr lost sight of them as dust rose up with the sudden howling wind.

There was a split second as Nikandr recognized the path of the speeding arrows. He expected one of them to punch into his chest, but the arrow never struck. It was the wind. Ashan had summoned the wind and fouled the shots.

Nikandr reached down, ready to lift Safwah in his arms if need be, but she was as strong a woman as he had ever seen. With his help, she reached her feet. As the wind roared and sand and stone bit their skin, she pointed toward the home Nikandr and Ashan had left only a short while ago. He slipped Safwah's arm over his shoulder and half-carried her as she walked. He could feel the warmth of her blood as it leaked from the place the arrow entered her back. It must have been excruciating, but the old woman merely gritted her teeth and hobbled stubbornly on.

Ashan followed, guiding the wind with his havahezhan, covering their retreat.

But the wind was now starting to die. It no longer bit as terribly, and the sound of it had ebbed.

"They're working against me!" Ashan yelled.

Nikandr shot a glance behind him and saw, through the haze of dust and sand, red forms running toward them—four of them, with veils covering their faces. Their swords were drawn, curving shamshirs that shone copper against the red tint of the dust.

Ashan faced them, his arms spread wide. He was trying to draw on another of his bonded hezhan, but nothing was happening.

And all the while the Kohori drew closer. They slowed now, spacing themselves wide.

Nikandr left Safwah and rushed to Ashan's side, pulling the short kindjal from his belt. "What do you want?" he called to the Kohori.

The approaching men did not respond.

A sharp whistle came from the right. Nikandr turned as the sound of running footsteps came to him. A flash of black. A sheathed sword spinning lazily through the air. He caught it, his own shashka. He pulled it from the sheath as Soroush rushed forward and met the nearest of the Kohori, his own sword bared.

Their blades clashed as Nikandr rushed forward, engaging the one closest to him. Steel rang as they traded fierce blows. An attack came in sharply toward Nikandr's neck. He beat the sword away and pierced the warrior's robes. The man grunted and retreated, his eyes fierce behind the veil across his face. A second joined him, and Nikandr was forced to retreat.

One of the four, however, was holding back. His arms were spread wide, as Ashan's were. His face turned up, and though Nikandr couldn't see his eyes through the dimness brought on by the cloud of reddish dust, he was sure his eyes would be vacant as he drew upon one—perhaps *more* than one—hezhan. He was countering Ashan, and soon, if they weren't careful, more of the Kohori would come.

They had to find Atiana and leave, and they had to do it soon.

Nikandr saw Soroush retreating from the swordsman with whom he was engaged. He no more than glanced at the Kohori with whom Nikandr was trading blows and Nikandr knew what he was going to do. Soroush darted in, sending a low attack toward the knees. The moment the Kohori moved to block the swing, Nikandr lunged, aiming for his chest. The Kohori leaned away just in time and caught the sword in his cheek instead. He reeled, trying to recover his defensive stance, but Soroush was already there. He stabbed the Kohori through his stomach.

It had all happened in an instant. Before the other two could recover, Nikandr and Soroush retreated, positioning themselves to protect Ashan. Nikandr could already see four more warriors coming, though. At a short bark from the Kohori, the two with whom Nikandr and Soroush were engaged glanced back and retreated two steps, waiting for their brothers to join them.

Six of them, Nikandr thought. Six, plus a qiram.

And then another resolved from the swirling dust. And this one was huge.

It was Goeh, Nikandr realized. Ancients protect them if they had to face that monstrosity.

The thought had no more blossomed in his mind than Goeh took one of the warriors ahead of him down with a huge swing of his sword across the man's thighs. The warrior dropped, screaming, while the other three turned to face him.

Again Nikandr felt something in his chest, a hollow ache that might never be filled. He glanced back and saw Safwah standing next to Ashan. By the ancients, the arrow that had been in her back was now out. She held it before her, the fletching near her chest, the head pointing toward their enemies.

And then she released it.

The dark arrow hung in the air for a moment, then sped forward as if shot from a musket. In the blink of an eye it covered the distance between Safwah and one of the warriors engaged with Goeh. It sunk into the warrior's back, exactly where Safwah herself had been struck.

The man cried out and fell to his knees. Goeh sidestepped, maneuvering so that this man prevented the others from reaching him, and then he released a primal cry and swung his blade across the man's neck. The warrior's head rolled from his shoulders, thumping against the earth as the body remained frozen in place for a moment.

As it slumped to the ground, the wind picked up once more, and soon it was much more fierce than it had been before. Sand tore into Nikandr's skin. The sound of it was like the crash of a mountain. He couldn't move. He couldn't speak. His breath was taken from him every time he opened his mouth. He could do nothing, and the only consolation he had was that the Kohori men were no doubt in the same state.

Nikandr felt a hand on his. Safwah's, or he was a fool. She placed someone else's hand in his—perhaps Ashan's, perhaps Soroush's—before leading him forward. They stopped twice, and when they did, she would leave him for a moment. Sand had worked its way into the corners of his eyes, beneath his eyelids. It was bitterly painful, and it forced him to keep his eyes shut tight. As difficult as it was not to know where they were going, he had to trust Safwah for now.

They resumed walking and this time didn't stop for a long time. Eventually they slowed and Safwah tapped his legs. "Steps!" he heard her shout. He climbed up onto what felt like stone steps, then onto wooden boards. And finally, at last, the wind died away.

He coughed, as did the others, as they entered a large space with shuttered windows. Inside it was dim as the darkest storm. The floor was covered in red dust. It was caked in their clothes and hair and their skin as well, making each of them—Ashan, Soroush, Goeh, and Safwah—seem distinctly alike, as if they'd all been sculpted from the same block of red desert stone.

"Atiana," was all Nikandr could manage to get out.

"We will search for her." Safwah bent over, clearly in pain. In a moment Goeh was by her side, helping her, but Safwah slapped his hands and waved him away.

"What's happening?" Nikandr asked. "Why are you fighting amongst yourselves?"

Safwah shuffled toward the rear of the one-room home and pulled away a horsehair blanket that covered the floor there. When the dark wooden floorboards were revealed, Nikandr could see the outline of a door that he assumed led to a tunnel. After seeing the Vale of Stars in the desert, he had no doubt this would lead to a series of interconnected caverns, perhaps the very same ones.

"There's no time to explain," Safwah said, "not now."

A form darkened the entryway. A Kohori man pulled a boy behind him. Sukharam. The man held weapons as well. Muskets and bandoliers and the two packs Nikandr had set on the table before rushing from the mudbrick home to find Atiana.

Sukharam was leaning on the man heavily, favoring one leg. Nikandr hadn't seen it at first because of the red dust, but an arrow shaft was sticking out from Sukharam's thigh. The shaft had been broken near the point of entry, but the rest was still embedded there. The bleeding, at least, seemed to be under control.

"Where's Ushai?" Soroush asked as he took Sukharam from the Kohori.

With Soroush's help, Sukharam hopped into the home. "I don't know." His voice sounded defeated, as if he felt responsible for her loss.

"We'll find her if she's to be found," Safwah said. She wavered, and suddenly tipped over. Goeh was there before she fell. He caught her and laid her gently on her side. He started ripping away the cloth around the arrow wound. "Go on," he said without looking at them. "We'll follow in a moment."

"We can't leave without Atiana and Ushai," Nikandr said.

Then Goeh did turn. His expression was fierce. "They will be found if the fates will it. Now go!"

"Come," Soroush said as he came to Nikandr's side. "We'll only be in their way. Let them find our loved ones for us, or we'll return if they're unable to do so."

Ashan took the ladder down in the darkness. Sukharam went next, with Ashan close at hand to help him in his descent. Soroush followed, but he paused half-way down, looking at Nikandr seriously.

Nikandr didn't want to leave. He wanted to return to the storm, to find Atiana, just as Soroush wanted to find Ushai. But they couldn't, either of them. There were larger things at stake now.

After one last glance to the doorway and the howling wind beyond, he nod-ded to Soroush, and followed him into the darkness.

CHAPTER THIRTY-TWO

When Nikandr reached the bottom of the ladder some three stories into the earth, it was pitch black. After a few breathless minutes, someone else began climbing down. It was Goeh. Hanging from his belt and shedding light as he descended were two siraj stones—blue instead of the pink Nikandr was used to. He was carrying Safwah over one shoulder. It seemed impossible, carrying a woman while navigating the narrow wooden ladder, but Goeh made it look easy.

When he reached the bottom, he set Safwah down onto her feet. Her eyes glistened with tears, and her jaw was set grimly against the pain. "Come," she said simply, taking one of the two siraj stones from Goeh and shuffling off into the darkness.

Nikandr went to help with Sukharam, but Ashan raised his hand. "He is my charge."

Nikandr nodded as Ashan slipped Sukharam's arm over his shoulder, and the six of them made their way through the dark and winding tunnel. They came to a fork, where Safwah led them down the leftmost one. At the next she took a right. They went lower and lower—much lower, Nikandr thought, than the Vale of Stars where he'd found Ashan and Sukharam.

"Quietly now," Safwah whispered. "Quietly." She glanced to one side, giving Nikandr the distinct impression she'd sensed they were no longer alone in this place.

They came to a room with many tunnels leading out from it—a dozen or more of them. Safwah didn't hesitate, she chose one to their right and led them deeper still. Unlike the Vale of Stars, it was clear that *these* tunnels had been formed by the hand of man. There were patterns in the stone, but they were much more subtle than those of the Aramahn, more primal somehow, as if the first men had created them, not the Kohori of today.

At last they came to a cavern. It opened up before Nikandr with an immensity that after the closeness of the tunnels seemed eager to swallow him. The cavern roof was easily taller than any of the island spires, perhaps twice as tall. The gemstones looked like nothing more than stars, except they were everywhere—on the cavern walls, on the ground beneath them, even along the lakebed where pale blue light glinted up from the depths.

Nikandr had to blink away the vision, for it made him feel dizzy if he looked at it for too long, as if he were floating among the stars, lost to the world forever.

Safwah stepped to the edge of the lake, bent down, and touched the glasslike surface of the water. The water rippled but then stilled, as if it had frozen in place at her touch.

"Stay close behind," she said. And stepped into the water.

Nyet, Nikandr thought. She hadn't stepped *into* the water. She'd stepped *onto* it. It was supporting her weight, without so much as a splash or a ripple.

Ashan and Sukharam followed, tentatively at first but then with growing confidence. Soroush went next, then Nikandr, and Goeh brought up the rear. It was the strangest sensation Nikandr had ever had, stepping out onto the surface of that lake. It gave ever so slightly, as if he were stepping upon the flesh of some strange, watery beast. He had the impression it would fail on the very next step, which made his gait odd and tentative, like a child stepping onto a frozen lake for the very first time.

The cavern was dead silent. The only sound he heard was the sound of their own breathing. That and the occasional echo from somewhere behind—perhaps the clink of a sword sheath as it caught against the stone of the tunnels, or the momentary rattle of arrows in a quiver.

The lake was wide—much wider than Nikandr had guessed. The largest of the hidden lakes of the islands were large indeed, but they were nothing compared to this place, this hidden reservoir in the middle of the desert.

At last they reached the far shore. They stopped along a short lip of stone that, as far as Nikandr could tell, held no form of escape. They were trapped. Perhaps Safwah merely wished to keep them here for a time while the pursuit chased them in the wrong directions, but it made Nikandr supremely uncomfortable.

When they'd all stepped onto the rocky shore, Safwah bent down and released a soft moan of pain as she touched the water's surface. The only discernible effect Nikandr could see was the smallest ripple that caught the bare blue light, and yet, as it expanded outward, he could feel within his chest an expansion, an easing of pressure he hadn't known was there. He breathed easier after that. Whatever she'd done, he trusted that she was keeping them safe.

They sat, all of them weary. Sukharam practically collapsed, even with Ashan supporting him.

"We'll see to the boy first," Safwah said. "And then I think it's time I shared with you a tale, some of which you may already know."

She and Ashan pulled up Sukharam's robes while Nikandr and Soroush held the siraj stones so the entry wound could be properly inspected. The arrow shaft was deep in his thigh.

Sukharam stared into Safwah's eyes with grim determination. He was poised—more poised than Nikandr had given him credit for—but he still glanced occasionally to his thigh and his breathing came in ever-shorter gasps.

Safwah gripped his hand in hers and spoke to him in Kalhani, "*Getham kal hiramal.*"

Sukharam visibly calmed. His breathing gained length if not steadiness, and a moment later, he licked his lips and nodded.

Safwah, as simply as if she were plucking feathers from a goose, placed one hand against his thigh and pulled the arrow out.

Sukharam did not cry out. He did not, in fact, seem to register the pain at all. If anything, he became *more* calm. Still, his forehead sweat, and his jaw was tight. He watched as Safwah set the broken arrow shaft aside and took a length of red cloth from a bag at her side and wrapped it around his leg.

Soon Safwah had finished dressing the wound. The moment she pulled his robe back down and smoothed the wrinkles, Sukharam laid his head down and fell asleep.

After leaving Sukharam to rest in peace, they sat upon the cold stone. When Goeh settled in beside her and set the siraj stones in the center of their rough circle, Nikandr realized just how much they looked alike. He thought back to the big man's face when Safwah had fallen. His look had been one of extreme concern, not over someone he knew, but someone he'd known his whole life.

By the ancients, Safwah was Goeh's *mother.*

The way he sat next to her now, the way he glanced at her, especially at the wound, made it seem obvious. But Safwah wouldn't allow herself to show weakness, and once she even sent a glare at Goeh, a look that told him to calm himself and stop worrying about her.

She began to speak not long after. "In the days of the sundering, there were three Al-Aqim. You know of them. In the early days, after the devastation, there were still many upon Ghayavand, those who wished to help, those who thought they might still turn the tide against the rifts that had been torn between our world and the next. It was not to be, of course. As days turned into weeks and weeks into months, hearts grew weary, and then despondent. Some left. Others came to Ghayavand, offering what help they could, but all looked to the Al-Aqim, who were gifted like no other. They were trusted still, and many thought they would some day lead us away from the edge of ruin.

"They did not. They created the abominations, the akhoz. The qiram who remained on Ghayavand, to their great shame, agreed to it, feeling there must be sacrifice if the world is to live. And yet, they knew it was wrong, and the more children that were given to the Al-Aqim, the more turned against them. They were largely silent at first, these men and women, but then their voices grew in number and volume. The Al-Aqim began to withdraw. They hid themselves away with their pieces of the Atalayina, hoping to study them and uncover the secrets they'd failed to find before the sundering.

"But the Al-Aqim were fools. They could not hope to find the secrets of the Atalayina separately. The stone needed to be mended. It needed to be whole before such a thing could happen, but the Al-Aqim began to distrust, not only the men and women who believed in them, but one another."

In the distance, there came a sound, so faint it was difficult to say what it might be. A rock falling. A creature stirring. A footstep. Safwah immediately went silent and all of them listened for a time. The sound was not repeated, and she went on, though quieter than before.

"There was a woman, Inan. Hers was the first of the children taken, whose name was Yadhan. The first of the akhoz. Inan gave her daughter willingly though many doubts warred with her loyalties to Khamal and the other Al-Aqim. As time went on, she became incensed—at herself, at the Al-Aqim, at even the fates—though she hid this from all, Khamal in particular, who she'd learned much from over their years together. Inan was wise. Inan had been born here, in Kohor, as had Sariya and Muqallad, and she knew much of the lore surrounding the Atalayina. She knew enough to bind it, but in order to do so, many would need to band together.

"One by one, then two by two, the qiram sided with Inan. They were known as the Tashavir—the stout, the resolute. Together they created the wards that still hold around Ghayavand. They muted the Atalayina, preventing the Al-Aqim from using it against them, and it bound the three of them to the island until such a time as the Tashavir returned to release them. Of all the qiram left on Ghayavand, Inan was the only one to stay behind so that she could deliver the news to Khamal and the others. What became of her, we do not know. We only know that she never returned to Kohor.

"But the Tashavir did return. They came to Kohor even as they spent themselves to hold the wards in place, hoping that they or others could learn enough that one day they could return to Ghayavand and close the rifts. But ideas..." Safwah was silent for a time, and Nikandr realized she was crying. She sniffed and wiped away her tears before going on. "Ideas are a strange thing. They are born of one mind but do not content themselves with this. Sometimes they spread like blooming fields of poppy—bright to look upon, and we are better for having seen them—but other times they spread like a dark plague, causing death wherever they go. The notion that had already sprouted from the Al-Aqim, that the sundering was no mistake at all, took root within some few of the Kohori, and from there it spread over time. The sundering was *meant to be*, some said, even if only to themselves. They were silent, these foolish men, these foolish women, but eventually their voices were raised. They said perhaps some should be sent to speak to the Al-Aqim, to treat with them.

"Foolishness," Safwah spat. Nikandr had the distinct impression she was no longer relaying a story. She was speaking to herself now, reliving the history of her people.

"As time went on, some of the Tashavir abandoned the cause, and the walls around Ghayavand weakened. It had taken many to form the spells around Ghayavand, but with the foundations crumbling, they knew they must take steps to preserve them. Decades might pass before a way to heal the rifts was found. Lifetimes. And so it was decided that the Tashavir who remained would hide among the mountains. Fifty-five traveled to the valley of Shadam Khoreh, and there they were entombed, their bodies preserved. They lived at the very edge of Adhiya itself, preserving themselves since the day they were buried. They were strong and bright, these flames of Shadam Khoreh. They sacrificed themselves that the world might one day recover from the days of the sundering."

"Forgive me." Ashan bowed his head reverently to Safwah. "But if this is so, why have you kept us from Shadam Khoreh?"

Safwah chuckled lowly. The sound echoed ominously against the walls of the cavern. "And now the other part of the tale comes. We who protect the old ways, the Keepers of the Flame, are now few. Then the daughter of Sariya came to this village. Kaleh, she named herself. And she brought a boy, but she told us he was dumb and mute. And it seemed so, for he never spoke. Not once. She asked us of the history of this place, slowly wheedling more information from us. She spent much time in the Vale of Stars as well, taking breath for days at a time."

At this, Nikandr looked over to where Sukharam lay, remembering the look on his face when he'd left the Vale of Stars. Had he seen what Sariya had seen?

"What I didn't know then, what none of us knew, was that she was working her way into our minds. One by one, she found us, the Keepers, and chained our memories. The others she may have bound as well, I do not know, but when they learned her true nature, they surely rejoiced. For Kaleh was not Kaleh at all. She was Sariya, one of the Al-Aqim returned, and for them—those who believed the sundering was no mistake at all, but the next step toward a rebirth of our world—it was a grand sign.

"Sariya took what she wanted from us. Knowledge of the Atalayina, knowledge of the Tashavir, but most importantly, the location of Shadam Khoreh, the valley where the Tashavir, fates willing, still remain hidden. She left us, but not before sending some away, and not before setting others to guard this village from presences like yours."

"If that's so," Nikandr said, "then why were we not simply killed when we arrived?"

Safwah nodded to Goeh. "It was Goeh who found you, and it was those loyal to us, the Keepers, that saved you at the edge of the valley. When you arrived, the others did not wish to raise suspicion, so they bided their time, waiting, hoping we would find nothing. That is why we pushed to use Atiana as we did. She awakened within us our memories."

"But Atiana knew nothing of Kaleh and Nasim's time here," Nikandr said.

"She didn't have to. She told us of Kaleh and Sariya and Nasim. She knows Sariya well, perhaps better than anyone alive. From her memories, from her understanding, our memories that had been hidden were returned to us. But when the others realized this, they knew they couldn't allow us to live. Nor could they allow *you* to live. They came for you, which is how I arrived at your home."

"But what happened to Atiana?"

Safwah shrugged. "They took her. I barely escaped with Goeh's help. The others may all be dead by now. Fates willing, it won't be so, but you"—she looked to each of them in turn—"may now be our last hope. You must go to the valley. We'll send help if we're able, but it may take days for us to find out who lives while the others search for us."

"Why would she have brought Nasim?" Soroush suddenly asked. He was staring at the lake over Safwah's shoulder, giving the impression he was speaking more to himself than anyone else. "Why bring one who is no ally of hers to such a place? Why not go herself?"

Ashan shifted where he sat. "Nasim was needed in Shadam Khoreh." He turned to Safwah. "Is it not so?"

Safwah searched Soroush's face, then glanced down at the siraj that lay between them as if searching for memories long hidden. "The tombs... They would not easily be opened by one such as Kaleh, even as powerful as she is. Nasim, however, is reborn of the Al-Aqim. Were he near, the tombs would open."

Nikandr shook his head. "But the Al-Aqim were the enemy of the Tashavir."

Safwah raised her hand to him as if scolding a child. "Not enemies. The Al-Aqim had been *allowed* to live. To consider what they had done. It was hoped that they would learn and find a way to repair the Atalayina and to close the rifts, and if they could do this, they would be able to leave Ghayavand and return to Kohor. The tombs would open for them, and the Tashavir would return to help as they could."

"And when the tombs have been opened?" Nikandr asked. "What will Kaleh do?"

"She will kill them," Soroush said, "one by one."

Safwah nodded. "That is what must be stopped. You must go to Shadam Khoreh. Find Nasim, but at all costs, you must save the Tashavir."

"And if we don't?" Nikandr asked.

"Then Kaleh will have what she wants. She will be able to return to Ghayavand, the Atalayina in hand, and rip the world apart." Safwah glanced back to Sukharam, who was still sleeping on the glittering stone. "Carry him. He'll sleep for a while yet."

She stood and moved to the cavern wall behind her. With but a touch the stone melted like ice, revealing another tunnel beyond. "Your ab-sair will be waiting for you at the end of this tunnel. The others will hound these caverns for a while yet, but they will expand their search to the desert, and when they do, you must be long on your way to Shadam Khoreh."

CHAPTER THIRTY-THREE

Styophan sat in the driver's bench of a tall coach. Edik sat next to him wearing his janissary's uniform. Behind the coach were thirty-seven of his men, marching two by two, their footsteps rising above the clop of the four horses pulling the coach and the jingle of tack and harness. Of the Haelish men who'd come with them there was no sign.

Styophan wore his commander's uniform. The rest wore the clothes of regulars. They traveled toward the city of Avolina. Its walls were made of stone, and it had the look of age about it. Avolina wasn't so old as Alekeşir or the cities of Old Yrstanla, but it was old enough that it had outgrown its original walls. It was this feature, along with one other, that had made Styophan choose it. It was large enough that it would have many men moving through it: men from the outskirts of the Empire; men from the warfront; men coming from Alekeşir with official news and supplies.

The other factor that had made them choose this route was the fact that the headwaters of the Vünkal, the very same river that bisected Alekeşir, ran through Avolina as well.

The coach rattled on. The men marched behind sloppily, exactly as they'd been ordered. Styophan could see janissaries manning the wall. One called another over and pointed to the field Styophan and his men were crossing. A moment later they called down to ground level, presumably to more soldiers who were hidden behind the half-timber buildings that stood outside the wall. Styophan stroked his two-week-old beard. He'd grown it and cut it in the fashion of the region—mustached with tails, long hair along the chin but shaved along the cheek and neck. He had to admit he looked the part, but many of the men didn't. They looked to him like streltsi posing as soldiers of Yrstanla, which was of course exactly what they were. Edik argued that the men of Avolina wouldn't suspect; they'd merely look down on these simple soldiers from the outlands, men who either weren't good enough to find posts in the cities or had been born far from civilization, both of which would be damning in their eyes.

Styophan hoped he was right, for already he was feeling the weight of the stares as the men on the wall studied their approach.

When they passed beyond a long building, a tannery from the smell of it, the city gate was revealed. It was open, but four men were standing at the ready, muskets in hand. He'd wondered for days if Avolina would have heard news of the coming war and the devastation at the fort.

Clearly they had.

"Hold," one of the soldiers said in thick Yrstanlan when they approached.

Edik pulled at the reins and the coach came to a stop.

The men came to a rest as well. They stayed in their rows, but they looked about, concerned, some of them wide-eyed, as if they were worried what was to become of them.

Good, Styophan said to himself.

"You look grim, you do," said the janissary as he looked Styophan up and down.

Styophan handed him the first of the notes he'd written before leaving the fort. "For the Kaymakam."

Styophan was ready for the man to lock eyes with him, to stare deeply into his soul, ready for him to peel back this simple deception to learn the truth. With that one look he'd know that these were men of the islands, not soldiers from the wide-open spaces of the Empire. Styophan readied himself to pull his pistol and fire, readied himself to order his men to storm over these few soldiers of Yrstanla.

But the janissary did *not* lock eyes with Styophan. He accepted the letter and inspected the seal carefully, then eyed Styophan as if he wondered how he'd come by such a thing. Styophan thought at first he recognized the seal itself. Each of the forts were given their own—he knew because he'd examined many that were left in the commander's desk—but a man like this probably wouldn't know them all.

"You've come all this way?" He looked beyond the coach and down the line of men. "All of you?"

Styophan ignored his questions. "The Kaymakam will want to see that."

"You've said as much." He looked for a moment like he was to pick a fight, but Styophan stared him down. The janissary blinked. He stared at the letter as if by doing so he could burn it, and then he barked, "Wait here," and left, storming past the other men as though each and every one of them had profoundly disappointed him.

Edik glanced sidelong at Styophan with a look that anyone else might interpret as relief. Styophan knew Edik too well, however. His was the face of a bloodthirsty man. Styophan had forbidden him from trying to seek retribution against the Haelish. Edik would never disobey, but neither would he forget, and if he could soothe the fires of vengeance by blooding the men of Avolina, he would gladly do so.

"Time enough in Alekeşir," Styophan had told him.

Now, as Edik stared coldly at the janissaries, he leaned back into the wagon's bench. It creaked loudly, the only sound besides a hammering that came from somewhere inside the walls.

The commander returned, but he hadn't more than framed himself in the gate than he waved his hand at Styophan to follow and walked back the other way. Styophan clicked his tongue and snapped the horses' reins, and soon the line was marching into Avolina. They passed homes of two and three stories. The city felt cramped, as did the streets, which were filled with people walking with baskets or children playing with barrel rings or men bearing lumber and tools. They parted for Styophan's coach, but did so only grudgingly.

Edik leaned closer and spoke under his breath. "They don't much like those from the edges of the Empire, do they?"

"Would *you* if they constantly failed to stop the barbarians from killing your women and stealing your children?"

"Point taken."

They passed a central square where a tall stone building stood—no doubt the house of the Kaymakam—but the soldier didn't stop there. He continued to the river an eighth-league further. There were warehouses here, and a dozen piers, some with ships, and two with low, flat barges on them.

Exactly what Styophan had been hoping for.

He stared carefully along the river, especially northward, but all he saw was a placid brown surface that twisted like a carelessly tossed rope toward the stone wall. Stout iron bars barred entrance from the water beyond, but they were cleverly set into the towers on either side to hinge inward and allow entry by river. Styophan doubted it saw much use, however. Avolina was the last large city along the Vünkal. Beyond, the river grew too narrow and shallow for use by any but the smallest watercrafts. It would be the southern river gate that saw use, for through it trade would come from Alekeşir and other cities along the Empire's largest river.

The commander stopped at a wide-open space along the main thoroughfare. He did not speak. He merely held his hands behind his back and stood at the ready, as if for inspection.

Minutes passed. Then more. Many came to see the men from the outlands that had gathered at the river. Men bearing carts filled with hay or potatoes or cages filled with chickens. Carpenters working on the roof of one of the warehouses stopped and stared. Urchins and children, many of whom showed signs of the wasting—dark circles beneath their eyes, thin, coughing—ran through the area, but more and more lingered near the edges of the street, sensing something was about to happen.

Then a procession of thirty soldiers came from the house of the Kaymakam. They marched with an odd gait—one leg arcing high, the opposite arm swinging up as the other, bearing the curved kilij swords of Yrstanla, swung back. The swords they bore were of high quality. The well-oiled blades gleamed under the sun. Each had a wheellock pistol at his belt, and their sheaths were a beautiful brown leather, tooled with the eight-pointed star common to the region. They moved in behind the lone officer, fifteen to a side, and waited, swords in hand, unmoving, their eyes staring beyond Styophan and his men.

"Trouble," Edik said softly.

Styophan shook his head furtively. "Sixty would be trouble. Thirty shows us they're not to be taken lightly. Thirty from his personal guard will show that the Kaymakam keeps his men well trained and at the ready. A show for the Kamarisi, whom he now knows we're off to see."

After several more minutes, a palanquin approached the river. It was borne by eight bald men, each of them nearly identical to the next. They marched quickly but steadily and set the palanquin down in front of the lone soldier, who bowed and stepped aside.

The cloth was parted by delicate hands adorned with golden rings, and out stepped a woman wearing a pristine dress made from fine cloth the color of wheat and snow. An intricate headdress draped her jet-black hair, which was pulled back into one long plait. She was not tall, but she strode forward with a confidence that commanded attention—the confidence of the royal born. Men like the Kamarisi had it. Nikandr and his brother Ranos had it. And this woman had it too. It was not something in their blood, but their upbringing, the expectation that when they spoke, men would follow. This woman had seen perhaps thirty summers, but her eyes had deep crow's-feet, as if the severe look upon her was one she wore even while sleeping.

She took Styophan in, her eyes resting on his eyepatch before speaking. "Your name."

"Hadeyn ül Fazel, Second Commander of Negesht."

Edik cleared his throat.

At this the Kaymakam snapped her head toward Edik. She looked him up and down, her sharp gaze lingering on the blood stain on his shoulder, before returning her attention to Styophan with a reluctance that spoke of just how spoiled and pettish she was. "This note says you've been summoned to Alekeşir. That you should make all haste."

"*Evet*, Kaymakam."

"Where were you raised, commander?"

"I've been stationed in Negesht for six years, but I come from Trevitze."

She stared at his lips, as if tracing the curve of his words. In all likelihood, she'd never left the region of Avolina, save perhaps for a handful of trips to Alekeşir. Still, Avolina was large enough that it would have received visitors from Trevitze.

She looked beyond him to the coach, to the men standing in line behind it. "*Two* barges," she spat.

"*Evet*."

Her next words came breathy and soft, and still they pierced the cold afternoon air. "Why? Why would Bahett ül Kirdhash send for a handful of broken men from the torn edges of our Empire?"

"It's not my place to say, Kaymakam."

He said the words with hesitance, and she took the bait.

"You *know*."

Styophan lowered his gaze, met her eyes briefly before looking down again. "*Hayir*, Kaymakam."

"Tell me, commander."

"I know nothing, Kaymakam. Truly."

She flicked one hand, and one of the janissaries strode forward. He had the look of grim determination on him, the look of deadly intent.

Styophan should have recognized it sooner. He should have sensed how mercurial this woman was. But he didn't, and before Styophan could think to stop him, the soldier had pulled the wheellock pistol from his belt and pointed it at Edik's head.

He pulled the trigger a split second later.

The wheel spun, shedding sparks.

The gun bucked with a cough of white smoke.

A flash of red exploded from the left side of Edik's head.

Something warm sprayed across Styophan's right ear and cheek and neck as Edik's body collapsed to the cobbled stones.

Inside, Styophan screamed. But outside he remained silent in his horror.

His head turned more slowly than the seasons to stare down at the ground.

Where blood poured from the shattered remains of Edik's skull and his eyes stared sightlessly toward the waters of the Vünkal.

CHAPTER THIRTY-FOUR

S tyophan felt something white hot form inside him. It surged up from his gut, fury and fear rising, mixing, until he wasn't sure which gripped him more fiercely. He stopped himself from reaching for his own pistol, but several of his men disobeyed orders and pulled their muskets to the ready position.

"*Hayir!*" he shouted.

In a blink the Kaymakam's janissaries had their wheellocks in hand and pointed at his men.

"*Hayir,*" he called, softer, praying to the ancients his streltsi would listen. They could overpower these men, but if they did, there would be no way to reach Alekeşir, not without the Kamarisi being alerted to their approach. And that would be disastrous.

He breathed deeply, assiduously avoiding looking to his right. By the ancients, Edik's hand was twitching on the ground!

Through all of this, the Kaymakam stared on placidly, unaffected by the bloodshed before her. She said nothing. She didn't need to. Her expression stated her demands for her.

Styophan swallowed once. He tried to speak, but failed for the growing lump in his throat. He tried again. "Lord Bahett ül Kirdhash made his way through Negesht, Kaymakam." He cleared his throat, well aware of how closely it echoed what Edik had done only moments ago.

"And?"

"A suurahezhan was summoned there, by men wearing red robes, men Lord Bahett had brought with him. They summoned it at the very doors of the keep. They—they lost control of it. It stormed through the keep, burning as it went."

Her eyes flicked toward the men, many of whom wore burned uniforms— uniforms they'd burned purposefully over campfires the night before they'd left the fort.

Styophan's eyes—ancients preserve him—flicked toward Edik again. Thank the souls beyond, he'd stopped moving.

Go well, dear brother.

"Lord Bahett left," Styophan continued, "with the Kiliç Şaik, nearly twenty of them, but he asked that we stay behind before following."

"Why?"

"To prevent the Haelish from following him. He lost a hand to them, and he worried they would soon storm over the walls, despite the protections of the Kiliç. Any who lived were to wait for three days and then follow him to Alekeşir."

"To what, reward you?"

Styophan bowed his head, the mere gesture filling his mouth with spit. "That is what Bahett told us, Kaymakam. He said we were owed. And since the fort was ruined, he ordered that it would be given to the Haelish should they wish for it. We'd have it back soon enough, he said."

The Kaymakam stared at him carefully, her once-placid eyes suddenly filling with interest. "He's done with his plans, then? To woo the Haelish kings?"

"As far as we know, the barbarians have retreated into their hills, and from where I stand, they can stay there until the end of days."

"And Bahett would leave them there? Return to his war in the east?"

Styophan looked down to the jeweled toes of her white leather boots. "Forgive me, Kaymakam, but his Lordship did not share his plans with me."

Styophan raised his gaze but did not meet her eyes. The Kaymakam glanced up to the center of Avolina, then to her left, toward the river and the barges. She was considering the orders Styophan had forged, and it was at this moment, even more than the moment the pistol had fired into Edik's skull, that Styophan realized he may have made a grave mistake. Bahett was not well loved, but all the Kaymakam knew he stood in the Kamarisi's favor. Disobeying him would be risky. Still, if she could embarrass him in some way, it might allow her to leverage it to her own favor. She might kill them all, have them hidden away in a mass grave to be forgotten by any who'd seen them, just to keep them from Bahett.

He considered ordering his men to fire. They could kill these soldiers. Every last one. And any others from the crowd who rose arms against them. But the moment he did, achieving their larger goals would become nearly impossible. His mind raced, searching for some way to tilt the Kaymakam away from her better instincts.

"There *was* one thing Bahett said," Styophan said, glancing down and away as if he were searching through his memories.

The Kaymakam stared, expectant, not dismissive.

"He said it while I was standing outside his office. I didn't mean to hear it—"

"Speak!"

"He said he would be calling for a council in Alekeşir."

A council would summon many of the Kaymakam to the capitol to speak with the Kamarisi. As it was among the Duchies of Anuskaya, Yrstanla held one yearly, but they were occasionally called at other times. The possibility introduced uncertainty, enough that the Kaymakam could not be sure what Bahett might do were he to learn that the men he'd summoned had gone missing near Avolina.

The Kaymakam measured Styophan anew. She'd already made up her mind, but something in her was reluctant to say it.

Then, without warning, she spun and strode to her palanquin. As she passed the janissary that had met Styophan at the gate, she said, "Give them their barges."

The palanquin was picked up and carried away, the soldiers falling into line behind like the body of a snake. The area felt empty and lifeless. The river looked dark, almost black, as though it were filled with blood.

"Wait here," the janissary told him, but Styophan hardly heard a thing. He could only stare at his hands, which were now shaking. He gripped them tightly and stiffened his jaw. He stared straight ahead so that he wouldn't pull his pistol and fire it into the back of the soldier.

Still, every step he took toward the barges felt like a deep and inescapable betrayal.

Twenty men—ten men per side—pulled at the barge's oars. They sliced into the dark waters of the Vünkal like a knife through oil. Ice rimed the stones at the very edge of the river, especially where the willow trees shouldered beyond the grassy banks and over the calm water. Styophan stood at the rear of the lead ship, staring at Avolina as it receded into the distance. Edik's body lay next to him, wrapped in tarp. They would find a place between here and Alekeşir to bury him properly.

Farther and farther they went, the river curving east, then south, until the tallest of Avolina's buildings were at last hidden by the snow-covered landscape.

Some distance behind the barge there came a rippling in the water. The surface of the river mounded as something swam quickly with broad, surging strokes. Styophan could see a hint of arms, of a head and torso, of legs snapping as a Haelish warrior stroked forward through the water. Eventually his head pulled up above the water. It was Datha. He immediately surveyed the area around him, and then, only after he'd assured himself there was no danger, he released a low, trilling whistle down toward the water.

"Hold," Styophan called to his men.

As they began rowing against the current to hold their position, another mound marred the surface of the Vünkal. Yet another followed, and another, and soon a dozen Haelish warriors had poked above the surface like otters. As they levered themselves up and over the edge of the barge, more warriors broke the surface near the second barge.

Datha now stood next to Styophan, cold water shedding from his frame. Across his chest and arms and face were bright swaths of blue paint. Styophan was surprised it had remained intact. They'd put it on hours before, well before he and his men had entered the environs of Avolina. It made some sense, though. The paint was infused with crushed azurite, which allowed jalahezhan to inhabit their bodies. The stone would need to remain in contact with their skin for the hezhan to remain in the material world.

It took a toll, however. This was a long time for the Haelish men to allow the hezhan to inhabit them. Datha's eyes were haggard, and his posture looked as though he were more than physically exhausted. It seemed, in fact, as though Datha were half a man.

Datha looked down at the body wrapped in the tarp. He met Styophan's gaze seriously, but with a clear look of regret. "The ways of war are covered in mist."

Styophan said nothing. He didn't want to hear mollifying words from the savages of Hael.

On the river, more and more warriors pulled themselves onto the barges.

But on the hill beyond, a form rode up.

Dear fathers, it was the janissary. The very one who'd led him into Avolina and later prepared the barges. He'd suspected something, and he'd come to watch their departure.

He was too far for Styophan to fire a musket. For probably the first time in his life, Styophan wished he'd been gifted with the powers of the qiram. He wished he could open up the earth and swallow the janissary whole, or summon a suurahezhan to burn him where he stood

Datha whistled three times, short and sharp, while pointing to the hill.

The warriors farthest behind the trailing barge turned and ducked beneath the water. They were lost from view for a moment but in the time it took Styophan to take two quick breaths they had reached the river's edge and were climbing onto the snowy bank.

The soldier from Avolina watched from the back of his horse, staring at the barges, too startled to move, but then he reined his tall horse over and kicked it into action.

The towering Haelish men sprinted after him, and Styophan could only stare in wonder. They sped toward the hill faster than a horse could gallop, and in moments they were over and beyond it. Shortly after a distant shout came. It was too soft to make out the soldier's words, but it sounded like a cry for help. It was cut off a moment later. Then came a deadly silence. Every man on the barge knew what had happened.

In short order the warriors returned, one of them leading the horse by its reins, and though the horse tried to tug itself free, it was eventually led into the river. Another warrior carried the limp soldier over his shoulder. It was easy to forget how large the Haelish were, but not when they carried a fully grown man and made him look like a boy. When they reached the bank and stepped into the shallows, one of the warriors drew his sword. The other, the one holding the horse's reins, ran his hand along its forehead. Styophan would never have guessed it, but the horse calmed, mere moments before the sword came down, severing its neck.

Styophan cringed at the sight of the head being dragged down into the water as two of the others dragged the body deeper into the water. He knew as well as everyone else, though, that there could be no evidence left behind, not if they were to reach Alekeşir and have any hope of completing what they'd sworn to do. The last of the Haelish carried the janissary down into the depths. They were gone for long moments, but a swath of muddy, bloody water rose up from the depths as they buried the bodies of man and horse alike in the riverbed. There might come a day when the bodies would surface, but in the meantime, a single janissary gone missing in Avolina would raise little concern in the capital of Yrstanla.

When the four warriors resurfaced and began swimming toward the barges, Styophan turned toward Datha. "Best you get into the hold." Styophan couldn't tell if Datha nodded or not, for he couldn't draw his gaze from the blood in the water.

Can a single man and a single horse bleed so much?

Datha left his side, calling softly for his men to join him in the barge's hold. Ahead, on the other barge, the Haelish warriors were doing the same, readying themselves for the two weeks of travel it would take for them to reach Alekeşir.

As Styophan ordered his men to stop rowing against the current and start heading downriver, the bloody water finally reached Styophan's barge, passing its wooden sides, caressing it like a dead lover. He felt like he should feel vindicated in some way, for Edik's sake.

He didn't, though. He felt foul.

As foul as the water flowing past him.

"Styopha."

Styophan woke and sat up immediately. It was Rodion, and his voice sounded urgent.

He pulled his eyepatch on and left the cramped confines of the hold, where fifty Haelish warriors and ten of his streltsi were sleeping. When he climbed the short ladder up to the deck, the yellow morning sun greeted him. To the south, however, was a sight that stopped him short.

He stepped up beside Rodion, gape-mouthed.

Alekeşir.

The land along the banks of the Vünkal was farmland dotted with plantation houses. Then came suddenly a press of fortifications and walls and towers and stone domiciles that spanned an area wider than Styophan had ever seen a city occupy. It seemed to go on and on. It was a league wide. By the ancients, it might even be two. How many people must live here? The sheer amount of resources it must take to sustain them…

To the right of the river's meandering path toward the city was a rise in the land. Not a hill, exactly, but a shallow plateau. On that rise stood a wall taller than the lower one that ran around much of the city. Towers were spaced along its length, and beyond Styophan could see minarets and massive domes. It was larger than anything he'd seen on the islands. Larger than Radiskoye by far. Larger even than Galostina.

This was Kasir Irabahce, the house of the Kamarisis, a place that had never been touched in battle.

And here they were, a handful of men hoping to find their way within her walls to kill the Kamarisi, to give the islands the time they needed to recover.

"What have we done?" Rodion said.

"Something foolish," Styophan replied without taking his eye from the vision before him. "Something foolish, indeed."

CHAPTER THIRTY-FIVE

Khamal walks through fresh green grass. Around him fields of it sway gently in the wind. Well beyond the fields is the deep blue sea of the ocean. He can smell the sea here. It feels right, as the sea is an inseparable part of this day.

On the mountain path ahead is Sariya. Her golden hair is pulled back, tied by a length of leather cord. Her dress—made from rough linen the color of sandstone—has intricate white thread-work at the hems of the sleeves and skirt and neck. Her fine sandals, like the robes, are new. They were presented to her by a craftsman before they'd left Alayazhar. Muqallad and Khamal had been presented similar style robes so that the three of them looked like brothers and sister walking their way toward the shoulder of the largest mountain on Ghayavand.

Ahead of Sariya is Muqallad. His curly black hair falls over his shoulders and down his back, and in his hands, cupped gently, is the Atalayina.

The three of them walk in lockstep, neither hurrying nor tarrying on their way to the site of the world's transcendence. Indaraqiram. It is upon them at last. He thought he might be excited when the day finally arrived, but he isn't. He is at peace, more so than he's ever been in his life.

Above them stands majestic Sihyaan. Today the mountain seems to be staring down with something akin to approval, and yet there is a massive flock of starlings weaving and churning through the sky above. Ill omen coupled with good. He might have hoped for clearer signs that the day will go well, but in truth he cannot ask for more than he's already been given. This is the way of life, after all—bad married with good, from one's first waking moment to that final, halting breath. It wasn't what happened in life, after all; it was how one reacted that mattered, so he would look to Sihyaan and in her imposing stare glimpse what might become of this world were he and the others to succeed.

At last Muqallad stops and turns. He holds out the Atalayina for Khamal to take. Khamal accepts it and stares into the deep blue depths of the stone before taking up the hike once more. It was decided that Muqallad would carry the stone from Alayazhar; Khamal would relieve him of it when they reached the foothills; and when they reached the most difficult portion of the trail, Sariya would carry it the rest of the way, to the peak.

The stone, as it has for these past many months, feels weighty in his hand, but there is more to it this day. He can feel something through it, a depth that has never been present before.

It knows, he suddenly realizes.

It knows what will happen this day.

But as they take the first of the hills that lead up toward the sharp peak of Sihyaan, he senses something else, or perhaps *someone* else. It feels as though another person holds it as well, as though he and they walk hand in hand, the stone clasped between them.

Like the starlings, which are now wheeling toward the sea, this feels like another omen. He opens himself to it. He accepts it, and as he does so, he feels a third. What it might mean, he doesn't know. Perhaps it's the simple fact that he and Muqallad and Sariya have become so intimate with this stone that he can feel their presence, especially with the two of them walking so close on the trail behind him. Or perhaps it's the fates watching from above, touching the stone and wishing him well.

He becomes so lost in his thoughts he loses track of time, so much so that when Sariya taps him on his shoulder, he realizes that *hours* have passed. The three of them now stand halfway up the mountain. The foot of the trail that leads to Sihyaan's steeper sections lies just ahead. How can this be? He told himself he would mark each step of this journey, and yet here he is, the last half-league little more than a dream.

"Are you well?" Sariya asks. Her smile is stunning, and Khamal feels a pride borne of working together with her for so long. She isn't fazed by what's happening, and why should she be?

"I'm well," he answers, and yet it is only when she stares down at the Atalayina with a bemused expression upon her face that he realizes he still holds it in his hand.

He smiles sheepishly and hands it to her.

This is the perfect day, he says to himself.

And yet... He feels a sense of longing when she takes it and walks ahead of him on the trail. Nothing he does seems to banish this one niggling thought as they take to the pathways along Sihyaan's broad shoulders.

It is the perfect day, he repeats.

Except now it feels like a hope, not a certainty.

Nasim woke with feelings of yearning still strong within him. Opposite a now-dead fire lay Tohrab, the Tashavir he'd saved from Sariya. Tohrab was sleeping, which was for the best. Even with Nasim's help he'd barely made it to the base of the mountain—the last, Nasim feared, that he would visit in this lost valley.

After adding dried sticks to the fire and stoking a meager flame back to life, Nasim pulled apart one of the pine cones he'd left near the fire to dry to liberate the nuts within. He chewed them absently while staring over the tops of the black pine trees to the mountain peak above. He couldn't help but think of Khamal's memories of Sihyaan. It was clear Khamal had been hiking to the peak to complete the ritual that would eventually cause the sundering. Nasim was desperate to know more, but he'd long ago learned that such memories were a gift. He could not question when he received them, or how much they revealed. He was simply glad they'd come, for each of them prepared him that much more for what lay ahead.

The peak above them—Malidhan, Tohrab had named it—was nothing like Sihyaan. Malidhan's was shaped more like a spearhead, and though Sihyaan was dark, she didn't have the feeling of ill intent Malidhan had. Sihyaan had always felt like a place where peace could be found no matter what the circumstances. Even the last time Nasim was there, even after the sundering, even after the pain and anguish Sihyaan had been witness to, she felt at peace with the world around her. Whereas Malidhan felt protective, isolated—not merely watchful or vigilant, but chary of being used.

Malidhan was unique among the mountains of Shadam Khoreh. It was the tallest and the only one which had snow gracing its peak. It wasn't much, just the very top, but it looked like the jewel of dawn in the setting of night's dark crown.

"Tohrab?" Nasim called.

Tohrab was sleeping next to the fire. It had been two days since the encounter at the last tomb. He'd wanted to take Tohrab to the peak immediately, but Tohrab was too weak. Nasim might have gone alone, but he couldn't afford to leave Tohrab here. So Nasim had brought him into the forest near the base of the tall peak and hidden them away in a copse of black pine.

"Tohrab," he called, louder.

The Tashavir had been difficult to speak to. He never seemed to understand what Nasim was saying, and when he did, his answers seemed steeped in the past. It was clear he thought little time had passed since he'd been interred, and no amount of explanation seemed to clear that up. It didn't help that Nasim knew too little of Kalhani. Tohrab knew some Mahndi, but whether his understanding was obscured by his addled state of mind or if it came from a true lack of knowledge of the language, Nasim couldn't tell.

Nasim had grown increasingly anxious over the last two days, fearing Sariya would rush toward this place, but it was likely she thought him dead. She'd buried him in stone, after all, and it may be she hadn't sensed their passage through the portal Kaleh had created at the last moment.

He feared that Sariya might know how to transport herself by using such a trick, but as far as he knew this was something unique to Kaleh. Sariya had not traveled so in the times Nasim could remember, and even Muqallad had seemed to rely on Kaleh's abilities, so it seemed safe to assume Sariya wouldn't be able to do so now. Besides, she had been taxed greatly by her assault on the tomb. She would have to recover, and hopefully that would give Nasim the time he needed.

Nasim reached down and shook Tohrab's shoulder. "Tohrab, we must—"

Nasim stopped, for Tohrab was shivering horribly. It wasn't the sort of shiver one gets when cold, that wracks the body as it tries to regain lost warmth; this was a shiver that ran through to the center of his soul, a shiver spurred by fear of the gravest kind.

Nasim knelt next to Tohrab and rolled him onto his back. He shook him harder now that he saw the amount of pain and anguish that was playing over the craggy landscape of his face. His skin was ashen. His eyes, sunken deep within their sockets, rolled beneath their lids, as from a dream. His cheeks stood out harshly, as did his brow bones and his jaw. Nasim shook him harder still, and finally Tohrab's eyes snapped open. They were haunted and troubled and filled with pain. Tears leaked from them from the moment they began taking in the dark clouds above and the pine forest that surrounded them.

"The rifts," he whispered in Mahndi, "they've grown so wide."

"They have, grandfather."

"They grow wider every day." His diction was markedly improved.

Nasim helped him to sit up. "They do."

Tohrab sat there, staring into his open hands. Every so often he would grip them and stare at fingers that were little more than skin on bone. From his brow he took the golden circlet, his wispy grey hair momentarily tugged by the motion. His eyes stared into the five stones in the circlet's settings. He rubbed his thumb over them as if to polish them, or perhaps to wipe away the unpleasant reality he now faced.

"The Tashavir," Nasim began tentatively. "You came here to protect Ghayavand, did you not?"

"All but one."

Nasim shook his head. "What do you mean?"

"My wife, Inan. We all considered her one of the Tashavir, but she remained. She felt duty bound to tell Khamal and the others what we'd done."

For long moments Nasim could only stare. "Your wife was Inan?"

"She was."

Nasim could still see her, burning at Khamal's feet after she'd told him what she and the others had done. They'd set the wards and trapped the Al-Aqim. She had once been a disciple of Khamal, and it was that betrayal, plus Inan's outward smugness, that had caused a rage to bubble up inside Khamal until he'd summoned a suurahezhan and burned her where she stood. Inan had somehow been pleased. Perhaps she'd felt it proper to die after giving her daughter, Yadhan, over to Khamal to become one of the misshapen creatures, the akhoz.

"You said you've had dreams from Khamal's life," Tohrab said. "Have you ever dreamed of Inan?"

"I have."

"Were any from the time after the Tashavir left Ghayavand?"

"Alas," Nasim said. "I've had none such." Fates curse him for a coward, he didn't have the heart to tell Tohrab that tale.

When Tohrab spoke again, his voice was as soft as the wind through the boughs of the nearby trees. "I would like to say it was true"—he levered himself up in slow and awkward increments and stared down at his circlet—"that we came here to protect Ghayavand, but that would be only half the truth, and the lesser of the two at that."

Strangely, sleet began to fall on the forest around them. The pellets struck Tohrab's head and shoulders. They struck his hands, making it look as though he were made of stone and bits of him were chipping away.

"And the other half?"

Tohrab looked up, holding Nasim's gaze. "We came here to hide from our own. We came because we could not trust those among us to hold faith forever."

Nasim stood and began gathering his things as the sleet rained down. "I don't understand."

Tohrab took one long, wheezing breath and placed the circlet upon his brow. "No matter. What's important is that Ghayavand is not yet lost. What's important is that there is still one. One more. The strongest among us, which is surely why Sariya did not assail this mountain first."

"She may be weakened now."

"And now so is Ahar. We came to this place and bound ourselves to it, as we had bound ourselves to Ghayavand. We drew strength from this valley, for such is the power of Shadam Khoreh, the valley in which the Atalayina was discovered. Through us, Ghayavand was protected, but through our shared bonds, the Tashavir protected one another as well." Tohrab looked up toward Malidhan. "When we buried ourselves within these mountains we didn't know whether some of us, after decades, after centuries, would die. We didn't know if our own will and the gifts granted by the fates would be enough. So we tied ourselves to one another. If one flagged, the others would lift him up. And so, were Sariya to have gone to Malidhan first, she, or you, might never have been able to enter Ahar's tomb, and even if you *had* entered, the others would have lent him their power."

"How then? How could she have taken the first, and the second?"

When Nasim had kicked dirt over the fire and Tohrab had picked up his walking staff, the two of them left the copse. Tohrab placed his hand on Nasim's shoulder for support as they walked uphill toward the path they'd picked out the day before. "She found the weakest among us. She found the weakest and she snuffed their flame, killing them in their tomb before moving on to the next, and the next. Each time she killed another, we were less able to help."

"And now there is only you and Ahar." Nasim shook his head. "So how? How can the walls around Ghayavand still stand with only two of the Tashavir left?"

"We may have created those walls, but they do not need our constant attention. We buttress them, that is all. It is Ghayavand itself, and this valley, Shadam Khoreh, that keep the walls strong. Still, there is no doubt the walls are weak. With so many now gone, they have given way in many places, and soon, Ahar and I will prove paltry indeed."

"And then?" Nasim asked. "Will Sariya's dream come true?"

"Her dream? You know her dreams, Nasim an Ashan?"

"She wishes to bring this world down that the fates may start anew."

"She told you this?"

"*Yeh*, on Galahesh. And it has been echoed by her every move since."

Tohrab was silent for a time. They hiked higher up the foothill, and again Nasim was struck by how much this echoed Khamal's memories of stepping up to the heights of Sihyaan.

"I fear Sariya is fooling herself," Tohrab said when the pine trees thinned and finally gave way altogether. They walked among a field of tall grass, and the sound of the sleet striking it was like the patter of rain on cobblestones. "I fear she has convinced herself of this because of the pain she now bears."

"You think she would allow the world to be destroyed for the part she played in the sundering?"

"Do you know how many died when the ritual failed? Do Khamal's memories tell you this?"

"Many in Alayazhar died, but I don't know how many."

"Tens of thousands."

Those words settled over Nasim as he looked out over the valley of Shadam Khoreh. Tens of thousands. The mountains ringing the valley no longer seemed like points on a crown. They seemed like men and women standing judgment.

And more stood behind, far into the distance until the haze of sleet robbed him of their sight.

"Tens of thousands," Tohrab repeated. "In an instant. Men, women, children. All because those three had thought to take us to a higher place. I am not removed from responsibility. No one on Ghayavand save the children were. But imagine how the Al-Aqim must have felt. They did not feel as though anyone else was to blame. They carried that weight on their shoulders—each of them differently. Who are you to say that Sariya was wrong to think the fates had willed the world to end? Who are you to say she is wrong now?"

"You're saying she's right?"

"I'm saying that Sariya stepped up to Sihyaan to bring about indaraqiram, and she nearly destroyed the world in one, quick instant."

Nasim's breath was coming faster now from the climb. The sleet fell harder, enough that many of the mountains were obscured, and it seemed to him that the forms he'd seen there had stepped back into the mist, taking their judgments with them.

"She is wrong," Nasim said.

"And Sariya believes just as fervently that she is right."

"Should I give myself over to her then? Help her in what she strives for?"

"You should trust to yourself. Listen to the fates, and the world around you. But don't let Khamal's memories or his desires affect you."

Nasim stopped at a rocky plateau, more angry than anything else. He thought surely Tohrab would help him, that he would have answers, but the truth was there were none. No one had them, except perhaps the fates themselves, and they were altogether too quiet for his liking. As his anger faded, he realized how right Tohrab was. Who *did* he have to rely upon? And who knew about the dark days after the sundering better than he did? No one. He could rely on no one else, and this in a way was freeing.

The plateau was black, not red like so many of the rocks down below, or dark grey, as it was higher on the mountain. It was black, and for this reason alone it gave Nasim pause.

"How close are we?" Nasim asked.

"I don't know. Ahar's tomb was built after mine. But it should be near." He looked around the plateau, and pointed to their left. "There are stairs worked into the mountain."

They took the stairs, climbing higher and higher, occasionally switching back and cutting along the steep slope at this midway point of the mountain. Then Nasim smelled something on the wind. A pungent smell, like garlic and ginger, but it was deeper and older, as if this particular scent had long ago been lost to the world. It was the smell of a vanahezhan.

And so it was that he knew—well before they'd reached the entrance to Ahar's tomb—that Sariya had beaten them here.

"We must hurry," Tohrab said before Nasim could voice his suspicions.

They moved quickly after that. It took several more minutes of climbing, but at last they reached a ledge of black rock overlooking the valley. A darkened tunnel was revealed in the rock face with a mound of broken stones at its entrance. The smell was stronger here.

Tohrab was desperate to reach Ahar. He shambled into the tunnel ahead of Nasim, but he'd gone no more than two steps when a gout of fire blasted outward from inside the mountain.

CHAPTER THIRTY-SIX

Along a dry trail in the Urdi Mountains, far to the south of Kohor, Nikandr slowed his mount until he was at the rear of their group. At the head of the line, Soroush and Ashan rode next to one another, speaking softly of Soroush's last circuit around the world. Sukharam, as he did so often these past few days, was staring into the distance—not watching the trail, not tending to his mount, simply staring, as if dreaming of another time and another place.

The mounts had been given to them by Safwah's allies—the Keepers of the Flame—those who believed in the cause of the Tashavir. Nikandr often wondered what happened to Safwah. Had she and others been killed for helping them? Had they been harmed? It was the day after they'd escaped from Kohor, and if what Safwah had told them was true they might reach the valley of Shadam Khoreh by sunset, but Nikandr still felt as though at any moment they'd hear the pounding of hooves behind them. Surely the Kohori would have guessed their destination by now, and if that were so they would have sent men flying southward to intercept them. Every rise they passed, every turn in the trail they followed, Nikandr felt as though red-robed warriors would lift from the very ground itself and fire arrows down upon them as they had against the janissaries.

But so far they hadn't.

Thank the ancients for small favors.

They'd agreed to speak only when absolutely necessary, so the ride was lonely, more lonely than at any other point on their long journey. Especially without Atiana. He felt like a coward for coming here to Shadam Khoreh, but what the others said was true. There was little they could do now. Their largest hope was in preventing Sariya from doing as she wished. Then they could return and discuss the terms for Atiana's release.

Near midday, Nikandr retrieved the stone of alabaster Ashan had given him in the Vale of Stars. He held it in the palm of one hand. He'd never tried to bond with a hezhan using stones as the qiram did—only his soulstone. That is, if what he'd done could even be considered bonding. He thought a circlet of some kind might be useful, but Ashan had assured him that simply holding it in his hand would suffice. So that's what he did. He held it loosely and stared up toward the blue sky, allowing his ab-sair to follow the others along the trail. He listened for the wind, which was faint but present as it flowed through the scrub bushes to either side of the trail. He felt it flow over his skin, watched it play with the clouds above. He did not call to Adhiya. He did not *try* to summon the hezhan he'd known for so many years. He merely allowed the world to take him, hoping the doors to the world beyond would open.

Minutes passed. The sound of hooves plodding against dry earth filled the air. He breathed deeply, hoping that he could see some small glimpse. Feel some small sign. But there was nothing. Each and every time he'd tried in the last few days, he'd felt nothing.

Ahead, Sukharam's mount turned and its back legs began skipping down the trail. In a few more moments, the mount would buck and try to throw its rider. Nikandr, releasing his breath in a huff, shoved the alabaster stone into the pouch at his belt and kicked his mount until he was riding alongside Sukharam. He took up the ab-sair's reins and held them out. "Control your mount."

Sukharam blinked and stared down at the reins. He accepted them, but shook his head vigorously, as if he sat at the very edge of exhaustion. Then he breathed deeply and stood straighter in his saddle and nodded to Nikandr with an apologetic look.

"In the Vale of Stars," Nikandr said to Sukharam, "you were entranced."

It took some time for Sukharam to respond. "I was."

"You said you felt Nasim."

"I did."

"But there was more. I saw it in your eyes."

"And why do you say that?"

It wasn't a denial, but mere curiosity as to how Nikandr knew.

"I don't know you well, Sukharam, but I know you well enough to see that you were shaken."

Sukharam guided his ab-sair around a large granite boulder that split the trail. The two of them passed on opposite sides of it like water in a stream. "I *was* shaken, son of Iaros."

"You can tell me of it. I won't judge you."

Sukharam laughed, making Ashan and Soroush turn in their saddles. "Will you not?" Sukharam asked when they'd returned to their low discussion. "It isn't weakness that holds my tongue. It's prudence."

"You don't trust me."

"I just don't know that it's wise to share it until I've learned more."

"It was something to do with the Atalayina, wasn't it?"

Sukharam seemed surprised by these words. "In a way, it was."

"In *what* way?"

"Suffice it to say that I may have more to learn from Nasim than I once thought."

Ahead, Soroush and Ashan had reined their ab-sair to a stop. They were both staring out over the distance ahead, and a few moments later, Nikandr understood why. He reined his own mount to a stop beside theirs, staring out over the wide valley below. In some ways it was the same as the rest of the Gaji—a low, level plain surrounded by mountains—but there was more to this place. It felt old. It felt as if this were the very birthplace of the world, as if this were the place the last of men would come when the world reached its final days.

Hopefully no time soon, Nikandr thought.

The peaks were tall here, proud, but there was a wariness to them, as if they thought ill of this intrusion into the land they protected.

"Where do we go?" Nikandr asked.

Sukharam pointed to their right, to the lone mountain that had snow upon its high peak. "There," Sukharam said. "To Malidhan."

No one questioned his judgment.

They rode down to the valley floor, for there was no other way to reach the mountain that Sukharam had pointed out. By common and silent assent, they pushed their ab-sair, not because they were afraid of the Kohori, but because they felt that something was wrong. This valley—the mountains, the valley, the air itself—made Nikandr feel as though something were imminent. He didn't know what, but he could tell the others felt it too. They rode more stiffly in their saddles. They glanced to their right, up toward the mountains, and to their left toward the wide valley floor with looks of concern, of wariness.

Nikandr had tried to feel for Nasim many times since leaving Galahesh. He'd expected nothing when he'd returned home to Khalakovo, but he'd hoped for months after reaching the shores of Yrstanla and then the Gaji itself that Nasim's presence would be known to him. It was that—despite the knowledge that Nasim had severed their bond when he'd plunged the khanjar into Nikandr's chest—which had convinced him that Nasim was dead. But now, with the knowledge that Sukharam had seen or felt him, Nikandr had harbored a hope that something still remained.

But he felt nothing. Nothing at all.

Ashan caught Nikandr staring up toward the snow-capped peak of Malidhan, and somehow he knew. "We'll find him," he said.

"I know."

As they urged their mounts higher along the dry terrain, sleet began to fall. Sleet. Here in the mountains.

The others were as confused as he was. Sukharam held out his hand, allowing it to fall against his palm as if he'd never seen it before. Soroush looked grim.

But Ashan...

Ashan seemed worried. He stared out toward the desert, where red dust was rising. Then he arched his neck back and stared up toward the white peak high above them.

"Hurry, everyone! Hurry!"

Moments later a blast of fire issued from a ledge high upon the mountain.

Nasim watched in horror as Tohrab flew outward from the mouth of the tunnel, carried by the massive blast of flame. He called upon the wind to cradle Tohrab, but before he could summon enough of it, Tohrab was gone over the edge of the escarpment.

Sariya was coming along that tunnel. She'd sensed them.

Nasim grew worried, for he'd dearly wanted to save Ahar, the strongest of the Tashavir, but the moment the flame had gouted from the tunnel, he'd realized Ahar was dead. They'd come too late. Sariya had beaten them here, destroying Nasim's hope to save another of the Tashavir.

Tohrab was now the last of them, and he too might now be dead or dying at the base of the cliff below.

He should have come more quickly. He should have taken the chance and gone ahead himself to protect Ahar.

But if he'd done that, it would have left Tohrab unprotected.

And a fine job you've done of protecting him, Nasim thought.

Sariya was coming. She was nearly ready to step from the tunnel, and Nasim was suddenly petrified. Spit gathered in his throat. His hands tightened into fists and his body began to shake.

"Stop it!" he shouted.

Sariya stepped from the tunnel, holding the Atalayina easily in one hand. By the fates who shine above, she looked older than only days before. She looked more mature, a woman who'd left all traces of childhood behind. She looked, in fact, more like Sariya than she ever had before, but there were still many traces of Kaleh, the confused girl who'd grown up on an island that sat between worlds.

She turned—this woman in Kaleh's frame—and leveled upon him a cold stare that shook him to his core.

"She will not save you," Sariya said with Kaleh's lips. "Not this time."

There wasn't a trace of doubt in those words. She was in supreme control. But how? How could she have regained her strength so quickly? How could she have come here and taken another of the Tashavir as weak as she'd been?

The answer lay in the glittering blue stone she held in her left hand.

The Atalayina was brighter than he ever remembered it being here in this valley. It was brighter even than on Galahesh, when the walls of Adhiya were so close he could almost touch them.

Sariya faced him, the hem of her simple yellow dress billowing and flowing in the growing wind. "Did you know it was you that gave me the clue?" The look on her face sent chills down his spine. "I remembered so little of the sundering. I'd thought for long years that the experience itself was too painful to look upon, even through the dim pane of our memories. But when you slowed the world around us"—she stared deeper into Nasim's eyes, as if trying to sift through *his* memories; it became so strong and felt so foul that Nasim took a step back—"I saw it once more. And I saw how to touch the Atalayina as we did that day. Do you remember, Khamal? Do you remember holding it? Do you remember the feeling that we held not a stone, but the world itself in our hands?"

Nasim wished he did, but he could only shake his head.

Sariya laughed. "You restored my memories to me and you don't remember yourself?"

The wind was growing stronger. It tossed her long brown hair about, pressed the fabric of her dress against her lithe form.

"There is only one left." She sidled toward the ledge where Tohrab had fallen, keeping her eyes on Nasim until she'd reached the very edge. Then she looked down, searching. A crease formed on her brow and her eyes snapped back to Nasim.

He wanted to draw upon the same powers he had in Tohrab's tomb. He wanted to stop her, to take away the Atalayina and drive Sariya from Kaleh's frame, but he didn't know how. He didn't truly know how he'd done it those other times. Even when he'd stood upon the Spar of Galahesh, the place he'd been most aware of it, he was unable to retrace his steps. It wasn't something one could teach, or that one could learn. It was more like the sensing of a limb—he didn't need to see his arm in order to move it. And yet now, when he needed help the most, the ability eluded him. Perhaps it was because he was weakened, or because Sariya was more aware of it and was preventing him from using it, or perhaps the death of Ahar or the power behind this growing wind was acting as a barrier. Whatever the case, he found himself cut off from it.

As his desperation grew, he became more aware of what was happening in the valley. The wind was only one of the symptoms. Since he'd arrived here, Adhiya had felt distant, but the feeling of it now was strong and growing stronger.

Sariya took one smooth stride toward him. "You can feel it, can't you?"

Nasim took a step back, drawing on this newfound power from beyond the veil.

With but a look, a wave of her hand, Sariya cut him off from it.

He coughed, not from the dust upon the wind, but from the sudden feeling of emptiness that yawned within him.

"The walls are falling." She looked out toward the desert plain. Much of it was obscured by dust, drawn up from the wind. It was coming this way. Moment by moment the wind became biting and the air became thick with a red haze. "The walls are falling here, as they soon will around Ghayavand. It's time to return, Khamal."

Nasim stepped back and fell. He struck his head on a rock behind him and winced from the pain as Sariya approached and held out her hand.

"Come," she said. "You know there's little time left. These winds will die, but not around Ghayavand. Those will build until they have consumed the world. Join me, and I will show you what the Al-Aqim may still do."

He stared at her hand.

It did not shake. It was as steady as a rock. As steady as the mountain beneath them.

He'd thought on this long and hard, how the world had lived. How it would die. He'd often wondered whether Khamal had thought like Sariya and Muqallad. There had been glimpses in the memories he'd inherited from Khamal—memories of doubts and uncertainty and wondering whether the sundering hadn't been a sign from the fates that the time was ripe to begin anew.

Sariya's eyes stared deeply into his. There was a part of him that didn't want to believe her. And yet, despite everything he'd told himself up until now, he did. She was right.

How could he not have seen it before?

Slowly, he reached up for her hand.

His fingers were mere inches from hers when a swath of red blossomed at a point just above and to the right of her heart.

A moment later the sharp report of a musket reached him.

Nikandr and the others pushed their ab-sair hard after seeing the flames from high on the mountain. They'd seen someone or some*thing* fly down from those heights and crash into the trees above them. They rode up, pushing their mounts harder than they had before, and soon they came to the place where the form had flown down.

"Go," Nikandr said to Ashan and Sukharam. "Do what you can. We'll continue up."

Ashan nodded as he and Sukharam rode their mounts deeper into the trees.

Nikandr and Soroush took their ab-sair as far as they could, but soon the way became too steep, the pathway too narrow, so they slid off their saddles and continued on foot, running up the steps that had been cut into the stone. The wind came stronger now, and it bit, the red dust and sand from the valley below rising and driving against them, making it difficult to see. Soroush wrapped the long tail of his turban across his face. Nikandr did the same with his ghoutra. Still, it was difficult to see far ahead.

They took a switchback, and Nikandr could see through the haze two forms standing at the ledge they'd seen from far below. One was Nasim. His back was to Nikandr, but it didn't matter; Nikandr could live to a hundred and never fail to recognize the younger man.

He cringed as Nasim fell and struck his head on a large rock.

While the other...

Nikandr shook his head.

"Can it be?" Soroush said beside him. "Sariya?"

Nikandr looked more closely. "It's Kaleh."

"She's too old," Soroush replied.

Indeed, she appeared years older than Nasim. She had been five years younger than Nasim when they'd left Galahesh.

"I don't understand it either," Nikandr replied.

Kaleh held the Atalayina in one hand, the stone a deep blue that stood out against the blowing red sand. Kaleh's other hand was stretched out toward Nasim. This was no simple offer of help, Nikandr realized. It was an offer of allegiance. It reminded him—as did Kaleh's physical appearance—of Sariya, of how she could with a simple twist of the mind make you believe that she was your ally, that she was in the right. Perhaps Nasim had somehow broken from her, and this one simple motion would bind him to her once more.

It was something he couldn't allow.

Nikandr looked along the path. It continued westward before curving back and heading up to the ledge where Nasim and Kaleh stood. He would never reach them in time.

"Nasim!" he called, but the blowing wind was too fierce for his voice to reach them.

Nikandr pulled his musket to his shoulder and sighted along its length.

The wind howled. The sand bit.

Nikandr breathed out.

And fired.

The musket bucked. A swath of red along Kaleh's shoulder.

She fell, lost from view.

Nikandr sprinted up the steps, Soroush close on his heels. The wind picked up. It pressed against them, threatened to toss them from the carved trail if they weren't careful.

They were halfway up the final stretch when the wind stopped. And the air became dead.

Sand began to fall, and with it came a sound like an early autumn drizzle over a field of blooming heather.

When they approached Nasim's fallen form, Kaleh levered herself up and stared at Nikandr and Soroush. The Atalayina was held tightly in her left hand. Her eyes went wide and she turned toward the center of the valley.

In the moments that followed, there came a low rumbling. Nikandr felt it deep in his chest, and in the pit of his stomach. He felt it on his skin, a tingling that seemed to cover every square inch of him.

Out over the valley he could see little more than a red-haze sky and the dark hint of trees below.

And then the wind rose and the world fell apart.

Nikandr was pressed against the hillside like a ship against rocks. A sound like the groaning of the earth itself stormed over the valley. It grew in intensity, drowning all other sounds.

The air was sucked from his lungs. The bones of his arms and legs and chest ached. His skull felt as though it were being pressed in a carpenter's vise. He couldn't move. Not an inch. He dare not open his eyes for fear they would be cut by stone and sand and the needles from the nearby pine.

He heard a groan. It was Soroush, and yet it took this to realize he was doing the same.

Another sound came, like mountains crashing, like worlds crumbling.

And then the pressure began to ease.

Slowly, it receded and the sound began to die away.

A whine came from the valley below and rushed upward.

"Quickly," Nikandr said, pushing himself to his feet. "We must make it to the top of the ledge."

Soroush nodded. His turban was gone. His long hair whipped in a wind that was rising to new heights. They'd only gone ten strides when a blast of sand and branches and ancients knew what else descended upon them. Nikandr could barely breathe. He held his sleeve to his mouth and felt for the next stair. The wind shrieked. Branches and stones tore at his exposed skin.

At last, he found the rock where Nasim had fallen. Nasim wasn't there, however, nor was Kaleh.

He continued, crawling forward lest the wind pick him up and throw him from the ledge.

"Nasim!" he yelled as he felt his way forward. "Nasim!"

He found more rocks along the grass-covered ledge, but nothing else. Nothing else.

He tried to open his eyes to see, but was blinded by the biting wind.

He scrabbled along, searching more frantically than before.

"Nasim!"

"Here," he heard faintly, somewhere to his left.

He moved, patting his hands before him.

He found a larger stone, and on its leeward side, he found Nasim huddling with his back against the mountain.

Nikandr grabbed a fistful of robes and pulled him away from his hiding place. Nasim stayed in a ball. Soroush was just behind, and together, the two of them dragged Nasim into the tunnel they'd seen earlier. They pulled themselves deeper and deeper into it as the wind continued to howl and scour and blind. All the while, Nasim coughed so heavily that Nikandr feared he was going to pass out. Long, wracking coughs overtook him, his entire body convulsing from it.

Ten paces they dragged Nasim. Then twenty. And finally they came to a place where the wind was no longer as fierce. They stayed there in the darkness—for little light entered the tunnel now—and waited, panting as the wind's anger slowly eased. Nasim's coughing eased as well, but it sounded wet now, perhaps from blood.

Nikandr took off his water skin and pressed it into Nasim's hands.

He heard him unstopper it and cough between sips.

The sun was beginning to shine through the haze of dust, and at last Nikandr could see Nasim. He was completely covered with fine red dust, as the rest of them had been not so long ago. Strangely, it felt good, as if the ancients had seen fit to tie them even in such a small way as this.

"Are you well?" Nikandr asked.

Nasim took another drink. He stared at Nikandr, then Soroush. Something passed across his eyes—pain mixed with confusion and gratitude—and then he nodded. "Well enough," he said in a croak.

He passed the skin to Nikandr, who took a long pull from it and handed it to Soroush.

"That was Sariya, wasn't it?" Nikandr asked. He'd heard the words from Safwah, but it was still hard to believe.

Nasim smiled. "I suppose in a way it was."

"Sariya and Kaleh," Soroush said, wiping the dust from his face with the palm of his hand. With the sun coming stronger now, he looked primal, like some ancient tribesman, half his face smeared by the deep red stains of blood, the other half covered by light red dust. Nikandr was sure he looked little better.

"*Yeh*," Nasim said, his gaze suddenly distant. "Sariya and Kaleh both."

"Did you see where she went?" Soroush asked.

Nasim shook his head.

"She may be dead," Nikandr said, "fallen from the mountain."

His words were more hopeful than he knew them to be.

"She's gone," Soroush said. "Gone with the Atalayina."

They were silent for a time. Then Nasim coughed and said, "We'll find it."

Soroush laughed at this, long and hard, like an old man amused by the callow thoughts of a child.

CHAPTER THIRTY-SEVEN

Nikandr helped Nasim to limp out from the tunnel and into a world completely different than the one that had been there before the storm. Trees were felled. Branches and boughs lay everywhere. The entire landscape was covered in a fine red dust. It made this place look completely alien, as if Nikandr had walked up the mountain and crossed a doorway to another world. The aether had been explained to him many times—by his mother, by his sister, by Atiana—but he'd never truly appreciated what had been meant by a world filled with but a handful of colors until he'd seen this.

Soroush ranged ahead, looking for Ashan and Sukharam, calling for them from time to time. Nikandr helped Nasim slowly down the steps. It felt good to be with Nasim again, to help him in some small way. Nasim was like a nephew to him now, family by deed if not by blood. As they neared the first switchback, a bird with russet wings and a bright yellow breast fluttered down and landed on the exposed roots of a fallen tree. It seemed to be watching Nikandr and Nasim approach, and it remained even when they came within a few paces of it.

Both of them stopped and stared, too intrigued to move past. The bird chirruped a song, a delicate thing that made Nikandr think of tall trees and hidden songbirds.

"It's beautiful," Nikandr said.

"It's a golden thrush." Nasim stretched his hand toward the bird with his forefinger crooked. "They used to come to Mirashadal on their migrations among the eastern islands."

The bird studied Nasim's finger. It twitched its head this way and that, shook its wings and then lay still.

"There aren't many on the motherland, but those who find them are said to have good fortune."

"Good," Nikandr replied. "We need a bit of that right now."

Nasim waited patiently, unmoving. Nikandr actually believed the thrush was about to leap onto his outstretched finger—it would stare at Nasim's finger, then flap, then stare again—but then it launched into the air and flapped southward and soon was lost among the sparse trees that still clung to the mountainside.

At last they came to the place Nikandr judged that he'd left Ashan and Sukharam to continue on up the mountain. It felt like days since he'd done so, and he wasn't entirely sure this was the same place at all, for the landscape looked completely different. Soroush was searching to the right of the path, so Nikandr left Nasim on the trail and searched along the left-hand side. He found one of their ab-sair a while later. It was dead, crushed by a fallen spruce. He continued and found another ab-sair standing among the devastation, unharmed except for some gashes across its withers and its broad, muscled chest. He found two more of their mounts a short while later, and then, when he was just ready to call for them again, he saw Sukharam, waving atop a pile of broken boughs and branches and other detritus.

"Where's Ashan?" Nikandr asked when he'd come close.

"He's below. Come." And with that Sukharam climbed down into the trees that—now that Nikandr was closer—looked like they'd been carefully placed to form a shelter.

Nikandr climbed up and then down through the hole where Sukharam had disappeared. There he found Ashan leaning over what Nikandr could only describe as the most ancient man he'd ever seen. His eyes were sunken, but they seemed alert. Tears leaked from them. If he was concerned by Nikandr's presence, he didn't show it. He merely moaned and repeated one word over and over.

"What's he saying?" Nikandr said, unable to make it out.

"*Abar*," Sukharam replied. "It means *gone* in Kalhani."

"Gone," Nikandr repeated, trying the word for himself. "What's gone?"

Ashan looked up. His eyes were wide, searching beyond the broken land around him. He was more shaken than Nikandr had ever seen him. "The walls," he said. "With the Tashavir dead—all of them except for Tohrab—the walls around Shadam Khoreh have finally fallen. All that remain now are the wards on Ghayavand. And when those fail, which they surely will, we'll see devastation like never before."

Nikandr didn't know what to say to that. He was right, of course, but he couldn't think clearly in the confines of this place.

"Come," Nikandr said, "there's someone you should meet."

Carefully, they hoisted Tohrab out of the shelter and moved down to level ground. By this time Soroush and Nasim were standing there waiting for them. Sukharam merely stared awkwardly, as if he couldn't quite believe that Nasim was alive. But Ashan's face changed. The horror of moments ago faded and was replaced with a smile like the break of dawn.

He strode forward and took Nasim into a deep embrace, swaying him back and forth as he began to laugh. As the laughter continued, Nasim looked shocked, and perhaps confused at such an emotional display. Who knew the last time Nasim had felt such a thing? Probably not since the two of them were together last. When Ashan's laughter finally faded, he pulled Nasim away and stared into his eyes. "It's good to see you," Ashan said at last.

"You as well," Nasim said softly.

Soroush cleared his throat and motioned to the ab-sair. "We should go."

It brought a measurement of sobriety to the group, and soon they were mounted up and riding back toward the Valley of Kohor.

Nikandr rode near the head of the group. Nasim sat behind him on the saddle, holding Nikandr's waist as the ab-sair plodded onward. It had been a day since the devastation at Shadam Khoreh, and still the ab-sair huffed noisily, clearing their nostrils of the red dust. Ashan and Tohrab came next on another ab-sair, and at the rear were Soroush and Sukharam.

They rode in silence down a path that would deliver them to Kohor by a more easterly route than the one they'd taken here. They didn't wish to risk coming across the Kohori unprepared, but they needed to go back for Atiana and Ushai.

They came to a curve in the trough they were following, a dry wash that looked like it hadn't seen water in months. When they took the curve, a landscape of scrub brush and brittle grasses met them. The land was peppered with boulders, especially along the left slope, where a wide swath of rock and stone had crumbled and fallen across their path. It was not insurmountable, but it would take time to cross, and they'd need to tread carefully, for the stones were uneven and sharp. Far ahead, beyond the slide, Nikandr saw the shoulders of the mountains fall away, revealing blue skies beyond. That was where Kohor lay, where Atiana was held prisoner. He only hoped when the Kohori learned of what had happened that they would listen to reason, that they would hear the truth in their words and not hinder them on their quest to close the rifts on Ghayavand. His stomach gave a twinge every time he thought about Atiana, the pain she'd surely endured.

They were approaching the rock slide, and Nikandr was just about to dismount when he saw movement from his left. No sooner had he turned his head than a figure rose from behind the fallen stones. Then another rose, and another. A dozen, each of them bearing a musket, which they trained on the six of them carefully. Nikandr's heart pounded in his chest. These were the janissaries, the very ones the Kohori had chased off of their eastern border. He thought they might have given up, or returned to Andakhara to resupply, or perhaps rally more men.

But they hadn't. They'd remained and bided their time.

And a moment later, Nikandr understood why. Beyond the men, standing and watching, was a tall woman. She wore the roughspun dress of the wodjana. She had known that they would come to this place, and she had led the Kamarisi's men here. By the ancients, he *recognized* this woman. She was the very one who'd come to Khalakovo and beseeched Ranos to treat with the Haelish Kings. She was the reason Ranos had asked Atiana's sister, Ishkyna, to fly west and speak with them. She was the reason Styophan had been sent afterward with gemstones and muskets and cannons, so that the Haelish could continue their long struggle with the Empire. How in the name of the eldest men could she have found her way here? And what might it mean for Styophan, for their cause in the west?

The wind began to pick up a moment later. Dust swirled at the base of the stones. It grew no more than this, for the leader of the janissaries, a man with a golden broach pinned to his white turban, fired his musket.

The ab-sair behind Nikandr released a long moan and collapsed to the ground. Ashan and Tohrab fell. Ashan managed to roll away, but Tohrab was still too weak, and he fell heavily to the ground.

"Do not summon hezhan," the commander of the janissaries said in Yrstanlan. "Do not summon hezhan," he said again in Mahndi as he pulled a flintlock pistol from his belt and climbed the mound of rocks. As he stepped carefully down the other side, he pointed the pistol at Nikandr. "Come down from those mounts."

Nikandr looked beyond him, to the blue skies of Kohor.

"Come down!" the commander shouted.

Nikandr complied. Nasim followed, as did Soroush and Sukharam.

In short order, all six of them had been locked in cuffs of heavy iron—around their wrists, ankles, and necks. The ones around their wrists were chained, but the ones around their ankles were left free so that they could ride. But the iron would serve to bind the arqesh. Ashan and Sukharam and Nasim and Tohrab— they were all of them gifted, but even they would not be able to touch Adhiya with so much iron around them. Nikandr harbored some hope that Tohrab, born of a different age, might be able to rise above these restraints, but one look at him told Nikandr otherwise. Tohrab was sunken, hunched over in his saddle as if he could barely remain upright, much less draw from the world beyond.

Where they would be taken now, Nikandr didn't know. To Andakhara. To Tethan Hohm. To Alekeşir. And there they would await a Kaymakam, or Bahett, or perhaps even the Kamarisi himself.

They were riding for nearly an hour when the commander looked sharply to his right, then behind him along the line of plodding ab-sair. He reined his mount to the side, looking severely at the landscape behind them.

He drew two of his men away and spoke to them in low, harsh terms. The two men scanned the landscape, as their commander had, and then they rode back the way they'd come.

It took Nikandr a few moments to realize what they were so excited about.

Somehow, improbably, the wodjan was missing. He remembered seeing her as the shackles were being secured, but he couldn't remember her taking a saddle, couldn't remember seeing her on any of the broad-chested beasts as they'd started riding north.

The two janissaries returned at nightfall. They reported to their commander, and he listened, his body going rigid at their news. Clearly they hadn't found her.

As the men began dismounting and setting up camp, the commander locked eyes with Nikandr.

Nikandr didn't know why he did it, but he found it vastly amusing that the woman from Hael had escaped. He laughed, good and long, for the first time in what felt like months.

He wondered if the commander would pull him down from the saddle, perhaps beat him for his impudence. But he did not. He merely set his jaw and pointed his gaze to the fore, as if he knew he deserved it.

PART II

CHAPTER THIRTY-EIGHT

Atiana lay against the floor of a pitch-dark cell. She took measured breaths, drawing in the mineral scent of the air, exhaling it as slowly as she drew it in. She was naked, her skin in direct contact with the cold stone. She tried to convince herself she was surrounded by freezing water, that a servant awaited her return from the aether, that above her lay the bulk of Galostina. But however she tried to fool herself, she knew it was not the same. It felt different. It smelled different. And by the ancients, it was too warm.

More than this, though, she *desperately* wanted to enter the aether—to find Nikandr and the others, to find Ishkyna, to summon what help she could—and desperation was one of the surest things that would keep a Matra from entering the midnight world.

Part of her wished for a censer, wished for a knife and coals so that she could burn her blood and cross over without the embrace of the frigid waters of the drowning basin. Another part was horrified at the thought. And another part still wanted to enter the aether as she had on the small island Duzol and in the city of Vihrosh on Galahesh. She'd done these things. Why couldn't she do it again? Why did she need water *or* blood?

She shivered.

The blood. Her own blood. How burning blood could allow her to cross over she had no idea. She wanted to believe that some combination of time and place and her own mindset had allowed her to cross over, and yet there was no denying what had happened.

She sat up, waited for the pain of remaining immobile for so long to pass, and then sat with her legs folded beneath her. Before she knew what she was doing, she'd pulled her hands over her head as if there were smoke rising before her now. She gripped her hands tightly to keep them from shaking.

She hadn't eaten in two days. She'd been given water, but very little. And yet she knew it wasn't these things that caused her mind to wander, to lose touch with the solidity of the world around her. It was the tūtūn. It had somehow remained within her ever since the ritual three nights ago. When her mind was at its weakest, she would slip into some memory, very often those that had run through her that night, and it would feel as though she were there, out in the desert, drawing smoke over her hair, or in the aether speaking with her sister. When she fell asleep she would wake to someone's voice, and it would take her long, panic-stricken moments for her to realize it was her *own* voice.

At times she would cry, but soon after she would force herself to stop. She would stand in her earthen cell, vowing to take whatever the Kohori had in store for her. She was a child of the islands, after all. What terrified her to the bone, however, was the thought that she was losing her own mind, because instead of fading, the memories of cutting her own wrist, of the sizzle as each drop struck the hot censer, of the acrid smell that lifted from it soon after, had come more often, and with greater intensity.

Light suddenly shone down upon her hands. She blinked from the intensity of it and saw with crystal clarity how badly her hands were shaking. She'd had no idea. She gripped them again as her breath released in halting increments, like snow as it slips in those silent moments before an avalanche begins.

But then came sound. A thump. Creaking.

The light dimmed, became brighter. The sounds approached, and she remembered that this place, this cell, was deep underground. Despite the pain it brought, she stared up into the bright light. There was a ladder there. Someone was descending. Who, she couldn't tell. Her eyes were watering, and blinking did nothing to help.

The person—a woman from the shape of her—reached the bottom of the cell and stared down at Atiana. After a few moments, she sat and leaned against the wall.

It was Ushai. She held a set of white robes, which she handed to Atiana.

Atiana accepted the robes, but did nothing with them. "What are you doing here?"

It made no sense. She'd been told that the others had left two days ago, the morning after she'd been put down in this cell. They'd answered few of her questions, but her query of where her friends and companions had gone had been answered coldly. "They left," the Kohori man had told her. "They attacked our people and left."

She thought surely *everyone* had left. Why, then, was Ushai still here?

"Can you climb?" she asked.

Atiana stared at her hands. They were shaking much less now. She licked her lips and nodded. "I think so."

"Then come."

Ushai stood and stepped up the ladder. Atiana pulled on the robes Ushai had given her and followed as best she could, but it was slow going. Her hands shook as she moved up one rung, two. Her feet slipped, until by the time she neared the top she was sure she would fall and crush her legs against the cold stone below. But she didn't fall, and Ushai helped her out into sunlight so bright it caused pain to look upon. She couldn't move. She couldn't do anything but hide her face in the crook of her arm.

Finally the pain eased and she was able to send quick glances to the landscape around her. She was outside the village. A hundred paces away were the first of the mudbrick homes with their thatched roofs.

Ushai stared at Atiana with an unconcerned look. She held her damaged arm close to her body, as if it had been injured. She stiffened when she realized Atiana was staring at it.

"Where are the others?" Atiana asked.

"I don't know," she said and walked away.

Atiana followed. They walked toward the center of the village. It took time as slowly as Atiana was moving, but eventually they passed the tall obelisk. It looked like a bloody finger pointing accusingly at the sky. Ushai continued toward a round building, the largest in the village. Two Kohori men, wearing the full red robes so that Atiana could only see their eyes, nodded to Ushai as she approached. She nodded back and passed through the open doors of the building.

Atiana had never been inside this place, but when she entered, she stopped and stared. Glittering stones had been worked into the brick in the patterns of the heavens. Larger bits of stone—most of them white, but some yellow or pink or blue—caught the light coming into the room from a hole in the ceiling. At the hole was a sculpture of mirrors crafted so that it spread the sunlight throughout the room, where it lit these manmade constellations from the nighttime sky. Atiana could nearly picture the blanket of stars that occupied the sky above, so different than what she was used to among the islands of the Grand Duchy.

In the center of the massive space was a stout table made of stone. Upon it, laid out over a black blanket, was a young woman. A beam of light shone down from above directly onto her face. Ushai led Atiana here, standing aside to let her look at the woman unobstructed. Atiana thought she should know her. She looked familiar. And yet, Atiana couldn't place her.

Beyond the table stood a brazier with hot coals glowing within it. The air above it wavered. What the Kohori might do with such a thing here, she had no idea. Near the brazier stood a pedestal with a fine red cloth thrown over it. Atiana wondered what lay beneath the cloth, but she was too transfixed by the vision of this place and this strange woman. She paced closer, moving over a stone floor inlaid with bits of glinting black stone. The woman. Her eyes were elegant. Her chin strong. Her hair was the color of rich, aged oak. She was so familiar...

At last Atiana reached the very edge of the table. There was a bandage wrapped around the woman's left shoulder. Blood seeped through, making Atiana wonder just how much blood she'd lost, how long she'd been unconscious.

"Who—"

Atiana stopped. No sooner had the word touched her lips than she knew.

It couldn't be. It was impossible.

And yet, there was an undeniable resemblance. She had Kaleh's eyes. And her nose and chin and lips. Her features were fuller—this was a woman grown—but there was no doubt that the youth Atiana had seen on Galahesh was hidden within those features. She'd seen her only eighteen months before, in Vihrosh. It was her hand, in fact, her touch, that had drawn her fully into Sariya's clutches. She'd been only eleven then. Eleven. And here she was now, a girl that looked as though she'd seen twenty summers.

"How?" Atiana asked.

"I do not know." She motioned to Kaleh's sleeping form, as if that were answer enough. "She was found by the Kohori to the south, near the edge of the valley. She was unconscious."

Kaleh's eyes moved beneath her lids as if she were having a terribly vivid dream. Her lips parted, and she began to speak. At least, Atiana *thought* she was speaking. She couldn't actually hear any words. Even when she leaned over so that her ear was just above Kaleh's lips, she heard only a low susurrus, like the whisper of the sea within the halls of Galostina.

"Has she awoken?" Atiana asked.

"Not since she was brought here."

Atiana's mind had been muddled in the cell. She'd been confused and off-balance from the climb and the light and the mystery of Kaleh. But her wits were finally starting to return to her. She stared into Ushai's eyes. "Where are the others?"

"I don't know."

"And yet you remain."

"I am here because I wish to be."

"You joined us to find Nasim and the Atalayina."

"Spoken like a woman of the Grand Duchy. Yours is not the only way, Atiana Vostroma. There are others, and the Kohori have opened my eyes."

A cold fury rose up inside Atiana. "You *abandoned* us."

"I left to find my own way. The world needs to be healed." She motioned to Kaleh. "Sariya has returned to them, just as they always believed."

"*You* can't believe it, though. You know what Sariya is like. She'll destroy us all if she has her way."

"I know that, and so do the Kohori. They're not so foolish as you believe. They were right about Sariya's return, and they were right about the Atalayina."

"She has it?"

Ushai paused, but then stepped over to the pedestal and pulled the red cloth away. Sitting upon the striated column of glittering granite was a stone of blue. Sunlight did not hit the Atalayina directly, and yet it still gathered much on its own, as if jealous of attention. Bright veins of silver and gold seemed lit from within, and in that instant, in this place deep within the wide, dry ocean of the Gaji, it looked deep, like a well one could use to peer to the center of the earth to see its soul.

Atiana stepped forward, suddenly and inexplicably nervous. She could feel the warmth from the glowing coals within the brazier to her right. She thought Ushai might stop her, but Ushai merely watched, her eyes passive, as Atiana approached the fabled stone of the Al-Aqim.

Atiana reached out a trembling hand. She touched the stone's cool surface, wondering what secrets lay hidden within, wondering indeed how they might be unlocked.

When she submerged herself into the waters of the drowning basin, as her skin was chilled and she neared the point at which she might slip over to the world between, she felt as though she could embrace one or the other—the material world or the aether—but not both. To try to remain grounded in the material world and the ephemeral world of the aether would doom her. She felt the same way now. Except instead of two worlds, she felt as though she were touching all three—the material world of Erahm, the spirit world of Adhiya, and the place between, the aether. She felt as though she could take a step in any one direction, and embrace any one of these worlds like never before. The material world of Erahm and the aether were two worlds she was familiar with; they caused her no fear. Adhiya, however, was something else entirely. Were she to take one more step toward it, she was sure she would be drawn into it, just as the hezhan did when they crossed over to *her* world. She would be lost, consumed by the hezhan that waited on the other side.

Atiana felt a hand on her shoulder. She turned and found Ushai staring at her with a look of mild concern, but when Atiana blinked and stepped away from the stone, her eyes relaxed.

"The two of them..." Ushai spread her hands wide like a havaqiram summoning the wind. Strangely enough, it was the ruined and shriveled remains of her left hand that motioned to the Atalayina, the one that had been burned trying to reach for a piece of that very stone. "The stone that came from this place at the dawn of time, and the woman who touched it on the day the world nearly broke. The Kohori would have her back, Atiana, daughter of Radia."

Atiana stared at Kaleh's young, smooth face. "And they want *me* to give her to them?"

"Just so."

Atiana struggled to understand. "Why would I do that?"

"Because you wish to know more. Because without Sariya's knowledge, the world might never be healed. And that knowledge is now more important than ever."

Atiana stepped up to Kaleh's side. "You want me to enter the aether."

Ushai stepped to the other side of the table. She regarded Atiana with heavily lidded eyes. She leaned down and from beneath the table—perhaps from a shelf Atiana hadn't noticed—retrieved a brass censer and a small, keen knife. She set the censer on Kaleh's stomach. The knife followed with a dull clink as it was set on top of the censer. "I cannot enter the aether as you can."

Atiana glanced back at the brazier, her mouth suddenly dry.

She'd done those things in the desert, finding her way to the aether with her own blood, but it had felt distant ever since reaching Kohor. It had felt like someone else had done it, not her. Even after the visions she'd had in the hut while taking in the smoke of the tūtūn, the memories of the Haelish ritual had felt distant, like a dream. But now it was all rushing back. The censer and the knife sat before her, rising slowly with Kaleh's breath, falling a moment later.

What she found might wake Sariya. It might give the Kohori what they wanted. But Ushai had the right of it. Atiana couldn't let this opportunity slip past. She had to know more about the stone.

As Atiana took up the bone-handled knife and the cool censer, Ushai smiled.

But Atiana grit her jaw. Ushai's approval felt foul, like a betrayal of all she'd ever known.

CHAPTER THIRTY-NINE

The brazier clacked as Atiana used the wide wooden handles to set it on the glittering stone floor. The sound of it echoed harshly in the immensity of the space. After taking a deep breath, she set the censer onto the coals and waited for it to heat. She held the knife in her left hand. Already her palm and fingers were sweaty. She swallowed as Ushai stood several paces away, staring down like an expectant mother.

Atiana pulled back the right sleeve of her coarse linen robes. She slipped the blade of the knife beneath the bandages, the ones that had been set days ago after Atiana and the others had arrived. She pulled the knife sharply along the light cloth, cutting it free.

She placed the knife near the other cuts and pressed it into her skin. The bright pain felt like the bursting of the sun from behind dark clouds. She watched as blood pooled in the cut, ran down the length of her wrist, and dripped down onto the censer.

The drops sizzled. The blood blackened. Smoke rose.

She felt sick, and still she squeezed her arm, forcing more blood to flow.

When the bleeding had slowed to a trickle, she leaned over the censer and pulled the rising smoke toward her. As the smoke sighed across the skin of her face, over her tightly bound blonde hair, she allowed her feelings of disloyalty to shed from her frame. She gathered more of the smoke with motions like a child trying to guide a dandelion seed drifting on the wind. She drew the smoke down along her chest, along her stomach and thighs. She drew it along her arms and across her fingers, never allowing her hands to touch. The feelings of fear, of being alone in this place without Nikandr, without any hope of her sister, Ishkyna, finding her, faded.

The feelings of isolation, however, she embraced, for this was the touchstone of the Matri. As important as it was not to fear the aether, it was important to understand its nature, and the aether brought nothing if not isolation.

The sounds of her breathing faded. The motions of her arm became rhythmic, trancelike.

And soon... Soon...

Atiana drifts in the dark. Before her is her own body, still rhythmically drawing smoke over her frame. She is white against a field of midnight blue, as are most things when viewed in the dark of the aether. Ushai stands near, watching, waiting.

And there is Kaleh.

She lies on the stone slab like an offering. She's outlined in white, but within her, subtler hues shift along her frame like sunlight against the bed of a shoal in calm seas. It's been six full seasons since Atiana saw her last, but she immediately recognizes Sariya's presence. It would be impossible not to. The two of them had seen one another's thoughts. They had warred against one another. Sariya had overtaken her with her subtle ways, making Atiana believe that Sariya's thoughts had been her own.

Atiana approaches, then stops short, shocked, for drifting from the wound on Kaleh's shoulder is a faint whiff of smoke. Like the dying breath of a snuffed candle the smoke rises and dissipates. Unlike the bright outline of Kaleh's form, it is darker than the near blackness of the aether's deep ocean blue. It flows from Kaleh's wound toward the Atalayina, and from there it is lost, drawn into some world known only to that ancient stone.

Never in all her years in the aether has she seen such a thing. She wonders if it was something she merely overlooked—its subtle nature would make it difficult to sense—but she has seen many wounded, and with more grievous wounds than Kaleh has now. It might be the nature of the Atalayina, a stone whose hidden powers are difficult to define, but she thinks not. More likely it's due to the ritual she performed to enter this place; the drawing of her own blood perhaps makes her more attuned to such things.

She approaches the Atalayina, hoping to learn more. Here, as well as outside the aether, the stone feels bottomless. There have been times when the aether pulled her consciousness wide that she felt similar things. The ocean depths, especially those to the north of Galahesh, brought on similar feelings, but the Atalayina is so much more. It feels as though the merest touch would draw her in, where she would fall until the end of time.

She will not be cowed, however. The stone is wondrous and intricate, but she refuses to bend to the fear that grips the center of her being.

She reaches out, brushes it.

And the moment she does, it embraces her. Unlike when she'd touched the stone before taking the dark, she feels not life, not Adhiya and Erahm, but the vastness of the aether. This does not cause her fear. She is instead awestruck by the immensity of it, the completeness of the void. Never has she felt so foreign a thing as this, and she wonders if this is how Ishkyna feels when she traverses the currents of the aether.

She rejects the notion as soon as it surfaces. Ishkyna felt life. Always life. She'd told Atiana this many times. This felt like the aether might have existed before Erahm itself was created. Before Adhiya was created.

It was like this, she thought, as the fates came into being.

Where then were they? It felt as though she should be able to, if not *commune* with them, at least *sense* them. But there was nothing. This was a void so complete that she wondered how anything could have come from it.

Slowly, reluctantly, she draws herself inward. She drifts away from the stone and returns to herself.

In this exact moment, Atiana's world goes white. It feels as though she's been laid over someone's palm, her skin slit open from chin to groin, fingers picking through the viscera within. She rigors so tightly that her bones must be breaking, her tendons tearing and ripping from joints that sear with pain. She wants to scream, but in some disconnected way she knows that she cannot. She is no longer tied to her body. She has been set aside as another pushes her way past.

Sariya.

She knows it is Sariya.

And she can do nothing to stop her. Nothing. All this time, and she is still powerless against her.

But there is another.

She is so near, so linked with Sariya, that it is hard to discern her form, to sense her presence at all, and yet even through the pain Atiana can see her like a deeper shadow lying within another.

There is no doubt that this is Kaleh. She pulls at Sariya, claws at her, draws her back toward Kaleh's own body. Sariya clings to Atiana, plunging her into a pain like being set afire. Only in those failing moments does she feel the burning pain along her wrist.

The small cut. She feels this, and her wrist and her hand. She senses the smoke that still drifts upward. There is something raw in this, something that taps the center of her soul, and it is this that she uses now. The smoke around her provides protection, for it is made of her own blood. It is *of* her. Sariya tries to prevent it, but Atiana retreats behind this barrier, and soon the battle has turned. Sariya is drawn further and further down by Kaleh, back into the sleeping form of the strange young woman on the stone slab.

Soon her presence is gone, locked away behind the trembling eyes, and Atiana is left alone in the aether, which now seems wider and deeper than it ever has before. She doesn't want to admit failure—there would be much to learn from Kaleh, or even Sariya—but she cannot hope to attempt such a thing. Not now. Not as exhausted as she is.

Atiana woke, coughing not from smoke but the crippling pain her body was experiencing. For a moment the pain was every bit as deep as it had been while in the aether, except now it felt much more a part of her, a reality upon waking from a dream.

She collapsed to the floor, stared up at the glittering ceiling above. The hole in the roof looked as though the sun had been broken into a thousand pieces, shattering into stars that splayed across the swath of the heavens.

Footsteps approached. Ushai stared down at her with disappointed eyes. She'd hoped that Atiana would draw Sariya forth.

Ushai leaned down, offering her good hand to Atiana.

Atiana slapped it away and stood on her own. "You used me. You wanted to deliver Sariya to the Kohori."

"That is what the Kohori wanted"—Ushai shrugged, glancing over to Kaleh— "but in truth I don't know which I hoped for. They are linked—mother and daughter—and I wonder if even the fates themselves foresaw this."

"You doubt that they did?"

"Years ago I never would have doubted the vision of the fates. Today, I am not so sure."

A low voice came from behind Atiana. "Can she control the child?"

Atiana turned and found a man standing at the entrance to the building. The last time she'd seen him near the obelisk shortly after waking in this village, his raiment had been fine, much finer than the rest of the other Kohori. Now, though, he wore a robe of deep red with thick black stripes at the sleeves, near his wrists, and along the hem near his ankles. This was Habram, the leader of the Kohori.

Those many days ago he had looked intense, but not cruel, not unkind.

Not so, now.

Now he looked angry at the mere presence of Atiana. His dark eyes stared into hers with a look that was not unlike those she'd seen on the faces of the Maharraht, especially those that had been captured and sentenced, except Habram's look was even more intense, as if he held Atiana accountable for all that had ever happened to his people.

The question he'd asked—*can she control the child?*—had been asked of Ushai. Atiana understood exactly what he'd meant. They'd wanted Atiana to control Kaleh so that Sariya might surface. But Atiana couldn't—at least not yet—and

Ushai knew it.

Ushai shook her head to Habram, after which Habram snapped his fingers twice. It sounded like the click a musket hammer made when it was pulled into place. Moments later two men in red robes entered. They approached her, and Atiana was sure they meant to kill her. She couldn't understand why, but there was no mistaking the cold look in their eyes.

She backed away, but the moment she did, they sprinted forward.

"Help me!" Atiana called to Ushai.

But Ushai merely stared.

The first of them snatched Atiana's wrist. She managed to pull it away, but he grabbed her again. Atiana used the palm of her hand to strike him on the nose. He seemed surprised, for he staggered back for a moment, but then the other man grabbed her, and together they led her away out of the building, through the village, and back to the deep cell where she'd been kept these last few days.

The sun was now high, and the heat of the desert was up. The landscape wavered in the distance like a dream. Beyond the hole the landscape was largely flat, but there was a small copse of trees in a depression in the land perhaps one hundred paces beyond, and it was here that Atiana's gaze was drawn. Something there had moved, she was sure of it, but now that she looked, she could see nothing.

The taller of the two men pulled back the wooden door over the cell and pointed to it. She refused him, however, hoping to get another look at the stand of small, withered trees.

"Go," the shorter one said, the one she'd struck. "Go, or I throw you in."

She took to the ladder, her eyes widening as she took in the landscape one last time. She continued down into the darkness, the chill of the space overtaking her as she did so. When she got to the bottom, the ladder was drawn up and the lid replaced, plunging this cold, lonely place into darkness once more.

As she sat there in the darkness, the scene of the desert played before her eyes. There, peeking out from a shadowed crook where two boughs met, was a woman.

The wodjan, Atiana knew. The woman from Hael. The one who'd come to her in the Gaji as they'd fled toward Kohor.

CHAPTER FORTY

S tyophan strode with Rodion down the widest thoroughfare in Alekeşir. Thousands of people on horses and carts and walking on foot flowed through the city, its lifeblood. In a city he was familiar with—like Volgorod—the people would be faceless, something he knew, something he was comfortable with. Here he was aware of so much more: the weapons the janissaries wore as they rode two by two down the city street, the children wearing cut-up blankets for winter boots who watched from the ends of alleys, the mistrustful stares of the people they passed. Styophan knew he was imagining much of the danger around him, but it would only take one—one person alerting the janissaries or the guardsmen of Kasir Irabahce—and all would be lost.

He and Rodion crossed a high, curving bridge over the Vünkal and continued deeper into the city, toward the kasir. The buildings here were tall stone edifices with wide steps and fat columns carved with rearing drakhen and falcons and horses ridden by men with tall spears. These buildings stood straight, shoulders squared, watching one another as if the people milling below were nothing they need concern themselves with. Ahead, the road met a circle bigger than some villages Styophan had been to. It connected the eight major arteries of the central city, and inside of it, at the center of a large green lawn, was a dome with stout fluted columns.

Styophan nudged Rodion, who walked next to him. "You see?" he asked in Yrstanlan.

Rodion looked ahead, confused at first, but then he eyed the open space within the dome. Standing there was a bronze statue of a man holding a spear in one hand and a sword in the other. The man stared outward toward the horizon, his face serene and confident, secure in the belief that none would dare challenge him. The afternoon sun against the white buildings around the circle made the bronze gleam. It was new, this statue, erected in Hakan's image after he'd died on Galahesh. He'd been taken by Muqallad and driven against an iron spike to forge the Atalayina anew. Quite a difference from the scene that stood before him.

Rodion rolled his eyes. "A bit grandiose, isn't it?"

"*Hakan* was grandiose. They're *all* grandiose."

"They say it's rebuilt each time a kamarisi dies."

Styophan nodded. "They take every last dram of bronze and build a new statue from the old."

"Subtle."

Styophan laughed. The Empire was nothing if not confident and full of symbolism. You may draw our blood, the statue said, but Yrstanla will survive.

As they came closer, Styophan could see the workmen behind the stout iron chains that barred traffic from reaching the green lawn around the dome. They were cleaning the steps with buckets and brushes. Several were running cloths along a set of steps near the very edge of the dome's floor that led to a podium. The podium itself was ornamented by stone and two men were painting it carefully in bright, gold paint.

"There," Styophan said softly.

Rodion stared at the podium, and then began taking in his surroundings, the streets leading in, the buildings that surrounded the circle. "He'll be difficult to reach."

This was the place where the Kamarisi came, twice per year, to address his people. He would do so two days hence, and it was the best chance they'd have to take him. If he managed to find his way back to Kasir Irabahce, it would be nearly impossible to reach him. It had to be here.

Still, it would not be easy. The Kamarisi was nothing if not concerned with imagery, with presence. It was said that the circle was filled with hundreds of janissaries, and most if not all of the Kiliç Şaik.

How they would reach the Kamarisi he had no idea. The words of the Haelish queen still haunted him.

When you go to Alekeşir, Elean had said, *the path will lead to your graves.*

A hulking wagon with a cage at the back rolled past Styophan, blocking his view momentarily. From within the cage, men and women with vacant eyes stared. All except a small girl with shorn hair and bright green eyes. Many wore clothing of fine weave. The girl herself wore a dress of rich silk. She could have been no more than six, and she was near to tears as she watched the city pass by around her. She locked eyes with Styophan, staring at his good eye, then his patch, then his good eye again. She pleaded with him to do something, anything, but moments later the wagon had continued around the circle, and she was lost from view. It left Styophan feeling like a coward.

"A cruel place is Yrstanla," Rodion said.

Styophan leaned over and spit. "Cruel, indeed."

He surveyed the lawn as a dozen janissaries rode by. It would be easy enough for Styophan and his men to position themselves among the crowd when the Kamarisi came to address the people of Alekeşir. The Haelish were another matter. They were tall and muscular. They'd stand out no matter where they were stationed.

"They'll have to be hidden," Rodion said, echoing Styophan's own thoughts.

Styophan stared across the grand circle, to the place where the wagon with the girl was now turning. The beginnings of a plan were forming. There would be many men here. Hundreds of soldiers, well trained, all bent on protecting the Kamarisi at all costs. But this was a place that hadn't been attacked in centuries. One Kamarisi had been murdered at this very place, but that had been generations ago, and it had been a betrayal from within, not an attack from an enemy of the state. They could not count on the Kamarisi's men being lax—they would all be well prepared—but if Styophan could attack to the fore, forcing the Kamarisi to retreat down one of these wide avenues, they might be caught in a place where they least expected an attack.

Two days, Styophan thought. They had two days to scout the surrounding area and make preparations.

Styophan and Rodion took the time to walk the entirety of the circle. Rodion stopped and bought two apples from a cart using a few of the Empire's coins they'd been given by Datha. He handed one out for Styophan, but Styophan wasn't hungry. He was too worried. Rodion shrugged and took a loud bite of his apple.

"I'm beginning to think those crones were wrong," Rodion said as he crunched on his apple.

"About what?"

Rodion leaned in and spoke more quietly. "With so many tall men at our side, and the Kamarisi here"—pointed with his apple toward the massive dome—"we may just pull this off."

"Have you already forgotten about Edik?"

Rodion shook his head. "I loved Edik like a brother, Styopha. You know this. But, ancients preserve him, he never knew when to keep his mouth shut."

They stopped as a palanquin borne by eight stout men shuttled past them and down a narrow street that curved as badly as the mighty Vünkal.

"I hope you're right," Styophan said.

They continued until they'd reached the very place from which they'd begun. Styophan was watching a vendor standing behind with a cart filled with sugared pistachios and almonds and some strange bone-white nut Styophan had never seen before. Styophan had seen him when they'd arrived at the circle, but now he was staring at the two of them and Styophan wasn't sure if he was suspicious or if he just wanted them to come closer to his cart.

"Styopha…"

Styophan was just about to walk over, to buy something if only to find out what he was about, when Rodion elbowed him in the small of his back.

Styophan turned toward the circle.

More janissaries were riding past, twenty in all. Unlike the ones that had ridden past earlier, these were dressed in full regalia, and they rode tall black horses, beasts whose coats gleamed under the high sun. These were men from the kasir or he was a miller's daughter.

Rodion, however, wasn't staring at the janissaries. He was staring to the rear of their line. Behind them came a wagon, and behind *it* were twenty more janissaries. Quite a guard for a few slaves or prisoners, but it was notable since the people in the cage were clearly being taken to Irabahce.

Styophan was just about to ask Rodion what he'd seen when the people in the cage registered.

Something black and bottomless opened up inside his chest and widened until it felt as though Styophan would fall inside.

How? he thought. How could they have arrived *here*?

At the front of the cage, holding the bars as the wagon rolled on, were two young men, both dressed in the robes of the Aramahn. One was Nasim, the boy who'd nearly caused the destruction of Khalakovo seven years ago. He'd seen him on the ship he and Nikandr had taken from Rafsuhan back to Khalakovo after Muqallad had fused two pieces of the Atalayina together. The other was Sukharam, the boy Nasim had brought back with him from Ghayavand.

Curled near their feet was a man lying down and facing away from Styophan. He seemed old and frail, for his robes hung loosely, revealing the curve of hip-bone and shoulder. Even his emaciated ribs showed through the cloth.

Toward the back of the cage were three more men.

Soroush Wahad al Gatha. Ashan Kida al Ahrumea.

And his Lord Prince, Nikandr Iaroslov himself.

They were all of them bound in iron. At their wrists, their ankles, and their necks were cuffs and collars of black iron. The janissaries knew, of course, the powers of these men, and had prevented their use with those dulling restraints.

His first instinct was to call out, but he realized how foolish this would be. The janissaries would not know that there were Anuskayan men in the city. They could not.

So his next fear was that Nikandr would recognize him.

"Say nothing," Styophan said.

He worried now that Nikandr *would* see him, that he would call or wave or do something else foolish, but on the opposite side of the roadway, the statue of Hakan had caught their attention—that or the sheer level of industry in and around the dome. They all stared that way, Ashan and Nikandr speaking with one another in low tones.

Just as they were passing, however, Nasim looked his way. His gaze darted to Nikandr, then back to Styophan, but he said nothing.

Thank the ancients for small favors.

All too quickly they were gone, but in their wake was a host of harrowing thoughts.

They couldn't go through with their attack, not as they'd planned it, for to do so would be to abandon Nikandr and the others. Nasim was the key to healing the rifts, and if what Nikandr said was true, so was Sukharam. He had little use for Soroush, but Ashan was known far and wide as a wise and powerful man.

These men were needed. The islands needed them. The world needed them. He couldn't have abandoned them even if Nikandr weren't here.

"Come," Styophan said. "We need to speak with Datha."

Rodion fell into step alongside him. "It isn't going to be pleasant, is it?"

"*Hayir*, it is not."

Styophan walked along the high bank of the Vünkal. He walked alone. He'd sent Rodion ahead, for he needed to think. Needed to figure out how he was going to tell Datha that they couldn't continue, not until they'd saved Nikandr and Nasim and the others.

On his right was a low wall, the top of a stone divide that separated the fish market and the warehouses from the quays and the water down below. The ships—barges and flat fishing ships and other light watercraft—bobbed as the lights of Alekeşir, vast Alekeşir, played over the water. Beyond the river, the city's landscape rolled like an inland sea. It was night, and the moon was but a sliver in the sky. Much of the city was lit softly by lanterns on tall posts—more of the ostentatious lifestyle of Yrstanla. Had this been Volgorod, the city would be near pitch dark. Not so in Alekeşir. No doubt the oil that filled those lanterns had traveled a thousand leagues from the sea, or overland from some distant corner of the Empire.

The market had closed, but there were still men talking. He heard a child giggling, then a squeal and another giving chase. Somewhere in the city, a dog barked until it yelped and fell silent.

Styophan stopped for a moment, allowing the sights and sounds and smells to wash over him. He'd been thinking of what to do ever since leaving the circle, but he'd come up with nothing. He didn't know how he could save Nikandr. He wasn't even sure that he should. Perhaps the wiser choice was to continue with their plans and kill the Kamarisi. Perhaps then, in the chaos, they could steal in to Irabahce and take Nikandr back.

When you go to Alekeşir, the path will lead to your graves.

But what of His Lord Prince? The wodjan said that they would kill the Kamarisi. Did that mean he should go on with that plan? Or did it mean he might save Nikandr and still kill the Lord of Yrstanla?

"It's not safe here after too long," called a rough voice.

Styophan turned and found the quay master, an old man with a limp and a crooked jaw, approaching him. His hair was long and curled. Greasy. He had not seemed like a man worthy of much trust, but neither had he seemed overly loyal to the Kasir. With the coin they'd brought with them, Styophan had figured it would be enough to buy several days silence at the least, and before today he'd figured that was all they would need.

The man approached and stood next to Styophan, looking out over the city, but not quite looking away from Styophan, either. He smelled of alcohol and garlic.

"I remember," Styophan said. "You told me when we arrived."

"From Avolina..." He let the words sit there between them.

"From Avolina," Styophan relied easily.

"Said you'd been sent by the Kaymakam. Waiting for orders to head toward the war in the east."

Styophan remained silent, but he turned himself toward the quay master, a not-so-subtle sign that he'd better get to the point.

He took the hint and squared himself up, and when he spoke again, it was with a notably softer voice. His voice creaked, though, as if he'd caught the cough but had never rid himself of it. "Might've been a messenger that came from Avolina this morning. Might've been asking for the soldiers who went through their city. Took two barges on the order of the regent himself. Said"—he took a deep breath and exhaled slowly—"they were looking for news on a young janissary that'd gone missing the day those soldiers left."

Styophan shrugged. "I don't know anything about that."

"Which is why I sent him to the southern quays. Said barges go up and down the Vünkal every day, but that none had stopped from Avolina at my docks. You know what he said to me after that?"

"I don't."

"Said they searched along the river. Said they found bits of his uniform. Tatters, he said, that caught up in the branches of some tree. A half-league further they found the head of his horse lying in the shallows. It'd been cut clean from its body. Clean, he'd said, as if from a single swing of a blade."

Styophan could feel himself breathing now, his chest expanding, contracting. The quay master was watching him closely for any sign that he'd known about this, but Styophan had been through much. He knew how to master his emotions. "What of it?" he asked.

"I don't get into people's personal matters as a rule. But this? I worked on a farm when I was young. I know what it takes to cut through that much meat. That much bone."

Styophan laughed. "Tales grow in the telling."

"That they do, but this one seemed to have a fair bit of truth in it. There aren't many who can do that sort of thing. But the Haelish?" He nodded grimly. "Maybe the Haelish could."

Styophan nodded in return, carefully preparing himself to snatch the knife from his belt if it was needed. He didn't want to, though—he'd seen enough killing on this ill-fated journey through Hael and Yrstanla—but he would do it in a moment if he thought this man would turn on him. "I imagine they could. They could cleave *me* in half. And you too." Styophan looked around theatrically, laughing again. "Do you think they're coming to tear the walls down?"

The quay master smiled. He looked out over the city again, as if he'd just shared something with an old friend—a strange story, a bit of gossip. "He comes back, you want me to clear him away?"

Styophan had paid him well for the berths that were furthest into the inlet by the warehouses—the ones most hidden from casual view both from the walkway above the quay and the river itself. He'd not told the quay master why, and the crooked old man hadn't asked, but he was no fool. He wanted to know if Styophan was nervous. He was baiting Styophan. If Styophan said he wanted to keep the messenger away, he'd know Styophan was guilty, and he'd tell the city guard. The kasir would know before the day was out about the strange barges on the river.

"*Hayir*," Styophan said while shaking his head. "Send him my way if you seem him again."

"Will do."

"Too bad about the horse," Styophan said as he walked toward the ramp leading down to the quay.

"*Evet*. Too bad."

CHAPTER FORTY-ONE

Datha met Styophan at the stairs to the hold. He led Styophan to a place on the floor where a horsehair blanket was laid out, and there Datha sat, motioning for Styophan to do the same.

Low-burning lanterns hung from the wooden beams, shedding meager light on the mass of Haelish men. *They're stacked tighter than cordwood*, Styophan thought. Most of the Haelish sat as Datha did, but others were up, hunched over from the low ceiling, walking back and forth simply to stretch their legs or to get some sense that they weren't trapped in this place until their true mission began. *Such men aren't made for life aboard a ship.*

The air smelled of man and piss and shit. At the far end, three of the men lay on pallets. They coughed and moaned, and though Styophan couldn't see them clearly, he knew that their eyes would be dark, the pits of their arms and knees blackened. They were close to death. He could hear it in the way they coughed. It was not only wet, but it went on and on. Soon they would start coughing up blood.

"There were none with the withering when we left," Styophan said to Datha. "And now there are three, laid low in less than a week."

Styophan shook his head. "A week…"

What were they to do when the wasting progressed so far in a mere handful of days? It used to be that it would take months for such symptoms as these men were starting to manifest. Was it now the same on the islands? Was it perhaps even worse? He couldn't help but think of Rozalyna. Had she been stricken? Was she already dead? And if the pace of the disease was accelerating, what it would be like in a month? In a year? Would men die in mere days? Would children fall in hours? Who would be left in this world if the disease continued unchecked?

Thankfully none of his own men had been infected so far. He knew that was merely the ancients shining down on them, but it could not last forever.

Something had changed in the world. He could feel it, and so could Datha. The very *air* felt heavier. There were times when Styophan felt it harder to breathe, harder to pick himself up and make his way through the hours.

"You wished to speak," Datha prompted.

Styophan realized he was staring at the sick men, and several of the Haelish warriors had stopped what they were doing and were staring back, their faces hard.

"I did," Styophan said, turning self-consciously to Datha. For a moment, Styophan could think of no way to begin. After a long, uncomfortable silence, he said simply, "The ways of the world are strange."

Datha frowned at this. "Something happened today? On your walk?"

Styophan nodded slowly, and seeing no way to approach it gently, went straight to the point. "I saw my lord, the Prince of Khalakovo, Nikandr Iaroslov. He was being taken in a cage to the Kasir."

"Your lord. Here."

"*Evet.*"

Datha rubbed the stubble along his cheek and laughed grimly. "Did he see you?"

"*Hayir*, but the boy, Nasim, the one I told you about, did. By now he would have told Nikandr."

"Strange days, indeed, Styophan."

"You see why I'm concerned. They cannot be left for the Kamarisi, or Bahett."

"Cannot?"

"Cannot," Styophan said. "We must save them, Datha. We must bring them to safety and return them home. My Lord left for the Gaji nearly two years ago to find Nasim, and now, at last, he has. He may even have found the Atalayina."

Datha frowned, all trace of humor gone. "And what is that to me?"

Styophan turned and pointed to the men at the far side of the hold. "Look to your warriors for your answer. Without ever having lifted a sword against the Kamarisi, they're dying. Your women and children are dying as well. Mine too. And it's because of the rifts. My Lord Khalakovo has gone to heal it, and Nasim is the key. If you abandon them now, you'll be turning your back on your own people."

"We came for a purpose."

"True, but things change in war. You adjust as the enemy adjusts. And make no mistake, the withering is an enemy every bit as dangerous as Yrstanla."

Datha's face reddened. The veins in his neck stood out. "The Kamarisi must die, and if we can find Bahett, he'll be put to the sword as well. Yrstanla must be taught that Hael is no plaything of theirs. They must learn that from this day forward, to touch our lands will be to lay the life of their greatest lords, even here in Alekeşir, on the block, and that we, the men of Hael, are the arm that holds the sword above their neck."

Styophan found himself breathing heavily, but if his blood was up, Datha was worse—his breath came in great gasps, his nostrils flared, and his eyebrows arched as if Styophan were a rat he meant to stomp.

"You cannot do this alone," Styophan said slowly.

Datha's breathing hitched. His eyes narrowed. "We could."

Styophan shook his head. "You *need* us, as we need you."

The meaning was clear to Datha. Styophan was not only threatening to withhold the help of his men. He was threatening Datha directly. If he didn't agree, it would be a simple matter of alerting the city guard. And then it would all be over.

Datha rose from the table, striking his head against the low ceiling. His back bowed as he stared down at Styophan. "You would break your vows?"

"My vows are to my Lord Duke and his family first," Styophan said as he stood as well. "All others come second."

In a blink, Datha had grabbed Styophan's shirt while drawing his knife with his other hand.

Styophan reached over Datha's massive hand and grabbed his two smallest fingers. He wrenched them up and away, and from there it was a simple matter to twist Datha's arm around.

Datha was quick, though. He crouched, relieving the pressure on his hand and yanked it away from Styophan sharply. Styophan lost his grip, and Datha spun, knife in hand. Styophan backed away as Datha rounded the table at which they'd been sitting.

"Think!" Styophan shouted. "We can find my lord, free him and the others, and still take the Kamarisi."

Datha either didn't listen or didn't care. He stalked forward as Styophan backed toward the stairs.

The other men made room, doing nothing to stop Datha or Styophan.

Datha swung the knife, but he overreached in the cramped space. Styophan grabbed his wrist and swung his arm high. He stepped to his right, preparing to bring Datha's arm behind his back, to force him to drop the weapon, but Datha was again too fast. He dropped the knife, grabbed Styophan's left arm, and yanked him sharply backward and down, forcing him down against the planks. Styophan tried to twist away, but soon Datha had slipped his arm around Styophan's neck.

Styophan reached for the knife, but it was too far away.

Stars filled his vision as Datha's arm tightened.

He couldn't breathe.

He tried to struggle away, but he could already feel himself weakening.

"Enough," a voice called.

Datha's arm did not relent.

"Enough!"

At this Datha finally pulled away, shoving Styophan's head roughly against the floor. Styophan immediately began coughing and sucking in breath noisily.

A hand grabbed his arm and pulled him to his feet.

He looked up and saw a face he recognized, but long moments passed before he understood.

It was King Brechan. Lord of the Haelish. He'd come to Alekeşir.

"How?" Styophan croaked.

"With bright paint and without my crown..."

Brechan left the rest unsaid. It seemed impossible. Styophan had thought Brechan a man impossible to miss. And yet he'd traveled with him all this way?

He had to admit he'd been concerned largely with his own men, making sure they were safe, especially after what had happened to his ships. He hadn't watched the ranks of the Haelish closely at all.

"Why have you come?"

Brechan did not smile, but there was a certain mirth in his eyes. Not to mention a deep-seated hunger. "I would taste the blood of a Kamarisi."

Styophan shook his head. This was a foolish thing, indeed, but he had to admit he wouldn't mind having a man like Brechan by his side as they made their way into Irabahce.

"You believe in this boy?" Brechan asked.

"I believe in my Lord Prince, and he believes in Nasim. That's enough for me."

Brechan eyed Styophan for long moments. He turned to Datha and regarded him as well. He looked the warrior up and down, as if weighing his argument. When he turned back to Styophan, his face was grim but resolute. He put out his hand like the thrust of a knife, holding it there until Styophan grasped his forearm and the two of them shook.

"Come," Brechan said, "there's something I would show you."

In an alley near the center of Alekeşir, not so distant from the dome Styophan had viewed earlier that day, King Brechan of Hael, dressed in a shapeless brown robe, knocked thrice upon a heavy, brassbound door. The air smelled of damp and mold. The door led into a building of stone, part of an old estate that now served as a winery. Its distinguishing feature—for it looked very similar to the other buildings in this quarter of the city—was a tall minaret that wound up into the star-filled sky.

Styophan waited, watching the darkened alley closely, ears peeled, as Brechan knocked again.

Styophan had been nervous every single step since leaving the barge. Nervous that the quay master would spot them, nervous they would stumble across the city guard, nervous the inhabitants of the city would wake and spy them walking along their streets and call the janissaries down upon them. But the city was strangely silent in the small hours before the sun rose. Most of the lamps had gone dark, leaving Alekeşir in near darkness save for the light of the waxing moon.

The door opened, creaking lightly. In the doorway stood a tall man—not nearly as tall as Brechan, but tall just the same. He wore simple brown robes and held a clay candle holder with two stubby candles burning within it. He looked to Brechan, then to Styophan, and finally he nodded and stepped aside.

Brechan led the way, walking into a hallway that flickered and waved under the light of the candle. Without a word, the robed man closed the door behind them and handed the candle holder to Brechan. After one final nod, he shuffled away as if longer strides would pain him.

"Come," Brechan said, and he led Styophan down a wide hall on their right that led to a set of tight, curving stairs. The stairs led up and up and up, and at the end of it they reached the minaret's belfry. Both of them ducked around the eight brass bells that occupied much of the tight space. Ropes slipped down from the yokes and through holes in the wooden floorboards. Styophan had heard these bells. They rang thrice per day at least, once at sunrise, once at midday, and once at sunset, each with its own distinctive ring.

From the open window Styophan could see the landscape of the city for leagues around. It was a study of shades in bistre and buttercream.

And Kasir Irabahce was laid bare.

"Do you see the tower of wives?"

Styophan looked across the expanse of the kasir. There were a dozen tall towers and minarets, but there was one near the center of the complicated cluster of buildings that was elegant. Even from this distance and in the dimness of the night, he could see the glint of gold paint as it shone off the balconies ringing each level.

"What of it?"

"There is a tunnel that leads there. If you want your prince, and your young Nasim, that is the way to reach them."

"It cannot be so easy as that."

"*Hayır*, not so easy as that. But there are women within the tower. Women with ties to Hael. They are not women the young Kamarisi trusts as yet, but they live within the tower, and if I ask for it, you will find your way in. From there, it will be a simple matter to forge a path to the smaller tower beyond it. The path is not straight. There will be blood. But I am sure you will find them there."

Fast-moving clouds swept across the moon, darkening the landscape, but

Styophan could see the tower Brechan was referring to: a squat tower perhaps four stories high. "You're sure?"

"The Kamarisi has always kept prisoners of import there."

"You've never been to Alekeşir," Styophan said.

Brechan had merely to look up to the roof of the bell tower, as if to show Styophan the reach of the Haelish kings, and the implications played themselves out. Styophan looked over the city, and suddenly Alekeşir took on a completely different complexion. How many who lived here had the blood of Hael running through their veins? How many silently refused to bend knee to the Kamarisi? Whether the reason was blood or money didn't matter. The point was that Brechan had power, even in the heart of the Empire. "Why, then, would you risk the attack during the Kamarisi's address as we'd planned?"

"Because attacking him there is something all will see. I would not have the Kamarisi's death hidden. I would not have them pretend that it was illness, or betrayal from within. I would have the entire Empire know that Hael has come. That our blades will be brought to bear against any who dare tread upon our lands."

"And you would give that up for my prince?"

Brechan paused, and when he spoke again, his words were grim. "*Hayir*, I would not."

The clouds had moved on, and Styophan could see the mischievous glint in Brechan's eyes. He was smiling a wicked smile, a smile that said he had plans, a smile that could easily turn to a snap and a growl.

"You're still going to the dome," Styophan said. "You're still going to kill the Kamarisi."

"*Evet*, son of Anuskaya." He slapped Styophan on the shoulder. Hard. "I am."

CHAPTER FORTY-TWO

I n the moments before dawn, Nikandr stared out through the thick iron bars of his cell and breathed in the chill morning air. The eastern sky was a burnished gold, the kasir and the towers of the city beyond dark as coal. He was sweating despite the chill.

In his right hand he held the alabaster stone given to him by Ashan. He'd been holding it so tightly for so long his hand hurt, but he didn't relax his grip. He refused to, because for the first time in over eighteen months, he could feel something.

He felt the wind, not merely on his face, or on the skin of his neck or the back of his hands; he felt it in his heart, in his gut. He felt it running *through* him, not merely around him. He felt the swells of air as low clouds blew across the city. As he knew his own mind, he felt the currents guide the flurry of snow over the orchards below. He felt the gust near the top of the wall beyond as a knot in his stomach. Strongest of all, though, was a kink of wind within a courtyard to his left. It played near the base of a tall tower. Snow was lifted like leaves on an autumn gust; it toyed for long moments along the circular black lines decorating the pavement.

It was a hezhan, Nikandr knew, and it was near to crossing over from Adhiya into Erahm. Its movements were rhythmic, though not in a way Nikandr was accustomed to. It twisted and rose, turned and disappeared, only to lift the snow near the sculpted trees that graced the yard. At one point it picked up five leaves. The snow described the rough shape of a man as the leaves circled the air like a crown. Nikandr could see the shape of a chest, shoulders, legs. Every so often he could even see the hint of an arm and a hand before a twist in the wind obscured it once more.

It strode across the courtyard, a king striding forth to meet his subjects.

Come, Nikandr called to it. *Take me.*

281

But the havahezhan did not.

Nikandr knew he was trying too hard, but he knew no other way to do it. This was a thing like breathing, like eating.

Nyet, he thought. *Not like breathing. It is like love or desire. How can I give those up?*

In a gust the hezhan was gone. Nikandr waited as the sun continued to rise, hoping it would return, but soon it was clear it had returned back across the veil to Adhiya. He loosened his grip on the alabaster stone, and the cramping in his hand eased. He could still feel the other hezhan, but they were distant now, and he was sure that if he'd had no success with one that had been so near, so tantalizingly close, he'd have no success with the others.

He held the stone between his thumb and forefinger, held it out through the bars of the window and thought about what Ashan had told him when he'd given him the stone. It lightens the mind, he'd said. It opens one up to the world.

Could it truly do so?

Nyet, he told himself. *That isn't the right question. Can it do so for* me? *That is the question.*

As he held it out at arm's length, he eased his grip until the stone barely remained in his grasp. It might easily slip from his fingers and fall to the ground below, lost to him forever. As he stared at it, accepting this, he lengthened his breath until inhalation and exhalation were the same. He breathed out as if it were his last dying breath, inhaled as if he'd been granted new life, each one longer than the last. The world at the edges of his vision began to fade, to darken, until everything had been distilled down to three things: his hand, the stone, and the sky beyond.

Something yawned open inside him. It felt as though the earth were splitting, ready to gobble him whole. He did not shy away from this feeling, for in the wind, not two dozen paces from his window, the snow was swirling. It gained shape as he watched, twisting and turning, losing form momentarily before gaining it once more.

It approached. Nikandr did not offer himself to the hezhan as he'd tried so often before. Instead he merely waited, accepting the widening of the divide within him. He could feel the heightened wind as it soughed through his fingers. He felt chill, but more than this, he felt as though he were reaching across the divide, reaching across the aether.

And it felt for the first time since the battle at the Spar as if a hezhan were reaching back. He could see—described only by a hint of eddying snow—an arm lift. He could feel it as well, a soul standing close to his. It was not the same hezhan as years ago. It was different, and for this he was glad. He felt as though he had *imprisoned* that one, where this one came willingly. They would trade of themselves, an accord that might last for a day, or a week, or a mere moment—he didn't care which, as long as he could feel the touch of a hezhan once more.

The hezhan was close now. It buffeted his hand, tickled the skin between his fingers. He could even smell it, a scent like burning mace.

Distracting him from this, however, was a sound that was faint but growing stronger—footsteps scraping upon stone. He ignored it, focusing on the stone and opening himself to the hezhan.

The hezhan, however, was now holding its position outside his cell window. The form before him bent and dissolved before coalescing once more into the hezhan-who-would-be-king. Nikandr thought surely it would dissipate as it had before.

But it didn't.

It reached out.

And Nikandr was certain it was ready to bond with him.

But then came the jingle of keys, the clank of metal, the clicking as a key was turned inside a lock. And before him, the twisting form burst like a crystal goblet upon a floor of white marble.

Behind him, the cell door creaked open, and the yawning inside him vanished. The hezhan was gone.

Nikandr drew his hand inside, and bent over, coughing from the sudden shift. Pain in his hand from a cold that was well past numbness blossomed. He gripped the alabaster stone tightly as the pain made him shiver.

"Stand up," said a voice in Yrstanlan.

He couldn't. Not yet. He cupped his hand gently with his other, trying to bring warmth to fingers that had turned blue.

"Stand up!" the guard said as he cuffed Nikandr's head.

The pain of it was nothing compared to the throbbing agony in his hand. He managed to stand and face the guard, but he couldn't help but cradle his right hand tenderly. The guard, a janissary with a red silk turban and fine white clothes, glanced down. He looked out through the bars of the window and frowned. With his broad mustache the look made him seem less like an enemy and more like an annoyed uncle. He strode to the window and swung the thick wooden pane shut.

"Did your hand wish to escape like a bird?"

"*Hayir.* I merely wished to look upon the city that has coveted our islands for so long."

The smile vanished, replaced by a disappointed frown and a jutting jaw. "Go," he said, pointing to the open cell door. "The Kamarisi will speak with you."

Nikandr was led to a grand hall filled with white marble columns and gold filagree and inlaid floors of mother-of-pearl and onyx and lapis lazuli. The hall was massive, one hundred paces if it was an inch. Above was a dome filled with bright paintings of gold and red. It showed the janissaries of old with conical helms and tall spears riding forth from a high gate—no doubt the gate that had stood as entrance to Kasir Irabahce for centuries.

Strangely, trailing down from the center of the dome, all the way down to the floor, was an iron chain with a spiked weight at the end of it. Standing next to this chain was a boy. He could be no other than Selim ül Hakan, the Kamarisi of Yrstanla. He wore robes of green silk with golden leaves worked into the cloth. The mantle he wore over his robes was a rich brown wool lined with white ermine. His almond-shaped turban was understated for the Kamarisi—or so it seemed to Nikandr. So many of the Kaymakam had large, olive-shaped turbans with tall plumes and ostentatious brooches. The Kamarisi's was simple silk, and the stone at the center was a large and beautiful emerald, but he wore no plume. *Perhaps he dresses more boldly when the Kaymakam come to call.*

To either side of the Kamarisi, standing near the pillars, were six bald men in simple kaftans. Nikandr thought the Kiliç Şaik would be present, but they were not. There were only the Kamarisi and these six men—slaves, surely, and most likely eunuchs.

Nikandr was led forward by the janissary, but he stopped when he reached the edge of a large circle exactly wide as the dome high above. The guardsman motioned Nikandr forward and then bowed to the Kamarisi and took his leave. The doors boomed shut behind Nikandr, leaving him alone with this young man, this ruler of a vast Empire, and his most trusted servants.

The Kamarisi waved to the space before him, the space opposite him on the circular design in the floor. "Come."

Selim was nine years old, Nikandr knew, but his voice made him seem older. He was also tall for his age.

Nikandr strode forward, the echo from his footsteps the only thing to fill this massive space. When he reached the circle, the Kamarisi motioned to the chain and the large weight at the end of it. One of the eunuchs slid across the floor and took up the chain. He brought it back to the edge of the larger circle and swung the chain fiercely, sending it swinging around the circle. The other five servants moved in, each taking some appointed place around the circle and pushing the weight as it swung by. Like this the chain moved around Selim and Nikandr, describing an endless arc.

"If you think to protect yourself from the Matri, there are none near enough to see you."

Selim had been watching the chain, but now he turned and faced Nikandr squarely. "Is the third sister of Vostroma not on our shores?"

He meant Atiana. It felt strange for the Kamarisi of Yrstanla to speak of her, even more so in avoiding the use of her name. Nikandr shrugged and nodded. "She is, but she's brought with her no drowning basin."

"And the first sister? What of her?"

Ishkyna. She could, of course, come this far, and had in the past, but she was most likely to the east, helping the Grand Duke, Leonid Dhalingrad, as he pushed the warfront westward.

"I doubt she is near, Kamarisi."

Selim, who came only to Nikandr's chest, took a step forward until the two of them were only an arm's length away from one another. "It isn't for the Matri that I do this in any case." Nikandr didn't understand at first, but then Selim spoke further. "They tell me you saw Kaleh in the Gaji."

"I did."

"Is it true? Is she one with Sariya?"

"That is what Nasim thinks."

Selim's eyes watched as the chain passed behind Nikandr. "And do you believe him?"

Nikandr shrugged. "I don't know. It seems far-fetched—I saw Sariya's dead body on Galahesh—but I would never doubt Nasim. And what she's done... It does seem beyond one so young as Kaleh."

"Your Soroush said you shot her, in Shadam Khoreh."

So he'd spoken to Soroush. Perhaps the others as well. "*Evet.* She dropped from the wound, but we couldn't find her body after the storm over the valley had passed."

Selim changed at these words. Up until this point he had seemed like a younger version of his father—not simply confident, but entitled—but now a bit of his youth began to show. He blinked his eyes and swallowed. His face looked hopeful, like a boy hoping to find some nod of appreciation from his father.

"Do you—" He swallowed and started again. "Do you believe her dead?"

"In truth, I don't know. If Sariya had assumed Kaleh, and we all believe she had, there's no telling what might happen were Kaleh to die. Perhaps she would move to another. Perhaps she would live in the aether as Ishkyna Vostroma does. Or perhaps she would fade and die, as do the Matri who become irretrievably lost in the aether."

Selim licked his lips while staring intently into Nikandr's eyes. "But what do you *think* happened?"

"Forgive me, Your Eminence, but you seem to be hoping for a certain answer. May I ask why you wish for it so dearly?"

"I..." He stopped and took a deep breath and released it in a huff. "When my father died, I was told of what had happened when Sariya came to Alekeşir in guise. She beguiled my father, as she did Bahett ül Kirdhash, as she did many others, including your princess, Atiana Vostroma."

Again Nikandr was surprised that he knew so much of Atiana—and himself—but of course the Kamarisi, even one as young as Selim, would have been briefed with much information from the islands, surely some even before his father had died.

"We had thought her dead, but we now know she returned here as Kaleh."

Nikandr shook his head. "She went to the Gaji, with Nasim."

"She did, but she came here first." Selim watched the iron chain pass beyond Nikandr's shoulders, and the way he was looking at it made it clear he dearly hoped it would help to protect him. "She found me. She took my mind, as she did my father. But that all changed two months ago. I've been thinking clearly for the first time in nearly two years, but I have no doubt that if Kaleh lives, that if Sariya returns, she will have me once more. I remember little of the days after Kaleh came to the kasir. I don't even remember her arriving. But I remember this, Nikandr of Khalakovo, she wanted Sukharam found. She wanted the rest of you as well, if that could be arranged, but in Sukharam she was clear. And she already had Nasim."

"Sukharam is gifted, as Nasim is. As Kaleh herself is."

"There's more. She wished for the war to the east to continue. She insisted that we not send so many resources that Leonid and his army and windships would be pushed back over the shores of Oramka and onto Galahesh. She *wanted* the war to remain on our lands." He waited for these words to settle. "Why?" He was desperate for this knowledge. The way he leaned forward, the way his hands grasped, the way his eyes pleaded, all of this spoke to his hunger for insight, perhaps so that he could have his Empire back, but more importantly, so that he could have *himself* back.

Of course the answer to his question was obvious. Sariya had gone to Shadam Khoreh to find the Tashavir, to destroy them one by one, thus lifting the wards they'd placed over the island long ago. She wanted the island for herself. She wanted to return with the Atalayina. And now she had it. She had everything she needed.

Before he could tell the Kamarisi of his fears, the doors to the room swung open and boomed against the walls. Two men wearing boiled leather armor stepped inside, leaving another standing in the doorway, taking in the scene before him.

Nikandr had heard stories of him from Atiana, of course, but he'd never seen him in person. This could be none other than Bahett ül Kirdhash.

CHAPTER FORTY-THREE

Nikandr knew little enough of Bahett, but no one else would dare interrupt the Kamarisi so. No one else would stride into the room as Bahett did now. What shocked Nikandr was the fact that his right arm ended in a stump. It was bandaged tightly, and Bahett seemed to be favoring it.

"Hold the chain," Bahett called.

The two armored men—surely men of the Kiliç Şaik—watched the eunuchs carefully. Their expressions were calm, but the heel of their hands rested on the steel-capped pommels of their swords, and they walked with a measured gait that spoke of their readiness, perhaps their willingness, to engage.

The eunuchs looked among one another. After some sort of silent agreement, one of them grabbed the chain and pulled it sharply to a stop. The sudden movement sent a wave up along the chain toward the top of the dome high above. As Bahett approached, the eunuch with the chain brought it to a rest near Selim, and then as one they bowed and backed away.

"Your Eminence," Bahett said as he approached. "The prisoners were to stay in the tower until my return."

Selim stared not at Bahett, but at the unmoving chain, as if now, without the protection it provided, he was afraid to say anything Sariya might hear. Gone was the bravado of moments ago. Gone was the soul of his father. These had been replaced with the callow self-awareness of youth.

Bahett came to Selim's side, placed his good hand around Selim's shoulder. "A Khalakovo in the halls of Irabahce, a man plucked from the wastes of the Gaji." As Bahett spoke, the Kiliç Şaik moved into place behind Nikandr. They stood a goodly distance away, but Nikandr didn't like them so near when he couldn't see them. "It's said," Bahett went on, "that you were betrothed to Atiana."

"I was."

"And that she was then promised to another. Grigory. A man you slew on the Spar."

"I didn't slay him. He died on a ship that crashed into the bridge."

Bahett went on as if he hadn't spoken. "And then she was betrothed to a third"—Bahett's smile widened for a moment—"yet she wasn't found in the mountain pass with you. Why is this, Nikandr Iaroslov? Where is Atiana?"

Nikandr was unsure where this was headed, but he didn't feel the need to grant Bahett any information related to Atiana, so he remained silent.

"She was with you when you entered the Gaji. She was with you when you left Andakhara, and when you reached the valley of Kohor. Is she there still? Has she remained with the crones of the desert?"

"You might better ask where your *own* wives are."

Bahett's wives had been held when the forces of the Grand Duchy had taken Galahesh, and as they'd moved on to Oramka and the mainland, requests to return them to Bahett—requests surely made by Bahett himself—had been met with denials by Leonid.

"My own wives? Those I left in Galahesh?" Bahett smiled a perfect smile. "I'll have more *wives*, Nikandr Iaroslov, but a princess of the islands? That is a rare jewel indeed." He stepped to the other side of Selim and looked Nikandr up and down. "So I can't have Atiana. Fair enough. But I have the six of you. That should be worth something."

He stomped one heel loudly, twice.

A moment later, two more Kiliç Şaik came. With them were Ashan and Soroush. Instead of the clothes they'd had when they arrived here in Irabahce, they'd been given simple white kaftans. Still hanging around their necks and wrists and ankles were their iron manacles they'd had since the desert. Nikandr they thought safe enough, apparently, but Soroush, a man they most likely knew to be burned of his abilities, they still kept in chains. Soroush's turban was gone as well. His long dark hair flowed over his shoulders and down his back, a stark contrast to Ashan's short, lightly curled hair. Together, the two of them looked like dawn and dusk—two things not wholly different from one another but opposed in many ways.

Bahett waved to a place on the floor. There Ashan and Soroush were brought to their knees by sharp swipes of sheathed swords against the backs of their knees.

"I have only three questions," Bahett said as if none of this were happening. He paused, tilting his head as if thinking of what to ask first, but Nikandr could tell he was acting. He'd been thinking about this meeting for a long while now, a long while indeed. "First, did you find what you wanted in the desert?"

He walked in a large circle around Nikandr. As he did, Nikandr saw the barely concealed look of terror on Selim's face. What hold the regent might have on the Kamarisi, Nikandr had no idea. Even with the threat of Sariya, Nikandr would have thought the Kamarisi would still hold sway over a man like Bahett.

Nikandr heard the snap of Bahett's fingers. A moment later, a whip sound filled the air, moments before something slapped against the flat of his back.

He groaned and arched as pain spread across his skin, just below his shoulder blades. One of the Kiliç had used his sheathed blade to strike him, and was poised to do so again. Nearby, Ashan stared at him with a compassionate expression. Soroush, however, looked on with hardly a hint of emotion. The only thing that betrayed him was a pinching of his brow.

"Did you find what you wanted in the desert?" Bahett repeated.

"I found some of what I was looking for."

"You found Nasim."

"*Evet*," Nikandr said.

Bahett had come full circle. He stood next to Selim once more. "Second. What did you learn of the Atalayina."

"Of the stone we saw no sign."

Bahett stared into Nikandr's eyes for a long time, weighing the truth in his words. He looked over Nikandr's right shoulder and gave a small nod.

Again came the whipping sound. And again the flat of a sword fell across his back.

He grunted through gritted teeth, nearly falling to his knees. But he pulled himself upright, refusing to grant Bahett the satisfaction of seeing him in pain.

"And where do you think it is now?"

"As far as I know, Sariya still has it."

Bahett smiled. He was a handsome man, but his smile made him seem small and petty. "And now we come to it. Where, good Nikandr, is Sariya?"

Of course. Bahett was in league with Sariya. Or he was beguiled. Either way, he would be desperate to know what had become of her.

Nikandr took too long considering, apparently. Bahett nodded once more to the Kiliç Şaik, and this blow came against his thighs. Despite himself, Nikandr fell to his knees, and this time the grimace on his face was slow in leaving. He found himself sucking in breath from the pain that radiated from his lower back and his legs.

"Will it hurt to answer such a simple question?"

"I shot her," he said, hoping to provoke Bahett into coming closer. If he was going to die, he'd like the chance of taking Bahett with him.

Bahett, however, seemed little concerned. "Did you?" He came to a stop in front of Nikandr. The two of them were close enough that Nikandr could smell the unguent that had surely been applied to his wound.

"I did. Just here." He pointed to his chest, near his left shoulder.

"Does she yet live?"

"I don't know."

"A man like you? A man of war? Do you not know when a shot will prove fatal?" Bahett's bloodshot eyes had become crazed. Had Nikandr not been standing right next to him, he would have said he was drunk or enraged from the drug-laced tabbaq that was common among the noble houses of Alekeşir. But his breath smelled not of alcohol, and his eyes held not the haze of drugs. This was a man that had been pushed to the edge. It might even have been the *loss* of Sariya that had caused it. Nikandr knew well the strength of Sariya's lure.

"She was some distance away, and the air was thick with dust from the desert. I couldn't say."

Slowly, the madness left Bahett's eyes. He breathed more easily and his shoulders unwound. "Well enough," he said simply. Then, at a thrust of his chin, the two Kiliç Şaik behind Soroush and Ashan stepped back. They pulled their swords from the sheaths at their belts and held them at the ready. "Choose."

The word struck Nikandr like the boom of a mainsail. "What do you mean?"

"Choose the one who will live."

Nikandr stared at Soroush, then Ashan. "I cannot choose."

"If you do not, you will see them both die."

"I *cannot* choose. I *will* not."

Bahett stepped forward, raising the arm that ended in a bandaged stump. "I lost this because of your man, son of Khalakovo. You sent him to the west, to the Haelish."

"Styophan?"

Nasim had told Nikandr of the man he'd seen in Alekeşir as they were being taken in the wagon toward Irabahce. *It was Styophan*, Nasim had insisted, though Nikandr had told him how far-fetched such a story that would be. And here was Styophan's name again. Could it be? Could he be in Alekeşir?

"*Evet*," Bahett said. "*Styophan*." He spat out the name. "Would you not pay your man's debts?"

Despite himself, a well of pride sprung up inside Nikandr. "Things happen in war, Bahett."

"They do." He glanced toward Ashan and Soroush, who knelt on the cold white floor. "They do." He stepped backward until he was once more standing by Selim's side. "You have taken much from me, and all I desire is but a word from you. Choose, Nikandr Iaroslov, and you may leave." Bahett waited for the words to sink in. "I'll give you a horse and what protection you'll need to reach the war front in Izlo, and you may go. From there you'll find your way to your Grand Duke. And all you need do is choose between these two men."

Nikandr stared at Ashan and Soroush. They stared back at him placidly, as if both were ready to die, except Soroush had a clear look of pleading, as if he dearly wished Nikandr would choose him. Ashan, on the other hand, merely smiled as if he understood what was to come and was ready for it. He did not relish it, as Soroush did, but he was just as prepared to die.

Nikandr shook his head. "I cannot."

"This is *difficult* for you?" Bahett stepped to his right, his boot heels clicking against the floor, until he was standing behind Soroush. "This man *murdered* your countrymen. Had he come to the shores of Galahesh and slew my kin, I would surely have taken up the sword and cut his head from his shoulders myself."

Nikandr's breath was coming faster and faster, and no amount of desire for it to slow had any effect.

"I've asked you twice," Bahett said, a gleam in his eye. He stepped back and snapped his fingers, and at this, the Kiliç Şaik drew their swords high. "I'll ask thrice, but no more." When he spoke again, it was with slow and deliberate care. "Which, Nikandr Iaroslov, shall you choose?"

Nikandr stared between the two of them, knowing full well he could not order either of their deaths. But when he was unwilling to reply, Bahett snapped his fingers and pointed to Ashan. "Kill him first."

"*Hayir!*" Nikandr called. "This is madness. Let them go, Bahett. I'll tell you what you wish to know."

"Which is little enough, indeed." He nodded to the swordsman, who raised his sword, but before he could bring it down, a voice called out.

"Stop!"

All eyes turned toward Selim, whose voice cut like a switch through tall, green grass. "You will stop." The words echoed in the massive room, making him seem small, and yet his voice was confident and clear. The voice of the Kamarisi.

Bahett's eyes narrowed at this. He stared down at young Selim with an expression that spoke not of amusement, but wonder, as if he'd thought Selim incapable of such protest.

"Kamarisi," Bahett said in silky tones. "By what right do you call on these men to stop?"

"They are my men."

"You are mistaken. These men protect the Kamarisi, and as you are too young to sit the throne, I have taken your place."

"You will not kill these men."

"I will do as I see fit. Even your brothers, as young as they are, recognize my right to do so."

Selim opened his mouth to speak, but stopped when he heard the word *brothers*. This was it, then, a threat on Selim's family, that kept Selim at heel. But it wasn't his brothers who were in danger, Nikandr suddenly realized. His brothers were in line for the throne. Since Bahett sat the throne, the Kiliç Şaik would take orders from him, but they would do nothing to harm the heirs of Hakan ül Ayeşe. But the life of his mother was an entirely different story. Selim had been born of Hakan's first wife, his ilkadin. She would be foremost on Selim's mind, and surely Bahett knew this well. He would have her in a special place, guarded always, so that should Selim step out of line, he could punish her for his crimes. He might do the same with Selim's sisters, perhaps the mothers of his brothers as well. Enough, and it would give Bahett more than enough leverage to control Selim.

Which was why this act of defiance on Selim's part was so very brave. It was a dangerous thing for him to do. Bahett might not kill his mother for this small infraction, but she would surely suffer, more than likely with Selim bearing witness.

Perhaps sensing how foolish he'd been, Selim searched the expanse of the room for some way out of this. "I would ask that you spare the lives of these men."

Bahett stepped away and regarded Selim anew. "*Spare* them... Your father, Hakan, would never have done so."

Selim stood up straighter. "My father would want them questioned more fully."

Bahett stared into Selim's eyes. He seemed to measure Selim. Seemed to weigh him. And then he nodded and smiled. "Perhaps you're right. Question them all you like"—Bahett spun on his heel and strode from the room, the Kiliç Şaik followed behind—"for in two days time, they'll be hung, every single one of them, from the gates of Irabahce as enemies of the Empire."

CHAPTER FORTY-FOUR

Nikandr was returned to his cell, and he spent the rest of that day alone. He hoped that someone would come to him, but no one did. In fact, other than the changing of the guards near midday, he heard no one at all.

Two days time, Bahett had said. He'd been angry, even petulant, when he'd given that declaration. Surely it had something to do with his missing hand. What had happened in the west, Nikandr wondered. Styophan had reached Haelish lands, clearly, but why had Bahett gone anywhere near there? Perhaps to survey the Empire's readiness. Perhaps the Haelish had already attacked— that was, after all, Styophan's entire purpose in treating with the Haelish kings.

But then a more insidious thought came to him. What if Bahett had learned of Styophan's mission? What if he'd gone to treat with the Haelish himself?

Could the Haelish be *allies* of the Empire?

It seemed impossible, but what other reason could there be for the regent of the Empire itself to have traveled there?

For the twentieth time that day he held his soulstone and called to Ishkyna, but as usual he felt nothing. He called to Mileva, who watched the eastern coast of the Empire from the island of Oramka. But it had been so long since they'd touched stones he knew she wouldn't hear him even if she had taken the dark.

At nightfall he took out his stone of alabaster once again. He held it softly between his fingers, doing much the same as he'd done that morning, but nothing happened. He felt Adhiya not at all. He relaxed his mind as much as he was able. He *offered* himself, as he should. But nothing happened. When the moon rose, he finally gave up.

His hands were numb. He was chilled to the bone and hungry. And still no one came. At some point he fell asleep but woke to the sounds of a key slipping into the lock. A moment later the door creaked open—

—and in padded the Kamarisi with a small candle.

Nikandr sat up in his narrow bed. "Does Bahett know you're here?"

Selim shrugged. "He may."

"And what do you think he'll do if he finds out?"

He shrugged again, the gesture of a boy, not a man. "He doesn't care that we talk."

There was nothing but the bed to sit upon, so Nikandr sat up and backed into the corner. Selim smiled and nodded and sat down.

"Why is it allowed?" Nikandr asked. "Why can he treat the Kamarisi this way?"

Selim leaned down and set the candle on the floor. The light shone upon his face in a ghastly way, making him seem aged and decrepit. "You know little of life in the capital."

"Enlighten me."

"My father was not well loved. He pressed the war to the west from the moment he took the throne to the day he died. His attention may have been diverted when the Spar was built, but he never let his interests in the west wane. And the Kaymakam hated him for it. They hate me for the same reason. None of them will lift a hand against me, and they will not openly allow Bahett to do me harm, but if something were to happen to me, none would cry, for it would leave open the possibility that they could take up the wreath of the Kamarisi and place it upon their head, for they are all of royal blood, even Bahett himself."

"Do they not wish to keep the throne from Bahett?"

Selim shrugged. "They do, but they all know Bahett doesn't want the throne. He doesn't love his life here in the center of the Empire, so far from his islands."

"Bahett would not content himself with Galahesh, not after wielding such power."

"*Hayir.* Not merely Galahesh. He wants your islands as well, Nikandr of Anuskaya. He wants his own empire to the east, and everything he's done so far has been leading to that. He drew heavily on our resources from the west, something my father would never have done. He focused on the east to slow the brunt of Leonid's fury, and since then he's allowed a slow withdrawal as the army of Anuskaya expends its energy trying to take more and more land before the worst of our forces can be brought to bear."

Nikandr chewed on these words. "Sariya hardly needs to control him, does she?"

"Perhaps, and perhaps not. She's been far afield, and she is not what she once was. I believe she thought Bahett could not remain under her control so long without incentive of his own. Bahett wanted the islands, so she offered them to him."

More and more pieces were falling into place. "Bahett is withdrawing the forces of Yrstanla on purpose?"

"Just so, and she's moving some key pieces to Ghayavand."

Nikandr had already been chill, but now he was cold, cold to the bone. "Why would she do that?"

Selim stared deeply into Nikandr's eyes. "Why, to give Bahett his islands."

Nikandr shook his head. "That cannot be the only reason."

"Beyond Bahett's goals, I don't know why she would do this. But I do know that some of the Kohori have been sent there."

"To what? Build a fleet?"

"Perhaps."

"One couldn't be built in so little time."

"I am telling you what I know, Nikandr Iaroslov."

Nikandr gave it more serious thought. Sariya had had months to build defenses. Build ships. Was she truly planning on attacking the islands for Bahett? Or was she preparing defenses for the eventual onslaught from the forces of Anuskaya? If that were the case, though, why build anything there at all? That would only bring attention to plans that she *should* want kept secret. Sariya was careful, though. Perhaps she didn't wish to leave anything to chance. Perhaps she was building a fleet there in case the Dukes of Anuskaya discovered her plans for Ghayavand and sent ships.

"There's little time left," Nikandr said. "The wards once held up by the Flames of Shadam Khoreh are gone."

"They are not all dead," Selim said.

"True, one of the Tashavir remains, but the spell erected in Shadam Khoreh has fallen. Tohrab says that the wards on Ghayavand will remain for days, perhaps weeks, but soon they will fail altogether. Clearly that is what Sariya has been planning for all along."

Through the cell window the sound of laughter came, then two women talking with one another loudly, as if drunk. From their tone—which was haughty and free of worry—Nikandr guessed they were two of the Kamarisi's wives returning to their tower. Heavy shadows from the lone candle played along Selim's neck as his throat convulsed. When he looked to Nikandr again, his momentary expression of worry was gone. "Time is growing short. Tomorrow I will address my people. Bahett will join me, and while we're gone, you and whoever you say should come with you will be released from your cells. You will be led to Bahett's apartments, and when Bahett returns from my address"—Selim's eyes hardened—"you will kill him."

"And what good will that do? Another regent will simply be appointed."

"There will be another, *evet*, but it will take time. And even if it were done the very same day, it would be better than what we deal with in Bahett. With

Bahett gone, I can do much."

"I need only to be released that I can return to the Grand Duchy and Ghaya-vand."

"You'll need a good deal more than that. Bahett thought Sariya would return, but he is no longer sure. He will move, now, after taking care of you and the others. He will go east himself to ensure that Ghayavand is ready. He will ensure that your Grand Duke is sufficiently baited, sufficiently angered, so that the way is paved. And if that happens your only hope is that Sariya truly *is* gone. A thin hope indeed, Nikandr Iaroslov."

Nikandr considered his words. There was a part of him that respected this young man, even though his father was an enemy of the islands—even though Selim himself would likely have been as well had Sariya not arrived in Irabahce. It was a bold plan he was offering, perhaps bold enough to catch Bahett and Sariya's other allies off guard.

"And what happens when Bahett is dead?"

"You'll be given stout horses and you'll ride eastward to rejoin your country-men. But there's more. And this is important. Sariya came to Alekeşir twice. Once nearly two years ago, shortly after the battle for the Spar. The second was a year later, just six months ago. She returned with red-robed men, the qiram of Kohor. She was shaken when she came. I know not why, but something she'd found in the desert had alarmed her. After she left, Bahett let something slip when he thought I wasn't near. Bahett was given a few of the Kohori, but most were being sent east, to Ghayavand. There they were making preparations."

"And why not?" Nikandr said. "We know she plans to return there."

"It's a trap," Selim said. "She plans to draw in the ships of Anuskaya, and when the time is right, the forces of Anuskaya will be baited. With such a threat on Ghayavand, your ships will be sent. Is it not so?"

Nikandr nodded, acknowledging the point. "If the threat is great enough."

"You cannot let this happen. You must convince your Grand Duke not to attack, for if they do, Sariya will have what she wants."

"And what is that?"

He shrugged. "I only know it is her desire. Prevent it, and then your Nasim and Sukharam can close the rifts."

"To do that we would need the Atalayina."

"Sariya will take it to Ghayavand. You must find her there and take it from her before all is lost."

Nikandr couldn't help himself. He started laughing. "Do you think all of this so simple?"

Selim smiled, but it was grim indeed for one so young. "We live in difficult times. The mountain is steep. Is that not what they say in Anuskaya? Well, it's true. The mountain *is* steep, and we must climb, together, you and I, or all will be lost. When Bahett is gone, I will send documents ahead, telling the commanders on the warfront to retreat. It won't last long, especially if the Kaymakam move quickly to replace Bahett, but it will be enough to give a pause in the battle, enough that you can convince your Grand Duke to give you men for an attack on Ghayavand. The rest will be up to you."

Nikandr shook his head and chuckled sadly. "You've no idea how stubborn Leonid Dhalingrad can be."

Selim stood and moved to the door. "You must convince him."

"Oh, I will," Nikandr said. "Believe me, I will."

"Tomorrow near dusk, Nikandr of Anuskaya. Be ready." And with that he left, locking the door behind him.

CHAPTER FORTY-FIVE

The air is thin and the sun is high when Khamal and the other Al-Aqim reach the final plateau. The crags of Sihyaan's sheer black cliffs make her look like the dark steps to the heavens themselves.

As Khamal wipes the sleeve of his white robes across his brow, clearing it of sweat, Sariya navigates the last of the climb. Muqallad comes after her. All of them are breathing heavily, but they have expectant glints in their eyes. It feels as though their past lives have been leading slowly but surely like the steps of a child over stones in a stream toward this very moment, the crossing of a threshold, the waking of the world to a new dawn.

And yet Muqallad and Sariya seem tentative. Perhaps now that the ritual is upon them they wonder whether the timing is right. Khamal has no such doubts. He is sure the fates are shining on them. He's never been more certain of anything in his life.

Muqallad points to a rock—grey, lifeless obsidian—that stands above the snowy grass. "Come."

As they gather around it, Muqallad reaches out and touches the stone. The currents of the aether shift, and a vanahezhan approaches. The stone melts before their eyes, reforming into a pillar as black as the darkest night. The top of it is smooth like glass, and a hollow is set into it, one that will cradle the Atalayina. Sariya sets the Atalayina there.

And the moment she does, the wind tugs at their robes. It twists their hair. The land around them—a plateau of knee-high grass—looks like a white, frothing sea in the dead of winter.

But then the wind dies, until Khamal can feel little save the score upon score of elder spirits that have gathered in this place. They are older than any Khamal has ever communed with. By the fates, they feel as old as the world itself, as if they were the first the fates had drawn forth from the firmament and the stuff of stars.

They know, he realizes. They know the end draws nigh, and they've come to watch. Or help.

Or hinder, Khamal thinks.

He pushes these fears away. They all knew the danger in coming here. It could be no other way.

The three of them hold hands. Muqallad stands on his left.

Strong Muqallad. Wise Muqallad.

And on his right is Sariya.

Thoughtful Sariya, she of subtle mind.

As one, the three of them nod. They tip their heads skyward. Their eyes relax, half-lidded, and they open themselves to the world around them. Khamal has never felt as at peace with the world as he does now. Everything else has paled in comparison, and it is not due to the Atalayina. It is not due to the other Al-Aqim. It is due to the world itself. It is ready. He knows this now.

Slowly, the walls between worlds peel away. Adhiya is so close to Erahm one might reach forth and part the veil with the brush of a hand. But it isn't proximity that they hope to bring about. It's unification. The aether must be banished that the worlds might merge, and this, they soon discover, is no easy task. As they hold one another's hands and draw upon the Atalayina, clouds form above. In moments the blue sky turns grey. They swirl as the ground rumbles, low and deep. The same is happening in Adhiya—the stuff of that world trembles at what is to come.

But there is more. Around the worlds, cradling them like the arms of a mother, is the firmament itself. And there...

There are those who watch. Those who've been waiting for this day for eons.

There are three.

The fates... The fates have come.

In anticipation they watch these three mortals who seek to alter the course the fates themselves have set.

Khamal did not know until that very moment that he's felt them before. Every time he's taken breath, every time he's communed with a spirit, every time he reached across the aether to the world beyond, they were there. They were watching, taking note, neither helping nor hindering.

Do they think him worthy?

Do they think the three of them worthy?

Khamal does not know. He hopes it is so.

And yet, even as these thoughts come, he feels in the fates something he never expected. It is barely present, like the scent of orange blossoms on the day's first breeze, but the longer they stand, staring up toward the sky, the stronger it becomes.

It is an ache. A yearning. A burning desire so strong the fates themselves can barely contain it.

Never in a thousand years would he have thought to find it so, but now that he has, he wonders how they could have hidden it from him all along.

Because he hadn't known. He hadn't known how to sense them at all, much less discern their mood. He'd been like a babe listening to the sounds of his parents, unknowing, uncaring that they're trying so desperately to speak to him.

The worlds touch. The veil begins to part. The aether itself becomes so thin that the currents begin to rip it, to tear it apart. The hezhan that had been waiting so eagerly step through. The disciples of the Al-Aqim, waiting in anticipation in Alayazhar, are drawn across and into Adhiya.

Neh, Khamal realizes. They are not drawn through. That distinction can no longer be made. In this place, on this island, the worlds are one.

And above—can it be?—the fates smile.

Khamal's heart fills with joy. It is this, more than anything, that convinces him that all is as it should be.

The worlds are beginning to tear.

And the fates are *smiling*.

Nasim opened his eyes.

He was cold as he had ever been. Again, as it had been since he'd woken from Sariya's spell, the dreams of Khamal were crisp and clear. He remembered them now as if they'd happened yesterday, or mere moments ago.

He shifted on the cot he'd been given the day before. When he did the chains that ran from the iron bands around his neck and wrists and ankles jingled. The iron was cold. It chafed the skin around his neck, especially near his left collar bone—a necessary consequence of the only position he'd found late last night that brought him some amount of comfort. He swung his bare feet over the edge of the cot and set them on the cold stone floor.

Across from him, Sukharam woke. He grimaced as he sat up, his chains clinking. It struck Nasim just how much Sukharam had grown over these past few years. When Nasim had found him in Trevitze, he'd been a callow youth, unaware of the world around him. It was understandable given the orphanage and the lack of influence from his Aramahn parents, but since then he'd grown in leaps and bounds. It had to do with the way he saw the world, the way he could peel back layers to find the soul within, not just with people, and not just with hezhan, but with the worlds themselves. He more than any other gave Nasim hope that they could still return to Ghayavand and complete what they had begun.

And yet Sukharam was staring at Nasim with eyes that barely concealed his disdain. He didn't trust Nasim—that much Nasim already knew—but what was worse: he didn't believe Nasim worthy of touching the Atalayina, didn't think him worthy of returning to Ghayavand to close the rifts. Sukharam had taken up the quest that Nasim himself had given him, and now he considered himself the only true judge of what was right.

Not so different from Muqallad, Nasim thought, though at least Muqallad had known his limits. Sukharam had yet to find them.

"I dreamed of Ghayavand again"—Nasim leaned over and strapped on his beaten sandals, the very same that had borne him across the wide expanse of the Gaji—"and this time I dreamt of the ritual."

At this, Sukharam sat up straighter. He knew Nasim rarely dreamt of the sundering itself. It had been something that he'd pressed Nasim about in the weeks before they'd reached Ghayavand.

"The three of them went to the top of Sihyaan," Nasim continued, "just below the peak, and there they used the Atalayina to begin the ritual. I felt the aether—" He stopped. Sometimes he recalled things so clearly that he had trouble distinguishing Khamal's memories from his own. "*Khamal* felt the aether parting. He felt the worlds touch. Felt the fates themselves watching."

"Would they not be drawn to such a thing?"

"You say it as if it's obvious. You say it as if you feel the fates each time you reach for the world beyond."

"Not every time." Sukharam stood and moved to the window, which had a thick wooden door over it. He unlatched it and pulled the door back, allowing frigid air to enter the room. "But there have been times when I've thought"—he turned back to Nasim—"where I've *hoped* that they were watching. It's something I've spent much time on, for it seems to me that the fates must help us close the rifts. It cannot be us alone. It cannot be a mere matter of manipulating the Atalayina, no matter how powerful it may be."

Nasim considered this. "After seeing those early moments of the ritual, I cannot help but agree, but I didn't see the end. Only the opening moments."

Sukharam frowned. "Get to the point."

Nasim finished tying his sandals and stood. "You cannot do this alone, Sukharam, and unless I'm wrong, we'll need one more. It must be three."

"I don't deny that, Nasim. I only question *your* presence." Before Nasim could protest, he continued. "You were an integral part of the sundering, so much so that I'm convinced that you should have no part in its redress. You are emotional and petulant. You are *incomplete*. How could I trust you to join me there?"

"Join *you*?"

"It is my fate. I've been sure of it since the day you plucked me from the great room in that orphanage. I will find the Atalayina, and I will go to Ghayavand. You may accompany me, Nasim, but you will not ascend to Sihyaan."

Nasim found his anger rising. "Do you know, then, how to touch the Atalayina? Do you know how to draw the worlds close? Are you so wise that you can reach up to the heavens and speak to the fates themselves?"

Sukharam's jaw grit. "I have done so already."

Nasim's words died on his lips as he tried to determine whether or not Sukharam was lying.

"In the valley of Kohor," Sukharam went on, "Ashan brought me to the Vale of Stars, and there the world opened up for me. I saw the place from which the fates look down." As he spoke, his eyes went wide, his expression beatific. "It was wide. Wider than I could ever have imagined."

"Think well on this, Sukharam. Even at the height of their powers, even with the Atalayina, even in the place they'd chosen, the center of the world itself, the Al-Aqim had difficulty. The fates were reticent. They do not wish to touch the world they set in motion, at least not directly. And it will be no different for you."

"I will manage."

"Do you know their minds then? Do you know their thoughts? When I felt them, through Khamal's dreams, they did not look upon the sundering unkindly." At this, all signs of Sukharam's self-assurance vanished, but Nasim pressed on. "They looked upon the ritual with smiles upon their faces, as if they'd been awaiting that moment from the very first days of the world."

Sukharam worked this through in his mind. "It cannot be. Khamal must have been mistaken. Or your memories... They're seen through the veil of the dead, Nasim."

"And yet they've never been wrong. Not once, Sukharam."

Sukharam stared at him, his eyes searching, as if he were trying to reconcile an understanding that moments ago he'd been entirely certain of.

And then the skin of his cheeks flushed red. His fingers began to quiver. He looked around the room as if he'd just woken to find himself here in this place. He turned sharply to stare out through the iron bars of the open window, his chains clinking as he did so. He looked up toward the heavens while swallowing heavily, as if something altogether unpleasant had suddenly become caught in his throat.

From outside their cell door, there came the sounds of chains clanking and the gritty slide of boots upon the winding staircase.

"Sukharam," Nasim said in a harsh whisper. "What's wrong?"

Sukharam turned to him as if he'd forgotten Nasim was there. His face was distant, his eyes wide.

"Sukharam, *quickly*."

But Sukharam only shook his head. A few moments later, the jingle of keys came, and a click, and then the door was swung wide. Tohrab shuffled through the doorway. His cheeks were sunken, his skin ashen, and he had a faraway look that Nasim hadn't expected. He didn't appear to be physically harmed, but he was staring at the wall blankly, not as though he were lost in thought, but as though he had no thoughts at all.

A man followed Tohrab into the room. Nasim expected a janissary from the kasir, but it was not. It was a man dressed in the red robes of Kohor. He had rings of gold along his ears and in his nose. His beard was long and brown. He was stout, his arms thick and hands gnarled. He looked more like an old oak than a man. Nasim realized he recognized this man. He'd seen him in Kohor when Sariya had first brought him there. Yet here he was in the heart of the Empire with the last remaining Tashavir in tow. "Come," he said to Sukharam.

Sukharam looked between the Kohori and Nasim, unsure of himself. It was a look Nasim was surprised to find no longer suited him. Sukharam had been so confident these past few weeks that seeing a bit of the boy he'd found in Trevitze was unnerving.

"What do you want with him?" Nasim asked.

The Kohori gazed upon Nasim with a jeweler's stare. "Mind your tongue, Nasim an Ashan."

With that he left with Sukharam, closing the door behind him with a boom.

CHAPTER FORTY-SIX

Nasim tried to speak with Tohrab—he called his name, asked where he'd been and what he'd seen, asked how he felt—but to none of these questions did the ancient qiram respond. He merely stood where he'd come to a rest and stared at the wall.

Eastward, Nasim realized. He was staring eastward, toward Ghayavand. He thought about trying to move him to the nearby cot, to allow him to lay down and rest, but for some reason it seemed important that Tohrab be left alone, at least for now, so Nasim gave him peace.

He waited for Sukharam's return, but the day wore on without his return. The sounds of the kasir rose up around the tower—the sound of a smithy's hammer pounding, the clop of hooves and the coming and going of the wives in their tower nearby, even the sound of barter somewhere in the distance—and still Sukharam did not return. Nasim grew worried. He wondered if the Kamarisi's men had found Sariya. She'd been lost in the storm, shot, if what Nikandr said was true. She might be dead, but that seemed far too convenient. Sariya was alive. Kaleh was alive. The only question was which of them had gained dominance over the other.

If Sariya hadn't been killed, and she'd resurfaced, she might very well have come here to the capital, or perhaps other men would find her and bring her here. But if *Kaleh* had won, where might she have gone? Perhaps she would return to Ghayavand—she seemed to lament it, after all—but what would that island be like now that the wards were tumbling down? Would he even recognize it if he made his way there once more? Even now, Ghayavand would be slipping closer and closer to Adhiya.

Nasim bunched his fists, stifling a primal scream. There was so little time left to them, and everything was going wrong. He had neither the Atalayina nor a way to reach the island, and even if he *did* reach it, he had no allies he could use to help close the rift. There was Sukharam, of course, but he had no desire to help Nasim. If it were up to him, Nasim would never touch the Atalayina again.

This only made him think more of Sukharam's reaction just before he'd left. What in the name of the fates could have unmanned him so? They'd been speaking of Nasim's revelations from his dream, of the ritual that had brought about the sundering. Nasim had told him how the fates had looked upon the ritual with smiles upon their faces.

He could still recall—it felt strange to have any direct knowledge of the fates even if it was through a dream—the feeling of expectancy from them, as if they were pleased indeed at all the Al-Aqim had done and what they were now doing.

It cannot be, Sukharam had said. *Khamal must have been mistaken.*

He was not. I felt it myself, Nasim had replied.

Your memories are seen through the veil of the dead, Nasim.

And yet they have never been wrong.

Those were the words that had given Sukharam pause. *They have never been wrong.* Why would they have caused him to go rigid with fear? And why would Sukharam have hidden it? He'd been fearful of the conclusion, but what was worse, he'd been afraid to share it with Nasim.

Late in the day, sounds came from the stairwell, but it was only food: a simple meal of round flatbread, herbed farmer's cheese and watered wine. As Nasim tore off a piece of the bread and chewed it absently, he wondered where the Atalayina was now. How odd, he thought, that all the pain and suffering the children of Rafsuhan had gone through to make the Atalayina whole. Could the stone have been fused another way? He didn't know. He doubted it. Strange are the ways of the fates.

As Nasim was drinking the last of the sour wine, he heard a moaning. He didn't realize at first that it was coming from Tohrab.

He set aside his food and moved to stand beside Tohrab. He was staring eastward, as he had been for hours, but his eyes looked sad, as if he were viewing not the stone, nor this tower, nor the horizon beyond, but the end of days.

"Tohrab," Nasim called.

The moaning quieted for a moment, and then died away, but only reluctantly, as if Tohrab were losing hope.

"Tohrab, are you well?"

Finally Tohrab tore his eyes away from the wall. They fixed on Nasim, reddened and moist with gathering tears. "I am torn in two, Nasim an Ashan."

"What? What is it?"

"The wards," was all he managed to say.

Nasim shook his head and put his hand on Tohrab's shoulder. He was forced to reach up with both hands, as the chain between his wrists was short. "They're gone, Tohrab. Aren't they?"

The way Tohrab was staring at him—as if he dearly wished Nasim could save him, knowing he could not—made Nasim realize just how much this was costing him. How much every *minute* was costing him, and *had* been since the devastation in Shadam Khoreh. Slowly, Tohrab shook his head.

"But the storm…"

Tohrab's jaw clenched. His lower lip quivered. "The outer wards failed. That was what you saw. But that was only half of our design. There was a larger purpose to setting those wards in the first place."

Nasim thought of Inan, the woman Khamal had murdered near the celestia of Alayazhar after she'd told him that he'd been trapped, that the Tashavir had set the wards against him and the other Al-Aqim. This man had been Inan's husband. He'd been Yadhan's father, the very first of the akhoz. And now here he was, hundreds of years later, speaking to the very one in whom Khamal had been reborn.

"You protected against the rifts as well."

"The outer wards did some of this, but there were more placed on Sihyaan, where the sundering began. Those still hold, Nasim. Through me, they hold, but it is no easy thing. And with these"—he lifted the chains around his wrists—"they do not affect me the same way they do you. Always we have fed the wards. Our souls, our minds. But the chains are dulling. That final ward is weakening even faster. And soon it will be gone."

"We'll find a way out, Tohrab. We'll speak to the Kamarisi and make him see reason."

Tohrab coughed. It was long and deep, the cough of those afflicted with the wasting. "Another day in iron and it will be too late."

"We will find a way to free ourselves."

"Even free of these chains, we have little time."

"I cannot—"

"Listen, Nasim. Listen to me."

Nasim heard the gravity in his voice and nodded.

"There are places of power in the world. You know this. It is from these that the ley lines flow. The islands are rife with such things, Ghayavand especially. It was why that island in particular was chosen by the Al-Aqim for the ritual. But there are other places here on the continent that hold power. Deep and ancient power. These places are connected in ways that are difficult to understand for some, but there are others who can feel them, who can manipulate them. Alekeşir sits on just such a place. Here, where two plains meet, where the mighty Vünkal crosses, is a nexus. And if we can find our way to it—"

"We can make our way to Ghayavand." Nasim knew it was so even as he said it. He'd seen it done before. He'd *felt* it. Kaleh had taken him by this method before, from Ghayavand to Rafsuhan. She'd done so again—or *Sariya* had done so—as they'd traveled to the Gaji in search of the secrets of Shadam Khoreh. And now Tohrab would do the same for them, if only they could escape the Kamarisi's tower.

"Will you need much time?"

"I?" Tohrab shook his head. "Not I, Nasim. We would not make it, as weak as I am. It must be you."

Nasim had often felt sensitive about what Khamal had done. In many ways he didn't *want* to know Khamal's thoughts, because in the years and decades after the sundering they had turned foul indeed, and yet this knowledge—which Khamal had surely known—felt like a thing that had been consciously hidden from him. It felt foolish to think so, but he felt insulted. Still, he was ready for this challenge, and he nodded to Tohrab. "But we cannot go without the others."

"*Neh.* You cannot risk so many. You can bring one other, but that is all."

"Only one?"

"One other. Three will carry enough risk as it is."

Nasim felt himself go cold. Who, then? Who would he bring? Sukharam was the obvious choice. He was necessary for the ritual they would perform together on the very same spot that Khamal and Muqallad and Sariya had three hundred years before.

He didn't want to leave Nikandr. There was still much to say to him that he'd never had the chance to. Nor, strangely enough, did he wish to leave Soroush behind. But leave them behind he would.

Ashan, however, was a different story. Ashan was wise. He brought calm to any situation, and those qualities would be treasured, especially as Nasim tried to convince Sukharam to join him on the path to Sihyaan.

"Two others," Nasim said at last. "We will take Sukharam and Ashan."

"That is unwise."

"Unwise or not, we will do it. I will not leave them behind."

"You will risk—"

"I will not leave them behind! Now tell me. Where can we do this? Where is the center of power?"

Tohrab swallowed. "There, Nasim, lies another problem."

"Why?"

"We may travel to Ghayavand, but we will leave in our wake a rift."

"A rift."

"One will form as we cross."

Nasim shook his head. "This makes no sense. Kaleh traveled like this many times with Muqallad."

Tohrab's ancient skin pulled back into a grim smile. The mere sight of it made Nasim shiver. "And where did Kaleh take him?" Tohrab asked.

"To…" Nasim stopped. The chill running through him deepened until he was shaking from it. "They went to Rafsuhan." He stood straighter. "There was no rift over Rafsuhan before they went there, was there?"

"There was not."

"But that took weeks. Months. This will all be over soon—we both know this. What will a few weeks matter if we can close the rifts on Ghayavand once and for all?"

Tohrab nodded. "You may be right. It may all be done soon. But the world stands at the brink. The rifts no longer form slowly. They no longer close as easily. Adhiya nearly touches Erahm where the rifts form, and when this one does, it will be like none other, save perhaps Ghayavand itself. Hezhan will cross. Men and women and children will die of the wasting in mere moments."

"Then we must find another way."

Tohrab's eyes became sad. His frown deepend, though whether this was in disapproval of Nasim or the choices left to them, Nasim wasn't sure. "Perhaps there is another. Perhaps. But Sariya, in Kaleh's form, approaches Ghayavand even now. She has the Atalayina, Nasim an Ashan. She has what she's been searching for over these past many months. She has what she's *murdered* for. And now she's ready to return to the place where the Al-Aqim nearly ruined the world. Would you risk that? Would you risk the fate of Erahm and Adhiya for those who live in this one place?"

Nasim suddenly felt more than this simple room bearing down on him. He felt more than the tower, or the kasir. He felt the weight of thousands, tens of thousands, who would be affected. The babes in the arms of mothers, the infirm in their beds, the hale in their fields of wheat, those who killed for coin. Vintners and chandlers. Whores and nurses. Beggars and money men. All of them would be affected. All of them would suffer. Even if he managed to do what he hoped atop Sihyaan, what would be left of Alekeşir?

"Why did you even tell me this?" Nasim asked.

"Because you should know."

Nasim moved to the window and opened it, letting the chill air in. He welcomed it, for his face was flush. Looking out through the iron bars, he could see the rolling landscape of Alekeşir beyond the walls of the kasir. "The fates are cruel."

Nasim heard a sad, gravelly chuckle coming from behind him. "Cruel indeed." Nasim turned back to Tohrab. "I won't do it."

Seconds passed in silence as the wind whistled through the trees outside. "Do you think that wise?"

"I don't care if it's wise. I won't allow so many to die. We'll find another way."

Tohrab nodded. "So be it, but I tell you this"—Tohrab coughed, and it took him long moments to recover—"Sukharam doesn't agree with you. We spoke while you were being questioned by the men of the tower. He wishes to go."

"Even knowing what will happen?"

"He considers the price worth it."

Nasim took a deep breath. "I'll speak with him."

CHAPTER FORTY-SEVEN

Atiana stared up into the darkness, her clothes piled next to her naked form. Her arms lay at her sides, her palms pressed flat against the stone. She'd been like this for hours, ever since finishing the meager meal of water and dried, salted meat the Kohori had lowered to her in a bucket.

She listened carefully to the sounds around her. At first she'd heard little—the whine of the wind above, the scrape of the guardsmen's boots, the occasional buzz of a desert scarab. She had not realized it before leaving with Ushai, but she now knew how different the desert felt. In the years leading up to the destruction of the Spar on Galahesh, she'd been able to sense the aether even while awake. At first it had felt like a mere yearning for the dark, but she'd come to realize that those times when she felt it strongest were the times when the aether was near. It was with her in Galostina, when she took to the long stairwell down to the drowning chamber, but she felt it at other times, too, and she'd begun to coax the feelings, hoping to touch the aether as Nikandr's mother, Saphia, was able to do.

She'd felt similar things few enough times since leaving Vostroma on their journey to the Gaji, and she'd been numb to it ever since approaching the mountains around the valley of Kohor, but in these last few days, the feelings had woken once more. She knew *something* had happened out there in the desert, she just didn't know *what*, nor the role Nikandr and Ashan and the others might have played in it.

It was this more than anything—her desire to know what had become of Nikandr—that spurred her to reach out for the aether now. And yet, although the aether was close, she couldn't quite touch it. It was as if she stood upon a threshold, unable to cross without the aid of drowning basins or the smoke from her own burning blood.

But then came movement, a shift of amber light. It came from her left. She turned her head—a strange feeling, as in the aether, she merely willed movement and it was so. Here she was still bound by her body, by her physical form.

She came to her knees and pressed her hands against the stone wall. Like coaxing herself back into a pleasant dream upon waking, she kept her breathing shallow and her eyes relaxed. She stared into the earth, well beyond the surface where her fingertips touched. She looked to the place where she'd seen the light.

And it came again. A burst of amber, like the arc of coruscating lightning running through a billowing bank of clouds.

For long breaths, it did not come again.

Still she breathed. Still she watched.

And then it came again, drifting further away now.

It was a vanahezhan, she knew, moving through the very bed of the desert. She could feel it in her fingertips as it slipped away, further and further, the yellow swath of light fading progressively more.

And then it was gone altogether.

This place had changed, she realized. It had changed greatly.

Nischka, what happened? she asked of the dark stone wall. *What have you done?*

She turned at the sound of scraping.

It had come from above. Something had moved, had shifted on the dry earth. And then she heard a groan followed by the distinctive sound of a body falling to the earth. It was no light sound, as of someone tripping. This was the full, solid thump that came when something of heft fell against the earth in one leaden motion.

Soon the door above her was pulled back and the ladder was lowered down. After slipping her clothes back on, she took the ladder warily up and into the dark desert night. The night was cold, and the breeze was brisk, but she felt it not at all. She was merely glad to be free of her imprisonment.

Nearby was the fallen form of one of the Kohori guardsmen in his dark robes. He lay there, unmoving, facedown in the dirt. Several paces away stood the woman. The wodjan, Aelwen. Even in the dim moonlight Atiana could tell her hair was unkempt and matted. She wore the same dress of buckskin tied with bits of bone that clacked when she moved.

The wodjan's eyes glinted fiercely. "There are things you must know." She moved to the fallen guard and squatted down. As she squatted, she moved back and forth, shifting her weight onto one leg and then the other as she peered closely at this man.

"What?" Atiana asked, tiring of her queer behavior.

"Help me with his clothes."

"Why?"

Aelwen stood, stared at Atiana. "The time comes nigh, Child of the Islands.

Would you worry over one that would draw your blood? Of one that would feed your homeland to the sea?"

Atiana had no idea what she was talking about, but she didn't like it all the same. There was something foul afoot. Still, Atiana couldn't allow herself to be taken by Ushai. She helped Aelwen to remove the man's robes, then his thin white shirt and sandals.

With that, Aelwen stood over him, her legs straddling his chest. "The Kohori are moving soon."

"Where?"

"Somewhere far away."

"*Where?*"

Aelwen turned and stared at her again. "You would know better than I. I only know that I go with you."

"You went with the men of Yrstanla."

"They wanted the boy. And your Prince."

"Nikandr?"

"As well as Nasim and Ashan. And now they have them. They take a different path than you and I, Atiana of Vostroma. We go together to a place we've never been, not in this skin. When we are done here"—she motioned to the body of the man lying at their feet—"I will find you again." She glanced up at the moon. "Time grows short."

Atiana grabbed the cool skin of Aelwen's arm. The wodjan stiffened, glaring fiercely at Atiana's hand, but Atiana held her tight. "Why have you come back?"

"Because I have seen it."

"Seen what?"

"You and I. Linked. A child of Anuskaya and a daughter of Hael. Together we may set the world aright."

"But what—"

"Enough," she said, yanking her arm from Atiana's grip. "There is much to do, and the Kohori do not sleep forever."

From her belt she retrieved something small, a tusk, perhaps. With this in hand, she slipped from her dress and let it fall to the ground. She stood naked, her thin, bony form catching the silver light of the moon. She pulled a stopper from the top of the tusk and squatted down. Something dark dripped down from the upturned tusk. Atiana thought surely it was blood, but then she realized it was glinting in the moonlight, like dust from the crushed remains of stars.

She rubbed it over his naked form—his arms and chest, his legs and groin. She took great care around his eyes and cheeks and lips. And then she pulled a knife from her belt.

She bent down, moving slowly back and forth, arms akimbo, knees jutting at awkward angles.

She drew the knife along his stomach, along his rib cage, and then she plunged it deep.

The man's eyes shot open. His pupils were dark wells surrounded by white. He looked around feverishly. Atiana thought he would cry out, but he uttered not a sound, and he moved not at all. Except for his eyes. His ceaselessly moving eyes.

Aelwen pulled the knife down toward his navel. The cut yawned open. Blood spilled. She reached in with her free hand. The knife followed, moving deep inside his chest, reaching up toward his heart.

His heart, Atiana realized.

She was cutting out his heart.

Spit filled Atiana's mouth. She swallowed reflexively. Her stomach felt as though a dark pit were forming beneath it.

The man's eyes widened further. They were filled with wonder, staring up at the gauzy veil of the heavens, as if he'd moved beyond the pain and was staring directly into the beyond. He shivered in eery silence, his whole body shaking like one does in the final days of the wasting.

Aelwen pulled out something dark. Something dripping.

Beneath her, the man stiffened. His shivering stopped.

And then Atiana heard a sound. A sigh. A release of breath as deep as a canyon.

Finally his eyes fell slack.

The wodjan saw this not at all, however, for she was transfixed by the heart she now held in her hand. After raising it up to the crescent moon, she brought it to her mouth and took one large bite. She chewed, took another bite, chewed again, repeating this until all of it had been devoured.

Atiana's hands were shaking. She could not look upon this any more. She bent over, breathing deeply lest she vomit on the desert floor. She could not look upon Aelwen, and so she missed the first signs of the transformation, but the strange movements before her forced her to look up.

Aelwen already seemed taller. The wodjan brushed her hands over her hair, again and again, and each time she did, more of it fell like sheaves of wheat from the sickle's swipe. It changed color as well, lightening until it was the same chestnut brown of the man's hair. It even took on the same light curl. Aelwen stretched her hands to the sky, and when she did, popping and cracking sounds rent the still desert air. She did not grow taller so much as widen, until her shoulders had become as broad as his, her hips and chest and torso. When she looked at Atiana again, she looked no different than he had, even down to his cock hiding in the dark bushy hair between his legs.

She pulled on his clothes and dragged him toward the stand of trees a hundred yards distant. She did it with such apparent ease it made Atiana shiver with sudden and inexplicable fear. What had she done? How had she come to trust this woman in any way, this heathen of Hael?

Aelwen returned and used her sandaled feet to brush away the blood on the desert floor. With the dirt as dark as it was here, no one would notice. No one would know that this man had been taken. No one would mourn his passing.

"Back down." Even her voice had changed to something resonant and scratchy. She moved to the hole in the earth and waved to the top of the ladder. "We'll speak again in the days ahead."

Atiana stepped onto the ladder and began to lower herself. Before the landscape was lost from view, she looked toward the trees.

I will mourn you.

She knew it was a foolish notion. The Kohori were cruel. Many would not think twice about killing her. But she couldn't help it.

I will mourn, she said one last time as she reached the cell and stepped away from the ladder.

Moments later, the ladder was pulled up and the door above her closed with a clatter, plunging the small space into darkness.

CHAPTER FORTY-EIGHT

Atiana woke with bright light spearing down into the earth.

"Up," someone barked.

The way that simple word had been spoken—like a hound with its hackles high—she knew something was wrong.

Her hands quavered as she climbed. It was lack of food and water, she knew. She squinted as she came to the top of the ladder, momentarily blinded by the bright sun. She shaded her eyes, looking at the feet of the gathered men. There were three of them, all dressed in the dark red robes of Kohor. They stood over the place where the guardsman had fallen last night. It had been real, hadn't it? It felt like a dream, for try as she might, she could see no sign of blood, no sign that he'd lain there dying beneath the stare of the sleepy moon.

The closest of the men stepped toward her. As he did, a black coil of rope twisted down from his hand toward the dry desert floor. He moved quick as a cat, snaking the rope around her neck.

"*Nyet!*" she called, but in a blink he was behind her, tightening the rope as she struggled to pull it away.

She kicked at him, but it didn't matter.

Soon, the blue sky began to twinkle in her vision. Points of light brightened as she struggled, growing as she gasped, until at last they overwhelmed both sky and sun.

Atiana woke to the sound of the surf. Slowly it rushed in, sighing, exhaling, until the next breath came. She smelled the salt of the sea, felt the spray against her cheeks and lips.

And she was cold. Not the cold of the Gaji, but the cold of the islands, the cold of the north. It felt as it had on the coast of Duzol, when she'd been shot by the musket. When she'd been waiting to die.

Was she dying now?

The sun was on her face, but she couldn't yet open her eyes. Her body seemed unready for it. But she could hear—more than she had even moments ago. The sound of footsteps—many of them—moving around her. They stepped over stones, shifting them, making them clack and scrape over the sound of the waves. She heard gulls as well, distant but clear.

At last she was able to open her eyes.

The sky above her was dark with grey clouds. The clouds of the desert had always been high and distant and uniform, painted with the flat of a knife. These clouds were tall and complicated, like the peaks and valleys of the island ranges.

To her right stood a dozen men and women in red robes. They were near the sea, all of them clasping hands with one another, their attention focused down toward the stones upon which they stood.

Atiana had no idea why. Nothing was happening.

But then the stones near their feet began to melt. They collapsed like sand beneath the pounding waves of the sea. The Kohori's boots sunk into the resulting slurry but they didn't seem concerned by it. They merely continued to clasp hands, eyes cast downward.

A shape rose up from the beach. It looked like little more than a peak of dark stone at first, but soon it had resolved into a wedge. More rose behind it. A ship, she realized. They were raising a ship of stone. The hull rose as if it were being lifted by the hands of giants. It was much larger than she'd thought. Much of it was hidden beneath the sea, but as the red-robed figures continued to watch, the ship lifted up and out of the white surf until the stern was floating in the water and the fore of the ship was beached, as if it had just landed.

A ship of stone made from rocks and pebbles of this place, this shoreline near the long line of looming mountains to the west. Suddenly she recognized it. She'd been here only two times before, on journeys along the easternmost edge of the Empire, but the Sitalyas were unmistakable, not only for the way the peaks marched into the distance, but for their sheer heights. The tallest of them—Nolokosta, distinct for its crooked white peak—could be seen for leagues in any direction.

By the ancients, the sea on her left was the Sea of Tabriz. She was nearer to her homeland than she'd been in well over a year.

But how? How could they have come so far in so little time?

The Kohori, clearly. She recalled Nikandr's stories of Nasim and how he'd been transported by Kaleh. If they'd been right, she'd done so again in taking him from the Straits of Galahesh to the mainland of Yrstanla. Such power, and it came, no doubt, from the ancient knowledge that Muqallad and Sariya had given her, knowledge the Kohori possessed as well.

Men and women began moving things into the ship as another rose from the surf beyond it, and another beyond that.

Atiana tried to lift her head, but the movement brought so much pain she set her head back down. A moment later, white pain blossomed in the place behind her eyes, a pain so bright and furious that it overtook her.

She woke some time later. She wasn't sure how long she'd been unconscious. The clouds were still grey. It seemed darker, so she guessed it was nearing dusk. To her left, a dozen ships were lined up along the beach. The surf rolled in, breaking like thunder against the ships and frothing white around the prows. Each of the ships' hulls had intricate designs carved into them—entwined roots or branches wrapping around twinkling stars. She had no idea how they would be brought into the water, how they would navigate across the sea. It seemed impossible. Ships of stone. But here the Kohori were, loading the ships, clearly preparing to sail for Ghayavand.

Atiana was picked up by a man. She didn't recognize him, but he was strong, and he was chewing something that smelled of anise. He handed her to another already inside the nearest of the boats. The one who carried her into the boat was a younger man with a stubbly beard and a scar running over his milky left eye. He carried her over to a pallet on the stone deck, set her down, and continued on about his business, accepting sacks of food and rope and wooden chests from those still outside the ship.

Atiana was able to pull herself up by the nearby gunwales and watch the other ships. There must be two hundred Kohori working at these ships. She looked for, but did not find, Safwah. Neither did she see Ushai. There were several women with veils across their faces, however. Ushai could easily be one of them and Atiana would never know it.

Soon it was done. Everyone was loaded. At the bow of each ship stood one qiram—some of them women, some men—each with arms spread wide and their heads lifted toward the sky. Another qiram stood on the deck near each of the ships' sterns, doing the same. Atiana managed to stand, holding tightly to the rough surface of the gunwale railing and staring out beyond the white, frothing waves.

Beneath them, the stones of the beach shook. The air rumbled with the sound of it. Atiana could feel it through her feet. The ship was lowering as if the beach itself were desperate to be rid of them. With one large surge they were drawn away by the receding wave into deeper water. The ships turned as if an unseen hand were guiding them until the prows were facing out toward open water.

Below the waves, large white shapes approached. They looked like massive spearheads with white cordage trailing behind. The forms thrust beneath the surface of the water, closer and closer until it seemed they were directly below the ships. Atiana's eyes went wide as one massive white tentacle with dozens of suckers along one side rose up near Atiana's ship. The tentacle quivered in the air, the surface of its skin turned from bright white to a grey not so different from the color of the ship itself. A second arm followed the first, the two of them latching onto the gunwales with a wet slap. They were followed by two more, then two more, until all six had latched tightly onto the prow.

Another white creature appeared ahead of the ship to her left. And more further down. Each rose their arms up and latched onto another ship, turning a deep and mottled grey as it did so.

Atiana could only stare in wonder.

These were goedrun, the giants of the sea, one of the reasons travel by water-borne ship had been abandoned by the Grand Duchy long ago. The high seas beyond the shallows around each of the Grand Duchy's islands, coupled with the threat of these and other creatures, made such travel too dangerous. Taking to the winds had been the obvious choice, especially with windwood so plenti-ful. But these qiram were unfazed by the dangers of the open sea. In fact, they seemed to welcome it. They would use the goedrun as their allies to tow these massive ships through the great waves.

The goedrun pulled them beyond the shallows, fighting the waves until they were into deeper water where the waves were not so great. Then the creatures began to haul them out toward the deep blue depths. Toward Ghayavand, Atiana knew. They were headed for Ghayavand.

In the days that followed, Atiana was asked to stay belowdecks. She was given a small, square cabin with a pallet and a chamberpot and little else save the mottled grey walls. There was no doorway, only an archway to the central pas-sageway that ran through the ship, but a Kohori man was stationed outside to make sure she stayed where she'd been assigned.

She had a horrible reaction to the cabin, however. It was the waves. The in-cessant waves. She didn't like windborne travel, but she liked waterborne even less, for this very reason. She'd always had strong reactions to it. She began throwing up within a few hours of staying in her cabin. She could keep nothing down. Not even water, and eventually Habram came to her. He stared down at her with his piercing look, his hawklike gaze, but eventually he seemed to gain some small amount of compassion. "You may come up to deck until it passes."

And she did, though it still took hours for the sickness to pass. She was al-lowed to roam the upper deck, but was not allowed to go anywhere belowdecks except back to her cabin.

She watched for Safwah, and for the Kohori man Aelwen had butchered before stealing his likeness, but she saw neither. She did, however, see Ushai.

She hadn't realized it at first, but Kaleh had been taken below the stone deck to the hold below, and Ushai had stayed there to tend to her. She came up one morning and spoke with Habram at the bow of the ship.

Atiana wanted to confront Ushai and Habram about their plans, but the men that had been set to guard her kept her amidships, refusing to allow her past.

"Do you fear to speak with me?" she called loudly.

Habram and Ushai turned at this. Habram merely stared, as if he'd never truly given Atiana due consideration before. But Ushai glared, as if she wished Atiana had been taken on another ship, or better yet, left behind entirely.

They finished their conversation, and Ushai returned belowdecks, while Habram went about his business.

The rhythm of the goedrun became ingrained in her. Atiana would stand at the gunwales, staring into the depths of the blue water, watching the wide arms sweep outward and then draw in like a bellows, propelling the great beast forward, and with it, the ship. She could feel the ship tilt slightly as the prow rose and bit into the waves, and then again as the prow dipped back down.

The goedrun were not tireless creatures. After hours on end, sometimes as long as a day, their progress would flag, and when that happened, the qiram would release it. Atiana could see it drift down into the depths as its many arms—once more the color of the frothing tips of the windswept sea—waved and were swallowed by the darkness. Another would come minutes later, spray lifting high into the air as a new set of arms grafted to the hull, and they'd be off once more.

Like this, the goedrun drew them across the sea. On the third day, Habram came and stood at Atiana's side as the sea drifted by them. He still wore his red robes, though the cowl was pulled back, revealing short brown hair and golden earrings that glinted in the sun as the wind tousled his hair.

He looked over to her, and though Atiana did not meet his eyes, she could tell that he was staring at the bruises that ringed her neck.

"My men should not have been so forceful."

Atiana watched a lone bird wheeling in the distant sky as the prow cut through the waves, waiting for him to get on with it.

Habram stared toward the horizon. "You came to find Nasim, did you not?"

"I did."

"And now he is gone. Taken from you by the fates. And yet Kaleh is here. As is Sariya."

"What of them, Habram of Kohor?"

He chuckled. "*What of them?* Do *all* those who live among the islands ignore the tidings of the fates?"

"I listen to my ancestors, for they guide me."

"And what do they tell you?"

"They tell me to keep my faith, for it is something that can never be taken from me, and to find a way to heal the world."

Habram paused. "Then they are wise. But know this, Atiana of Vostroma, our paths need not cross. We seek the same thing."

"And yet you think Sariya will guide you there."

"I do. It was written by the fates before the Tashavir ever left Ghayavand."

"You were not there on Galahesh. I know her mind, Habram. She wanted the world to end. She wants it still. And if your hope is that she will take the Atalayina and walk to the shoulders of Sihyaan and mend what she and the Al-Aqim tore, then you are gravely mistaken. Worse, you are a fool."

"When she came to Kohor," Habram said without a hint of annoyance in his voice, "she did not at first trust us, as we did not trust her. She took our minds, something I'm told you're familiar with, and she found where the Tashavir were buried. Only after she'd learned this did she see that some would be loyal to the Al-Aqim. She remained with us for several months, and most of that time was spent in the Vale of Stars. She found something in that place, something that changed her. I could see it in her eyes. I knew it would happen—for such were the prophecies—but it was still wondrous to behold."

"That was no prophecy, Habram. That was a twist in history. Nothing more."

"What if I were to tell you she found something there that convinced her she could not bring about indaraqiram, that she no longer believed in the path she once followed?"

Atiana turned toward him and waited until she'd met her gaze. "I would laugh in your face."

"And yet you believe that Kaleh can help to heal the rifts?"

Atiana ran her hands along the stone of the gunwale, brushing away some of the sea salt that had collected there. "Ashan seems to think so."

He pursed his lips and then smiled, as if he knew something she didn't. "I'll offer you this bargain. Take to the currents of the dark once more. Go to Kaleh. Try to free her. If the fates will it so, she will be yours."

"And if Sariya rises instead of Kaleh?"

Habram's smile widened, the crow's-feet along his eyes deepening. "Then we wil have our answer, won't we?"

Atiana turned back toward the sea. Below the ship, white arms waved like the branches of a willow. "I will try to summon Kaleh from the depths of her mind. And I will try to smother Sariya while doing it. You know this."

"I do."

"I will kill her if I can, Habram."

Habram nodded.

"I will require the Atalayina."

"Of course."

As the ship was pulled over a large wave, Atiana's stomach lurched. She glanced toward the hatch that led down into the hold. "I will not attempt it while we're at sea. When we reach Ghayavand, I will make preparations."

"Very well," he said, and with that he walked away.

It left Atiana feeling strange. She was alone here. Alone save for the help of a heathen wodjan.

Then I'm alone indeed, Atiana thought.

CHAPTER FORTY-NINE

In a dank cellar filled with five rows of wine tuns, Styophan and Rodion followed the man in brown robes. He was the same one who'd opened the door at Brechan's knocking the previous night, and he carried a bronze oil lamp in his shaking right hand. The flame wavered as he shuffled along the stone, but at last he stopped at a tun along the far wall. He leaned hard against one corner, and something groaned. It swung away with a thumping creak to reveal the entrance to a tunnel that looked no wider than Styophan's own backside.

"You want my men to go into *that*?" Styophan took the lamp and crouched down, putting the guttering flame of the bronze oil lamp he held near to the hole. It was dry. He could say that much, but it was hardly the width of a man's shoulders. And who knew what it would be like as they continued on?

The lanky man—Thirosh was his name—stood a few paces away, stretching his jaw while using one hand to smooth down the stubble on his cheeks and neck. The lines along the sides of his mouth and across his brow deepened as he leaned down and frowned into the tunnel. "Like it or not, that's the tunnel that'll take you to Irabahce."

"That's no tunnel," Rodion said. "That's a burrow." He looked at Styophan soberly. "That's a bloody trap," he said in Anuskayan.

Thirosh's frown deepened even further. "It's no trap," he countered in Yrstanlan. "It'll take you to the tower of wives. Use it if you like."

"When's the last time anyone's used it?" Styophan asked.

"I sent my son through early this morning. It took him time, but he says it's clear."

Rodion shook his head. "Clear for ten-year-olds, maybe."

"Go or don't," Thirosh said, "but if you're not going it's best you return to your barges now before the sun comes up."

Styophan didn't like the looks of it. A child might make it through, but his men? How was Mikhalai—broad Mikhalai—going to make it through there? He'd caused enough pain and death on this trip to last a lifetime, but what was he to do? What real choice was there? "We'll go. Send down the rest."

"Well enough." Thirosh left them, his shoes scraping against the cellar floor as he walked to the stairs.

The others had been left upstairs in the courtyard until Styophan and Rodion had had a chance to look over the entrance. Two by two, they started coming down. He'd left only three at the barges. Three that had been taken by the wasting in the past few days, men that were already bad enough along that they'd be a liability, not merely from weakness, but from their incessant coughing. With Edik's death in Avolina, they were now forty-six strong.

It would have to be enough, Styophan thought. Forty or five hundred, what mattered was that they gained the element of surprise and held off the guards in Irabahce until they could escape with Prince Nikandr and the others.

With his men gathered, Styophan walked past them, staring each in the eye before moving on to the next. "The janissaries of Irabahce are well trained," he told them. "They're hand-picked, some say by the Kamarisi himself. The Kiliç Şaik may be there as well. Fine swordsmen, every one of them. I saw them myself in Hael. But I tell you this. They haven't seen the likes of Khalakovo. Not on these shores, not within those walls."

Some men nodded grimly at this. Others grit their jaws. Others merely stared. But he could tell. They were ready. They were ready to repay Alekeşir for what had happened on Galahesh, for what had happened when the Kamarisi's ships stormed over the straits and destroyed many of the spires on Vostroma, even for what had happened centuries ago in the war of independence.

"They will today," Styophan continued, "for today we go to find our prince. We go to bring him home once more. We go, but the mountain is steep."

"Then we climb," came the refrain.

"The winds blow!" Styophan called.

"Then we suffer!"

"The blade is sharp!" he bellowed.

"Then we bleed!"

Styophan slapped his fist to his chest. His men did the same, the sound echoing in the confines of the cellar.

"Then come! But carefully, men. For we go to shed the blood of Yrstanla."

Rodion led the way with a hooded lantern no larger than his fist. It had only a few hours of light, but it would bring them to the far side of the tunnel.

Once Rodion's legs were lost in the darkness, Styophan entered and began crawling along. He could see Rodion's outline ahead lit by the small lantern. The air had smelled cool and earthy in the cellar, but here it smelled of minerals.

He could taste it on his tongue. He heard those behind him entering the tunnel as he progressed, but with his body so tight against the tunnel he couldn't so much as look behind to check on them.

The ancients smiled on them for a time, for the tunnel widened, enough that they could make good progress. But not long after, the tunnel closed in again. There were places where it was so tight they came to an utter halt as first Rodion, then Styophan, then Mikhalai and the rest squeezed their way through. Like an impossibly long earthworm, they stretched and crawled, they tightened and lengthened in strange ways, crawling along their endless hole, bit by bit, coming closer and closer to a place that had never witnessed battle from an outside enemy.

But they will today, Styophan thought.

He had hoped that they could storm into the tower and take Nikandr and the rest before anyone was the wiser. But he knew in his heart it wouldn't be so easy. Swords would be drawn. Lives would be spent.

Do not fear, My Lord Prince. Your men are coming for you.

By now Brechan and Datha and the Haelish would be preparing for their push into the city. They'd received robes from Thirosh, enough for all his men. When the time came, they would leave the barge, two by two, three by three, and if the quay master was there to witness it, they would kill him, quick and simple.

They would weave through the streets by different routes, moving calmly but steadily until they surrounded the dome from which the Kamarisi would speak. Then, when they heard the silence, when they heard the rise of the Kamarisi's young voice, they would tighten the noose and attack. There would be many men set to protect the Kamarisi, but those men would have no idea what they were up against. The soldiers of Yrstanla would fight, but they would lose, and their Kamarisi would die.

Styophan didn't know if their sacrifice would be worth it in the end, but there was little doubt that the address would draw attention away from Irabahce long enough for Styophan to make his way in, somehow find Nikandr, and carve their way out again.

Ahead, the way sloped down. They crossed a place that was wet and slick, but little more than this. It was easy to slip past, but by the time he did, his janissary's uniform and the layers beneath were damp, and it started to rob him of warmth.

Behind him, he heard men coughing. He heard some talking until he passed an order back for silence. He'd told them as much before they'd left the barges, but this was a strange place. The constant darkness made him feel alone, as if this were little more than a grave and the world above had already forgotten about the men who crawled below.

For hours they continued. Styophan's shoulders and arms became sore from the slow but constant dragging. He found himself looking forward, hoping to steal a glance ahead to see if they were nearing the end, but he saw only Rodion outlined in golden light, and the few times he did manage to sneak a look, he saw only a glimpse of the tunnel wall, the blackness beyond.

He resolved himself to creeping forward, gathering himself, creeping forward more, over and over, mindlessly.

But then Rodion stopped. "I think I see something," he whispered back. "The tunnel widens a few yards ahead."

"Pistol at the ready," Styophan said.

Rodion reached into his woolen coat and pulled out his wheellock pistol. Styophan did the same. They passed the word back that the end was near, and then, at word from Styophan, they moved forward as quickly and as silently as they could.

"*Quiet now.*"

The soft voice, clearly a woman's, called from the end of the tunnel. Surely this was one of the women Thirosh's son had gotten word to the night before, but Styophan couldn't shake the feeling it was a trap, that they'd been betrayed before they'd even made it into the tower of wives.

Rodion left, and at last—it had felt like days in that tunnel!—Styophan crept out and stood. Several paces from Rodion was a tall woman, nearly as tall as Styophan. She had chestnut hair and bright eyes and delicate lips. There was a clear resemblance to some of the women he'd seen in Hael, not the least of whom was Queen Elean, but in the set of her eyes and her strong cheekbones and the color of her skin he could see the women of central Yrstanla.

"There were to be two," Styophan noted.

"I am Nabide. Serin is watching the door to the tower. But come. Only you, or one other. There is a problem."

She started to walk away but Styophan grabbed her by the elbow.

She spun, her eyes afire, and snatched her arm away.

"*What* problem?" Styophan asked.

"Your prince has been taken from the tower."

"Where?"

"Come, and I will show you."

Styophan nodded for Rodion to join him. Together they climbed up the nearby stairs. They went up one level to another cellar, but in this one there were windows set into the upper reaches of the stone walls. There was a curving stairwell here that led up into the tower, but Nabide took them instead to a rich oak cabinet built beneath the curving slope of the stairwell. Inside the cabinet was a lantern turned low. She set it to burn higher, and Styophan saw another, hidden stairwell built inside the larger one. It was very tight and he had to twist his shoulders in order to make the climb. He used his hands to guide him, as Nabide did ahead of him, and they went up and up—how many stories Styophan didn't know—and eventually they came to a balcony that ran around the top of the tower. There was a low parapet to which Nabide crawled. Styophan and Rodion dragged themselves forward with as much care as Nabide had until the entirety of the kasir's grounds was revealed to them.

To the south, ahead of their position, was a massive stone building with a white dome and golden statues.

Rodion's eyes were wide. He looked breathless, and not from the climb. "Just look at it."

Indeed, Styophan thought. This one building was larger than any structure he'd ever seen. It dwarfed anything Volgorod had to offer. Even the State House in Evochka, the largest single building the islands had to offer, would be consumed by this monstrosity. And the embellishments. Golden statues of horses charging, of drakhen rearing, of men with wings and women with shield and sword.

Beyond the kasir, a variety of towers were spread about the grounds. Most were minarets like the tower of wives, but there was one simple round tower, ancient by the looks of it, as if it among all the buildings of Irabahce had been built first. Beyond the buildings were lawns of green grass, ordered rows of trees, vineyards, mazes, ponds. It was easily ten times the size of Palotza Radiskoye.

"Look to the red building."

Styophan saw it, a squat but wide building made from a stone the color of coral.

"That is Bahett's home. From there he conducts the business of the Empire in Selim's stead."

"What of it?"

"Your prince and another, an Aramahn with a black beard and a ruined ear, were taken there by the Kamarisi's eunuchs."

"Why?"

"We do not know, but the rest remain in the tower that Brechan told you of." She pointed to the grey tower. There was a lot of ground between the two buildings, and it was not an easy path. There were walls and buildings between the two.

"We have some time yet," Styophan said in Anuskayan. "We'll wait. If they return, we'll go as planned, but if not, we'll divide the men, Rodion. Vasiliy will go to the grey tower, while you and I go to find our prince."

"*Da*," came Rodion's reply.

CHAPTER FIFTY

"I must return, or there will be questions," Nabide said to Styophan, "but I've made arrangements. The cellars will remain safe. One of us will return if we hear that your prince has been returned to the tower, but do not let midday approach."

"Why are you doing this?" Styophan asked.

She seemed surprised by the question at first, but then her gaze bore into him, and her look became grim. She pointed out to the red building where Nikandr had been taken. "The same reason as you."

"You may die."

Her smile softened, but her eyes were no less determined. "My entire life has been leading toward this one moment."

Styophan saw in her the fierce resolve that he'd seen on the battlefield many times. She would most likely die when all was said and done, but she didn't care. Her mind was on her people—the people of Hael, no matter that she had the blood of Yrstanla running through her veins.

Styophan nodded to her, and she nodded back.

"Go with her," Styophan said to Rodion. "Tell them what's happened, and prepare them." He pointed out to the kasir grounds. "Break them into two, thirty with you and the rest for Vasiliy. Explain the lay of the grounds to all of them, especially the stables there." He pointed to the long wooden structure to the west of the kasir grounds. "We'll meet there when we have what we've come for."

Rodion nodded soberly. "We'll be ready." And then he and Nabide took the stairwell down.

Styophan waited as the sun rose and Kasir Irabahce came to life. Servants moved about the grounds and among the buildings. It was a hive of activity, surely due to the celebration planned for the Kamarisi's return. These men and women were going on their way, oblivious to the fact that the Kamarisi would most likely never return to the kasir.

Styophan was well aware of the fact that the time for the Kamarisi's address was fast approaching. He could see, far to his left, the dome where Brechan and Datha and the rest of the Haelish men would descend.

"Come, My Prince," Styophan whispered to the chill morning air.

But he did not, and it was less than an hour until the Kamarisi would speak. Perhaps Nikandr was being held so that Bahett could interrogate him or arrange for Nikandr's ransom with the forces of Anuskaya. Why Soroush had been brought as well he had no idea, but it was clear Nikandr wouldn't be returning to the tower.

He crept back down to the stairwell and made his way to the cellars. There, Vasiliy and Rodion waited.

"They're ready?" he asked them both.

"*Da*," came the sharp reply.

Styophan stepped forward and hugged Vasiliy's stout form and kissed his cheeks. "I go to find our prince. Wait ten minutes, or until you hear signs of resistance, and then take the tower. We'll meet at the stables."

Vasiliy nodded. "Go well, Komodor."

"Go well." Styophan then nodded to Rodion, who in turn nodded to the lanky Yasha, and so on down the line. The men prepared their wheellock pistols. Styophan did the same, and then took to the stairs, his men following smartly behind.

Near the top of the stairs, standing with the door nearly closed, was Nabide. She'd been peeking through the crack in the door, but as Styophan came she turned to face him. "Take the leftmost path around the tower to reach Bahett's home. Go through the tree garden there and you'll find a small gate that leads through the wall. It skirts the grounds where the Kiliç Şaik practice their swordplay, but most have gone with the Kamarisi and Bahett into the city."

"You have our thanks."

"Keep your gratitude. I don't do this for you." And with that she pushed open the door and walked out, leaving it open behind her.

Styophan continued up the stairs and into an ostentatious hallway of striated white marble and rich tapestries. To his right was a set of two ornate doors. He rushed through these into the gravel yard outside and then ran, pistol in hand, as low and as silently as he could. His men did the same, spreading out into a formation three men wide and ten deep.

He'd not gone twenty paces when a door opened at the far side of the yard, a door set into a long, low house of granite with a green slate roof and a chimney that coughed smoke. Through the doorway stepped a boy carrying a basket filled with steaming buns covered loosely by red-banded cloth.

The boy stopped dead, hand still on the handle. He stared at them, a look of confusion on his young, round face, but then his eyes fixed on Styophan's gun.

"Get back inside," Styophan said softly, "and don't come out again."

The boy didn't move.

"Get back inside, boy." And then Styophan ran past, his men following.

They continued beyond the bakery to an empty yard of benches and standing stones and winter bushes thick with clinging snow. Ahead lay the grey tower where Nasim and the others would be. He continued along a well-worn path through a small copse of laurel trees that bent toward one another, forming a tunnel. On the far side, once they rounded the tower, they were faced with a long wall that cordoned off this section of the grounds from the larger, more grand buildings of state.

The iron gate Nabide had told them about was twenty paces along the wall, but Styophan paused at the edge of the trees, for in the field to their right there were seven men dressed in the hardened leather armor of the Kiliç Şaik. Two of them were practicing, though it was vicious—the clack of their wooden swords cutting through the crisp air while the five others watched. Styophan breathed, counting the seconds, wondering when the boy would raise the alarm. But no sounds came from behind them, and soon, one of the swordsmen struck a point against the other's thigh.

The two men parted and bowed to one another, and then the seven of them fell into step and began walking toward their barracks, which were just north of the stables. Styophan had no idea how many Kiliç Şaik might remain here in the kasir, but he prayed to the ancients that they were few.

When they'd gone far enough, Styophan moved along the wall to the black gate. As he reached for it, a bell—like those near the helm of a windship—sounded from somewhere behind him. It rang over and over as men began to cry out, "To arms! To arms!"

Styophan rushed through the gate, but as he did he glanced toward the Kiliç Şaik. They'd turned and were already running toward their position.

Inside the gate was an immaculate lawn with a dusting of snow that led to the building of red stone. Three servants stood there looking toward the sounds of alarm, but as soon as they saw Styophan and the others, they bolted for the kasir's massive, domed building.

Styophan turned to Yasha. "Take twenty men. Set up an ambush there." He pointed to the row of bushes that ran along this side of the wall. "Pistols first, Yasha, then swords. Don't treat them lightly."

Yasha nodded and set himself to the task, choosing men and positioning them.

Styophan chose one desyatnik—Rodion and Mikhalai and seven more—and led them into the red building. The entrance revealed a hallway that ran the entire length of the building. Along both sides of the hall were niches with marble statues on pedestals, regal statues of the long line of the Kamarisi. Between the niches were doors leading to various rooms, offices perhaps, or rooms where the Empire kept records.

To his left and right were stairs leading up. No doubt he would find more of the same there, and on the third floor as well.

Styophan nodded to Rodion who immediately said, "*Da*," and took three men down the hall, pistols and swords at the ready. "Nikandr Iaroslov!" he called as he went. "Nikandr Iaroslov! The men of Khalakovo have come!"

Styophan continued up the stairs to his right. When he reached the top of the landing, he nodded to Mikhalai. Mikhalai took three more men down a hall that was nearly the same as the one below—opulent and ostentatious—calling out Nikandr's name.

Styophan headed up the stairwell, but before he'd gone ten steps, two janissaries in ceremonial garb holding tall spears appeared at the top of the stairs. Styophan fired at the nearest of them. The wheel spun, shedding sparks, and the gun bucked, but the shot merely caught the soldier in the shoulder.

Damn my eye.

Two of his streltsi discharged their weapons, and the janissaries fell, clattering down the marble stairs to the landing.

After a nod of thanks Styophan leapt over the janissaries and took to the last of the stairs up to a room with couches and fig trees in marble planters. On the far side of the room were two ornamented doors that Styophan could only assume led to Bahett's private rooms. He stepped forward and kicked the center of the doors. With a crunch the doors flew wide.

From the nearby window Styophan heard the sound of gunfire.

Yasha and the Kiliç.

"Nikandr Iaroslov!" Styophan called. The grand room before him was a wide-open space with rich carpeting and tall windows and a gold filigreed ceiling. But it was empty. "Nikandr, My Prince! Khalakovo has come!"

He moved to another door and found it unlocked. The next room was smaller than the previous one, but no less rich. A large bed was set against one wall. A marble fireplace dominated another. Rich paintings lined the walls, including one of Bahett himself—still with two hands—standing tall in silk finery and a wide turban with a bright emerald brooch and a tall plume of vermillion and carmine.

"Nik—"

Styophan stopped, for a door opened, and from it strode Prince Nikandr. He held a knife in his hand, his own kindjal. He was staring at Styophan as if he were a ghost.

But then the sounds of battle came—guns no longer, but the ring of steel on steel—and Nikandr's eyes hardened. He turned back to the room in which he'd been hiding, a dressing room from the look of it, and waved someone forward. Soroush Wahad al Gatha stepped out, staring at the streltsi gathered before him in much the same way Nikandr had.

Styophan waved him toward the doors. "My Lord Prince, please, come."

Nikandr stared at the door, then looked to the painting of Bahett. "Styopha, what's happened?"

"We've come to take you east, back to Anuskaya."

Nikandr shook his head. "Bahett was to return here after the address."

And then Styophan understood. Nikandr had come to murder Bahett. "No longer, My Prince. The Haelish will be moving against the Kamarisi even now."

From the windows, the cries of men rose higher.

"My Lord, please." Styophan motioned Nikandr toward the door. He looked haggard and confused. Styophan was nearly ready to take him by the arm and drag him from the room when Nikandr's eyes widened. He stepped back and met Styophan's gaze. "The Haelish are here?"

Styophan nodded. "They go to kill the Kamarisi. With any luck, Bahett will be taken as well."

Nikandr shook his head. "Styophan, they can't. We *need* Selim. We need him to send orders east."

And now it was time for Styophan to be confused. "It's already too late, My Lord."

"*Nyet*. We must go there. They cannot kill the Kamarisi."

Styophan couldn't believe his ears. "There's nothing we can do about it now."

Nikandr's jaw worked as he looked to the streltsi, then to the nearby window, where the sound of swords still rang.

"How many men?"

"My Lord?"

Nikandr's face grew angry. "How many men do you have?" he shouted.

"Forty-six." He nodded toward the window. "Perhaps fewer."

He glanced at Soroush, who nodded in return.

"Come, Styopha," Nikandr said. "We go to Alekeşir."

CHAPTER FIFTY-ONE

Nikandr ran with Styophan and Soroush and the streltsi of Khalakovo, down the stairs from Bahett's apartments. At the landing halfway down to the second level, two janissaries lay sprawled across the white marble. Blood slicked the floor around them. Like a river across a snowy landscape a trail of blood led down the marble stairs. Nikandr stopped to take up a sword from one of them. As they continued down he hefted it several times, getting the weight of it. The kilij had a strange balance to it, but he had practiced with them in the past to get their feel. On the second floor they found Mikhalai and two more soldiers, and finally they reached the ground floor, where Rodion and his men joined them. It was strange indeed to find these men here, men he and his brother, Ranos, had sent to Hael, but now that they were here it felt good indeed. They felt like his kindjal, familiar and deadly, for these were fighting men.

As they left the building, he saw on the snow-covered lawn a dozen streltsi locked in battle with the Kiliç Şaik. The snow around them was matted with blood and mud.

Nikandr flew down the steps, the others coming close behind. As they approached the skirmish, several of his streltsi discharged their wheellocks. The sound of the wheels spinning while sparks flew rose above the clang of swords, and then came the cracks of pistol shots. Five of the Kiliç Şaik took wounds to their shoulders or chests, but only two of them dropped.

And then they were locked in battle. Nikandr took one who fought with tall Yasha. The Kiliç saw Nikandr and retreated slowly, trading blows until he was next to one of his brother swordsmen. Then the two of them fought together, helping one another to fight off Nikandr and Yasha and Valentin.

One of them released a flurry of blows against both Yasha and Nikandr, but he was tiring from the effort.

It was all a ruse, though.

In a blur he spun away and swung low, taking Valentin's left leg clean off at the knee. In one fluid motion he was back fighting Nikandr and Yasha as his brother in arms beat off Valentin's final desperate sword stroke.

It was now Yasha and Nikandr against these two men. A few of the Kiliç that had caught pistol shots had finally succumbed to their wounds. A few others fell to the swords of his streltsi—who were dressed in the uniforms of the Empire's western territories—but more of Nikandr's men fell as well, faster than the Kiliç.

Something dark flew above the wall to Nikandr's left. Another came, but the moment Nikandr turned his head to see what it was, the Kiliç ahead of him pressed. He had seemed to be flagging mere seconds ago, but now it was all Nikandr could do to fend him off. His blows rang down hard, beating against Nikandr's sword arm.

Nikandr leaned back from a blow instead of blocking, did so again when the Kiliç advanced, and then caught him with his sword too wide. Nikandr swept his sword up, catching his enemy across the wrist. The Kiliç retreated immediately. Blood spilled from the wound. After beating away one last desperate attack, Nikandr stepped in and drove his sword through the Kiliç's exposed gut.

Chaos raged around him.

Styophan and his cousin, Rodion, were fighting with Soroush. Yasha had stepped to Nikandr's right to intercept one of the enemy, who was trying to flank Rodion.

Rustam, a young strelet with black hair and a wickedly fast sword arm, fell to the ground to Nikandr's left, blood pouring from a deep wound in his neck. The Kiliç he'd been fighting, who had just taken a deep wound to his thigh, retreated.

Rustam, however, had taken a deep stab through his chest. He looked up to Nikandr, his eyelids tightened in pain. As blood flowed freely over his janissary's uniform, he flipped his shashka around and held it for Nikandr to take. "Use a proper sword, My Lord Prince." No sooner had Nikandr taken it than Rustam's head fell back, his green eyes staring sightless toward the sky.

Another shape flew over the wall, landing at the top before dropping down and into the field of battle. More of the Kiliç. They were launching themselves over the wall to engage. There were a dozen of them now, fighting Nikandr's fifteen. Even as he crossed swords with one of them, more of his streltsi fell.

This was a battle they could not win, not if more of the Kiliç came while his own continued to fall.

"Together, men! Pull together!"

The men withdrew while sliding in toward one another, and soon they had something resembling a line. But they were only ten now, against the dozen Kiliç.

Nikandr glanced back. They were only halfway across the lawn. The relative safety of the building might as well have been leagues distant.

Another strelet fell as a sword cut fiercely down across his shoulder and into his rib cage.

Nikandr slipped on the slick ground. He fell and scrabbled away.

The Kiliç he was engaged with advanced quickly, bringing his sword up high.

Nikandr managed to beat away two strokes and roll away from a third. But the fourth caught him at an odd angle, and he lost grip of his shashka.

His left hand was already reaching for his kindjal, but he knew it would be too late.

The roar of a single, desperate soldier made the Kiliç turn.

Yasha, brave Yasha, swept in and rained blows down on the Kiliç. The enemy was fast, but Yasha was a blur. He forced the Kiliç back, shouting all the while. Then Yasha caught the Kiliç with a deep cut to his arm. He followed it immediately with an advance and a thrust of his sword through the Kiliç's chest. Yasha's shashka bit deep, cutting through the hardened leather armor.

Nikandr had no sooner made it to his feet than another Kiliç came in from behind.

"Yasha!" Nikandr shouted.

He tried to intercept the Kiliç, but he was too late. The Kiliç caught Yasha across the back of his calves.

Yasha fell, grimacing against the pain with clenched teeth. He tried to keep his sword high, to block the next blow, but could not. He dropped his guard and lowered himself to his hands.

The Kiliç raised his sword high—

"*Nyet!*" Nikandr cried.

—and brought it down across his neck.

Yasha's head rolled away as his body collapsed.

Nikandr released a guttural cry and fell against the Kiliç. He brought his sword down again and again, a rain of blows that the Kiliç could not fend off. At the last the Kiliç's sword came up too late and Nikandr caught him against the top of his brow, the sword cleaving his skull. The Kiliç's body spasmed and fell to the ground, twitching.

Nikandr surveyed the field, his breath coming in heaving gasps. By the ancients, there were only seven of them left including Soroush, and the Kiliç Şaik had ten. And even as he watched three more passed through the iron gate.

They had to run. They couldn't stand against so many.

Just as he was about to call for retreat, the report of a pistol rang across the bloody lawn.

One of the Kiliç that had just run through the gate grabbed for his back and fell heavily to the ground.

Another pistol fired, and another Kiliç dropped.

At the gate stood two streltsi. They ran forward fanning wide as more streltsi came behind them. These men bore wheellocks as well. Once they'd cleared the wall, they stopped and aimed. The wheellocks spun, sending sparks into the air, and the pistols fired. The last of the newly arrived Kiliç fell to the earth, and then over a dozen men of Anuskaya came charging, pulling swords with one hand, holding pistols in the other, shouting at the top of their lungs. Nikandr took up the call as well, as did the men around him. Even Soroush joined in as he beat away the attacks from two of the Kamarisi's swordsmen.

Soon the battlefield became little more than wrathful cries and the ring of steel and spinning wheellocks and the sharp smell of gunpowder.

None of the enemy retreated. Perhaps they hoped that more of their own would come, or perhaps they hoped to take down as many of the enemy as they could in order to protect their kasir. Whatever the case, they fought to the very last man.

When the last of the Kiliç had finally fallen to a sharp thrust from Styophan, the men of Anuskaya stood at the ready, waiting, as if they all expected the enemy to stand up, or for more to leap over the wall, but none did, and they moved quickly to help those of their fallen who were still alive.

It was only then that Nikandr realized Ashan was among those who'd come at the last. Ashan had his circlet and bracelets back. He had his stones as well. He must have found them in the tower before coming here.

While the men cared for the wounded, Nikandr waved Ashan and Soroush and Styophan over. "Three are missing," Nikandr said to Ashan. "Where are Nasim and Sukharam and Tohrab?"

Ashan looked back toward the grey tower, the top of which was barely visible over the wall. "I've not seen them since we arrived and I was placed in one of the uppermost cells. They were not in the tower when we searched. We looked in every cell."

Over Styophan's shoulder, the bulk of the men were helping the wounded. He did a quick count. There were perhaps twenty still able to fight. Twenty. How in the name of the mothers and fathers was he going to save the Kamarisi with only twenty men? And how was he going to save Nasim and Sukharam at the same time?

He told Ashan quickly of what Styophan had told him, that the Kamarisi had become an unexpected ally, that the Haelish were even now ready to attack and kill him. "The Haelish," Nikandr said to Styophan. "Will they listen to you?"

"If we can find King Brechan, he will hear our plea, but I can't say what his answer will be."

That was their only hope, then—to find Brechan—for they would never be able to fend off the forces the Kamarisi would have amassed there.

Nikandr turned to Ashan. "Can you find Nasim and Sukharam?"

Only moments ago, Ashan's alabaster stone, the one set into the circlet upon his brow, had been dull and lifeless. Now it was glowing—not brightly, but enough to make it clear that Ashan was now bonded with a havahezhan. "I will find them, son of Iaros, if they can be found at all."

Nikandr stepped in and hugged him. "Five of my men will go with you. The rest will wait for you in the stables."

Ashan tried to smile, but his eyes took in the carnage around him. "Go, Nikandr. Save the Kamarisi if he can be saved."

CHAPTER FIFTY-TWO

Nikandr rode atop a tall black stallion with Styophan beside him on a roan mare. The rest of his men—eighteen in all—rode behind, the thunder of their hooves ringing through the city as the citizens of Alekeşir, those few who remained in the streets, noted their passing with widened eyes. Their destination, the massive dome at the center of the city, was easy enough to see, but the streets of Alekeşir were confusing and difficult to navigate. And strangely enough, there was a cloud of birds high above the city, circling slowly, directly above the dome. Perhaps here in the capital the birds had learned that crowds might leave scraps of food.

Nikandr might have chosen to go straight east along the main thoroughfare—it would have brought them to the dome faster—but their purpose was not to blunder onto the grounds of the dome, but to remain hidden for as long as they could, and most importantly, to find Brechan before he attacked. They would have no chance of doing this at all had Styophan not known their basic plan. Brechan was coming in from the north with his most trusted men, and they were the ones who would wait for the Kamarisi to be flushed toward them by the others, who would sweep in toward the dome from the south.

Nikandr was well aware that noon had passed. He was also aware that the conflict at the kasir might have caused the Kamarisi to have been alerted. But even if men from the kasir had gone to the dome, they most likely would alert only Bahett, not the Kamarisi, and knowing Bahett, he would consider the threat to the Kamarisi minimal. Plus, in the end, Bahett wouldn't much care if Selim was killed. He would remain regent one way or the other.

They came to a square where the top of the white dome was in clear view of a row of two- and three-story buildings.

"Here," Styophan said as they came to a halt. "We should fan south from here."

The square was deserted. This close to the dome, anyone refusing to attend the address would be punished severely, which had left the streets blessedly empty. This was part of the old city, and as such the streets were narrow and serpentine. Six of them led from this old square with a well at the center. It was as likely a place as any for the men of Hael to have come. From here they could easily spread out to cover the entire area directly north of the dome.

"Good," Nikandr said. "Styophan and Soroush, with me. The rest, spread out in threes." He pointed to the two northward streets. "Even there in the event they were late in coming."

The men did so while Nikandr, Styophan, and Soroush headed directly south toward the dome. As they rode, Nikandr heard a young man's voice calling over the eery silence of the city. By the ancients, it was Selim. He was still giving his address. They'd come in time, then.

"Why wouldn't they have attacked by now?" Nikandr asked.

Styophan spoke softly. "Perhaps they wanted the Kamarisi's speech to be delivered in full before they took his life."

Nikandr nodded, granting him that. The Haelish might indeed wish to embarrass the Empire by waiting for this speech of power and permanence to be complete before they drew blood from the very one who'd spoken the words.

At an intersection, Nikandr looked down a narrow alley and saw three of his streltsi riding along another street. He saw no fear in their eyes. They were ready, these men, ready for whatever would come. Nikandr waved and they waved back, and then they all continued on. Selim's voice was coming clearer now, though he couldn't yet make out the words. Surely the address was coming to a close. It was well past the noon hour.

Nikandr watched among the stone buildings, down the alleyways and arches. The darkened doorways and the occasional plum or lemon tree in the small yards that could contain them. They were nearing the point where the sound of the horse's hooves might be heard by the people in the circle by the dome. Nikandr was ready to call for a halt when Styophan pointed ahead to a doorway that was partially open.

The sun was bright enough that he couldn't see into the shadows, but Styophan was already snapping the reins of his horse and moving ahead of the group. He didn't call, but he waved his hands above his head, waiting for the person within to recognize him. The door opened a moment later and a tall man with broad shoulders stood in the doorway. The man remained as Styophan and the others approached, but Nikandr could see now that he was jittery, as if he had smoked too much of the foul black tar the drug dens of Alekeşir were famous for, but his eyes were too sharp—angry even—for that to be the reason.

Styophan slipped down from his horse and approached the doorway. "We must speak with Brechan."

"The time for that was last night, Styophan of Anuskaya."

"The time is now." Styophan turned and motioned to Nikandr. "We've found our prince, but there is reason to keep the Kamarisi alive."

The Haelish warrior regarded Nikandr impassively and shook his head. "No reason Brechan will hear."

"Let *him* be the judge, Datha. This could be the ruin of us all. The withering. The rifts. The deaths of so many in Hael. It will not stop unless we can reach the islands, and Selim has promised help."

"Lies," Datha said. "Lies for the benefit of the Empire."

"I have no love for Yrstanla. You know this. So believe me when I say I would do nothing to help them. It is *they* that will help *us*. There is little time left, Datha. I only wish to speak with him."

Datha stared down at Styophan with uncaring eyes.

Styophan, however, stepped toward the towering Haelish man. Nikandr had no idea what he was doing until his hand had shot out and punched Datha in the throat.

Datha doubled over, holding his throat and reaching for Styophan at the same time, but Styophan had stepped back, forcing Datha to stagger forward in order to reach him. The moment Datha did, Styophan ducked and slithered behind him, catching Datha's leg in a twisting move that brought the big man crashing down to the dirt road. In a blink Styophan had Datha's arm behind his back and his pistol to the back of Datha's head.

With his black eye patch and grim expression Styophan looked like death itself. "You may not care if you die this day, but when the gun goes off it will alert the Kamarisi and his guard. Now tell me where he is."

Datha's answer was to face downward, and lift his head *into* the barrel of Styophan's gun, daring Styophan to pull the trigger.

Nikandr slipped down, ready to order Styophan to hold, but his words died on his lips, for just then shadows played across the ground in front of him and behind him and all around. A flapping of wings came. A white-breasted jackdaw came to rest on the edge of the roof of the building to Nikandr's left. Another came, and another, then dozens descended. But it wasn't the birds that drew Nikandr's attention. It was the girl that walked down the street, partially hidden by the shade of an ancient, slouching pistachio tree that hung over the stone wall of a hidden yard. She had straight, jet-black hair, and she wore a flaxen dress with simple-but-elegant embroidery around the hem and sleeves. She walked not as a normal child might, but with a strange, shambling gait.

The akhoz, Nikandr thought. *The akhoz are here.*

But when she stepped into the stark sunlight, he realized the girl's condition had nothing to do with those strange, twisted creatures from Alayazhar. Her eyes were half-lidded, but at least she *had* eyes, and her skin… Her skin was the normal olive hue of a child from the Empire's heartland, not the sickly grey of the akhoz.

Soroush slipped down from his horse and pulled his wheellock, but he paused as well. Even Datha seemed confused, for he turned his head to look at the girl, then arched awkwardly to take in the strange birds that were still collecting all around them. Except for the flapping of their wings they made not a sound, not the squawk or quorks the jackdaws would normally make. They merely stared, their collective eyes watching as the girl approached.

Some that stood in her way jumped and flapped to one side as she approached. They seemed *of* her, somehow. Connected in some way Nikandr couldn't understand.

But then he felt through his soulstone something he hadn't felt in months. "Ishkyna."

Hers was an imprint he knew well at this point, but it felt different, as if his memories were of a girl and here before him was a woman fully grown. The realization was unnerving, for it meant that Ishkyna had widened once again her already considerable powers.

"Ishkyna," Nikandr said again, stepping forward.

The girl turned and looked to a nearby street that angled off the one they'd been riding along. She spoke with the voice of a little girl, but it came out in a croak, as if she were sick and hadn't used her voice in days. "The King of Hael is two streets over, hiding behind a mule cart, waiting for their signal."

"And when will that be?" Nikandr asked.

"Why, no time at all, Nischka."

Before Nikandr could ask her what she meant, the rattle of musket fire came from the direction of the dome.

"Mount," Nikandr called, running to his horse and swinging himself up and into the saddle. "Head down the street there." Nikandr pointed to a narrow street that went westward up a steep hill.

Styophan remained, holding Datha's arm tight.

"Leave him be," Nikandr called. "One more won't make a difference."

Styophan glared down with his one good eye and released Datha. Then he mounted as well, and soon they were riding toward the street Ishkyna had indicated. As Datha sprinted southward, pulling a long, wide sword from inside his robe as he went, Nikandr guided his horse forward and reached down to the girl.

Ishkyna, however, merely stared westward, perhaps toward the king, perhaps to something Nikandr would never have the ability to see.

"Come, Ishkyna. Quickly, now."

He shook his hand in front of her face, but the moment he did, the girl collapsed to the ground. She lay there motionless. Nikandr had no idea whether she was alive or dead.

The sound of gunfire grew, as did the shouts from the crowd. The streets were going to be utter madness in moments. The girl would be trampled.

Nikandr slipped down from his horse and carried the girl over to the edge of the road and laid her against the worn stone of the building there. She was still breathing, thank the ancients, and she'd be in plain sight here. Hopefully someone would find her and care for her.

He vaulted back onto his horse, grabbed the reins, and kicked the black stallion into action. It responded well. This was a horse of war. It was jittery from the sounds that were now coming closer, but not from nerves. This was a horse used to the smell of blood and the sounds of battle. He caught up with the others, who were waiting for a sign. As if in answer to their call, a swarm of jackdaws swooped down from above the height of the nearby homes and swept along the road heading south.

They followed the birds, turning right, then left, up an alley filled with the stink of a tannery, all as the first of the refugees from the Kamarisi's address came running along the roads. The crowd was still thin, but the streets would be teeming in moments.

The sight of the jackdaws caused the Alekeşiri to stop in their tracks. They stared at the black, writhing vision before them—it looked more like a swarm of bees than a flock of birds—and then backed away as the birds flew overhead, revealing the eighteen pounding war horses riding down the street toward them.

They parted like kindling beneath the blade of a hatchet.

Nikandr and his men came to a wide thoroughfare, one of the major streets running north to south through Alekeşir, and here the birds swarmed over one figure.

"That's him!" Styophan called over the din of hooves and the growing alarm of the crowd. "That's Brechan."

They headed straight for him, but as they did, Nikandr saw the mass of people and horses and soldiers coming down the street toward them. Somewhere, a woman screamed for her child. Citizens fled before a vanguard of janissaries on horses, and behind came a group of Kiliç Şaik. They surrounded a golden chariot pulled by two white horses with grey manes.

It was the Kamarisi, Nikandr realized. Selim ül Hakan was coming, and Bahett was with him.

CHAPTER FIFTY-THREE

Nikandr watched as Styophan kicked his horse, urging it toward Brechan. Styophan slipped down and shouted to the Haelish King as the sounds of panic and screaming became first loud and then deafening.

The janissaries had seen Nikandr and his streltsi. They were still dressed in the uniforms of Yrstanla, but somehow they knew. Their commander was pointing. His men trained their muskets a moment later.

And then a man—seven feet tall if he was one, wearing a simple brown robe—swept in front of the charging horses, grabbed the reins of the lead horse, and yanked the horse's head down so sharply the beast tipped forward and tumbled onto the stones of the street. The Haelish warrior was lost from view as several horses behind tumbled over the first. More and more crashed into the fallen beasts, and the screaming of horses rose above the din of the crowd and mingled with the smattering of gunfire that was raining down not just on Nikandr and his streltsi, but three Haelish warriors, who were just now charging with great swords drawn into the crowd.

"Ishkyna!" Nikandr called. "Stop them!"

The jackdaws had flown up above the buildings, but at Nikandr's words they swept in around the Haelish men, who had already started swinging their swords, cleaving the soldiers of Yrstanla in their saddles or the legs of the horses they rode. Blood poured along the cobbled street like barrels of spilled ink.

As the hundreds—thousands—of black birds wheeled around the Haelish, they became confused. They batted at the birds, trying to carve a path to the Kamarisi, but the janissaries had recovered and they were firing en masse into these three hulking men. It was hard to discern, but Nikandr could see what looked to be chips of stone flying from the men as the shots bit into them. He knew it wasn't stone, however, but skin.

Closer, Brechan stood and shoved Styophan away. His face was angry. He looked to his men. More of the Haelish had come now. Four more rushed in from a street Nikandr and his streltsi had ridden down a short while ago, and behind Nikandr six more advanced along the wide thoroughfare. The Kiliç Şaik beyond the line of janissaries had turned to face another threat—surely more of the Haelish, probably those that had flushed the Kamarisi in this direction toward Brechan and the others.

As the jackdaws spread out to harry the approaching warriors, Styophan shouted something to Brechan. Brechan drew his sword and rounded on Styophan.

Nikandr raised his pistol to fire on Brechan, but before he could the Haelish King stopped. He became stock-still. His face went vacant, but then it regained some of the emotion it had had only a moment ago—not the anger, but certainly the grim determination.

He turned and bellowed to his men. His words—spoken in Haelish—carried over the sounds of battle. The jackdaws flew higher and hovered like a black fog over the street as Brechan called again. He called out again, louder still, and his men turned toward him, their faces confused.

The fighting continued beyond the tight grouping of the Kamarisi's guard, but closer, to this side of Selim and Bahett, the janissaries stopped. They watched, and a tenuous but mutual detente settled over this place in the heart of Alekeşir.

Nikandr kicked his horse forward, raising his hands in an appeal for calm. Heads began to turn toward him. The hostilities would end. At the very least he'd be able to speak for a moment with Selim to have him order his men to stand down.

This was when Nikandr caught movement along the top of a three-story building to his left. It was Datha. He was no longer wearing the brown robes he'd had on earlier. Instead he had only the soft leggings of the Haelish. Scrawled across his bare chest were primitive patterns drawn with glittering red paint. He called out a strange and throaty ululation as he leapt from the building and dropped onto one of the Kiliç Şaik. He'd chosen the only one wearing white armor, surely the leader of the Kiliç. Datha drove his sword straight down through him. It entered at the space between his shoulder blades and pierced his body like a pig on a spit. The rear legs of the horse the Kiliç had been riding collapsed. It neighed as it rolled, the other horses skittering away, and for a moment Datha was lost.

"Stop!" King Brechan called in Yrstanlan.

But Datha wouldn't. He'd come to slay the Kamarisi, and even the words of his king would not stay his hand.

Nikandr pulled his pistol and trained it on the Haelish warrior. Those few janissaries still watching somehow seemed to know that Nikandr was trying to stop him, and they did not raise their muskets against him. The others fired at Datha. The Kılıç Şaik closed, but Datha was simply too near. He leapt up to the chariot that carried the Kamarisi and grabbed Selim's head by his hair.

Nikandr pulled the trigger. The wheel spun, sending sparks flying.

The pistol roared, kicking the palm of Nikandr's hand.

The shot caught Datha on the crown of his head. A chunk of something the size of a peach pit flew from Datha's head. Blood followed the chunk of Datha's skull in an arc as his hair burst into flame.

Datha screamed in triumph and surprise and pain as the muscles along his arms flexed and he drew his sword across Selim's neck.

Nikandr swore that in that final moment Selim looked straight toward him, his eyes wide with shock and fear. And then his body tilted and fell away from his neck.

Blood rained down from Selim's disembodied head while Datha screamed and went rigid. The Haelish warrior's body tightened. Fire gouted from his mouth, from his eyes and ears. And soon his whole body was engulfed in flame.

Nikandr could think of no other than Stasa Bolgravya, the Grand Duke who years ago had been consumed by a suurahezhan as it stepped onto the deck of his yacht. Here again Nikandr could hear the screams of man and spirit alike, a sound that somehow bridged the gap between worlds.

Bahett scrambled off the imperial chariot. The Kılıç Şaik backed away.

And the janissaries turned toward Brechan and the Haelish. Toward Nikandr and his countrymen.

Brechan looked into Nikandr's eyes. "Run," he shouted, and then drew his sword and charged into the line of janissaries, swinging as he went.

The other Haelish followed, and the battle that had paused resumed.

Nikandr reined his horse over and kicked it into motion. "Ride, men! Ride!"

No sooner had he said these words than he saw more riders coming down the street behind them. Dozens of janissaries, and more riding along from the narrow street Nikandr and the others had used to reach this wide thoroughfare. Where they'd come from he had no idea. Perhaps some had circled around while they were fighting. Perhaps they'd come from some nearby post. It mattered little. What mattered was that they were surrounded.

Nikandr was ready to try to drive through them. Ishkyna must have sensed his thoughts, for the jackdaws returned, driving against the bulk of the soldiers ahead of them.

The cloud swooped in, clawing at faces and pecking at eyes. Many were hampered, but many more were not. Musket shots came raining in. A streltsi to Nikandr's left went down. And two on his right. Those that still had loaded weapons returned fire. The rest pulled shashkas and prepared to engage.

But before they could close, the jackdaws scattered. They flew upward in one sweeping motion that reminded Nikandr more of a dancer swinging a veil than it did a flock of birds.

Then the ground tipped and Nikandr's horse fell.

He was thrown wide as his horse struck the ground hard.

It was then that he felt it. The world around him rumbling. The ground itself moving, shifting, bucking as if it were little more than the skin of some titanic creature long since forgotten by the minds and hearts of men.

The sound of crumbling stone rent the air. One of the nearby buildings shuddered and then collapsed to the street, the stone blocks crashing into a spray that caught the janissaries. Another building fell behind Nikandr, taking many of his men with it. Just how many Nikandr wasn't sure, for the dust that billowed up was impossible to see through.

All around there came the cries of men, barely louder than the crumbling of the world.

Nikandr managed to stand. "To me!" He limped forward, low to the ground, squinting against the fine dust in the air. "To me, men of Anuskaya!"

"Here, My Lord Prince." It was Styophan.

The ground continued to buck as he moved forward. He was thrown to the ground several times, but he warded with his hands and kept moving. He found Soroush, who was helping Styophan to his feet. Their horses were gone, and both men were bleeding.

"To me!" Nikandr called again as he helped Soroush with Styophan.

Slowly, the rumbling started to die away, but another building crashed somewhere back toward the chariot. The cries of misery mixed with the sound of crashing stone, and Nikandr wondered idly whether Bahett had just been killed.

It matters little now, he thought. They had failed, but now they must escape.

Slowly they gathered horses. There were enough, for they found only two other men. A mere five had survived from the eighteen they had started with.

"By my father, I've made a mess of things," Nikandr said as they led their horses tentatively away. They passed several janissaries, some fallen, others helping their brothers in arms, but none made a move to stop them. They simply peered through the settling dust, eyes wide in wonder and fear at the world around them.

They mounted once the rumbling had stopped and rode hard northward, planning to head back to the Kasir to find Ashan and Nasim if they could be found, but when they came to a bridge that led over a canal filled with brown water and detritus, he saw a gallows crow standing on the edge of it. It fidgeted as they approached, as if Ishkyna were having difficulty maintaining control.

"East," the crow said before cawing several times. "You must head east."

"Nasim and the others—"

"Gone, Nischka. They're all gone."

"Gone where?"

"I don't know, but I felt them, moments before the quake. They entered a rift at the kasir, and then I felt them no more." It cawed again and flapped into the air before turning round and alighting onto the same spot it had been only moments ago. "Flee, Nikandr. This place is not safe. The rift they opened has already widened, and it will quickly grow worse."

And then the crow launched itself into the air and winged down the canal toward the mighty Vünkal. He could barely see the muddy river through the dust that had drifted over the city like a pall.

CHAPTER FIFTY-FOUR

Sukharam was returned to Nasim's room after darkness fell. He was still in his manacles. He sat and looked over to Tohrab as the door was locked and the guard's footsteps faded away.

Tohrab sat on his bed, his back against the cold stone wall, staring eastward. It was a grim stare, as if he feared he hadn't the strength for what lay ahead, but it was also determined. This was a man—if he could still be called such—that had withstood the forces of the rifts for centuries. True, he'd had his brothers and sisters to help him, and clearly every single day that passed cost him dearly, but he had strength yet. Such was the power of the men of old.

"Where did they take you?" Nasim asked Sukharam.

"To the Great Hall. Bahett wished to speak with me." He said these words in a voice that was distant, as if he too were thinking about another place and another time.

"What about?"

Sukharam lifted his head and regarded Nasim. "What do you think? He wanted to know of our plans. Of Sariya. Where I thought she was now. He wanted to know of the Atalayina, whether Sariya had managed to unlock its secrets."

"And what did you tell him?"

Sukharam's face became harder, which in the moonlight made his skin look like marble. "There was little harm in telling him the truth."

"Was there not?"

"You would rather I suffered before telling him? Or have you adopted the ways of the Landed?"

"The Landed... Listen to yourself. Are you Maharraht to speak of them so?"

Sukharam opened his mouth to speak, his face dark and angry, but then he calmed himself and lay down facing the wall. "Go to sleep."

"Sukharam?" When he didn't turn around, Nasim continued. "Why were you afraid when we were speaking of the fates?"

"Nasim, I'm more tired than I've ever been."

"This is important."

"Many things are important."

"*Yeh*, but this—"

"We can speak of it in the morning. For now, just leave me be."

Nasim waited, hoping Sukharam would change his mind. He wanted to press, but that would only make Sukharam angrier. "Very well," Nasim said as he lay down. "We'll speak in the morning."

Nasim tried to fall asleep, but couldn't. His mind was filled with everything around him. Tohrab's suffering. Sukharam's secrets. But more than anything, the uncertainty over their future.

Finally, near dawn, he did manage to close his eyes.

And when he opened them again, Sukharam was gone.

The sun was already high. He'd slept for hours, and Sukharam's bed was empty. His manacles lay upon the rough grey blanket, broken.

"Tohrab," Nasim called.

Tohrab was still sitting where he had been when Nasim had nodded off. His lips pressed tight. His eyes fixed on the far wall.

Nasim shook his shoulder. "Tohrab! Sukharam is gone."

Tohrab met Nasim's gaze, but his eyes were glazed, and he didn't speak. He merely stared, as if he no longer had the ability to do anything beyond holding the last shreds of the wards together.

"Did you hear me? Sukharam is gone."

When Tohrab spoke, the words came slowly. "Did I not tell you it would be so?" He was clearly in pain. Nasim wished there was some way he could share the burden, but he didn't know the first thing about the wards, and Tohrab could most likely spare neither the attention nor the strength to teach him.

Nasim picked up the manacles, which looked to have been melted along a thin line near the lock. "He burned his way out. A suurahezhan, through iron. How, Tohrab? How did he do it?"

For the first time, Tohrab seemed truly present. He stared at the manacles, then took in the room around him, and finally he looked up to Nasim with a look of clarity he hadn't seen since Shadam Khoreh. "Bonding through iron is difficult, but not impossible."

"How, then?" Outside the cell door, Nasim heard sounds, perhaps from the level below them. "Tohrab, we have to stop him."

"The chains," Tohrab said. "They bind you to this place, to the earth. It is there that you can find your way to Adhiya. A suurahezhan can reach you through such a link. Find one, Nasim. Find one and use it as Sukharam has."

Nasim stared at the black iron around his wrists. He'd never considered that it might be defeated, and so had never tried. He felt for the link Tohrab spoke of, but sensed nothing whatsoever. The chains were an anchor, dragging him down, rooting him in place, deadening the way to Adhiya.

"You feel the heat, Nasim. You see the wavering in the air. Look beyond, and you will see the flames."

Nasim shook his head, spread his feet wider. He felt the stone of the tower beneath him. Felt the earth below it, solid and deep. When he focused on the chains, any sense of this vanished. He took a deep breath and closed his eyes. He spread his hands wide at his side and tried again.

This time, he felt not only the tower, not only the earth below, he felt the other buildings in the kasir. He felt the long curtain wall that surrounded it. He felt the stones set into the roads of the city and the thousands of buildings that made up Alekeşir. If he had allowed it, this expanding awareness would have continued to the landscape beyond, toward the mountains to the east and the desert to the south, to the hills of the Haelish that lay westward or the cold wastes of the north. But he reined his awareness in. He drew it toward the tower, and when he did, he felt the ways in which he was rooted by the iron chains. And with that understanding he also felt its weakness: narrow veins where the iron was imperfectly forged. It was there, through those narrow openings, that Adhiya could be found.

He touched that part of him that was aligned with fire, hoping the suurahe-zhan would find him through these narrowest of openings. It took time, but eventually he sensed one. The smell of cardamom came to him as he beckoned it forth, and eventually a bond as tentative as a butterfly's kiss was forged through the gaps in the chain. He gave of himself while asking the suurahezhan to heat the chains. This did little at first, and Nasim could barely feel it feeding on him. But the heat the hezhan granted to the chains made the gaps widen, which allowed him to draw more heat. A sensation grew within him. It was unlike the nausea he'd felt so often when he was young. Those days were gone; Nikandr's taint had been removed from him on the Spar of Galahesh. It was more like an exuberance that also enfeebled, like walking along the heights of an impossibly tall mountain.

He'd been freed of his bond with Nikandr for years, but only recently had his mind been wrested from Sariya so that he could *feel* a bond with a hezhan. It was ... wonderful. Had he truly never felt this way before? He could remember nothing but discomfort, nothing but pain and confusion and disorientation. He'd wondered in the dark days of his childhood how men like Ashan could willingly bond with hezhan, but he wouldn't have questioned their actions had he known how *good* it felt.

"Nasim!"

The world around him went cold.

He looked down to his hands and saw glowing metal melt and fall away. Some of it pooled in his hands. He lifted them and stared at the glowing, molten metal. He allowed it to fall to the floor of the tower as he felt the suurahezhan—an ancient creature, indeed—slip back toward the aether to the world beyond. He kept it close, however. He was not yet ready to release it, no matter that he'd been weakened by its touch.

He stared down. At his feet was a pile of slag—the color of it glowing red, then burnt rose, then charred grey—and around it, smaller spatters of dull grey metal, the very same color the manacles had been moments ago.

"Nasim."

Nasim looked over at Tohrab, who even through his pain was staring at him with eyes of wonder.

Outside, the sun was higher still.

By the fates, how much time had passed?

"I must ask you to do so again," Tohrab said, holding up his own manacles.

Nasim drew on the suurahezhan once again and grasped Tohrab's chains, but as he did, he felt another suurahezhan slipping across the aether even then, bonding with a nearby qiram.

It was Sukharam, and Nasim knew with certainty the reason. Sukharam was readying his passage to Ghayavand.

Tohrab's eyes said that he felt it too. They begged him to move faster.

Nasim bent his will to the iron chains. The magic of the suurahezhan again slipped over them like water on oiled canvas. But this metal was of poor quality, and he knew now how to foil such stuff. He was careful that he didn't burn Tohrab, so it took time, but soon enough the manacles split and fell away.

The lock to the door, he found, had been melted, but it was simply a matter of melting it again. This time, he moved as quickly as he could. In moments, the wood of the door was smoking and the glowing, molten metal was pouring from the hole where the lock once was. Then he and Tohrab were out and navigating the steps down. He wanted to free Ashan and Nikandr and the others, but he could spare no time. He had to stop Sukharam. Once that was done, he could return to free them.

They left through the door at the tower's base and headed across the snow-covered yard toward the southeast portion of the kasir's grounds. That was where Sukharam was. He had bonded with another hezhan, this one a vanahezhan, a spirit of the earth, and even now he was drawing forth another.

Five, Nasim thought. He was going to bond with five of them.

Sukharam must have known he was coming, for Nasim felt him speed up his process. He bonded with a spirit of life, and then a water spirit, and finally a havahezhan, a spirit of wind.

Nasim wanted to run, but Tohrab was already flagging. He staggered forward until Nasim put Tohrab's arm around his shoulders and helped him forward.

He'd not gone ten strides when something opened up inside him. He knew immediately what it was. Years ago, when Kaleh had done the same thing, he'd had no idea what to look for. But now it was as intimate as an itch beneath the skin. Sukharam had just opened a hole in the earth, one that would lead him to Ghayavand.

He would have to summon spirits as Sukharam had. It might make things worse here, but he couldn't allow Sukharam to reach Ghayavand's shores alone.

Luckily, such a thing was child's play. There were so many hezhan near that he need only call and he found many willing to bond. He chose carefully, taking only those powerful enough to do his bidding, but not so powerful that they would widen the rift any further—or worse, cross over to Erahm.

Fire he had already. Earth was next, then water and air, and finally a spirit of life. The feeling was heady and eerily similar to what he'd experienced on Oshtoyets years ago when Soroush had fed him the elder elemental stones.

Tohrab was still leaning on him for support, but he seemed to find some inner reserve. His breath came in long rasping wheezes, but they moved with speed, a shambling run, toward the orchards. They came to a clearing with a pond at its center and a hillock on the far side. Sukharam stood near the top of this, hands wide, face turned up toward the sky. Near his feet was an open maw, a tear that exposed dark earth and mottled stone. It was still widening as Nasim and Tohrab approached, but he'd no sooner stepped onto the gravel path that lined the pond than Sukharam stopped and turned.

He raised his hand and a wind buffeted Nasim. It roared in his ears and pushed him backward. It came on so fiercely and so quickly that he didn't have time to do anything but raise his arms and ward his face against the hail of rocks that lifted from the path and struck him. Finally he was able to draw upon his havahezhan to quell the winds. Sukharam tried over and over to lift the wind once more, but Nasim stopped him at every turn.

A wave of water rushed forward. It slipped over the bank of the pond and snaked toward him. With a wave of Nasim's hand the effect ceased and the water splashed to the ground and drained back toward the pond.

These were merely delaying tactics, Nasim knew. Sukharam was keeping them at bay until the earth widened sufficiently. Nasim couldn't make it there in time, so he furthered the effect. He forced the earth to open *wider*.

Sukharam didn't realize what he was doing until it was wide enough to swallow a house. Without turning back, he stepped into the breach. As the earthen maw began to close, Nasim ran forward, struggling to keep the rift open. It wasn't going to be enough, he realized. He wouldn't reach it in time.

"Nasim!"

He turned and found Ashan standing by a handful of streltsi.

The look on Ashan's face was one of horror at what was happening, but he was also helping Nasim to hold the gateway open.

"Go!" Ashan said to the streltsi. "Find your prince as he bid you."

The streltsi standing there looked amongst themselves. "Where will you go?" one of them shouted above the sound of the rumbling earth.

"To Ghayavand. Tell Nikandr we go to Ghayavand."

The streltsi nodded and were off, heading back toward the bulk of the kasir, while Ashan stepped forward, the stones in his circlet and on his wrists shining more brightly than Nasim had ever seen them.

Together, Nasim, Ashan, and Tohrab made their way to the rift. It was nearly closed, but there was room enough yet.

No sooner had they stepped down into the earth than it pressed in. In an instant Nasim felt his bonds release. He was alone in the dark, and for a moment he feared he'd made a grave mistake. He feared Sukharam had gone and the gateway had already closed, leaving him breathless seven feet below the surface of the ground.

But then he felt disorientation, a shift in the world around him. A shift in the aether as well. It felt different than before, as though the transition was taking longer than it had with Kaleh.

When the earth above him opened, it was to a blanket of stars.

Nasim pulled himself up, helped Ashan and Tohrab to do the same. His joints ached. His mouth felt like dried leather.

How long he'd been in that place he couldn't guess. Surely it had been at least several hours.

"By the fates," Ashan said.

He was staring up at the sky, at the constellations that shined down on Ghayavand. When Nasim did the same, he realized they weren't right. It had not merely been a handful of hours. It had been *weeks* since leaving Alekeşir.

CHAPTER FIFTY-FIVE

The breeze smelled fresh of the sea as Nasim and Ashan led Tohrab through the streets of Alayazhar. Morning sunlight angled in against the city, making the gutted stone homes and buildings look like they were tipping to the ground. Nasim and Ashan were tired—they'd walked nearly every waking minute since crawling up from the hole in the ground well before dawn. But if they were tired, Tohrab was nearing collapse. He shuffled, stumbling occasionally before straightening and continuing on. Nasim and Ashan had both pleaded for him to allow them to help, but Tohrab had refused them.

"Your mere touch draws my concentration from where it's needed," he'd said. "I will hold for a while yet. But you must leave me be."

So they'd continued on, hoping Tohrab was right, for he had no idea what would happen when the final ward failed altogether.

"It's so desolate," Nasim said.

Ashan, walking next to him, took in the city. They were walking through the center of the old city northward toward the crescent bay. "It has been so for some time, Nasim."

"I'm not talking about the days before the sundering."

"You speak of the akhoz?"

Nasim nodded and waved to the city around them. "They're gone, Ashan. All of them."

They'd spoken of how the akhoz had been made. In the days following the sundering, after other attempts at halting the spread of the rifts had failed, children and suurahezhan had been bonded to one another by the Al-Aqim. They had used the broken pieces of the Atalayina to fuse the two together, and when they had, they'd created a grounding of sorts, and it had for centuries slowed the spread of the rifts. The tragedy was not that the children had been used in such a way, it was the fact that both spirits—the soul of the child and the

353

suurahezhan—had forever been lost to the cycle of death and rebirth. Both had been fated to death, true and final death, when the ritual had been completed. Though their existence had been miserable, it gave Nasim no solace that they had now been freed from it. They would never return to Erahm, never slip back to Adhiya. They would never learn and grow, and so their destiny of eventual enlightenment had been robbed from them, a fate infinitely worse.

Unlike the last time he was here, the streets were completely free of akhoz. Their aching calls no longer haunted the city.

In their place, however, was a strange feeling of discomfort. Nasim knew it was from the closeness of Adhiya. He could feel the hezhan there, some hoping to cross when the veil grew thin enough. Occasionally he would feel one slip through—most often havahezhan in the sky above them—but when they did they often slipped right back through the same rift that had delivered them. The rifts were not so deep that they could cross at will.

It won't be long, though.

"They were wretched creatures," Ashan said. "I'm glad they no longer suffer."

"As am I. Yet still, the world seems poorer for their absence."

They came to a crumbling bridge. Below, the stream that once ran through the city was dry. Nasim and Ashan walked over it easily, but it took Tohrab long minutes to make the twenty steps needed to cross to the other side. Nasim was about to ask him again if he could help, but Tohrab, sensing it, raised his hand and shook his head. His deep-set eyes were pinched in pain or concentration or both, and his hands quavered, but he continued on.

"Men are driven to desperate things in times like those," Ashan said when they'd started making their way once more.

"But they were learned," Nasim replied. "They were wise. We are meant to heal, not harm."

To Nasim's surprise, Ashan didn't respond. He merely walked beside Nasim, the soles of his boots scraping over the remains of the stone road.

"You no longer believe those words?" Nasim asked.

"I do, but I say them from the comfort of the life I've led and the time in which I've lived. I've often wondered what I would have done in their place."

"You?" Nasim laughed. "I can't *escape* such thoughts."

"You are not Khamal."

"I know that, Ashan, but I feel his fears and hopes. I feel his desperation. I can only think that they were blinded by the failure of the ritual. They were more desperate than they realized."

They came to a bend in the street, and before them, down a hill and near the rocky shore, were the remains of Sariya's tower. It had crumbled to nothing, a mere remnant of the proud, white tower Nasim had seen when he was here last.

Ashan looked up to the ridge on their left that overlooked the city. There the remains of the celestia could be seen. They lay like the bones of a drakhen collapsed from hunger. The celestia had been Khamal's demesne, and the tower had been Sariya's. There was only one remaining, though it was a place to which Nasim didn't relish returning. The village of Shirvozeh to the east of Alayazhar. It had been used by many before the sundering, but after the three Al-Aqim had been trapped on the island, Muqallad had claimed it for his own. Nasim had traveled there two years ago. It had been the place he and Rabiah had come to free Ashan. It had been the place Ashan had been taken and tortured by Muqallad. Nasim would go elsewhere, but the village and its lake were still a place of power on the island.

And, he told himself, he would not allow Muqallad power beyond his death. If the village was the place he needed to find answers, he would go there and hopefully free it from Muqallad's taint.

"I wonder where she is," Nasim said as they passed the fallen white stones of Sariya's tower.

"I wonder as well. But more, I wonder where the Atalayina is."

Nasim had been so close to it in Shadam Khoreh. He should have grabbed it when Sariya fell. But he'd been so disoriented by the storm. He'd simply been glad he was still alive.

"It will find its way here," Nasim said.

"If it hasn't already."

"*Yeh*," Nasim said, laughing. "If it hasn't already. The ways of the fates are strange."

Nasim felt Ashan's hand on his shoulder. The old arqesh rubbed him affectionately, as a father might his son. "Strange, indeed."

Tohrab had begun walking past Sariya's tower. He was headed not along the road toward Shirvozeh, but the trail that led down to the seashore.

"Tohrab?" Nasim called.

"I must take rest." He did not turn as he spoke. He merely kept treading forward with his slow, shuffling gait. "Go to Shirvozeh. You will find me on the rock"—he raised his hand and pointed—"there."

Nasim shivered. He was pointing to the rock where Khamal had sacrificed one of the akhoz. It had been in preparation of leaving the island. Of tricking Sariya and Muqallad to murder him so he could be reborn.

Reborn as me, Nasim thought.

For a moment he struggled to recall the boy's name.

Alif, he finally remembered. Alif. One of the survivors of the devastation after the sundering. It had been that reason—his status as an orphan—that had made Khamal choose him over Yadhan for that ritual. *A poor reason, indeed.*

As they watched, Tohrab reached the trail and headed down, but before he was lost from sight completely, he turned his head and said, "Hurry, Nasim. Hurry." And then he was gone.

"Come," Ashan said.

Nasim nodded, and they were off.

They reached Shirvozeh hours later when the sun was near its zenith.

The entrance stood open. The tall metal doors that once hung there were gone. They trekked down through the tunnels. Nasim could have taken them through the darkness to the lake from memory—such was his memory of this place—but Ashan found a siraj stone within one of the dark rooms they passed, and he used it to light their way.

Eventually they came to the stairway that led them to the dark lake. When they reached the massive cavern that housed the lake, however, Ashan gasped. Gone was the black water. All that remained was a dry cavern with a rocky bed. The water had drained. Nasim didn't understand the power of the lakes, but he knew that the same thing had happened to many Aramahn villages over the centuries, and when that happened, the Aramahn eventually left.

Nasim stepped to the edge of where the water once was and stared out over the field of dark grey stones. "Sukharam said that my memories of Khamal were being viewed through the veil of the dead. I told him they'd never been wrong, and he became stricken. He was terrified, Ashan. I've never seen him so scared."

Ashan squatted and ran his hands over the line on the stones that had once marked the water level. "I think it has something to do with his time in Kohor. When he left the Veil of Stars, shortly before we traveled to the valley of Shadam Khoreh... To say he was unsettled would be to trivialize it. He was shaken to his core. He was wide-eyed, but he wouldn't speak of it, not yet." Ashan paused his inspection to peer into the darkness. "He'd been making strong progress, reaching further each night as he took breath. Perhaps he'd managed to reach the heavens. He might even have managed to feel their intent. But when he left, that memory may have faded like a dream. Perhaps it resurfaced when you spoke with him in Alekeşir."

"The question, then, is what did he see?"

Ashan shook his head. "The fates. Their will. Their anger. Who can know?"

That was exactly why they'd come to this place. They had to know more, and it was time for Nasim to unearth the answers that had been eluding him for years.

He moved several paces away from the lake and lay down. Ashan knelt and cradled Nasim's head between the palms of his hands. Ashan took a deep breath and released it, as if by doing so he were releasing all his troubles as well. Ashan had always been good at such things, a skill Nasim was extremely envious of. How could a man who dealt with things of such import take them so much in stride?

Perhaps one day I'll manage the same.

"Close your eyes," Ashan said. "Think of that day. Relive it. I'll guide you, but keep within the dream as long as you can."

Nasim nodded and began taking longer and longer breaths. Soon, his inhalation and exhalation were the same length. They were long as the night. The feeling of the round stones against his back faded. Then the chill of the air. Then the feeling of Ashan's warm hands against his cheeks and ears.

And finally, that fateful day from the life of another man returned to him, brighter than ever before.

As the ritual begins, Khamal looks into the eyes of Muqallad and Sariya. They nod to one another.

At last, after all these years, it has begun in earnest.

The world opens up around him, not simply the mountain with its crisp spring air, not simply the island and the sapphire waters that surround it, but the firmament above and the heavens beyond. The aether and Adhiya are drawn in as well. In this moment, all worlds have become one.

And Khamal feels all of it.

He feels the fates as well.

They are smiling, and with this, they give their tacit approval.

They *approve* of this grand undertaking.

Together, Khamal draws Adhiya closer, as Sariya draws the aether and Muqallad draws Erahm in around them. The Atalayina brightens. It moves beyond its deep blue to a cerulean glow, then the bright blue of the sky, then a white so bright it is difficult to look upon. And yet it is not warm—it is cool and getting colder.

It is then, when the stone becomes painful to touch, that Khamal realizes the mood of the fates has changed. No longer do they smile. They are discomforted yet still expectant. The three of them have anticipated this for eons. He can feel it in his bones.

He looks to Sariya and Muqallad. They sense it every bit as strongly as he does—he can see it in the way Sariya's brows pinch, the way Muqallad's jaw grits—but there is nothing to do now but rededicate themselves and draw upon the Atalayina further.

The stone becomes colder still, the cold of the deepest winter, the cold of the frozen north seas. His hand is numb. The brightness of the stone shines red through his skin, revealing the hint of bones beneath.

Dear fates, the pain of it.

Should the fates not help? Should they not lend their strength in this time of change?

Neh, Khamal realizes. Indaraqiram, the rising of the soul of the world, is a mortal thing, a threshold only men can cross, a goal set against the children of the fates when they were first made from the raw elements of Erahm and Adhiya. The fates will not interfere when man has nearly completed all they were meant to do.

And yet Khamal can't help but fear that something is terribly wrong. Should the fates not rejoice when indaraqiram finally comes?

They should, and yet he feels none of this from them, only a grim determination, a feeling of release—of *release*, as if they are tired of this world, tired of the burden that they've borne for generations beyond count.

How long we have waited. How long we have prayed for the will of man to rise above all that assaults them.

This is wrong, Khamal realizes.

It's all wrong.

Khamal opens his eyes as the pain from the cold stone moves further up his arm. It goes beyond his shoulder and takes him deeper into the place of pain than he has ever been.

There is a ringing in the air, a high-pitched cry, and he realizes it is his own lament, his own pain, and that of his brother and sister. The three Al-Aqim have come to this place to take the world beyond, but now they know—all three of them—that this... this tragedy... is something the fates had been hoping for. Pleading for.

As much as the fates pulled the strings of man, they did not have control over this: their own death.

They had not considered their task a burden in the early days of the world. For long ages their will was strong, but when the cycles of man rose and fell with collapses from disease, from war, from a struggle with the worlds themselves, they grew weary. And then desperate for release.

The fates are dying, Khamal realizes. *They are dying, and there's nothing we can do about it.*

He feels them slipping away. They fade even as the worlds approach. This will not be indaraqiram. This will be the very end of the world.

He feels Sariya and Muqallad. They know. They weep as he weeps—for the fates, for the end of the world—but just as he is they are caught like flies in amber.

A guttural scream rises up inside Khamal and finds release in the thin air of the mountain at the center of the world's destruction. It is nothing to the tearing of the world around him, but it gives him strength. He pushes the worlds away. Sariya and Muqallad feel him doing this, but they merely watch.

"Help me!" he cries.

They do not. Their hearts are broken, and the fates begin to slip away. Perhaps they go to worlds beyond. Perhaps they go to the place where those who have reached vashaqiram—true enlightenment—go. Perhaps they will simply be gone, leaving the world bereft of their guiding hand.

It is nearly too much. Khamal does not know what the world will be like after this day. It will be cast adrift. Rudderless.

It is nearly too much to bear, and yet he knows he cannot abandon it. He loves it too dearly. He pushes harder as the worlds close in. He screams, releasing his soul into this one, final effort.

And slowly, the worlds stop. They begin to recede. They take their rightful places once more.

But there is something terribly, terribly wrong.

There are tears in the aether. Tears that allow Adhiya to touch Erahm. It is not as it should be, but before he can try to heal it, the world around him begins to shake. The air above him is afire. The island itself shifts. And the spirits begin to cross through the tears between worlds.

It will not stop, he realizes, not here. It will move beyond to the rest of the islands. It will consume them, and then it will move to the mainland itself, the motherland where life itself began.

He cannot allow it, and yet he is powerless to stop it.

He feels a hand against his. Sariya. Or Muqallad. He can't tell which. And then another joins in. At last they understand what is happening, enough to help him stop it.

Yet even as they do, they feel the faint and final notes of the fates. They slip to their final resting place, wherever that may be, and are lost to the world.

This is when the blinding white stone between them shatters.

CHAPTER FIFTY-SIX

Atiana was sitting on the deck of the ship of stone with her back to the
gunwales when one of the red-robed Kohori on deck stood and began
pointing over the bow. "Land!" he called.

Atiana pulled herself up, shading her eyes against the bright sunlight as she
looked to where the man was pointing. The day was bright, the sky cloudless,
and in the distance was the top of an emerald island.

Ghayavand.

It was hard to believe. They'd been on the sea for nearly three weeks, one long
day melding into the next, the monotony of the sea making the days seem ach-
ingly long. But here they were at last.

It's beautiful, Atiana thought, this place that had been the source of such pain.

Without warning, the white arms of the goedrun released the ship and slipped
down into the deep blue sea. The sudden absence of the surging motion felt
strange after having felt it every waking moment for the past ten days. The
goedrun released the other ships as well, and soon they were all floating and
drifting with the waves.

The qiram near the prow, the one who had released the goedrun from their
ship, remained where she was with her arms spread wide. Habram, who was
standing amidships, went to her. He waited patiently for her to drop her arms,
to turn and speak with him. When they were done, he spoke orders in Kalhani. Atiana could only pick out a few words. *Many* and *qiram* and a word that
sounded like the Mahndi word for *rift*.

The men and women on the ship began making preparations, many going
belowdecks, others packing away food and utensils and other things that had
been used during their sea journey. They were taken the rest of the way by a
strong wind summoned by the Kohori. As they approached the rocky shore of
Ghayavand and passed beyond a lush green promontory, Atiana saw far to the

east a line of objects floating in the sky. They were clearly anchored—she could see the lines that moored them in place—but they were nothing like typical windships. They were bulbous, with the heavier end oriented toward the sea and the tapered end pointing up toward the blue sky. They reminded her of conch shells, except she could tell that they were made of some fibrous material like wood or vines. There were at least two dozen, and perhaps more beyond the curve of the island.

"What are those?" Atiana asked Habram, pointing toward the ships, if they could be called such.

Habram turned to her with a serious look, but he did not reply. Atiana looked at them again, floating on the wind at the end of their tethers. A shiver ran down her frame. She liked the look of those ships not at all.

As they approached the island, Atiana felt the hairs on the back of her neck rise and stand on end. Her skin prickled along her arms. Even without the benefit of the aether, she could feel the hezhan here. They crouched at the edge of her perception, hungering for a taste of Erahm.

They beached a short while later. Many Kohori worked to unlade the ships, but others traveled inland, including Habram and Ushai and Kaleh, who was borne on a stretcher by two Kohori men in red robes.

Atiana was allowed to remain beneath the trees. No guards were set to watch her, but she knew that there would be some deeper in the forest watching her closely. Any attempt to flee and they would soon have her back. Atiana looked for Aelwen among those who were unlading the ships of stone but didn't find her.

An hour later, Habram returned and asked that Atiana accompany him. They traveled inland for nearly a league. The Atalayina was in a pouch at Habram's belt. Atiana could not see it, but she could feel it, especially in this place. The Atalayina had arrived at the very site where the world had nearly been destroyed three hundred years ago, and now it felt wild, a creature alive, not some dormant remnant from the forging of the world.

They came to a clearing where many tents already stood. These were military tents, set in three long rows with one larger tent set apart from the others. From the tall central pole of the large tent flew the pennant of Yrstanla, an ivory drakhen rearing on a crimson field.

As they approached that tent, several guardsmen moved forward to meet them. They wore fitted leather armor. These were the Kiliç Şaik. Which could only mean that the Kamarisi was here. No sooner had the thought blossomed than Bahett ül Kirdhash stepped out of the tent. He was dressed in a fine silk kaftan with high boots of soft leather and a turban of gold with a large ruby brooch pinned to the center. He seemed exactly like the Bahett she remembered until she realized his right arm ended in a stump. It was bandaged heavily in silk the color of sand, as if Bahett couldn't bear his wounds to be wrapped in poorer cloth.

"Here you are at last," Bahett said in Yrstanlan as he came to a stop.

"What are you doing here?" was all Atiana could think to ask.

Bahett smiled, showing his perfect teeth. "Please," he said, bowing and motioning with his good left hand. "Let us speak in peace."

Habram was led away, while Bahett himself brought Atiana inside his tent. Rich carpets lay over the ground, and pillows were strewn over much of the center.

"Sit," Bahett said sharply.

Atiana would normally have refused to obey such a presumptive command, but there was something about Bahett, a desperation in his gaze she couldn't remember him ever having before. He had always been one to hide his true intent. If he had become so strained that he would allow his composure to break, she would not test him, not until she knew more. She sat in the pillows as Bahett went to an ornate chest near a simple table and chair. He retrieved from the chest a small wooden box, no larger than a closed fist, and then he came and sat a respectful distance away from her.

He set the box between them on a pillow of golden thread, but otherwise drew no further attention to it. He didn't have to, though. Atiana could feel something inside. The aether here was terribly close—close enough to touch—but what could affect the aether in such a way that she could feel it without taking the dark? She might have said the Atalayina, but this felt different. It felt more immediate, more dangerous, like the exhilaration of seeing an old enemy.

"You've come a long way," Bahett said simply.

"As have you." Atiana couldn't help but glance down at the stump where his right wrist used to be.

It did not go unnoticed. He glanced down as well and the space between his eyebrows pinched, as if he were reliving the event. She nearly asked him what had happened, but she thought better of it, and a moment later the look was gone and he was once again staring into her eyes with a composed, almost gentle, look.

"The trip through the Gaji was risky," he said. "I might have called it foolish, but here you are, and Sariya has returned to me as well."

"You sent those men to find us."

"I did."

"And yet you are allied with the Kohori."

"Now, *evet*, but not then. They have come to see, as I did long ago, that Sariya will bring us peace."

Atiana couldn't help but laugh. She thought she would regret it, but Bahett merely shook his head and nodded to the box.

"Open it," he said.

She took it and slid the top off of it. A golden light was revealed within. It glimmered brightly, scintillated as she turned the box this way and that. It was like the siraj stones of the Aramahn, but it was of a color and quality she'd never seen. It was small, no larger than a chickpea. And, she realized, it did not touch the blood-red cloth that lined the box; it floated at the center.

Bahett reached in and took it. He gave it a spin between them, and there it remained, floating in the very place Bahett had released it into the air.

Atiana couldn't help but be reminded of her time in Sariya's tower in Baressa. She'd done much the same with the piece of the Atalayina that Atiana had brought to her. The feelings of peril she'd experienced before opening the box intensified. It felt not unlike those moments in the aether when she sensed another presence. She knew someone was near without yet knowing who.

"This is Sariya's," Atiana said with certainty.

Bahett waggled his head, the ruby brooch glittering beneath the golden light. "Much more than that, Atiana. For all intents and purposes, this *is* Sariya."

Atiana could hardly tear her eyes away from the spinning stone. "She nearly died on Galahesh, did you know? You and the other Matri had nearly smothered her. That, plus the unhealed wound from Ushai's blade, which had nearly killed her once already. But she was resourceful. She still had her tower, the spire she'd had Hakan build for her in the forest, and she had placed some of herself in this stone. Sariya called to me when the bridge was destroyed. She guided me to her stone, even as she took Kaleh's form and brought Nasim to the Gaji. *This,*" Bahett said, motioning toward the stone, "is her grounding here in this place. Her anchor to the material world. Without it, she would surely slip to the other side and be lost to us."

"You care that she will be lost to us?"

"I do, Atiana Radieva. I do. There is a problem here among the islands. The rifts will not stop, and Sariya is the last one alive who can tame them."

"She will not *tame* them."

Bahett breathed in deeply as if he were trying to keep his composure. "She will, and I've brought you here to convince you of it."

"I won't be, Bahett. She hasn't changed her mind. She still seeks indaraqiram."

"She does not, and perhaps I've misspoke. It is not *I* who will convince you, but Sariya herself."

"She is trapped."

"Just so, but you can reach her in the aether. You can find her as you have before. Go. Speak to her, and you will know whether she is telling the truth."

Atiana paused, debating on whether or not to say more, but this was not the time to mince words. "And there is you."

"You think you cannot trust me. But know this. Sariya and I have come to an understanding. I have agreed to help her, and she has agreed to leave my mind my own."

"She would not keep such a promise. Not for long, in any case."

"True." He reached forward and caught the spinning stone. "But through this, I can *feel* her intent. Were she to break our compact, I would crush it, and Sariya would be drawn to the other side as quickly as a fallen star." Bahett's expression turned to one of pleading. It was an act, but she could see the fear in his eyes as well. "Take the dark, Atiana. Look into Sariya's soul, and you will find that I speak the truth."

"She took me before, Bahett. You know this. I thought I knew her mind—I was *sure* of it—but I did not. She fooled me, well and truly."

"But then you didn't know she was spying upon you, learning the ways of your mind and the Matri. You know her well now, and you won't be easily tricked."

That was true enough, and still, part of her was screaming for her to deny Bahett. This was something Sariya desperately wanted. Or at the very least that *Bahett* wanted. And yet what could she do otherwise? She did not wish to leave Sariya to her own devices. She wanted to weigh the truth in her words. But how could she trust her own judgment in the presence of Sariya?

"I will contact Ishkyna and Mileva," Atiana said at last. "They will not be fooled even if I am."

Bahett nodded and placed the glowing stone back into the wooden case. It was an awkward thing, as Bahett had only one hand, but she made no move to help him. As he slid the lid closed, he smiled and said, "Very well."

Bahett called for Habram. A short while later he came with Ushai and led her back into the nearby forest. They walked through the sparse rake pine before coming to a clearing, in the center of which was a conical hillock with an obelisk standing at the peak. The obelisk looked to be made of obsidian, though it was mottled grey, not the deep black of the spires.

Near the base of the hillock, lying on a bed of brown pine needles, was Kaleh. After motioning to her, Habram and Ushai continued up to the top to inspect the obelisk. Atiana knelt near Kaleh. She brushed the hair from her eyes and stared at the young woman's face, realizing that she looked older than she had mere days ago. By the ancients, the things this girl had seen. The things she was going through even now. Atiana knew the battle she was waging within her mind. The girl was strong indeed to hold Sariya off for so long. Then again, Sariya had been dominant for nearly two years. It would wear on her to fight for so long, while Kaleh could wait, bide her time. She had probably found weaknesses in Sariya during that time, weaknesses she was exploiting even now.

It was telling that Kaleh had not gained dominance, though. The two of them were at a stalemate, and now it would be up to Atiana to decide their fate.

After a time, Habram and Ushai returned. Ushai had a look of grave concern on her face as she looked on Bahett, and when she stared into Atiana's eyes, her look grew even more dire. But then she pulled herself taller, as if she'd come to some serious decision about her own fate, and walked into the woods while Habram came close and squatted near Kaleh's side.

"What is this place?" Atiana asked, jutting her chin toward the hillock.

"It is one of the places where the Al-Aqim and the Tashavir tried to stem the tide of the growing rifts after the sundering. There are dozens like them across the island, near the shore."

"They failed."

"True, but that was merely one attempt of many, before they stumbled on the children, the akhoz."

"I thought they'd all died."

"The akhoz?" Habram shrugged. "Who knows. In Alayazhar there may be one or two who still wander the forgotten streets."

Ushai returned with a censer and wood. Habram took these from her and set them near Atiana. He began to draw from a suurahezhan to light the wood aflame, but Atiana waved him away.

"*Neh*," she said. He looked at her, confused and cross, but she continued, "This place... It... I will not use my blood. Not yet."

He stood and stared down at her, then looked around the clearing and regarded Atiana anew, as if he'd just now realized that he'd woefully underestimated her.

"Very well," he said carefully.

"The Atalayina," Atiana said.

A Kohori man had just come to the clearing carrying a hinged wooden box. Atiana had to keep herself from staring at him.

It was the man Aelwen had killed. Or, rather, it was Aelwen herself in the Kohori's form.

It was strange seeing her—him—in this place, as if what had happened in the desert had merely been a dream. In fact, she was not even sure it *had* happened until Aelwen looked over at her with grim purpose. She said nothing, but her face had an expression of desperation on it, as if she were no longer sure of the path she was following.

Habram waved him over and motioned to the ground near Atiana. Aelwen set the box down and opened the lid, revealing the blue stone, the Atalayina with its striations of gold and copper and silver. The way it twisted the sunlight was hypnotic. It felt eager for Atiana to begin.

Soon enough, Atiana thought.

She set the box between her and Kaleh. She was careful not to touch the stone itself, but the smooth edges of the wooden box.

When she closed her eyes, the frame of mind she sought came easily. She'd done so a thousand times before in the drowning chamber, and more recently with the rising smoke from her own burning blood. She'd done it on Oshtoyets as well when she'd caught a musket shot in the chest, and again on Galahesh when Sariya had caught her in her grasp. Yet those times outside the drowning chamber had always seemed like flukes, things she could never have repeated. Now she knew they were all facets of the same jewel. All of them—the drowning basin, the smoke, hovering near death—they had all borne her toward the aether until she'd been close enough to touch it. Here, the aether was so close no such ritual was needed. She need merely strip the world away until she could sense the veil that separated Erahm from the dark of the aether.

The Atalayina, strangely enough, was no settling force. It still felt eager—too eager—and that was a disturbing notion, indeed, in this place of all places.

But she was able to set these thoughts aside.

And soon... Soon...

CHAPTER FIFTY-SEVEN

A tiana floats before Kaleh. She sees her in the dark, a diaphanous white against the depthless blue of the aether. She sees Habram and Ushai and Aelwen who ate the heart of a Kohori man. She feels the strange intent of the Atalayina. But more than anything, she feels the chaos of the rifts. They are so near they lash at her. And yet she does not fear. Her time on Galahesh taught her well. The wild currents of the aether running through the straits two years before were every bit as strong as the aether that swirls over Ghayavand now.

She draws away from Kaleh, allows herself to feel more of the island, and through this she is able to sense its center. There is another place like this one, a hillock with an obelisk. It stands on the shoulders of Sihyaan, the tall mountain peak near the center of the island. It was there that the sundering occurred three centuries before, when the world was nearly undone.

It may still be undone, Atiana thinks.

Slowly, she expands her awareness, widens her mind until it encompasses the island itself. She can feel the rifts deeply now, and they make it difficult, even painful, for Atiana to cast her mind beyond.

Mileva, she calls. *Ishkyna.*

She hears nothing, so she presses harder, casts her mind farther. She moves beyond the Sea of Tabriz toward Vostroma, toward Yrstanla as well, until she is spread as wide and as thin as she has ever been. She feels the dark depths of the sea, the wide plains of the Motherland, the very currents of wind, and she wonders: is this how Ishkyna feels every moment?

It is through this one small musing that she senses Ishkyna's presence.

Ishkyna, she calls again. *Ishkyna, hear me.*

Ishkyna doesn't respond, however. She, too, is spread far and wide, and it reminds Atiana of the first days after Ishkyna had become lost in the aether.

Atiana calls again and again, and she begins to worry.

She cannot hear you, sister. It is Mileva. *We are lucky she's still with us.*

For a moment, Atiana's heart fills with joy. She hasn't spoken to Mileva since she left Vostroma.

What's happened? she asks at last.

She was near Alekeşir helping Nikandr to escape when a rift was torn wide. We nearly lost her then and there.

A strange mixture of relief and worry roils within Atiana. She still doesn't understand how Ishkyna was saved, how she survives in the aether though her body lies dead in the mausoleum far beneath Galostina. It feels as though every moment will be Ishkyna's last, and it only becomes worse when there's some strange event like this one.

And Nikandr?

He survived, though where he is now we don't know. What of you, sister? You've reached the shores of Ghayavand.

I have, and I need your help.

Atiana explains everything, her conversation with Bahett, Sariya's plans, her fears over being fooled by Sariya once again.

It's dangerous, Mileva says. *We may gain more by simply slitting her throat.*

We may, Atiana replies, *but what if we're wrong?*

What if we're right?

That is why you must help. If Ishkyna cannot come, we will call on Saphia.

She is not in the dark.

Then Paulina.

They cannot come, Atiana. They are not strong enough to reach Ghayavand. It will be you and I or it will be none.

Then come, sister. Help me. The time here grows short. I can feel it.

Mileva paused, but not for long. *Very well, sister. Let us see what Sariya is about.*

Atiana draws herself back. She moves down toward Kaleh, who struggles every bit as much as she had in Kohor. How she can keep this up day after day Atiana has no idea. She wonders if either of them really knows who or why they're fighting. Perhaps they both feel trapped by the other. Perhaps they both feel like they've won.

Atiana can feel Sariya now that she's come close. Here, too, Galahesh has prepared her well. Had the two of them not been so entwined in the days and final hours before the Spar had been destroyed, she might not have known how to find Sariya, how to discern her from Kaleh, but now it's child's play.

Together, Atiana and Mileva probe Kaleh's mind. She seems deadened, a common enough thing. When people sleep and do not dream their mind is deadened like Kaleh's is now. It's simply a matter of finding her somewhere within the darkness and drawing her forth. When they approach and attune themselves to Kaleh's mind, Atiana senses thoughts, and when she comes closer still, she begins to sense the edges of a dream. She smells flowers. She feels tall stalks of grass brush against her skirt. She feels the wind as it blows against a field of ivory brightbonnets.

Atiana knows she's being drawn into Kaleh's dream, but she allows it. She can feel Mileva's mind near hers. It feels like it did when they were children, when the three of them—Atiana, Mileva, and Ishkyna—shared a bed and they would hold one another's hands to fend off fears of the darkness. As Kaleh's dream brightens in her mind, she allows Mileva's hand to slip through hers.

Running through the field below her is a girl. She runs with abandon, her head turned toward the sky, her fingers touching the tips of the flowers, chasing bees from their bells.

As Atiana walks toward her, she slows.

Then stops.

Then turns to regard Atiana coolly.

She is seven, perhaps eight years old. Her face is the face of a child, full of innocence, but it is dark as she watches Atiana's approach.

The wind picks up. The skies darken.

"I mean you no harm," Atiana says.

"I know."

This is Kaleh as she truly is, Atiana realizes, or at the very least as she sees herself. "Do you know why you're here?"

The girl takes in the landscape around them. The wind kicks up, tossing Kaleh's light brown hair and making the brightbonnets wink as they toss to and fro.

"Here in this place? Or on the island of Ghayavand?"

"You know that we've arrived..."

"I know much, daughter of Radia. I know why you've come."

"I was taken here."

"So you would not have come had the Kohori not taken you?"

"I would have come by a different road."

"Yet you've arrived at the same place."

"Without allies. Without my love."

Kaleh's innocent face brightens, and she begins skipping around Atiana. "Are they necessary for you to do what you must?"

"And what is that? What *must* I do?"

"Kill Sariya. Free me. Summon your Matri here. Who knows but you and the fates?" Kaleh stops and pulls up one of the brightbonnets. She begins plucking tiny petals from around the bonnet's black eye, tossing them to the wind.

As Atiana watches, she wonders if she should kill Sariya. She isn't opposed to it, but she also wonders what has happened between these two. It seems important, as does the existence of this very place. It is very much like the place of Sariya's making that Atiana was drawn into while on Galahesh. She found Nasim there, and she witnessed him liberate the third and final piece of the Atalayina.

She draws upon the Atalayina now, and finds that she can change things here, much as Sariya and Kaleh do. She calms the wind until it is little more than a soft summer breeze. With the chill wind gone, Atiana can feel the sun kissing her skin.

Kaleh stares up to the sky, squints at the brightness there, then regards Atiana anew. "You've come far," she says, "though not nearly as far as your sister."

"Tell me why you're hiding in this place."

Kaleh smiles wryly. "You think I'm hiding?"

"Aren't you?"

"I'm trying to find Sariya. I've lost her."

Atiana takes in the landscape around them. "Is she stuffed into one of the bells you're plucking? Is she hiding in the weeds?"

Kaleh's smile widens, and for a moment she looks much older than her apparent years. "There's more than one way to catch a bee."

Atiana begins to broaden her mind, perhaps doing the very same thing Kaleh is doing. "Has she become so afraid of you, her own daughter?"

"*Neh*, it isn't me she's afraid of. Nor is she afraid of you, or the Kohori."

"Then what?"

"That *is* the question." With all the tiny flowers gone, Kaleh throws the stalk away and plucks another. This she hands to Atiana, and then takes Atiana's hand and begins leading her downhill. "You grew up on the islands?"

"On Vostroma," Atiana replies, confused by the sudden change in mood.

"What was it like, growing up with two sisters and a brother?"

Atiana shrugs. "It was..." She pauses, not because it is odd to speak to this girl of her family—though it is—and not because she doesn't wish to share—for some reason, here in this place, she doesn't mind—but because it strikes her just how innocent those days now seem. How much they've all changed. Atiana foolishly thought that none of them would take to the drowning chamber, and now all three are more powerful than any Matra in memory. They nearly lost Ishkyna—in many ways she *is* lost—but she has attained a freedom that she hasn't had since childhood, when their mother gave them free reign of Galostina.

She hopes that Ishkyna looks upon her ethereal state as a gift. She tries to ask her of it, but Ishkyna always refuses to speak of it.

And then there is Bora. By the ancients how she misses him, misses the *old* Borund. He used to watch over them, but now he acts as if the three of them are little more than a burden, servants to order about as he does everyone else.

"At the time it felt like a struggle, but now I look back and all I can think is that I wish I had it back."

"Do you think about dying?"

"Of course I do."

The grip of Kaleh's hand tightens. "I can think of nothing else."

Atiana glances down and sees tears running down Kaleh's face. She stops and pulls Kaleh around. "What is wrong, child?"

She looks over the field around them, stares down at Atiana's hands that hold her own. "You know by now I age differently than you."

The nod Atiana gives her is a strangely difficult thing to do. It's as if she's condemning this girl to the fate she's been handed.

"It's speeding up. I can feel it." A tear drops onto Atiana's hand. Its warmth fades as the tear tickles down the back of her hand. "Soon I'll be as old as you. Then as old as your mother. And then..."

"How has this happened?"

The shrug Kaleh gives her is one of childish innocence. The confusion and worry in her eyes runs so deep that Atiana pulls her into a tight embrace, holds her as she continues to cry.

"The fates work strangely, Kaleh, but you'll return to us brighter than before."

When Atiana pulls away at last, the fear in Kaleh has ebbed. "You don't believe that."

"I know nothing, Kaleh." She presses her fingers against Kaleh's chest. "Listen to your heart, and it will guide you, and perhaps one day you can come to Vostroma. I'll show you the palotza, and introduce you to my sisters and my brother."

Like the rising glow of a candle, a smile comes over Kaleh, but a moment later her gaze shifts to something over Atiana's shoulder. Like a hare that has sensed danger, her whole stance changes. "Can you feel it?"

Atiana expands her awareness, but feels nothing.

"Come," Kaleh says.

Without ever taking her eyes from the landscape ahead, she holds Atiana's hand and begins walking once more. They head down toward a stream and a low stone bridge that crosses it. It leads to a path on the other side that runs uphill toward a ridge. Atiana can feel something beyond it, and as they take to the bridge and cross the gurgling stream, the presence grows. "It's Sariya, isn't it?"

"She's been gone a long time. But I wonder if she's come because of you."

"Why would she care if I've come?"

"I wonder that myself, daughter of the islands."

As they climb the slope and approach the ridge, the sky darkens, and nothing Atiana does can clear the clouds away. Rain begins to fall. It seeps into her clothes, chilling her instantly.

Before they gain the ridge, Atiana begins to suspect what she will see. And then she is sure of it.

And yet, even knowing this, a chill sweeps over her when they gain the ridge at last and look down to the valley below.

There, nestled in a copse of larch, is Sariya's tower.

CHAPTER FIFTY-EIGHT

Nikandr woke to the sound of pounding hooves. He threw off his blanket and sat up, looking wildly about, wondering where the sound had come from, but then he realized it had all been a dream.

The stars shed faint light across a moonless sky. The coals in the campfire cast a ruddy glow against the sleeping forms of Styophan and Mikhalai and Rodion. Styophan was asleep as well, but the patch over his right eye, which in the dim light looked like a deep and bottomless pit, made Nikandr feel as though Styophan were staring right through him.

Soroush was sitting up with his back to an ancient yew. His black beard framed his long face in stark relief, as the golden rings in his ruined left ear glinted in the dim light. "They're not coming," he said in Anuskayan. He was smoking a long pipe he'd found in the saddlebag of the horse they'd taken in Alekeşir. The smell of it filled the windless night.

"I know." Nikandr levered himself up and stoked life back into the fire with a stick.

Nearby, Mikhalai wheezed. He coughed a deep cough and then fell back asleep. Soroush and Nikandr eyed one another. They were all too familiar with the sound of that cough. Nikandr himself had coughed like that for months. He'd had the wasting then, years ago, when he'd first met Ashan and Nasim. How long ago those days seemed. Yet when Mikhalai wheezed, or when Nikandr saw the dark, sallow skin around his eyes, they seemed like only yesterday.

"It's coming on much faster than I've ever seen." The firelight played over the skin of Soroush's face. It reminded Nikandr of Datha, of the way the flames had burst forth from his mouth and eyes and had consumed his skin.

Nikandr shrugged. "The rifts," he said, as if that were answer enough.

Mikhalai coughed and shifted in his sleep.

Soroush drew on the pipe, the bowl brightening momentarily, and exhaled slowly. "Soon he will slow us down."

"I will not leave him behind."

"I don't mean to leave him unaided. We have things of value. We can find those who would treat him kindly until he dies."

Nikandr wanted to say that there were those who recovered, but the words were hollow. They were words he'd used for himself, words he'd used for his sister, Victania. And they were true enough seven years ago. No longer. Now, those who fell to the wasting died, and did so much faster than they ever had before. Still... This...

They were only seven days out of Alekeşir, and he wasn't sure if Mikhalai would live to see another seven.

"I wonder what it's like on Ghayavand," Nikandr said.

For a time the two of them merely stared into the low glow of the fire. Nikandr couldn't help but think of the island. With the lines between worlds already blurred, what would it be like now?

"Do you really think Nasim made it to Ghayavand?"

Nikandr had suspected as much as soon as Ishkyna had told him that a rift had opened on the grounds of Kasir Irabahce. Kaleh had done the same years ago. And where would they have gone but Ghayavand? "They must have. If they didn't, our cause is already lost."

Soroush was quiet for a time, his eyes searching through the darkness, and when he spoke, his voice was distant. "I wonder sometimes if the fates hadn't meant for the world to end those many years ago during the sundering. I wonder if the failing of the Al-Aqim to bring about indaraqiram was in the eyes of the fates a failure to bring about the end of our world."

"So that they could what? Make it anew?"

"It is told so, in the ancient texts, and in the songs of our grandmothers."

"But the fates see all, do they not?"

"*Nyet.*" Soroush had been about to draw on the pipe again, but he stopped and stabbed the mouthpiece at Nikandr. "They do not. They guide us, certainly. They see into the distance, well beyond the horizon. But their concerns are not with us and us alone. They worry over Adhiya. They worry over the heavens. They set the world in motion, but they do not guide our every move."

"Is this the same man I spoke to on Rafsuhan?" Then, nearly two years ago now, Soroush had lectured Nikandr on the fates. He'd scoffed at Nikandr's own beliefs in the ancients, his forebears that watched from the world beyond and sheltered both those they'd left behind and their children. And here he was now, wondering just how much the hand of the fates could really be seen in this world.

Soroush stared into Nikandr's eyes. "Am I to close my eyes to the world, son of Iaros? Am I to stop learning?"

"What, then? Do you think we're headed toward ruin? Do you think Sariya will have her way?"

"I think the fates have seen fit to watch the world wither for three hundred years, and I suspect they're willing to let this play out."

"Perhaps they tire of their place in the heavens. Perhaps, like an old man too infirm to leave his chair by the fire, they merely wish to pass."

The old Soroush would have taken offense at this, but the Soroush that sat beneath the centuries-old yew merely turned toward the fire and drew breath from his pipe. "Perhaps you're right. And if that's so, we are on our own. You. Me." He nodded his head toward Mikhalai, who had fallen into a fitful sleep. His breathing came heavy though. It was a familiar pattern. Soon he would wake again, coughing.

"I will not leave him behind," Nikandr said. "He may make it home. He deserves the chance to die on the islands where he was born."

Soroush nodded. "I understand."

He didn't agree, but he understood, and for now that was good enough.

As they rode the next day, Nikandr couldn't stop thinking about Mikhalai. They made decent enough time, but the following day, the broad-shouldered strelet was indeed riding more slowly. He would devolve into coughing fits and riding, of course, did nothing to help. They would stop and give him water and a bit of time to recover, and then they'd be off again, but within a few hours, sometimes less, it would start again.

Nikandr didn't want to consider what Soroush had said, but what sort of life was this? He had so little time left. Why use it up by riding along a road that could lead only to his death? Why not give him a day or two of comfort before he died, no matter that it made Nikandr feel like a coward?

The next morning, Mikhalai was gone.

Nikandr remembered waking in the middle of the night from Mikhalai's coughs. They'd died off as Mikhalai walked away from camp, but Nikandr was so groggy he'd thought that Mikhalai had merely left to spare them the burden of listening to it. But now it was clear he'd snuck away. Strong Mikhalai. Perhaps he'd heard Soroush and Nikandr talking, or perhaps the thought had come to him on his own. Either way, he'd done what he thought best for his prince and the others.

As Styophan and Rodion finished packing their things and mounted, they looked to Nikandr.

"It's better for him this way," Nikandr said.

Styophan bowed his head. "Of course, My Lord Prince."

"He might not have finished the day's ride," Rodion added.

They went on ahead, catching up with Soroush, while Nikandr mounted his own horse. Nikandr sent one last glance toward the woods where he'd heard Mikhalai coughing.

"Go well, brave soul," he whispered, then whipped the reins.

Two weeks out from Alekeşir, as Nikandr coaxed a fire to life for evening camp, he felt something from his soulstone, a presence, one of the Matri, but not Ishkyna. A moment later, a rook flapped down through the winterdead trees and landed on the fallen log he was sitting on.

By the ancients, it was Yrfa, his mother's favorite rook.

The bird cawed once, then clucked and pecked the soft white bark. Nikandr could only stare for a moment. This was like a memory, so long had it been since they'd spoken. And the feeling in his chest. It was like the brightness of spring after long, dark winter.

Despite himself, a broad smile came over him. "It's good to see you, Mother."

Styophan, who was nearby tending to the horses while Rodion and Soroush hunted, bowed his head and took his leave, grabbing their water skins and heading for the nearby stream.

The feeling in Nikandr's chest broadened as the rook looked him over, its head swiveling in twitchy movements. "Nischka," the bird called in a long, low moan. "You've been gone too long, my son."

Too long, indeed, Nikandr thought. The war and the recovery of the islands had taken the Matri's attention, and by then Nikandr and Atiana and the others had traveled too far. Then, the only one who could find them was Ishkyna, but she was too often needed closer to Anuskaya, and so communication had been sporadic at best.

Years ago it would have been impossible for a Matra to have traveled this far, and even more difficult for her to assume a rook while doing so. But then the Spar on Galahesh had been built. Since then, since Muqallad and Sariya's failed ritual, the ruined center of the bridge had been rebuilt, and the fluctuations of the aether had settled to the point that the Matri *could* cross. They *could* assume rooks and speak from distances much greater than they'd ever thought possible. Strange, Nikandr thought, to have profited from that bridge, a thing that had been created to destroy not merely the islands, but the entire world.

The rook flapped closer, and Nikandr ran his fingers down its neck, as his father once had. "I'm returning home, Mother."

As welcome as his mother's presence was, it highlighted something that had been missing since the earthquake in Alekeşir. "I thought Ishkyna would have returned long before now."

"Ishkyna is not well."

Nikandr waited for further explanation, but apparently he wasn't going to get it. "What happened?"

The rook cawed. "She'll be fine, Nischka. It's you I'm worried about."

"Me? Why?"

"Because you go into the jaws of the wolf."

Nikandr adjusted the kindling, stoking it higher. "Leonid Dhalingrad is no wolf."

"He is the Grand Duke."

"And he murdered my father."

The bird nipped Nikandr's wrist and then hopped away. "We'll not have this argument again. The time hasn't yet come to deal with Leonid. He's too well protected at the warfront."

Nikandr took a deep breath. He knew that when he saw Leonid again he would want to take his revenge on him. He'd felt the fool for months after leaving Galahesh two years before. He'd suspected what Leonid had done—a musket shot from a friendly position was indistinguishable from one shot by the enemy—he'd just been so surprised by it. Killing another duke was a bold and cowardly move, even for Leonid, and for days afterward he had come to doubt his instincts, but the more he thought about it, the more he knew he was right. The man who had examined his father, a well-known physic from Volgorod, had said that the musket shot had entered between Iaros's shoulder blades. And several men that Nikandr had talked to who had seen him fall had said that he was facing the line, rallying the men of Khalakovo and Mirkotsk and Rhavanki forward.

He'd been shot from behind, where only the men of Anuskaya had been positioned. The only question remained was who would do such a thing? The answer was simple: the man who stood to gain the most.

"Things will only get worse if Leonid leaves the warfront."

"You've come to accuse him, then? To attack him in front of the entire stremya?"

"I've come to give them warning."

"What warning, Nischka?"

"We cannot go to Ghayavand."

The rook was motionless for long moments, its black eye blinking every so often. "Why?"

"Because Sariya wishes us to go there. The Kamarisi told me himself."

"*Selim* told you, or Bahett?"

"It was Selim." Nikandr told her of their strange conversation beneath the dome with the eunuchs and the twirling iron chain. He told her about Selim's suspicions of Sariya, how Bahett was hoping to sweep over the islands as the forces of the Grand Duchy were occupied with the land war with Yrstanla, how

Selim suspected the Kohori were on Ghayavand and how he had planned to help Nikandr before he was killed.

The rook cawed raucously. To anyone else it might sound as if the animal was frightened or alarmed, but Nikandr knew it was the sound of his mother laughing. "Selim tricked you. The Kohori *are* on Ghayavand. And they've already attacked the islands."

Nikandr stared at the rook. "What?"

"Mirkotsk and Khalakovo and Vostroma were attacked two days ago. And yesterday it was Dhalingrad and Nodhvyansk. Each time strange ships came, ships formed in the shape of a spearhead. They came and they rained fire down on the villages, killing dozens in each, wounding hundreds more."

Nikandr stood and paced on the opposite side of the fire. "Why? Why did they attack? Did they take anything? Gain some advantage over us?"

"These may be the first volleys in a war against us, Nischka."

Nikandr stopped his pacing and faced the rook across the burgeoning fire. "It's a trick. Sariya's luring us. She wants us to come to Ghayavand."

"You don't know that."

"I know her better than most, Mother. Better than you. Certainly better than Leonid."

The rook pecked at the smooth bark of the log and cawed. "They're making preparations even now. We saw them, Nischka. Me and the other Matri, including Leonid's wife, Iyana. He will never back down now, and I don't know that he should."

"We can prepare our ships. We can wait. But we cannot go to that island. It is exactly what Sariya wants. Again."

"Why? Why does she want this?"

Nikandr could only shrug. "I don't know."

The rook cawed and arched its neck back. "It was a trap she laid for you, and you've fallen into it."

"*Nyet,*" Nikandr said. "I've never been more certain of anything in my life. Sariya wants the men of Anuskaya to come to Ghayavand. And it isn't so that she could give Bahett what he wants. Sariya is drawing us there."

"Then I ask you again, why?"

"I don't know, but we cannot give her what she wants. Give me time to go there. Let me and my men go and discover her plans."

"You and your Maharraht?"

Nikandr glanced through the trees beyond the rook where Soroush had gone. "He is not Maharraht. Not any longer."

"He isn't Maharraht *for the present*. There's a difference."

"I won't defend him to you. He has saved my life many times over."

"Do not trust him, Nischka."

"On Soroush, I keep my own counsel."

"Well enough"—the rook cawed and hopped along the log—"but you overlook the obvious. Leonid will believe none of this."

"Of course he won't."

"Then why go? Skirt the warfront, Nischka. Go to Trevitze. I'll prepare a ship for you there."

"I can't. Sariya can't be left to her own devices. I will go to Ghayavand, but not before making sure Leonid leaves Ghayavand alone."

"You have a plan, Nischka?"

"I do, Mother, and I need your help."

CHAPTER FIFTY-NINE

Nikandr heard sounds of battle hours before he saw it. He and the others rode well off the road along the grassy plains dotted with bushes that were thick with ice. A freezing drizzle had swept over the plains last night. When the sun had risen, they'd found themselves in a wonderland of grass blades trapped in crystal.

There was no wind to speak of. Which made the sounds of their travel conspicuous, especially during the lulls in battle in the city ahead. Near midday, however, the sounds of battle stopped. As the minutes passed, Nikandr was sure the hostilities would resume. Even if one side or another retreated, the other would press. Why would they simply stop in the middle of a bright day?

Soon they came to a rise, where they could see the city of Izlo below them. A pair of horses galloped out from the walled city, moving westward along the road Nikandr and the rest had left. The riders saw Nikandr and his three companions—one of them even pointed, warning the other—but they didn't change course. They simply kept riding. Most likely these were men heading toward Alekeşir with news. Strange that there were no lines of streltsi to stop them, nor any mounted hussari to keep them from riding as they willed. He wondered if it had anything to do with the attacks on the islands.

Far to their right, to the south of Izlo, a line of Anuskayan soldiers and cannons could be seen. "You should not come," Nikandr told Soroush.

Soroush smiled, the earrings on his ruined left ear glinting as he took in the forces of Anuskaya. Then he tipped his head back and laughed. A good, deep laugh that Nikandr hadn't heard from him—or anyone, for that matter—in months. "I fear you're right, son of Iaros." He pointed beyond Izlo. The land in this part of the world was largely flat, but in the distance a clump of snow-topped hills rose above the land like scheming lords. "I'll wait for you for three days there. Come to the base of the hills and I'll find you. If not, I go to Ghayavand."

Nikandr felt uncomfortable saying farewell. They'd been companions now for over two years. He'd saved Soroush's life several times and Soroush had done the same for him. They might never see one another again. There was still a question hanging between them. The Maharraht... Would Soroush return to them once this was all done? Maybe he would, and maybe he wouldn't. The question, for the time being, was immaterial. Soroush was dedicated to closing the rifts, as Nikandr was. They could take up that question when—if—they made it through this alive.

He urged his horse forward and clasped arms with Soroush. "Go well, son of Gatha."

"Go well," Soroush returned.

Next Nikandr guided his horse over to Styophan's. He held Styophan's gaze. It was impossible to look at Styophan's face, to see the black leather patch over his eye, and not be reminded of all Styophan had done for him, for Khalakovo, and for the Grand Duchy. He nodded, and Styophan nodded in return. Nikandr then took in Rodion, weighing him and finding a stout soldier ready to follow his commander wherever he was needed. He nodded once more, Rodion returning the gesture, and then pointed east. "Go with Soroush. Follow the line of hills toward Trevitze. The *Zhostova* will find you, three or four days from now."

Nikandr had told his mother to summon the ship for Styophan. Fitting since it was one of the five ships he'd commanded on his way west to Hael. Nikandr needed someone on Ghayavand. Nasim might already be there. The Kohori and Sariya were headed there. And that meant Atiana would be there as well.

Styophan nodded. "If she's on the island, I'll find her. And Nasim and Ashan if I can."

"Ancients preserve you," Nikandr said.

"And you."

The two of them leaned in and kissed cheeks. Nikandr did the same with Rodion, and then the three of them—Soroush, Styophan, and Rodion—were off, riding northward so that they could skirt the city before heading east toward the hills.

Late that night, while Nikandr sat by a small fire less than a quarter-league from the camp, he heard footsteps approaching. He stood and whistled like a woodland thrush, the kind that run thick through the islands in the summer. A return whistle came, and soon Nikandr saw him, a soldier of Vostroma wearing a long cherkesska, black boots, and a grey kolpak hat.

Nikandr stared openly. "Andreya?"

It was. Andreya Antonov, the polkovnik of Vostroma's stremya, and one of Grand Duke Leonid Dhalingrad's inner circle. He approached and dropped a sack near the log Nikandr had been sitting on. His beard had grown longer, not to mention greyer, but he still had that steely look. Most odd was the fact that he was wearing the uniform of a sotnik. It looked worn, but it wasn't cut in the style of Andreya's younger days as a junior officer, which meant he'd *borrowed* someone else's. Andreya Antonov, reduced to sneaking through his own camp to meet with Nikandr, someone he clearly did not trust to speak with his Duke.

Nikandr couldn't help it. He burst out laughing before he could stop himself. This pleased Andreya not at all, but before he could object, Nikandr stepped in and hugged him vigorously and kissed his cheeks as if he were Nikandr's own brother. "By the ancients it's good to see you."

Andreya frowned when they parted. "I wish I could say the same. Your arrival at the warfront is a strange one, Khalakovo."

Nikandr smiled. "My *journey* has been strange. Why would the ancients see fit to change that now?"

"And where have the ancients led you?"

Nikandr opened the sack and found the uniform he'd requested. He slipped out of his coat—the coat of a janissary—and started pulling off his shirt. "To a desert so vast it would swallow the islands. To the very heart of the Empire."

"And now you wish to speak not only to My Lord Duke, but to the Dukes of Bolgravya and Lhudansk and Mirkotsk as well."

"I do."

"A smarter man than I might think you were conspiring."

"A *mistrustful* man, Andreya." He pulled off his boots and baggy sirwaal pants and quickly took up the pants from inside the sack. The night wind was freezing against his skin, but it felt wonderful to rid himself of the garb he'd worn in the desert. It felt as though he were becoming a man of the islands again. "I merely wish to speak to the men who make the decisions for our good state."

"And yet you've excluded our Grand Duke."

"All will be revealed to Leonid in good time. For now, let's say that this is a matter that only certain dukes need consider."

"And what is that, Nikandr? What should they consider?"

"I'll speak to Your Lord Duke and no other, Andreya."

"You'll speak to me if you wish to see him on your terms."

"I will not. What I learned in Alekeşir concerns us all. All of Anuskaya. And Borund will learn of it first, he and the others I've asked for." Nikandr paused. "Assuming they wish to hear it."

Andreya took in a deep breath and exhaled, his breath lit by the meager firelight. "Very well."

With that he turned and walked away.

Nikandr finished pulling on the uniform, that of another sotnik, and ran to catch up to Andreya. They trudged over the even terrain and in short order came to open land. Ahead, spread over acre upon acre of landscape, were ordered rows of tents, campfires with men huddled around them, stands of muskets resting nearby. To the left, visible largely because of the whiteness of its walls, was the city of Izlo. Nikandr would have expected to see lanterns here or there in the city, but there were none. It made it seem more a forgotten ruin than a besieged city in the plains of Yrstanla.

Soon they were among the tents. Many of the men were sleeping, but there were those that remained awake, nursing the fires, passing cups around the circle. Some looked up, but few did so for long. Near the center of the camp was a large circular area where nine large tents stood. A tenth, much larger than the others, sat at the center, the command tent where Leonid would be. The others would be the tents of the duchies. One would be for Khalakovo, though Nikandr knew that Ranos was elsewhere. He'd been stationed on Galahesh with what remained of Anuskaya's common fleet. Exiled, in effect, perhaps due to Nikandr's reputation or because he'd disobeyed Leonid in sending Styophan west.

Hopefully he was already on his way here. If Mother had reached him, if he believed the words Nikandr had told her to relay to him, he would come.

Andreya led Nikandr to the tent of Bolgravya. Andreya went first and Nikandr stepped in after. In the center of the tent, to the left of the long central pole, a brazier burned low, casting the gathered dukes in light like the dying of autumn. There was Yevgeny Mirkotsk, a man who had always stood by Khalakovo, as his father had, and his father's father. He watched Nikandr's entrance with something akin to disfavor. Although he was a strong ally of Ranos's, he had never quite approved of what Nikandr had done on Oshtoyets. No matter that it had likely saved the lives of many of his men; no matter that it had closed the rifts that would soon have threatened the islands of his homeland. To him, Nikandr was too entwined with all that had happened then—and since—to completely trust him.

Nikandr nodded to Yevgeny, who nodded in return.

Next to him stood Konstantin Bolgravya, a man only a handful of years older than Nikandr. He looked healthy, and his bright eyes seemed accepting, almost pleased, of Nikandr's presence. Strangely enough, Konstantin was probably his closest ally in this tent. He'd asked Nikandr to save his brother, Grigory. Not directly, of course. He wouldn't have placed himself in a position where Nikandr could have said no directly. Instead he'd sent his lover, Mileva Vostroma, to pose the question for him. Nikandr had agreed, because it had given him a slim ray of hope to make his way to Galahesh to save Atiana. He'd even found Grigory, but Grigory had refused Nikandr's help. In fact, he'd imprisoned Nikandr and then abandoned him to die for having the impudence to bring a note penned by Konstantin himself, a note that had somehow heightened the embarrassment of being saved by Nikandr, whom Grigory hated above all others. Grigory had later died at the Spar on Galahesh, but he'd died bravely. He'd commanded the ship that had crashed into the Spar, breaking it and killing Muqallad, effectively saving Galahesh, the islands, the entire world from Muqallad's plans. As strange as it was—and as hard as it was for Nikandr to admit—Grigory had died a hero. Konstantin had somehow seemed relieved when he'd learned of it, and he had thanked Nikandr in private.

Nikandr nodded to Konstantin, who returned the gesture with a reticent yet heartfelt smile.

Yegor Nodhvyansk watched as Nikandr stepped toward the warmth of the low fire. Nikandr remembered how Yegor had acted as the voice of reason on Khalakovo when the southern dukes—especially Leonid Dhalingrad and Zhabyn Vostroma—had begun to toss accusations at the feet of Nikandr's father. It had happened after the Grand Duke, Stasa Bolgravya, had been killed by an elder suurahezhan on Radiskoye's eyrie, and tensions had been running hot. Yegor was older now, perhaps wiser in some ways, less willing to stick his neck out. Nikandr could only hope he could once again show his good judgment. Plus, Nikandr had learned while speaking to his mother that Leonid's rule had not been kind to Nodhvyansk.

When Nikandr nodded to Yegor, the duke merely stared back with emotionless eyes.

And then there was Borund.

The image of the seven mahtar of Iramanshah hanging from ropes in the garden of Radiskoye flashed through Nikandr's mind. Borund had ordered their deaths, and yet he'd been strangely protective of Nikandr. Nikandr was sure he'd somehow maneuvered the situation so that Nikandr could be ordered to the warfront, to help protect the Grand Duchy against the ships Sariya had just unleashed against the Grand Duchy.

Another image came. An image of his dog, Berza, being shot while bounding across a meadow of flowers and heather. A shot that had come from Borund himself. How far they'd come since their childhood, when they'd been fast friends. The mantle of leadership will do that, Nikandr's father used to say.

Nikandr reached the edge of the circle, giving Borund the final nod. "My Lord Dukes."

At a wave from Borund, Andreya bowed and took his leave. A rook, sitting atop an iron perch at the back of the tent, began flapping its wings. The dukes turned to look, but the rook merely tucked its head into its wing as if it were having a bad dream.

Borund waved to the low seat at Nikandr's side.

Together, the five of them sat.

That was something, at least, the fact that they were treating him as an equal, for now.

A bone mazer filled with vodka sat on the arm of each chair. In unison they picked up the mazers and raised them to one another.

"*Budem zdorovy,*" Nikandr said before downing the vodka in one burning mouthful.

"*Budem,*" the dukes responded in kind, raising their mazers before downing them as well.

"You may wonder why I've asked to speak with only the four of you."

"Because we're the only ones who will listen," Borund said, "but we won't listen for long, Nischka. Get on with it."

"What I tell you first you may speak of freely outside of this tent."

Yevgeny bared his teeth, fighting the burn of the vodka he'd just swallowed. "And what you say after?"

"In good time, My Lord Duke. I come with news from Alekeşir, from the Kamarisi himself." The dukes looked among one another, confused. Yevgeny even looked angry. But Borund seemed calm, more calm than Nikandr could ever remember him being.

He told them the same things he'd told his mother, how the Kamarisi, before he'd been killed by Datha in the streets of Alekeşir, had told him of Bahett's plans, how Sariya had arranged for it all with the men and women of Kohor, how strange new ships had been built on Ghayavand. He mentioned the attacks on the islands as well, for if he left it for them to say, it would be a mark used against him.

"So you know that our islands are being attacked," Yegor said.

"I do."

Yegor sat more stiffly in his chair. "Then what, good Khalakovo, would you have us do now?"

"I would have you wait. Do not fall into the trap Sariya has laid for us."

"You would leave us defenseless," Yevgeny said.

"*Nyet.* Prepare the fleet. Position our ships to meet the threat. But under no circumstances can we approach Ghayavand."

"Because Sariya wishes it..."

"Because she has been working these past two years to orchestrate that very thing."

"You said she was in the Gaji."

"She was, but before going there she spent time in Alekeşir, enthralling Hakan's son before taking Nasim to Shadam Khoreh. There were those in Kohor who became her allies as well, and many were sent to Ghayavand to begin preparations."

Borund leaned back in his chair, which creaked beneath his stout frame.

"There is one difficulty, of course."

"You speak of Leonid."

Borund nodded, his jowls folding as he did so. "Our Grand Duke."

"He is our Grand Duke, but he does not rule in your stead. You are all the dukes of your own islands, are you not?"

"That may be," Borund said. "But we are now at war, and we defer to Dhalingrad to lead us."

"Leonid is foolhardy."

"He's taken us deep into the Empire's territory."

"We all know that Yrstanla was woefully unprepared after Hakan's gambit on Galahesh failed. Any one of you could have taken us this far, but I daresay you wouldn't have done so as quickly. You wouldn't leave our lines of supply so open to attack."

None of the dukes nodded, none of them said a word, but Nikandr could tell he'd scored a mark. They knew as well as he did how vulnerable the islands now were. It was only because the Empire had wasted their resources in Hakan's blindness that the islands hadn't been attacked on another front. That and the fact that the Maharraht had been decimated by the events on Rafsuhan and Galahesh.

Borund, apparently uncomfortable with the silence, shifted in his chair and said, "We defer to the Grand Duke."

"Only until Council is held."

"The Mantle is not passed on at Council, Nikandr."

"It once did. Else why is there a vote of confidence the opening day of each Council? The Covenant of Anuskaya details that the vote shall be made, each year, or when five of nine demand it."

Yevgeny seemed to be the uncomfortable one now. He was a man built on tradition and ceremony, and that made him uneasy with change. "No one has paid attention to such things for a hundred years."

"And yet it is there, so that if the Grand Duke takes us to a place of woe or desperation, he can be unseated." Nikandr paused for a moment before continuing. "For the good of the Grand Duchy."

Yegor said, "But he hasn't done such a thing. Not yet."

"He will. When he learns of the ships on Ghayavand, he will send our entire fleet to root it out, for it will not only expose his mistakes, it will shine light upon them. He'll wish to correct it before anyone says anything against him."

"As he should," Yegor replied.

"In other circumstances, I would agree. But not in this. It will spell our ruin." Nikandr raised his hand to them, seeing all of them ready to speak. "You may put little trust in me. None of us has seen eye to eye at various times in the past, and I've not helped, as brashly as I've acted. I grant you all this, My Lord Dukes. But you must agree that I've always worked to protect our Grand Duchy. I love our islands above all else. These have been strange times to live in. The blight. The wasting. The rifts. At first we all doubted their existence. I was no different from you. And now we all acknowledge them as truth. As things to be respected, even feared. We all agree that if we continue on the same course as we have been, the islands are doomed. Is this not the very reason Leonid has pushed so hard to gain a foothold on the Motherland? He fears we'll soon lose the islands entirely. And he would be right if the rifts were simply left to spread on their own. But they are *not* being left alone. Sariya has plans for them. And she is dearly hoping we'll fall into her trap. Do not do so, My Lords. Do not give her what she seeks."

"Which is what?" Borund asked.

"Can it be anything less than what she and Muqallad sought over the Straits of Galahesh? She hopes to bring about indaraqiram."

In the silence that followed, Nikandr looked to each of them. The brazier had died further, making each of the dukes look as though he'd been dipped in blood.

"Leonid may agree with you, Nikandr." This came from Konstantin, an ally Nikandr had never expected to find among the southern duchies.

"And he should be given that chance. Grant me an audience with him tomorrow, and I'll present these choices to him."

"And if he doesn't agree?" Borund asked.

"Then I ask that you call Council and vote him down."

The dukes shifted in their seats.

"You don't have the votes," Borund said.

"Not yet, but Ranos is on his way. He'll be here in two days if all goes well."

As the reality of this struck the gathered dukes, the tent went deadly silent, which was good news for Nikandr. He thought they might force him from the tent, refuse to listen to him, perhaps drag him before Leonid to explain himself—no matter that he was next in line for the Scepter of Khalakovo. The fact that they were quiet meant they were considering, and if they were considering, they would see just how reckless Leonid had been. Most of all, though, they would realize just how dangerous a gamble it was. Send in ships, and they risked losing all. Wait, and it would give Nikandr and others time to find Sariya and remove her from Ghayavand.

"Go to your brother's tent, Nikandr. We will discuss it. We'll tell you of our decision in the morning."

Nikandr stood and bowed to them. He felt confident that he'd won them over. But as he left the tent and the cold of night swept over him, and their looks of doubt began playing within his mind, he wondered if he'd misplaced his trust.

But what was he to do? He had to trust. The Grand Duchy was not built on one island alone, nor one man.

CHAPTER SIXTY

Nikandr was led to the tent of Khalakovo, and inside, he was surprised to see Isaak, his father's seneschal, sitting with bent back at an impossibly small desk, writing a letter. A lantern hung from the roof of the tent, lighting Isaak's wrinkle-lined face with deep shadows and golden light.

"Isaak, what in the name of the ancients are you doing here?"

Isaak turned in his chair and took him in with a perturbed look on his face. His long white beard waggled as he spoke. "Don't use their name in vain, and I could ask the same of you."

"I've come to prevent our Grand Duke from making a grave mistake."

"*Have* you?"

"I have." Nikandr moved to one of the many cots in the darker portion of the tent, pulled off his cherkesska and sword belt, threw them down, and fell into the cot, not even bothering to remove his boots.

"Boots off, My Good Prince. You may leave them by the door."

"I'm no longer a child," Nikandr said, his eyes covered by the arm he'd draped over them. All of the stress from the Gaji, from Shadam Khoreh, from Alekeşir and the chase here toward Izlo, all felt as though it had been building and was shedding from him only now—now that he'd reached a touchstone from his childhood.

"Then you should know better. Off with your boots or it's off with your head." A phrase Nikandr hadn't heard in twenty years. He couldn't help but smile. "And then get you some rest. You look like you've one foot in your grave."

Nikandr took off his boots as he'd been bade, set them by the door and fell back into the cot. The last thing he heard before he fell asleep was the soft *scritch scratch* of Isaak's writing.

When he woke, it was to someone shaking his shoulder.

He jerked upright and found the tent occupied by a stout man with a long beard with a white streak running down the middle. On his head was a pale blue kolpak trimmed in black fur. In the center of it was a brooch of a rearing bear, the sign of Dhalingrad. Nikandr hadn't seen him in years, but once he'd wiped the sleep from his eyes he recognized him. Vadim Dhalingrad, Leonid's second son.

Two streltsi stood behind him. Both with hands upon their belted pistols.

Nikandr looked to them coolly, then met Vadim's gaze.

"Up, Khalakovo."

"Would you like some tea, Vadya?"

Vadim reared back his hand to slap Nikandr, but Nikandr was too quick. He leaned back, making Vadim miss, and then rolled backward off the cot.

By the time he'd risen to a stand, the hands of the streltsi had shifted from merely resting on the butt of their pistols to gripping them.

"I wonder if you could take me to see the Grand Duke. There is much we must speak of."

Vadim, ten years Nikandr's senior, went red in the face. He looked as though he was ready to draw the shashka that hung from his belt, but Nikandr was within easy reach of his own sword. As good as Vadim was reported to be, he wouldn't draw his sword here, not against someone as good with a blade as Nikandr was, and not when he'd clearly been sent by his father to fetch Nikandr.

Without a word Vadim strode from the tent, leaving his men to wait for Nikandr.

Nikandr pulled on his sword belt and boots and cherkesska, and then stepped out of the tent and into the cold morning air. They were entering the deepest part of winter, but still, Nikandr was surprised at how raw the wind was. The mainland was often warmer than the Grand Duchy, but this rivaled anything winter among the islands had to offer. He didn't have to travel far, however, only to the large command tent.

Inside, the dukes were gathered. Yevgeny and Konstantin and Yegor and Borund. Andreyo Rhavanki had been struck by the wasting, but his son, Alaksandr, stood in his place. Had Andreyo Rhavanki been present, Nikandr might have summoned him to the meeting last night as well; but as sick as he was, barely able to recognize the loved ones who tended to his needs, getting Alaksandr on his side would be all but impossible.

At the center of these men was a large wooden chair. Heodor Lhudansk stood to one side of it, Aleg Khazabyirsk to the other. These two duchies had allied themselves most closely with Dhalingrad. At one time both had been allies of Nikandr's father, Iaros, but after Stasa Bolgravya had died on Khalakovo's eyrie, their allegiance had slowly but surely shifted toward the south, and to Leonid Dhalingrad especially.

In the chair—a throne in effect—sat Leonid. He looked even more twisted and bent than Nikandr remembered. His white beard hung down his chest and pooled in his lap like a sleeping cat. He stared as Nikandr approached and bowed, more than displeased at how shallow it had been.

"The Grand Duke wishes to speak with me?"

It took Leonid several wheezing breaths before he spoke. "You leave the war for a mission of your own choosing. You see fit to be gone for seven seasons. You make your way to Alekeşir and back. And when you return, you do not make the leader of this war, the leader of your sovereign state, aware of your presence."

"I thought it best not to disturb His Imperial Highness."

Leonid's breath rasped in, his breath rasped out, and all the while his eyes bored into Nikandr. Did he have the wasting, Nikandr wondered, or was it a less deadly malady? Whatever the case, he looked shrunken and small, like a wet possum staring at him with blackened eyes. This was a strange reality to be faced with. In his mind, he saw the Leonid of old. He had never been physically imposing, but his sharp tongue and his unbending will had always marked him as one to think twice about crossing.

That man is still there, Nikandr reminded himself. He couldn't underestimate Leonid's ability to inflict harm.

"You thought it best not to disturb, yet thought it wise to speak with other dukes before coming to me."

Nikandr knew a meeting such as this had been a likelihood. Matri would be watching the camp at all hours. Any of the Matri allied with Dhalingrad might have seen Nikandr speaking in Borund's tent and informed the Grand Duke. The Matri wouldn't know what Nikandr had spoken of—they couldn't hear while in the aether—but Leonid wouldn't rest until he was satisfied he'd learned everything, and that made him more dangerous than ever.

"I wished to tell them news, Highness, news of the ships that can be found on Ghayavand even now. Dozens of them. Ships of war. Ships flown by the powerful qiram of Kohor. Ships massing at the command of Bahett ül Kirdhash."

"At *Bahett's* command…"

Nikandr nodded. "The Kamarisi is dead, killed by one of King Brechan's own. But the events on Ghayavand were set into motion long ago by Sariya." He went on to tell his tale once more, though this time the reaction was infinitely different. When he'd told the dukes last night, they'd listened, even if there had been a note of mistrust in their eyes. As he told the Grand Duke, however, Leonid's eyes narrowed. His nostrils flared. It seemed all he could do to keep his lips from rising in disgust. Yet when he'd finished, Leonid did not bark. He did not dismiss Nikandr's words. He merely nodded, as if he were giving the story due consideration.

This was not merely unexpected. It gave Nikandr pause. Leonid had never believed in Nikandr's mission to the Gaji. He'd thought Ranos foolish to allow it. But in the end he hadn't forbidden Nikandr from going, most likely because he thought Nikandr would never return.

If reports were to be believed, however, Leonid had been furious over Ranos's orders for Styophan. He hadn't thought the Haelish worth treating with, and even though Khalakovo's ships weren't needed against Yrstanla—nearly all of the Empire's ships had been decimated in a furious storm before the events at the Spar—he'd inflicted harsh levies against Khalakovo and demanded all of Khalakovo's fighting ships be stationed on Galahesh as recompense. Ranos had fought to keep as many ships as he could near Khalakovo's shores should the remains of the Maharraht resume their attacks, but it had still left Khalakovo woefully unprotected.

For as long as Nikandr had known him, Leonid had been a man quick to pick up the sword when pen would do, and yet here he was, listening calmly to Nikandr's story, even nodding from time to time, as if caught up in the tale.

This was how Nikandr knew that something was terribly, terribly wrong.

When he'd finished, Leonid ran his hand down his white beard. He adjusted it until it ran just so down his chest. Then he shifted in his chair and regarded Nikandr anew. "The boy you left to rescue. He is dead?"

"Nasim," Nikandr said. "Ishkyna believes he left through a portal, as Kaleh did when she fled Galahesh with Nasim."

"And Alekeşir. What state is it now in?"

"Decimated, Your Highness. Half the city is destroyed and little now remains of Irabahce. I've never seen the like."

"And what now, Nikandr Iaroslov? Where would you go? What would you do?"

"I would go to Ghayavand."

Leonid smiled, a wicked looking thing as Nikandr had ever seen. "To see if they have made their way there. Your Kaleh and Nasim."

"As it please Your Grace."

"And the Kohori. You say they're on the island."

"They are, but they are baiting us—"

Nikandr stopped, for Leonid had raised his hand. "They are baiting us, as you say, so that we will come to them."

"The Matri have seen it."

"Saphia, your mother, has seen it."

"Others can make their way now. The path is not so treacherous as it once was with the outer wards now fallen."

Leonid smiled. It was a humoring gesture, but for anyone who looked upon him, he would seem accommodating. Nikandr prayed the gathered dukes could see the lie in his eyes, in the way he smiled. This was not the Leonid Nikandr knew. It was all an act for their benefit.

Somehow he knew what Nikandr had asked of the other dukes. He knew of Nikandr's plans. And he was pretending to consider Nikandr's warning so that they wouldn't find him unreasonable. So that they wouldn't call for Council.

I've been betrayed, Nikandr realized.

Nikandr searched the eyes of the other dukes. Borund looked confused. Konstantin as well. Yegor looked curious, as if he'd figured it out and was trying, as Nikandr was, to piece things together.

But Yevgeny. Yevgeny Mirkotsk—his father's closest ally for decades—met Nikandr's eyes and then looked down.

As if he were embarrassed.

Nyet, Nikandr thought. Not embarrassed. Ashamed.

He'd told Leonid. He'd gone to him after Nikandr had pleaded for his help and told the Grand Duke everything. Nikandr couldn't believe it for a moment, but now it only made sense. Leonid treated the duchies that didn't fall in line ruthlessly. The effect of his new levies hadn't affected Khalakovo as much as the other duchies for the simple fact that Khalakovo was resource rich, especially with windwood. With the number of ships lost in the battles with Yrstanla two years ago, dozens of new ships had been commissioned, and Khalakovo had received the lion's share of the contracts.

Mirkotsk had not been so lucky. They'd become the convenient substitute for Leonid's anger. Yevgeny had done the only thing he could—he'd caved to curry favor. And now, with Yevgeny gone, Nikandr no longer had the votes. Council or not, Leonid would have his way.

Unless, Nikandr thought…

Unless Leonid were thought of as unreasonable. That was half the reason the dukes hadn't committed last night. They wanted to give Leonid a chance to show what stuff he was made of. Well, Nikandr knew what he was made of. Hatred and anger and bile. That was what roiled inside Leonid Dhalingrad. That and a desire to retain the mantle of Grand Duke at all costs now that it had finally landed on his shoulders.

"That is the extent of it, Your Grace," Nikandr said at last. "Leave Ghayavand alone. Watch for them if you will, but leave the rest to me. Grant me a ship and I'll take the men of Khalakovo to the island." Leonid opened his mouth to speak, but Nikandr talked over him. "Do not worry over the ship. Ranos will be bringing one here shortly."

Leonid's black eyes narrowed. "And who granted him leave to come?"

"I did. I knew His Grace would see the wisdom in my decision, so I bid him come."

"*Your* decision."

"By Your Grace's leave, of course."

Leonid stood, an act that looked as painful as it was slow. The other dukes watched the exchange uncomfortably. All except Borund. Borund was watching Nikandr with the look he'd had on Radiskoye, the one that had pleaded with Nikandr to remain quiet. It had been moments before he'd ordered the hangman to release the lever on the nearby gallows, condemning the seven Mahtar of Iramanshah to swing in the wind with ropes around their necks.

As Leonid shuffled forward, Borund gave Nikandr another warning. He shook his head, almost imperceptibly.

But Nikandr didn't care. He couldn't let this go, not now, and not for a man like Leonid Dhalingrad.

"Your Grace shouldn't trouble himself in his state," Nikandr said. "If you'll grant me leave to go, I'll begin making preparations. I merely need a writ with your seal, if you please."

"Enough!" This came from Leonid's son, Vadim. He took two long strides forward, and this time he pulled his black-handled kindjal from its sheath at his belt.

Nikandr made no move to retreat. He'd take a cut from Vadim if that's what it came to—the image it would leave on these dukes would be valuable, indeed—but Leonid raised his hand and pressed it against his son's broad chest before Vadim could get close enough to strike.

"All is well, my son." Leonid turned to Nikandr and with an effort that seemed almost insurmountable pasted on a smile. "All is well." His eyes wavered as he spoke, the left one ticking, as if Leonid could hardly believe the words coming from his own mouth. "You've done the Grand Duchy a great service, Nikandr Iaroslov, and you've done well to bring this news to us, the dukes of the Council. We will consider what you've said, and in due time, we'll give the proper orders."

He stepped forward and patted Nikandr on the shoulder. Nikandr wanted to say more. He wanted to force Leonid's hand, but he couldn't think of a way to do so without damaging his own cause.

"Rest now," Leonid said as he passed. "Rest, and you'll know our decision soon enough."

And then the Grand Duke left. Vadim followed, glaring with hate-filled eyes at Nikandr. And then the other dukes began filing out.

Soon Nikandr was left alone with Borund, the tent silent as a mausoleum. "Why did you do it?" Borund asked. "You should have waited to speak with me."

"You?" Nikandr laughed, the sound of it grim and humorless. "The man who sat on Khalakovo's throne, bleeding us dry for your father?"

"Whether you believe it or not, what I did was necessary for the Grand Duchy.

Not Vostroma. Not Khalakovo. But for the Grand Duchy."

"This is necessary, too."

"Which is why I listened. But Yevgeny…"

"I know," Nikandr said, "and now I've made a mess of things."

"*Da*," Borund said. "You have."

CHAPTER SIXTY-ONE

As cold rain continues to fall, Atiana stares at the white tower nestled in the copse of larch trees. "Have you seen this before?"

"Once, but only in the distance. I chased it, but when I came to the hill where I'd seen it, it was gone." There is something in Kaleh as she watches the tower. It isn't fear—Kaleh has been through too much to be afraid of Sariya—but respect, certainly, and an expectancy that makes Atiana think that she is glad this will soon be over, one way or the other.

Atiana touches Kaleh's shoulder. "I will go to her."

"Then I will go as well."

"*Neh*," she replies. "Keep watch, but do not approach. We cannot allow her to take us both."

Kaleh looks between the tower and Atiana. "Once you're inside, I won't be able to help you. You'll be on your own, truly."

Atiana searches for Mileva, but cannot sense her. "I know."

As Atiana walks down the hill, the smell of the brightbonnets fades. The rain turns to hail, pelting her mercilessly as she treads onward. Halfway down she turns to look for Kaleh, but the girl is gone. For reasons Atiana can't fully express, this lightens her heart.

When she reaches the copse of larch, the hail eases and turns to rain, then stops altogether. Above, the sun shines down from between two banks of clouds. It brightens them but does little to brighten Atiana's heart. *This is dark business, for which rain is better suited.* As she nears the tower and rainwater patters down from the branches of the larch, the door at the base of it creaks open.

The moment she steps across the threshold, however, the rain picks up again, harder than before, and a streak of lightning strikes the field she'd been walking across moments ago. It blinds her as the pounding of thunder reverberates through her chest and limbs and even her teeth.

Better, Atiana thinks grimly. *A meeting such as this calls for thunder.*

Inside, as she suspected, the room at the base of the tower is bare and empty. She goes up the stairs that hug the interior wall. Level after level is empty, just as it was below. When she reaches the seventh floor she finds Sariya standing on the far side of a room with rich rugs layering the floor. If the position of the lowering sun can be believed, Sariya is staring through the northern window. It feels strange to admit that north and south exist in the world of dreams, but it cannot be ignored. Directions have too much meaning for the Aramahn and even more for Sariya, the last of the Al-Aqim.

As she steps forward, Atiana feels a probing. Sariya reaches beyond these walls as well, perhaps wondering how Atiana came to this place. Sariya doesn't turn as Atiana reaches the middle of the room. She speaks not a word. She doesn't have to. There is an undeniable feeling of sisterhood between them. They have been enemies, true, but the two of them understand the aether like few ever have. They have also shared their lives with one another, albeit unwillingly, when Sariya became lost in her tower on Galahesh. In some ways Sariya knows Atiana better than anyone, even Nikandr or Mileva or Ishkyna. It's an uncomfortable conclusion, especially when Atiana stands in a world of Sariya's own making.

"I was trapped on this island for centuries," Sariya says, "and yet those days feel shorter than the handful of years I've been gone from Ghayavand."

Sariya turns, and Atiana gasps.

There are changes about Sariya… She had always been so beautiful, so youthful, that it seemed as though nothing could take those qualities from her, but here she stands, her skin lusterless, her eyes sunken. Deep wrinkles form in the skin around her lips as she smiles, and she looks down at herself, as if to acknowledge all that Atiana sees.

Again, Atiana feels her probing. She goes farther now, perhaps searching for Kaleh, searching for the bounds of her imprisonment.

"Your Nischka did this to me. Did you know?"

Atiana shakes her head, failing to comprehend how anything Nikandr might have done could have resulted in this.

Sariya glances to the eastern window on her left. "Did you know that Nikandr came to me? Here in this very room?"

"Not in this room," Atiana replies. "It was in your tower in Alayazhar."

Sariya laughs, more the croak of an old crone than the sound of a vibrant woman. "Make no mistake. It was here."

"*Neh*," Atiana replies, her voice stronger than Sariya's. "This is a vastly different place than the tower you created on Ghayavand. That was a place that gave you knowledge and strength. It was the place where you learned the secrets of the world, where you returned after taking breath on Sihyaan. It was a place that nurtured you for years before the sundering, and for decades afterward. *This* place"—Atiana waved to the room around her—"this is a place of decay. *It* draws from *you*, not the other way around. This will become your grave, daughter of Vehayeh."

"Do you think so?" She turns back to the window, the northern, the direction the Aramahn associate with winter, with end of life, but also rebirth. "I wonder."

Atiana approaches and stares through the window. There she sees not the empty landscape she expected, but a boy sitting on a mountaintop with his back to a pillar of obsidian nearly hidden by tall grass. Sage-colored moss grows on the face of the exposed stone, making it difficult to recognize, but it is not so different from the one that she'd seen on the hillock before she'd taken the dark.

It takes her long moments to realize the boy is Sukharam.

"Why does he cry?"

"Why, indeed?" Sariya glances her way, regards Atiana from head to foot. "Do you know that after I woke from the sundering, I remembered almost nothing from the ritual? I recalled only white light, the shattering of the Atalayina. I knew we had failed, and little more. But there was a lament within me, Atiana, daughter of Radia. A lament so deep it nearly smothered me." Sariya turns away from the window and stares into Atiana's eyes, and Atiana wonders about her apparent age. In this place, Sariya controls all. She can make herself as young as she wishes to, as Kaleh can, so why doesn't she? What has changed: her ability to control her appearance or her will to do so?

"At the time," Sariya continues, "I thought our collective failure was the sole source of our pain—not merely our failure to reach indaraqiram, but that we'd torn the veil between worlds."

"And now?"

"Now?" Sariya takes in a deep breath, and her eyes go distant. "It was all there before us. We had only to look." Tears well in her eyes and slip down her cheeks. "I nearly died on Galahesh, at the foot of the Spar. It brought me to the very edge of the veil, not between Erahm and Adhiya, but between our worlds and the heavens above. I looked beyond the veil, and I saw it." Her lips quiver. "The fates. They had gone, fled to another realm. Either that or we killed them that day. The reality of it matters little. What matters, daughter of Radia, is that we failed. We failed ourselves. We failed the Aramahn. We failed you and the people of the desert and those who live on the wide plains of Yrstanla. We failed, for without the fates, the world is truly doomed." She points out the window, where Sukharam is staring up at the sky in pain and bewilderment. "He knows that now. That is why he cries. He has realized the world can no longer be saved."

Atiana shakes her head. "It *can* be saved."

"Do you think so?"

"It must be so."

"And why is that?"

"We have lived three hundred years since the sundering. If the fates were dead, all would have been lost long before now."

"If you take a man from the helm of a windship, does it begin to list that very moment? Does it immediately fall to the ground? Or does it continue along its path until eventually crashing to the earth?"

"We have the ancients."

"*Yeh*, your ancients. They protect you, do they not?"

"They do!"

"And who protects *them*? Who do you think were there when the first of your ancients crossed to the other side?"

"The fates may have given us life, but we decide our *own* paths."

Sariya nods. "That doesn't contradict their ways, Atiana. They granted us free will. But there are many paths to the same place, are there not? So it is with the fates. We choose, but they guide what choices are available. Whether you like it or not, we cannot go on forever without them. The *world* cannot go on."

"So what will you do? Remain here in this place, locked in Kaleh's mind, refusing to let her go?"

The smile on Sariya's face is humoring. "*Neh*, I will not do that."

"Then release her."

"If I do that now, I *will* die, and I would see the end of the world. Kaleh will remain mine." The way Sariya speaks those words... They seem distant, as if she is looking not to the days ahead, but to the eons beyond.

"I will fight you."

"You are welcome to try. But you will have to find me first."

Suddenly the probing, which hasn't ceased since Atiana first felt it, grows much stronger.

And then there is nothing.

And Sariya is gone.

Atiana is left alone in the tower, which is now bare and nearly ruined. Through the window she sees not Sukharam but the same landscape she saw upon entering. And then she hears a rumble, a sifting of dirt and stone.

She flees down the levels of the tower as more of it crumbles and falls away. She reaches the doorway ahead of the tower's collapse—clearly Sariya doesn't wish for her to die—but it's still a shock. As the rubble settles and a cloud of dust rises into the air and drifts on the wind, it feels final. It feels like a note heralding the end of all things. Sariya may get her wish after all, Atiana realizes. She removed the world of the Tashavir, and now, with the wards gone, she will simply watch as the rifts open wide and the end of the world comes at last.

Is she right? Could the fates truly have died when the sundering occurred?

It doesn't matter, Atiana decides. She cannot simply wait for the world to end. She won't.

"She's gone."

Atiana turns and finds Kaleh standing behind her. "What?"

"I can no longer feel her at all. She's escaped, Atiana Radieva."

Atiana goes cold. The probing. Sariya was searching for something, not merely reaching out for the boundaries of her imprisonment. And then it all falls together.

She was tricked from the beginning.

It started with Habram and Bahett and their pleas to have Atiana merely speak to Sariya. They had allowed Atiana to demand help. And that connection, her own connection to Mileva, is what allowed Sariya to escape.

Rarely has she had difficulty leaving the aether, but it is so now. She tries to pull back, to rise above the currents of the dark to reach her own form, but finds she cannot.

She rails against her bonds. She reaches out for Mileva, for Kaleh. She searches for some way to escape.

But there *is* no escape. She has been trapped as surely as Sariya had been only moments ago.

CHAPTER SIXTY-TWO

Atiana walks along a gully. By her side, a stream gurgles on its way toward a forest of impossibly tall trees. As she jogs into the trees, a fecund scent fills the air. There is no wind. The trees, their leaves and branches, move not at all. She goes further into the forest and finds a place where there are walkways and homes within the trees above. This is the village of Siafyan on the Maharraht island of Rafsuhan. Atiana has never been to Siafyan, but she flew through it in rook form when Nikandr rescued Soroush from the floating village of Mirashadal and brought him there.

How long ago that seems now.

Atiana has been trapped in Kaleh's dream for what seems like days. She knows Kaleh has been driven into hiding. She just has to find *where*. She decides she's been looking in the wrong places and starts to push herself to touch Kaleh's mind, to find her greatest fears, her greatest source of pain. Those are the places she will find Kaleh.

And she *must* find Kaleh if she's ever to leave this place, for Kaleh, much like Nasim, is bound up in this tale of the sundering, and unless Atiana is sadly mistaken, Kaleh will have more to say about it before all is done.

She wanders aimlessly though the village, calling Kaleh's name, and then continues to the forest beyond. She realizes she's walking toward the clearing. She had never seen this place of misery, but Nikandr had told her about it—the clearing where the children, the akhoz, had been sacrificed by Muqallad. The akhoz were chained to posts and burned while Bersuq held the two pieces of the broken Atalayina. Their sacrifice, the heat from their dying souls, had fused the two pieces together, and Muqallad had moved on, leaving them like the forgotten embers of a still-warm fire.

Atiana has often wondered how Kaleh viewed that time and that place. Did she justify the pain and anguish of the children as a necessary inconvenience?

Or did she see herself in the eyeless faces of those children?

How confusing it must have been for her to have aged so strangely. She was clearly a gifted child. Yet still, a child—no matter how smart and how perceptive—cannot absorb years upon years of experience.

She arrives at the clearing.

Ashes layer the ground. The blackened stumps of the posts, as high as Atiana's knees, stand from the bed of ashes like the clawing fingers of the dead. As Atiana approaches a wind picks up. White ashes are drawn up toward the sky, higher and higher until they're lost among the low clouds. It looks as the roiling column of fire did, except this is grey, completely devoid of color, like a distant memory half remembered.

Atiana waits for Kaleh, thinking surely the ashes must be a sign, but Kaleh doesn't come, so she continues on into the woods. She allows her mind to wander, but she knows there is a place she is being taken—by her own mind, by Kaleh's, she doesn't know. She cares only that for the first time since being trapped here, she has some sense of direction.

She wanders through the damp wood and comes to a mound of earth overgrown with moss and littered with red and yellow leaves. Nearby she hears the slow ticking of the bark beetles. She becomes aware of the beating of her own heart. Moments ago, she felt it not at all, and now she can think of little else.

This is the place, she realizes.

She puts her hand against her chest. For long moments she can feel only the pumping of her own blood, but then she feels another pumping in time with hers. It's beneath the hillock. There is a heart beating somewhere beneath the earth.

She approaches. Kneels next to it. Places her hands against the soft earth. She lowers herself until her cheek and ear are pressed against it.

And she listens.

She hears it—*THOOM-thoom, THOOM-thoom*—and if she remains perfectly still, she can feel minute vibrations against her cheek. This happened to Nikandr as well, but that was in the real world. This is different. This is a place of Kaleh's own making.

"Kaleh," she whispers. "Can you hear me?"

The beating does not change.

"Kaleh, hear me," she says louder. "Sariya is gone. She's on her way to Sihyaan."

Still the beating remains the same.

"She goes to tear the rift open. All you've done. All you've worked toward in trying to stop her. It will mean nothing if she reaches the mountain before we do. Come, Kaleh. Join me, and together we will stop her."

She waits. The sound of the beating heart slows. And then the earth beneath her cracks. As Atiana steps back, the crack widens like overbaked custard, revealing dirt so black it looks like the night itself lies below this thin crust of earth. In the center of the gap lies a girl in a simple white dress. The dress is wet and smeared with mud, as is her white skin. The sound of the beating heart—muted moments ago—is now loud, like the rhythmic fall of a wood axe.

Kaleh looks up—not the woman, but the girl Atiana had seen when she first entered this place. "She cannot be stopped."

"She can, and you will do it, for there are no others."

She is silent for a time, as if considering Atiana's words. She looks down at her hands, which are cupped tightly around something. Atiana is sure it is the heart, yet when Kaleh opens her hands, there is nothing there. Kaleh herself seems confused by this. She stares up at Atiana as the sound of the heart slowly fades.

"There is Nasim."

"*Yeh*," Atiana says, smiling. "There is Nasim."

"And Sukharam."

Atiana reaches down, offering Kaleh her hand. "And Sukharam."

She pulls Kaleh up and together the two of them leave that place. At first she isn't sure where to go, but she's learned much from Sariya, even if Sariya never meant to teach her. She knows the lay of this land as well as she knows the islands of Anuskaya, but more than simply *knowing* this place, she understands how to manipulate it, at least to a degree.

Ahead lays a dark patch of forest. She leads Kaleh there, heading toward the darkest huddle of trees. Branches bar her way, but she parts them and finds beyond a field of grass that ends in a sharp cliff. The smell of the sea is strong and the winds are up. Beyond the cliff's edge are the dark waters of the Sea of Tabriz. This is Ildova, her favorite of the islands in the Vostroman archipelago. To her right, sitting at the very edge of the cliff like a lone seabird is a squat tower of mottled grey fieldstone. She begins walking there, but realizes that Kaleh has remained in the darkness of the trees, watching the way ahead with mistrustful eyes.

"Come," Atiana says, taking her hand.

And Kaleh does. They head for the tower, which appears deserted. When Atiana opens the weatherworn door, the hinges groan. Once they're inside, Atiana closes the door with a boom. The sound of the sea fades. The wind has left their cheeks red, but the air is already beginning to warm.

Atiana sets her hand on the wrought-iron door handle. "Are you ready?"

Kaleh looks at the door, swallowing, her nostrils flaring. Her eyes dart between Atiana's hand and the grey wood of the door itself, but then she seems to gather herself, and she nods.

After one last squeeze of Kaleh's hand, Atiana opens the door.

When Atiana woke, she was lying on a bed of pine needles. She could feel them pricking the skin of her palms. At first she thought she was home on Vostroma, but it was too warm for that. Then she thought she was in the great Gaji desert, breathing in the heavy smoke of tūtūn.

Nyet. Not tūtūn. Blood. Smoke from her own burning blood.

She turned her head—a simple enough thing that still took every ounce of her will—and there she saw the pine trees, the hillock, and Kaleh lying next to her. Two men were talking at the top of the hill, near the half-hidden obelisk. One was Habram, dressed in his red robes. The other, his back to her, was Bahett. A warm wind—so warm it felt as though the world was beginning to melt—blew over the island, causing Habram's robes and the tall feather attached to the front of Bahett's turban to flutter.

Atiana blinked, for the two men seemed to be limned in silver. The edges of their clothing, the contours of their faces, the subtle shift of shade along their ruddy skin. It was as if she were looking at them through crystal dipped in moonlight. She knew immediately it was the aether. She'd woken, but she hadn't yet left it.

The feelings of dizziness grew. The feeling was akin to what had happened at the Spar on Galahesh. She'd shifted between worlds, but this was different. She was seeing both worlds at the same time.

Suddenly Bahett turned. His gaze dropped to Kaleh, who lay just to Atiana's side. Atiana looked at her as well. Her breath came slowly, but she seemed as peaceful as Atiana ever remembered her being.

The Atalayina and the wooden box that held it were gone. Not surprising, since…

Sariya… Where would Sariya have gone? She had been freed, of this Atiana was sure. But who might she have taken?

It wasn't difficult to answer this question. She recalled Ushai's look when she'd come down that hill. She'd seemed so fatalistic—concerned but determined—and Ushai was one of the very few besides the Matri that had learned to navigate the aether. Of course it had been Ushai.

Atiana searched for her, but she was nowhere to be found. She started at movement in the trees, however. Aelwen, the Haelish wodjan, stood there watching Atiana from behind a large tree. She knew something. Atiana could see it in her eyes. She tried speaking to her as she would the Matri. *Aelwen*, she called. *Aelwen, hear me.*

"You've been gone a long time."

Atiana turned, nearly throwing up from the movement, and found Bahett walking down the hill toward her. Habram walked by his side, watching Atiana carefully.

"Have I?" Atiana said. Her words were slurred horribly. With great care she was able to turn on her side and eventually sit up. When she looked back to the woods, Aelwen was gone.

Bahett smiled, his movements bleeding silver. "Two full days."

Atiana shook her head, finding even that simple motion nauseating. And then Bahett's words sunk in. Two days... How long had it been since Sariya had taken Ushai's mind and left?

"What do you think now, Atiana of Vostroma?" Habram said to her.

He was talking about their conversation on the ship of stone. They'd spoken of Sariya and her purpose. Habram had said that Sariya had returned to mend what she had broken. Atiana had thought him a fool, and yet he'd given her the chance to find Sariya within Kaleh's mind. He'd given her the chance to stop Sariya, trusting to the fates that the last of the Al-Aqim would not only be saved, but healed.

Atiana took a deep breath and stood. "I think that you're utter fools to trust her."

Habram's expression of smugness faded, but it was Bahett who stepped forward and struck her across the face. "That will be enough," he said coolly.

Pain blossomed across her cheek and jaw, and with it came an anger that rose up from somewhere deep inside her. That this man of Galahesh, of Yrstanla, a man responsible in part for the deaths of hundreds of Vostromans, thousands of Anuskayans, would strike her dredged up something she hadn't known was there.

When she spoke again, she spoke in Anuskayan. "You're not worthy to touch the blood of Vostroma. And this is only the beginning."

The world around her went dark—the midnight blue of the aether—while Bahett was lit in ghostly white. She reached out with her mind as easily as she did in the aether and descended upon him. She *felt* his fear even as she saw it in his eyes. She pressed down upon his mind, smothering him as he tried to escape. It was an easy thing. Easier even than assuming the rooks of the Grand Duchy. They at least were used to such things. They sensed the Matra's approach and fought for their own minds. Bahett had no such defenses, and he succumbed all too easily. But instead of merely being content to take control of his form, she continued to press, continued to rend. She could feel his desperation, could feel his will to live.

Some of the world's color returned. The sound of the wind through the trees reached her ears. Bahett lay there, twitching, white foam emanating from his mouth as his eyes fluttered, unable to focus.

Habram stared down, his throat constricting reflexively over and over again. He looked up at Atiana, and when their eyes met, there was fear there, and that turned to desperation. Before she could stop him, Habram wrapped his hands around her neck. "Release him!" he shouted.

Atiana looked down, and the world gained all its color. The sound of blood rushing through her ears nearly overwhelmed her.

Habram tightened his grip on her throat. "Release him!"

"I have!" she choked out.

For just one moment, Habram relaxed his grip and stared down at Bahett as the reality of what had just happened dawned on him.

Atiana could hardly keep her eyes from Bahett's twitching form.

But truly, he was Bahett no longer.

Now he was no one. He was nothing.

As the light within him faded, Atiana felt pain pierce her skull and drive down through her jaw. She didn't know what it was at first. But then she realized. Bahett was dying. Even now, he was dying, and she was somehow still connected to him.

Habram, his eyes crazed, reached around the back of her neck and grabbed a fistful of her hair. And then he pulled the curved khanjar from his belt. Atiana knew he was going to kill her, but just then she could do nothing to prevent it. Her pain was too great.

A blur rushed in from her right. Someone collided with both her and Habram, and she was thrown to the ground. All around her was a mass of limbs. A line of bright steel slid across Habram's arm.

Atiana rolled away and found Habram locked in battle with Aelwen, who still held the form of the Kohori man. It was clear, however, that Aelwen was severely outmatched. She was no swordsman. Already Habram was testing her weak defenses with precise strikes.

The pain in Atiana's head was crippling. She could hardly move, but perhaps that was for the best. Bahett lay just next to her. She reached over, trying to pull the ornate knife from his belt, but all she could manage to do was place her hand on his chest. By the ancients, his heart. Even through the pain she could feel it beating. It felt like the heartbeat she'd heard in Kaleh's dream. It was slow and getting slower. His body still worked even while his mind had become a gutted shell.

Die, she thought. *Please die.*

Finally she was able to grasp the hilt of the knife and pull it free of its sheath.

Aelwen shouted, a man's voice for all who heard it, but Atiana could hear the Haelish woman calling from somewhere deep inside. Aelwen fell, a bloody wound to her thigh. She gripped it tightly as Habram approached.

Habram towered over her, but then stopped. "Nasrad?"

Nasrad... That must have been the man's name, the man Aelwen had killed to take his form.

Nasrad's face changed. It softened, became more rounded. His black hair lengthened and took on a brownish tinge. His arms lost definition. His hips widened. His chest rounded as breasts took form. And soon it was not Nasrad at all who stared up at Habram, but Aelwen.

Atiana managed to get to her feet. Her shaking hands warded before her, helping to maintain her balance, and she managed to remain standing. She stepped forward, sure that she would fall before she reached Aelwen, sure Habram would turn and drive his sword straight through her.

But Habram paid no attention to her. He'd become enraged. He was hammering down blow after blow against Aelwen, as if by killing her he would somehow have Nasrad back.

That was when Atiana stepped in and drove the knife into Habram's back.

He screamed and reached behind him as Atiana stepped away. He managed to grip the hilt of the knife, but his fingers slipped from it. He tried again, and managed to pull the knife free. Blood poured from the wound.

He turned on Atiana, his eyes wide in surprise and pain and rage.

Atiana retreated, but Habram was still fast.

Before he could chase her more than three steps, Aelwen was behind him swinging the sword across the backs of his legs.

He fell and twisted around to meet this threat, but by then Aelwen had the sword high. She screamed and brought it down. It fell through Habram's chest with a sickening crunch.

For long moments Atiana and Aelwen stood there, watching as Habram's arms reached for the blade. His fingers touched it, then ran down its blood-slicked length to where steel met skin. He touched where his lifeblood spurted like a newfound spring. He stared up at the sky, face ashen, and then finally went still.

Atiana and Aelwen stared into one another's eyes. The two of them had killed this man. His blood was on both their hands, and that felt like a strange and unwelcome bond indeed.

Before Atiana could think what to say to her, Kaleh, lying mere paces away, bolted upright and drew in one long, gasping breath. Her eyes were wild with fear.

"It's all right," Atiana said to her, taking her hands. "I'm here."

Kaleh looked up at her, looked at Aelwen, and slowly her fear began to fade.

"We must go," Aelwen said in Yrstanlan.

"*Evet*," Atiana replied, "but where?"

"To Alayazhar," Aelwen said. "I heard Sariya speak it through Ushai's lips. She goes to Alayazhar."

CHAPTER SIXTY-THREE

Nikandr pulled his mare—a proper pony of the islands—to a stop along the eastern edge of the camp. He watched as strelet after strelet marched east along the road to Trevitze. The day was grey, and many of the men—nearly all of them wearing the colors of Dhalingrad or Lhudansk or Khazabyirsk—glanced at Nikandr with mistrust in their eyes, some even with open hatred. The sotni, marching at the head of their men, would salute with a raise of their hand, but only because he was a Prince of the Realm and it was required of them.

It had been three days since the meeting with the Grand Duke. No one had spoken to Nikandr since, and every time he'd tried to gain an audience, he'd been rebuffed. Even Borund told Nikandr to wait, that no decisions had yet been made.

"But the men," Nikandr had told him.

"We have to man the ships, Nikandr."

A few ships had been stationed in Trevitze, but there were dozens more flying from Galahesh, each manned by skeleton crews. The streltsi would board them, and they'd be off to Ghayavand. Leonid had already made his decision. He'd made it the moment he learned of the threat posed by the Kohori and their ships. The only question that remained was what to do with Nikandr.

Nikandr spurred his pony into a trot. After another sotni passed, he rode across the muddy brown trail and into the white, snowy field beyond. Ahead were the line of hills where Soroush was hidden. Assuming he was still there, of course. Hopefully he'd left for Ghayavand, where he could do some good. It was where Nikandr would go soon, but only after speaking with Ranos, who should arrive today.

Against a pewter sky Nikandr caught the sight of black wings. He felt his mother's presence through the soulstone hanging around his neck. Yrfa, his mother's favorite bird, winged down and alighted on his shoulder. The rook cawed several times, the sound loud in Nikandr's ear. "We've made a mess of things, Nischka."

"*Nyet. I've* made a mess of things."

They were alone in the field, the road far behind Nikandr. It felt as if he were riding over the fields of Uyadensk, and that in an hour or two he could be home in Radiskoye. How he longed to return there. The roads he'd traveled had made him weary. The odds continually being stacked against him and the others. Why couldn't Leonid see that he was only trying to protect the Grand Duchy?

The rook made a clucking sound. "I would hear the tale, Nikandr. I need to know more."

After taking a deep breath, he went on to tell her everything, how Leonid had reacted, how Yevgeny had betrayed him, the long days since. When he was done, she was silent for a time. "I thought it would be Konstantin that turned on you."

"Not Borund?"

"Borund was always living beneath his father's shadow. Much of what he did when Nasim came to our shores he did to impress Zhabyn. Now that Zhabyn is gone and Borund rules alone, he's more likely to return to his younger self."

Nikandr couldn't deny it. Borund had acted like he wanted to help Nikandr but couldn't, knowing it would be too difficult given his duchy's ties to Dhalingrad.

"There is still time for Leonid to reconsider. Yevgeny as well. Ranos is on his way now. He may convince the others that what you say is true, that Leonid can no longer be trusted."

"And what of Ghayavand?" he asked. "Have you been able to reach it?"

"I've tried many times, as have the other Matri, but things have become difficult, even with the wards now gone. I was able to approach once, but only for a few moments. The ships are still there, Nikandr. They are ready, two score or more. Let Ranos come and speak with Yevgeny. He may be able to turn him to our cause."

"He won't," Nikandr said. "Not now that he's committed himself to Dhalingrad."

"Men can change their minds, Nischka."

"Perhaps, but not Yevgeny. Not in this. Mirkotsk is too desperate."

"He has always thought well of Ranos. Yevgeny sees much of your father in him." *But not me*, Nikandr thought. "When Yevgeny sees his strong neighbor willing to stand up against the Grand Duke, he will do so as well."

"Perhaps," Nikandr said, but he doubted it. He doubted it very much. As well liked as Ranos was, he'd never quite had the savvy of their father, Iaros, in convincing others to join him. But perhaps he's learned. Nikandr might not be giving Ranos the credit he deserved. He'd had nearly two years to settle the mantle of Khalakovo across his shoulders. The notion cheered Nikandr. He'd wanted to reunite with Ranos—it had been too long since they'd seen one another—but now he had hope as well.

"Did you search for Atiana?" he asked.

The rook cawed and nipped at his ear. "Of course. I felt her, Nischka. She's alive, but her presence was faint. I know not where she is."

"And Ishkyna?"

"She'll go when she can. Mileva is strong, and her bond with Atiana will help. She'll search in Ishkyna's stead."

Far in the distance, a ship dropped down from the clouds—Ranos's ship, following the line of hills westward.

It was then that Leonid's words returned to him. *Rest, and you'll know our decision soon enough.* The words hadn't sat well when Leonid had said them, but it was somehow worse now that Ranos was here.

Without knowing why, he urged his pony into a trot. Then a canter.

And then he was galloping across the snow-covered field.

"Go, Mother," Nikandr said to the rook, which winged through the air just ahead of him. "Warn Ranos. He's in danger. Tell him to leave the ship as soon as he can. Take a skiff down to land."

The rook cawed over and over and then circled round. "What is it, Nischka?"

"I don't know! Just tell him!"

Nikandr thought she would deny him, but he could feel her alarm growing through their shared bond, and surely she felt his. The rook flapped up and away, moving quickly toward the ship.

Nikandr rose up in his stirrups. He whipped the reins against the pony's flank, pushing her harder than he'd ever pushed one before. And the mare responded, perhaps sensing his desperation. They flew across the field, the pony instinctively maneuvering around the dips and depressions in the land.

The rook grew smaller and smaller until it was an indistinct flutter of black against the high grey clouds. Then it suddenly veered away. Nikandr thought it was being attacked, but his mother must have realized she'd never make it in time. She'd abandoned the rook. She would assume one of the crewmen on board and warn Ranos that way, regardless of the insult or injury it might cause to the one she'd assumed.

The galleon floated lower.

Then Nikandr heard the report of gunfire. And shouts.

A skiff drifted away from the ship. The ship was close enough now that Nikandr could see men standing at the gunwales. They were pointing muskets at the skiff. They fired. Perhaps they struck whoever they'd been firing at, perhaps they didn't—Nikandr couldn't tell—but it was clear that the ship's havaqiram, the Aramahn windmaster, was using his abilities to catch the skiff in a twist of the wind.

The skiff drew closer to the ship's hull.

And then a form leapt from within the skiff, not *toward* the ship, but out and into the wind.

A black cherkesska fluttered as the strelet's form picked up speed. Faster and faster he plummeted, and still some of the men on board the ship fired down at him.

Nikandr eased his grip on the reins. The mare slowed, more out of need than Nikandr's command. The mare huffed with breath.

Far ahead, a quarter-league or more, the strelet's black form struck the field and was lost from sight, hidden by the snow and the tall grass.

Smoke now trailed up from the ship.

Smoke. From the stern. Where the ship's magazine was located.

No sooner had the thought occurred to him than the stern exploded in a blast of red fire and white smoke.

Wood and canvas and rigging flew outward. A dozen black forms with fluttering coats flew wide of the ship—they looked like rooks taking wing—and the only thing Nikandr could think of was that Ranos was one of them. He watched in horrid fascination as more of them plunged down. Nikandr didn't know which he wished for more, that Ranos was already dead or that he would gain a few meaningless moments as the ship plunged toward the ground.

The bulk of the ship listed as it lost buoyancy. The bowsprit tilted starward.

Nikandr reached out through the alabaster stone Ashan had given him. Never had his need been so great. He tried desperately to bond with a havahezhan—he swore he felt some near—but none of them would approach, and the broken remains of the ship gained speed, plummeting faster and faster.

"*Please*," Nikandr said.

But the hezhan kept their distance.

And the galleon crashed to the ground, the wood and smoke and fire still contained within the ship billowing outward.

The sound of it fell over the field like a pall. Nikandr felt it in his chest, against the roof of his mouth, as if the lives of the windsmen and streltsi aboard that ship were passing through him to reach the land beyond.

In the moments that followed, a memory of Ranos came to Nikandr like the strike of a bell. The two of them had been young. They'd snuck into father's throne room. Only then had Ranos shown Nikandr the key he had tucked away on a chain around his neck. It was the key to the massive chest where the scepter of Khalakovo was kept. They'd lifted the heavy thing out and taken turns sitting on the throne, each pretending to be the Duke while the other took knee on the floor below. Nikandr had dropped the scepter when he'd gotten up from the throne for the last time.

Nikandr had stared at the scepter. At the ruby that had broken off and skittered away across the floor. Ranos had warned him to be careful. He was just going to put the scepter away.

Father had been furious. Mother as well, and she'd asked who had done it. Ranos told them that he had, and he'd apologized a dozen times. Nikandr had been too scared to admit the truth, and Ranos had suffered for it. They'd both been whipped with a switch, but Ranos had been forced to work in an abattoir in Volgorod for a month. He'd come home each day, his face sickened. No matter how much Nikandr asked, he refused to tell Nikandr of the things he'd seen and heard. Nikandr had promised himself that he'd repay Ranos some day. He'd tried to find ways to do so in the weeks and months that followed, but in the way of these things, the memory eventually faded and then lay forgotten in the recesses of his mind.

He knew why the memory of taking the throne had resurfaced now, but he refused to think about that. All he could think of was the fact that he *had* failed to repay Ranos. What had Nikandr ever done but bring grief to Ranos?

"I'm sorry," Nikandr whispered to the wind as finally, mercifully, the sound over the field faded. In one fell swoop this idyllic place had been transformed into a burial field.

Nikandr hadn't realized, but his pony had come to a rest, its barrel chest working like a bellows. The reins hung limp in his hands. He urged the pony back into motion, but he allowed it nothing faster than a walk. The sight of the ship laying like some dead, forgotten beast was too much. He couldn't look upon Ranos. Not now.

But there was another he *would* look upon.

He steered the pony beyond the wreckage. He thought he knew exactly where the strelet had fallen, but it still took him long minutes of searching. At last he found him hidden among the tall grasses, the body of the man who'd leapt from the skiff. The man who'd been trying to escape.

His cherkesska was cut and stitched in the style of the south, but that meant little. He needed more. Nikandr dropped down and searched the still-warm body. He searched inside the man's shirt, found his soulstone. It was the typical oval shape, and rounded like a grape cut in half, but the setting itself had the stylings of Dhalingrad.

Still not good enough.

He needed something to tie him to Leonid.

He searched the pockets in his cherkesska and pants. He looked through the leather bag at his belt, hoping to find a note. There was nothing. Leonid wouldn't have given this man orders by note in any case. It would have come from his wife, the Duchess Iyana, and no other. She would have found him on the ship's detail, which, even though Ranos commanded it, would have been stocked with several men like this one, spies for Dhalingrad, trusted men who could be called upon should Leonid have need of them.

Over the field, men were coming. The streltsi who'd been marching west, they were coming to see what had happened, to look for survivors.

Nikandr had to find something quickly. He even pulled off the man's boots, hoping to find something hidden away. But there was nothing.

He fell back onto his rump, resting his hand on the pommel of his shashka. Nothing. There was nothing to tie this man to the one who'd truly committed these murders.

He looked down at his hand.

The one gripping his shashka.

Twisting the sword back and forth, he could see the inscription that ran along the guard. *For the Sons of Khalakovo*, it read. Many of the swords made by the smiths of Radiskoye read as such. It referred not to the soldiers who wore them at their sides, who fought with them, but for the children they protected, the sons and daughters of Khalakovo's seven isles.

Nikandr looked to the other man's sword. He slid it from its sheath, looked along its length and on the guard. It was a serviceable sword in good condition, but was otherwise unremarkable.

Then Nikandr noticed his kindjal. It looked to be of fine craft indeed. The hilt was the deep, dark brown of walnut. The stars of Dhalingrad, their house sign, were worked intricately into the brass rivets, and the sheath was made from fine, worked leather that showed the night sky above Palotza Iyavodska, the seat of House Dhalingrad. Nikandr pulled the weapon free to reveal the bright blade. It was worked as well, and clearly by a master craftsman. It had the same design as the sheath, but it also had an inscription.

For a trusted man of Dhalingrad, it said, and there, below it, was his name. *Leonid Roaldov Dhalingrad.*

A cold anger settled in Nikandr's chest, in his very core.

The wind over the field picked up, swirled around him.

It became so strong the snow lifted from the nearby grass to form a circle around him, a wall that for a moment seemed as impenetrable as stone.

Beyond the wall of swirling snow, the streltsi stopped. None dared approach as Nikandr slipped the kindjal into his belt and picked the man up. He hefted him over his pony's saddle and swung up behind him, ignoring the stares of the gathered streltsi. They parted as he rode through, their arms warding the wind from their faces.

Nikandr kicked his pony into a trot, moving beyond the staring men and toward the main encampment. The wind began to scour the field. His coat was open, flapping. The wind coursed over the skin of his neck and face. It no longer felt cold. It felt warm. Like a summer breeze.

Part of him wanted to turn back, to find Ranos and say his goodbyes. But those words could wait. The reckoning with Leonid could not.

As he approached the camp, he could see the central tents. Nine surrounding the one in the middle. The pennants atop the central poles snapped in the wind. The walls of the tents bowed inward. Here, too, the gathered streltsi stood and watched. Some ahead saw Nikandr coming and ran to the command tent. By the time Nikandr rode his pony into the clearing within the outer row of tents, many of the officers of the stremya had gathered. Konstantin Bolgravya and Yegor Nodhvyansk were there as well.

"Dhalingrad!" Nikandr shouted toward the main tent.

The men standing there spoke low to one another.

"Dhalingrad, show yourself!"

Borund approached. "Nikandr, what are you doing?"

"Something I should have done on Galahesh, Bora."

From the command tent came Leonid's tree of a son, Vadim Dhalingrad. He was followed by more officers of Dhalingrad—a polkovnik and several polu-polkovniks—and then Leonid himself. The Grand Duke was holding a short knife in one hand. Blood coated the blade. It coated Leonid's left hand as well. Drops of bright blood spotted the lower length of his long white beard. What in the name of the ancients had he been doing in that tent? Carving a goat?

The men between Leonid and Nikandr parted. More dukes stepped forward, Yevgeny Mirkotsk and Heodor Lhudansk and Aleg Khazabyirsk. Alaksandr Rhavanki, standing in for his father, came last. It was a council of sorts, and for this Nikandr was glad.

Borund, seeing there was nothing to be done—not now—stepped back, giving Nikandr the field.

The wind had settled—Nikandr had allowed it to do so—but it waited, begging for leave to howl among these gathered men. Nikandr allowed the body of the strelet to fall on the ground. It dropped onto the muddy earth and lay there, dead eyes staring up toward the sky.

"Your man, Dhalingrad."

Leonid did not so much as glance at the body. He merely stared, bloody knife in hand. "A disgraced member of my family, Khalakovo. What of him?"

"This was the man sent on the ship with my brother, Ranos, the man sent to bring that ship down before Ranos could step foot upon these lands."

Leonid's eyes thinned. He looked like a rat, standing there squinting at Nikandr. "The Matri have informed us of the ill news. An accident, as can happen on a ship from time to time."

"Yet it happened on *that* ship, *this* day, just as my brother, the Duke, was coming to speak to you of your orders for our fleet."

"Was he?"

"*You know that he was!*" Nikandr's shouted words settled over the dukes.

"I know nothing of the sort. Your brother had been ordered to remain on Galahesh should he be called upon to defend the realm."

"He was coming here so that Council could be called, something you well knew, Dhalingrad." Nikandr leaned over and spit down upon the fallen strelet. "That was why you sent your knifeman. To ensure that Ranos never arrived. You feared for your seat. As you should."

"A fallen windsman proves nothing."

Nikandr pulled out the knife and held it up for all to see. "This man tried to escape with a skiff and was shot at before leaping to his death. Moments later, the ship's magazine exploded, dooming every last man on board. Leonid *knew*." Nikandr said this to the crowd, but especially the dukes. "He knew Ranos was coming to take up Council, to vote for the seat of Grand Duke. There are other dukes here that know the same. And Leonid knew fear. He has acted brashly, My Good Dukes. He ordered the death of one of our own because he feared the loss of his mantle."

Some of them believed his words. Nikandr could see it on their faces: Konstantin and Yegor and even Yevgeny. But others did not. They watched him with mistrust in their eyes and the set of their jaws. Borund, however, had a look of regret, as if he dearly wished he could believe Nikandr, but could not.

"These men know," Leonid said, stepping forward. He pointed to Nikandr with the tip of his bloody knife. "They know the treason you've committed. They know the men you call your *allies*." Leonid turned back to Vadim and said, "Bring him."

Suddenly the reason for the blood on Leonid's hands became vitally important. The pieces of the puzzle began falling into place. And so Nikandr knew, well before Vadim returned, who he would bring from the tent, but he still wasn't prepared to see him like this: turban gone, hair snarled and matted, blood painting his chest from a wealth of cuts, none deep enough to mortally wound. Steam rose from his scalp and his bloody, sweaty skin.

Soroush looked up, lips quivering, eyes unable to focus. Then he seemed to recognize Nikandr, and his expression turned to one of shame, as if he'd failed Nikandr by being captured.

Soroush was a careful man. He wouldn't have been found or caught easily. Leonid must have sent one of the Matri to find him.

The shock of seeing him like this was beginning to wear off, and the implications were setting in. *Treason*, Leonid had said. They had found the man who had once commanded the northern tribes of the Maharraht. No matter to them that Soroush had foresworn those destructive ways. No matter that Soroush had helped to save them all on Galahesh. Leonid would use him to hang Nikandr. He would then take Khalakovo as Zhabyn Vostroma had once done, but this time there would be no giving it back. Nikandr's family would be murdered, any who could be found—Saphia, Victania, Ranos's son and daughter, any who posed a threat—while men of House Dhalingrad would be set in their place.

Nikandr realized the connection he'd had with the havahezhan had faded. The spirit was now crossing back over to Adhiya. He tried to summon it, to bond with it once more, but it did not hear him, or did not heed. Either way, he was soon there, alone, in the camp of the Grand Duchy.

It created in him a desperation he'd never felt before, a desperation to save his family and the world in one fell swoop.

He kicked his pony into action. The mare jolted forward as Nikandr pulled his shashka free. He swung it up over his head, oblivious to all else, focusing only on Leonid and his white beard and his bloody red hands.

Leonid's eyes went wide.

Nikandr saw a flash of movement on his right side.

Something rose up in a blur and struck him across the head.

He fell backward off his pony and into the mud.

As darkness swept in around him, as the shouting of the men faded, the face of the man that had swung the musket fixed in his mind.

Borund.

It was Borund.

Once again betrayed by Borund.

He embraced this singular thought—*betrayed by Borund once again*—as the darkness finally took him.

CHAPTER SIXTY-FOUR

When Nikandr woke and lifted his head, the mere motion summoned a series of painful waves that crashed against the side of his skull. Slowly the pain receded. He tried to touch it, but his wrists were weighted down. He was in heavy chains that clinked and rattled as he moved. He sat up on the cot, realizing he was in a tent. Khalakovo's tent. But now it was completely bare. The chains around his hands and ankles were wrapped around the central pole.

He bent over so that his hands could reach his head. A gentle touch to the crown of his head produced more pain. He found dried blood and a wound that felt as big as a galleon.

He fell in and out of sleep, but some time later, the flaps to the tent opened, and two men of Dhalingrad stepped in. Nikandr didn't recognize them, but they wore the stars of a polkovnik.

"Come to take me to the dance?"

The first one, a man with jowls and greying stubble, frowned and stepped forward. "Watch your tongue, Khalakovo, or I'll give you a lump to match the one the Prince of Vostroma gave you."

"You would strike a Prince of the Realm?"

"Prince no longer," he said as he unlocked the chains. "Now you're a traitor, like your brother before you."

Strangely, this brought no sense of anger to Nikandr. If anything, it calmed him, for he knew the end was near. He had failed, but he would join his family in the afterlife. He would look upon them and tell them his tales, such as they were, and he would help Khalakovo from beyond, no matter what Leonid Dhalingrad might do to him here.

The streltsi led him outside. The entirety of the camp seemed to be abandoned, and he soon found out why. Beyond the next rise, thousands were gathered around a lone oak tree in the middle of a wide field. They parted as Nikandr came. So many, Nikandr thought. Leonid wanted to gloat before he saw Nikandr swing, but he wanted it on display as well. He wanted every man present to see Khalakovo brought low.

The soldiers parted, many watching with hard stares, though some few looked upon with something akin to sympathy. Or perhaps it was worry. Worry over what this meant, not merely for Khalakovo or Dhalingrad, but for the Grand Duchy itself.

At last, Nikandr reached the place where Leonid and his son stood. The dukes were gathered as well. They stared on with faces of stone. Nikandr met Borund's eyes, and Borund stared back. He blinked, then glanced to Leonid as if he were now unsure about what he'd done. Had he thought that Nikandr might not be hung? Perhaps so. Perhaps he'd thought he was protecting Nikandr in his own way, as he'd done on Radiskoye.

The streltsi used the chains to drag Nikandr to the tree. Soroush, standing naked and shivering, was already there. Strung around his neck was a rope that went up and over a low-hanging bough. The other end was tied to the horn of a pony's saddle. Another pony waited next to it, and another rope, similarly tied, stood waiting, swinging in the breeze next to Soroush. Two polkovniks held the ponies' reins, calming them, preventing them from bolting, but as Nikandr was maneuvered into place, one of the ponies stamped. The other followed suit, as if they couldn't wait to run and string the two of them high. Soroush didn't look at Nikandr. He didn't look at anyone. He stared at the horizon, drawing the world around him like a blanket, as if he was barely able to keep in the pain from the dozens of wounds he'd sustained.

As the rope was slipped over Nikandr's head and tightened snugly around his neck, the eyes of those gathered bore into him. Leonid, wearing the mantle of Grand Duke, a heavy black cloak with golden trim, stepped to the center of the circle, just before Nikandr. His face was sour, as if something distasteful were stuck between his teeth. "Your final words," he finally said, as if even a trifle such as that were something too precious for Nikandr.

"A moment." The voice had come from among those gathered at the front. The crowd began to murmur.

"Silence!" Leonid's son, Vadim, called.

The crowd calmed, and all looked to Yevgeny Mirkotsk, who had been the one to speak. All except Leonid. He barely turned his head, as if Yevgeny were little more than a mewling child. "Speak your peace, Mirkotsk."

"You've hung a rope around the neck of a duke."

"Around the neck of a traitor," Leonid corrected.

"A duke deserves a trial."

Leonid turned to face Yevgeny fully now. "It has already been decided."

"New information has come to light. Soroush helped us on Rafsuhan. He helped us on Galahesh. He helped Nikandr and Atiana to save thousands of lives, perhaps tens of thousands."

"Who told you this?"

"I did," a deeper voice said.

Nikandr blinked. It was Borund. *Borund* had come to his defense.

"And what do you know of it?" Leonid spat.

"I have men who saw what happened on the Spar. Soroush was there, and he helped defeat Muqallad. The reasons he did this are known only to him, but the fact remains."

"That he did so proves nothing. He was in league with Muqallad, as we all know."

Borund pulled himself taller. "If that had been so, he would have admitted as much to you."

"He did admit it."

At this, a rook came flapping down from somewhere above in the tree. It cawed as it soared over the crowd and landed on Borund's shoulder. "He did not," the rook said.

Leonid stared warily into the rook's black eye. "Who speaks?"

"It is I, Radia Anastasiyeva Vostroma."

All around heads bowed to the Matra, but still a murmur ran through the crowd. This time Vadim did nothing to stop it—Radia, like Borund's father, Zhabyn, had always been a friend to Dhalingrad.

The rook craned its neck and pecked at the medals on Borund's chest. "Your questions were heard, Dhalingrad. As were his answers."

"What of it? The Maharraht lie as easily as you or I breathe."

"And yet no lies passed his lips. You asked of his involvement with the Maharraht, before and after the incident with the boy, Nasim, on Duzol. You asked of his involvement with Nikandr on Rafsuhan, how his brother, Bersuq, was taken by Muqallad, and how he took his people to Iramanshah afterward. You asked of his involvement in saving Nikandr on the shores of Yrstanla, and how he brought the kegs of gunpowder to the Spar. On it goes, Dhalingrad. His involvement with Nikandr since. Their time in the Gaji, their travels to Alekeşir, the chase they led here. And all the while he told the truth, even when you asked him of those he killed in the name of his war."

"Just so!" Leonid said, spittle flying as he spoke. "Did you hear him admit how many died? Dozens by his own hand! Hundreds by his command!"

"All the more telling that he told the truth, and that he told the truth after. He gave no indication that he was planning more such attacks. He gave no indication that he was plotting against the Grand Duchy, nor that he would ever do so again. And he gave no indication that Nikandr was doing such. And upon this you pressed him mightily, Leonid. You know this. As do I, for I heard his words. I heard his pain."

"What care you of Soroush Wahad al Gatha?"

"I care nothing for him. I care that a Prince of the Realm has been strung up like a fish, ready to be hung from a line like a baseless criminal. And I care that you have hidden much from the dukes in order to do it."

"This is a time of *war*, Matra."

"The Covenant governs us all, even in times of war."

"Play with words if you like. These men will not unseat me. They know the sort of man the leader of the Maharraht is." Leonid's voice rose in volume and pitch as he looked about the gathered dukes. He scanned each of them in turn: Konstantin, Borund, Yegor, Heodor, Aleg, Alaksandr. And finally Yevgeny. His eyes bore into him as he sneered. "They know what he's capable of. They know the sort of man he is, and those who associate with him. That he gave no confession means nothing. It means nothing more than that the Maharraht are singular of mind and purpose, and that even by pain of blade or hammer they are not swayed. *That* is how he hides the truth of his allegiance." Leonid pointed toward Nikandr without taking his eyes from Yevgeny. "*That* is how he hides his alliance with this so-called Prince of Khalakovo."

The rook took wing, cawing so fiercely Nikandr thought Radia had been rejected from its form, but then it landed on Borund's shoulder once more and regarded Leonid. "A prince must have a trial."

"He will not," Leonid replied.

"He will," Yevgeny said.

Yevgeny was resolute; his voice spoke it like a clarion call. Borund was as well. And Konstantin and Yegor. But with Nikandr's own vote thrown in doubt, it was four against four. And when that was the case, the Grand Duke's voice cast the deciding vote. It would take only one more, but Alaksandr was standing in for his father, and Heodor Lhudansk and Aleg Khazabyirsk were too closely aligned with Leonid to vote against him.

Or were they?

Heodor was a man who put the law of the land above all else. It was why his own allegiance had shifted. Years ago, he'd brought a trade dispute to Nikandr's father, Iaros, claiming that, under the agreement, the taxes being levied against the windwood supplied to Lhudansk were too dear. Iaros had denied Heodor, claiming new agreements superseded it, but Heodor had insisted. It led to a severing of ties and had pushed Heodor to side with first Stasa Bolgravya as the Grand Duke and then Zhabyn Vostroma.

But it was that very narrow way of reading such things that Borund and the others might have counted on. Indeed, Heodor was watching Leonid fiercely beneath his black, bushy brows.

Leonid must have sensed the shift in the wind as well, for his face grew red. "You would deny me?"

The dukes were silent, waiting for Leonid to back down. As they stared on, as the wind blew through the bare branches of the tree above, Leonid's face calmed. His skin lost its hue. And a cold calculation entered his eyes.

Before Nikandr knew what was happening, he'd pulled the ornate wheellock pistol from his belt. He whipped around and pointed it at the rightmost pony.

Then he fired.

The bullet took the pony in the rump. The pony jolted forward.

Nikandr grabbed the rope with both hands a mere moment before he was hauled up.

The screaming of the pony was quickly drowned out by the rush of blood through his ears, and then a high-pitched tone that sounded like a call from the world beyond. He saw the grey sky above through the black of the branches. He saw the beating of wings, the rook taking flight, though why it would do such a thing he had no idea.

Though he fought to keep the noose from cinching, it had been pulled tight when the pony had bolted. He was still rising into the air until at last he could go no further. The bough prevented him. But that only pulled the rope tighter.

He heard voices above the ringing. Or thought he did.

They sounded like his father. Like Ranos. Like the calls of those taken by the wasting. *The rifts*, they said. *Why haven't you closed them?*

He could feel more as well.

A hezhan. Standing just on the other side of the divide between Erahm and Adhiya. It was there to welcome him, he was sure, to the life beyond. And yet it was close enough to touch. He could feel its expanses, feel the way it caressed the wind of the world.

He could feel the stone of alabaster in his cherkesska pocket, a source of power, a way to ease his path to Adhiya. But he didn't need it anymore. He knew with certainty what would happen when he called to the hezhan.

Come, he said to it. *Come, and you shall taste of this world.*

And this time, it did.

It's like the feeling he has when he reunites with Atiana. A love deeper than he can hold in his mind at the mere thought of her. It is only when he sees her, smells the scent of lilies in her hair, feels the first touch of her hand upon his skin, that it all comes rushing back.

And this hezhan…

The one he was bonded to before was completely different. This one is deeper. Older. The tree his body hangs from is but a child compared to it. The nearby city of Izlo is little different. This spirit is older than the hills in which Soroush was found, older than the nearby river that wends its way across the landscape.

Welcome, Nikandr calls to it.

He hears no response, but he feels its glee. It rejoices as it embraces the material world. And Nikandr rejoices as well. Never has he felt Adhiya so clearly, not even while he was on Rafsuhan trying to heal the children there. This is deeper, as if he's *in* Adhiya already.

Am I dead? he wonders. *Have I crossed over?*

He feels the wind as it courses through the branches of the tree, as it makes the ancient oak sway. And now, at last, he draws upon it. He calls it down upon those gathered. It howls with glee. It revels in the men who cower from it, at the ponies who fear it.

The rope around his neck tightens. It will soon snap his neck.

But only if he allows it.

He directs the wind, forces it against his swinging frame. It lifts him, carries him like a newborn babe up and over the thick lower bough. The pony, temporarily freed of restraint, bolts forward. Like a daisy tied to a summer ribbon, Nikandr is dragged along with it, still aloft, until he calls on the wind again. He calls upon a gust to blow against the pony, to tip it over, so that he can pull the rope free.

Stars swim in the air before him, and for long moments his breath refuses to return to him, but the stars begin to fade as the wind bears him down to the ground.

Movement draws his attention.

There, at the tree, Soroush swings, as Nikandr had moments ago. This time when he calls upon the wind it is no different than a lift of his arm, a cupping of his palm to cradle Soroush over the bough and set him down on the ground.

He turns now toward the assembled men. The dukes are upon their knees covering their faces as snow and mud are lifted and driven against them. None can look upon him, so strong has the wind become.

Good.

Let them cower.

He strides toward Leonid, who lies upon the ground, his arms over his head. He allows the wind to wane here at the center of things. Around him it still howls, but here, like the calm eye of a monsoon, the wind blows as idly as a springtime breeze.

"Stand," Nikandr calls to Leonid.

It takes Leonid long moments to pull his arms away, to regard Nikandr. When he does it is with a look of naked contempt. "Unmasked at last," he says as he props himself onto his heels and stands.

Nikandr waits until he's recovered himself, until he pulls himself taller. "You killed my father. I would hear it before this is done." Leonid glances to those around them. "Only the two of us can hear one another."

"Your father?" At that Leonid begins to laugh, and he seems unable to stop it. "Allow him to sweep in and take the mantle from me? You're joking, child. And you! A duke? You're but a mewling prat traipsing among your betters. A lover of motherless whores and beggars. And when this wind dies, which it shall, whether I live to see it or not, you'll be taken from this world and forgotten by all who knew you."

Nikandr feels something rise in his throat. He swallows, trying to clear it. Fails. For months after his father's death he wanted nothing more than to stick a knife in Leonid's side and watch him bleed, as his father bled. But now is not the time to call upon that score. As much as he hates it, he needs Leonid. He needs him to call off the ships, for only in that might they affect the outcome of what's happening on Ghayavand.

"You're taking us into ruin," he finally says, "and I won't allow it."

"*You* won't allow it? You're the very one who led us to this place."

"If you believe that, you're as blind as you are brash."

"It's clear to anyone who considers what you've done, where you've been, and with whom." He waves his hand around him. "And there's this."

"This? This is a gift from the ancients, who sent Nasim to us to protect us. They sent Ashan as well. And Soroush." Nikandr waves behind him toward Soroush, who is still coughing on the windswept ground. "You cannot have him. He will come with me. And you will be voted down. The tide has turned against you, as you well know. We will call off the fleet, and I will go to Ghayavand to see if there is still time to heal the world."

Leonid laughs. "You can't call the fleet away. They're filled with *my* men, Khala-kovo. Mine… Your mother, or the three sisters, or Radia… Send all the rooks you wish. None of them will force the ships to turn course." He laughs harder. The wrinkles around his eyes deepen as he squints in genuine amusement. It makes him look like a wizened apple. "The ships left Galahesh *days* ago. They will reach Ghayavand soon, and when they do, they will lay the Kohori to waste."

Nikandr feels his heart drop within his chest. "You must stop them. You must call them away."

Leonid, wind whipping his white beard in the air around him, raises his chin. "*Never.*"

With that word, something inside Nikandr snaps. All of the effort he and the others have put forth in trying to save what they could, the emotions Nikandr buried in order to prevent himself from drawing steel against Leonid. All of it comes bubbling up in a fount of seething anger.

The wind at the center of the storm rises, becomes a gale, becomes a tempest. The air itself turns atavistic and hungry. It steals breath, steals life, Nikandr's included, but he's prepared for it.

Leonid is not.

This wicked, pathetic little man wards with his arms, trying to bat away some unseen foe. He stumbles, rises again, tries to break for the edge of the howling wind, but he doesn't make it two steps before the wind throws him backward.

He falls, slipping in the mud and slush. He claws at the ground, clutches at the trampled grass. For long moments he writhes, unable to breathe, and then, at last, he falls still.

And the wind dies away.

Nikandr was so taken by the visage of Grand Duke Leonid lying dead on the ground before him that it took him long moments to realize the havahezhan had retreated. Not *left*, but retreated. It was close enough to call, and Nikandr would when the time was right.

The lack of wind felt strange, as if a friend with whom he'd been holding hands was suddenly and inexplicably gone. He looked around him, took in the devastation. As far as the eye could see the camp was ruined. Tents fallen. Gear scattered. Ponies running wild in the distance.

And streltsi. Hundreds. Thousands. Watching him with naked fear.

The dukes watched him with wary expressions on their faces. They took him in—he and Leonid—but none approached. None but Vadim, but he was tackled as Soroush bulled into him from behind and restrained him.

None moved to help.

Slowly, Borund approached. Others closed in behind him. The circle of men that was once so wide was now closing in around Nikandr like a fist.

Nikandr was sure they were going to take him, place him in chains and bring him back to the islands or elsewhere to await a trial, but when Borund spoke, he spoke these words, "What do you need, Nischka?"

Confused beyond reason, Nikandr shook his head. "What?"

"What do you need, to take you to Ghayavand?"

CHAPTER SIXTY-FIVE

S tyophan pulled the spyglass up to his good eye, his left, and peered down its length. He stared out over the expanse of the sea to the island of Ghayavand, a virescent gem against a bed of blue. The *Zhostova* ran low to the waves, the seaward mainmast mere yards above the churning sea. Styophan scanned the island carefully, but so far there was no sign that they'd been seen.

Which was well and good, for yesterday, he'd spotted the ships on Ghayavand's northern shore. Luckily the day had been cloudy and dark, and they'd not been spotted themselves. There had been strange ships in the distance. They looked like living things shaped like the tips of spears, and yet they had floated in the air like windships. He knew not what they were, but he knew enough to avoid them.

"You plan to moor near Alayazhar?"

Styophan brought the spyglass down and turned. It was Anahid, one of the two qiram that had joined him on this journey. As the wind played with her long black hair, throwing it across the shoulders of her coral-colored robes, an opaline gem glowed softly in the circlet she wore over her brow.

"I do," Styophan said. "From what we know, Sihyaan is the place they will be focused on, not the city, which now lies dead."

"There is dead and there is dead," Anahid replied.

She'd warned him of going there several times already, but he'd already made up his mind. "You've become superstitious."

Anahid stared out over the water. Against the surrounding green landscape Alayazhar and the gutted white shells of buildings stood out like bones upon new summer grass. "I merely respect the power of that place. It is the source of much of our misery."

"You sound like you hate it."

Styophan expected her to deny it, but instead she glanced up at him and for the first time in memory was unable to hold his gaze. "It is our people's darkest stain."

"It happened three hundred years ago."

"It was yesterday," she shot back. "We inherit the sins of our former selves."

"You inherit their virtues as well."

She tried to smile. "Sometimes I wonder."

Styophan took her hand and squeezed it. "You do."

Her smile faded, and she took her hand back from him, but not before giving his hand a squeeze back. "We're getting close," she said, glancing out over the water.

A short, uncomfortable silence followed, but when Styophan ordered the ship brought down, all returned to normal.

They moored on the beach beneath the city. He'd chosen this location not only because it hid their approach, but because the beach was low enough that the ship would be hidden from much of the nearby landscape.

He and three sotni—thirty men in all—treaded across the beach. The tide was low. Mossy green rocks lay beneath the sun as crabs scuttled among them. They were headed toward the trail that led up to the city proper, but before they'd gone a hundred paces, Styophan saw movement. On a massive rock near the shoreline, cloth fluttered. He couldn't see what or who was atop the rock, but it looked strange indeed.

He called a halt and climbed to the top of the stone, and there he found the desiccated creature Nasim had saved in the Gaji. Tohrab, Nikandr had named him. He was staring up toward the sky, his breath coming slowly as the wind tugged at his robe and made it flutter.

"Are you well?" Styophan felt the fool for asking such a thing, but he didn't know what else to say.

Tohrab didn't move, didn't speak.

In the center of his chest Styophan could feel a thrumming. The rock below him seemed to shudder with it. It made the very waves of the sea and the air around him seem alive.

Styophan came closer and crouched down. He shook Tohrab's shoulder. "Are you well?" he asked, louder than before. Tohrab's skin was so white, so thin. It looked like rain-drenched paper left in the sun to bleach. How this miserable soul had made it this far he had no idea.

Slowly, Tohrab's wrinkled eyes opened. He regarded Styophan with a look of profound confusion and pain. But in his eyes there was a timelessness, and a determination the likes of which Styophan had never seen. In those eyes Styophan could believe that he alone was holding the final wards together. It would take an immense reserve of will and power, but if what Nikandr had said was true, one of the Tashavir would have it.

"How can I help, grandfather?" Styophan asked.

"Who are you?" the Tashavir said, his voice reed thin.

"A friend."

Tohrab slowly and with obvious pain pulled himself to a sitting position. "You cannot help."

"Where is Sukharam? Where are Ashan and Nasim?"

Tohrab's eyes went distant. "The time has nearly come. She approaches."

Styophan turned and followed Tohrab's gaze toward the city. Nothing had changed, however, and he saw no one approaching.

"*Who* is coming?"

As the water below drew back, Tohrab drew in breath with a slow wheezing sound, and when the waves crashed against the rocky beach, he released it again.

Styophan shook him, and still Tohrab didn't answer. "Tohrab, *who* is coming?"

"Styopha?"

Styophan turned. Rodion was staring toward the base of the cliff below the city. Many people were hiking down a trail that led from the city down to the sand. At the head was a woman. Dozens followed her, men dressed in red robes and flowing scarves that covered their faces.

"She comes for me." With great effort, Tohrab pushed himself up off the stone. "Do not fight her. Go to the city. There is another that needs your help."

"Who?"

Tohrab's lips were pulled back into a grim line. He drew breath, released it with the sound of the waves. "They will not harm you. Not if you give them wide berth."

"I've come to help you."

"You cannot help me. The time has finally come. What the world will do, it will do. Now go."

"I cannot. My Lord Prince has sent me here to find you, you and the others."

Tohrab did not speak again—he did not so much as glance his way—but just then a wind picked up and pushed Styophan so hard he was forced to the very edge of the dark stone. He tried to remain in place, but the wind shoved him off. He fell hard to the beach, rolled and came to his feet, but by then the wind was picking up, sending sand and pebbles against him and his men. Despite the men baring their muskets before them to ward the magic of the hezhan away, they were forced, step by step, away from the stone and toward the cliffs. Tohrab was doing this, he knew. He thought he was fated to die, but Styophan still didn't understand why he wouldn't allow them to help.

By now the woman in white and the men in red had closed the distance. The woman was near enough now that Styophan recognized her. It was Ushai, the woman who'd betrayed Soroush and Nikandr and the others in the heart of the Gaji. Her left hand hung useless and scarred at her side. Her right hand gripped the Atalayina. Styophan had never seen it himself, but he'd heard the stories. Even through the haze of the biting dust and stone it glowed blue under the sun, and it glittered like gold.

Ushai stared directly at Styophan. Her face was emotionless, but there was threat in her eyes. *Approach*, they said, *and I will kill you.*

Tohrab had known this, of course. He'd known the odds were too much against them. Part of him still wanted to raise his pistol and fire on Ushai. Part of him felt cowardly for not doing so.

As if Tohrab had heard his thoughts, the wind picked up, driving saltwater and pea-sized rocks against them.

"To the city!" Styophan shouted.

If the miserable creature on that stone wanted to die, there was nothing he could do about it. Not any longer.

They marched as well as they were able, ducking their heads as they went, and soon they'd lost all sense of unity and they started running as quickly as they could toward Alayazhar. Finally, as they reached the path toward the city, the wind eased, but the sand still swirled high above the water, enough that he could see little but a hint of the darkened stone.

They marched to the top of the path. No sooner had Styophan stepped foot on the level ground near the buildings of Alayazhar than a howl reverberated over the island. Styophan felt it through the soles of his boots as it rang through air and land itself. Down on the beach, the sand had begun to settle. The howl faded until the only thing he could hear was the patter of rocks and sand below. The world around them had suddenly become as still as the making of the world.

On the beach, the sand drew inward toward the rock. And then it blasted outward.

"Away!" Styophan called. "Away from the cliff!"

The land around the black rock undulated as if it were made of so much water. The wave expanded, eating the distance between the shore and the cliffs. The ground below Styophan shifted and buckled. Part of the cliff—including the pathway—fell away, taking men with it. They cried out not in pain but in shock.

The voices died away as his men fell, surely to their deaths.

Styophan was thrown to the ground. He scrabbled away from the edge, but more and more of the cliff began to ablate like a fortress of sand built by the hand of a child. Those who had managed to remain standing helped the others to regain their feet.

Slowly the sound died away, and the rumbling beneath him quieted. The edge of the crumbing cliff stopped only paces away from where he stood. Styophan's mind and heart told him not to approach the edge, but he forced himself to go step by tentative step to search for his fallen men. His heart pounded like a skin drum as he inched to the edge and looked down. There was no sign of his men. Nor was there any sign of Ushai. Or the men in red robes.

But Tohrab, he could see. As the sea churned white waves around him, he lay on the rock, unmoving. He'd found his peace at last, but his death meant the last of the wards had probably fallen.

It won't be long now, he thought.

"Styopha." It was Rodion, and there was confusion in his voice.

Styophan turned and found three women approaching.

By the ancients, one of them was Atiana Vostroma.

She was walking toward him with a Haelish wodjan on one side and an Aramahn on the other, neither of whom he recognized. Atiana's blonde hair was pulled back into a ragged tail, and the shayla dress she wore was dirty and threadbare, but there was a determination in her eyes that Styophan could feel in his chest. It reminded him of Nikandr.

"My Lady Princess," Styophan stammered, "how did you find us?" She had only to wave at the beach for the ridiculousness of the question to hit him. "I mean, how have you come to be here?"

"I could ask you the same, but there isn't time. You saw Ushai, did you not?"

Styophan glanced back toward the beach, still half expecting the ground beneath him to give way and swallow them. "She found Tohrab on the beach below. She killed him. Or rather, he allowed himself to be killed." He paused, feeling wholly inadequate before this Princess of Vostroma. "We could do nothing against them."

"I came too late myself," she replied. She looked over his men. "But I believe the ancients have watched over us all. You've done well to reach these shores, and I have great need of you now that you're here."

Styophan snapped his heels and bowed his head. "You have only to name it."

"Ushai goes to the mountain." She raised her arm and pointed southwest. "To Sihyaan. We cannot allow her to reach it, Styophan Andrashayev, or we will be lost, not merely those on this island, or even those in the Grand Duchy, but everyone, everywhere."

Even as Atiana spoke these words, Styophan saw the strange, spear-shaped ships rising into the sky. Only a few at first, but then more and more. And then he saw the reason why. Far to the southwest, he could see incoming warships.

Nikandr had failed, he realized. The ships of the Grand Duchy were coming.

"Best we hurry," Styophan said in Anuskayan.

"Best we hurry," Atiana replied.

CHAPTER SIXTY-SIX

The darkness around Nasim was impenetrable, and yet his mind was consumed by a white flash, a shattering stone.

The moment he'd seen it—when he'd *remembered* that it had happened—a bottomless pit had opened up inside him. Down it went, deeper than the darkness between the stars.

The knowledge of what had truly happened that day washed over him like a dark and hungry wave.

He screamed. Screamed until his throat was raw. His fingers curled into fists, nails cutting skin, and body tightening until he shivered from the pain.

That one moment consumed him. It wasn't the shattering stone, nor the blinding white flash, but the utter emptiness he'd felt in the space of a blink beforehand.

He wanted to tell himself that these were *Khamal's* memories, that he needn't accept them as his own, but he knew this to be foolish, utterly foolish, and he refused to deceive himself any longer. These memories were his as well.

He was Khamal, and Khamal was he.

It was something he should have reconciled with long ago. Perhaps he would have saved himself a lot of pain.

As his cries subsided, and his body began to unclench, part of him wanted to immerse himself in the pain. Part of him hoped this would go on until he could no longer *feel* the pain. But he knew that would never happen. He would feel this until his dying day. And then, at last, he would be gone, forever. Khamal had seen to that when he'd sacrificed the akhoz, young Alif. It had allowed Khamal to escape the island and the wards of the Tashavir, but in doing so, it had committed his undying soul to this one, final life. It had grounded Nasim to the material world. He would never again return to Adhiya. He would never reach vashaqiram, one's own state of enlightenment, nor would he see the world

430

reach its higher plane of existence: indaraqiram.

But this?

A white flash.

The breaking of the Atalayina.

How could anyone go on toward enlightenment, whether they believed in the ways of the Aramahn or not?

Nasim felt a tender hand stroking his hair. It was such a familiar gesture. Ashan had done it for him over and over again after he'd rescued Nasim from the Maharraht. In those days it had merely allowed him to slip back into a state of directionless confusion. He'd been caught between Adhiya and Erahm, unable to distinguish between the two.

How he wished he could return to those days.

For a time, he simply lay there in the cavern by the dry lake of Shirvozeh. The siraj stone lit Ashan's kind face. In the vastness of the cavern, the stone cast his brown hair in a numinous light, making him look half man, half hezhan.

"Can you hear me?" Ashan asked softly, still stroking his hair.

As Nasim rolled over, the stone beneath him felt different. It felt meaningless, as if this place were merely the center of some grand experiment that had failed.

"It's all wrong," Nasim said, more to himself, or perhaps to the vastness of the cavern. "We've been wrong all along."

"Wrong about what?"

Nasim shifted away from Ashan. He didn't wish to say the words—to voice it would make it real. But of course the notion was foolish. A child's reasoning. His insignificant voice would change nothing. "They're gone, Ashan."

"Who's gone?"

"The *fates*. They…" He didn't know how to say it.

"Come," Ashan said as he took Nasim's arm. "Let's get you up into the light."

Nasim pulled his arm away. "I don't need light! On the day of the sundering, Ashan, they were there. Watching."

"The fates?"

"*Yeh*." The memory was so clear, Nasim felt as though it were happening all over again. "They were waiting. They'd *been* waiting since the moment the Al-Aqim were born, and they'd been holding their breath every moment since." Nasim felt sick. "They *wanted* the sundering to occur, Ashan."

Ashan's face pinched into a frown. He was already shaking his head. The siraj—which had moments ago made him seem like so much more than a man—now made him seem pale and sick, a man in the throes of the wasting.

"You must listen, Ashan. You may try to reason this away, but you must set those thoughts aside. The fates sat idly by as the ritual took place. They could have stopped it had they chose, but instead they did nothing. And then"—Nasim was unsure how to say it, so he said it as simply and as truthfully as he could manage—"they were taken by the ritual. The very moment the Atalayina tore the first of the rifts between worlds, they were freed. They stepped beyond this life. To another. To their death. Who knows? But they are gone, Ashan. Lost to us. And they *have* been since that very moment."

Ashan stared deeply into Nasim's eyes, a parent suddenly embarrassed by his son. "You're wrong," he said. His voice was resolute, but his hands shook; his eyes quavered with indecision.

"I am not."

"There was much happening. The Atalayina shattered. This is known."

"The Atalayina shattered not from the ritual, as we'd always assumed. It shattered from the passing of the fates."

Ashan's face grew angrier by the moment. "You are viewing this through the memories of a man that has been dead for decades. And even then, his memories of the event were centuries old. *Centuries*, Nasim!"

"Those moments are as clear to me as this conversation is now. The fates are dead, Ashan."

Ashan took a step forward. They were of a height, but he still towered darkly over Nasim. "You've no idea what you're saying!"

"The fates are dead!"

Before Nasim knew it, Ashan's arm flew up and struck him across the face. Pain flared along his cheek and jaw. The darkness blossomed with stars. He worked his jaw, tasted blood from the cut on the inside of his cheek, but he did not cower. He turned back to Ashan and faced him, as resolute as the mountain above him.

Ashan struck him again, but this time it was weak. Nasim could easily have blocked it, but he let the blow fall. Ashan's lips trembled. He swallowed uncontrollably, his eyes tearing as they searched Nasim's face, searched the darkness beyond.

"You are wrong." The words echoed in the cavern as Ashan shoved Nasim away and stumbled into the darkness toward the stairs.

Nasim let him go. This was a difficult thing, especially for one who believed in the fates as strongly as Ashan did. It was no less so for Nasim, but it was a puzzle over which his mind had been working for months, even years. For Ashan it would be like dropping into the frigid waters of the Great Northern Sea, something impossible to prepare for. Strangely, to have someone else react so strongly to this news gave Nasim a sense of grounding. Having someone else to explain it to—even if he didn't fully understand it himself—give it form.

He waited for a time near the lake. He wanted to give Ashan the time he needed, but he also needed to do something while he was still here in this place of power. He reached out to Adhiya. It was close enough to touch, and through this bond he could feel the outlines of the aether, a gauze as thin as a burial shroud. From there, with these realms in hand, he reached up toward the fourth. The heavens. The place where the fates reside.

Or *did* reside.

This had been what Khamal and the other Al-Aqim had done. He remembered how euphoric it had made Khamal feel. What Nasim felt now was wholly different. He felt only emptiness and despair. These were things he remembered now from his childhood. He had known, even then, but he hadn't understood. How could he have? He'd had no context, no true understanding of his prior life. His soul had felt it, though, and it had been part of the pain and anguish he'd experienced nearly every moment of every day.

As painful as this was, as alone as it made him feel, he held tightly to it. This was the true state of things. At last, he understood. It was why the rifts had continued to spread, no matter what the Al-Aqim did, no matter what the collected arqesh had tried to do. Even the akhoz, and the wards, desperate attempts at stemming the tide, had only delayed the inevitable. It was clear now that they would never succeed. The Atalayina may find its way here to Ghayavand. He and Sukharam might wield it. But what would they do then? The rifts would never remain closed. Never.

Perhaps this was why the Al-Aqim had fought, why they'd been driven mad. It hadn't been in their waking thoughts, but it must have been there in the small places of the mind where one hides his secret shames. That was why the three greatest arqesh the world had ever known had been reduced to squabbling. It had perhaps been why Muqallad and Sariya had been so driven to end the world on Galahesh. Their disgrace had resurfaced in ugly and destructive ways. This had been true even of Khamal, whom Nasim had defended too often.

But what now?

What could he do?

Nasim picked up the siraj.

What *was* there to do?

The Atalayina was powerful. It was powerful indeed. They might try to mend the rifts. It might hold for a year, perhaps two? Wasn't that time precious? Wasn't that better than giving the world over to annihilation?

He trekked up through the empty halls and corridors of the village, his soft footsteps echoing in the utter silence. When he reached the entrance and stepped out into the light he found Ashan standing on the dilapidated bridge, staring down toward the chasm below. Nasim moved to stand beside him. So often Ashan had felt like his father. Not now, though. Now he seemed like a wayward orphan in need of *Nasim's* help. He seemed small and confused and—for the first time since Nasim had met him—lost. Their roles had suddenly reversed, and for a moment it was discomforting.

But all have times when help is needed. Ashan was no different, and if he needed someone to lean on, Nasim would be there for him.

Nasim traced Ashan's gaze to the gorge below. He was staring at the very place Nasim and Rabiah had climbed down years ago when the akhoz had chased them. It all seemed so inconsequential now.

But it hadn't been, he realized with sudden clarity.

It had been supremely important.

Nasim felt himself go cold.

It had been one step in a chain of events that had led Nasim here. If Rabiah had not died, who knows what might have happened? Perhaps he never would have been able to enter Sariya's tower, not without Rabiah going first. Not without Sariya becoming distracted by her presence.

His fingers and toes began to tingle.

This impossibly long chain of events... It could mean only one thing. He was no longer willing to entertain the possibility that the fates simply wished to pass, that they'd abandoned the world, for in that lay desperation and hopelessness.

He stared up toward the pewter sky, wishing he could look beyond the clouds to the heavens beyond.

Ashan looked over at him. "Nasim, what is it?"

Nasim barely heard him. He took in the land around him. Looked toward the northern horizon where he could see the deep blue of the sea between two tall hills. It all looked so different now. Down by the lake it had felt as if nothing mattered, as if it had all been sacrificed the moment the fates had moved on, but now it felt like *all* of it mattered. Every single piece.

What else could explain everything that had happened since the sundering? It would be like releasing a dandelion seed to the wind, to have it travel the world and return to you. It would be like stacking a thousand sticks end-on-end to build a tower of them. The impossibility of it all made him wonder if he was wrong, but it was his very reality—that he'd made it here, that the Atalayina had been fused, that the world itself had still *not* fallen to the rifts—that made him realize that he must be right.

"Nasim, tell me."

"Come, Ashan." Nasim began walking along the bridge, his mind alive with possibility. "We must find Sukharam."

Ashan hurried to catch up. "Where?"

Nasim pointed to the tall black mountain near the center of the island. "Sihyaan," he answered. "We will find him on Sihyaan."

CHAPTER SIXTY-SEVEN

Nasim hiked up the slope of Sihyaan. Ashan came behind as the wind blew fiercely, blowing the tops of the trees, knocking branches and even trees down across their path. Eventually they left the trees, and the bulk of Sihyaan—from here little more than an angry black beast—stood before them, but it felt as though the mountain itself would soon rise and walk the earth and crush the world that stood before it.

A strange scent laced the air. It was something he hadn't experienced in years, not since before Soroush had awoken the elders through his ritual on Duzol seven years ago.

Had it been so long already? There were days it felt so near, and others where it felt like lifetimes.

The scent was one of brine and blood and the bitter smell of a lightning strike. It was the smell of ache and yearning and anger. It was the smell of Adhiya. It was wrapped up with the life of the boy he'd been, a boy trapped between worlds. A boy of both, and of neither. He couldn't remember ever recognizing the scent in a conscious way—it had been the air he'd breathed from the moment he'd been born—but now, smelling it again, it made his heart race. Made his breathing quicken like a frightened hare. He found himself glancing downslope to his right, or upslope to his left, wary of he knew not what.

"Can you smell it?" he asked Ashan.

Ashan was tight and wary. "What is it?"

"The world beyond. We're close enough now to touch it."

To his right, beyond the forest, beyond the grassy foothills, beyond the white city of Alayazhar, a storm raged, a dark cloud the color of granite rising and swirling into the sky like an elder wind spirit.

They continued, much faster than before.

Far ahead, near the southern shoreline, strange shapes began to lift into the

435

sky. From this distance they looked like dark teardrops floating against a slate-grey sky. They looked not like windships that had been framed by the hand of man, but like things grown. Surely the Kohori had had a hand in their making.

"That bodes ill," Ashan said, pointing beyond the shapes.

Nasim looked closer. On the horizon were dark marks. Windships approaching from the south. They were ships of the Grand Duchy, sent, no doubt, by the bellicose Grand Duke that sat the throne of Anuskaya. "Sariya planned for this."

"Without a doubt," Ashan replied, "but why?"

Nasim could only shake his head. He had no idea.

They continued hiking uphill as fast as they were able. The slope was not yet steep, but it made Nasim's lungs burn and his legs feel twice their size. Ashan was breathing so hard Nasim worried over him. He was about to call for a rest when they came across a body, a man's, shriveled and blackened so badly it was clear he'd been burned. His arms and legs were pulled tightly to his chest, like a shivering child. There was a golden circlet on his brow with five stones set into it.

Nasim reached down and pried the circlet from around his head. It came only as the skin beneath it crumbled in charred chunks. There was a feel about this, a certain scent in the very air around this place. "What could have made him do it?" Nasim asked as he wiped the soot from the stones.

"Sukharam?" Ashan asked. "You're sure?"

"I am. He's become desperate." Nasim set the circlet gently on the burned man's chest. "I wonder if it's too late now to reach him." He had hoped to find Sukharam, to convince him to help, but now Nasim wasn't at all sure that was the right course. As much as Sukharam doubted Nasim's place on Sihyaan, Nasim now doubted his. He was powerful, true, but brash. Too brash.

"Come," Ashan said, still breathing hard. "Time grows short."

They pressed harder after this, attacking the hill with a desperation that matched their fear. But soon Ashan could no longer keep up.

"Go on," Ashan said. "Find him."

Nasim nodded, outdistancing Ashan quickly. But he stopped when he reached the second body, another dressed in the red robes of the Kohori. He was not burned. The ground was trampled nearby, and beyond that, near a stand of trees, were three skiffs. Nasim wondered vaguely how the man had died, but his thoughts were interrupted by the third body, and the fourth and the fifth. From there he found more and more—dozens, he realized, lying in the grass like the forgotten baubles of a child.

Nasim was ready to collapse, but he couldn't stop now. He drew on a dhosha-hezhan to speed himself along. As he did, however, he felt a shift in the aether. It was Sukharam. He could feel him over the rise ahead. What shocked him was the sheer breadth of Sukharam's power. It felt as if the entire island had come alive, and it struck within him one of Khamal's memories. When the Al-Aqim had come to this place, it had felt the same way.

He found Sukharam over the next rise standing a hundred paces away. He had both hands pressed against the top of an obsidian pillar. It was *the* pillar, the one the Al-Aqim had used to break the world. Sukharam's head was tilted toward the sky, his eyes pressed tight, as if he were having a nightmare.

Then, around Sukharam and the pillar, the tall grass flattened. The effect spread like a growing wave from a pebble in a pond. When it passed Nasim, he felt something deep within him, a lament that made him cower and fall to his knees. In that moment, he could feel what Sukharam was feeling. He was reaching toward the heavens. He was searching them, looking desperately for the fates.

He would not find them, however, for they were dead. The fates had chosen to move on. Whether it was their choice or some collective will of the world, Nasim didn't know, but they were well and truly gone.

Sukharam's body went rigid. He shivered with rage and fear. He released a cry that seemed to rend the world.

Nasim approached, hoping Sukharam could be brought back from the edge of pain. "Sukharam."

When he came within a dozen paces of the pillar, Sukharam's eyes shot open. He fixed them on Nasim. His face was red. His hands were at his sides, balled into fists. In that moment, he looked like nothing more than the boy Nasim had found in Trevitze.

Nasim raised his hands. "Sukharam—"

"*You* did this. You and Sariya and Muqallad."

"We did."

For a moment, Sukharam seemed surprised by Nasim's candor, but then his face hardened once more. "You brought the very fates down from their place in the firmament."

"How? How could we have done it, Sukharam? Had the fates willed it"— Nasim motioned to the pillar—"the Al-Aqim would never have reached this place. I remember more of that time now. Khamal touched the fates. He felt their desire. They *wanted* to leave."

Sukharam took one long step toward Nasim, thrusting his finger like a knife. "Liar!"

"I do not lie. They left. They arranged for it to be so. But listen to me, Sukharam. All may not be lost. We can find Kaleh. We can find the Atalayina—"

Before he could finish, Sukharam raised his hand above him and drew fire around it. The flames roiled around his hand. It was all Nasim could do to draw upon a vanahezhan to lift the earth between them as a bolt of flame shot toward him. The flame baked the earthen wall, the grass sizzling as smoke and ash burst upward in a fan.

"Sukharam, don't!"

Again flame shot forward, and again Nasim blocked it.

A gale of wind roared and knocked Nasim off his feet. He tried to stand, but the wind kept him down.

Nasim drew more heavily on the vanahezhan, lifting more of the solid earth. The wind flagged for a moment, but then shot in from another direction. Nasim opened the earth below Sukharam's feet, wide enough to swallow him, but not enough to kill. He needed Sukharam to see beyond his rage.

The wind lifted one final swirl of black earth before going still.

Nasim came to his feet only to find the grass sprouting around his ankles and shins and knees. Nasim tried to slow the growth with a dhoshahezhan of his own, but Sukharam's bonded spirit was already too near, and it was powerful.

Spirits were gathering now, drawn by the battle and the qiram that called for them. They crowded around, sensing a crease through which they could slip into the material world.

"Can't you feel them?" Nasim shouted. "You're going to tear open a rift!"

The ground shook. Movement like a serpent slithered beneath the earth. The ground lifted, cracked like brittle skin, and Nasim was thrown. He flew through the sky, landing heavily on one shoulder. His arm went numb for a moment as he rolled over and reached his feet.

In the place he'd stood only moments ago stood a vanahezhan. It towered over Nasim, its blackened face with glinting eyes staring down at him. Its four arms unfurled and spread wide as it stalked forward, all as Nasim tried desperately to send it back from whence it came.

"Sukharam, don't do this!"

But already another hezhan was lifting beyond the first, and another further down the hill.

The wind picked up the dark earth from the passage of the vanahezhan. It swirled in the sky above, just as a twinkling of light coalesced above it.

"Sukharam! Too many are crossing!"

Sukharam, however, was content to let them come, perhaps embracing this final end. But Nasim did feel one who *was* helping him. As the vanahezhan bore down on him, as Nasim scrambled away, he felt Ashan commanding the vanahezhan. He could not force it back—Adhiya was simply too close to do that now that it had crossed—but he could bond with it.

And he did.

The vanahezhan turned just as a complex structure of shifting white light, slid downward. The vanahezhan lifted two of its arms, blocking the blinding streak of lightning that unfolded down toward Nasim. The coruscating lightning forked and drilled into the vanahezhan's arms, which burst, unable to absorb the sheer power being released. The debris struck Nasim across his chest and face. A bitter clay smell filled the air.

Nasim retreated as the vanahezhan's arms reformed. Earth extended outward—an oozing mud that hardened when the arms had taken shape once more.

Ashan was bonding with more of the hezhan that were crossing: a suurahezhan, its flaming form lifting into a shape that made it look as though it were taking breath; a dhoshahezhan, one that was just crossing over above Nasim; a jalahezhan, its watery form taking shape from further down the slope. Nasim did the same—bonding with the dhoshahezhan that had attacked him, and the havahezhan near it—but it wouldn't be enough. There were already too many spirits crossing, and more were coming closer every moment. Soon, dozens would cross, and then all would be lost.

That was when Nasim felt a drifting of the worlds. In this place, the aether widened, making it more and more difficult for the spirits to cross. Fewer and fewer crossed, and soon, the hezhan, no matter how eager they might be, could no longer reach the material world. A long moment paused, a moment of relative silence. The divide grew so wide that the hezhan began slipping back across to Adhiya. The dhoshahezhan winked out of existence. The havahezhan gave one last curl of wind that rose higher into the sky, and then was gone. The suurahezhan consumed itself, the bright heat falling against Nasim's skin to the point of pain before it vanished in a cough of smoke. The dhoshahezhan crumbled into heaps of black earth and grass, and the jalahezhan lost form, the water splashing noisily against the earth below them.

And then Sukharam and Nasim and Ashan were left staring at one another, wondering what had happened.

But Nasim already knew. Her touch was unmistakable.

He looked down the slope, past Ashan.

A woman strode forward with men in red robes trailing behind her. He was surprised to see, however, not Kaleh but Ushai, holding the glowing Atalayina in her good right hand.

He knew this wasn't Ushai, however.

This was Sariya. And she'd come to finish things.

CHAPTER SIXTY-EIGHT

A cold rain fell hard and relentless as Nikandr, holding tight to the sail lines of a skiff that bucked in the heavy winds, flew over the Sea of Tabriz. The skiff could hold twenty, but instead held only three others: Soroush, Borund, and Sayyed, Vostroma's most skilled dhoshaqiram. Soroush and Sayyed both wore the woolen robes of the Aramahn while Nikandr and Borund wore heavily oiled cherkesskas.

Despite the objections from the others, Nikandr stood while summoning the wind. "Conserve your strength," Sayyed had told him. But the lines in Nikandr's hands were the only things keeping him awake. Were he to sit on one of the thwarts he would surely fall asleep, and that was something they could not afford. Not now that they were so close to the end of their journey.

Nikandr spotted something in the seas far ahead. At first he thought it was nothing. A low, black cloud. A patch of rain. But then he recognized it for what it was. With skies the color of ash and a sea of solid pewter, the gloomy hint of an island could be seen through the rain. It was Ghayavand, where all of this had begun, where it would end as well, one way or another. The mere sight of the island made his heart speed up, but it was the burgeoning feeling in his chest that made his eyes lose their heaviness, that made him feel real hope for the first time in days. *Is it truly you?* He took his soulstone out from inside his shirt and held it in one hand. They were still leagues from Ghayavand's shores, and already he could feel her presence. He'd abandoned Atiana in Kohor, yet here she was, so close he wanted nothing more than to guide the skiff straight to her.

But he couldn't. Not yet. *Hear me, my love.* He gripped the stone tighter. *I'm on my way.*

"The island's ahead," Nikandr said, pointing to it. "Just there."

Borund scanned the skies around the island with a leather-and-brass spyglass as rain pelted down against his brown hair and curly beard. He held the glass with fingers that had once been fat, but were no longer. His time at the war-front had seen him lose two stones at the least. "If they're there, the rain's too thick to see them."

To the fore of the skiff, and windward, the sky was dark and angry. "They must be close," Nikandr said. "Perhaps the storm's delayed them."

Borund took his eye away from the spyglass long enough to look to Sayyed. "What say you? Can you feel anything?"

The old Aramahn, dressed in robes of orange and copper, shook his head. "I feel *too* much." His sodden grey beard waggled as he spoke, but he didn't seem bothered by the weather, nor had he been since they'd taken to the winds. "It's become difficult to control the dhoshahezhan." He glanced up beyond Nikandr, to the sky above. "You must feel the same."

Nikandr shook his head. "I do not." It felt strange to say so, knowing how difficult it was for Sayyed, how difficult it *should be* for him, but the truth was that it wasn't. He was still bonded with the very same havahezhan he'd found on the plains of Yrstanla.

Just then Nikandr felt something spread across the sea. His bones ached from it, just as they had in Shadam Khoreh when the wards had fallen. The same was happening now. The inner wards, he realized. They'd finally given way, which meant that nothing now stood between Sariya and her ultimate goal.

"Give me the glass," Nikandr said.

Borund handed it over.

Nikandr scanned the skies ahead, and for long minutes saw nothing, but then, as the rain lightened, his heart sank. Dozens of windships, small as blackbirds, were sailing the wind near the island. He could tell by the very shape of them that they were ships of the Grand Duchy. Despite the sleepless nights of flying, despite pushing themselves to the very edge of exhaustion, they'd arrived too late.

As he watched, the distant thunder of cannons came to him. The battle was beginning in earnest.

Nikandr handed the spyglass to Borund, who took it and scanned ahead, his lips set in a grim line. "What shall we do?"

"We go on," Nikandr said, his heart beating harder and harder. "There may yet be time to call a retreat."

Borund nodded.

They moved as quickly as they were able. In their patch of sea, the rain lessened and then ceased altogether, the water collecting and draining through the holes in the bottom of the skiff. The wind that Nikandr called forth bore them forward with speed, driving them like an appleseed through pinched fingers. They were hit with one last downpour of rain, but when they were through, they were near the island at last.

The weather was kinder here. The clouds were not so dark, and the sky was clear of the heaviest rains. The ships of the Grand Duchy were arrayed in force, but standing opposite them were things he'd never seen before. He'd been told about them, though. His mother had warned him about them. As she had said, they were shaped vaguely like spearheads, but they were massive. Thick branches radiated out from the base and swirled up about one another to the top of the queer, floating vessels. They were smaller than ships of war, but not by much. The branches near the tops were delicate, almost vine-like, but the boughs near the base looked stout indeed.

The cannons of several Grand Duchy ships were concentrating fire on one of them. Though branches shattered with each shot that blasted into it, the structure remained strong, protecting whatever lay cocooned within.

In a flurry, dozens of cannons released their shots simultaneously, part of some orchestrated attack on the part of the Grand Duchy's commander. Branch by branch, the closest of the tree-ships was torn apart. Enough of the limbs were blasted away that it revealed a hollow interior, where a red-robed qiram stood with arms held wide. It was a gesture that seemed so familiar, but it looked foreign on the man from the desert wastes of the Gaji. More shots struck home until the craft could no longer sustain its loft. It plummeted down toward the seas near Ghayavand, the branches unfurling as it went. The qiram's robes fluttered about his frame and his arms flapped like a grouse shot through the heart. Soon the tree crashed into the sea, and the Kohori was taken down into the water by the ceaseless, churning waves.

That the forces of the Grand Duchy were taking their time Nikandr could understand. They had strong crews that fired crisply and accurately. They could afford to wait and pick apart the enemy ships. The forces of the Kohori were a completely different story. They gained nothing by waiting.

"They've been *ordered* to wait," Nikandr said. "They're waiting for a signal. I must go to Sihyaan, Borund, but first"—he pointed to the largest of the Grand Duchy's ships, a sixteen-masted galleon—"we must bring you there."

Borund nodded, and Nikandr drew the wind to carry them there, but just then, over the tall mountain of Sihyaan, clouds began to swirl. Moments later a blue light shot straight upward and pierced the clouds. It was brilliant and difficult to look on directly. It shined blue, like threads of pure moonlight that had been woven into a tight, bright beam.

That was when the first of the tree-ships began flying toward the ships of Anuskaya. It took salvo after salvo from a dozen ships but the stout lower branches moved and twisted so that they stood in the line of fire. Musketry was brought to bear as well, the combination of the two shattering branches, their remains fluttering downward like flocks of starlings. Yet as the branches shattered, more grew from the base, taking their place, providing protection.

As the tree-ship continued on its course toward the galleon, more Kohori ships followed, each toward a different Grand Duchy windship.

"Retreat," Nikandr called to the wind, dearly wishing they could hear him. "Retreat!"

But it was too late.

When the first had come within a hundred paces of the galleon, the branches unfurled and grew at an alarming rate. Thin vines wrapped around the galleon's bowsprit, then the foredeck, and then they reached the rigging with a speed that made Nikandr and every other man on the skiff draw breath. The vines thickened as they crept over the ship, grabbing men and pinning them in place.

Nikandr heard their cries among the sound of cannon-fire—men shouting in alarm, then screaming in pain until their cries were eventually cut short.

By the ancients, the life is being squeezed from them. They're all going to die.

Sariya, in Ushai's form, stepped up the mountain. Nasim tried to bond with another hezhan—there were so many near—but the Atalayina prevented him. It prevented Sukharam as well. His face grew angry and red. He released a primal cry into the air, the pent-up frustration of a young man who could do nothing against the forces arrayed against him. And then he charged Sariya.

"*Neh!*" Nasim cried.

Sukharam ignored him. He hadn't taken three strides when a bolt of blue-white lightning shot out from the Atalayina and struck him in the chest.

Sukharam was driven to the ground.

Nasim ran and dropped to his side. The smell of burned cloth, of singed flesh, filled the air. His robes at the center of his chest were charred and smoking. Sukharam's mouth was open, his jaw slack. His eyes stared unseeing into the cloudy sky. Nasim took Sukharam's hand in his and checked for his heartbeat, feeling nothing.

"Wake, Sukharam!"

He squeezed Sukharam's hand, pressed his ear against Sukharam's chest, and there, faintly, heard his heart beat. His chest rose as the blood *thrummed*. Thanks be to all that was good, he yet lived, but his pulse was weak and his breath was terribly shallow.

"Sukharam, wake." Nasim shook him, first gently and then vigorously, and finally slapped him across the cheek. "Wake!"

Sukharam's eyes fluttered open.

He stared into Nasim's eyes with a confused expression. And then his eyes softened. "Has the end come?"

Nasim shook his head, nearly laughing from nervousness and joy. "Not yet."

Sariya strode past them. One of the red-robed men of Kohor grabbed Nasim. Another other pulled Sukharam upright and held his arms tightly behind his back. The men faced Nasim and Sukharam toward Sariya, as if insisting they watch. The rest of the Kohori fanned out, circling around the obsidian pedestal, and when they came to a rest, they faced Sariya.

Sariya stood at the pedestal, the Atalayina held above it with a steady hand. Only when the last of the Kohori were in place did she set the Atalayina on the pedestal. She breathed deeply, spread her arms wide with her palms lifted toward the sky. Above, the clouds churned and swirled. The Atalayina glowed a brilliant blue, so bright it was difficult to look upon.

Sariya, who was using Ushai's body as a vessel, went rigid. Her whole frame shook. Nasim and Sukharam and the Kohori all stared in awe as a beam of light shot upward toward the clouds. Where the beam touched the clouds, they parted, but instead of showing the blue sky beyond, a blackened sky was revealed, a sky dark as the dead of night. The beam continued up and up and up until at last it was swallowed by the darkness.

In the distance, the sounds of cannon-fire grew. Muskets joined in, distant snaps of gunfire among the boom of the cannons. The windships of Anuskaya had closed with the living ships of the Kohori. Men were dying now. Many of them. And it made a certain sort of sense as Nasim felt the worlds close in. Adhiya drew near, at least in this one place. The aether as well. It felt as though the three were now one. Three facets of the same jewel.

Neh. Not merely three. There were other facets as well. The heavens beyond. Nasim could feel those as well, for the Atalayina was opening a pathway to them. Sariya was reaching up to touch the very heavens, as he'd known she would. He'd realized it on the bridge outside of Shirvozeh. The fates had abandoned the heavens in preparation for others to take their place, and Sariya was now fulfilling that promise, a promise made three hundred years before.

Sariya didn't want to destroy the worlds.

She wanted to *replace* the fates.

With the Atalayina and with the knowledge she'd gained in Kohor and elsewhere, she was the only one who could open the pathway to the heavens where the fates once lived.

She was not quite there, however. The path was not wide enough for her to ascend. But then souls of the fighting men of Anuskaya began to slip through from Erahm to Adhiya. More and more fell, their undying spirits slipping over to the world beyond, and it widened the gateway above.

The deaths were unfortunate, Nasim thought, but necessary, for the pathways *had* to open. There was no other way for Sariya to take her place in the heavens.

Atiana sits cross-legged in the grass below the shoulder of Sihyaan.

Kaleh stands nearby, watching. The young woman will go with Styophan and the streltsi of Khalakovo, who stand at the ready nearby. She might stay to help protect Atiana, but truly, her place is with Nasim and Sukharam.

Aelwen busies herself with a fire. What she's doing, or why, Atiana no longer cares.

"Go," Atiana tells the streltsi.

Styophan nods to his men, and they begin marching at the double, muskets at their sides, all of them wary-eyed, all of them in awe of what's happening around them. Styophan pauses, however, staring down at her with his one good eye, as if he's unsure of her orders.

"I will give you a sign if I can," she tells him, "but use your best judgment." He nods, but before he can follow his men, she speaks on. "You have been a good soldier, Styophan Andrashayev. A good son of Khalakovo."

This makes him pause. His nostrils flare for a moment. The veins on his forehead stand out. His eye searches hers, perhaps weighing the sincerity in her words. And then he is off, following his men. Kaleh takes one last look, and then pads off as well, trailing quietly behind the men of war.

No sooner have they left than a bright blue light streaks up and into the billowing clouds over Sihyaan, parting them and revealing a darkness that is nothing like the aether. It is not the midnight blue she has always seen. It is black—a depthless black—and wider than the worlds. It feels as though it will widen like some unspeakable maw until it swallows them all.

She begins to float upward toward it without even realizing it's happening. She fights to remain in place, but soon she is flailing, trying ineffectually to keep from being drawn toward it.

Sister! Atiana, you must regain yourself!

Atiana hears the words, but can think of little but the blackened sky and the hole between worlds. It is like nothing she's ever sensed. It is not of Adhiya, nor Erahm, nor the aether itself. It is of something *other*, though what, she cannot guess.

You are a Matra of the Grand Duchy!

Atiana knows this voice, but cannot place it. It is too distant, her mind too fixated on the depths of the darkness above her. But then an earthy scent of incense comes to her. It fills her mind and grounds her, pulls her back and away from the gateway. It is Aelwen, she realizes. She's burning something to keep Atiana grounded. How Aelwen might have known of the danger Atiana has no idea, but she has since given up on trying to understand the ways of the wodjana.

Control yourself, a voice says.

The voice is Ishkyna's. The mere realization shakes her, as does the growing presence of others. Mileva is with her. Saphia Khalakovo is here as well, along with her daughter, Nikandr's sister, Victania. More and more minds make their presence known—not merely the Duchesses, not merely their daughters, but many others, two score or more, resting within their drowning basins throughout the islands. Some are near and some are far. Some are strong while others maintain tentative holds on the aether. They have come in the hour of Atiana's greatest need, though she could not have hoped for it.

They all take a moment to bond with one another. Atiana strengthens those who are weak, sharpening their hold on the dark. Their consciousness expands beyond anything Atiana has ever felt. It encompasses the entirety of the seas and the islands that lie within them. Even Yrstanla feels small compared to this.

But they all know they've spread themselves too far. With Atiana now guiding them, they tighten their focus, drawing in toward the Sea of Tabriz and Ghayavand within it, and finally to the mountain of Sihyaan and Sariya who stands upon it, drawing on the power of the Atalayina.

It is the stone that holds their collective attention.

In the aether it is not merely bright; it saps their souls. It makes one ache in a way that Atiana can't quite comprehend. It's as if a part of her is slipping away toward Adhiya even now, and she knows it's the same for the others. Already she feels some of them, the weakest, are losing their hold. They try to buoy one another, but it isn't enough, because the first of them, the Duchess Ekaterina Rhavanki, slips toward the blackened void.

Save me, sisters!

They reach for her. They try to keep her in place, but in her desperation Ekaterina loses control. A primal scream resounds through them. It fades, though slowly, and then the Duchess is completely and utterly gone.

Styophan motioned for his men to slow. Further away, partially obscured by the tall grasses in which he crouched, Rodion waited for a sign. Styophan took a deep breath. He was well aware that he and Rodion were the only two soldiers left from their mission to Hael. He was surprised they'd survived Alekeşir, but the ancients—and perhaps the fates—work in strange ways. In truth he wasn't worried over his own life. Nor was he worried over Rodion's. They had both been ready to give their lives for Anuskaya from the moment they accepted the mission westward. He simply didn't wish to throw their lives away—or worse, for his actions to help the enemies of Anuskaya in any way.

Motion at Styophan's left side caught his attention. Kaleh crouched there, watching the way ahead warily, not with a look of fear, but of resolve. They were as ready as they were going to be. Styophan nodded to Rodion. Rodion returned the nod and then was off, slipping low and quickly through the grasses with his nine men.

Styophan then took Kaleh and the rest of his men—twelve more—toward a depression in the land, a natural place from which to begin their attack. They moved quickly, all of them spying the rise above them. The men of Kohor were facing inward, watching those at their center instead of facing outward toward any threats that might present themselves. He didn't understand why, but he wasn't about to question it. At the top of the rise was Ushai. Nasim and Sukharam were held nearby by two of the Kohori men whose red robes flapped in the fierce wind.

Styophan waited, staring at the empty black hole in the sky. The world felt as if it were ending, here and now. He could feel it on his skin, a prickling that felt like death's hand clutching for him.

Atiana was to give him a sign that she was ready, but they'd agreed that he would go if he felt it necessary. He could wait no more. He brought his musket to his shoulder, sighted along its length, aiming carefully at the one who held Nasim. And then he pulled the trigger.

The musket kicked. The Kohori man fell, clutching his side. The sound of more musket shots rattled the air, followed by the grunts and cries of their enemy. Few of them fell, however. One dropped and was lost among the grasses, then another further along the slope. The rest, however, seemed to be affected only momentarily by the musket shots that had struck home. They turned, drawing their swords and scanning the ground around them.

That was when Styophan and his streltsi stood and charged.

"For Anuskaya!" they called in unison.

Nikandr watched in horror as the galleon was taken by the twisting and thickening branches. The crewmen screamed in pain. Some died from the constricting vines. Others still lived, but they were trapped, pinned in place by the will of the Kohori.

The other windships desperately tried to stop the advance of the tree-ships. As each one approached and its branches unfurled, cannon-fire would blast a few of them free, sending them down toward the roiling sea, and when the branches reached the ship, the streltsi and windsmen aboard would hack at them desperately with shashkas and axes. Some even threw themselves at the branches, grabbing onto them and weighting them down so they couldn't grab the ship.

All of it only served to delay Sariya's forces. Sooner or later, the vines would gain a foothold on the ship, and then they would split and grow and spread throughout the ship, grabbing men and rigging and sails alike. And then they would squeeze, gripping the windship like a hand crushing an overripe peach.

Most of the Anuskayan ships had not yet been trapped. They were spread out in a ragged line, firing at the enemy, hoping to save those ships that had fallen to the animated trees.

"Son of Zhabyn," Sayyed said as he gripped Borund's wrist. "They're being taken." He pointed up to the impenetrable darkness. "For that."

Nikandr realized it was true. He could feel their souls slipping toward the passage between worlds. Sariya was using their deaths to widen it.

Borund pointed to one of the largest of the nearby warships, a ship that flew the black and orange of Bolgravya. "Quickly, Nischka, take me to them. Take me there, then go."

Nikandr nodded. The ships had to be made to flee. It was the only way to stop Sariya's plans. He summoned the wind to bring their skiff toward the Bolgravyan ship. The streltsi there trained muskets on Nikandr—one of them even fired, the shot punching through the canvas over Nikandr's head—but then Borund stood and waved at them. "Stand down!" he called. "Stand down! The Duke of Vostroma commands you!"

And the men of Bolgravya did.

Nikandr brought the skiff in until the crew could pull them in with ropes. When the skiff had been brought tight against the gunwales, Borund stepped across, and Soroush rose to do so as well. "I can do little on the island, son of Iaros. But here, I may be able to help."

"How?"

"The men of Bolgravya," Soroush replied. "They may not believe Borund, but they might believe me when I tell them that the Kohori, all of them, are willing to die this day. With luck, we will draw them all away. Now go."

Soroush stepped onto the ship's deck and kicked the skiff away.

Nikandr waved to Soroush. Soroush nodded in return and then was off, following Borund to speak with the kapitan of the ship.

Nikandr summoned the wind and guided the skiff toward Sihyaan. The Kohori ships were moving quickly now. More were pressing in toward the windships of Anuskaya. Nikandr could feel them drawing upon their bonded spirits, working to keep the hezhan at bay, carefully drawing upon their powers while preventing them from entering this world.

All it would take, though, was a tug, a pull, and in this Nikandr saw an opportunity. He drew those havahezhan toward Erahm. It felt as if a thread were running from him to the gathered spirits, and when they felt him tugging, they were drawn toward and into the material world.

Two of them crossed, then three and four, each manifesting within one of the Kohori tree-ships. He could see them, twisting and swirling within the protected center. One of the Kohori raised his hands, trying to regain control, but he was drawn up through the branches and tossed to the wind. He flew down toward the sea as the hezhan slipped through branches and twisted toward another of the floating ships.

Nikandr had pushed too hard, though. He was having a fight of his own now. His havahezhan, perhaps emboldened by the crossings of the others, fought him, trying to reach Erahm itself.

Nikandr pushed back desperately. He couldn't allow the hezhan to cross. Not now.

But then something caught Nikandr's eye. The boughs and branches of one of the nearby tree-ships had unfurled, had spread wide, and the red-robed qiram within was staring straight at Nikandr. He was drawing on something, but Nikandr knew not what. Not until the skiff began to creak and tick. The wood dried and warped. It crumbled, just as Nikandr's ship, the *Gorovna*, had when he'd first traveled to Ghayavand.

And soon, the entire skiff was soft as dry-rotted timber, and Nikandr and Sayyed fell clean through the hull.

Atiana tries desperately to hold the Matri in place. They strengthen one another, and in this Ishkyna is the strongest of them all—she touches each of them, after all, as much a part of the aether as its midnight-blue essence—but she is also the most vulnerable.

Careful, sister, Atiana tells her. *Do not spread yourself so thin.*

I know my business, Ishkyna replies. *See you take care of yours.*

Ishkyna is strong, as are many of the other Matri, but soon more begin to slip toward the void. Iriketa Bolgravya, the daughter of the Duchess Alesya, is taken. And then Alesya, in trying to save her daughter, is swept up and lost as well.

Suddenly Rosa Lhudansk cries out. Fear and desperation run through them all, but Rosa is voicing it for them. It is a grave mistake. To give voice to one's fears is to be lost in the aether, especially here in so violent a place. She is soon lost, her mind drawn away until they can feel her no more.

Atiana feels herself beginning to worry, and there lies danger. She cannot allow it—none of them can—or the aether will have them all.

They are forced to draw away from the Atalayina. Only then are they able to gain some sense of stability. They all know it may be fleeting, but for now, it is enough.

With the desperation gone, Atiana can sense what's happening beyond the shores of Ghayavand. The men of Anuskaya are dying. Their souls are being lifted and are passing through the gap between worlds. They go to Adhiya, surely, as all souls do, but they're also widening the gap above.

Surely this is what Sariya wanted all along. But why? Atiana doesn't understand.

She knows that they must close it, however. The only question is how.

The Atalayina is the key, of course. It is allowing Sariya to open the way to the heavens.

Near the stone, Nasim is still held in place. But he is screaming. He's looking around wildly—to the skies more often than not—and she knows he's trying to tell them something.

Hold, sisters. Hold a moment longer.

And then she slips into the mind of the robed Kohori man who's holding Nasim. The warrior from the desert fights her, but he is easy to overpower. He wasn't expecting this and his mind is in rapture now that Sariya is so close to undoing the world.

Through the man's ears she can hear Nasim shouting among the crack of gunfire and the clash of swords.

"You must keep the way open!" he cries.

She releases Nasim, and he stumbles away. He looks back at her only for a moment. "Quickly, Matra," he says. "Prepare your sisters. We need but little time, and you must give it to us!"

And then he faces Sukharam and spreads his arms wide. As Atiana slips back into the aether, the other Kohori releases Sukharam—Ishkyna's doing. Nasim gathers the currents of a havahezhan, which cast a blinding white against the aether's midnight blue. The scent of burning mace and cloves comes strongly. She even sees the form of the wind spirit coalesce around Nasim. An instant later, a wind pushes both of the Kohori men away like leaves in the gales of autumn.

For a moment she doesn't understand what Nasim meant. *Keep the way open.* But she need only to look at the blackened hole in the clouds above and it all comes clear, or enough of it for her to understand Nasim's intent. She'd been wrong. She and Nikandr and all the others—they'd been wrong about Sariya. She wasn't trying to destroy the world. She was trying to save it. She can hardly believe what she and the other Matri are about to do, but it's clear that it *must* be done.

For a moment, she stares in wonder at Nasim. So much has this young man been through. Returning to the world by the hand of Khamal. Coming to his own mind with the help of Ashan and Nikandr. He's hardly had the chance to live, and now comes this. She dearly hopes he is ready for what is to come.

Go well, she wishes him, and then rejoins her sisters.

When the Kohori men had been blown far down slope, Nasim lowered his hands. He turned to Sukharam, ready to ask him of Kaleh, if he'd felt her, but he stopped, for he sensed her nearby. There was fighting all around. Men firing muskets and pistols, more fighting with swords, but among them strode a young woman. She looked so much older than when he'd seen her only a few short weeks ago.

Her hair was long and brown. It flowed in the fierce wind as she stepped lithely among the fighting men. She went untouched, as if she knew what they would do and when they would do it.

In this moment, in this place, she was her mother's child.

Indeed, as she strode forward her eyes fixed on the Atalayina. Her look spoke of hunger, as though she would swallow it if she could. But she could not. They were each and every one of them caught up in the stone's great pull.

When at last she reached their side, she looked at Sukharam and then Nasim in turn. Her gaze felt weighty, as if she looked well beyond the years the three of them had lived. "My mother is trying to ascend."

Nasim nodded. Sukharam, however, seemed unsure of himself.

"You know it to be true," Kaleh said to both of them, "and you know she must succeed." She paused. "And we must follow."

Sukharam glanced at Sariya, shaking his head. "*Neh.* We must stop her."

"It's too late for that," Nasim said, "and well you know it. The way has been opened, and now there is only one choice left to us."

Sukharam balked, his jaw grinding as he worked through the implications, but when he looked to Kaleh, he must have seen something within her, something that lent him courage, for his eyes softened and his breath released. "I'm scared," he said.

"As am I," Kaleh said.

"As am I," Nasim said. And it was no lie. He had no idea what lay in store for them, for any of them, but he would do this, for though Sariya opened the way, though she was the first to cross, she could not be left on her own to rule the ways of the world.

Together, they held hands—Kaleh between Nasim and Sukharam—and walked toward Sariya. Even in this cold place, Kaleh's hand was warm.

Through the eyes of Ushai, Sariya stared at them. "My children."

"We are not your children," Kaleh says.

"But you are," Sariya replied. "You all are."

Nasim stepped toward her. Sariya looked ready to say something, perhaps to warn him away, but she must have seen something in Nasim's eyes that gave her pause, for the words died on her lips.

Nasim knew he could not have found the way to the heavens on his own. And neither, he suspected, could Sukharam or Kaleh. The three of them were powerful, but they had not the years of study and meditation that Sariya had, nor the intimate knowledge of the Atalayina and its inner workings. They needed her, but that didn't mean they would leave her to her own devices. The three of them—he, Kaleh, and Sukharam—had been chosen, or perhaps they'd chosen their own way. Whatever the case, they would follow Sariya. It was the only way to ensure that the world would be cared for properly. The fate of the worlds could not be left to one and one alone. There had to be more, as surely the fates had wished.

"Go, Sariya Quljan al Vehayeh, but know that when you do, you will not go alone."

Sariya's face had been supremely confident moments ago, but now that mask of confidence began to crack. Her brows pinched. She gazed upon the sheer blackness above, working Nasim's words through her mind, working them against the plans she'd laid so meticulously these past many years.

And then understanding came to her. Nasim knew, for her searching eyes went still. She went utterly rigid. She even began to shake. Sariya, shaken like a newborn foal.

She pulled her gaze down and stared into Nasim's eyes. Her lips trembled. She looked as though she were about to speak.

And then her mortal shell—Ushai—collapsed in a heap.

She was gone, and she hoped to leave them all behind. Already Nasim felt the way closing, but indeed, as he had bade them, the Matri fought to keep the way open. Nasim moved to the obsidian pillar where the Atalayina rested. Sukharam and Kaleh followed, for they knew as well as Nasim did that the way would not remain open for long. The stone glowed beautifully. It was so bright it felt as though it could swallow him in place of the blackness above. Together, they tried to ascend, as Sariya just had. They worked with one another, searching for the heavens above. They could feel it, tantalizingly close, but the moment they tried to ascend they knew that the way was too narrow. Sariya was working against them now from the other side.

CHAPTER SIXTY-NINE

Nikandr fell through the sky with bits of the skiff trailing above him. He called upon the wind to save him, but the hezhan was already too close. He couldn't draw it closer without pulling it across.

So he did.

He abandoned himself. He gave himself completely to the hezhan.

He felt it cross over, even as he plummeted downward. The rocks were below. The rocks and the frothing surf. But he accepted this. For once, he felt truly like a part of the world, a part of *both* worlds, and if this was his time to cross, then so be it.

The wind whipped harder as the havahezhan gathered around him. It held Nikandr like a babe and bore him aloft. He pleaded for it to save Sayyed, to bear him as well, but it was too late. Sayyed crashed into the rocks below, little more than a swath of red against black rock and frothing surf.

Grimacing, Nikandr asked that he be carried north toward Sihyaan. The hezhan complied, the roar of it filling his ears, and together they flew over the forests of Ghayavand toward the dark peak ahead. The blue light of the Atalayina was still bright, and as he came closer he saw Ushai standing there, the brightness of the Atalayina casting her skin in a blue-white glow. She looked like a ghost, a woman already halfway to the world beyond.

Around her, men were fighting, the streltsi of Khalakovo and the warriors of Kohor. The desert men were vicious fighters with a sword in hand, but those he'd sent with Styophan were the best soldiers Khalakovo had to offer, as skilled with sword as they were with pistol or knife.

Nikandr found Styophan, who was engaged side-by-side with another strelet against two Kohori swordsmen. Near them, a Kohori was engaged with two streltsi. The Kohori wielded his shamshir masterfully, beating off swing after swing while preventing the two soldiers of Anuskaya from flanking him.

But then he made a mistake. He slipped on the uneven ground, leaning too close to the nearest strelet.

As the hezhan carried Nikandr lower and lower, he realized it was all a ruse. "Watch him!" he cried, but they couldn't hear him, not from this distance, and not with the roar of the wind around him.

The strelet's shashka came down. The Kohori snaked to his right, the blurring blade narrowly missing him. He spun and brought his sword down in a two-handed chopping motion across the strelet's shin, cutting cleanly through the leg just below the knee.

The other strelet overcompensated. He came in hard, but his bull rush was defended masterfully. Three quick parries were followed by a sharp thrust to the strelet's neck, then deep through his chest.

Both streltsi fell, one holding his neck as blood spurted through his fingers, the other trying desperately to slow the blood pouring from his severed leg.

Closer now, Nikandr dropped from the air, drawing his shashka before his feet had even struck solid ground. The Kohori was looking for a new enemy. He saw Nikandr down the hill, saw the threat of the hezhan, but Styophan was closer, and his back was to the Kohori.

As the Kohori ran toward Styophan, Nikandr raced up the slope, hoping to intercept, but he already knew he'd never be able to reach Styophan before the Kohori cut him down.

The bond Nikandr now shared with the havahezhan was unlike anything he'd felt in the past. Only the wind spirit that had attacked him on the deck of the *Gorovna* those many years ago came close. The bond with a hezhan that had crossed was more intensified, which only made sense with the aether no longer acting as a veil between them. With the bond so much stronger, so too was the spirit's ability to draw upon Nikandr's soul. And so even as the hezhan did his bidding, as it blew down against the desert warrior, Nikandr's knees were made weak. He quivered, not from pain, but from this ancient spirit using him up. He felt like fruit left drying in the sun.

Still, his sacrifice had the desired effect. A great gust of wind pulled warrior's legs out from underneath him. He fell clumsily to the ground, yet moments later the wind began to deaden and the Kohori returned to his feet. He was working against the spirit with his own hezhan, but he couldn't hope to fight a spirit that had crossed over for long, not with a spirit still trapped in Adhiya.

Nikandr charged, if only to distract him. They traded a flurry of blows, the ring of their steel mixing with the sounds of swords and dying around them. Nikandr's rage over these past many months returned to him. His frustration at having lost Nasim, his feelings of impotence as the events in the Kohor valley, then Shadam Khoreh and Alekeşir unfolded. But now he had blade in hand

and the ability to help Nasim see this through. He channeled all of this into his battle with the Kohori, who was a better swordsman than Nikandr had ever seen. Back and forth they moved, parrying, feinting, cutting viciously in a furious dance before having to cede ground back.

And all the while the two havahezhan fought as well—a similar back and forth, each trying for supremacy over the other. It was clear, though, that Nikandr's was winning. The wind was beginning to rise. It wouldn't be long before Nikandr's won altogether and then Nikandr could do as he would with this man.

The Kohori knew it too. He brought his sword down against Nikandr's defenses—three sharp strikes that forced Nikandr back. The moment Nikandr stepped back, the Kohori did so as well. He raised his hand, and flame formed in his open palm.

Nikandr wanted to bid the havahezhan to help, but the bond he shared with it was too tenuous. He could no longer maintain the bond and fight this man at the same time.

So he released it. He let it go where it will, if only to have the energy to defend himself.

Nikandr advanced quickly. He used his shashka to slap the Kohori's curved shamshir out of line, then flicked the tip of his sword toward his neck. The Kohori retreated, raised his free hand high. The roiling ball of flame was now the size of Nikandr's head. Nikandr backed away, preparing to leap, but when the Kohori brought his arm forward, Nikandr already knew it was headed straight for him.

It streaked toward his chest, but made it only halfway when it was caught in a powerful eddy of wind. The havahezhan had placed itself between them and trapped the flame within it. In the time it took Nikandr to breathe in, the flame was drawn up to a single orange thread and snuffed into a thin line of black smoke. The hezhan fell upon the Kohori then, drawing wind and grass mercilessly upward as it tried to steal the warrior's breath away. The Kohori was working against the hezhan to free himself, but Nikandr didn't allow him that luxury. He stepped forward and drove his sword deep through the Kohori's chest until the tip buried itself in the earth below him.

No sooner had Nikandr yanked his sword out than the havahezhan fled. It slipped up and away and with one final gust shoved Nikandr unceremoniously backward and onto his rump.

Nikandr scanned about for more of the enemy, but thank the ancients they had all been killed. Styophan was now striding toward him, sword in hand, watching the fallen warriors for hints of movement. He'd lost his leather eyepatch somewhere along the way, revealing the mass of scars where his right eye used to be. As he came closer, his gaze fell to the dead Kohori near Nikandr's feet. "You have my thanks, My Lord Prince."

Nikandr waved his thanks away, pointing toward the pedestal and the Atalayina and those gathered around it.

Standing opposite Ushai—who by now Nikandr understood must be Sariya—were Nasim and Sukharam and Kaleh. They were speaking, trying to reason with Sariya, perhaps. But then, as Nikandr neared the slope below the glowing Atalayina, Sariya's face went ashen and she collapsed in a heap.

Nikandr and Styophan traded glances. Neither had any idea what had just happened.

They strode together with the other surviving streltsi toward Ashan, who was just then approaching the pedestal where Nasim, Sukharam, and Kaleh stood. Sukharam and Kaleh watched Ashan approach with uneasy looks on their faces, but Nasim couldn't seem to pull his gaze from the impossibly dark hole far above them. So intent was he that Nikandr looked up as well. The gateway, Nikandr realized. It was smaller than it had been only moments ago.

"Nasim?" Ashan called. "Nasim, hear me. The way is closing."

Nasim pulled his gaze down from the heavens and stared at Ashan, then Nikandr and the streltsi. "It is, and the Matri cannot hold it open."

"Perhaps not the Matri," Kaleh said, "but Sariya managed it."

"Through death," Sukharam replied. "She did so through death."

"Not through death," Ashan countered with a smile. "Through rebirth. Those souls were not lost. They went to the world beyond, and they will return to us brighter than before."

And suddenly it struck Nikandr—what Ashan was saying, what he truly meant. The old arqesh was offering his own life and Nikandr's and the lives of the streltsi so that Nasim and the others could ascend.

Nasim stared, unable to give an answer to Ashan's offer. How could he? How could he ask this man—his father, more than any other—to do this for him?

"You need not say it," Ashan said, sensing Nasim's thoughts. "In fact, you shouldn't." He then turned to Styophan, all but ignoring Nikandr. "But I will not take life unless it is offered."

Styophan took a long step forward so that he was now closer to Ashan than Nikandr was. He looked over his men, weighing them, then looked to the sky, over Ashan's shoulder where the battle was dying. "This will save the islands?" he asked. "It will save the world?"

Ashan's smile widened, showing his stained and imperfect teeth. "It may very well do so."

Styophan looked to his men again, asking each for his assent. Each and every one of them nodded to him. And then Styophan nodded to Ashan.

Only then did Ashan turn to Nikandr, smiling his crooked smile. "Your timing is ill, Nikandr son of Iaros."

"What do you mean?"

"The lives of these men, and my own life, will be enough. There is another you should find further down the mountain."

He meant Atiana, of course. Nikandr could feel her through his soulstone. "If this is needed, then I will go. I am a Duke of the Realm."

And now it was Styophan that stepped forward. He nodded to Ashan, and then his men. Ashan nodded back and led the streltsi up toward the Atalayina.

"Our story should be told, My Lord Prince."

"It should, and you should be the one to tell it. Go home, Styopha. Go home to your wife. Raise children and tell them what we did this day."

Styophan shook his head sadly. "This I cannot do."

"It wasn't a request, Styopha. It was a command."

Styophan smiled. He embraced Nikandr, kissed him on both cheeks, then held him at arm's length. "Then just this once, My Lord Prince, I must disobey." And with that he snatched Nikandr's wrists in an iron grip and nodded to someone over Nikandr's shoulder.

Not all of the streltsi had gone, Nikandr realized. One had remained.

Styophan held Nikandr in place, but Nikandr was able to turn his head to see Styophan's cousin, Rodion, snaking his arm around Nikandr's neck. In the blink of an eye Rodion had locked the one arm with the other and pulled tight, cutting off Nikandr's breath.

Nikandr raged. He fought against Rodion's hold. He tried to drop his weight to throw Rodion off balance, but he was strong and so was Styophan.

Blood coursed loudly through his ears. Stars filled his vision.

"Forgive me, My Prince."

Nikandr wasn't even sure who had spoken those words.

All too soon the darkness swept in.

Styophan checked to make sure Nikandr was still breathing, then he stood and walked with Rodion to the circle that was now forming around the Atalayina and the black pedestal upon which it rested. Nasim and Sukharam and Kaleh all stood in the center. His streltsi were already in a larger circle around them, but Ashan was taking care to place each man just so. Styophan watched as Avvakum took his place, then Roald and Rabyn and Estvan. As Ashan finished with each soldier, Styophan looked to them, waiting until they met his eye. He nodded to them, one by one.

He was so proud—more than he could ever express—and yet there was part of him that felt as though he'd utterly failed, a part that yearned to protect them even now. But that was not the way of things. The ancients were holding out their hands, summoning the living to take their place among the dead. They would, these soldiers, these sons of Anuskaya. They would protect their families from beyond these shores, adding to the wisdom that had been collected over the course of ages.

Ashan came to Rodion next, and here Styophan nearly broke down. The wodjana had predicted this. He remembered Queen Elean's words with crystal clarity. *When you go to Alekeşir*, she had said, *the path there and the path beyond will lead to your graves.* He didn't mind dying. Everyone dies sooner or later. He only wished he could have seen Roza one last time, could have held her in his arms once more. *Goodbye, sweet love.* And now he did break down. He wished that he could be reborn, like the Aramahn believed. He wished that Roza could one day be too, and that they could find one another again.

Perhaps we will. Ashan came and stood before Styophan. *Perhaps we will.*

Ashan moved him back and to his right. He took Styophan's shoulders and adjusted his stance, grinning his infectious grin even at a time like this. Styophan wiped away his tears and managed a smile. He was sad, but there was no doubt this was a time for happiness as well. What they did would heal the world. What greater gift could he give Roza and the children she would one day have?

Finally, Ashan was done, and he stepped into place across from Nasim. After one last smile just for Nasim, he placed his hands to his side and lifted his gaze to the sky.

And Styophan did the same.

Nasim swallowed hard, trying to clear the growing lump in his throat. He held hands with Sukharam and Kaleh as Ashan guided the streltsi in a wider circle around them. He was glad that Nikandr would live. It felt as if a part of him would remain behind, and that gave him some small amount of comfort.

He looked to the streltsi. Some watched him, particularly the one-eyed strelet, who regarded Nasim with something akin to reverence. Others were too lost in the moment to do so. He was as proud of these men as anyone he'd ever known. They would return to this life much brighter than before, and for this he was glad. When Ashan had finished arranging the last of them, he took his place in the circle. He stood opposite Nasim, a conscious choice, one last gift before he and Nasim parted ways. Tears formed in Nasim's eyes. They flowed down his cheeks as Ashan nodded, giving him comfort.

"Go well," Ashan said to Nasim.

"Go well," Nasim replied.

And with that Ashan spread his hands wide. He closed his eyes, turned his face up toward the sky. The soldiers of Anuskaya, though they knew they could not help him, did the same.

And then the first of them burst into flame. The soldier shivered from the pain, but did not cry out. He merely grit his jaw and stared up, trusting that his sacrifice was worth it.

Another burst into flame, and another, and through it all Nasim realized he could feel the world as he rarely had before. He felt its inner workings, as though he could unravel it bit by bit had he so chose.

It had been the same on Mirashadal, when Kaleh had murdered Fahroz, and again on the Spar, when Nasim had stabbed Nikandr in the heart, and once more in the depths of Shadam Khoreh.

And now here.

It took only a nudge, a mere push of his will.

And the world slows.

Flames continue to form on the soldiers of Anuskaya. None of them make a sound. It is bitterly strange to stand there as men are dying from fire and the only sound the wind through the grass and the flames themselves. Nasim grips the hands of Kaleh and Sukharam tightly. Too tightly, he realizes. As the three of them breathe in time, as the men of Anuskaya burn, he relaxes. He loosens his grip. He falls into the world around him.

Soon only Ashan remains untouched.

Still he smiles. Still he holds Nasim's gaze, offering him guidance and protection even at the last.

Nasim wants to open his mouth, to offer some word of thanks.

But to do so would distract too much.

As the hint of orange flame curls around Ashan's arms, as they lick at the hem of his robes, Nasim turns his head skyward. He looks to the narrowing circle of black.

The way is widened as the first of the streltsi dies. As his soul is lifted and borne to the world beyond. The second goes, and the third. One by one, the streltsi are taken.

Ashan goes last. He holds on until the end to make sure all others have crossed before allowing himself to be borne upward.

It is enough. Nasim's awareness spreads. He feels the land itself and the fires that lie beneath. He feels the roiling sky above and the falling rain to the west. He feels the life around him. The swaying grasses, the stoic trees. The streltsi. The Matri. The hezhan.

He feels Soroush, who flies on one of the few Anuskayan ships that remain.

He feels Atiana, who kneels upon the fields below Sihyaan's broad shoulders.

He feels Nikandr, with whom he shared his life for a time.

But more than anything, he feels the place above. It is dark, and he knows not what to expect. He worries that he will not be up to the task, that he will fail to guide the world properly or that he will allow Sariya or Kaleh or Sukharam too much sway, if not now then millennia from now. But in some ways this feels like the way things should be. He should not approach his charge with absolutism, but with open arms. He does not know if Kaleh and Sukharam feel the same. They may or they may not. This is the nature of things. After all, even the fates may not know all that lies ahead, with the world, with one another.

He can but try. And with that, he is ready.

After one final breath, he closes his eyes.

And he ascends.

CHAPTER SEVENTY

Nikandr woke as the hole above was beginning to close. He stood on shaky knees, looking to the place where Nasim and the others had gathered around the Atalayina. They were there still, but they had all fallen. Nasim and Sukharam and Kaleh. Ashan and Styophan and the streltsi. Many of their bodies were still aflame, though none of them now moved. The smell of it sickened him.

He waited for the fires to die down, the only sound the wind through the tall grasses. He had no idea what he was waiting for, what he was hoping for. Perhaps some small sign. Some sign that Nasim had made it, that the others had as well, and that their sacrifice had been worth it. That the rifts had been healed.

In this he was disappointed, for nothing happened. Eventually he worked up his courage enough that he could step up to the ring of blackened bodies. He spent a long time near Ashan, thinking over his time with the kindly arqesh. He did so again near Styophan. Then Rodion and each of the others that had given of themselves so bravely.

Go well, he wished them all.

Then he moved beyond them and crouched next to Nasim. As he smoothed Nasim's brown hair back, he wondered where Nasim might be now. Tears fell along his cheek and dripped onto Nasim's face, but he quickly wiped them away. He understood Nasim in a way that no one else did, and for this he felt rich indeed. Nasim might have left this world, but he would live on through Nikandr. And perhaps, in some small way, Nikandr would live on through Nasim.

Nikandr stood and stepped to the pedestal, where the Atalayina still lay. It was lustrous as ever—gold and silver veins twinkling in the deep blue stone—but it felt lifeless now. A relic. A thing no longer useful to the world. He picked it up, and the surface was cold to the touch.

"You should hurry."

Nikandr spun and found a woman standing outside the ring of burned bodies. It took him long moments to recognize her. The wodjan. The one from the Gaji. The one who'd taught Atiana her strange, heathen ways. The one who'd come to Radiskoye those many months ago.

"Why?" Nikandr asked.

"Your Atiana." The wodjan turned and pointed down the hill. "You will find her there, beyond that ridge. She has been in the dreaming place for a long time, and she will not wake."

Nikandr bolted in the direction she'd pointed. *Dear ancients, please don't take her as well.* He crested the ridge and found her there, lying among the grasses.

He dropped to her side and shook her. "Atiana!" He shook her harder. "Atiana! Please wake!"

He tried for long minutes, calling her name. She breathed, but did not open her eyes. Did not call his name nor squeeze his hand.

She might be lost, he realized. Like Ishkyna, or worse. Her body might wither and die and her soul go wherever souls go when a Matra loses herself.

All of the energy left him then.

He held her tight in his arms, rocking her back and forth, as he hummed an ancient song. It was the tale of Anuskaya, the one every child was taught when they were young. It was all he could think of, but it felt right. As he was stroking her hair, he heard something flutter onto the matted grasses nearby. It was a bird with russet top feathers and a bright golden breast. A thrush. Just like the one he and Nasim saw in the valley of Shadam Khoreh.

He looked to it, confused, wondering if it could possibly be the same one. There were markings along the left side of its neck, three dots that together looked like a small black clover. It turned its head this way and that, hopped closer, and then it was up and away, flying westward toward Alayazhar.

The moment the bird flew out of sight, he felt Atiana's arm twitch.

He sat upright immediately. He stared into her eyes but did not stop humming. He continued to rock her, and eventually she twitched again.

Then her cheek moved. And her lips.

And at last her eyes fluttered open. She stared up into his eyes and with no hint of emotion on her face said, "You'll wake the dead, humming like that."

He stared at her for a moment, uncomprehending, and then burst into laughter.

He held her tight to his chest, still rocking her, as his laughter filled the fields of green.

EPILOGUE

Nikandr walked over smooth, river stone gravel in the garden of Palotza Radiskoye on a day that was unseasonably warm. It had been so warm, in fact, for so many days, that the snow had melted around the palotza grounds. They were in the dead of winter, and yet the air smelled of early spring, and it was strange indeed to see the grounds clear when normally they'd be fighting to keep the paths clear of snow.

On Nikandr's right was Atiana. She wore a green silk dress with small pearls in the pattern of a field of brightbonnets. She'd had it commissioned for this very day. He'd asked her why she'd chosen a field of flowers, but she'd merely smiled and said it was a dream she'd had. Her hair was stunning. One long braid wrapped her head like a circlet, while locks of hair were pulled and layered beneath, accentuating the beautiful colors of ivory and amber and cream. Strands of golden chain, bejeweled with citrine, were woven among the braids. It was beautiful, but he had to admit he could think of little else but pulling the hairpins and letting her hair fall over her bare shoulders.

Nikandr could hardly complain over her new attire, trussed as he was in a new cherkesska and a shirt that was altogether too fine for his liking. He was the Duke of Khalakovo now. He knew appearances had to be maintained, but it still irked.

At least he'd been able to wear his own boots. They were polished to a fine black sheen, but they were his, and they were comfortable, which tonight would be an important thing indeed.

To his left was Soroush. He wore the double robes of the Aramahn. The inner was burnt umber, the outer a rich bistre that reminded Nikandr of a forest of black walnut he and Soroush had ridden through on their way from Alekeşir to Izlo. Soroush wore his black, almond-shaped turban, the ragged tail falling down his chest in the style of the Maharraht. It was strange to see him like this, as if he were caught between his past and his future, but in truth everyone was caught this way, between old and new. It was true that it had always been so, but in the days since the restoration—as some had begun to call it—the idea felt more powerful than ever. The rifts were not completely healed. That might take months or even years, but they were healing, and one day soon the worlds would be back on their proper path.

Soroush had returned along with Borund on one of the few Anuskayan ships that had survived the attack over Ghayavand. Borund, with Soroush's help, had convinced the kapitan of the Bolgravyan ship that they needed to retreat. Nikandr knew now that it had almost cost them everything. There needed to be deaths so that the gateway to the heavens would open. Had Nikandr succeeded in stopping the fleet, the gateway might never have opened.

The ancients work in strange ways, indeed.

Nikandr and Atiana had returned south with Borund to Vostroma as the remaining Matri spread word to the corners of the Grand Duchy. After a week on Vostroma—days in which Atiana helped Borund to put the House of Vostroma back in order—the two of them had flown to Khalakovo.

Council was called. The dukes had returned from the war front. Most had arrived only in the last few days. On the morrow, they would all discuss the passing of Leonid and who would take the mantle of Grand Duke. But not tonight. Tonight was a night for a different occasion.

The three of them continued toward the eyrie. On the perches were four yachts—some of the precious few remaining windships in Anuskaya. Moored to the last perch was a simple skiff, laden with supplies. It was there that they went, coming to a stop in silent agreement only when they'd come alongside the skiff.

"Where will you go?" Nikandr asked Soroush.

Soroush glanced eastward with a wistful look. The golden earrings pierced along the ruined remains of his left ear glinted beneath the lowering sun. "Wherever the winds take me. It's been too long since I've circuited the world."

"Will you return to the islands?" Atiana asked. "Tell us what you've seen?"

The look Soroush gave her was one of wry amusement. "I may come, but let's see who remembers the name of Soroush Wahad al Gatha by the time I do."

From the palotza came another Aramahn. Anahid, wearing bright yellow robes. Having already said her goodbyes, she walked to the skiff and stepped down into it, waiting for Soroush to finish so they could be on their way.

Atiana squeezed Nikandr's arm, and then stepped forward, hesitating for a moment before taking Soroush into a long, heartfelt hug.

"Go well," she said simply.

"And you," Soroush replied.

And then Atiana was off, as simple as that.

Nikandr understood. They owed Soroush a great deal. And yet he'd taken much from the Grand Duchy. It was as bittersweet for Nikandr as it was for her. In some ways he didn't want Soroush to leave. He'd come to value his advice, his opinion. He even enjoyed the stories of Soroush's travels before he'd turned to the Maharraht. But in other ways he would be glad when Soroush was gone, because in him there were too many reminders. Of his days leading the Maharraht. Of the Battle of Uyadensk and the ritual on Oshtoyets. Of the horrors on Rafsuhan.

Not least were the memories of what had happened on Ghayavand. Ashan's death. And Nasim's ascension, if that was what had truly happened.

"Do you think he passed on to the heavens?" Nikandr asked.

They'd spoken of it many nights since the restoration four weeks ago.

"I do," he said. "Do you truly have doubts any longer?"

"It's just... It seems so..."

"Improbable?"

"Impossible."

Soroush shrugged. "For a time, I thought the same. But look around you. The very world is impossible. It should not be, yet here it is."

"I suppose you're right." Nikandr smiled and motioned toward the skiff. "I've set a cask of araq to aging in the cellars. When you return, come to Uyadensk, and we'll open it."

"It may age a very long time indeed."

"Then it will be that much finer when we drink it."

Soroush seemed put off by this offer, as if he'd had no intention of returning, but then he nodded. "That will be a fine day, Nikandr, son of Iaros."

"It will indeed, Soroush, son of Gatha."

They embraced, the two of them kissing cheeks in the manner of the islands, and then Soroush stepped down into the skiff.

"One more thing," Nikandr said.

Soroush turned, expectant, while Nikandr reached inside his cherkesska pocket. He pulled out a leather bag tooled with the curving designs of the Aramahn. He held it out for Soroush.

Frowning, Soroush pulled at the strings holding it shut and pulled back the flap to reveal the bright blue stone within. He took the Atalayina out and stared at it, shaking his head. "This cannot be given to me."

"It is yours now, Soroush. If you judge that someone else should have it, then so be it."

Soroush's jaw worked. He swallowed several times, and his eyes glistened. "Thank you," was all he said.

"Go well, Soroush."

"Go well, Nikandr."

And then they were off. Anahid guided the skiff up and away from the eyrie, allowing the prevailing winds to bear them eastward.

In some ways, Nikandr envied them—it would be wonderful to see more of the world—but in another, he was glad to remain exactly where he was. He'd come home. He'd seen much of this world, and he'd come to realize how much he loved Khalakovo. It would take the rest of his life, but he would relish learning more of it. He'd found his place in the world at last.

He turned and began walking back toward the palotza, wondering what would become of the world now. It was a question that had haunted him since Ghayavand. From talking to the others, he'd pieced together much of what had happened in the two years since Galahesh. Sariya had clearly planned carefully for her time on Ghayavand. She'd known since reaching the Valley of Kohor that she would ascend to the heavens, and she'd made careful plans before doing so. She'd returned to Alekeşir. She'd manipulated the powers of the world—the Haelish, Yrstanla, and lastly, Anuskaya—so that they were a shell of what they once were. Nikandr suspected it was so that each would have time to reflect on what had become of them. They'd have time to heal the wounds that they'd caused one another as well so that perhaps, in time, accords could be formed. Lasting peace could be formed.

At least he hoped it was so.

With Nasim beside her, and the others, he thought it might.

But it was not completely up to the fates. The will of man was a factor as well. Each had a say in their own fate and the collective fate of all. Nikandr would remember this, and if he was able he would strive to forge a better world.

As always, when he thought of such things, he thought of his brother. *Would the scepter was still yours, Ranos.* It wasn't the responsibility he minded—he'd been brought up in the halls of power, after all. He would shoulder it and hope to do as well as Ranos and their father, Iaros, had done. What he wanted—what he missed so dearly—was to ride with Ranos one last time, to hunt pheasant or grouse or ride the winds around Khalakovo as they'd done when they were younger.

But it was not to be. His brother had joined his father, and in this he found some small comfort. Father missed him as well. So let them rest. Nikandr would join them soon enough.

He stopped as he caught movement from the corner of his eye.

By the ancients who protect...

It was the golden thrush, sitting on a branch of one of the carefully shaped evergreen bushes in the garden. It stared at Nikandr intently. It called its beautiful song and then went silent. The clover-shaped mark was there, just below its beak on the left side of its neck. It was the very one he'd seen on Ghayavand, and surely the same one he and Nasim had found in Shadam Khoreh. Could it be any other?

As Nasim had done, Nikandr reached his forefinger out slowly. The bird sang again, staring sidelong, fluttering its wings and puffing up the golden feathers along its breast. He thought surely it was about to leap onto his outstretched finger—it would stare, then flap, then stare again—but then it launched into the air and flew up and over the walls of Radiskoye. And soon it was gone altogether.

Nikandr released a pent-up breath and stared into the brilliant, cloudless sky. In some ways he wished he could stare beyond it, to the heavens above. But in another, he was glad to be where he was. Home. With those he loved and who loved him.

"Nischka?" He turned and saw Atiana standing outside the thick palotza doors. "It's time for our dance."

After giving the depthless sky one last look, he strode toward her.

Indeed.

It was time to dance.

On Elemental Spirits
and the Use of Stones

The Aramahn harness the elements by drawing spirits, or hezhan, close to the material world and bonding with them. They do this by way of specific stones, each of which is aligned with one of the elements. The men and women who are able to do this are called qiram. The specific name of the qiram is altered based on the type of spirit they're able to bond with. Thus, a qiram who bonds with spirits of earth, vanahezhan, are called vanaqiram. Those who bond with spirits of fire, suurahezhan, are called suuraqiram.

Earth
Gem: jasper
Spirit: vanahezhan

Air
Gem: alabaster
Spirit: havahezhan

Fire
Gem: tourmaline
Spirit: suurahezhan

Water
Gem: azurite
Spirit: jalahezhan

Life
Gem: opal
Spirit: dhoshahezhan

The people of the Grand Duchy cannot bond with spirits. However, they do have magic of their own. They use chalcedony, and it can range in use by the peasantry to honor their dead to more formal use by royalty. The Matri use the stones in order to anchor themselves while in the aether. They also use them to find others with whom they've recently "touched stones." Chalcedony grants no direct control over the elements, but the Matri do guide the ley lines that run between the spires in order to create stronger, more predictable currents for the ships to sail along.

ON THE PRIMARY DIRECTIONS
OF WINDSHIPS

The windships in the Lays of Anuskaya are in some ways similar to their waterborne brethren. However, they are buoyant, and they never touch the water, docking at great eyries built onto the faces of cliffs instead of docks by the sea. They also have masts not just directly upward from the deck, but in all four of a ship's primary directions.

The list below gives some grounding in the terminology used by the windsmen of the Grand Duchy.

bow: the front end of the ship.
stern: the rearmost portion of the ship.
fore: toward the foremost portion of the ship.
aft: toward the rearmost portion of the ship.

starward: upward from the deck of the ship, toward the sky and stars.

seaward: downward, named so because the windships often fly above water.

landward: to the left while facing the fore of the ship, where the side windships tie up to a perch or a dock.

windward: to the right while facing the fore of the ship, named so because the wind is in this direction when the windship is moored.

mainmast: the central mast in any given direction. Thus, the mainmast that points down toward the sea is called the seaward mainmast, and the one pointing upward is called the starward mainmast.

foremast: the mast nearest the bow. Similar to the mainmast, the foremast can be modified to indicate which direction is being referenced (i.e. the landward foremast).

mizzenmast: the mast aft of the mainmast.

keel: refers to the obsidian cores of the ship's four mainmasts. Another length of obsidian is laid through the ship from stern to bow. The ley lines are captured by these three components of the keel, orienting the ship in a certain direction and allowing it to maintain that position as it sails forward like a waterborne ship through the sea.

rudder: a complex set of obsidian cylinders at the center of the ship, the nexus where the four mainmasts meet the obsidian core that runs lengthwise through the ship. These three sets of cylinders are adjusted by the pilot at the helm.

helm: the helm contains a set of three levers. These levers alter the set of the rudder, allowing the keel to set itself against the ley lines and turn the ship freely along all three axes: roll, pitch, and yaw.

GLOSSARY

Adhiya: the supernatural world of the hezhan; the world beyond the material world.

Aelwen: the wodjan that found Atiana in the desert and taught her to use blood to touch the aether.

aether: the realm that separates the physical realm, Erahm, from the spiritual realm, Adhiya.

akhoz: children that have become twisted by the Al-Aqim on the island of Ghayavand. Their eyes have closed over with skin, and they breathe fire, as they're bonded with suurahezhan.

Alif: the akhoz that Khamal chooses to perform his ritual on the beach below Alayazhar.

Ahar: one of the Tashavir buried in the valley of Shadam Khoreh.

Ahya Soroush al Rehada: deceased daughter of Rehada and Soroush. Died on the shores of Bolgravya.

Al-Aqim: the three arqesh who created the rift over Galahesh. Sariya, Muqallad, and Khamal.

Alayazhar: the largest city on Ghayavand, now in ruins.

Aleg Ganevov Khazabyirsk: the Duke of Khazabyirsk.

Alekeşir: the capital city of Yrstanla, one of the world's oldest cities.

Alesya Zaveta Bolgravya: wife to the former Grand Duke, Stasa Bolgravya.

Alhamid: Hakan ül Ayeşe's great-great-grandfather, a Kamarisi of Yrstanla.

Anahid: Nikandr's dhoshaqiram, the cousin of Jahalan.

Andreyo Sergeyov Rhavanki: the Duke of Rhavanki.

arqesh: an Aramahn qiram who has mastered all five disciplines (water, earth, fire, air, and life), and who has also reached a higher level of enlightenment.

Ashan Kida al Ahrumea: one of the arqesh (master of all disciplines) among the Aramahn.

Atalayina: a legendary stone used by the Al-Aqim in their failed attempt to bring about indaraqiram on the island of Ghayavand.

Atiana Radieva Vostroma: daughter of the Duke and Duchess of Vostroma. Nikandr's betrothed.

Avayom Kirilov: a kapitan of Bolgravya's staaya.

Avil: a strelet of Khalakovo who travels with Nikandr.

Avolina: a city to the northwest of Alekeşir, in the heartland of Yrstanla.

Bahett ül Kirdhash: the Kaymakam of Galahesh.

Behnda al Tib: the largest village of the Hratha in the islands to the south of the Grand Duchy.

berdische axe: a tall axe which streltsi use to rest their muskets against for higher accuracy.

Bersuq Wahad al Gatha: Soroush's brother, burned to death in a ritual on the island of Rafsuhan.

bichaq: slightly curved knife, used primarily in Yrstanla.

Borund Zhabynov Vostroma: eldest child and only son of Zhabyn and Radia Vostroma.

Brechan son of Gaelynd: King of Kings among the Haelish.

Brunhald: a one-footed rook belonging to the Bolgravya family. Alesya Bolgravya assumed Brunhald shortly before assuming Atiana before the Battle of Uyadensk.

cherkesska: long black coat worn by the streltsi of the Grand Duchy.

Cyhir: one of the akhoz that aids Nasim.

Datha: a stout Haelish warrior of Clan Eidihla.

Devrim ül Mert: seneschal to the Kamarisi, Hakan ül Ayeşe.

desyatnik: the lowest rank of officer in the Grand Duchy's staaya, typically responsible for ten streltsi.

dhoshahezhan: a spirit of life.

dhoshaqiram: one who bonds with dhoshahezhan and draws upon their power to wield or alter life in the material world.

dolman: a dress commonly worn by the women of northern Yrstanla, along the coast of the Sea of Tabriz.

dousing rod: a rod with a circle at one end of it, made of iron, used to sap the ability of the Aramahn qiram to bond with the hezhan.

drakhen: large amphibious lizards that sometimes make their home on the rocky beaches of the islands.

Dyanko Kantinov Vostroma: the boyar of Elykstava and the posadnik of Skayil.

Ebru: Bahett's second wife, the woman second in power to Meryam.

Edik: a soldier assigned to Styophan on his trip westward to Hael.

Ekaterina Margeva Rhavanki: the Duchess of Rhavanki.

Elean: the wife of Kürad, queen to the people of Clan Eidihla.

Erahm: the physical world.

Evochka: the capital and largest city in the Duchy of Volgorod. Situated near Palotza Galostina on the island of Kiravashya.

eyrie: the places where windships are moored, typically built onto cliff faces with many perches available for windships.

Fahroz Bashar al Lilliah: a former mahtar of the village of Iramanshah. The woman who taught Nasim after he was returned to himself in the ritual performed by Soroush.

Galostina (Palotza Galostina): the seat of power for the Vostroman family.

ghazi: the local militia in much of the southern and eastern reaches of Yrstanla.

Ghayavand: the island that was once a place of learning for the Aramahn. It became a wasteland when the Al-Aqim attempted a ritual to bring about indaraqiram.

Gaji: a large desert in the southwestern reaches of the Yrstanlan Empire.

Galahesh: a semi-autonomous island that sits between the islands of the Grand Duchy and Yrstanla.

goedrun: large sea creatures with squid-like tentacles that often prevent sea travel.

Goeh: one of the Kohori, and the man who finds Nikandr and Atiana and leads them safely to Kohor.

Gravlos Antinov: a shipwright. Oversaw the design and construction of the *Gorovna*.

Grigory Staseyev Bolgravya: the fourth son of Stasa Bolgravya. Brother to the Duke, Konstantin Bolgravya.

Habram: the leader of the village of Kohor.

Hael: the kingdom of the nomadic Haelish people, which lies to the west of Yrstanla. The Haelish have been locked in a bloody war with Yrstanla for decades.

Hakan ül Ayeşe: the former Kamarisi of Yrstanla, now dead. Selim's ül Hakan's father.

havahezhan: a spirit of wind.

havaqiram: one who bonds with havahezhan and draws upon their power to wield or alter wind in the material world.

helm: the helm contains a set of three levers. These levers alter the set of the rudder, allowing the keel to set itself against the ley lines and turn the ship freely along all three axes: roll, pitch, and yaw.

Heodor Yaroslov Lhudansk: the Duke of Lhudansk.

hezhan: souls or spirits in the world of Adhiya.

Hratha: the southern sect of the Maharraht. They have largely focused on fighting the southern Duchies of Anuskaya.

hussar: the cavalry of the Grand Duchy.

Iaros Aleksov Khalakovo: the former Duke of Khalakovo. Nikandr's father.

ilkadin: the first wife in a harem, which are common among the lords of Yrstanla. The ilkadin sit in a place of power in the household of an Yrstanlan lord.

Inan: Yadhan's mother. The one who instigated the push to cast a spell over Ghayavand and the Atalayina.

indaraqiram: the state that the Aramahn believe the world will one day reach when all its people become enlightened through individual vashaqiram.

Irabahce (Kasir Irabahce): the imperial palace of Yrstanla, home to the Kamarisi.

Iramanshah: an Aramahn village on the island of Uyadensk.

Iriketa Alesyeva Bolgravya: daughter and youngest child of Stasa Bolgravya.

Isaak Ylafslov: the steward of Palotza Radiskoye.

Ishkyna Radieva Vostroma: daughter of Zhabyn and Radia Vostroma. One of three triplets, sister to Atiana and Mileva Vostroma.

Iyana Klarieva Dhalingrad: the duchess of Dhalingrad.

Jahalan Atman al Mitra: Nikandr's former havaqiram (wind master). Killed in a skirmish against windships from Yrstanla.

jalahezhan: a spirit of water.

jalaqiram: one who bonds with jalahezhan and draws upon their power to wield or alter water in the material world.

janissary: the soldiers of Yrstanla.

Jonis: a young windsman that joined Nikandr on the *Yarost*. He has sharp eyes and was often asked to keep watch.

Kaleh: Sariya's daughter, found by Nikandr on the island of Rafsuhan.

Kalhani: an ancient language of the Aramahn. The precursor to Mahndi and many other languages of Yrstanla.

Kamarisi: the supreme lord of Yrstanla. In essence, the Emperor.

kasir: the term for palace in Yrstanla. The kasirs of the Empire tend to be much more ostentatious than the palotzas of the Grand Duchy.

Katerina Vostroma: a Matra of Vostroma; Zhabyn Vostroma's sister.

Kaymakam: a major lord under the Kamarisi. Bahett, who is the Lord of Galahesh, is a Kaymakam, but there are many others who rule beneath the Kamarisi.

keel: refers to the obsidian cores of the ship's four mainmasts. Another length of obsidian is laid through the ship from stern to bow. The ley lines are captured by these three components of the keel, orienting the ship in a certain direction and allowing it to maintain that position as it sails forward like a waterborne ship through the sea.

Khamal Cyphar al Maladhin: one of the three arqesh who lived on Ghayavand. Along with Muqallad and Sariya, Khamal caused the sundering three hundred years ago and had been trapped on the island.

khanjar: curved daggers used by the Aramahn and Maharraht.

khedive: the lord of a city in the Yrstanlan empire.

kilij: blade with a distinct curve near the middle, used primarily in Yrstanla, especially by the janissaries.

kindjal: the traditional knife of Anuskaya.

Kiravashya: the largest island in the Duchy of Volgorod. Home to the capital city of Evochka and Palotza Galostina.

Kirzan: the large building at the center of Baressa's bazaar, the old seat of power on Galahesh, abandoned after the treaty was signed with Anuskaya after the War of Seven Seas.

Kohor: the birthplace of Sariya, and the village where legend says the Atalayina was first found.

kolpak: a tall rounded hat typically worn by the streltsi.

Konstantin Staseyev Bolgravya: the Duke of Bolgravya. The first son of the former Grand Duke, Stasa Bolgravya.

korobochki: brightly painted blocks.

kozyol: goat, used as a curse, or a derogatory term.

Kseniya Zoyeva Nodhvyansk: the Duchess of Nodhvyansk.

kuadim: an Aramahn teacher.

Kürad son of Külesh: the King of Clan Eidihla, a tribe of the Haelish people.

Kuvvatli Mountains: the mountains that separate Hael from the bulk of Yrstanla.

Landed: a term that originally applied to those who hold land in the Grand Duchy of Anuskaya. Over time, it came to mean anyone who hails from the Grand Duchy.

Landless: a term used by the people of the Grand Duchy for the Aramahn. It refers to the way the Aramahn view land, that it is owned by no one, but also the way they move throughout the world, rarely staying in once place for long.

landsman: a general term for the men who work the eyries, lading and unlading windships.

landward: to the left while facing the fore of a ship, where the side windships tie up to a perch or a dock.

Leonid Roaldov Dhalingrad: the Duke of Dhalingrad.

ley line: lines of power that run between islands. Windships harness the ley lines to orient their ships with their obsidian keels. The Matri use their abilities to groom the ley lines so that travel between the islands becomes easier.

Maharraht: a splinter sect of the Aramahn who have forsaken their peaceful ways in order to drive the Landed from the islands they once had free reign over. Their ultimate goal is to regain control over the islands, but also to prevent the Grand Duchy from abusing and taking advantage of the Aramahn.

Mahndi: the modern language of the Aramahn and Maharraht.

Mahrik: a strelet of Khalakovo who travels with Nikandr.

Mahtar: an elder, a leader of the Aramahn villages.

Majeed Bassam al Haffeh: a man close to Fahroz on the floating island of Mirashadal, one of the mahtar of the village.

Malidhan: the mountain peak where Ahar, the most powerful of the Tashavir, is kept.

Matra (plural: Matri): a woman who has the ability to submerge herself in ice cold-water to enter the aether, where she can communicate with other Matri and see ghostly images of the material world.

Meryam: Bahett's current ilkadin, his "first wife."

Mikhalai: a soldier assigned to Styophan on his trip westward to Hael.

Mileva Radieva Vostroma: daughter of Zhabyn and Radia Vostroma. One of three triplets, sister to Atiana and Ishkyna Vostroma.

Mirashadal: the floating village of the Aramahn. The place Fahroz takes Nasim after he was healed on the island of Duzol.

Mount: the large hill that houses Kasir Yalidoz in the city of Baressa.

Muqallad Bakshazhd al Dananir: one of the three arqesh who lived on Ghayavand. Along with Sariya and Khamal, Muqallad caused the sundering three hundred years ago and had been trapped on the island.

Muwas Umar al Mariyah: a gifted jalaqiram.

Nabide: one of the two wives who let Styophan and the others into the tower of wives in Kasir Irabahce.

Nasim an Ashan: an orphan boy with strange powers.

Nataliya Iyaneva Bolgravya: wife of Borund.

Negesht: a fort in the wilds of western Yrstanla.

Nikandr Iaroslov Khalakovo: youngest son of the Duke and Duchess of Khalakovo.

palotza: a castle or palace, typically quite large, within the Grand Duchy.

Polina Anayev Mirkotsk: the Duchess of Mirkotsk

polkovnik: the highest rank of officer in the Grand Duchy's staaya.

polupolkovnik: the second highest rank of officer in the Grand Duchy's staaya, below only the polkovnik in the chain of command.

privyet: Anuskayan for hello or good day.

qiram: an Aramahn with the ability to bond with hezhan, giving them the elemental abilities of the spirit.

Rabiah Wahid al Aahtel: one of Nasim's disciples that he brings with him to Ghayavand.

Radia Anastasiyeva Vostroma: the Duchess of Vostroma.

Radiskoye (Palotza Radiskoye): the seat of power for the Khalakovan family.

Rahid Umar al Gahana: one of the more powerful men from the southern sect of the Maharraht known as the Hratha.

Ramina: the northern city on Galahesh, the one closest to Oramka and Yrstanla.

Ranos Iaroslov Khalakovo: eldest son of Iaros Khalakovo. Became the Duke of Khalakovo on Iaros's death.

Rehada Ulan al Shineshka: an Aramahn woman. Nikandr's former lover in Volgorod.

Rodion: Styophan's cousin and one of the soldiers assigned on Styophan's trip westward to Hael.

Rosa Oriseva Lhudansk: the Duchess of Lhudansk.

rudder: a complex set of obsidian cylinders at the center of the ship, the nexus where the four mainmasts meet the obsidian core that runs lengthwise through the ship. These three sets of cylinders are adjusted by the pilot at the helm.

Safwah: an old woman and a powerful qiram from Kohor. Safwah is Goeh's mother.

Saphia Mishkeva Khalakovo: the Duchess of Khalakovo.

Sariya Quljan al Vehayeh: one of the three arqesh who lived on Ghayavand. Along with Muqallad and Khamal, Sariya caused the sundering three hundred years ago and had been trapped on the island.

Sea of Khurkhan: the sea south of Galahesh, northwest of Nodhvyansk, and southeast of Yrstanla.

Sea of Tabriz: the sea between Yrstanla and Anuskaya, bounded by the empire to the west, Khalakovo to the east, and Volgorod to the south.

seaward: downward, named so because the windships often fly above water.

Selim ül Hakan: the new Kamarisi of Yrstanla. Hakan ül Ayeşe's eldest son. Although he holds the title of Kamarisi, Bahett ül Kirdhash has been appointed regent until Selim is old enough to rule the Empire at the age of fourteen.

Serin: one of the two wives who let Styophan and the others into the tower of wives in Kasir Irabahce.

Shadam Khoreh: the valley in the Gaji Desert where the Tashavir, the followers of Inan who trapped the Al-Aqim on the island of Ghayavand, reside.

shamshir: a curved sword used primarily by the Maharraht.

shashka: a lightly curved sword used primarily in the islands of the Grand Duchy.

Shirvozeh: the Aramahn village to the east of Alayazhar, on the island of Ghayavand. It became the seat of Muqallad's power when the three Al-Aqim became trapped on the island.

Siafyan: a large village with massive trees and hanging walkways running between them on the island of Rafsuhan.

Sihyaan: the tallest mountain on Ghayavand and the site of the ritual that caused the sundering.

Sihaş ül Mehmed: an envoy who goes to treat with the Grand Duchy.

siraj: the Aramahn lanterns, made of stone that glows.

Sitalyas: the mountain range to the west of Trevitze.

Skolohalla: a formal meeting of the Haelish Kings and their nomadic tribes.

Soroush Wahad al Gatha: leader of the northern sect of the Maharraht.

sotni: a unit of one hundred soldiers.

sotnik: an officer of the Grand Duchy, responsible for one hundred men.

Spar: the large bridge built by Yrstanla over the Straits of Galahesh.

spire: a tower of obsidian used by the Grand Duchy to control the ley lines between the islands. The Matri groom the ley lines using the spires and their abilities in the aether.

starward: upward from the deck of ship, toward the sky and stars.

strelet (plural: streltsi): the military men of the Grand Duchy.

szubka: hat worn by the women of the Grand Duchy.

staaya: the ducal (Royal) air fleet of the Grand Duchy.

Stasa Olegov Bolgravya: the former Grand Duke, killed on Khalakovo when a suurahezhan, a fire spirit, attacked his yacht as it docked at the eyrie of Radiskoye.

Styophan Andrashayev: the sotnik of the streltsi who accompany Nikandr.

Sukharam Hadir al Dahanan: one of Nasim's disciples that he brings with him to Ghayavand.

suurahezhan: a spirit of fire.

suuraqiram: one who bonds with suurahezhan and draws upon their power to wield or alter fire in the material world.

Svoya: the southern city on Galahesh, the one closest to the islands.

Syemon: an old gull who serves on the ship, *Strovya*.

taking breath (or, to take breath): the Aramahn act of meditating, where they try to become one with their surroundings, to understand more about themselves or the world.

Tashavir: powerful and ancient qiram from the time of the sundering. Followers of Inan who trapped the Al-Aqim on the island of Ghayavand.

Thabash Kaspar al Meliyah: the leader of the Hratha.

Thirosh: the man who runs a winery in secret for King Brechan of Hael. An ally of the Haelish in Alekeşir.

Tohrab: one of the Tashavir buried in the valley of Shadam Khoreh. Also Inan's husband, the father of Yadhan.

Trevitze: the city where Nasim finds Sukharam.

Udra Amir al Rasa: Nikandr's dhoshaqiram (master of the stuff of life).

Urdi Mountains: the mountains separating the Kohori Valley from the Valley of Shadam Khoreh.

Ushai Kissath al Shahda: one of Fahroz's most trusted servants. She travels the world, hoping to find Nasim.

ushanka: squat woolen hat.

Uyadensk: the largest island in the Duchy Khalakovo. Home to Palotza Radis-koye and the capital city of Volgorod.

Vaasak Adimov Dhalingrad: the envoy of Zhabyn, sent to Baressa to negotiate for him before his arrival.

vanahezhan: a spirit of earth.

vanaqiram: one who bonds with vanahezhan and draws upon their power to wield or alter earth in the material world.

vashaqiram: a state of pure enlightenment. The state of mind most Aramahn search for.

Victania Saphieva Khalakovo: the only daughter of Saphia and Iaros. The middle child.

Vihrosh: the old name for Baressa, and now the section that lies to the west of the straits.

Vikra: one of the rooks of Vostroma, the one Atiana favors the most.

Vlanek: the acting master of the *Yarost* on Nikandr's journey across the Sea of Khurkhan.

Volgorod: the capital and largest city in the Duchy of Khalakovo. Situated near Palotza Radiskoye on the island of Uyadensk.

Wahad Soroush al Qediah: Soroush's first son, his second child.

windwood: a variety of wood that is specially cured so that it becomes lighter than air. All windships are made of windwood.

windship: one of the ships made of windwood that flies with the help of havaqiram to harness the wind and dhoshaqiram to adjust the heft of the ship's windwood.

windsman: general term for a man who crews windships.

windward: to the right while facing the fore of a ship, named so because the wind is in this direction when the windship is moored.

wodjan: a mystic among the Haelish people. The wodjana are able to scry using their own blood or the blood of their enemies.

Yadhan: the first of the children to become akhoz on Ghayavand. She was taken by Khamal.

Yalessa: the handmaid that most often attended to Atiana in the drowning chamber.

Yalidoz (Kasir Yalidoz): the palace in Baressa, on the island of Galahesh, home to Bahett ül Kirdhash.

Yasha: a soldier assigned to Styophan on his trip westward to Hael.

Yegor Nikolov Nodhvyansk: the Duke of Nodhvyansk.

Yevgeny Krazhnegov Mirkotsk: the Duke of Mirkotsk.

Yrfa: Saphia Khalakovo's favorite rook.

Yrstanla: an Empire situated on a large continent to the west of the islands in the Grand Duchy.

Yvanna Antoneva Khalakovo: Ranos's wife.

Zanaida Lariseva Khazabyirsk: the Duchess of Khazabyirsk.

Zanhalah: the woman who helps Nikandr to heal Soroush's son, Wahad.

Zhabyn Olegov Vostroma: the former Duke of Vostroma, killed in the war with Yrstanla.

Afterword

Like many works of fiction, The Lays of Anuskaya was years in the making. The creation of a new world and the story that lives within it often begins well before the first words hit the page. It was no different here. The genesis of The Lays of Anuskaya can be pinpointed to a trip to Scotland I took with my wife in 2004. We went on a whirlwind tour of the UK and Ireland, and one of the stops was Edinburgh, where we visited the National Gallery of Scotland. While there, I was struck by many of the beautiful paintings, especially some of the paintings from the Dutch masters on display, and I thought, I'm going to write a story from these. I had no idea what the story might be—only that I wanted to gather certain works as inspiration and use them to help seed the story I was about to embark upon.

Little did I know what sort of people the characters in those paintings might become—not only Nikandr and Atiana, but Nasim, Ashan, Rehada, Soroush, Victania, and Iaros. Over the years, what started out as a story that was important for me to write became one that was deeply personal. The story of these characters became so much a part of me that I felt real feelings of loss when the story was done and turned in. It was wonderful to have the story complete and ready to go out in the world and into readers' hands, but I also knew I would miss these many characters.

One thing that strikes me, now that the tale has been written, is the personal journey I've taken over the course of the many years it's taken me to start, publish, and shepherd this project to market. I was not a neophyte author when I started working on The Lays of Anuskaya, but neither was I seasoned. I grew immensely as a writer during the telling of these tales. I grew and changed as a person. My daughter was just a baby when I started, and now she's seven. My son is only three, and so was many years in my future by the time I put hands to keyboard. The world has changed around me and changed *me* as a result.

481

And through it all I've been chipping away at this tale, hoping it will find a home out there in the world. That has been one of the more gratifying parts of this journey. I truly enjoy interacting with those that have read and found these books fun to read. It's a very gratifying thing for the writer, because let's face it, even with social networking, writing is a terribly lonely profession, and it's wonderful to speak to people that relate to what you've written, and also to find like-minded souls.

I also look back over the journey told within the pages of the book and find myself deeply gratified with how it turned out. Tolkien once said that writers are like archeologists. The tales are there to be found and told and we authors simply uncover the truth of it, slowly but surely. I like that take on it, because it speaks to the internal consistency writers are looking for in a story. But it sure does pay short shrift to the work we put in to flesh out the world, the magic, the characters, and the plot.

As I write, the story seems so full of possibility. It could go so many ways as it begins to unfold and various people and places and plot points come to me. But like concrete the story eventually begins to set. It feels more solid. Less *able* to change. Until eventually it's fixed and feels more like a window to another world than an unending set of possibilities. That's what this story has become to me now. A real world. A whole world. One that started before I began writing and will continue well beyond it.

That is my fervent hope for you as well, that you find this world wondrous and unique and complete.

Another thing I've rarely talked about is the fact that 9/11, the Iraq War, and the surrounding conflicts were one of the primary sources of inspiration for this story. Like so many people—not just Americans, but people all over the world—I was greatly affected by the events of 9/11. There was rage and confusion and a deep desire to "get to the bottom of it," to understand why the perpetrators of that crime had done what they'd done. The more I searched for answers, however, the more I realized that it's an endless story with endless causes and endless consequences.

Look, I'm a pragmatist. I know there are hard truths in our world, and I'm fully aware that there are legitimate reasons to use violence to achieve an end, but it also seems that too often violence (or the threat of violence) is the first thing we reach for in our arsenal (a funny word to use when you're trying to broker peace, but somehow it seems apropos; and by the way, when I say we, I mean the entire human race). So much of our politics is posturing and refusing to give in for fear of being seen as weak or "appeasing" the enemy. This is true of many conflicts around the world and was true of the conflict in the Middle East, and as I watched it unfold, it built within me a frustration that was hard to reconcile. It was in that frustration that the seeds of *The Winds of Khalakovo* were laid down. Those seeds started to bear fruit as I fleshed out the conflict that's told in the story, one that has roots in generations past but that's coming to a head just as *Winds* opens.

The heart of the story—a tale of irreconcilable differences—didn't change very much in the telling. It continued to be the primary driver of what happened, but I was able to show that some people, if they try hard, can meet somewhere in the middle, and I was able to bring that new perspective to several different characters. That was one of the more gratifying things for me, to show a tale in which the characters learn and come to understand another culture from a perspective that was beforehand very limited. As you now know, not everyone ended up agreeing with the other side—that wouldn't be a truthful story—but they certainly understood more if nothing else, and all of that came from my inner desires for us, in this world, to do the same.

I recently (it's May of 2013 as I type this) stopped by John Scalzi's The Big Idea to help promote *The Flames of Shadam Khoreh*. The notion is you talk about the big idea in your book. Its central theme. Most people talk about a single book, but I chose to talk more about the series as a whole.

So what's the Big Idea? The Lays of Anuskaya isn't *about* our world. It isn't *about* the conflict in the Middle East. But it was born there, certainly, and so it's hard to escape some parallelism. I suppose if I had to formulate the roiling of inner desires that led to these books, I'd say it's a plea for us to look further than today.

It's a plea for peace, as told through a tale of war.

ACKNOWLEDGEMENTS

Books are not written alone. They have many supporters, some silent, some vocal. This is my attempt to thank as many of them as I can.

To my wife, Joanne, who carves out time for me to do this crazy thing I love, thank you so much. This thanks also extends to my children, Relaneve and Rhys. Every single ounce of effort I put into you is rewarded by the pound.

To Ross Lockhart, I've said it in private, but I'll say it here as well. Your help to me in the process of getting this trilogy from its raw written form to final product has been invaluable. Thank you for being a champion of this work, both within the halls of Night Shade Books and in the wide, scary world of publishing.

To my agent, Russ Galen, as time goes on, I respect your insight more and more. Thank you for believing in me enough to take on a fledgling writer and shelter him forward to an actual, honest-to-goodness writing career.

To the people of Wellspring II Electric Boogaloo (Brenda Cooper, Debbie Daughetee, Kelly Swails, Holly McDowell, Kameron Hurley, Greg Wilson, Vincent Jorgensen, Grá Linnaea, Stephen Gaskell, Eugene Myers, and Chris Cevasco), thank you so much for reading those early pages and sending the ship off in the right direction. To Debbie and Brenda go an extra helping of thanks for reading the entire novel, warts and all. What I had was roughly formed clay, and you helped me turn it into a sculpture. Full manuscript reads of such a long book are golden, and you have my deep gratitude for taking it on.

I'd also like to thank a few of my many mentors who've helped me along the way. To Orson Scott Card, thank you for running your Literary Boot Camp in 2005. I learned so much, not only from your books on writing, but from your incisive talks and comments on writing. And to my Clarion instructors, Chip Delaney, Michael Swanwick, Joe and Gay Haldeman, Nancy Kress, Holly Black, and Kelly Link, thank you for running the most intense six weeks (writing-wise) of my life. No one can fully appreciate what Clarion gives them while they're there at the workshop. It takes years afterward to absorb it and put it into practice. But your efforts were greatly appreciated. Clarion took me farther than I ever imagined it would.

To Holliann Russell Kim, I don't know what I would have done without you. I'm so grateful you were there all the way. Thank you for taking this journey with me, and for lending your keen eye to these sorry pages.

To Aaron J. Riley, thank you for taking a few notes and some words and turning them into such a gorgeous cover.

To Ryan Leduc, thank you for your generosity to Worldbuilders and for providing the inspiration for Rodion Ledokov, a fine addition to this tale.

For last, I save Paul Genesse, who has always been such a great supporter of this story and who helped immensely with this final book, particularly getting the ending to the point where it would honor not just the threads playing out in this novel, but the entire trilogy and beyond. My thanks, Paul, for your friendship, encouragement, and advice.